W9-BSH-001

To my own Merrilee:
Martha Lee

And to Laurelin:
Tina

And the ichor and the thee's and thou's
are respectfully dedicated to
Ursula K. Le Guin

THE IRON TOWER

The Dark Tide

The Dark Lord stirs from his slumber, his power building to new heights, dimming the very sun, and waking legends to walk the land. It is the long-feared time of reckoning!

Galen, High-King of Mithgar, sounds a desperate call to the Warriors of the Light. And Tuck and his fellow Warrows—small but fierce fighters with the gift of Sight—join with the ever-growing army of Dwarves, Elves, and human warriors to stem this deadly tide of destruction the final conflict has begun . . .

Shadows of Doom

At Gûnnaring Gap, the valiant Riders of Valon began their charge. And though Challerain Keep lay in ruins, and treachery led to the capture of Princess Laurelin, heroes strode forth from the ranks of Men, Elves, Warrows, and Dwarves to turn the tide of doom. And across the land ruled by unnatural dark, freedom flickered and burst into flame. . . .

The Darkest Day

It is the time foretold, when the Dark Liege Gyphon will return from exile to subdue all creation to his vile domination. In the Iron Tower, Modru works his magics to summon his implacable lord. And across Mithgar, the Warriors of the Light are massing for their final assault on the Powers of Dark. Their state is desperate, for if they fail there comes the unending Darkest Day. . . .

THE IRON
TOWER

Dennis L. McKiernan

For the First Time Complete
in One Volume
and
with a New Foreword
by the Author
(previously published as three
separate titles in the *Iron Tower Trilogy*)

A ROC BOOK

ROC
Published by New American Library, a division of
Penguin Putnam Inc., 375 Hudson Street,
New York, New York 10014, U.S.A.
Penguin Books Ltd, 80 Strand,
London WC2R 0RL, England
Penguin Books Australia Ltd, Ringwood,
Victoria, Australia
Penguin Books Canada Ltd, 10 Alcorn Avenue,
Toronto, Ontario, Canada M4V 3B2
Penguin Books (N.Z.) Ltd, 182–190 Wairau Road,
Auckland 10, New Zealand

Penguin Books Ltd, Registered Offices:
Harmondsworth, Middlesex, England

Published by Roc, an imprint of New American Library,
a division of Penguin Putnam Inc. These are authorized reprints of hardco
editions originally published by Doubleday and Company, Inc.

First Roc Printing (*The Iron Tower* omnibus), December 2000
10 9 8 7 6 5 4

The Dark Tide copyright © Dennis L. McKiernan, 1984
Shadows of Doom copyright © Dennis L. McKiernan, 1984
The Darkest Day copyright © Dennis L. McKiernan, 1984
All rights reserved

RoC REGISTERED TRADEMARK—MARCA REGISTRADA

Printed in the United States of America

Without limiting the rights under copyright reserved above, no part of this
publication may be reproduced, stored in or introduced into a retrieval
system, or transmitted, in any form, or by any means (electronic, mechanical,
photocopying, recording, or otherwise), without the prior written
permission of both the copyright owner and the above publisher of this book

PUBLISHER'S NOTE
This is a work of fiction. Names, characters, places, and incidents either are
the product of the author's imagination or are used fictitiously, and any
resemblance to actual persons, living or dead, events, business establishments
or locales is entirely coincidental.

BOOKS ARE AVAILABLE AT QUANTITY DISCOUNTS WHEN USED TO PROMOTE
PRODUCTS OR SERVICES. FOR INFORMATION PLEASE WRITE TO PREMIUM
MARKETING DIVISION, PENGUIN PUTNAM INC., 375 HUDSON STREET, NEW YORK,
NEW YORK 10014.

If you purchased this book without a cover you should be aware that this
book is stolen property. It was reported as "unsold and destroyed" to
the publisher and neither the author nor the publisher has received any
payment for this "stripped book."

who decided it should be a trilogy (trilogies were a big thing back then). And so it was done that way: three books to tell the tale. But you know, I always felt that the story should have been published as written—as a single book and not three. Well, here we are finally: *The Iron Tower* all in one book; whole at last. And with this tale now in print as it was written, as it was meant to be read, let us all get comfortable in our favorite rooms, in our favorite chairs or lounges or beds, in whatever and wherever are our favorite places to read, and open the pages to the (oh-so-familiar, for some of us) opening words and experience all over again the tale for the very first time.

—Dennis L. McKiernan
Tucson, Arizona, 2000

Journal Notes

Note 1:
The source of this tale is a tattered copy of *The Raven Book,* an incredibly fortunate find dating from the time before The Separation.

Note 2:
The Great War of the Ban ended the Second Era (2E) of Mithgar. The Third Era (3E) began on the following Year's Start Day. The Third Era, too, eventually came to an end, and so started the Fourth Era (4E). The tale recorded here began in November of 4E2018. Although this adventure occurs four millennia after the Ban War, the roots of the quest lie directly in the events of that earlier time.

Note 3:
There are many instances in this tale where, in the press of the moment, the Dwarves, Elves, Men, and Warrows spoke in their own native tongues; yet, to avoid the awkwardness of burdensome translations, where necessary I have rendered their words in Pellarion, the Common Tongue of Mithgar. However, some words do not lend themselves to translation, and these I've left unchanged; yet other words may look to be in error, but are indeed correct. (For example, DelfLord is but a single word, though a capital L nestles among its letters. Also note that waggon, traveller, and several other similar words are written in the Pendwyrian form of Pellarion and are not misspelled.)

Note 4:
The "formal" speech spoken at the High King's court is similar in many respects to Old High German. In those

cases where court speech appeared in *The Raven Book*, first I translated the words into Pellarion, and then, in the objective and nominative cases of the pronoun "you," I respectively substituted "thee" and "thou" to indicate that the formal court speech is being used. Again, to avoid over-burdening the reader, I have resisted inserting into the court speech additional archaic terms such as hast, wilt, durst, prithee, and the like.

THE IRON TOWER

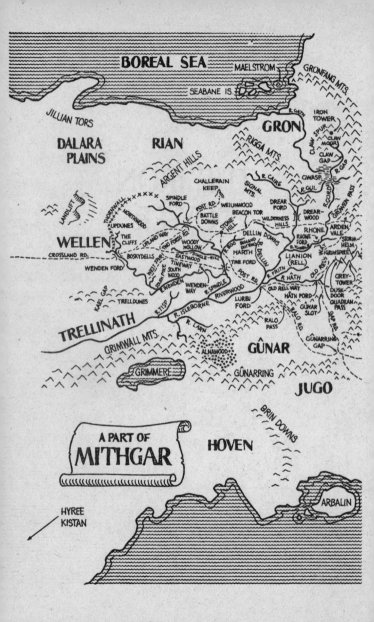

BOOK ONE

The Dark Tide

Contents

Foreword Anew   ix
Journal Notes   xiii
Map   xvi

BOOK ONE   The Dark Tide
  1. The Well-Attended Parting   3
  2. Retreat to Rooks' Roost   21
  3. Spindle Ford   42
  4. Challerain Keep   71
  5. The Dark Tide   116
  6. The Long Pursuit   182

BOOK TWO   Shadows of Doom
  1. Captive!   215
  2. Grimwall   244
  3. The Struggles   301
  4. Myrkenstone   336
  5. Drimmen-Deeve   348
  6. Shadows of Doom   374

BOOK THREE   The Darkest Day
  1. The Gathering   431
  2. Encounter at Gûnarring Gap   464
  3. The Valanreach Long-ride   466
  4. The Iron Tower   489
  5. The Darkest Day   505
  6. The Journey Home   574
  7. The Raven Book   605

Foreword Anew

When I first decided to write high fantasy set in my own world of Mithgar, I knew that I would include Elves and Dwarves and High Kings and brave warriors and Wizards and Rucks and Trolls and Gargons and other beings fair and foul in tales set in hazardous times. And surely Elves and Dwarves and nobility and warriors of renown and other such heroes were and are needed in a high fantasy—at least in my version thereof—and I knew they were extraordinary and quite remarkable folks who would step forward to deal with whatever perils might threaten the world . . . and as such would play great and noble roles in any adventure I would write.

Yet, I also believed I needed a folk to be a key part of a story who weren't great warriors or High Kings or noble Elves or resolute Dwarves, but rather those who could represent "everyman, everywoman, everyperson;" I needed someone with doubts and weaknesses and lack of lore, someone like "me," someone with whom the reader could identify, yet also be someone with "heart" and grit and determination (as I believe we all have within us).

I could have chosen any number of folk to represent us, but I also felt, in addition to those named above, that a mythical, high-fantasy land needed some kind(s) of wee folk as well. Oh, I knew that ultimately I wanted to write about Pysks and other Hidden Ones—all more or less Fairy Folk—but I needed a less mystical people to represent you and me, someone less fey to represent us all. Some kind of wee folk, I believed, could in fact fulfill that need. But, to represent us, unlike the wee folk of other authors, of other tales, I wanted that someone to be able, when pressed, to do whatever was needed in the defense of all he or she holds dear. Hence, the Warrows of *The Iron Tower* and *The Silver*

Call and other Mithgarian sagas were born. And in many instances throughout the tales, driven by circumstance and peril and need, the naïve Warrows—our surrogates, our everypersons—become the most effective warriors, the most lethal killers, of all, even though they never seem to lose their innocence. After all, the quintessence of Warrows is the same as our own—you and me and Joe down the street and Martha and Giles and whoever else you'd like to name; at core, we ourselves are Warrows . . . with our weaknesses and naïveté and doubts and strengths . . . but most especially our "heart."

Hence, given the foregoing, unlike hobbits and kender and other such wee folk, Warrows are quite deadly, quite lethal when pressed, just as we ourselves could be in the same circumstances. Oh, don't take me wrong: I love the wee folk of other authors' tales, especially the hobbits of J.R.R. Tolkien's magnificent saga, *The Lord of the Rings;* and let me acknowledge here and now that a couple of things within *The Iron Tower* (and *The Silver Call*) are written in homage, in tribute, to Tolkien . . . in particular, the title(s) of the opening chapter(s), as well as parts of the journey(s) through the Dwarvenholt of Kraggen-cor, of Drimmendeeve, of the Black Hole. Wonderful tale tellers like Tolkien come along not once in a generation, but rather once in a lifetime, and then only if we are lucky. Fortunate are we that he set his story down in writing; fortunate are we also that his work lives on after he himself is gone. Like other authors, I can but pray that my own efforts will live on after me; though when I began I never expected such.

Little did I know some twenty-odd years ago that *The Iron Tower* would transform my life forever, would lead to a career change and to an age-spanning series. For me, Mithgar is a wonderful place—even though quite perilous at times—and I am so glad to have journeyed therein. Glad, too, am I that so many of you—new readers and old alike— have chosen to travel across Mithgar at my side. A simple "thank you" doesn't seem nearly enough to express my gratitude for your company, yet it will have to do, for I can think of nothing else to say that would better convey my heartfelt appreciation.

Let me also say that when I first penned *The Iron Tower,* I wrote it as a single story. It was my editor at the time

"And that is what Evil does: forces us all down dark pathways we otherwise would not have trod."

—Rael of Arden
January 10, 4E2019

CHAPTER 1

The Well-Attended Parting

With a final burst of speed, the young buccan Warrow raced through ankle-deep snow, his black hair flying out behind. In one hand he carried a bow already nocked with an arrow, and he sprinted toward a fallen log, clots of snow flinging out behind his flying boots; yet little or no sound did he make, for he was one of the Wee Folk. Swiftly he reached the log and silently dropped to one knee, quickly drawing the bow to the full and loosing the arrow with a humming twang of bowstring. Even before the deadly missile had sped to the target, another arrow was released, and another, another, and another—in all, five arrows were shot in rapid succession, hissing through the air, striking home with deadly accuracy.

"Whang! Right square in the center, Tuck!" cried Old Barlo as the last arrow thudded into the mark. "That's four for five, and you would'er got the other, too, if you'd'er held a bit." Old Barlo, a granther Warrow, stood up to his full three feet two inches of height and turned and cocked a baleful emerald-green eye upon the other young buccen gathered on the snowy slopes behind. "Now I'm telling all you rattlepates: draw fast, and loose quick, but no quicker as what you can fly it straight. The arrow as strays might well'er been throwed away, for all the good it does." Barlo turned back to Tuck. "Fetch up your arrows, lad, and sit and catch your breath. Who's next now? Well, step up here, slowcoach Tarpy."

Tuckerby Underbank slipped his chilled hands back into his mittens and quickly retrieved his five arrows from the tattered, black, Wolf silhouette on the haycock. With his breath blowing whitely in the cold air, Tuck trotted back through the snow to the watching group of archers at the

edge of End Field, where he sat down on a fallen log,
standing his bow against a nearby barren tree.

As Tuck watched little Tarpy sprint toward the target to
fly arrows at the string-circle mark, the young buccan sitting
beside him—Danner Bramblethorn as it was—leaned over
and spoke: "Four out of five, indeed, Tuck," Danner said,
exasperated. "Why, your first arrow nicked the ring. But
Barlo Stingy won't give you credit for it, mark my words."

"Oh, Old Barlo's right, you know," replied Tuck. "I hurried the shot. It was out. He called it true. But you ought
to know he's fair, Danner. You're the best shot here, and
he says so. You're too hard on him. He's not a *stingy,* he
just expects us to get it right—every time."

"Humph!" grunted Danner, looking unconvinced.

Tuck and Danner fell silent and watched Old Barlo in-
struct Tarpy, and they carefully listened to every word. It
was important that they as well as the other hardy youth
of Woody Hollow become expert with the bow. Ever since
the word had come from the far borders of Northdell that
Wolves were about—in autumn no less—many young buccen (that time of male Warrow-hood between the end of
childhood at twenty and the coming of age at thirty), in
fact most young buccen of the Boskydells, had been or
would be in training.

Even before the onset of winter, which had struck early
and hard this year, killing most of the late crops, wild
Wolves had been seen roaming in large packs up north;
and strange Men, too, were spied in the reaches across the
borders beyond the Thornwall. And it was rumored that
occasionally a Warrow or two—or even an entire family—
would mysteriously disappear; but where they went, or just
what happened to them, no one seemed to know. And
some folks said they'd heard an awful Evil was way up
north in the Wastes of Gron. Why, things hadn't been this
bad since the passing of the flaming Dragon Star with its
long, blazing tail silently cleaving the heavens, what with
the crop failures, cattle and sheep dying, and the plagues
that it had brought on. But that was five years ago and
past, and this winter and Wolves and strange happenings
was now.

                    *   *   *

And down at the One-Eyed Crow, not only was there talk of the trouble in Northdell, but also of the Big Men far north at Challerain Keep, mustering it seems for War. At the moment, holding forth to a most attentive Warrow audience was Will Longtoes, the Second-Deputy Constable of Eastdell, who, because of his dealings with the *authorities*—namely various Eastdell Mayors and the Chief Constable in Centerdell—appeared to know more than most about the strange doings abroad:

"Now I heard this from young Toby Holder who got it in Stonehill—them Holders have been trading with Stonehillers ever since the Bosky was founded, they came up there in the Weiunwood in the first place, they say—anyway, the word has come to Stonehill to gather waggons, hundreds of waggons, and send 'em up to the Keep."

Hundreds of waggons? Up to the Keep? Warrows looked at each other in puzzlement. "Whatever for, Will?" asked someone in the crowd. "What can they want with hundreds of waggons?"

"Move people south, I shouldn't wonder, out of harm's way," answered Will.

What? Move 'em south? With wild Wolves running loose and all?

Will held up his hands, and the babble died down. "Toby said rumor has it that, up to the Keep, King Aurion is gathering his Men for War. Toby said the word is that the Big Folks are going to send their Women and youngers and elders west to Wellen and south to Gûnar and Valon, and even to Pellar." As Will took a long pull from his mug of ale, many in his audience nodded at his words, for what he said seemed to fit in with what folks had heard before.

"But what about the Wolves, Will?" asked Teddy Cloverhay of Willowdell, who was up in Woody Hollow delivering a waggon load of grain. "I mean, wull, ain't the Big Folks afraid that the Wolf packs will jump their travelling parties, it being winter and all, and the packs roaming the countryside?" A general murmur of agreement came from the listening crowd, and Teddy repeated his question: "What about the Wolves?"

"Wolves there may be, Teddy," answered Will, "but Toby says the Big Folks are preparing for War, and that means they're going to be sending some kith away to safe havens, Wolves or not." Will took another pull on his ale. "Anyways, I reckon that the Wolves won't tackle a large group of travellers, the Wolf being what he is, preying on the weak and defenseless and all."

"Wull," responded Teddy, "there ain't many as is weaker than a younger, or some old gaffer, or even a Woman. Seems to me as they wouldn't send them kind of folks out west or south to fend against Wolves."

Again there was a general murmur of agreement, and Feeny Proudhand, the Budgens wheelwright, said, "Teddy is as right as rain. Folks just don't send their kin out agin Wolves; not even the Big Folks would do that. It sounds like *Word from the Beyond,* if you asks me."

Many in the crowd in the One-Eyed Crow nodded their agreement, for people in the Boskydells tend to be suspicious of any news coming to them from beyond the Spindlethorn Barrier, from Foreign Parts as it were. Thus the saying *Word from the Beyond* meant that *any* information from beyond the borders, from Outside, was highly suspect and not to be trusted until confirmed; certainly such news was not *Sevendell Certain.* In this case, the *Word from the Beyond* had in fact come from beyond the Thornwall—from Stonehill, to be exact.

"Be that as it may, Feeny," shot back Will, fixing the wheelwright with a gimlet eye, "the Holders are to be trusted, and if young Toby says he saw the Stonehillers gathering waggons to send up to the Keep, and preparing for a stream of Big Folk heading to the south, down the Post Road, then *I* for one believe him."

"He *saw* them?" asked Feeny. "Well, that's different. If Toby says he actually *saw* them; then I believe it, too." Feeny took a pull from his own mug, then said, "I suppose it's the Evil up north."

"That's what they say," spoke up Nob Haywood, a local storekeeper. "Only I talked to Toby, too, and he'd heard that the Big Folks are saying that it's Modru's doings!"

Ooohh! said some in the crowd, for Modru of Gron strode through many a legend, and he was always painted the blackest evil.

"They say he's come back to his cold iron fortress way up north," continued Nob, "though what he's doing there, well, I'm sure I don't know."

"Oi then, that explains the winter and the Wolves and everything!" exclaimed Gaffer Tom, thumping the iron ferrule of his gnarled walking stick to the floor. "The old tales say he's Master of the Cold, and Wolves do his bidding, too. Now everybody here knows it started snowing in September, even before the scything, and certainly before the apple harvest. And the snow's been on the ground ever since, with more coming all the time. And I says and everybody knows that ain't altogether natural. Besides, even before the white cold came, there appeared them Wolf packs, up Northdell way for now, but like as not they'll be near Woody Hollow soon. Oh, it's Evil Modru's doings, all right, mark my words. We all know about him and his mastery of the cold and the Wolves."

A hubbub of surprise mingled with fear rose up in the room, for with these words Gaffer Tom had reminded them all of the cradle-tales of their youth. And the Gaffer had voiced their deepest fears, for if it truly was Modru returned, then it was a dire prospect all of Mithgar faced.

"Not Wolves, Gaffer," said Bingo Peacher, a hunter of renown, sitting in a shadowed corner with his back to the wall. "Modru, he don't command wild Wolves. Nobody commands Wolves. Ar, maybe now and again there are tales of Wolves helping the Elves, but even the Elves don't *tell* 'em what to do, they *asks* them to help. Oh, Wolves is dangerous, right enough, and you've got ter give 'em wide berth, and they'll do the same for you unless they're starving—then look out. Ar, I don't doubt that Modru is behind all this cold weather, and that's what's driven decent Wolves south where their food has got to, or where they can raid some hard-working farmer's flocks, but that don't mean that Modru gives Wolves their orders. Wild Wolves is too independent and don't bow down to no one, not even Modru. Oh no, Gaffer, it ain't the Wolves that Modru commands; it's *Vulgs*!"

Vulgs? cried a few startled voices here and there, and the faces of most of the listeners turned pale at the thought of these evil creatures. Vulgs: Wolf-like in appearance, but larger; vile servants of dark forces; savage fiends of the night; unable to withstand the clear light of the Sun; evil ravers slaughtering with no purpose of their own except to slay. Grim fear washed over the crowd at the One-Eyed Crow.

"Here now!" cried Will Longtoes, sharply. "There ain't no cause to believe them old dammen's tales. They're just stories to tell youngers to get 'em to behave. Besides, even if they were true, well, you all knows that Modru and Vulgs can't face the daylight: they suffer the Ban! And Adon's Ban has held true from the end of the Second Era till now—*more than four thousand years!* So stop all this prattle about Modru comin' to get us." Will had put up his best show of confidence, but the Second-Deputy Constable of Eastdell neither looked nor sounded sure of himself, for Gaffer Tom's and Bingo's words had shaken him, too. Many was the time as a youngling he'd been told that Modru and his Vulgs would get him if he didn't mind his manners; and, too, he recalled the fearful saying: *Vulg's black bite slays at night.*

"Think what you will," replied Gaffer Tom, pointing his cane at Will, "but many an old dammen's tale grows from the root of truth. Like as not the early winter here in the Bosky has brought the Wolves, and maybe even some Vulgs, too. And like as not they are the cause of the *Disappearances.* Who's to say it *ain't* Modru's doings?"

As the Gaffer's cane thumped back to the floor for emphasis, nearly all the folks in the Crow nodded in agreement, for Gaffer Tom's words rang true.

"Well, early winter or not," replied Will, stubbornly, "I just don't think you ought'er go around scaring folks, what with your talk about a hearthtale bogeyman, or Vulgs. And as to the Wolves, we all know that the Gammer began organizing the Wolf Patrols up in Northdell, 'cause they're the first ones as is had to deal with them. And the Gammer has asked Captain Alver down to Reedyville to take over and lead the Thornwalkers. What's more, archers are being trained, and Wolf Patrols organized, and Beyonder Guards set. All I can say is Wolves and any other threat will soon fear Warrows, right enough."

The folks in the crowd murmured their endorsement of Will's last statement about old Gammer Alderbuc, past Captain of the Thornwalkers; and many in the crowd had praised Gammer's handpicked successor, Captain Alver of Reedyville; and all were confident in the abilities of the

Thornwalkers, for many of those there in the Crow had been 'Walkers themselves in their young-buccan days. And although these facts concerning the Thornwalkers were well known throughout the Boskydells, still the crowd in the One-Eyed Crow had listened to Will's words as intently as they would have were they hearing them for the first time, for Warrows like to mull things over and slowly shape their opinions.

As to the Thornwalkers, ordinarily they were but a handful of Warrows who casually patrolled the borders of the Boskydells; and, like the Constables and Postal Messengers, in times of peace they served less as Boskydell officials and more as reporters and gossips who kept the outlying Bosky folks up on the Seven Dells news. But in times of trouble—such as this time was—the force was enlarged and "Walking" began in earnest. For, although the Land was protected from Intruders by a formidable barrier of thorns—Spindlethorns—growing in the river valleys around the Land, still those who were determined enough or those who were of a sufficiently evil intent could slowly force their way through the Thornwall. Hence, the patrols and guards kept close watch on the Boskydell boundaries, "Walking the Thorns" as it were, or standing Beyonder Guard, making certain that only those Outsiders with legitimate business entered the Bosky. And so the Spindlethorn patrols, or Thornwalkers as they were called, were especially important now, what with Wolves crossing into the Land and strange Folk prowling about. Why, indeed, that was the reason Old Barlo was training a group of archers: to add to the Thornwalker ranks.

"Wull, all as I can say," replied Gaffer Tom from his customary chair in the One-Eyed Crow, "is that the 'Walkers is got a fight on their hands if we're dealing with Modru's Vulgs. Them archers had better learn to shoot true."

And shoot true they did, for not only was Old Barlo a good teacher, but Warrows, once they set their minds to it, learn quickly. Over the past six weeks, Old Barlo had had them shooting in the bright of day and in the dark of night, in calm still air and through gusting winds, through blowing dim snow and across blinding white, from far and from near, at still targets and at moving ones, on level ground and uphill and down, in open fields and in close brambly woods. And now they were learning to shoot accurately while breathless and panting after sprinting silently for a good distance. And the young buccen Warrows had learned well, for the shafts now sped true to the target, most to strike in or near the small circle. But of all of Barlo's students, two stood out: Danner was tops, with Tuck a close second.

"All right, lads, gather 'round," cried Old Barlo, as Hob Banderel, the final shooter, came puffing back from collecting his arrows. "I've got something ter say." As soon as the students were assembled around him, Old Barlo continued: "There's them as says there's strange doings up north, and them as says trouble's due. Well, I don't pretend to ken the which of it, but you all know Captain Alver asked me to train as good a group of bow-buccen as I could, and you was selected to be my first class." A low murmur broke out among the students. "Quiet, you rattlejaws!" As silence again reigned, Barlo went on: "You all know that more Thornwalkers is needed in the Wolf Patrols and for Beyonder Guard, them as can shoot straight and quick. Well, you're it!" Barlo looked around at the blank faces staring at him. "What I'm trying to say is that you're done. Finished. I can't teach you no more. You've learned all I can show you. No more school! Class is dismissed! You've all graduated!"

A great yell of gladness burst forth from the young buccen, and some threw their hats in the air while others joyously riddled the Wolf silhouette with swift-flying arrows.

"Did you hear that, Danner?" bubbled Tuck, jittering with excitement. "We're done. School's out. We're Thornwalkers—well, almost."

"Of course I heard it," gruffed Danner, "I'm not deaf, you know. All I can say is, it's about time."

"Hold it down!" shouted Old Barlo above the babble, as he took a scroll from his quiver and began untying the green ribbon bound around it. "I've got more ter say!" Slowly the hubbub died, and all eyes turned once more to the teacher. "Wag-tongues!" he snorted, but smiled. "Captain Alver has sent word," Old Barlo waved the parchment for all to see, "that Thornwalker guides are to come and take each and every one of you to your companies. You've got one more week to home, then it's off to the borders you'll go, to your 'Walker duty."

To the borders? One more week and away? A thick pall of silence blanketed all of the students, and Tuck felt as if he'd been struck hard in the pit of his stomach. *One week? Leave home? Leave Woody Hollow? Why of course, you ninnyhammer,* he thought, *you've got to leave home if you're joining the Thornwalkers.* But, well, it was just that it was so sudden: one short week. Besides, he had only thought about *becoming* a Thornwalker, and he'd not really envisioned what that meant in the end, leaving his comfortable home and all. Tuck's spirit rallied slightly as he thought, *Oh well, after all, a fellow's got to leave the nest sometime or other.* Tuck turned and looked to Danner for reassurance, but all he saw was another stricken Warrow face.

Tuck became aware that Old Barlo was calling out assignments, posting Warrows to the Eastdell First, and the Eastdell Second, and to other companies of the Thornwalker Guard; and then his name was being shouted. "Wha—what?" he asked, his head snapping up, recovering a bit from his benumbed state. "What did you say?"

"I said," growled Old Barlo, stabbing his forefinger at the parchment, "by Captain Alver's order, you and Danner and Tarpy and Hob are posted to the Eastdell Fourth. Them's the ones what are up to the north, between the Battle Downs and Northwood along the Spindle River, up to Spindle Ford. The Eastdell Fourth. Have you got that?"

Tuck nodded dumbly and edged over to Danner as Old Barlo resumed calling out assignments to the other Warrows. "The Eastdell Fourth, Danner," said Tuck. "Ford Spindle. That's on the road to Challerain Keep, King Aurion's summer throne."

"Like as not we won't be seeing any King on any kind of throne, much less the High King himself. And we won't be doing too much Wolf patrolling either, if we're stuck at the ford," grumped Danner, disappointed. "I was looking forward to feathering a couple of those brutes."

As Danner and Tuck chatted, two other Warrows made their way through the crowd and joined them: Hob Banderel and Tarpy Wiggins. Of that foursome, Danner was tallest, standing three feet seven, with Hob and Tuck one inch shorter and Tarpy but an inch over three feet. Except for their height, as with all Warrows, their most striking feature was their great, strange, sparkling eyes, tilted much the same as Elves', but of jewellike hues—Tuck's a sapphirine blue, Tarpy's and Hob's a pale emerald green, and Danner's, the third and last color of Warrow eyes, amber gold. Like Elves, too, their ears were pointed, though hidden much of the time by their hair; for, as is common among the buccen, they each had locks cropped at the shoulder, ranging in shade from Tuck's black to Hob's light ginger, with Danner and Tarpy both being chestnut-maned. Unlike their elders, they each were young-buccan slim, not yet having settled down to hearth and home and four meals a day, or, on feast days, five. (But, as the elders tell it, "Warrows are small, and small things take a heap of food to keep 'em going. Look at your birds, and mice, and look especially at shrews: they're all busy gulping down food most of the time that they're awake. So us Wee Folk need at least four meals a day just to keep a body alive!")

"Well, Tuck," said Hob, "it's the Eastdell Fourth for us all."

"Four always was my lucky number," chimed in Tarpy. "Fourth time's the charm, they say."

"No, Tarpy," put in Danner, "*third* time's the charm. Fourth time is *harm*."

"Are you sure?" asked the small Warrow, fretting. "Oh my, I hope that's not an omen."

"Don't let it bother you, Tarpy," said Tuck, aiming a frown at Danner. "It's just an old saying. I'm sure the Eastdell Fourth will be good luck to us all."

"Well, I think it will be the best Thornwalker company of them all," smiled Hob, "now that we're in it, that is."

At that moment, Old Barlo again called for quiet, interrupting the babble among the graduates. "Well, lads, you're about to shoulder an important duty. One week from now you'll be on your way, and I wish I was going with you, but I've got to stay behind to get another group ready. Besides, the 'Walkers needs them as is spry, which I ain't anymore. So it's up to you, Thornwalker Warrows, and a finer bunch I've never seen!"

A cheer broke out, and there were scattered shouts of *Hooray for Old Barlo!*

"There's just a couple of more things I've got to say," continued Old Barlo when quiet returned. "We meet in the Commons at sunrise next Wednesday, and you'll be off. Pack your knapsacks well; take those things we talked about: your bows, plenty of arrows, warm boots and dry stockings, down clothes, your Thornwalker-grey cloaks, and so on. The 'Walker guides will bring food, and ponies for them as needs 'em for the faraway trips." Old Barlo paused, looking over his charges, and before their very eyes he seemed to grow older and sadder. "Take this week to say goodbye to your friends and family, and any damman you may have about," he said quietly, "for like as not it'll be next spring or later before you'll be to home again."

Once more Tuck felt as if he'd been kicked in the stomach. *Next spring? Why, he wouldn't even be home for Yule, or Year's End, or . . . or . . .*

"Cheer up, lads!" Old Barlo said heartily, " 'cause now it's time for your graduation present. We're off to the One-Eyed Crow, where I'll set up a round of ale for each and every one!"

Again there was a cheer, and this time all the young buccen shouted *Hooray for Old Barlo!* three times. And they tramped away, singing rowdy verses of *The Jolly Warrow* as they marched down from Hollow End toward the One-Eyed Crow.

The week was one of poignant sadness for Tuck; he spent the time, as many of his comrades did, saying goodbye. It was a goodbye not only to his friends and acquaintances, but also to the familiar places he'd frequented throughout his young life in and around Woody Hollow: the Dingle-rill, now rimed with ice; Bringo's Stable, with its frisky ponies; Dossey's Orchard, where many a stray apple had come into Tuck's possession; Catchet's Market, full of the smells of cheese and bread and open boxes of fruit and hickory-cured bacon hanging from overhead beams; Gorbury's mill, grumbling with the groan of axles and the burr of wooden-toothed gears and the heavy grind of slow-turning water-driven millstones; the Rillbridge, under which was some of the best jiggle-bait fishing in the Boskydells; Sugarcreek Falls, where Tuck's cousins from Eastpoint had taught him to swim; and the High Hill on the Westway Trace, from which all of Woody Hollow could be seen. These places, and more, Tuck visited, moving quietly through the snow to stop at each and fill his being with its essence, and then after saying goodbye he would sadly trudge on.

But the place to which Tuck turned the most was The Root, his home, with its warm, cozy burrow rooms, the smell of his mother's cooking, and all the familiar objects that it seemed he'd never really looked at before. And to his mother's surprise he actually straightened his cubby; and without bidding from his father, he split a cord or two of wood, laying in a good supply outside the burrow kitchen door before he was to be off. Each evening he sat before the fireplace, having a pipe with his sire, Burt, a stonecutter and mason, while his dam, Tulip, sewed. And they quietly talked about the days that had been, and the days that were, and the days that were yet to come.

Tuck spent some time with Merrilee Holt, maiden Warrow, dammsel of Bringo Holt, the farrier, and his wife, Bessie, who lived four burrows to the east. Merrilee and Tuck had chummed together since childhood, even though she *was* four years younger. Yet in these last days, Tuck saw for the first time just how black her hair was, and how blue her eyes, and how gracefully she moved; and he marvelled, for it seemed to him that he should have *noticed* these things before. Why, back when he had first begun Thornwalker archery training, and she had insisted that he teach her, too, he should have seen these things about her—but he hadn't. Instead, they'd laughed at her struggle to pull an arrow to the fullest. But even when she became skilled, using Tuck's old stripling bow, still at the time he'd seen only her accuracy and not her grace. And why was it only in this last week that he realized that she alone really understood him?

"You know that I'll not be here for your age-name birthday," Tuck said on the last wintery forenoon as they tramped through the snow on the Commons, trudging toward the Rillbridge. "I'm disappointed that I'll miss your party when you officially become a young damman."

"I'll miss you, too, Tuck," answered Merrilee, sadly.

"Well, be that as it may," said Tuck, "here, I've a present for you. Early it is, yet likely I'll still be at the Spindle Ford when you pass from your maiden years." Tuck handed her a small packet, and inside was a gilded comb.

"Oh Tuck, what a wonderful gift," beamed Merrilee. "Why, I'll think of you every day—every time I use it." Carefully Merrilee put the gift away in a large coat pocket, saving the paper and ribbon, too. They both stopped and leaned over the rail of the Rillbridge, listening to the churn of the millrace and watching the bubbles of air darting under the ice, seeking escape but being carried along by the fast-flowing stream.

"What are you thinking, Tuck?" asked Merrilee, as the bubbles swirled by below.

"Oh, just that some people go through life like those bubbles down there, caught in a rush of events that push them thither and yon, never able to break free to choose what they would. I was also thinking that many of us are blind until we've but a short time left to see," he answered, then looked up and saw that Merrilee's eyes had misted over, but she smiled at him.

The week had fled swiftly, and now it had come to the last hours of the last day. Once more Tuck found himself with his parents before the fire at The Root.

"Merrilee and I went down to the Rillsteps today," Tuck said, blowing a smoke ring toward the flames, watching it rend as the hot draft caught it and whirled it upward. "Thought I'd give them one last look before leaving. Danner was there, and we talked about the times we'd played King of the Rillrock. He always used to win, you know. No one could dislodge him from that center stone, Rillrock. He'd just knock us kersplash right into the Dingle-rill, shouting, 'King of the Rillrock! King of the Rillrock! Danner Bramblethorn is the King of the Rillrock!'"

"His sire was like that, too," said Tulip, looking up from her stitchery. "We used to think that he was *glued* to that rock. Many a time your own dad was tumbled into the Rill by Hanlo Bramblethorn."

"Hmph," grunted Burt Underbank, pausing in his whittling, inspecting the edge of his knife, "that's right. He did. Fought like a cornered badger, he did. Against all comers and all odds. Harrump! Took us all down a peg or two. Seemed to think that rock was his own personal property

instead of part of the east public footway across the Dingle-
rill. From what I hear, Danner's even better at it than
Hanlo was."

"What makes Danner that way, Dad?" asked Tuck. "I
mean, it seems he's always got to be the best at what he
takes up. Why is he that way?"

"Like sire, like bucco, I always say, Tuck," answered
Burt.

"No, Dad, I mean, what makes people the way they are?
What makes me," Tuck paused, then found the word he
was searching for, "easygoing, while Danner is, uh . . ."
Tuck couldn't seem to come up with the appropriate word.

"Pugnacious," said Tuck's mother.

"More like quarrelsome," said his father, "if he's anything like Hanlo was."

"Well, all I know is that he always wants to be King of
the Rillrock at anything he does," said Tuck, puffing another smoke ring at the hearth.

"I think people are born to their nature," said Mrs.
Underbank.

"I think it's the way they're raised," said Tuck's sire.

They sat and gazed at the fire for moments as the flames
twined and writhed and danced, casting flickering shadows
throughout the parlor of The Root. Burt threw another log
on the pyre. They watched as sparks flew up the chimney,
and the flaming wood popped and cracked as it blazed up.
Then the flames settled back, and once more the quiet was
broken only by the faint creak of Tuck's rocker, the snick
and slice of Burt's knife against the whittling stick, and the
pop and whisper of Tulip's needle, puncturing cloth and
pulling bright floss through taut linen stretched drumhead
tight within the embroidery hoop.

"I saw two more strangers today," said Burt after a moment. "More Thornwalkers, I think. Went riding down to
the stable, each leading a string of ponies. That's seven, no,
eight so far." Burt stopped his whittling and leaned forward
to tap the dottle from his pipe against the hearth. Then he
settled back, stuffing the warm clay into a pocket of his
unbuttoned vest. "You all set, Tuck?" he asked for perhaps
the tenth time that day and the fiftieth time that week.
"Tomorrow's the day."

"Yes. I'm ready," answered Tuck, quietly.

The sound of Tulip's sewing stopped, and she sat in her chair by the soft light of the warm yellow lamp and looked down toward the needlework in her lap. But she stitched not, for she could no longer see what to do through her quiet tears.

Dawn found grey-cloaked Tuck wandering through a milling, chattering crowd in the Woody Hollow Commons. It seemed as if the entire population of the town had turned out in spite of the cold to see the Thornwalkers off. A lot of folks had come up from Budgens, too, for a few of their buccoes had been trained in Old Barlo's class and would be off to Thornwalker duties this day, also.

Tarpy and Hob had managed to find Tuck, and now they were looking for Danner. But before they could find him, Geront Gabben, the Woody Hollow Mayor, standing up on the Commons' platform, rang the fire gong for quiet. As soon as he got it, he sallied forth into a speech of indeterminate length.

"My friends, on this most auspicious of occasions," he began, and such a beginning should have tipped off most of the Warrows that Geront was in a talkative mood. But perhaps because this was a farewell parting for the Thornwalker young buccen, the Warrow citizenry only thought that this was a "fare-you-well" speech, and Warrows do love speeches—short ones, that is. And so, some in the crowd cried out, *Tell it to 'em!* and *Hear! Hear!* and Mayor Gabben, encouraged, pressed on. Tuck listened intently for a while, but finally his attention began to stray. It seemed that the Mayor couldn't decide whether this was a sad and solemn occasion or a happy, ribbon-cutting ceremony as he swung back and forth between the two and droned on and on. But when folks in the crowd began to call out, *What's your point, Geront?* and *Let's get on with it!* and other not so subtle notices of restlessness—to the extent that the Mayor began to feel somewhat chivvied— Geront, puffing and fuming, rambled his speech down to an unsatisfactory ending; and at last he introduced Old Barlo, which brought on such a loud and prolonged cheer of relief that it left Geront with the grand delusion that in some mysterious fashion his speech had been a smashing success after all.

Old Barlo mounted the platform and got right to the matter at hand. "Folks, it's time these here brave lads," *Yay*!—he was interrupted by a lengthy cheer—"time these brave lads were on their way. There's no call to delay them further, 'cause the Thornwalkers (*Hooray*!), the Thornwalkers has got crossings to guard (*Rah*!), borders to protect (*Rah*!), and Wolves to repel." *Hip! Hip! Hoorah!* Barlo waited for the cheering to subside, and, casting a gimlet eye at Geront, he continued. "And they can't do them duties if they've got ter stand around here listening to speech making and cheering crowds!" *Rah! Rah! Old Barlo!* Then Barlo pointed to the first Warrow in a line of eight strangers standing quietly to one side, all dressed in Thornwalker-grey cloaks. "Them as is assigned to the Eastdell First, there's your guide." The first Warrow raised his hand. Barlo then pointed to the second grey-cloaked 'Walker. "Eastdell Second," Barlo called out, and that Warrow held up a hand. "Eastdell Third," came the next cry, as Barlo continued down the line.

When Eastdell Fourth was called, Old Barlo pointed to an emerald-eyed Warrow with fair hair who was holding a string of seven ponies—five riding and two pack ponies, their coats heavy with winter shag. Tuck, Hob, and Tarpy made their way to the guide, and from the far side of the Commons came Danner. With a deep bow, Tuck introduced himself and named his companions.

"Patrel Rushlock at your service," spoke the guide with an infectious grin and a sweeping bow of his own. Patrel was small—even shorter than Tarpy, who, for the first time ever, felt as if he simply *towered* over another young buccan, though he was but one inch different. Yet, somehow—perhaps because of his bearing—Patrel seemed neither diminished nor overshadowed by the four taller, Woody Hollow buccen.

"Let's fix your knapsacks to this pack pony," said Patrel, getting right to the matter at hand, "then each of you pick out one of the riding mounts for your own. The one with the white face is mine. But heed this: keep your bows and quivers. We may need them before we come to Ford Spindle," he said ominously, momentarily frowning, but then his face brightened and the wide grin returned. "If you have a flute or pipe, or any other tune maker, keep it, too,

and we'll have a ditty or three to cheer us along the way."
Tuck then saw that a six-stringed lute was strapped across
Patrel's shoulders to hang at his back.

Shortly, they, as well as the Thornwalkers of the other
Eastdell companies, were ready to leave. All turned to say
that one last goodbye to young dammen and maidens, sires
and dams, brothers and sisters, grandams and granthers,
aunts and uncles and other relatives, friends and neighbors,
and additional assorted buccen and dammen who had come
to see them off and who were collected in knots and rings
and clumps, Warrows with stricken and worried and crying
faces, and cheery and smiling ones, and proud and stern
and grim looks, also.

"Harrump! Take care of yourself, lad," said Burt to his
only bucco, "and watch out for the wild Wolves. Make 'em
fear the sight of an Underbank—harrump!—or any other
Warrow, for that matter."

"I will, Dad," answered Tuck, and quickly he embraced
his sire, then turned to his dam.

"Wear your warm clothes, keep your feet dry," said
Tulip as she clasped Tuck to her. "Eat and, and . . ." but
she could say no more through her tears. She held on
tightly and softly cried until Burt gently disengaged her
embrace from Tuck, and Tuck quickly swung astride the
dappled grey he had chosen as his mount.

A friend gave him a pouch of Downdell leaf, "The best
there is"; another friend handed him a new white-clay pipe,
"Smoke it well"; while a third gave him a small tin box
with flint and steel and shavings of touchwood, "Keep your
tinder dry."

Merrilee Holt, who had shyly hung back, squared her
shoulders, stepped forward, and held an elden silver locket
up to Tuck. "Would you wear my—favor?" the Warrow
maiden asked. Speechless with surprise, Tuck nodded
dumbly, and he leaned down for Merrilee to slip it over
his head. As she did so, she whispered in his ear, "Take
care, my buccaran," and kissed him on the lips, to the raucous whoops of some of the striplings nearby. But Merrilee
simply stepped back to the crowd, her eyes glitter-bright
with tears.

"Hey, Tucker," spoke up his cousin Willy, stepping to
the pony's side and holding up a new, blank diary and a

pencil, "keep a journal, hey? Then when you get back you can read to us of all your adventures, hey?"

"All right, Willy," said Tuck, stuffing the gift into his jerkin along with the leaf and pipe and tinderbox. "Thanks. I'll try." Then Tuck smiled, raised his hand, waved to all those who had come to see him off, looked again at his parents with their arms about one another, and last of all looked at Merrilee, who brightly smiled back. At a nod from Patrel, Tuck and his companions, who also were finished with their farewells, urged the ponies forward. They wove through the waving crowd and out of the Commons, riding toward the North Trace up through the Dinglewood, aiming for Spindle Ford.

As the ponies trotted away from the heart of Woody Hollow, the five riders—Tuck, Danner, Hob, Tarpy, and Patrel—could hear Woody Hollow Mayor Geront Gabben leading the townfolk in a rousing cheer: *Hip, hip, hooray! Hip, hip, hooray! Hip, hip, hooray!* And someone began ringing the fire gong.

The Sun crept upward in the morning sky as they rode farther and farther from Woody Hollow. The sounds of the cheering crowd and clanging gong slowly faded away to disappear altogether in the snow-blanketed quiet of the Dinglewood, and all became silent except for the creak of leather saddles and harness, the muted sounds of pony hooves stepping in the snow, and an occasional muffled snuffle from one, or perhaps four, of the riders.

CHAPTER 2

Retreat to Rooks' Roost

The bright light of the mounting Sun fell aslant 'cross the white, glistening snow. From the glitter, tiny evanescent shards of sparkling color winged to the eye, as if reflected from diminutive fragments of shattered jewels nestled among the fallen flakes. The cold crystalline air was calm, and in all the wide Dinglewood nothing seemed to be astir except for a jostling flock of noisy ravens squabbling over a meager breakfast up among the barren trees on Hawthorn Hill. Down below, wending slowly along the North Trace were five Warrows astride five ponies, leading two more of the animals laden with gear.

Patrel, riding in the lead, turned and looked over his shoulder at the glum faces of the four young buccen behind. For the past six miles no one had said even a single word; and for a group of Warrows to remain silent for two solid hours, well, that's no mean feat. Deciding that this dolorous mood had lasted overlong, Patrel shucked his mittens and unslung his lute; he plucked a few strings, strummed a chord or so, and tweaked a tuning key or two this way and that.

"Hey," said Tarpy, his utterance breaking the muteness to fall upon startled ears, "give us a happy tune; we need it." And Tarpy clucked his pony forward till he rode beside Patrel. At Patrel's nod, Tarpy called to the others: "Hoy, you grumlings, clap your heels to those ponies and gather 'round."

Tuck, riding last and leading the pack ponies, was jerked out of his gloomy thoughts by Tarpy's call. Clicking his tongue, he urged the grey forward. "Come on, Danner," he said as he drew even with the young buccan, "let's go."

"What for?" asked Danner, mumpishly. "He's just going

to twang that stringed gourd of his, and I don't feel at all like a song."

"Perhaps that's just exactly what we do need," answered Tuck. "Even if it's just a song, still we'll cheer up a bit, I'll wager. And right now I could do with a bit of cheering up, and so could you—so could we all."

"Oh, all right," grumped Danner, agreeing more to keep Tuck quiet than for any other reason, and he kicked up his pony. In moments, Tuck, Danner, Hob, and Tarpy were all riding grouped around Patrel. "All right, lads," grinned the small Thornwalker, looking aflank, "it's time you learned what the Thornwalkers are all about." Patrel plucked a chord or two, checking a last time the tune of the lute, and then his fingers began dancing over the strings as he sang a lively, simple, Warrowish tune.

> *We are Thornwalkers,*
>   *Thornwalkers are we;*
> *We walk around the miles of bounds*
>   *To keep the Bosky free*
> *Of Wolves and Vulgs and great wild dogs*
>   *And other enemy;*
> *We are Thornwalkers,*
>   *Thornwalkers are we.*
>
> *We are Thornwalkers,*
>   *Thornwalkers are we;*
> *We've trod the Thorns from night to morn*
>   *Through Bosky history.*
> *Our ears can hear, and never fear,*
>   *For keenly do we see;*
> *We are Thornwalkers,*
>   *Thornwalkers are we.*

Patrel began the third verse, and this time Tarpy and Hob joined in, thinly singing the refrain: *We are Thornwalkers, Thornwalkers are we.*

> *We are Thornwalkers,*
>   *Thornwalkers are we;*
> *The Seven Dells, well I can tell,*
>   *All of them we do see,*

> *To north and east and south and west,*
>   *Wherever they may be;*
> *We are Thornwalkers,*
>   *Thornwalkers are we.*

"Come on, you sickly sparrows," urged Patrel, pausing, "you can chirp louder than that." And with a wide smile, he struck up the tune again and sang another verse. This time four other voices picked up the lilt of the rustic song, and even though they sang *tum-tiddle-tum* in the places where they could not guess the words, still their timber strengthened.

> *We are Thornwalkers,*
>   *Thornwalkers are we;*
> *We walk along the Spindlethorn*
>   *Wherever it may be,*
> *Through fens and fields and woods and hills*
>   *'Long rivers bound for sea;*
> *We are Thornwalkers,*
>   *Thornwalkers are we.*

On the last verse, all the Warrows were grinning broadly and singing lustily, and to Tuck's surprise Danner's voice was the heartiest of all.

> *We are Thornwalkers,*
>   *Thornwalkers are we;*
> *And finer scads of sturdy lads*
>   *No one will ever see;*
> *We guard and ward and work so hard*
>   *To keep the Bosky free;*
> *We are Thornwalkers,*
>   *Thornwalkers are we—Yo ho!*
> *We are Thornwalkers,*
>   *Thornwalkers are we—Hey!*

And with this last *Hey*! Patrel planged his lute with a loud discordant *twang*! and all the Warrows broke into guffawing laughs. The somber mood was gone.

"So that's what we Thornwalkers do, hey?" asked Hob,

merrily. "Guarding and warding. It sounds as if we'll be busy."

"Oh no," grumped Danner, "not if we're stuck at Spindle Ford. I expect it means we'll spend a lot of time sitting around waiting for something to happen, but it never will."

"Well that suits me just fine," chimed up Tarpy. "I'd rather sit around a warm campfire, sharing a pipe or song or tale, than to be out in the cold looking for Wolves and Vulgs and great wild dogs."

"And the other enemy," added Tuck. "Don't forget the *other enemy* the song spoke of—*Wolves and Vulgs and great wild dogs and other enemy.*" Tuck turned to Patrel, "What does the song mean—*other enemy?* Where did the song come from in the first place? I've never heard it before, and I think I'd better write it down in my new diary— my cousin Willy will really like it. Besides, a song that good deserves to be spread about, and, well, it seems to me as if we should have heard it before."

"Oh . . . ahem . . . well," stammered Patrel, somewhat flustered and flushed, fumbling embarrassedly as he refastened the strap to sling the lute across his back once more. "I'm pleased you liked it. And you haven't heard it before because it's new. I mean, well, I made it up myself as I rode down to collect you four."

"Made it up yourself?" burst out Tarpy. "I say! I thought only minstrels and harpers did that sort of thing. You aren't a minstrel now, are you?"

"My Aunt Oot used to make up songs now and again," interrupted Hob, "mostly in the kitchen. Songs about food and cooking. Rather pleasant. Nothing jolly like yours, though."

"Tell us about the words, Patrel," said Tuck. "I mean, tell us how you came up with your song."

"There's not that much to say," answered Patrel. "You all know that the Thornwalkers help to protect the Bosky— a big responsibility that is, too, for it's a wide Land. Seven Dells: North, South, East, West, Center, Up, and Down. Ringed 'round by the Great Spindlethorn Barrier. Bounded by two rivers, the Wenden and Spindle, and by the Northwood and the Updunes."

"What is this," grumbled Danner, "a geography lesson?"

"No," laughed Patrel. "Well, perhaps a touch of both geography and history."

"Come on, Danner, let Patrel speak," said Tarpy, his Warrowish nature astir to listen to things he already knew. "Besides, I've always wanted to learn where harpers get their tunes."

"Argh!" growled Danner, but he fell silent.

"But, Tarpy, I don't know where harpers get their tunes," protested Patrel. "I only know where mine come from. It's very simple. The mission of the Thornwalkers is to patrol the Dells and the Spindlethorn Barrier, to guard against unsavory Beyonders coming into the Bosky for ill purposes, and to repel Wolves, or great wild dogs."

"What about the Vulgs?" asked Hob.

"Yar! And the *other enemy*," snorted Danner, sarcastically. "I'll give you an *other enemy*!" He leaned over toward Hob and made a face. "Boo!"

"Danner!" burst out Tuck, exasperated. "If you don't wish to listen, then ride on ahead."

"Just who do you think you're ordering about?" bristled Danner. "I—"

"Hold it!" shouted Patrel, his own fiery temper rising. Then, as he got control of himself: "Let's not get to squabbling among ourselves." He turned to Danner. "Just what point are you trying to make?"

"Well," grouched Danner, "just what *other enemy* could be a threat to the Bosky?"

"How about Vulgs?" shot back Hob.

"And Rūcks, Hlōks, and Ogrus," chimed in Tarpy.

"Ghûls," added Tuck.

Danner looked disgusted. "You left out Colddrakes! And Modru! And bloody Gyphon himself!" he snapped. "And it seems you've also forgotten High Adon's Ban! And that's why there isn't any *other enemy*: the Ban!"

Amid the burst of babble that followed, Patrel's clear voice cut through, bidding silence, and when it reigned: "Danner's got a good point there. Now hush and let him speak."

Danner looked somewhat flustered as all Warrow eyes fastened in silence upon him, but he was not speechless: "Well, you all know what the old tales say." Danner's voice took on the rhythm of a chant, as if he were reciting a well-learned school lesson. "When Gyphon challenged Adon for control of the Spheres, War broke out in the three Planes: Upper, Middle, and Lower. Here in Mithgar the struggle was mighty, for Modru, Gyphon's servant, was supreme and his Horde was nearly without number. Yet the Grand Alliance opposed them, not realizing that the outcome here in the midworld would tip the balance of power in the Upper and Lower Planes, too.

"And so it was that the Grand Alliance of Men, Elves, Dwarves, Utruni, Wizards, and Warrows fought on the side of Adon in the Great War against Gyphon, Modru, Vûlks, Ghûls, Hlōks, Ogrus, Rūcks, Vulgs . . . and some Dragons."

"Here, in the Middle Plane, by an unexpected stroke the Alliance won; Modru lost. And so it was that Adon won and Gyphon lost on all three Planes. As forfeit, Adon banished from the light of day, on pain of death, all the Folk who aided Gyphon in this Great War. From those of the Dragons who opposed Him, Adon took their fire, and now they are Cold-drakes and also suffer the Ban.

"And it is said that Adon's Ban *shall rule for as long as night follows day, and day follows night.*

"He banished Gyphon, too, 'beyond the Spheres,' though no one I've asked knows where that is.

"Modru himself fled through the night from the Wastes of Gron to the far frozen land beyond. The tales tell that he lives there because in the winter the nights are long, very long, and the Sun, his bane, is feeble for six months each year. Yet in the summer Modru must hide away, for then the days are long and the Sun rides high, and the Withering Death is ever at hand."

Danner then paused, looking at the others, and his voice took on a pedantic tone. "So you see, *that's* why the Bosky has little to fear from *other enemy*: His Ban would slay them!" Danner looked at the other Warrows, challenge in his eye, but no one there gainsaid him, and the ponies wended slowly northward.

"Ah, Danner, you are right," said Patrel after a bit. "Yet remember this: Adon's Covenant kills only if they get caught in the Sun, but not at night. And other Thornwalkers have reported fleeting glimpses from afar of great black beasts, like Wolves, but dire, running through the dark."

"Vulgs," breathed Hob.

"Perhaps," answered Patrel. "If so, then they must lie up in the cracks and splits of the land when the Sun is on high, and thus the Ban strikes them not. As for Rūcks, Hlōks, and Ogrus, or Vûlks and Ghûls, or Cold-drakes, I think none are here in the Bosky, though they, too, could escape the Sun in the same manner. Yet we are a far distance from the mountains they haunt: the Grimwall, the Rigga, and the Gronfangs."

"But Vulgs run fast and far, they say," said Tarpy, "and perhaps they've run all the way to the Boskydells."

"Yes, but what has driven them to come to the Bosky now?" asked Tuck. "It's been a long span since the end of the Great War. Why have they come at this time? And to the Bosky?"

"If!" exclaimed Danner, compelling their attention. "If it's Vulgs and not Wolves. Who's to say it wasn't Wolves, or even wild dogs, seen from afar by the Thornwalkers, instead of Vulgs? Look, the Ban has held good for two whole Eras. Why should Vulgs show up now?"

"Ah! There's the rub," responded Tuck. "Why, indeed, now?"

The ponies plodded forward, and the Warrows rode on in silence for a bit, pondering the puzzle. "The only thing that comes to mind," continued Tuck, "is that it is said Gyphon, just as He was vanishing, swore a bitter vow to Adon, claiming that He would be back."

" *'Even now,'* " Danner quoted, his voice sepulchral, " *'Even now I have set into motion events you cannot stop. I shall return! I shall conquer! I shall rule!'* That's what the old tales say Gyphon last spat at Adon, then He was gone, beyond the Spheres, banished. But He was wrong, for He hasn't returned. In four thousand years He hasn't returned. That's how long they say it has been. And for those same four thousand years, no Rūck, no Vûlk, ah, fie! Nothing! Nothing suffering the Ban has threatened the Bosky! Ever!"

Again silence descended upon them, and each rode immersed in his own thoughts. Finally, Patrel spoke: "Maybe so, Danner. Maybe you are right. But they say Vulgs now push through the Spindlethorns. And no one says why."

*   *   *

Northward they wended throughout the day, at times riding, at other times walking and leading the ponies, sometimes stopping to eat, or to take care of other needs, or to feed grain to the mounts, or to break through the ice on a woodland stream to refresh their canteens and to give the ponies a drink.

The large, thickset trees of the Dinglewood bordered close upon the trail, their grey bark and stark branches casting a somber pall upon the North Trace.

A pall, too, seemed to have dropped over the Warrows, and little else was said that day as they pressed on through the silence of the barren forest. The Sun slowly crossed the cold sky, and its rays did little to warm the travellers. When the orb sank below the western horizon, darkness found the five young buccen huddled around a campfire on the far edge of the Dinglewood, some thirty miles north of Woody Hollow.

They drew lots to see in what order the watch would be kept, with Tuck pulling the mid-of-night turn. As all prepared to bed down, except Hob, who had the first watch, Patrel said, "Tomorrow night we all sleep in a hayloft—Arlo Huggs' hayloft. I stopped at his place on the way to Woody Hollow. He has a farm along Two Fords Road, about twenty-five miles north of here. Arlo said he'd be glad to put us up in his loft, and his wife, Willa, said she would feed us a hot meal, too." This last brought drowsy approval from all but Hob, who merely smiled as he threw another limb on the fire and began his tour.

It was midwatch when Tuck was awakened by a prod from Danner. "It's your turn, Tuck," said Danner, gruffly.

Tuck threw some branches on the fire and gathered more wood from the pile to have at hand to ward away the cold. Danner was still sitting on a log near the blaze, glowering mumpishly at the flames.

"Get some sleep, Danner," sighed Tuck. "Perhaps you'll not be so grumpy if you get enough rest."

"What do you mean, grumpy?" flared Danner, glaring at Tuck.

"You've got to admit, you were somewhat of a grouch today," answered Tuck, distressed, wondering how this conversation had gotten off on the wrong foot.

"Look, Tuck," shot back Danner, "my philosophy is this: I'm like a mirror—I only give back what I get."

They sat without speaking a moment, as the fire popped and cracked. "Well, Danner, I think you ought to consider this: you either can be like a mirror or like a window; but remember, only the window lets light in." Tuck then stood and began his rounds, and Danner took to his bedroll, a thoughtful look on his face.

After a turn around the camp, Tuck came back to the log, and by the moonlight and firelight he began recording in his new diary the day's events in terse sentences or cryptic notes, except for Patrel's song, which he wrote out in full. He would jot down a few words, then tour the perimeter, returning to write some more. And that is how he passed his watch, writing in his journal, as the Moon slid westward to be hidden by clouds moving to the east. It was a diary he planned to keep up throughout the next few months—the record of his travels.

The next morning dawned to falling snow. After a light breakfast of dried venison and bread, and grain for the ponies, the five broke camp and headed once more to the north. A breeze blew from the west, carrying eddying flakes aslant across their path, and they rode with their cloaks wrapped tightly around them and their hoods up. Through the falling snow they went, and their mode of travel was much the same as the previous day's, only now they trekked 'cross open land, having left the Dinglewood behind. The North Trace continued to carry them toward Two Fords Road, but the route was becoming harder to follow as the thickening snow obscured the path. Hence, slowed by the storm, it was not until midafternoon that they finally struck the main artery toward Spindle Ford.

"I sure am looking forward to that hot meal and hayloft you spoke of last night," said Tarpy to Patrel as the Warrows slogged through the snow, now calf-deep, leading the ponies and giving the animals a respite.

"Ha! Me too!" answered Patrel. "I hope Willa won't mind if we are a bit late, and keeps the meal hot. I judge we'll get to Arlo's well after dark."

"Blasted storm," carped Danner, then fell silent as they trudged on.

*   *   *

Patrel's words proved to be accurate, for it was three hours into the night when they came at last to the edge of Arlo's farm. The wind had risen, and a mournful wail could be heard as it keened through a nearby stand of timber. With their backs to the gust, the five Warrows turned down the lane leading to the Huggs' stone field house.

"Hold!" said Patrel above the wind moan, his voice tight with apprehension. "Something is wrong."

"What?" asked Hob. "What's the matter?"

"There's no light in the house." Patrel reached for his bow. "Ready your weapons."

"What?" asked Danner, unbelieving. "Bows?" Then he saw Patrel was serious and, shaking his head, followed suit.

"Maybe they've just gone to bed," spoke up Tarpy, but took up his bow just the same.

"No. There should be a light. They were expecting us," answered Patrel. "Take care. Let's go."

Arrows nocked, they proceeded toward the dark house, on foot, leading the ponies. Off to the side, the barn loomed like some great dark beast. Now they could hear an ominous banging above the moan, as from a loose shutter blowing in the wind. Closer they came, and now they could see that the windows of the house seemed open, for curtains were blowing in and out. Tuck's heart was pounding, and his lungs were heaving in ragged gasps. He felt as if he could not get a firm grip on his bow. It took all of his courage to force one foot ahead of the other. Motioning Tuck and Danner to the left and Tarpy and Hob to the right, Patrel stepped toward the porch. As he put his foot on the top step the door burst open with a *Blam*!

Tuck's heart gave a great lurch, thudding in his mouth, and he realized that he had a deadly aim centered on the doorway's gaping blackness. The bow was fully drawn, and Tuck could feel the fletching of the arrow against his right cheek as he held steady, ready to release. And for the life of him, Tuck could not recall taking the pull. *And nothing came through the doorway.* Just as abruptly, *Wham*! the door slammed to. *Whack*! It whipped open again and *Blam*! shut once more as the wind swirled again.

"Lor!" said Tarpy, relaxing his pull a bit, as they all did, "I thought—"

"Hsst!" Patrel cut off Tarpy's words and motioned them to go forth.

Tuck and Danner went around to the left of the house and Tarpy and Hob to the right, while Patrel stepped through the front door. As they went along the side of the house, Tuck saw that the curtains were indeed whipping and flapping in and out of the windows, for the glass was shattered. *Bang! Blam!* They could hear the front door slamming to and fro. On they went, coming to the kitchen door, splintered from its hinges and hanging awry. Into the house they went just as Patrel, already in the kitchen, managed to light a lamp. *Whack! Slam!*

The glow revealed a shambles: overturned chairs, a shattered table, broken crockery, an upside-down bench, smashed glass—ruin. Snow blew in through the broken door and past torn curtains across the sills of the shattered windows. Tarpy and Hob at last entered and looked about as the wind moaned and gnawed at the destruction. "We took a quick check of the barn," said Hob. "Empty. No livestock. It's gone." *Thwack! Whack!*

"What's happened here?" asked Tarpy, as Danner lit another lamp.

"I don't know, yet," answered Patrel. *Blam! Whack!* "Hob, will you latch that infernal front door? Tarpy, pull the shutters to. Although the glass is broken, they will keep most of the snow out. Danner, use your light to help Tarpy. Tuck, add the light of another lamp or candle to mine. We'll see what we can make of this."

As Tuck found one more lamp and lit it, Patrel propped the kitchen door in its jamb, for the most part sealing out the wind and snow. They then opened what turned out to be the pantry door; Patrel took a quick look inside. "Nothing. No one," he said to Tuck. "Let's look—"

"Ai-oi!" came a call from another room, and Patrel and Tuck rushed to find Danner kneeling with his lamp, Tarpy and Hob peering over his shoulder in the fluttering light.

"What is it?" asked Tuck, and then he saw—blood. A lot of blood. And in the center, a huge paw print.

"Wolves," hissed Tarpy.

"No," said Danner, grimly. "Vulgs!" And off in the distance, mingled with the moan of the wind, came a single, horrid, prolonged, savage wail.

* * *

"The Vulgs smashed through the windows and doors," said Patrel when they all had gathered again in the kitchen following a thorough search. "See, the broken glass flew inward, as if the evil creatures hurtled through."

"Yar, and the kitchen door," put in Danner, gesturing at the panel propped in the opening. "Remember, it was broken inward, too."

"What about Farmer Arlo and his wife? Where are they?" asked Tarpy, his eyes wide and glittering in the lamplight. "We've looked everywhere."

"It's another *Disappearance,*" whispered Hob, and Tuck felt his heart plummet.

"No, Hob, say instead a Vulg slaughter," said Patrel, his voice grim as he peered at the stricken faces of the others, his own a sickly, ashen grey. "This time it's not just a mysterious disappearance. This time all the evidence cries out wanton murder, Vulg butchery."

"If it's murder," asked Tarpy, tears brimming, one hand with a sweeping gesture indicating the vacant shambles they stood amid, "then where is . . . where are . . ."

"The bodies," spoke Danner, harshly, his jaw clenched in anger. "What did the bloody Vulgs do with the bodies?"

"I don't know," answered Patrel. "All the other disappearances I've heard about left no traces of any kind. Just this one. It's as if . . ."

"As if Farmer Arlo put up a fight, and the others didn't," put in Tuck. "The others must've had no warning. Arlo managed to bolt the doors, but the Vulgs prevailed."

"Arlo and Willa are probably out there somewhere," gritted Danner, "covered by the snow." The sound of Tarpy's soft weeping was lost in the moan of the wind, and Tuck bleakly peered without seeing through the kitchen window shutters out into the dark night.

"Well," asked Hob, after a long moment, "what do we do? Search for them? Though I don't see how we can find them in the snow in the night."

"Let's go after the Vulgs," demanded Danner, raising up his bow, his knuckles white with anger.

"No," said Patrel. "Neither search nor hunt. We've already looked over the immediate grounds with no results, and the Vulgs are beyond our vengeance by now. No, here we stay and rest, and tomorrow we press on to Spindle Ford, warning the countryside as we go."

"Faugh!" snorted Danner, raising his bow. "I say let's get the brutes!"

"Danner," Patrel's voice had an angry bite to it, "until we get to Spindle Ford, you are in my command. I'll not have you out chasing around in a blizzard at night looking for Vulgs long gone. I say we stay here, and what I say goes."

"Oh no," said Tarpy, peering around desperately. "Not here. I can't stay here. Not in this wrack. Not when there's blood on the floor in there. Not in this house."

"How 'bout the hayloft?" asked Hob, throwing an arm around Tarpy's shoulders and cocking an eye at Patrel, who nodded. "Yes, we'll stay there," continued Hob. "Besides, we've got to get the ponies into shelter and fed and watered." He took up a lamp. "Come on. Let's see to the ponies."

And so they all went, Hob in the lead with Tarpy shivering beside him, Danner and Patrel glaring at one another, and Tuck bringing up the rear.

They kept the same order of watch as they had the previous night, and though Tuck didn't see how he was going to get any sleep, it seemed as if he had just lain down when Danner shook him awake. "Time to get up," said Danner. "Bring your blanket; it's cold." He climbed back down to the floor of the barn.

Tuck struggled down the ladder from the loft, blanket over one shoulder. As he stepped from the bottom rung, he saw that Danner was refilling one of the lamps with oil and trimming the wick with his knife. "Need any help?" Tuck yawned. At Danner's negative shake of his head, Tuck asked, "Any sound of Vulgs?"

"No," replied Danner. "The wind died about an hour ago, and the snow's stopped, too. And there's been no sound of Vulgs, Wolves, or anything else from out there. Blast! I've pinked my thumb." Danner sucked on his thumb and spat, while Tuck finished trimming the lamp wick. "We should be out there, you know," grumbled Danner between sucks, "hunting Vulgs."

"Come now, Danner," replied Tuck, lighting the new

lamp and extinguishing the old, "you heard Patrel. We can't go blundering around at night in the dark looking for Vulgs."

"Well let me leave you with this thought, Tuck," shot back Danner. "Night is the only time you *can* hunt those slavering brutes." And Danner disappeared up the ladder into the hayloft.

Why, thought Tuck, *he's right! The Ban! They won't be about in the daytime.*

Later, during his watch, Tuck scribbled in his diary as the last entry for the day: *How true will be our aim in the dark?*

Morning discovered the Warrows back on Two Fords Road, travelling north toward the Spindle Ford. At first light they had taken one last look about the Huggs' farm, but they found no sign of Arlo or Willa. Patrel had then tacked a note to the front door warning any who came to the stone field house about the Vulgs. Then the young buccen had mounted up and ridden away.

Two miles north, they came to another farm and spoke to the crofter there. Dread filled the eyes of the family upon hearing of the Vulgs and the fate of the Huggs. The tenant, Harlan Broxeley, sent his sons upon ponies to warn the nearby steading holders, with Patrel's request to "pass it on." Patrel and the others were loath to leave the family alone, but Mr. Broxeley said, "Don't you fret none. Now that we are warned, me and my buccoes can hold 'em off till dayrise. Then the Sun'll stop 'em. Besides, we ain't the only family near about, and you five can't protect us all. You've got to get this word to the Thornwalkers so as they can do something about it." With that and a warm breakfast, the five young buccen went on northward, bearing the news toward Spindle Ford and the Eastdell Fourth.

All day they rode north, stopping three more times to start the word spreading. Dusk found them eight miles south of the ford. "Let us press on and get to the ford tonight," said Patrel, grimly. "I'd rather we were not camped out in the open." So onward they went, as darkness fell and the Moon rose to paint black shadows streaming away into the night.

Through the enshadowed land they rode. A mile passed,

and then another. Of a sudden, Tuck's pony snorted and shied, tossing its head. Tuck looked sharply into the blackness but saw nothing, and the other ponies seemed calm enough. Onward they rode, Tuck's own senses now alert. "What's that up ahead?" asked Tuck, pointing to a tall spire looming up through the darkness and into the moonlight.

"It's the Rooks' Roost," answered Patrel, on Tuck's left, "a great pile of stone that happens to be where Two Fords Road and the Upland Way come together. It means, when we get there, we'll be just five miles from the Thornwalker camp at the ford."

Toward the junction they rode. The Upland Way was a main route running aslant across the Boskydells, joining the Land of Rian in the north to that of Wellen in the west. Two Fords Road ran north and south—up from the Bosky village of Rood and north to the Spindle River. It was called Two Fords Road because it crossed the Dingle-rill at the West Ford and passed into Rian at the Spindle Ford.

As they came closer to the Rooks' Roost, by the bright moonlight Tuck could see that it was higher than he first had thought, rising perhaps fifty feet into the air, a great jumble of rocks and boulders placed there in ancient times by an unknown hand to stand ominously in the night. As the ponies plodded onward, Tuck felt as if this looming pile somehow boded doom.

Without warning, again the grey pony shied, scudding to the left. "Hey! Steady," commanded Tuck, looking to the others, but now their ponies, too, were skittish. *What's happening?* he asked himself, and then he gasped in shocked fear: off to the east a great black shape slunk through the shadows, keeping pace with the Warrows. "Vulg!" he cried to the others, his voice tight with dread. "In the field to our right! Just beyond arrow range!"

"Stay close!" shouted Patrel. "Keep riding!"

Danner, in the rear with the frightened pack ponies trailing him, grimly called out, "Two more behind us! No, three!"

"Left! Look left!" came Tarpy's startled voice. "Lor! Another one!"

The Vulgs trotted without effort. Their evil yellow eyes gleamed like hot coals when the Moon caught them just so, and slavering red tongues lolled over wicked fangs set in crushing jaws. Hideous power bunched and rippled under coarse black fur as the beasts slid through the shadows.

"Cor! Let's ride for it!" shouted Hob, clapping his heels to his pony. But Patrel reached over and grabbed the pony's bit strap.

"Whoa! Hold it! Don't panic. Stick together. When I give the word we ride for the Rooks' Roost. As long as they stay their distance, we'll just keep trotting for our goal. We've got less than a quarter mile to go." Patrel nocked an arrow, but as if that somehow were a signal, with blurring speed the Vulgs closed in. "Fly!" cried Patrel. "To the Rooks' Roost! Ride for your lives!"

With shouts and cries, the young buccen all clapped their heels to the ponies' flanks, but the steeds needed no urging, for they had taken full flight. Yet the hideous great Vulgs closed the distance with horrid quickness. Tuck wanted to cry out in fear; instead, he leaned forward and urged the grey onward. Toward the rock pike they raced, yet faster ran the Vulgs. Tuck could hear Danner shouting a challenge of some sort as the ground flew by. The Vulgs drew abreast, and Tuck could hear guttural snarling and see the gleam of fangs. They were now less than a furlong from the Rooks' Roost, closing the distance rapidly. Tuck thought of winging an arrow at the beasts but knew that his aim would be unsteady from the back of a running pony: *The arrow as strays might well'er been throwed away,* he seemed to hear Old Barlo's voice cry, and so he held his shot. Yet a Vulg closed in and slashed at his pony's hind-quarters; Tuck clubbed at it with his bow, and the brute shied back as the pony plunged on.

Tuck looked ahead just in time to see Hob's steed go tumbling down, screaming, hamstrung by the Vulgs, but Hob was thrown free. Tuck tried to turn his pony but was past the fallen Warrow ere he could do so. He heard Danner yell and looked back to see Hob on his feet with a Vulg slashing at him just as Danner rode by and reached out an arm. Hob caught at it and swung up and onto the pony behind the other buccan. Yet the Vulg snarled in rage and leapt at the twain, and Hob screamed horribly as the cruel fangs rent the Warrow's side and leg, though still he kicked out and the Vulg fell back. Danner's pony bolted forward at an even faster clip, in spite of bearing double, and temporarily gained a pace on the Vulg. Yet the slavering creature once more closed the gap, and with a great snarl and jaws wide it leapt at the two. *Hsss, thwock!* An arrow sprang full from the beast's left eye, and with a sodden thud it fell dead to the earth! Tarpy had gained the Rooks' Roost and had let fly with the shot of his life!

Tuck thundered up and leapt off to follow right behind Patrel as they scrambled onto the lower tier of stone to join Tarpy, and he turned to see Danner and Hob come at last. On, too, came the dire Vulgs, but Patrel let fly and struck one a glancing blow on a foreleg, and its yipping howl caused the others to sheer off the attack.

As their mount skidded to a stop, Danner and Hob jumped off. But with a moan, Hob collapsed unconscious to the snow, a dark stain spreading from under him. Down leapt the others to aid, but Danner hoisted Hob across his shoulders. "Climb!" he snarled, and started forward.

Tarpy ran and snatched up Danner's bow and quiver. "What about the ponies?"

With his free hand, Danner shoved Tarpy toward the rocks. "Climb, you fool, they're after Waerlings, not horselings!" But Danner was only partly right, for as the buccen scrambled up the rocks of the Rooks' Roost, the frightened ponies scaddled off into the night. Yet two ran right into the jaws of the evil Vulgs, and their shrill death cries sounded like the screams of dammen. And the blood of the Warrows ran chill.

It took all the energy of the other four to lift Hob's dead weight up to the top of the Rooks' Roost, but at last they were there. The Vulgs loped around the base of the jumble but did not attempt to climb it. And the Moon shone brightly down upon the land.

"He's still alive," said Tuck, raising his head from Hob's breast. "We've got to do something to stop this bleeding." But in his mind whispered words from the old hearthtale: *Vulg's black bite slays at night.*

"Make a tourniquet for his leg," said Patrel, "and press a bandage to his side." And so Tuck and Tarpy tended to Hob as Danner stared in hatred down at the Vulgs.

"Look at them," he spat, "just sitting there now, as if

they were hatching a vile plan, or waiting for something to happen, three evil brutes."

"Three!" exclaimed Patrel. "There should be four! Where's—" They heard the click of claws scrabbling up the stone on the opposite side. " 'Ware!" shouted Patrel and rushed over in time to see a great Vulg leaping up through the shadowed stones toward the crest. As Patrel drew an arrow full to the head, he heard Danner cry, "Here come the others!" for the remaining three beasts were streaking for the mound.

With malevolence in its yellow eyes, the lone Vulg swarmed up the stone. Patrel loosed the bolt to hiss through the air, but with a twist the Vulg leapt sideways, and the shaft but struck it in the loose fur above the shoulders. Howling and snapping at the quarrel, the Vulg fell scrambling down the side of the pile, while the other three again veered off the attack, bounding down from the stones and beyond arrow range.

Patrel and Danner watched as the four Vulgs collected together. The fifth one—the one slain by Tarpy's shaft through the eye—lay like a black blot in the snow. So, too, did the three slain ponies: Hob's steed, a pack pony, and one other mount—Tarpy's. Of the other four steeds, there was no sign. "We're in a tight fix here," said Patrel, watching the Vulgs. "I just hope our arrows last till dawn." Danner merely grunted.

Tuck and Tarpy had returned to Hob, laying their bows aside. "Maybe this will staunch the flow," fretted Tuck as he tourniqueted Hob's leg. "We need something to press against his side."

"Here, take my jerkin," said Tarpy, peeling off his quilted jacket and stripping his shirt. "Cor! It's cold," he shivered, and quickly redonned his wrap.

Tuck folded the jerkin and pressed it to the wound in Hob's side. The young buccan moaned and opened his eyes; pain crossed his features. "Hullo, Tuck," he gritted, "I've made a mess of it, haven't I?"

"Oh no, Hob," answered Tuck, smiling. "Sure, you've got a bit of a scratch, but that's not what I'd call making a mess of it."

"Where are the Vulgs? Did we get any?" Hob tried to

struggle up, his breath hissing through painclenched teeth. "Is everyone all right?"

"Coo now, Hob," Tuck gently pressed him back. "Stay down, lad. Everyone's fine. Tarpy, here, feathered one of the brutes—the one that scratched you. That's one Vulg that'll never bother anyone again."

"Tarpy?" The small Warrow knelt by Hob's side, and the wounded buccan squeezed Tarpy's hand. "Fine shot, Tarpy. I thought I saw one of 'em drop just before I faded out." Another wash of pain moved across Hob's features, and but for his ragged breathing he was silent a long moment. "Where are we? And where are the Vulgs?"

"We're on top of the Rooks' Roost," answered Tarpy, "and a great heavy thing you were to lug up here, too. All the rest of us had to climb while you, bucco, got a free ride."

"Sorry to be such a lazybones. But the Vulgs, what about the Vulgs?" whispered Hob, his voice sinking low.

"Ah, Hob, don't you worry your head about them," answered Tuck. "They're below where they'll stay." Hob closed his eyes and made no response.

Tuck pressed his cheek to Hob's forehead. "He's burning up, Tarpy, as if fevered."

"Or poisoned," added Tarpy.

Slowly the night crept by. One hour and then another passed with no movement either by Vulg or Warrow. In an effort to save Hob's leg, every so often Tuck would loosen the tourniquet to let circulation into the limb. Yet there seemed to be a fearful loss of blood whenever this was done, and so Tuck was both loath to do it and loath not to. He was just preparing to loosen the tourniquet again when Danner cried, "Here they come! All four!"

Tuck snatched up his bow and joined the other three to look down and see the Vulgs streaking toward the mound. Up they leapt, toward the line of archers.

"Take this, night-spawn!" grated Danner. *Thuunn*! went his bowstring as he loosed the arrow. *Hsss*! It sped toward the lead Vulg scrabbling up the rocks. *Thock*! The shaft drove full into the creature's breast, piercing straight to the heart. The beast fell dead in a black heap. Howling in fear and frustration, the others fled downward.

Tuck watched until they again were back out on the land
away from the Roost. Then he turned and cried in dismay,
"Hob!" The wounded Warrow was on his feet, swaying,
trying to answer the call to arms. Tuck sprang toward him,
but ere he could reach the buccan, Hob fell with a sodden
thud. "Oh Lor, his wounds are gushing," sobbed Tuck,
tightening the tourniquet and pressing Tarpy's jerkin back
to Hob's side.

"Tuck, it's so cold . . . so cold," said Hob, his teeth
chattering. Tuck shed his own cloak and spread it over the
buccan, but it seemed to do little good.

The silver Moon sailed across the silent heavens, and the
bright stars glimmered in the cold sky. Three Vulgs stalked
around the base of the dark spire while the Warrows atop
watched grimly. And there was nothing that they could do
to staunch the wounds of evil Vulg bite, and Hob's life
slowly leaked away among the cold, dark rocks. In less than
an hour he was dead.

Just before the dawn came, the Moon set, and the three
Vulgs fled in the waning night. At day's first light, a dark
reeking vapor coiled up from the bodies of the two slain
Vulgs as Adon's Ban struck even the corpses of the creatures, and two withered dry husks were left behind, to
crumble at the wind's first touch.

Atop the Rooks' Roost, Tuck and Danner, Patrel and
Tarpy all wept as they gathered stones for Hob's cairn.
They washed him with snow and combed his hair and composed his hands across his breast. His Thornwalker cloak
was drawn about him, and his bow was retrieved and laid
beside him. And then they slowly and carefully built the
cairn over him. And when it was done, in a clear voice that
rose into the sky, Patrel sang this verse.

> *The Shadow Tide doth run*
> *O'er boundless Darkling Sea*
> *'Neath skies of Silver Suns*
> *That beckon endlessly.*

> *Reach out thy ship's wings wide,*
> *Ride on the gentle wind,*

Sail with the Shadow Tide
To shoreless Time's own end.

Alone thou sailed away
Upon the Darkling Sea,
Yet there shall come a day
When I will sail with thee.

All then wept long for the young buccan with whom they would never Walk the Thorns. But at length the tears faded to silence, and weary, drawn faces gazed into the bleak morning. Yet a fell look of dark resolve slowly came over Tuck's features, and he wiped away a final tear and knelt upon one knee and placed his hand upon the cairn and said unto the grey, unyielding stone, "Hob, by all that I am, the Evil that did this shall answer to your memory." And so swore them all.

At last the Warrows stood and took up their bows. With a last sweeping look around, their eyes briefly lingering upon the barrow, they climbed down from the Rooks' Roost—known ever after as Hob's Cairn—and, shouldering the backpacks retrieved from one of the slain ponies, on foot they set off northward for Spindle Ford.

CHAPTER 3

Spindle Ford

Just before noon, cold and weary, Tuck, Danner, Tarpy, and Patrel trudged into the Thornwalker encampment set in the fringes of the Spindlethorn Barrier at Spindle Ford. *Hai roi! Patrel! Ho! Where's your ponies? Welcome back!* and other cries were called out as the four came among the tents and lean-tos and made for the headquarters building, one of only two permanent structures there, made of hewn, notched logs, stone, and sod. The other building was a goodly sized storehouse. The welcoming cries quickly faded as the realization that something was amiss came to those encamped, for Patrel's smile was absent, and the four strode grimly onward without returning as much as a nod. *Hey! Something's afoot!* A substantial following was tagging along by the time Patrel and the others stepped through the rough-cut door and into the headquarters.

The interior was but a single room that somehow seemed too large for the building that contained it. The floor was made of thick, sawn planks, and a stone fireplace stood at the far wall. There, two Warrows dressed in Thornwalker grey relaxed in wicker chairs while having a pipe together. One looked to be in his prime buccan years; the other was old, a granther. Both glanced up from their deep discussion as the four entered. Recognition flooded the face of the younger of the two, and he leapt to his feet. "Patrel! Welcome back. These are the recruits, I take it. Ho, but wait, I see only three. Where's the fourth?"

"Dead. Vulg slain." Patrel's voice was flat and bitter.

"What? Vulg?" The old buccan snapped, thumping his cane to the floor and rising. "Did I hear you say Vulg? Are you certain?"

"Yes sir," answered Patrel. "We were set upon by five at the Rooks' Roost, where our companion, Hob Banderel,

42

was slain. But that's not all: it looks as if the brutes got Arlo Huggs and his wife, Willa, too."

At Patrel's words, the elder buccan's face fell, and he sank back into his chair. His voice was grim: "Then it is true: Vulgs roam the Bosky. What fell news. I had hoped it were not so."

Silence reigned for a moment, then the elder looked up and gestured with a gnarled hand. "Patrel, you and your three friends come and sit by the fire. Tell us your tale, for it is important. Have you eaten? And introduce us. This here is Captain Darby, Chief of the Eastdell Fourth, and I'm Gammer Alderbuc, from up Northdell way." Hasty introductions of Tuck, Danner, and Tarpy were made.

As the three young buccen bowed, they saw before them Captain Darby—square-built, slightly shorter than Tuck, with hair nearly as black, though his eyes were a dark blue. He had about him an air of command. Yet, as arresting as Captain Darby's appearance was, Gammer Alderbuc's was even more so, and the eyes of the trio were irresistibly drawn to him. Old he was, a granther, yet his gaze was steady and clear, peering from pale amber eyes 'neath shaggy white brows that matched his hair. He could not have been any taller than Patrel's diminutive three feet, but he was not bent with age, and though he bore a cane, he seemed hale. This was the Warrow who had first taken action to muster the Thornwalkers and to organize the Wolf Patrols when Northdell crofters began losing sheep and other livestock because the unnatural winter cold had driven Wolves into the Boskydells. At the time, he had been the honorary First Captain of the Thornwalkers, but he had stepped aside, declaring that it was a task for a younger buccan, Captain Alver of Reedyville in Downdell. And so it was that Captain Alver assumed command of all the Boskydell Thornwalkers.

At the bidding of Captain Darby, the four young buccen shed their backpacks, cloaks, and down jackets and drew near the fire in wicker chairs. Patrel began telling their tale in short, terse sentences, starting with the events at the Huggs' farmstead and moving on to the attack of the Vulgs at the Rooks' Roost, his voice hesitating only when he told of Hob's death. Tears brimmed in Tuck's eyes.

The tale done, Patrel's voice fell quiet, and no one spoke

for a moment while all reflected upon what had been said. At last Captain Darby broke the silence. "When you four came through the door," his eyes touched each of them, "I thought, *Ah, here is Patrel and the recruits,* but I was wrong, for you are not raw recruits. Instead, you are now four blooded warriors, Thornwalkers all, who have met a foul enemy and given good account of yourselves—at high cost, to be sure, yet it is a price that sometimes must be paid whenever emissaries of fear are challenged. I am proud of you all."

"Hear, hear," said the Gammer, thumping the floor with his cane.

At that moment, hot food, sent for earlier by Captain Darby, arrived. Adjourning to the table, the four gratefully dug in. It was the first meal they'd had since the previous afternoon, their parck pony, the one with the provisions, having fled from the Vulgs the night before. Little was said during the meal, for Captain Darby bade them to eat while the food was hot. But when at last they pushed away from the table and resumed their places near the fire, filling clay pipes with some of Tuck's Downdell leaf, the talk turned again to the Vulgs.

"Ye've done the right thing, raising the alarm through the countryside," said the Gammer. "Now the brutes'll meet prepared Warrows. And that ought to put a stop to the disappearances."

"On the morrow I'll dispatch heralds to all nearby Thornwalker companies," said Captain Darby, "and start the word spreading. It won't be long till the whole Bosky knows."

"Uh . . . Captain Darby," said Tuck, "would it be possible to send a patrol out to look for the ponies that survived? My grey seems to have gotten away, and one pack pony, with Patrel's lute strapped to it. Two others fled, also."

"My chestnut," said Danner.

"And my piebald," added Patrel.

Tarpy said nothing, for, full of good food and drawn up to a warm fire, exhausted by the all-night battle with the Vulgs, he had fallen asleep, his pipe slipping from his lax fingers to drop to the plank floor.

"You must be weary," said Captain Darby, his eyes soft upon the sleeping young buccan. "Patrel, take your comrades to the tents of your squad. Get some rest. Tomorrow We will begin search patrols into the countryside, looking not only for your steeds, but also for places where Vulgs may hole up during the day. Ah, but if we only had Dwarves as allies, then could we root out the underground haunts of these beasts. Tomorrow we also shall begin night patrols, Vulg hunts, and Thornwalks to keep more of the beasts out." Captain Darby stood and gestured for the four young buccen to seek out their tents and sleep.

They awakened Tarpy and donned their jackets and cloaks, gathering up their packs and bows. "Wait," said the Gammer, "I've something to say." The granther Warrow got to his feet. "When I organized the Wolf Patrols, I thought that it was only them raiding flocks that we had to deal with—and perhaps in the beginning that was true. And we've done a fair job at that: most Wolves in Northdell have come to fear the sight of Warrows. Oh, we know that it's only the strange winter that has driven them to kill livestock—they are only trying to survive—but it's been touch and go for many a Northdeller, and I expect more Wolves to push through the Barrier ere this winter ends, for it's bound to get worse. Before you know it, the other Dells will likely feel the bite of Wolf jaws; though that may not be, for the Wolves have made themselves scarce since the Patrols started and now seem to leave the livestock alone—in which case we'll leave them be, too.

"But, none of us thought that we'd be dealing with Vulgs. Oh, to be sure, there's been talk of Vulgs in the Bosky for two or three weeks, but it's just been tavern talk heretofore, rumors. Ah, but now you four have proven it to be more than just ale tales: it's fact, not fancy.

"Thanks to you, the Bosky will be warned, and the four Warrow kindred will ever be in your debt, for the preservation of the Warrow Folk is what the Thornwalkers are all about. Look around you. This very building symbolizes the four kindred. The logs represent the trees where dwell the Quiren Warrows, my folk, and I dare say ancestors to Tarpy and Patrel; the stone represents the field houses of the Paren Warrows, perhaps kith to Danner, here, by the

look of him; the wicker comes from the fens of the Othen
Warrows, like Captain Alver down in Reedyville; and the
sod represents the burrows of the Siven Warrows, Captain
Darby's folk, and it seems Tuck's, too. But whether Bosky
folk live in tree flets, stone field houses, fen stilt houses, or
burrows, none are safe where the Vulg walks, for Vulgs
slink in secret through the night.

"But now, the secret is out. We know what we are dealing with, though we don't know why they've come to the
Bosky. Be that as it may, I for one thank you for all the
Warrow kindred." And the Gammer bowed to the four and
clasped each one's hand.

When the Gammer took Tuck's hand, the young buccan
said, "Sir, please do not forget, our slain comrade, Hob
Banderel, for he was there, too."

"I haven't, and I won't," said the Gammer, solemnly.

"Thank you, eld buccan," said Tarpy, last to shake
hands.

"Eld buccan?" laughed the Gammer. "Nay, bucco, it's
been seventeen years since my eighty-fifth birthday. Next I
know, you'll be shaving another twenty-five years off o'
that, calling me buccan. Nay, the clock doesn't run in that
direction, and it's seventeen years a granther am I. But I
thank you just the same, Tarpy Wiggins, for you almost
make me feel spry." Amid a round of quiet smiles, the
Gammer herded the four out of the building.

As Patrel led the weary Warrows to the tents of his
squad, they could hear Thornwalkers calling farewell to
Gammer Alderbuc as the granther prepared to ride back
to Northdell, to set out on his journey back to the town of
Northdune along the Upland Way. They could also hear
Captain Darby giving orders to summon the squad leaders
to the headquarters building to tell them of the Vulgs in
the Bosky and to lay plans.

Late in the night, Tuck woke up from deep slumber, still
exhausted. Yet he stayed awake long enough to update his
diary by the flickering yellow light of a lantern. Then he
fell back into troubled, dream-filled sleep—but what he
dreamt, he did not recall.

*   *   *

"Time for duty, slugabeds." Patrel shook Tuck awake. "It's midmorn. Stir your bones, break your fast, meet your squadmates." Danner and Tarpy sat up, rubbing sleep from their eyes. "I've got our orders. We stand the early nightwatch at the ford—sundown to mid of night."

With Danner grumbling and Tuck and Tarpy yawning great gaping yawns, Patrel led them to a common wash-trough where they broke through the thin layer of ice to splash frigid water on their faces. "Brrr!" shivered Tarpy. "Surely there's a warmer way to get clean."

"Oh yes," answered Patrel, pointing to one of the tents, white wisps of steam leaking here and there from seams. "There is the laundry and bathing tent. Our squad gets to use it on Tuesdays."

"Tuesdays?" asked Danner. "Is that all? I mean, just once a week?"

"Yes," laughed Patrel. "But by the time you've chopped the wood for the heating fire, hauled water from the spring for the tubs, and done all the other work needed to get a bath and do your laundry, then once a week will seem often enough for that privilege."

"What other chores will we have?" asked Tuck, rubbing his face on the common towel and passing it on to Danner, who looked at it with some dismay before using it, too.

"Well, each squad is fairly self-sufficient," answered Patrel. "At times, on rotation, each of us will cook for the other members of our squad, and sometimes for Captain Darby, too, though we all pitch in every day to clean the pots and pans. And occasionally we'll help lay up supplies in the storehouse. Everyone cuts firewood, not only for the squad's needs, but for headquarters, too." Patrel continued to name the other chores they would perform, and it soon became clear that each Warrow was expected to care for his own needs, in the main, but that there were several jobs shared by all.

Patrel's squad consisted of twenty-two young buccen, including Tuck, Danner, and Tarpy, who were introduced at the breakfast campfire. The three were accorded smiles and nods and a friendly wave or two. Little was said as they ate, and Tuck's eyes were drawn to the Great Spindlethorn Barrier looming near. Dense it was; even birds found it difficult to live deep within its embrace. Befanged it was, atangle with great spiked thorns, long and sharp and iron-hard, living stilettoes. High it was, rearing up thirty, forty, and in some places fifty feet above the river valleys from which it sprang. Wide it was, reaching across broad river vales, no less than a mile anywhere, and in places greater than ten. And long it was, stretching completely around the Boskydells, from the Northwood down the Spindle, and from the Updunes down the Wenden, until the two rivers joined one another; but after their joining, no farther south did the 'Thorn grow. It was said that only the soil of the Bosky in these two river valleys would nourish the Barrier. Yet the Warrows had managed to cultivate a long stretch of it, reaching from the Northwood to the Updunes, completing the Thornring. And so, why it did not grow across the rest of the Land and push all else aside remained a mystery, though the grandams said, *It's Adon's will,* while the granthers said, *It's the soil,* and neither knew the which of it for certain.

Here at Spindle Ford, as well as at the one bridge and at the other fords on the roads into the Boskydells, Warrows had worked long and hard to make ways through the Barrier, ways large enough for commerce, for waggons and horses and ponies and travellers. Oh, not to say that the Barrier couldn't be penetrated without travelling one of these Warrow-made ways, for one could push through the wild Spindlethorn. It just took patience and determination and skill to make it through, for one had to be maze wise to find a way, usually taking days to wriggle and slip and crawl the random, fanged labyrinth from one side to the other. And never did one penetrate without taking a share of wounds. No, even though Warrows seemed skilled at it, and legend said that Dwarves were even better, still ways through the Barrier must needs be made for travel and commerce.

But the work was arduous, for the Spindlethorn itself was hard—so hard that at times tools were made of its wood, such as arrow points and poniards, fashioned directly from the thorns. And the wood burned only with great difficulty and would not sustain a blaze. Yet again and again, over many years, Warrows cut and sawed and chopped and dug, finally forming ways through the Barrier. And as if the Spindlethorn itself somehow could sense the commerce, the ways stayed open on the well-used routes; but on those where travel was infrequent, the 'Thorn grew slowly to refill the Warrow-made gap. Some had, in fact, been allowed to grow shut. But here at Spindle Ford, the way had remained open, looking to all like a dark, thorn-walled tunnel, for the Great Barrier was thickly interlaced overhead.

All these thoughts and more scampered through Tuck's mind as he took breakfast and gazed at the Barrier looming at hand. But his reflections were broken as he took on a share of the after-breakfast cleanup chores. Then Patrel spoke to the others of the events at the Huggs' farm and the fatal attack of the Vulgs at the Rooks' Roost. And when Patrel came to the end of the account, Tuck noted that he and Danner, Tarpy, and Patrel, were being eyed with a high respect akin to awe.

Patrel assigned one of the squad members, Arbin Digg—a slightly rotund brown-haired blue-eyed young buccan from Downyville—to show Tuck, Danner, and Tarpy where things were around the camp, and especially to show them Spindle Ford.

"Ar, so you actually fought with Vulgs, and killed some, too," said Arbin as they strode toward the gaping, tunnel-like hole arching away into the Spindlethorn Barrier toward the Spindle River and the ford. "Good show. Gilly, over in the third squad, he thought he might've seen one about two or three weeks ago, but he wasn't certain. Here now, let me ask you, are they the great brutes we've all heard about?"

"Nearly as big as a pony," answered Tarpy, "though who'd want to ride one, I can't say."

"Asking a Vulg for a ride would be like begging a Dragon to warm your house in the winter," snorted Danner. "He'd warm it, all right—right down to the very ashes."

"Are you saying that the only way you'd get a ride from a Vulg is on the inside?" Arbin asked.

"Perhaps, Arbin, perhaps," responded Danner, "though I don't know what they ordinarily eat. The ones we met seemed to kill just for the joy of slaughter."

"Wull then, I don't believe I'll ask a Vulg for a ride," said Arbin, "or a Dragon to warm my house, either." He led them into the Barrier.

Although the day outside was bright, the light sifting through the entangled Spindlethorn to the roadway fell dim unto the eye, and the sounds of the Warrow encampment faded away and were lost. Only the muffled footsteps sounded within, and Tuck had visions of walking in a dagger-walled cave.

"They say in the summer when the leaves are asprout that torches are needed to light the way through, just as if it were night," said Arbin, looking at the tangled thorn-weave overhead. He had shown them the brands set in rows at the entrance—wooden stakes, with oil-soaked cloth layered over one end, to be used as torches for wayfarers to light their way through at night. "In autumn, when the leaves fall, they make a roof in places. Snow, too, can pile up and make solid ceilings overhead here and there. But sooner or later, leaves or snow, it works its way through, and the road must be cleared at times."

On they walked, through the wan light, a mile, then two. Ordinarily they would have ridden ponies to their posts, but first-timer Thornwalkers always were taken afoot, to get the "feel" of the passage. At one place, Arbin pointed out sections of a large movable barricade, now set to the side, made of Spindlethorn. "There's one of the barriers. I suppose we'll be putting it in place one of these days, and start warding it, now that there seems to be trouble Beyond, Outside. It's one of several Thornwalls that we can put up, though only two, one on each side of the ford, are actually in place now." Arbin pointed ahead. "Ah, look, the end is in sight."

Ahead they could see an archway of brightness, where the daylight shone at the end of the Spindlethorn tunnel. Shortly they came to the Beyonder Guard barrier, and with shouts of greetings all were welcomed by ten Warrows warding there. At roadside, a string of ponies stood, munching grain from nosebags. Arbin explained to the guards that they'd come to see the river and beckoned the three to follow him, slipping through the thorns of the barricade where it was slightly ajar. "This here is the aft-guard. Over there is the fore-guard, where there's another wall like this one, just on the other side of the river, just inside the tunnel," he said, as he led Tuck, Danner, and Tarpy out blinking and watery-eyed into the daylight.

All told, two and a half miles they had walked, and had come at last to the edge of the river, the shallows of Ford Spindle. Wide it was, and ice-covered, although here and there, bath upstream and down, dark pools swirled as the river rushed and bubbled over and around upthrust rock, the churn keeping the water ice-free.

Across the ford they could see the mouth of the tunnel as it continued on through the 'Thorns growing on that side, where the Barrier reached another two miles before the Realm of Rian began.

Out onto the ice Arbin led them, to stand at river's center. They looked up and down the frozen length to where it curved away beyond seeing, a white ribbon wending between two looming, fifty-foot high, miles-wide walls of thorn. Overhead slashed a bright blue ribbon of sky, impaled upon the long spikes, tracing the course of the waterway.

"It's a wonder, ain't it?" asked Arbin, pointing both ways at once, his arms flung wide. "Kind o' gives me the shivers." Tuck had to agree, for a more formidable defense he had yet to see. "Come on, buccoes," said Arbin, "I'll show you the fore-guard."

On they went, over the ford to just inside the tunnel, where they came to another barrier. Ten more of the squad stood at this post, the barricade shut, though a small crawlway twisted through, with a barrier set to drop and plug it. Ponies stood near.

"Who's up the road?" Arbin asked one of the warders.

"Willy," came the reply.

Arbin turned to the three. "The Beyonder Guard always has a point buccan, one with sharp eyes, good hearing, and a swift pony, out at the far edge of the Spindlethorns, out where the Bosky ends and Rian begins. If someone approaches, then he'll come pelting back here ahead of 'em to warn us. If it looks like trouble, and if there is time, then we'll open the wall and in he'll gallop and we'll slam shut the barricade behind him. But if they're right on his heels, then through the crawlway he'll scoot and we'll drop the thornplug to stopper it. O' course, the aft-guard will be signalled so that they can prepare, too.

"If it's a fight, then we climb up on these stands and shoot down at them, though we've never had to do that yet. Meanwhile, the aft-guard will send a fast rider back to warn the camp and to bring reinforcements. If by some chance the foe breaks through here, then there's the aft-barrier on the other side of the ford where we'll get to. Beyond that is another one, and finally the Deep Plug back at the campsite. And the Deep Plug will cork up this tunnel till Gyphon, Himself, comes back."

At the mention of Gyphon's name, Tuck felt a deep foreboding, and a cold shudder ran up his spine as if from an icy wind blowing. But Tuck said nothing of this dark portent, and soon they turned and walked back the way they had come.

That night, Tuck, Danner, and Tarpy were assigned with seven others to the barrier on the near side of the ford. A fire was built out beyond the open barricade, out where it would cast light upon anyone coming across the shallows, and the buccen alternately took turns standing guard and warming by the fire. On Tuck's turns to warm himself, he jotted notes in his diary by the firelight.

At mid of night, the watch was changed, and Patrel's squad rode back to the campsite, Tuck, Danner, Tarpy, and Patrel himself riding double with other Warrows of the squad.

The next morning, Tuck's grey pony and Danner's chestnut were found by a patrol from the fifth squad, but as of yet there was no sign of Patrel's piebald or the pack pony.

Tuck, Danner, and Tarpy had spent the morning studying, memorizing a section of a map; and at midday the squad Walked the Thorns in that area, going some five miles to the north by pony before returning, searching diligently but vainly for splits and cracks in the land where Vulgs might lie up during the time the Sun was on high. They kept their eyes out for Wolves, too, but saw none. And they inspected the Barrier for breaks, but of course there were none.

Again at night they stood Beyonder Guard at the ford, but nothing of note occurred.

For six more days the routine did not vary, except Tarpy was called upon to cook for the squad. As usual, the food was jovially vilified by all, except, since it was Tarpy's first go at cooking, the jokes were a bit more gentle than would be the case were he a cooking veteran.

Patrel's piebald pony came wandering alone into the camp on the following day, seeming no worse for the wear. As chance would have it, on this day the fourth squad, Patrel's, was to begin Wolf Patrol, roving wide across the countryside and looking for sign of Wolf, and now Vulg, too. The trio of Danner, Tuck, and Tarpy were pleased, for they had studied hard and the features of the maps were firmly implanted in their memories, hence they were to be permitted to join the wide-ranging search. But Tuck was to be disappointed, for he was to be left behind. He had forgotten that he was the cook for the day, and his duty was to prepare a hot meal for the squad's return at dusk.

All day Tuck jittered about nervously, fretting about Danner and Tarpy and Patrel and all of his other squadmates, wondering if they were safe and if they had seen any Wolves or Vulg sign or had found any Vulg lairs. And the day dragged by on leaden feet. At last it was dusk, and Tuck had the meal hot and waiting, but still they had not yet returned, though other squads had.

An hour passed, then another, and Tuck worried about the food and felt anger that they hadn't come to eat it when it was first ready. But then he thought how foolish it was to get upset over a meal when someone could be hurt or a fight with Vulgs could be raging. But most of all he fretted and paced and stirred and took the cauldron off the cooking irons only to put it back on when it had cooled a bit.

Finally they came, plodding wearily into camp. Tarpy was first. He slid off the back of his new white pony and tiredly removed the saddle, blanket, and harness and slapped the steed on the rump, sending it scudding into the rope pen to the awaiting hay. The others, too, came stringing in to do likewise.

"We found the pack pony," Tarpy said to Tuck as he dished up a hot, steaming, thick stew into Tarpy's mess kit. "Dead. Vulg slashed. Patrel's lute smashed beyond repair. We searched for hours but found no Vulg dens. Ah, me, but I'm tired."

*　　　*　　　*

Another ten days passed, and each day the young buccen saddled up and scoured the countryside, tracking down rumors of Vulg sightings or starting at farms where Vulgs had slaughtered livestock or had been seen, but to no avail. Neither Vulg nor Wolf was spotted. Someone suggested that perhaps the Vulgs were lairdd inside the Barrier, and special missions to examine the 'Thorn forayed out repeatedly, to return scratched or pinked by the spikes.

"Ah, it's no good," said Tarpy, dabbing at a puncture wound in his forearm as the squad sat at supper. "It's like trying to search out an endless maze. If they're in there, then it's one puzzle we won't solve in a lifetime."

"It's a puzzle all right," said Patrel, "for surely we should have sighted some by now. Oh, perhaps not Wolves, for they have gotten wily and now hunt their normal game in the woods. But our night patrols should have turned up a Vulg or two by now, and our day patrols, at least one den." Patrel fell into thoughtful silence.

"What's needed here," said Danner, "is for us to lay traps for them. Or to wait for them to come to us. We need some kind of bait, or an advantage of some kind."

"How about dogs?" asked Tuck. "I'll wager that dogs'd find the lairs."

"Ar, they tried dogs over at the Eastdell Second," said Patrel, "and they had no more luck than we. You know, it's as if the Vulgs came to the Bosky on some *mission* and, having accomplished it, are now gone. But what that mission may have been, I cannot say."

Neither, of course, could anyone else say, and again Tuck felt the icy fingers of an unknown doom walking up his spine.

The next day at sundown, they returned from patrol to find the camp all astir. A waggon train of refugees from Challerain Keep had passed through, following along the Upland Way; their goal was the Realm of Wellen to the west. Danner, who had cook duty, described the train.

"Long it was, perhaps a hundred or so waggons, loaded with food and household goods, and driven by *Men,* mostly oldsters, and *Women,* with their offspring, too. Big, those Folk are—nearly twice my size, and I'm no tiny dink like Tarpy, here.

"And the escort, soldiers on horseback, with helms and swords, and spears, too. Lor! Big horses, big Men." Danner paused in reflection, and it was the first time in Tuck's memory that he'd ever seen Danner impressed. "It took nearly two hours for the train to pass through," continued Danner, "and the Captain of the escort, well he was closeted with Captain Darby for most of that time. Then he just up and rode off as the last waggon trundled through. And then they were gone." Danner took a bite of bread and chewed unconsciously, his amber eyes lost in elsewhen thought.

A hubbub of questions and comments burst forth from the squad, washing over Danner, and Tuck was caught up in the fervor, his own supper forgotten, more than a little envious that he'd missed seeing the train. But before Danner could respond to the babble, Patrel came to the fireside and called for quiet.

"Captain Darby will speak to us tonight, in less than an hour, so eat up and finish the meal chores quickly. We are to assemble shortly at headquarters. Hop to it, now, for we've little time as it is."

Hurriedly, Tuck wolfed down his meal, cleaned his mess kit, and pitched in with the pots and pans. Soon the chores were done, and the squad collected with the others at the main building. Captain Darby was there, his face enshadowed by a lantern swinging from a pole by the door. He spoke to a few nearby, then sprang upon a bench and overlooked the company. The night was cold, and a light snow had begun to fall. Warrows stamped to keep their feet warm, and their breath rose up in a great white plume as if from some huge aggregate creature. Squad call was made, and each was there except the third squad, who had Beyonder Guard duty.

"Buccen," Captain Darby began, his voice raised so that all could hear, "some of the rumors are true: There *is* trouble brewing up north, beyond the Keep. High King Aurion prepares for War: *War with Modru, the Enemy in Gron.*" A collective gasp of dismay welled up from the assembled Warrows, for this indeed was dire news, and many muttered grim words and spoke with their squadmates. Captain Darby let the talk run on for a bit, then held up his hand for silence. When it returned he continued.

"I had a long talk with Captain Horth, leader of the waggon train escort. He said that the call had gone forth for the allies of the High King to rally to his aid. Why the summons has not yet come to the Bosky, neither he nor I can say. But I believe that it will, and so we must begin to think upon going. Those who will it may take their leave and join the Allies at the Keep. Yet the Bosky must not be left unguarded and undefended should the foe come nigh, hence that, too, must be considered."

Again a babble rose up from the assembled young buccen. *Leave the Bosky? Fight a War way up north? High King's call?* Tuck, too, felt a wrenching at his heart, just as he had when Old Barlo had told him he would be leaving Woody Hollow, but this was even more unexpected. He had never dreamt that he might be asked to fight the foe in a strange land, especially when the Bosky itself was in danger from Vulgs. Yet how best to avenge Hob—face the enemy here, or in a far Land? For it now seemed certain that the High King's summons would come to the Boskydells, and Tuck would have to answer to his conscience no matter which way he chose. He was caught up in a dilemma: Could he leave the Boskydells to answer the High King's muster if Modru's Horde marched this way? But on the other hand, could he refuse the High King's call to colors at the Keep? For if he and enough others answered the summons and went north, perhaps the Enemy in Gron could be defeated ere War came south. What to do? *Torn between love of home and duty to King,* Tuck realized, but knowing this did not help resolve the question.

"What about Modru? How do they know it's him?" someone called to Captain Darby, breaking Tuck's train of thought. Again a hubbub arose, but it quieted when the Captain raised his hands. "Captain Horth said that there's a great wall of darkness stalking down the Land from the north. Eerie it is, and frightening, too, like a great black shadow. And inside the darkness is bitter winter cold and the Sun shines not, though it rides the day sky. And there be fell creatures within that blackness, Rūcks and such, Modru's lackeys of old, a gathering of his Horde. And it is reported that some skirmishes with the Enemy's forces already have occurred."

Shouts broke out among the Warrows. *Black shadow?*

*Rūcks and such? Modru's Horde? This is awful! Legends
come to life!*

Again Captain Darby called for quiet, but it was a long
time coming. At last, though, he said, "Hold on, for we
know not whether these things be true, or are common
events made dire in the telling. The black wall, for instance,
could be but a cover of dark clouds. It does not have to
be Modru's hand at work. But even if it is, till the High
King calls we will concentrate on the defense of the Bosky,
by Beyonder Guarding and Vulg Hunting. Yet when King
Aurion's muster is sounded, then you must choose. But for
now, we Walk the Thorns." Calling his squad leaders to
him, Captain Darby leapt down from the bench and
strode inside.

Tuck, Danner, and Tarpy trudged back to their tent, each
immersed deep in his own thoughts, and Tuck's entry into
his diary that night took longer than usual.

The next day the squad was assigned Beyonder Guard,
this time on the late night shift, mid of night till sunup. As
was the case with this shift, on the day before beginning
the duty the squad was given no daylight assignment so
that they would be rested and alert when their late assignment began. Hence, they lazed the day away in small tasks
and idle talk—talk that inevitably turned to Modru.

"Why now?" asked Tarpy. "I mean, well, after four thousand years, why does Modru threaten now?"

"What I'd like to know is, what kind of creatures are in
his Horde?" queried Arbin, as he fletched another arrow,
sighting down its length. "I know about Rūcks, Hlōks, and
Ogrus, or at least what the tales tell. They're supposed to
be all alike, just different sizes. The Rūck is the smallest,
a bit larger than we—say, four foot tall; the Hlōk, big as a
Man, I hear tell; and the Ogru, or Troll, as the Dwarves
call him, twice Man-size."

Danner, who was the only one there who'd recently seen
a Man, and who knew how *big* they were, snorted. "Hah!
Twice Man-size? I think the old legends exaggerate. Why,
that'd make the Ogru the greatest creature on the land."

"Except for Dragons," chipped in Tuck, "but none of
those have been seen for five hundred years or so—or so
they say."

"You're forgetting one Dragon that's been seen recently," smiled Arbin.

"What do you mean?" spoke up Tarpy, puzzled. "What Dragon has been seen recently?" He appealed to the others with outstretched hands, palms up.

"The Dragon Star!" shouted Arbin in glee, having lured Tarpy into his word trap. Tarpy made a face, and the others smiled ruefully, shaking their heads.

"Now there's a thing folks will talk about for ages to come," said Delber, a fair-haired young buccan from Wigge, "the Dragon Star."

Delber was talking about the great flaming star with its long burning tail that had come blazing out of the heavens five years past, nearly to strike the world.

For weeks before, its light could be seen, appearing at sunset, and it burned through the night. Night after night it grew brighter and larger, plunging through the star-studded sky. And its fiery tail, called "Dragon's Breath" by some, and "Dragon's Flame" by others, grew longer and longer. An awful portent it was, for the hairy stars had presaged dire events since the world began. On it came, rising each night, inexorably sweeping closer. Now it was so bright that it could be seen even in the dawn light, as it set while the Sun rose.

But night was its true Realm, for then it silently clove the splangled sky, looming ever larger, ever brighter. And then folk noted that it seemed to be changing course, shifting, for slowly its tail swung behind till it no longer could be seen, *as if the Dragon Star had turned and was hurtling directly for Mithgar.*

Some folk prepared for the cataclysm: cellars were dug, and food was canned and stored away. The sale of charms against the Dragon Star became brisk, though even the sellers said they were not at all certain that the amulets would work. And it was commonly told that Mithgar was doomed. And onward it came, now an enormous blaze in the night.

And then the last night to live arrived, but in spite of the impending death of the world, most Bosky folks had worked their fields and livestock and trades as usual, though the taverns after the Sun set seemed more crowded than was ordinary.

That night the great Dragon Star rushed across the sky of Mithgar, so bright that books could be read by its light. As if in escort, myriads of blazing, burning points of light seared and streaked across the heavens, brighter than the brightest fireworks. Huge glowing fragments were seen to splinter from the Dragon Star and hurtle down through the sky toward the ground, and great, loud blasting booms shuddered over the Land, breaking windows and crockery. One great flaming piece, gouting fire and rucketing boom after boom, seemed destined to destroy the Bosky, but it seared a great blazing south-to-north path, hurtling to smash somewhere far beyond the Northwood, in Rian or perhaps even further.

People wept and cried out in fear, and some swooned while others drank in the taverns. Some fled to their burrows, and others took to their cellars. But most simply sat and watched and waited, with their arms around their buccarans or dammias, or about their sires and dams, or their buccoes and dammsels, or granthers and grandams, or uncles, aunts, cousins, or other relatives or friends, for they knew nought else to do.

Yet the mighty Dragon Star hurtled not into Mithgar, but instead rushed past. Still, its great glowing tail long washed over the world: it was said to the vast woe of Mithgar. For days upon days the bright glow of the Dragon Star could be seen in the sky, in the daytime now as it sped for the Sun. And the Sun at last seemed to swallow it, but later spat it out the other side. And the Dragon Star hurtled back into the heavens, now chasing its own tail, or Breath, or Flame, as the case may be, growing fainter every day, until at last it was gone.

For weeks afterward, a day did not pass that the Sun and sky did not show sullen red in the fore-dusk—blood red, some claimed. At night, great blowing curtains of shifting light glowed and shuddered in the sky—Mithgar's Shroud, some called it. A caul fell upon the face of the Moon and did not fade for weeks. And a raging fever plague swept the Land; many died. Milk soured, cows went dry, crops failed, hens stopped laying, dogs barked without reason, and once it rained without letup for eight days. It was said that two-headed calves and sheep without eyes were born, and some claimed to see snakes roll like hoops.

Wherever Warrows gathered, great arguments arose. Many believed that *all* of these strange things were the doings of the Dragon Star. Others said, "Rubbish! Most of these happenings are ordinary events; we've seen 'em before. And some o' these stories are just wild tales. Only a *few* things might be laid at the feet of the Dragon Star."

Slowly the Land returned to normal: the plague abated and finally died out, Mithgar's Shroud and the bloody sunsets gradually disappeared, cows came afresh, hens laid eggs, and the crops grew. But no one who had seen the Dragon Star would ever forget it; it would be an event talked about for generation upon generation, until it, too, joined the other epic tales and legends told 'round the hearth, as it was now being talked about around the Thornwalker campfire.

"Yar, I seen it," said Dilby Helk, peering at the other squad members, "but who didn't? I can 'member sitting on the hilltop near our farmstead with my elden grandam. And she said, 'No good'll come of this, Dilbs,'—she always called me Dilbs—'mark my words. It means the death of the High King, or something else just as bad, or worse.' And I said, 'What could be worse, Granny?' And her face went all ashy and her voice all hollow, and she said, 'The Doom of Mithgar.' Wull, I'll tell you, I was ascared!" Dilby's eyes were wide and lost in the memory, then he shivered and looked up at the others and gave a nervous laugh. "Ar, but the High King's alive and Mithgar's still here, so I reckon as she was wrong."

For a moment no one spoke. Then Tarpy said, "Maybe she was right, what with Modru stirring up north. Perhaps the Dragon Star came to forewarn us of that."

"What if it was a sending of Adon?" speculated Arbin. "He might have tried to tell us of this coming War, but we just couldn't read His message."

"Ar, sending!" burst out Danner, disgusted. "Why not say it was sent by Modru? Or even by bloody Gyphon, Himself? Hah! The Doom of Mithgar, indeed."

"Yes, Mr. Danner High-and-Mighty. Sendings!" cried Arbin, his face flushed with anger. "Don't look down your crusty beak at me! Everyone knows about sendings and omens. Plagues are sendings of Gyphon, the Great Evil. If not from Gyphon, then plagues come from His servant

Modru, the Enemy in Gron. And as to omens, well just look the next time you see a flight of birds, for they tell of fortunes, sometimes good, sometimes bad. So you see, Mr. Wise Danner, the Dragon Star could well have been a sending of Adon."

Now Danner's ire, too, was up. "Ask yourself this, Arbin Oracle: If I shied a rock at a bird on a limb, and somewhere else you saw it flying in fright, what would it auger, what great omen of fortune would it tell you? Would it be a sending of Modru, or Gyphon, or one of High Adon? Answer me this, too: If Adon wanted to say something, why wouldn't He just come right out and say it plain? Why would He cast it in runes that nobody can read? Sendings! Omens! Faugh!"

Arbin leapt to his feet, his fists clenched, and so, too, did Danner. And it would have come to blows except Tuck stepped in between and gently pressed Arbin back, saying, "Hold on, now, and save your fighting for Modru." He turned to Danner and placed a hand on his forearm and said, "Squabble with Vulgs, not Warrows." Danner shook off Tuck's grip and, glowering at Arbin, sat back down. Talk ceased.

The tense silence was finally broken by Tarpy. "Look, we can't have you two buccoes forever glaring at one another like circling dogs. Let's just leave it at this: Sometimes events seem like sendings and omens, sometimes not, and who's to say the which of it? Perhaps some things *are* portents while others are *not*, even the flights of birds—there may be times that they mean something and other times not. Yet I think none of us here will ever read a winged augery. But this I say: Until we know the truth about sendings, omens, whatever, there's got to be room for different beliefs and respect for the right to hold diverse opinions." Little Tarpy glared at Danner and Arbin, both of whom towered over him. "Have you got that? Then formally put your wrath behind you." Both Danner and Arbin stood, albeit somewhat reluctantly, and stiffly bowed to one another, to the smiles of the other squad members.

Tuck and Tarpy and eight others were assigned to the fore-barricade while Danner was among those that drew the aft-gate for their Beyonder Guard duty. Just prior to mid of night, they rode down the long black tunnel of thorns to their posts, greeting the squad there with *Halloos* and *Hai-rois* and *Ai-oi, where you been? Have you bitten any Vulgs lately? What's the news from Modru?* and other such banter. The relieved squad mounted their own ponies and rode back toward the encampment, leaving Patrel's squad to stoke the fires and prepare for the long watch. The fore-barrier was opened, and Dilby rode out to relieve the point-watch at the far side of the 'Thorn. After a while they could see the approaching torch of that young buccan, and as he rode up to the fore-barricade it was opened long enough for him to pass through on his way back to camp. Tuck watched as he rode across the frozen river and was passed through the aft-barricade.

An hour dragged by, and then another, and few words were spoken. In the main, the gurge of swift water under ice and the pop of pine knots in the fire were the dominant sounds of the night. All of the ponies and half of the young buccen dozed while the other half drank hot tea and kept a sharp watch out. Another hour passed, and Tuck, on rest, was just nodding off when Tarpy shook him awake. "Tuck! Look sharp! Dilby comes, and he's riding fast!"

Tuck scrambled up, and Warrows nocked arrows and stood ready, their senses alert. Arbin scuttled out the crawl-way, kicked up the fire in front of the barricade to better see by, and scurried back through, making ready to drop the Spindlethorn plug into the crawlway if necessary. The signal was given to those across the ford to close the aft-barricade. They could see Dilby's torch bobbing closer and now hear the pony's hoofbeats as it raced toward the barrier. Patrel came running across the river, arriving just as Dilby pounded up.

"A rider comes!" Dilby cried. "At speed! Sounds like a horse, not a pony. Let me in!" Quickly they opened the barricade and shut it just as fast once Dilby was through. He threw a leg over the pony and leapt to the ground, giving his report to Patrel as the others took up their posts on the ramparts of the barrier. "I was at the point and thought I could hear something coming up the road, far off. I put my ear to the icy ground, nearly froze it, and listened. The sound became plain—a horse, I think, at speed, running along the road, headed for the ford."

"Oi! A light!" cried Delber, and all peered beyond the barricade to see a torch, its light growing swiftly. Now they could hear the pounding of hooves, this time horse rather than pony. On it came, growing louder, until a black foam-flecked steed, ridden by a haggard Man, burst into the fire-light to thunder to a halt at the barrier.

"In the name of the High King, open up, for I am his herald, and War is afoot!" cried the Man, holding his torch aloft so that all could see that indeed he was garbed in a red-and-gold tabard, the colors of High King Aurion.

"Your mission?" called down Patrel.

"Ai! Modru gathers his Horde to fall upon Challerain Keep," cried the messenger, his horse curvetting, "and I am sent to muster this Land, for all must answer to the call if the Realm is to brave the coming storm. And I am told to show you this"—he held up a leather thong laced through a hole in a coin—"though I know not what it means."

The eyes of all the Warrows on the barricade widened in alarm, for it was a Gjeenian penny, the cheapest coin in the realm, a symbol hearking back to the Warrows Tipperton Thistledown and Beau Darby and the Great War of the Ban. There was coin just like it in the Centerdell town of Rood, to be sent to the King should the Bosky be in desperate straits. And none on the barrier ever thought to see such a dreadful sign.

"Open the barricade," ordered Patrel, and Tuck and Tarpy and two others leapt down to do so. "What news?" he called as the four set aside their bows to move the barrier.

"Darkness stalks the north. Prince Galen strikes within the Dimmendark. Young Prince Igon has slain Winternight Spawn. And Aurion Redeye fortifies the Keep," answered the herald.

The barrier at last was open, and the Kingsman rode through, but at the sight of the yawning black maw of the thorn tunnel on the far side of the ford, he paused and sighed. "Ah, Wee One," he called up to Patrel, "riding through this Great Thornwall is like passing through the very gaping Gates of Hèl."

"Would you have a hot cup of tea before going into

those gaping Gates?" asked Tuck, looking up, marvelling at how huge both horse and Man seemed to be.

"Would that I could, but I must away," smiled the Man down at Tuck. "And shut that thorngate soon," he gestured at the barricade behind, "for I ken something follows me."

At a light touch of spurs to flank, the black steed trotted forward out of the mouth of the Thornwall and onto the frozen river, gingerly stepping toward the far bank, the strike of iron-shod hooves knelling through the ice. The Warrows watched his progress toward the far side and signalled the Beyonder Guard at the aft-gate to let the Man pass.

And thus it was that while all eyes were riveted upon the Man, a great snarling black shape hurtled through the open fore-barrier, racing to overhaul the herald. *"Vulg!"* cried Tarpy, snatching up his bow. Yet ere he could nock an arrow, the black beast was beyond range, but Tarpy sprang after.

"Close the barrier! More come!" shouted Patrel, and several leapt down to do so, while others spun to see three more hideous Vulgs speeding toward the barricade. *Thuun! Hsss! Thuun! Ssss!* Arrows were loosed at the creatures as the thorngate slammed to, walling them out.

Tuck, too, had snatched up his bow and raced after Tarpy, fumbling for an arrow as he ran. The Vulg was swift and closed upon the Kingsman with blinding speed.

" 'Ware!" shouted Tuck as he pounded onto the ice, five running strides behind Tarpy.

The herald turned in his saddle to see what was amiss just as the great black Vulg sprang for his throat, and but for Tuck's warning he would have been slain then and there. He threw up an arm to ward the beast, and the Vulg hurtled into him, knocking him from the saddle, though his left foot was caught in the stirrup. The Vulg rolled on the ice, and his claws scratched and clicked as he scrambled to his feet, and his baleful yellow eyes flashed evil. The horse screamed in terror and reared up and back, dragging the Kingsman under. Tarpy had reached the steed and grabbed at the reins, and Tuck slid to a stop over the Man as the Vulg bunched and leapt at Tarpy, snarling jaws aslaver. *Thuun! Sssthwock!* Tuck's arrow buried itself in the Vulg's chest, and the beast was dead as it smashed into the horse, knocking its feet from under. Squealing, the steed crashed down onto the ice. Rending cracks rived the surface, and a great jagged slab tilted up and over. Tuck, Tarpy, and the Man—each desperately clawing at the canting ice—the screaming, kicking horse, and the dead Vulg all slid down to be swept under by the swift current. *And the slab slammed shut behind them like a great trapdoor.*

The icy shock of the frigid water nearly caused Tuck to swoon, so cold it was that it *burned.* But ere he could faint, the racing current rammed him into a great rock, and the jolt brought him to. Up he frantically swam, to collide with the underside of the ice, and he all but screamed in terror. His fingers clawed at the hard undersurface in panic as the merciless torrent swept him along. He needed to breathe but couldn't, for the bitterly cold water was everywhere, though breath raced by only inches away. Numb he grew, and he knew he was dead, but he held on until he could last no more. Yet, *lo!* his face came into a narrow pocket of air trapped between hard ice and gushing water, and he gasped rapidly, his cheek pressed against the ice, his panting breath harsh in his ears. He clutched helplessly at the smooth frozen undersurface, trying to stay where he was, but there was nought to grasp and his fingers no longer did his bidding.

He was swept under again, dragged down away from the ice, his saturated clothes weighing him under. Again the frigid current whelmed him into a great rock, and he was slammed sideways into a crevice, jammed there by the surge at the riverbed, far below the surface. He reached down and numbly felt a river rock and forced his fingers to close, to grasp it up from the bottom, and he clawed his way up the crevice. He would try to hammer through the ice, though he had little hope of succeeding.

Up he inched, buffeted by the whelming surge, pressed into the cleft of the great rock, nearly pinned by the force. Up he struggled, straining every nerve, every sinew, his lungs screaming for air. Up, and his grip failed him and the rock plummeted, whirling away from his benumbed fingers, but the furious battle upward went on. Up he clawed, and against his will his lungs heaved, trying to breathe, to find air and draw it past clamped lips. He knew he could hold out no longer. *No!* his mind shouted in anger, and with all his might, all his energy, he gave one last desperate surge upward. He came into the sweet night air, and his lungs pumped like bellows, for he had come up in one of the dark gurgling pools where ice had not yet formed.

With enormous effort he crawled onto the great stone thrusting above the water and lay against the icy rock, gasping for air. He could no longer feel his hands, and uncontrollable shudders racked through his body. He was cold . . . so cold . . . so bitterly cold, and he knew that he was dying. Yet from the depths of his being he willed himself to get up, to stand, but he only managed to roll over onto his side. He lay there panting, with his cheek pressed against the cold, hard stone, and only his eyes moved at his will.

Down between the great walls of thorn looming darkly upward he could see a ring of torchlight, perhaps one hundred yards away, at the ford. But one torch was much nearer, darting from place to place. Closer it came, held high. It was Danner! He came searching the pools! Tuck tried to speak, to call out, and his voice was but a feeble croak, lost in the churn. Again Tuck called, this time louder, though still faint. Danner jerked about and held up his torch to see the Warrow crumpled on the rock, and he darted to the pool, stopping at the edge of the ice.

"Tuck!" he cried, "I've found you! You're alive!" His voice sounded as if he were weeping. "Har! Yar!" he shouted at the others, his cry loud between the thorn walls. "This way! Hoy! Bring rope!" He turned back to Tuck. "We'll throw you a line and pull you out of there."

"I can't use my hands," Tuck managed to say. "They don't work anymore. I can't even sit up." And Tuck found that he was sobbing.

"Don't worry, bucco," Danner said, "I'll come and get you." Danner began stripping his clothes, muttering angrily to himself: "Witless fools! Trying to flip that slab back over." Other young buccen came pelting up, wondering in their eyes at the sight of Tuck. "I told you!" spat Danner. "Search the pools! Some now stay with me! The rest search for Tarpy . . . and the Man! Who has the rope?" They stood agape a moment until Patrel barked out orders, and four stayed with Patrel and Danner while the others began the search.

Danner tied the line to himself, and Patrel and the other

four took a grip on it. Then the young buccan plunged into the water, crying out with the shock and pain of the cold, but swiftly he reached the rock, the current carrying him. Up onto the stone he clambered, shivering uncontrollably, his teeth achatter. Pulling in some slack, he sat Tuck up and looped the line over him, using a great slipknot. "All right, bucco," his voice diddered with the cold, "in we go now. The current will carry us out of here."

Tuck was of no help, but Danner managed to get the two of them into the bitter rush, and Tuck lost consciousness. With Patrel and two others anchoring the line, paying it out, Danner kept Tuck afloat while the swift current carried them onward to the downstream rim of the frigid pool, where waited Argo and Delber, who pulled first Tuck and then Danner up onto the ice. Hurriedly, his feet trailing behind, they half carried, half dragged Tuck back to the fire, where they stripped his clothes from him and warmed him and wrapped him in two blankets taken from the bedrolls behind the ponies' saddles. Danner, too, moaning with the cold, came to the fire, limping, with Arbin helping him. He, also, was first warmed, then wrapped in blankets by the fire. Tuck came partly awake, and hot tea was given to both, Patrel holding the cup to Tuck's mouth, urging the buccan to sip.

A time passed, and Tuck was now sitting. His hands were beginning to tingle needle-sharp when at last the other buccen returned from the search. Tuck looked up as Dilby came to the fire. "Tarpy?" Tuck asked, and he burst into tears when Dilby shook his head, no.

When Captain Darby and the healers came, sent for by Patrel, both Tuck and Danner were taken by pony-cart back to the Thornwalker campsite. Neither said much on the trip, and in the tent Tuck was given a sleeping draught for his painfully throbbing hands and fell into a deep, dreamless state. Yet Danner awoke after but a few hours of restless sleep to see Tuck awkwardly gripping a pencil and determinedly writing in his diary. *He's putting it all down in his diary, you know, to get it out of his mind,* muttered Danner to himself, and he fell once again into troubled slumber.

* * *

Tuck awoke to Danner shaking his arm. "Up, bucco. They've gone off without us, as if we were sick or something," said Danner. "Well, we've got to show 'em we're tougher than they think. How are your hands? It was my feet that nearly gave out on me."

Tuck flexed his fingers. "They feel just a bit strange, somewhat like they're swollen. But that's all." He looked up at Danner and their eyes met, and Tuck began to weep.

"Come on, bucco," said Danner, his own voice choking, "don't go into that now."

"I'm sorry, Danner, but I just can't help it." Tuck's voice was filled with misery, and his tear-laden eyes stared unseeing into a private horror. "I can't wrench my mind away from it—the Man, the horse, Tarpy, all trapped beneath the ice, struggling for air, beating at the frozen surface. Oh, Lor! Tarpy, Tarpy. I close my eyes and see his face under the ice, his hands clawing, but he cannot get out." Sobs racked Tuck's frame, and Danner, weeping too, threw an arm over Tuck's shoulders. "If only I hadn't shot the Vulg just then," Tuck sobbed, "it wouldn't have struck the horse and the ice wouldn't have broken and . . . and . . ." Tuck could not go on.

"Hold it!" exclaimed Danner, leaping up and facing Tuck, his sorrow turning to anger. "That's stupid! If you hadn't feathered that brute when you did, then it would have bitten Tarpy's head off! Don't blame your fool self for an accident of misfortune. You did the right thing, and I mean *exactly* the right thing. It could have been you drowned under the ice instead of Tarpy—or the Man. Any one or all three could have come up in a pool like you did. No, Tuck, chance alone slew our comrade, and chance alone saved you, so if you want to blame someone or something, blame chance!"

Tuck, shocked from his grief and guilt and self-pity by Danner's angry words, looked up at the other buccan. A moment passed, and the only sound was Danner's harsh breathing. And then Tuck spoke, his voice grim. "No, Danner, not chance. I'll not blame chance. Chance did not send that Vulg after the Kingsman. 'Twas Modru."

Captain Darby called the Thornwalker Fourth together at the Spindle Ford, and a service was said for Tarpy, and for the unnamed herald. And through it all, Tuck's eyes remained dry, although many others wept.

And then Captain Darby spoke to all the company: "Buccen, though we have lost a comrade, life goes on. The High King has called a muster at Challerain Keep, and some from the Bosky are duty-bound to answer. I will send couriers to start the word spreading, and others then will respond to the call. Yet some must go forth now and be foremost to answer. It has fallen our lot to be the first to choose, and these are the choices: to remain and ward the Bosky, or to answer the King's summons. I call upon each now to consider well and carefully and then give your answer. What will it be? Will you Walk the Thorns of the Seven Dells, or will you instead walk the ramparts of Challerain Keep?"

Silence descended upon the Thornwalkers as each considered his answer—silence, that is, except for one who had already made up his mind. Tuck stepped forward five paces until he stood alone on the ice. "Captain Darby," he called, and all heard him, "I will go to the High King, for Evil Modru has a great wrong to answer for. Nay! two wrongs: one lies atop the Rooks' Roost, the other sleeps 'neath this frozen river."

Danner strode forward to stand beside Tuck, and so, too, did Patrel. Arbin, Dilby, Delber, and Argo joined them, and so did all of Patrel's squad. Then came others, until a second squad had formed. More began to step forward, but Captain Darby cried, "Hold! No more now! We cannot leave the ford unguarded. Yet, heed this: when others come to join our company, then again will I give you the same choice. Until that time, though, these two squads will be first, and the High King could not ask for better.

"Hearken unto me, for this shall be the way of it. Patrel Rushlock, you are named Captain of this Company of the King, and your squad leaders are to be Danner Bramblethorn of the first squad and Tuckerby Underbank of the second. Captain Patrel, as more squads are formed, they shall be dispatched to your command. And this is the last order I shall give you: Lead well. And to the Company of the King, I say this: Walk in honor."

The next morning, forty-three grim-faced Boskydell Warrows rode forth from the Great Spindlethorn Barrier and into the Land of Rian. They came out along the road across the Spindle Ford, each armed with bow and arrows and cloaked in Thornwalker grey. Their destination was Challerain Keep, for they had been summoned.

CHAPTER 4

Challerain Keep

North, then east rode the young buccen, the Warrow Company of the King, along the Upland Way, the road into Rian. They were striking for the Post Road, some twenty-five miles hence, the main pike north to Challerain Keep. Tuck spent much of the time riding among the members of his new squad, getting acquainted. Some he knew from days past, others he did not. Quickly he found that they had come from all parts of Eastdell—from the villages of Bryn and Eastpoint, Downyville, Midwood, Raffin, Wigge, Greenfields, Leeks, and the like, or from farms nearby. Other than Tuck, no one else in his squad was from Woody Hollow or even from its nearby neighbor, Budgens, though one young buccan was from Brackenboro. Yet soon the Warrows were engaged in friendly chatter and no longer seemed to be strangers. Why, Finley Wick from Eastpoint even knew Tuck's cousins, the Bendels of Eastpoint Hall.

They rode through a snow-covered region that slowly rose up out of Spindle Valley to become a flat prairie with but few features. Behind, they could see the massive Barrier clutched unto the land, looming sapless and iron-hard in winter sleep, waiting for the caress of spring to send the life juices coursing through the great tangle, to set forth unto the Sun a green canopy of light-catching leaves, to send the great blind roots inexorably questing through the dark earth again. Immense it was, anchored from horizon to horizon and beyond, a great thorny wall. Yet as the Warrows rode, distance diminished it until it took on the aspect of a vast, remote hill, stretched past seeing. At last it sank below the horizon, and although Tuck rode in the company of friends, still he felt as if he had been abandoned. Yet whether it was because the loss of the Thornwall meant that he'd truly left the Bosky behind, or whether he felt exposed and vulnerable because he now rode upon an open plain, he could not say.

Ahead, here and there, lone barren trees or winter-stripped thickets occasionally appeared, but they, too, were slowly left behind on the snow-swept prairie. A thin, chill wind sprang up, gnawing at their backs, and soon all cloak hoods were up and talk dwindled to infrequent phrases and grunts. On they went, stopping once to feed the ponies some grain and to take a sparse meal. At times they walked, leading the steeds, giving the animals some respite.

On one of these "strolls in the snow," as Finley called them, Tuck found himself trudging between Patrel and Danner. "I hope this blasted cold wind whistling up my cloak is gone by the time we make camp," said Danner. "I don't fancy sleeping in the open in the wind."

"I don't think we'll be in the open, Danner," said Patrel, "if we reach the point where the Upland Way meets the Post Road, as planned, for that's at the western edge of the Battle Downs. We should be able to find the lee of a hillside there, out of the wind, and make the best of things."

Tuck nodded. "I hope so, but if we don't and if the wind doesn't die down, it doesn't give us much to make the best of, does it now?"

Patrel shook his head, and Danner looked at the sky. The wind mouthed at the edges of their hoods, and the ponies patiently plodded beside them. "Say," asked Danner, "how long will it take us to reach the Keep?"

"Well," answered Patrel, "let me see. One day to the Battle Downs, and then six more along the Post Road north to Challerain Keep. If the weather holds—by that I mean, if it doesn't snow—we'll be seven days on the journey. But, with snow, it could be . . . longer."

"Seven days," mused Tuck. "Perhaps that'll give me enough time to get skilled with my new bow—if I practice every morning before we set out and every evening before bedding down." Tuck's bow had been swept away, lost under the ice of the Spindle River when the Kingsman's horse had crashed through and Tuck had been dragged down by the whelming current. Another bow had been drawn from stores, one that most nearly matched Tuck's old one in length and pull. Yet Tuck would need practice to get the feel of it and regain his pinpoint accuracy.

"Look, Tuck," said Patrel, "I've been meaning to tell you something, but I just haven't been able to muster my courage to the point where I could. But it's just this. I'm dreadfully sorry about Tarpy's death, and I know how close he was to you. He was a bright spirit in this time of gloom, a spirit we will sorely miss in the dark days to come. But I just want you to know that I'll try with all my being to make up for the horrible mistake I made, the mistake that got Tarpy slain."

"What?" cried Tuck, dumbfounded. "What are you saying? If any is to blame, it is I. I shot the Vulg. The horse would not have fallen but for that. Had I only acted quicker, the Vulg would have been slain ere he sprang."

"Ah, but you forget," answered Patrel, "had I but ordered the gate shut immediately after the Kingsman rode through, then that Vulg would have been slain outside the barricade as were the three beasts that raced but Vulg strides behind."

"Nay!" protested Tuck, " 'Twas not your fault. If I had—"

"Ar!" interrupted Danner, scowling, his voice harsh. "If this and if that, and who's to blame. If I'd only ordered the gate shut; if I'd only listened to the Man's warning; if I'd only watched the road instead of the Man; if I'd only seen the Vulgs sooner; if I'd only shot sooner. If! If! If! Those are just a few of the ifs I've heard, and without a glimmering doubt there's many a more where those came from. Tuck, you had the right of it yesterday, though you seem to have lost it already, so I'll remind you: the only one to blame is Modru! Remember that, the both of you! It is Modru's hand that slew Tarpy, none other, just as he slew Hob." With that, Danner leapt upon his pony's back and spurred forward to the head of the column, shouting, "Mount up! We've a ways to go and little time to do it in!" And so went all the Company, eastward along the Upland Way.

The Sun had lipped the horizon when the Warrows came into the margins of the hill country called the Battle Downs, a name from the time of the Great War. They made camp on the lee of a hill in a pine grove and supped on a meal of dried venison and crue, a tasteless but nourishing waybread, and they took their meal with hearty hot tea. After supper, Tuck cut some pine boughs and lashed them together in a large target bundle, and long into the evening, by flickering firelight, the pop of the fire and the sigh of the wind were punctuated by the sounds of bow and arrow.

The next dawn, many were awakened by the *Shock! Shwok!* of Tuck's practice, and they wondered at his dedication, for they could see that his arrows struck true. "Cor," breathed Sandy Pender of Midwood, helping to retrieve the bolts, "but you're a fine shot. Perhaps even as good as Captain Patrel."

"Danner's the one you ought to see shoot," said Tuck. "He'd put us all to shame." Back went Tuck and continued his drill, standing far and near, uphill and down. He stopped to eat breakfast while his pony took some grain, and then he resumed. But at last it was time to get under way, and the Warrows mounted up, urging the ponies out of the grove to take up again the journey, now travelling north along the Post Road.

Midmorn it began to snow, though there was no wind, and the horizon was hidden behind a thick wall of falling flakes. The Warrow column pressed doggedly on, the hill margins of the Battle Downs off to their right, and the long flat slope of land toward the far Spindle River on their left. Dim grey silence fluttered all about them as they rode.

Still the flakes fell as the blear day trudged into the afternoon. Tuck was riding at the head of the column when he looked up to see horses and a waggon loom up through the snow. It was the fore of a refugee train, and the young buccen rode off to one side heading northward while the horses plodded and the wains groaned southward. Both Men and Warrows eyed each other as they passed, and Patrel spoke briefly with the Captain of the escort. The waggon train was nearly two miles long, and it took almost an hour for them to pass one another, for the last wain to disappear south in the snow as the last Warrow vanished north.

"They're headed for Trellinath," said Patrel. "Old Men, Women, and children. Across the Bosky, then south through Wellen and Kael Gap. Ah, me, what an arduous journey for them." Tuck said nought, and north they rode.

Four days later they camped for the evening in the last northern margins of the Battle Downs. They had ridden north for two days, swung east for two more, and now the road had begun to swing north again. They had settled up in a stand of cedar, perhaps a furlong from the road. The Sun had set, and a full Moon rode the night sky. Tuck had finished his archery practice and was sitting by the campfire writing in his diary.

"Two more days, perhaps three, and we'll be there, eh, Patrel?" he asked, pausing in his writing. At Patrel's nod, Tuck jotted a note in his journal and snapped it shut, putting it into his jacket pocket.

Shortly, all except the sentinels had bedded down. But it seemed to Tuck that he had no more than closed his eyes when he was awakened to a darkened camp by Delber. *"Shhh,"* cautioned the Warrow, "it's mid of night and something comes along the road."

Tuck silently moved through the campsite and awakened others, and bows were made ready. Now could all hear the jingle of armor and clatter of weaponry amid the thud of many hooves. Below, a cavalcade of mounted soldiers cantered north through the bright moonlight. The Warrow company watched them pass, and made no signal. When they were gone, a new fire was kindled, and the young buccen went back to sleep.

All the next day they rode, and there was much speculation about the night riders. "Nar, I don't think they were forces of Modru, even though they did ride at night," said Danner. "Men they were, riding to the Keep."

"Yar, answering to the King's call, like us," said Finley. "Besides, were it Modru's forces, I think as we would'er sensed it. They say as the Ghûls casts fear."

"Oh, it's not the Ghûls that cast fear," chimed up Sandy, contradicting Finley, "it's Gargons. Turn you to stone, too, they say." At the mention of Gargons, Tuck's blood ran chill for they were dire creatures of legend.

"Wull, if it's Gargons as cast fear, what is it that the

Ghûls do?" asked Finley. "I've heard they're most terrible."

"Savage, horse-borne reavers they are," answered Sandy, "virtually unkillable, for it is said that the Ghûls are in league with Death."

"Ar, that's right," said Finley, "now I remember. But I seem to recall that they ride beasts like horses but not horses. And don't the Ghûls just about have to be chopped to shreds before they die?"

"Wood through the heart or a pure silver blade," murmured Tuck, remembering fables.

On they rode, all through the day, stopping but briefly for rests. The Sun swung through the high blue sky, but the land below was cold. The snow scrutched under the ponies' hooves, and the Warrows put up their hoods and looked upon the bright white 'scape through squinted eyes and saw only unrelieved flatness.

Slowly the Sun sank, and when night came they camped in a small ravine on an otherwise featureless plain of Rian.

The next day the land slowly changed into rolling prairie as the Warrow column went on. Occasionally they passed a lonely farmstead, but only one—a mile or so east of the road—had smoke rising from the chimney, and they did not ride to it.

That night they camped in the southern lee of a low hill where stood a copse of hickory, the thickset small trees harsh and grasping in the winter eve. The young buccen had settled in but an hour or two when drumming hoofbeats ran toward the north and a lone rider hurtled past on the nearby road. Again they did not hail. Yet, Finley was dispatched up the hill to the crest to watch the rider in the bright moonlight, to see him on his way.

"*Ai-oi!*" cried Finley from the hilltop. "This way, buccoes. We've arrived!"

All the company scrambled up to Finley, and he was pointing to the north. "There she be." And a hush of awe befell them.

The land fell away before them, beneath the light of the Moon. Along the road sped the rider, now but a fleeting dark speck on a shadowy blanket of silvered white. Yet off to the north all eyes were drawn, for glimmering there, perhaps ten miles away, like a spangle of stars mounting up a snow-covered tor springing forth from the argent plains, winked the myriad lights of their goal—Challerain Keep.

"Lor, but it's big. Look at all those lights," breathed Dilby in the silence as they stood and gazed in wonder at the first city any of them had ever seen. "Why, there must be hundreds, no, thousands of them."

"Mayhap we look upon the campfires of an army as well as the homelamps of a city," said Patrel.

"More like several armies, if you ask me," said Danner. "See, to the right are what look to be three main centers, and to the left, two more. I make it to be five armies plus a city."

"Well, we will find out tomorrow when we ride in," said Patrel. "But if we are going to be bright for the King, then it's to bed we must go."

Tuck reluctantly turned and went with the others down to the hickory thicket, to the Warrow encampment. His being was filled with the excitement of watching distant fires and speculating upon the Folk gathered about them. His mind was awhirl with thought, and he paused to scribe in his diary. Yet when he set it aside and took to his bedroll, sleep was a long time coming.

All the young buccen were eager to set out the next day, to gaze upon Challerain Keep, and to move through its streets. "Coo, a real *city*," said Argo as they broke camp and mounted up and rode over the crest of the hill to see from afar the terraced buildings mounting up toward the central Keep. "What will a village bumpkin like me, straight from the one street of Wigge, do in a great place as that is like to be? No matter where you turn, there'll be streets running every which way. And shops and buildings and everything. What with this, that, and the other, it'll be as confusing as the inside of the Barrier, and like as not we'll be lost before it's over."

Tuck felt as if Argo had voiced the silent thoughts of each and every Warrow. "You're right, Argo, it will be confusing to us all, but exciting, too. Hoy! Let's kick up this pace a bit!" They clapped heels into pony flanks, and, shouting with laughter and anticipation, the young buccen raced galloping down the white slopes, powdery snow billowing and pluming up from the ponies as they plunged through the deep drifts onto the great long flats leading toward the distant city. The pace slowed once they regained the Post Road, and steadily they went north. Slowly, ever so slowly, the distance diminished, but their excitement grew.

Long ago, in very ancient times, there had been no city of Challerain; it was merely the name given to a craggy mount standing tall amid a close ring of low foothills upon the rolling grassland prairies of Rian. Then there came the stirrings of War, and a watch was set upon Mont Challerain. Various kinds of beacon fires would be lit as signals, to warn off approaching armies, or to signal muster call, or to celebrate victory, or to send messages to distant Realms. These tidings were sent via the chain of signal fires that ran down the ancient range of tall hills called the Signal Mountains and south from there over the Dellin Downs into Harth and the Lands beyond. War did come, and many of those signal towers were destroyed, but not the one atop Mont Challerain.

After the War, this far northern outpost became a fortress—Challerain Keep. And with the establishment of a fort, a village sprang up at the foot of Mont Challerain. Yet it would have remained but a small hamlet, except the High King himself came north to the fortress to train at arms; and he established his summer court there, where he could overlook the approaches to the Rigga Mountains, and beyond, to Gron.

Year after year the King returned, and at last a great castle was raised, incorporating the fort within its grounds. It was then that the village grew into a town, and the town into a city. The city prospered, and it, too, was called Challerain Keep. This it had been for thousands of years.

As the Warrow column gradually drew closer, they began to discern some details of the city. The mount shouldered up broadly out of low rolling foothills upon the prairie and rose eight or nine hundred feet above the plain. At its peak stood a castle: rugged it looked, even from afar, not at all like an airy castle of fable, but rather like one of strength:

crenellated granite battlements loomed starkly 'round blocky towers. The grey castle stood within grounds consisting of gentle slopes that terminated in craggy drops stepping far down the tor sides until at last they fetched up against another massive rampart rearing up to circle the entire mount. On these Kingsgrounds there were many groves, and pines growing in the crags, and several lone giants standing in the meadows, many trees bereft in winter dress. There, too, were several buildings, perhaps stables or warehouses—the Warrows could not tell—and, of course, the citadel itself.

Below the Kingsgrounds began the city proper. There stood tier upon tier of red, blue, green, white, yellow, square, round, large, small, stone, brick, wooden, and every other color, shape, size, and type of building imaginable, all ajumble in terraced rings descending down the slopes. Running among the homes, shops, storehouses, stables, and other structures were three more massive defense walls, stepped evenly down the side of Mont Challerain, the lowest one nearly at the level of the plain. Only a few permanent structures lay outside the first wall.

Out on the crests of hills to the east and west sprawled the encampments of massed armies, yet there seemed to be less activity than could be expected from the extent of the bivouac—fewer Men and horses, as it were, for the number of tents.

All this and more the Warrows saw as slowly they came toward the hills and unto the city. Finally, in late morning, the company rode up among the sparse buildings flanking the Post Road to come at last to the open city gates, laid back against the first wall with a portcullis raised high. Fur- and fleece-clad, iron-helmed soldiers from the nearby camps streamed to and fro. Atop the barbican stood several Men in red and gold—the gate guard—and one leaned on his hands on the parapet and looked down upon the Warrows with wonder in his eyes. And he called to his companions, and all looked in surprise at the small ones below.

"Ho!" called up Patrel. "Which way to the castle?" he asked, then felt very stupid, for, of course, the castle was at the very top of the mount. Yet the guardsman merely smiled and called back that all they had to do was stay upon the Post Road and it would bear them there.

In through the twisting cobblestone passage under the wall they rode, looking up at the machicolations through which hot oil or missiles could be rained down upon an enemy. At the other end of the barway another portcullis stood raised, and beyond that the Warrows rode into the lower levels of the city proper, and the smells and sounds and sights of the city assaulted them, and their senses were overwhelmed, for they had ridden into an enormous bazaar, the great open market of Rian at Challerain Keep.

The square was teeming with people, buyers and sellers. Farmers from nearby steads were selling hams, beef, sausages, bacon, geese, duck, and fowl of other sorts. They offered carrots, turnips, potatoes, grain, and other commodities. And many customers crowded around the stalls, purchasing staples. Hawkers moved through the crowds selling baskets, gloves, warm hats, brooms, pottery, and such. A fruit seller peddled dried apples and peaches and a strange orange fruit said to come from far south, from Sarain or Thyra or beyond. The odor of fresh-baked bread wafted o'er all and mingled with that of hot pies and other pastries. Jongleurs strolled, playing flutes and harps, lute and fifes, and timbrels, and some juggled marvelously. Here and there soldiers and townsfolk warmed themselves over fires of charcoal set in open braziers and talked among themselves, some laughing, others looking stern, some nodding quietly, others gesticulating.

Through the ebb and flow of the crowd rode forty-three Warrows on ponyback, hooves clattering on the cobbles. The eyes of the young buccen were filled with the glory and marvel of it—why, this was perhaps even more exciting than the Boskydell Fair—and they looked in wonder this way and that, trying to see *everything*. They were so overwhelmed that they did not note that townsfolk and soldiers were staring back at the Warrows in amazement, too, for here come among them were the Wee Folk of legend with their jewel-like eyes.

At last the column rode out of the market square. Now they moved between the shops of crafters—a cobbler's shop, a goldsmithery, mills, lumberyards and carpentries, inns and hostelries, blacksmitheries and ironworks and armories, kilns, stoneworks, and the like. And above many of the shops and businesses were the dwellings of the owners and workers. And the cobbled Post Road wended through this industry, spiraling up and around the mount, climbing toward the crest. Narrow alleyways shot off between hued buildings, and steep streets slashed across the Road. But for the signs at each corner, the Warrows easily could have been lost in the maze of the city. Following the well-marked Post Road, they clattered through the streets of shops and warehouses and workyards, yet as they rode they noted that many of these businesses stood abandoned.

Again they came to a massive wall and followed the road as it curved alongside the bulwark. At last they came to a gate, and it, too, was guarded but open. Through it and up they rode, now among colorful row houses with unexpected corners and stairs mounting up, and balconies and turrets, too, their roofs now covered with snow, bright tiles peeking out here and there. Yet here also, buildings stood empty. But where there were people, they stopped in the streets or leaned out of windows to watch the Wee Folk ride by.

Here there were but a few hawkers: a knife sharpener; a charcoal vendor; a horse-drawn waggon hauling water from the prairie wells up to households on the mount to augment the fluctuating supply provided by frequent but highly variable summer rains and winter snowmelts, caught by the tile roofs and channelled into catchments.

Once more they passed through a barway under a great rampart—the third wall—and again they wended among houses, now larger and more stately than those below, yet still close-set. Again there was an aura of abandonment, for people were sparse and homes unattended.

"Hey," said Argo to Tuck, "have you seen all these empty houses?" At Tuck's nod, Argo went on. "Well now I ask you, how can the market down at the first gate be doing such a brisk trade in an almost deserted city?" Tuck, of course, had no answer, and on they rode.

At last they arrived at the fourth wall, the one encircling the Kingsgrounds. When they came to the gate, the portcullis was down, although the massive iron gates themselves were laid back against the great wall. Up to the portal they rode and stopped, the clatter of pony hooves on cobbles ceased, and in the airy silence Patrel hailed the guard atop the barbican: "Hoy there! Guardsman!"

"State your business," called down one of the Men.

"We are the Company of the King," cried Patrel, and all the Warrows sat proud, "and we've come from the Boskydells in answer to his summons."

Impressed though he was by the very fact that he looked upon Wee Folk, still the Man atop the wall smiled to himself that such a small ragtag group would give themselves the auspicious title "Company of the King." Yet from legend he knew that another small group of these Wee Folk, these Waerlinga, had played a key part in the Great War; thus he was not at all prone to scoff at them. "One moment," he called. "I'll get my Captain."

The Man disappeared behind the merlons, and the Warrows sat calmly waiting. Shortly, another Man appeared, calling down, "Are you warriors come to serve the King in this hour of need?"

"Yes," called Patrel back up to the tower, but in a low voice he said to Tuck and Danner, "though *warrior* is perhaps too strong a term." Then again he called up, "We are the Company of the King, Thornwalkers of the Boskydells, Land of the Barrier. We answer to the King's call, though the herald who bore us that message is dead, Vulg slain."

"Dead? Vulg slain?" cried the tower commander. "Enter. I shall meet you." He turned to the guard squad and ordered, "Open the waybar," and disappeared from view as Men rushed to winches. With a clatter of gears, slowly the portcullis was raised until at last it was up.

The column rode into the passage under the wall and waited until the second portcullis was raised, too, and at last rode out into the Kingsgrounds, where waited the guard Captain. "I will take you to Hrosmarshal Vidron, Kingsgeneral, Fieldmarshal. He must be told of the death of the herald. It is he you want to see, in any case, for he commands the Allies if the King himself cannot take to the field. Now, follow me, we go to the Old Fort." The Man leapt upon the back of a dun-colored horse, and along the cobbles of the Post Road they clattered, at times mounting up along craggy bluffs, drawing ever closer to the Keep.

Now the fortress in all of its massive strength could be seen. Grey it was and ponderous, with great, blocky granite buildings with high windows and square towers. Crenels and merlons crowned the battlements; massive groins supported great bastions outjutting from the walls. Stone curtains protected hidden banquettes, where would stand defenders in the face of attack. In awe rode the Warrows, never having seen such might, and Tuck wondered what his stone-cutting sire would say were he here.

At last they came to the fifth and final wall, the last rampart ere the castle itself, and the massive main gate was shut. They did not go to this portal, however, but instead rode northward alongside the bulwark, striking for the north wall, for there was the Old Fortress, now incorporated into the barrier itself.

As the company slowly rounded a bastion upon the northwest corner, thin wind sprang up, and the young buccen raised their hoods. Yet they heard the drum of hoof-beats and across the slope below saw a spear-wielding youth bestride a galloping charger bearing down upon a pivoting Man-shaped target, wooden shield on one side, extended arm and chain mace upon the other. *Chunk!* The spearlance was driven into the shield by the full weight of the running War-horse, and the target whirled under the impact, violently whipping the wooden mace ball at the passing warrior's head. But the young Man ducked under and was borne away by his courser, leaving the target spinning behind, the ball cleaving nought but empty air. Finally the target gyred to a stop, the pivot coming to a rest in a shallow groove so that the silhouette was square to the list. Again the youth and steed charged upon thundering hooves. *Thunk!* The spear crashed into the shield, and the mace spun and slashed in vain.

To one side and just upslope stood a pavilion, and several Men were gathered about a table, occasionally looking to the north and gesticulating, pointing, and arguing. *Thunk!* The horse and warrior raced cross-slope. As the Warrow column drew near, they came under the winter limbs of an ancient oak tree. Their guide said, "Stop and dismount here. Which among you is Captain? Good! Come with me."

Patrel dismounted and signed Tuck and Danner to accompany him. Following the Man, the three bow-carrying Warrows strode off toward the pavilion, leaving the two squads behind looking at the huge battlements of the massive north wall and speaking in hushed tones. *Chunk!* sounded the spear on target.

Striding down to the tent, Tuck could now see that the

Men were gathered about a table strewn with maps and scrolls; some lay flat with the corners held down by improvised paperweights—a helm, a dagger, a small silver horn, a cup. Again some Men pointed at the maps while others stared northward, and they seemed to be arguing a point. Tuck glanced north, too. Here, high on the mount, he could see miles upon miles of unrelieved snow stretching forth upon the plains below; a low, dark cloud-bank clung to the far horizon. *Thunk!*

The young buccen came unnoticed to the edge of the group and stopped where the guardsman indicated. The guide then made his way to the warrior at the head of the table, a large, robust Man, black hair shot through with silver, with a close-cropped silver beard. The Captain of the tower guard said a word or two, and Marshal Vidron's eyes flicked over the hooded three and briefly up to the forty under the oak. *Thunk!* The target spun wildly under the impact, mace lashing air.

"Faugh!" growled Vidron, glancing back at the small trio. "Saddle me not with infants!"

"Infants? Infants?" cried Patrel, wrath rising in his voice. "Danner! Tuck! Arrows!" and swiftly the three nocked arrows to their bows.

"Hold!" cried one of the Men, grasping the hilt of his sword and drawing it, stepping between Vidron and the young buccen.

But Patrel looked angrily about and cried, "The whirling mace!" and turning, let fly at the spinning target. *Thock!* His arrow struck home, *intercepting the hurtling wooden ball in flight!* Now it gyrated wildly, yet *Thunk! Thock!* Tuck's and Danner's shots followed, and *two more arrows struck the flying ball!* Stunned, the Men were speechless as the Warrows turned back to face them in ire.

"Ai-oi!" shouted Vidron in wonder, "these *infants* have fangs!" Then he burst out laughing loud and long, and in spite of themselves the Warrows smiled at his pleasure. "Hai!" cried the Valanreach Fieldmarshal, "I, Hrosmarshal Vidron of Valon, name you Captain of the Infant Brigade!" He swept up the small silver horn from among the maps and scrolls and strode forward, presenting it to Patrel as a token of his newly bestowed rank. The Warrows and all the Men laughed in great humor as Vidron hung the horn from Patrel's shoulder by the green-and-white baldric. "Someday I shall tell you the history of that trumpet, lad," said Vidron. "It is a noble one, for it was won from the hoard of Sleeth the Orm by my ancestor Elgo, Sleeth's Doom."

"Aye, we know that legend, Sire, for it is famous and told as a hearthtale," answered Patrel. "Elgo tricked Sleeth into the sunlight, and the Cold-drake was done for."

Patrel excitedly examined the bugle. He saw it had riders on horseback engraved upon it, running round the flange of the horn bell among the mystic runes of power. Patrel then set the horn to his lips and blew a clarion call that rang bell-like upslope and down, and spirits were stirred and hearts leapt with hope. And the Warrow company under the oak sprang up and would have come running, but Danner waved them back. Patrel looked upon the trump in wonderment. "Ya hoy! A fine badge of office is this!" he cried, beaming up at Marshal Vidron.

Patrel saw before him a Man in his middle years, with eyes of black and a sharp penetrating gaze. He was clothed in dark leathern breeks, while soft brown boots shod his feet. A fleece vest covered his mail-clad torso, and his silver and black hair was cropped at the shoulders and held back by a leather band upon his broad brow. White teeth smiled through his silver beard. A russet cloak hung to the ground, and a black-oxen horn depended at his side by a leather strap over one shoulder and across his chest.

"From where do you hail, lads?" asked Vidron, not expecting the answer he got.

"From the Boskydells, Sire," answered Patrel, throwing back his hood.

"Waldfolc!" cried Vidron in amazement, and now he looked sharply at all three and at the company upon the slope, at last seeing the color and tilt of gemlike eyes and the shape of sharp-pointed ears, finally recognizing the Wee Folk for what they were.

"Ai, but I knew the Land of the Waldana was nigh, yet little did I think to see you Folk here. Ho, but I thought you mere lads from an outlying village, and not Waldana from the Boskydells, or even from the Weiunwood near. But today, it seems, legends bestride this mount. Our liege will want to see you, as will his younger son, whose target you just bested. Yet wait! He bears your arrows now."

Toward them galloped the horseman of the spear, and he carried the three arrows plucked from the wooden ball of the target mace. Up he thundered, checking his great roan horse at the last moment with the cry "Ho, Rust!" And the red steed skidded to a halt, while in one and the same motion the young Man of fifteen summers sprang down. "Who winged these arrows?" he asked, then his eyes alighted upon the three bow-carrying young buccen. *"Waerlinga!"* his voice rose in surprise. "Was it you who loosed these quarrels?" He raised the arrows in a clenched fist. "Hai! What splendid marksmanship! Would that I could shoot as well. Ai, but what are Waerlinga doing here?"

"My Lord," spoke up the Captain of the gate guard, "they hail from the Boskydells and bear dire news. I know not their names."

"Captain Patrel Rushlock of the Company of the King at your service, Lord," said Patrel, bowing most formally. "And these are my companions and Lieutenants, Tuckerby Underbank and Danner Bramblethorn, Vulg slayers, Modru foes. My company of Thornwalkers are there, up-slope, awaiting the orders of the King."

"Oi! Warriors of the Thornwall, Vulg slayers, hail and well met." The youth's spear was raised in salute, and his eyes touched them all in admiration. "Here, take back your bolts of doom. Spend them on the night-spawn instead of riddling my hapless wooden foe. And you've come to the very storm front itself if you stand against Modru, for his Horde swirls and gathers as a winter blizzard about to strike. But ho, my manners: I am Igon, younger son of King Aurion."

Prince Igon! Tuck's stunned thoughts were set awhirl as he bowed to the young Man before him. Prince Igon stood tall and straight and gazed at them out of clear grey eyes. His hair was dark brown and fell to his shoulders. He was slender as is wont for one of his tender years, but he seemed to conceal a strength beyond his form. A scarlet cloak fell from his shoulders, and light mail gleamed on his breast. His breeks and boots were rust red, and in his hand he held the lancing spear. Upon his head was a leather and steel helm, embellished with black-iron studs. His face was handsome.

Tuck's thoughts were broken by Vidron's bold voice: "Captain Patrel, what is this dire news you bear?"

"Marshal Vidron, the herald sent to the Bosky was pursued by Vulgs and slain at the very gates into the Seven Dells. His message came, but barely," answered Patrel.

"When was this?" asked Prince Igon, casting a look of significance at Vidron.

"Why, let me see." Patrel paused. "I make it ten days past." He turned to Tuck and Danner, who nodded in confirmation.

"And this was the first summons to your Land?" asked Vidron, a frown upon his features.

"Why, yes," answered Patrel, puzzled at the direction these questions were leading. "None else came ere him."

"*Rach!* Then it is so!" gritted Prince Igon, smiting a fist against the table, setting the scrolls ajumble. "Modru sends his Spawn to intercept and slay our heralds. Captain Patrel, he was the second messenger to be dispatched to your Land. I fear our Kingsmen to other Realms have been intercepted, too, for few have answered the call, and the camps below stand half empty."

"But wait," interjected Danner, "last night we saw the campfires of five armies. Surely that is enough soldiery to withstand a thrust by Modru?"

"Ah, you saw but a ruse in the dark to deceive the night spies of the Enemy," rumbled Vidron. "At night we have the look of five armies, yet the Men of less than three. And even five armies are not enough to withstand *that*." Vidron pointed at the far horizon.

Tuck looked, this time closely, and saw that what he had thought was but a low dark bank of distant clouds to the north in fact were not clouds at all. Instead it seemed to be . . . it looked like . . . an immobile solid black wall, rearing up a mile or more to swallow the sky, the darkness fading at the towering limit of its ebon reach.

"Wha—what is that?" asked Tuck, his mind recoiling from the unnatural sight, fearful of the answer.

"Ah, that we do not know," answered Prince Igon, "though some call it the Dimmendark. A sending of Modru, it is, and the land beyond lies in eternal night—

cold, cold night—Winternight. In the day when the Sun is
on high, I have ridden my horse into the Dimmendark, and
it is like passing from bright day through twilight and into
Winternight. There in that spectral dark the land about can
be seen, as if in strange werelight; yet the Sun above is but
a wan paleness, dim, so dim, only faintly can the orb's disk
be descried. And at night, the stars glimmer not, and the
Moon cannot be seen, yet the werelight shines. And in
these glowing lands of winternight gather Modru's Spawn,
and they roam freely—Rukha, Lōkha, Orgus, Ghola, Vulgs,
and perhaps other things as yet unknown, for there Adon's
Ban strikes not."

"Ar, wait a moment," interrupted Danner. "That can't
be so, for Adon's Ban shall rule for as long as night follows
day and day follow night: that is His Covenant."

"My trusty Waldan," said Vidron, "you forget: in the
Dimmendark eternal Shadowlight rules. Hence, there day
does not follow night, nor does night follow day. *There, the
Covenant has been broken.*"

Broken? The Eternal Ban broken? Tuck felt as if his
heart had flopped over, for now Modru defied even High
Adon. How could a meager number of Men and a handful
of Warrows hope to withstand a might such as that?

"Ah, but for now, cast aside the thoughts of Winternight
and the Dimmendark, and of Modru's Horde, too," said
Prince Igon, "for there is nought we can do to change a
jot of it at the moment. Instead, come, bring your company
of Waerlinga. You must be hungry. I'll take you to the Old
Fortress for a meal while Marshal Vidron ponders your
assignment. And I'll take you to my sire, for the High King
would meet with Waerlinga, and he would hear your tale
of the Vulg slaying of the herald."

Nodding to Kingsgeneral Vidron and his staff, Prince
Igon walked with Tuck, Danner, and Patrel, and the Captain of the gate guard, back to the oak where the Prince
was proclaimed to all the young buccen to their delight. A
rousing cheer burst forth when it was announced that they
were going for a hot meal, and amid happy chatter they
mounted up to follow Igon. Waving goodbye to the guard
Captain as he departed for the gate, the Warrow company
trailed the Prince on his steed, Rust, as he rode for a point
midway along the north wall. Through a postern he led

them and across the cobbled courtyard of the Old Fortress, at last coming to some stables.

After seeing to the needs of their mounts, the young buccen were led by Igon to empty barracks, where they stowed their gear from the pack ponies. The Prince then took them to a mess hall for the promised meal and broke bread with them. Igon was astonished by their gusto, for they were such a small Folk—their feet dangling and swinging as they sat on the Man-sized benches, their eyes more or less just above the level of the tabletop—yet they packed away food like hungry birds, and in fact chattered like magpies at a feast. All about them Men paused to stare and smile. But the Warrows paid heed only to the meal, for to them it was indeed like a feast, the first hot food they'd had in eight days, and they happily made the most of it.

"This is where you'll take all your meals while you are at the Keep," announced Igon, and the company heartily approved. The Prince turned to Patrel. "Now, Captain Patrel, you and your Lieutenants and I shall go and seek out my sire, for he will want to hear your full tale, as I do. As to your company, I can arrange for a guide to show them about, or they can rest in the barracks."

"Cor!" proclaimed Argo, "what with my belly full, it's me for a nap on that soft cot back there in the barracks, and a welcome relief it'll be from the hard ground or cold snow, for a change."

"Har! Me too," spoke up Arvin. "I've been looking forward to resting my bones ever since I laid my eyes on that beautiful mattress." There was a general murmur of agreement. "But first, in the back room I spotted a tub or three, and it's me for a hot bath."

Bath! cried several voices at once, and it was a mad scramble as Warrows rushed helter-skelter from the mess hall to be first in the tubs, and Tuck found himself wishing he could go along, too.

Laughing, Prince Igon stood to lead Patrel, Tuck, and Danner in search of the King.

Through labyrinthine corridors of hewn granite blocks the young Prince took the three Warrows. The long passages were dimly lighted by slotted openings to the outside day. Under massive archways and past great pillars they strode, the young buccen's mouths agape as they peered up at huge shadowy cornices with carven gargoyles staring stonily down. Up long flights of stairs they went, and then back down. Tuck was bewilderingly lost and wondered at the route they had taken, deciding he should have spent more time seeing to the way and less time peering into dark corners at stone carvings. At last they rounded a corner to come to a short passage leading to massive, iron-bound, studded oaken doors. The hall was flanked by pike-bearing Kingsguards in scarlet and gold, who struck clenched right fists to hearts when Prince Igon hove into view. Returning the salute, the Prince strode past with the young buccen in tow, stepping to the oaken portals. Igon grasped a door ring in each hand and pulled; the great doors divided in twain, and though massive, each panel easily and noise-lessly swung outward, coming to rest against the stone of the passage. Through this entry he led the wondering Warrows.

They saw before them a great long chamber beringed by pillars spaced along the walls. There, too, were huge hearths, most without fire. Along the tapestried walls, staffs jutted out, from which depended the flags of many different Kingdoms. Overhead, great wooden beams spanned from wall to wall dangling chain-hung braces of night lamps, the chandeliers now dark, for daylight streamed in through high windows. Three broad steps down began the great stone center-floor, smoothly polished stone, ringed around by raised flooring for banquet tables. The amphitheater swept forward till it fetched up against four steps leading to a throne dais. Upon the top step sat a flaxen-haired lass listening to the deep converse between a golden-haired stranger and High King Aurion himself.

As young Prince Igon waited to be noted and summoned, he murmured to the Warrows. "On the throne sits my sire, but whom he converses with, I know him not. The Lady is Princess Laurelin of Riamon, betrothed of my brother, Prince Galen. The other maidens are her Ladies-in-waiting." Tuck then saw three young Women sitting on a bench, partially hidden by a pillar.

The High King, though he was seated, looked from afar to be a Man of middling height. One of his eyes was covered by a scarlet patch, the result of a blinding wound taken in his youth during an expedition against the Rovers of

Kistan. Because of the patch, many villagers called him
Aurion Redeye; and he was much loved, for though his
spirit was bold, his hand was gentle. Although silver locks
fell from his head, it was said that his grip was stronger
than that of most Men. He was dressed in scarlet, much
the same as Igon, but trimmed in gold. When Tuck looked
at him he thought of iron.

On the other hand, Princess Laurelin looked to be but a
slip of a girl. Dressed in blue, she sat upon the step, her
arms clasped about her knees, her face turned toward the
King such that Tuck could not see her features. But her
wheaten hair was beautiful to behold, for it fell to her hips.

Lastly, the stranger: Something there was about him, for
as the day shone through a high portal down upon the
throne dais, it seemed that he was wreathed in a nimbus
of light, his golden hair gathering sunbeams. Grey-green
was his cloak, as if it were woven of an elusive blend of
leaf, limb, and stone—and his boots, breeks, and jerkin
were of the same hue.

The King looked up, and his face broke into a smile.
"Igon, my son!" he called, and beckoned the youth to him.

The Prince said, "Come," and he led the Warrows down
the steps and across the center floor to the foot of the
throne dais, where he stopped and bowed. "Sire," he said,
"I present Captain Patrel Rushlock and his Lieutenants,
Danner Bramblethorn and Tuckerby Underbank, Waerlinga three from the Land of the Thorns."

"Waerlinga!" breathed King Aurion, rising to his feet as
the Warrows deeply bowed. "Welcome, though I would
that times were better." His voice was firm, and his one
eye glittered blue and clear.

Igon turned to the Princess as she gracefully rose to her
feet. Slender she was, and small. "My Lady Laurelin," he
said, inclining his head. Decorously she curtsied as the Warrows bowed to her. Tuck looked up and gasped in wonderment, for she was most beautiful—high cheekbones, wide-
set grey eyes, delicate lips—and her dove-grey eyes caught
his and she smiled. Tuck blushed, flustered, and looked
down at his feet.

King Aurion presented the golden-haired stranger. "Lord
Gildor, once of Darda Galion, the Larkenwald beyond the

Grimwall, now a Lian Guardian who brings us news from
Arden Vale and from the Weiunwood, though grim it is."

Tuck again gasped, this time in astonishment, for the
bright Lord Gildor was an *Elf,* with green eyes atilt and
pointed ears 'neath his yellow locks. In the shape of these
two features, eyes and ears, Elves are much the same as
Waerlinga. Yet, unlike the Wee Folk, Elves are tall, being
but a hand shorter than Man. In this case, the slim, straight
Gildor stood at the same height as the young Prince Igon.

King Aurion stepped down to the Warrows. "But come,
let us sit and talk. You must be wearied by your travels,"
he said, and led them all to a small throne-side alcove,
where they each took a comfortable seat.

"Grim news?" asked Prince Igon, turning to the Elf. "It
seems to be a day of ill tidings, for the Waerlinga's news
is dire, too. What sinister word do you bear, Lord Gildor?"

At a nod from King Aurion, Gildor spoke: "The Dimmendark marches down the Grimwall Mountains, the
abode of ancient enemies, freeing them from High Adon's
Ban. Even now Arden Vale lies deep in Winternight, and
the 'Dark stalks south, into Lianion called Rell, and, on
the far side of the Grimwall, it sweeps along the margins
of Riamon. I fear Modru has in mind to strike at Darda
Galion, for this he must do ere plunging into Valon, and
beyond to Pellar. But though my heart calls me to rush to
aid Darda Galion, here I have come instead, for here I can
best serve Mithgar, at Aurion's side." Gildor fell silent and
for a moment nought was said, and Tuck saw that others,
too, had had to choose between love of home and duty to
the Realm.

"You know that you have my leave to go," said Aurion,
but Gildor gave a faint shake of his head.

"Your pardon, Lord Gildor," said Patrol, "but it was said
that you bear news from the Weiunwood, home of our
distant kin." Weiunwood lay to the east of the Battle
Downs, some thirty leagues south of Challerain Keep.

"Ah yes," answered Gildor. "Your Folk of the Weiunwood have allied with the Men of Stonehill and a small
band of Lian Guardians from Arden. Even now, hidden
holts are being prepared and plans laid for battle should
Modru's Horde come."

"Who leads the Warrows?" asked Danner.

"Arbagon Fenner," smiled Gildor, "and a feisty Waerling is he." But the young buccen shook their heads, for none knew him. "The Men are led by Bockleman Brewster, owner of the White Unicorn Inn of Stonehill. Young Inarion leads the Elves."

King Aurion spoke to the Prince. "And your ill tidings, Igon: what grim news do you bear?"

At Igon's indication, Patrel spoke to the King. "Ten nights past your herald arrived at the Boskydells, bearing word of the muster here at Challerain Keep. Unbeknownst to us, pursuers followed, and while crossing Ford Spindle he was Vulg attacked. Though the foul beast was slain by Tuck, here, still your Man's horse fell to the ice and broke through, and herald, horse, dead Vulg, Tuck, and one of our comrades named Tarpy were all swept under the ice by the swift river current. Only Tuck survived, thanks to Danner's clear thinking in that time of crisis." Patrel paused, and Tuck could feel the Lady Laurelin's soft gaze upon him, sympathy in her eyes. "Though your herald is dead, still the word goes forth across the Bosky," Patrel continued, "borne by the Thornwalkers; hence, in this, Modru has failed to stop the call from spreading through the Seven Dells. Four Vulgs did he send to haul down your messenger; we slew them all. Yet I am told by Prince Igon that this was the second herald sent to the Boskydells, and that Modru's hand must have stopped the first. That explains why the word came late, for Warrows in the Bosky had wondered why no call had come, though rumors of War nested in every tavern. I wonder if other messengers to other Lands have failed to reach their goals, but instead have been intercepted and slain by the foul beasts of Modru, like the Vulgs we slew."

"Aye," said King Aurion, and though his mood was somber, still he looked with admiration upon these casual Vulg-slaying Waerlinga in Thornwalker grey. "Many a herald did we send, but few nations received our first summons, though here and there now the muster begins. We are reduced to playing a sham at night to make our forces appear larger than they are, though whether or not the Enemy is deceived I cannot say. We will know that we have succeeded if we are given enough time for our armies to come ere the storm strikes.

"Yet it is not only armies we await at the Keep. Waggons have been summoned to bear our loved ones to safe haven, whether or not they desire to go." Aurion cocked his shaggy white brow at Laurelin, but she did not look at him, keeping her eyes instead upon her folded hands.

"My Liege," her voice was soft but unyielding, "I cannot flee whilst my Lord Galen yet roams the Dimmendark. He is my betrothed, but even more so, he is my beloved, and I must be here when he returns."

"But you must go, Laurelin," said Prince Igon, "for 'tis your duty to see to the needs of the people above all else, and your presence will buoy up their hearts and spirits in a time of great distress and darkness."

"You speak as if Duty o'errules all else, my Lord Igon," said Laurelin, "even Love."

"Aye," answered Igon, "even Love; Duty must go before all."

"Nay, Prince Igon," interjected Gildor. "I would not gainsay thee, yet I think that Honor must go above all, though each of the three—Love, Duty, Honor—must be tempered by the other two in the crucible of Life."

"Naytheless," said King Aurion, touching his brow above the eye-patch, "when the waggons arrive, refugee trains will be formed to take the old, the halt and lame, the children, and the Women hence from here, including you, my daughter-to-be." Laurelin would have protested but the King held up his hand. "It is my royal edict that this thing be done, for I cannot wage a War where the helpless and innocent are caught in the midst of raging combat. I cannot have my warriors battling with one eye on the foe and the other upon their loved ones, for that is a road to death.

"Yet this I will do, though it goes 'gainst my better judgement: You may delay your departure till the very last caravan, but then you must leave with it, for I would not have you fall into the Enemy's clutch." The thought of Laurelin in the grasp of Modru made Tuck shudder, and he futilely strove to banish the image.

"But now, my friends," said King Aurion to Lord Gildor and the Waerlinga, "you must excuse my son and Princess Laurelin and me, for, you see, this is the final market day, the last before all are evacuated from the city—if the dratted waggons will ever get here, that is. We three must needs

make an appearance at the bazaar, for, as Prince Igon has
so succinctly put it. 'tis our duty. The folk expect to see
their good King Aurion Redeye, and the handsome Prince,
and their Lady-to-be."

"So that's the answer!" burst out Tuck, striking the table.
"Oh . . . er . . ." He was embarrassed. "I mean, well, we
were wondering at the large crowd in the market square,
what with the city being half deserted, as it were. Now you
have answered our question: it is the *last* market day, for
some time to come, I ween . . . sort of a 'Fair' one might
say, though a dark event it is you celebrate."

"With darker days yet to come, I fear," sighed the King,
standing, and so they all rose. He turned to Lord Gildor
and the three Waerlinga. "I thank you all for your news,
though ill tidings it is. We shall speak again in the days
ahead. My Lady." He held out his arm, and Princess Laurelin took it. He led her from the hall, and they were followed by the Princess's Ladies-in-waiting.

"I'll meet you at the gates," called Igon after them and
turned to the Warrows. "But first I must lead you back to
your barracks. Lord Gildor, are you quartered?"

"Yes, the King has given over the green rooms to me,"
answered the Elf. "Here, I'll walk with you as you go, for
it is on the way."

The next morning at breakfast, again the Warrow company chattered like magpies as they ate, for they had much
to talk about. Tuck, Danner, and Patrel had spoken to all
at length the previous day upon returning from the King,
and the news they bore fired the furnaces of speculation.
But though the ore they smelted was high-grade, much
dross was produced for every pure ingot. The gathering
War dominated all thought, and the conversations turned
ever to it, as iron pulled by lodestone.

Patrel's meal was interrupted by a page, summoning him
to attend Hrosmarshal Vidron. As before, Patrel took Tuck
and Danner with him. Again they were led through a maze
of passages in the labyrinthine Keep, yet this time Tuck
paid more attention to their route, recognizing parts of it.
They were brought up the steps of one of the towers and
left on a bench at the door outside the Kingsgeneral's quar-

ters. They could hear angry voices behind the door, muffled, but the words were distinct.

"I say, Nay!" cried a voice. "I remind you, I and my Men are not in your command. Instead I take my instructions directly from the King and none else. And we are sworn to but one duty, and that is to protect the person of the High King. I will not remove any from that charge and place them at your behest, Fieldmarshal."

"And I tell you, Captain Jarriel, it is already decided!" thundered the Voice of Marshal Vidron. "You will reassign forty Men from the duty of guarding Challerain Keep to field duty under my command."

"And what? Replace the forty with those pip-squeaks? With those runts?" Captain Jarriel shot back. "You lief as well just hand the King over to Modru himself, for all the good those mites will do under an attack."

"Hey, he's talking about us!" exclaimed Danner angrily, leaping to his feet; he would have stormed through the door except he was restrained by Tuck and Patrel.

"May I remind you, sir," boomed Vidron, "that these Folk are renowned for their extraordinary service to the Crown. Or have you forgotten their role in the history of the Ban War, the Great War itself, when last we faced the Enemy in Gron, the very same Enemy, I might add?"

"Faugh! Hearthtales and legends! I don't care what fables you might believe about these Folk, for I intend to take this matter up with the King, himself. Then we shall see!" The door was flung open, and a warrior in the red-and-gold tabard of the Kingsmen strode angrily out and past the Warrows to disappear down the tower steps.

Just as angrily, Danner strode through the open doorway and into the Fieldmarshal's quarters with Patrel and Tuck behind. Vidron was sitting on the edge of his bed, pulling on a boot while an orderly hovered nearby.

"Pip-squeaks and runts we are?" Danner demanded. "Just who was that buffoon?"

The Kingsgeneral looked at the spectacle of a fuming Warrow: feet planted wide apart, clenched fists on hips, jaw thrust out, all three feet seven inches aquiver with rage. And then Vidron burst out laughing, falling backward on his bed, his foot halfway into the boot. Great gales of laughter gusted forth, and every time he tried to master his guffaws they would burst out again. Tuck and then Patrel and finally Danner could not help themselves and they laughed, too. At last Marshal Vidron struggled upright. "By the very bones of Sleeth, each time I meet you three, humor drives ire from my heart. It is not every day that I am brought to task by an angry Waldan, bearded in my very den, as it were. Ah, but you are good for my spirit."

"And you, sir, are good for ours," replied Patrel. "Yet Danner's questions remain, and I'll add my own: Why have you summoned us?"

Grunting, Vidron pulled the boot the rest of the way on and stood. The orderly held the Fieldmarshal's jacket as Vidron slipped his arms in. "Well, Wee Ones, for your information, that 'buffoon' is Captain Jarriel. His company wards the Keep, the castle itself, that is, and guards the person of the King. A loyal Man, he is, and one I would gladly have in my command, but he stubbornly sees only one way to perform his charge of office. Because of his duty, he disagrees with the assignment. I have for your company of Thornwalkers, yet had he but listened, I would have told him that High King Aurion himself suggested your assignment."

"And what, prithee, is it that we 'pip-squeaks' and 'runts' are to do?" asked Patrel, smiling.

"Why, patrol the Keep. Guard the King. Keep watch from the ramparts of the castle," answered Vidron.

"Just a moment, now," objected Danner. "We are here to tackle Modru, not to hide away behind the walls of some remote castle."

"Ah, as much as we all would like to brace that foe, each and every one of us cannot," said Vidron. "Heed me, Danner: think not that there is but one way to perform a duty, for to do so would make you the same kind of 'buffoon' as is Jarriel. Hearken unto this, too: by your company of *Waldfolc* warding the castle, forty Men can be freed to take the field against the Enemy, and forty Men on horseback can range farther faster than forty Waldana on ponies, whereas forty Waldana on Castle-ward, clear of eye and skilled in archery, are as good as, nay, better than forty Men in the same assignment. It is as simple as that."

Danner seemed unwilling to accept the argument until Patrel spoke. "Well said, Marshal Vidron. And if I have

understood you aright, the King has so ordered, correct?"
At Vidron's nod, Patrel said, "Then it is settled. To whom
shall we report for duty, and when?"

"Why, to Captain Jarriel, of course, and this morning at
that," answered Vidron, pulling a bell cord. "Now, now,
before you object, Jarriel is a fair Man, just stubborn. Give
it a try. Should it become unbearable, try harder—then see
me. After all, by then I'll need a laugh or two. Ah, here is
your page now."

With misgivings, the Warrows left Hrosmarshal Vidron's
quarters, following the page to Captain Jarriel's command
post, located centrally within the castle at the junction of
two main corridors. They had to wait a short while, for
Captain Jarriel was not there.

"Perhaps he is seeing King Aurion," suggested Tuck, but
there was no way of knowing. At last the Captain arrived,
and the Warrows were summoned. Tuck expected Danner
and the Man to exchange angry words, but, true to Vidron's
appraisal, Captain Jarriel spoke only of duty to the King
when he met with the Warrows, dealing with them as if the
dispute had never occurred.

A page was assigned to show all the members of the
Waerling company the ins and outs of the castle. They were
to become familiar with its layout, at least the major corri-
dors and rooms, as well as the ramparts and battlements.
Then they would take on duties alongside the Men of the
Castleward.

All that day and the next, every moment was spent learning the environs of the Keep. Also on the second day, they
visited the King's armorers to be measured for corselets
made of overlapping boiled leather plates affixed to padded
jerkins, these to wear as armor while guarding the walls of
the Keep. On the third day, the day watch on the north
wall was assigned to Tuck's squad, while Danner's took on
the south rampart.

"Har!" barked Argo as they overtopped the ramp alongside the bastion gorge and came upon the banquette behind
the crenellated battlement. "I said it before and I'll say it
again: these walls were not meant to be patrolled by Warrows. Cor, I can't see over the merlons at all, and only by

walking along the weapon shelf can I look out through the crenels."

"Ar, but what would you see?" asked Finley, who then answered his question: "Nothing but that black wall out there, and who wants ter see that? Nar, we're here to feather the Horde, if and when they try to climb these walls." Finley walked over to a set of machicolations, sighting through the holes where they would rain arrows down along the ramparts should the enemy attempt to scale them.

Tuck spaced the young buccen along the stone curtain, relieving the Men warding the north wall. True to Argo's word, they walked along the weapon shelf to see out upon the land. And far to the north, darkness loomed.

Even though the Sun marched across the sky, still time seemed suspended, for nothing moved upon the snowy plains beyond the foothills. It seemed as if the Land held its breath, waiting . . . waiting. And Tuck's eyes were ever drawn toward the far Dimmendark.

In midwatch, Patrel came to take the noon meal with Tuck. And as they sat eating, Tuck said, "I keep thinking about Captain Darby's words back at Spindle Ford, when he asked for volunteers to answer the King's call. 'Will you Walk the Thorns, or will you walk instead the ramparts of Challerain Keep?' That's what he asked us. At the time I didn't consider his words prophetic, yet here I am, upon the very walls he spoke of."

"Perhaps there's a bit of a seer in each of us," answered Patrel, taking a bite of bread. He chewed thoughtfully. "The trick is to know which words foretell and which don't."

They ate in silence and gazed upon the land. At last Patrel said, "Ah, it looks so dangerous, that black wall out there. And who knows what lurks in the darkness beyond? But this we must do: tonight, and every moment off duty that can be spared, have your buccen fletching arrows, for there may come a time when we will need all the bolts we can get." Tuck nodded without speaking as he and Patrel watched the brooding land.

The Sun continued its slow swing across the sky, and in late afternoon Princess Laurelin and one of her Ladies came to the north battlement. The Princess stood gazing far over the winter snow, her eyes searching along the edges of the foreboding black wall, the distant Dimmendark. She was wrapped in a dark blue cloak, its hood up, concealing her face so fair, though a stray lock of her flaxen hair curled out. She seemed to shiver, and Tuck wondered if the cold stone chilled her, or was it instead the far dark loom.

"My Lady," he said approaching her, "there is a warm charcoal fire along the wall a bit, yet the view to the north is the same." He led her and her Lady-in-waiting to the brazier where the hot coals burned.

Laurelin warmed herself and then stepped to a nearby crenel. Long she looked, and Tuck stood on the shelf at her side gazing northward, too. At last she spoke: "There was a time, a happier time, when on clear days a low range of hills could be seen to the north. The Argent Hills, my Lord Galen called them. Often we stood upon this very wall and spoke of living alone in a cottage by a stream in the pines there. Daydreaming. Now the Argent Hills can be seen no longer, for they have been swallowed by that terrible blackness. Yet I know that they are still there, behind the dark wall, just as is my beloved." Laurelin turned, and she and her Lady went back to the narrow span leading into the castle. Tuck said nought as he sadly watched her go. And behind to the north, the Land waited in airy silence.

The next evening, Laurelin again came for her sunset vigil along the north wall, searching the plains and horizon just before the dusk, while Tuck stood quietly by.

Long moments fled, and the plains were empty of returning warriors. At last Laurelin spoke: "Ah, but I do not like looking for my Lord out over the barrows of dead heroes. He stands in harm's way, and gazing past graves would seem to portend no good."

"Graves, my Lady?" Tuck's voice was filled with puzzlement.

"Aye, Sir Tuck, graves." Laurelin pointed down into the foothills near the north wall. "Do you see that tumbled ring of stone jutting up through the snow? It stands in the center of the barrows of nobles and warriors felled in Wars past."

Tuck looked, and in the deepening shadows he saw snow-covered rounded mounds of elden turved barrows. But his eye was drawn to the center of all mounds, where an ancient ruin of fallen stone lay ajumble—a ruin that once was a ring of tall standing stones. And in the midst of the ring . . . "My Lady, what is that in the stone ring's center?"

"A crypt, Sir Tuck, a crypt, hidden in summer by a tangle of vines and in winter by a blanket of snow." Laurelin's eyes grew reflective. "Lord Galen took me once to see it— the ancient tomb of Othran the Seer, according to legend, Othran who came from the sea, they say, a survivor of Atala, lost forever. But that is only legend, and none knows for certain. Yet the worn carvings in the stone are arcane runes of an elden time, and only the Lian Guardians are said to have read them, for the Lian are skilled at tongues and writings."

"Runes?" Tuck blurted, drawn by the mystery of a lost language.

"Aye." Laurelin thought a bit. "My Lord Galen says that there is an eld inscription:

> *Loose not the Red Quarrel*
> *Ere appointed dark time.*
> *Blade shall brave vile Warder*
> *From the deep, black slime.*

Those are the words the Elves are said to have ciphered from yon stone."

"What do they mean?" asked Tuck. *"Red quarrel, vile Warder, appointed dark time."*

"I cannot say," laughed Laurelin, "for it is a riddle beyond my knowing. Sir Tuck, you ask me to answer an enigma that has stumped the sages ever since Elf first came upon the crypt in elden times, since Man first settled these lands and chose to place his barrows around an ancient tomb, even then a ruin, in the hope that the wraith of the mystic seer of Atala would give guide to the shades of Man's own fallen heroes."

Tuck looked down upon the tower in wonder as Laurelin spun forth the eld tale. Slowly the shadows mustered unto the low foothills, and when the Princess fell silent, darkness covered the land. Finally Laurelin bade Tuck goodeve and disappeared into the castle. Tuck watched her go, and then his vision was drawn again toward the darkness where stood the jumbled ring of stone. And he pondered the riddle of the carven runes, etched words of a long-lost tongue.

On the third evening Laurelin, looking down at Tuck, asked the small Warrow, "Do you have a beloved? Oh, I think you must. Do I see a sweetheart's favor around your neck?"

Tuck fumbled at Merrilee's silver locket, lifting the chain over his head. "Yes, my Lady," he answered, "only, in the Boskydells a sweetheart is called 'dammia,' er, I mean, I would call her 'dammia' while she would call me 'buccaran.' That is what we Warrows name each other, uh, Warrow sweethearts, that is. And yes, this is my dammia's favor, given to me on the day I left my home village of Woody Hollow." Tuck handed her the locket and chain.

"Why, this is beautiful, Tuck. An ancient work. Perhaps from Xian, itself." Laurelin pressed a hidden catch and the locket sprang open. Tuck was dumbfounded, for although he had touched the locket often, he had not known that it actually opened. "My, she is very pretty," said Laurelin, looking closely. "What is her name?"

"Merrilee," said Tuck, his hands atremble, yearning to take the locket back to see what face it held.

"A lovely name, that." Laurelin glanced to the brooding north. "My Lord Galen wears mine own golden locket at his heart, but no portrait has it, just a snippet of my hair. It must ever be so, that warriors in all times and all Lands have carried the lockets of their loved ones upon their breasts. If not lockets, then other tokens do soldiers bear into danger, to remind them of a love, hearth, home, or something or someone else dear to their hearts." Laurelin clicked shut Tuck's silver locket and handed it into his trembling hands, and turned once more to look beyond the abutment and across the winter plains.

Tuck eagerly fumbled at the locket, discovering at last that it opened by pressing down upon the stem where attached the chain. *Click!* The leaves of the locket fell open in his hand—mirrored silver on the left, and a miniature portrait of . . . it *was* Merrilee! *Oh, my black-haired dammia, you are so beautiful.* As he stood upon the cold granite rampart, all of his loneliness, his longing for quiet evenings before the fire at The Root, and his love for Merrilee welled up through his very being, and his vision blurred with tears.

"Ah, Sir Tuck, you must miss her very much," said the Princess.

Blinking back his tears, Tuck looked up to see Laurelin's sad grey eyes upon his blue ones. "Yes, I do. And, you know, I didn't realize just how much until I saw her portrait just now." Tuck shuffled his feet, embarrassed. "You see, until you opened the locket, I didn't know she was there, all the time secretly next to my heart."

Laurelin's laughter had the ring of silver bells chiming in the wind, and Tuck smiled. "Ah, but Sir Tuck, did you not know?" asked the Princess. "We Women and dammen do practice our secret arts to remain in the hearts of our Men and buccen." And they laughed together.

Yet in the waning light of day and by candleflame throughout the night, again and again Tuck gazed at Merrilee's likeness, for now it seemed she was closer to him, and he could not seem to get his fill of her image. The young buccen of his squad smiled to see him peering at the locket, but Danner merely snorted, "Faugh! Moonstruck calf!"

The next afternoon when Laurelin came to the north wall, there was a deep look of sadness about her, and desperately she scanned the sullen horizon.

"My Lady, you seem . . . disturbed." Tuck looked out over the remote snowy plains.

"Have you not heard, Sir Tuck?" Laurelin turned her gaze to him, her grey eyes pale. "The waggons arrived yestereve. Even now a first caravan presses south, and a second one forms. A train will leave each day, bearing Women and children, oldsters and the infirm, until we are all gone. And my beloved ranges far north, and I fear I will not get to see him ere I must board the last wain of the final caravan."

"And when might that be, Princess?" Tuck turned to Laurelin, and her face was shadowed within her hood.

"The first day of Yule," said Laurelin, forlornly. "That day, too, I become nineteen."

"Ai!" exclaimed Tuck. "The last of Yule is my dammia's birthday, and for her it is an age-name birthday, too. It's when Merrilee turns twenty, no longer a maiden but a young damman she becomes. Oh my, but neither she nor you have been given much cause to be merry."

"High King Aurion has granted me but one more day of vigil after this eve. But on my birthday, the shortest day of the year—First Yule, just two days hence—the last waggon train departs, bearing south to Pellar. And I go with it, to Caer Pendwyr." The Princess looked crestfallen.

"Ai-oi! But it *is* your birthday," said Tuck, attempting to brighten her spirit. "At least we have that to celebrate, though I have no gift for you, nought but a smile, that is."

Tentatively the Princess smiled back, brushing aside a stray flaxen lock. "Your presence alone is gift enough, Sir Tuck. Yes, your presence gladdens me. Please do come to my birthday feast tomorrow night on Yule Eve. High King Aurion holds the celebration in the Feast Hall, and all the Captains are to attend. Ah, but they are such stern warriors, all cheerless but for Marshal Vidron, Igon, and, of course, the King himself."

"But, my Lady," protested Tuck, "I am no Captain. I and Danner are but Lieutenants. It is Captain Patrel you would invite."

"Nonsense!" Laurelin tossed her head. "I'll invite whom I please. After all, it is *my* birthday we celebrate. Yet, would it make you happier, I invite all three—Captain Patrel, Sir Danner, and yourself, Sir Tuck."

"But we have nought to wear except our rude clothes, not fine jerkins nor shiny helms nor—" Tuck's protests were interrupted by a stamp of Laurelin's foot.

"But me no buts, Sirrah!" she exclaimed, her sad mood now replaced by one of amused determination. A smile played at the corner of her mouth, her eyes twinkled, and her mode of speaking now dropped into that of formal court parlance: "I shall see to the petty details of thy raiment. Tomorrow eve, gather thy two friends unto thee at the change of watch. I will meet thee here at the wall, as is my wont, and then we will get thee hence to be fitted, for I have secret knowledge of the whereabouts of clothes just thy size but fit for a Prince. Then thou shall be dressed for my party, be it one of farewell or of a birthday anniversary or simply a celebration of the coming Yule."

Tuck threw up his hands in surrender, resigned to the

inevitable, and the Princess laughed at the look upon the face of her diminutive, newfound confidant. Then, while Laurelin spoke of Lord Galen and Tuck listened, the Warrow and Princess gazed over the waiting snow until it became too dark to see.

During the early part of the next day-watch, one of Laurelin's Ladies-in-waiting came first to Tuck, then to Danner, and lastly to Patrel and took their measurements with a tailor's tape. Yet when queried by the curious Warrows as to what was to be done with the figures, the Lady merely smiled and answered not their questions.

That day all three were the targets of the jests and japes of their fellow Warrows: "Ar, keeps yer thumbs out o' the soups if you please, me buccoes," said Dilby. "Mind your p's and q's, and stay off the Ladies' toes when you dance," laughed Delber. "Watch out for lettin' your little fingers droops as you takes your tea," cautioned Argo. "Mind you now, eats with your knifes and forks, and don't go tearing into it with just yer little teeths like a common hanimal," added Sandy. Throughout the day the good-natured remarks assaulted Tuck's, Danner's, and Patrel's ears, accompanied by raucous guffaws.

An hour before sunset, Laurelin came alone to stand at the wall and search for sign of the return of her betrothed. Long she sought, but again the vigil bore no fruit, for the expectant plains lay empty as great flat shadows mustered upon the distant prairie. The darkening land seemed poised upon the brink of doom, yet nought stirred in the deepening gloom. As the last of the Sun dipped below the horizon, the ward-relief appeared, and so, too, did Tuck and Danner and Patrel. Sadly, Laurelin turned away from her watch, for this was her last night. Tomorrow would see her depart south, and who, then, would look for her beloved? She sank to a ledge and put her face between her hands and wept silently.

Laurelin cried as Tuck, Danner, and Patrel stood helplessly by, not knowing aught else to do. At last Tuck took her hands in his own and said, "Fear not, my Lady, for as long as I can I will come hence to be your eyes, to watch in your stead. And when Lord Galen comes at last, I will tell him of your lasting love." And Laurelin clasped Tuck to her and wept even more so. And he held her and soothed her while a tear ran down Patrel's cheek, and Danner, in dull rage, looked out over the empty stillness toward Modru's black wall.

After long moments, Laurelin's tears began to subside, and she looked at the three Warrows and then quickly away, as if afraid to catch their eyes with her own. "I am shamed by my outburst, for often I have been told that a Princess should not be seen to weep, yet I could not help myself. Oh my, I seem to be lacking a kerchief."

Patrel stepped forth and gave her his own. "A gift my Lady, for it is your birthday eve."

"I have acted more as if it were a funeral, keening my lamentation," said Laurelin, wiping her tears away, gently blowing her nose.

"Then, Princess, I suggest we give over this whole night to the singing of dirges," smiled Patrel, and Laurelin laughed at the absurdity. "If not dirges, then, let us instead celebrate, for I know where they're holding a party tonight, though we have nought but rags to wear."

Again Laurelin laughed, and she rose up and clasped one of Patrel's hands and twirled him about. "Ah yes, such lowly beggar's garb you wear," Laurelin crowed, "yet I know where we can remedy that, and then perhaps all four of us can slip into that party of yours and not be cast back out the door. Come." And smiling secretively unto herself, the Princess led the three Warrows into the castle, to the old living quarters of the royal family, to a long-abandoned room. Inside was a waiting valet, there to attend the three young buccen, much to their surprise.

"I shall return in a trice," said Laurelin, mischievously. They heard the sound of a distant gong. "Hasten, for the guests now gather and we would not be late to the feast." She slipped out the door and left them with the valet.

In an adjoining room three hot baths had been prepared in great copper tubs, and the Warrows wallowed and sloshed in the soapy suds. But they were soon herded out by the servant, who bade them to hurry and dry themselves for betimes the Princess would return. They found awaiting them soft silken garments, both under and over—stockings and shoes and beribboned trews, blue for Tuck, scarlet for Danner, and pale green for Patrel, with jerkins to match—

and they fit as if sewn for them by the royal tailors. As fine as these clothes were, the three young buccen had a greater surprise in store, and they were astounded.

The valet presented them with three corselets of light chain mail. Silveron was Tuck's, amber gems inset among the links, with a bejeweled belt, beryl and jade, to be clasped about the waist. Danner's ring-linked armor was black, plain but for the silver-and-jet girt at his middle. And Patrel was given golden mail with a gilded belt: gold on gold. Helms they wore, simple iron and leather for Tuck and Patrel, a studded black one for Danner. And at the last they were given cloaks, Elven-made, the same elusive, grey-green color as was worn by Lord Gildor.

They gaped at each other in astonishment. "Why," said Danner, "we look like three warrior Princelings!"

"Just so," came a tinkling laugh. Laurelin had returned, now dressed in a simple yet elegant gown of light blue that fell straight to the floor from a white bodice. Blue slippered feet peeked under the hem. Her hair was garlanded with intertwining ribbons, matching those crisscrossing the bodice. A small silver tiara crowned her head.

"You *do* look like Princelings," she said, "but that is befitting mine escorts, warriors three."

"But how . . . where?" stammered Tuck, holding out his arms and pirouetting, indicating the raiments and armor upon Danner and Patrel and himself. "Tell me the answer to this mystery before I burst!"

"Oh, *la!*" laughed Laurelin, "we can't have you bursting on my birthday eve. As to the mystery, it is simple. Once apast, my Lord Galen showed me where first he and then Igon quartered as children. Here I knew were closets of clothing worn by the seed of Aurion. And I thought surely some would fit you three, and I was not wrong. But happiest of all, here, too, was the armor of the warrior Princelings of the Royal House of Aurion. The silver you wear, Sir Tuck, is from Aurion's own childhood, handed down to him from his forefathers. Silveron it is, and precious, said to be Drimmen-deeve work of old. And, too, Sir Tuck, I chose the silver armor for you because you wear your dammia's silver locket." Laurelin smiled as Tuck blushed before the other young buccen.

The Princess then turned to Danner. "The black, Sir

Danner, comes from Prince Igon's childhood, made just for
him by the Dwarves of Mineholt North, who dwell under
the Rimmen Mountains in my Land, Riamon. It is told that
the jet comes from a mountain of fire in the great ocean
to the west."

Laurelin spoke to Patrel. "Your golden armor, Captain
Patrel, is Dwarf-made, too, and came from the Red Caves
in Valon. It was my beloved, Prince Galen, who wore it as
a youth, and I hold it to be special because of that."

Princess Laurelin turned again to Tuck. "There, you see,
the riddle is now solved, though simple it was, and hence
you must not burst after all. You are, indeed, wearing clothing and armor fit for Princelings, yet they never graced a
more fitting trio." The Princess smiled, her white teeth
showing, and the young buccen beamed in response.

Again they heard the tolling of a distant gong. "Ah, let
us begone," said Laurelin, "for the time is upon us. Captain
Patrel, your hand please." And thus they went forth from
the abandoned quarters and through the corridors and
down the steps to the great Feast Hall: Captain Patrel, in
golden armor, with the hand of the beautiful Lady Laurelin,
gowned in blue; black-armored Danner to Patrel's right;
and silver-armored Tuck to Laurelin's left. Each of the
Elven-becloaked Warrows strode with a helm under one
arm, and a silver horn of Valon on green-and-white baldric
hung at Patrel's side. And when they came through the
main doors and into the long Feast Hall, all the guests rose
and murmured in wonderment, some at the great beauty
of the Princess, others at the Waerling warriors by her side.

Across the wide floor they strode, unto the steps of the
throne dais, and thereupon sat Aurion Red-eye; scarlet-
and-gold raiments were upon him, and he looked every
inch the High King. To his right stood youthful Prince Igon,
in red, and Lord Gildor, in grey. To Aurion's left stood
Hrosmarshal Vidron, dressed in the green-and-white colors
of Valon. The Warrows bowed low, and Laurelin made
a graceful curtsy. Aurion acknowledged their courtesy by
inclining his head, and then he rose and walked down to
the Princess and took her hands in his and smiled.

Then Aurion turned to the guests. His voice was firm
and all heard his words: "This is the eve of the twelve days
of Yule, a time of celebration, for it marks the ending of

an old year and the beginning of the new. Tomorrow, First Yule brings with it the shortest day and longest night as the old year lays dying, and some may take that as a bleak omen in these dark times. Yet I say unto ye all, First Yule is also a time of new beginnings. Hearken unto me, though Twelfth Yule is reckoned as the first day of a new year, I ween that First Yule marks its true beginning; for it is thereafter that the days grow longer as the land begins the slow march toward the shining days of summer, and that is a bright omen of hope.

"But First Yule also has brought us great grace and beauty—the Princess Laurelin. If there be omen seekers amongst ye, look upon this Lady in blue, and ye can do nought but see good fortune in your rede."

King Aurion led the Princess to a throne to one side, where she was seated and flanked by the armored Waerlinga. The King turned to his guests and proclaimed, "Let the celebration begin." And there rose up a great cheering in the Hall that made the very rafters ring.

Spectacle and entertainment filled the Hall as the grand party got under way, with jugglers and wrestlers, dancers and buffoons, prestidigitators and a Man who spewed fire from his mouth, and others, all strutting in file through the doors and around the floor to be seen before they were to perform.

Next, servants bearing platters laden with food paraded into the Hall. There were roast pig and lamb, beef and fowl, and vegetables such as carrots, parsnips, beans, red cabbage, and peas, and great pitchers of frothed ale and dark mead, and apples and pears, and even the strange new fruit from Thyra, orange and tangy and full of juice.

The tables were set and groaned beneath the weight of the feast. The Warrows' eyes grew big at the heaped mounds of food, for trenchers were they all, but never had they seen such a spread of banquet.

The King stood and escorted Princess Laurelin to the royal table, and Prince Igon, Lord Gildor, Marshal Vidron, and Tuck, Danner, and Patrel accompanied them. The Princess was seated, and King Aurion raised a horn of honey-sweet mead; so did they all. "Yule and Lady Laurelin!" he cried, and a great shout went up: *Yule and Lady Laurelin!*

And the Princess's eyes were bright with tears as she signed for the feast to begin. And so it did.

Food and drink and entertainment occupied Tuck's senses as the party pulsed into the night . . . and good conversation, too:

"We celebrate this same festival in my Land of Valon," said Marshal Vidron to Tuck as they watched a juggler. "Only there we call it Jöl rather than Yule. But that is because the old language, Valur, still names many things in the Valanreach, though the Common Tongue, Pellarion, makes up our everyday speech. Ah Valur, a language rich in meaning, once spoken by many, but now known only to my countrymen. Yet Valur will live forever, for it is our War-speech, the battle-tongue of the Harlingar, the Vanadurin, Warriors of the Reach!" Vidron raised his cup in salute and took a great gulp of mead.

"Yule has had many names in many tongues," said Lord Gildor, his Elven eyes aglitter, "yet it always has been the same twelve days of winter festival throughout the years. And though days, months, and years mean little to my Folk, memories are important to us. And many a happy memory centers about Yule, or Jöl, Yöl, Üle, or whatever it may be called. Yes, I can remember a time such as this when it was still called Gēol, and we celebrated even though Modru threatened the Land in that Era, too."

"You can *remember*?" exclaimed Danner, hushed awe in his voice. "But that was . . . that was back before the Ban, four thousand years . . ." Danner's words trailed off in wonder.

"Yes," smiled Gildor, his voice soft, "I can remember."

A roar went up from the guests, and nothing more was said as they watched wrestlers grapple on the central floor. At last, one of the young soldiers hefted the other and spun him about and flung him to the mat, pinning him. Great shouts of praise rose up from the assembly.

"Ah, if I am not mistaken," said Aurion to the Princess, "that young Man, the victor, is from Dael in your Land, for I have seen him wrestle before. He has great strength and agility, as many in Riamon do."

Laurelin smiled brightly, but behind her eyes loomed sadness. "What a grand party," she said to the King, "yet many of this gay troupe will be on the waggons with me on the morrow."

"And I ride with the escort," said young Igon, glumly, "when I think it would be better that I return to the Dimmendark to stand beside Galen against the foe."

"My son," said Aurion, "I need you in Pellar. You but ride with the escort to Stonehill, beyond the range of Modru's Vulgs. Then you will leave the train behind, and with six fast companions you will go apace to Caer Pendwyr to rally the Kingdom to our aid."

"Sire, I will obey thy command," replied Igon, his speech now courtly, "though I think thee but try to place one of thy heirs temporarily beyond harm's way." King Aurion's face flushed, and he glanced at Vidron as if to a conspirator. Prince Igon spoke on. "I think others, Captain Jarriel for one, can do this deed thou hast given me as well as I if not better, whereas I have fought and slain foe in the bitter Winternight and that is what I am suited to do. Aye, 'twas perchance by accident that we stumbled across the enemy, still that does not alter the fact that Galen and I slew five between us. It is this task I would return to: to stand with Galen against the foe."

"Son, you spoke that others could do this deed I have given you," responded Aurion, stonily, "and you name Captain Jarriel, for you know I send him south as your counsel. But this I say unto you: Captain Jarriel cannot command the jealous generals of rival factions to set aside their pettishness. Only one of the Royal Family can fire the will of the armies with the resolve and unity needed to meet and do battle with Modru's Horde. And that is the command I have thrust upon you: to muster the forces and return unto me with them."

"The commanding of that army, Sire, should be Galen's task, not mine, for he is elder, by ten years," answered Igon.

"But he is not here!" snapped the King, his voice rising, the flat of his hand slapping the table, setting cups atumble. Then his look softened, and his speech became as courtly as was Igon's. "Ah, mine son, in thy veins flows the same blood as mine own, yet thine is made hot by youth. I know thou wouldst sally forth to join thy brother and meet the foe, for that is a hard thing to resist. Yet set aside thy

rashness at this time, and see that a royal hand is needed
to bring mine Host northward apace. Thou knowest that
the first heralds were Vulg slain, and perchance the second,
and only slowly doth the word go forth unto the Land.
Hence, the muster has not yet truly begun. This, then, is
the eleventh hour of our need. Thou, or Galen, or I must
go and return with that which will whelm the Enemy." King
Aurion placed a hand upon Igon's. "Fate hath decreed that
it is thou who must gather mine Host, for Galen is to the
north, and I must remain here to take the field if Modru
comes. This, then, is my charge unto thee: Bring unto me
mine Host."

The youth bowed his head to the King and placed his
free hand upon Aurion's. "Sire, I am at thy command,"
said Igon, acceding to Aurion's reasoning. And the King
stood and raised up Igon and embraced him, and then they
each drained a horn of mead.

Prince Igon turned and spoke to the Princess. "It seems,
my Lady Laurelin, that we crue to be travelling companions, at least for a while. Hear me now: I take upon myself
a sword-oath to ward you to safety on our travel to Stonehill; let the Enemy in Gron beware."

Laurelin smiled radiantly up at him. "I am most pleased
to have you as a protector, Lord Igon, though I would that
neither of us had that journey to make."

The feast went on. A sleight-of-hand artist made doves
appear from kerchiefs, and flowers from empty tubes, to
the delight of all. Then one came who swallowed swords—
making Tuck's stomach queasy—and threw knives with
wondrous skill. Finally a harper played, but his song was
of love lost and sad unto the heart. Patrel looked at Laurelin and saw that tears glistened upon her lashes, and he
nudged Tuck and Danner, who saw her sadness, too.

The small gold-clad Warrow took a great draught of ale
and called the harper to him. "Have you got a lute?" Patrel
asked. "Good! May I borrow it?" In a trice the Wee One
held a fine lute in his hands, and he turned to the Princess.

"My Lady, it is nearly mid of might, and in but a few
moments you will be nineteen. We of the Boskydells have
nought to give you as a present on this your birthday eve,
yet there is a happy song, really nought but a ditty, that
perchance will cheer you. It is called *The Merry Man in*

Boskledee, and practically every Warrow in the Boskydells knows it and the dance that goes along. I propose that Tuck and Danner and I perform it as the Warrows' gift to you."

Tuck and Danner were both thunderstruck. Had Patrel actually proposed that *they* sing a simple Warrow song before all of these *Warriors*?

"Patrel!" hissed Danner, "you can't be serious. This hardly seems the time or place for a nonsense tune."

"Nonsense!" roared Vidron, his mood jovial. " 'Twere no better time than now for a happy jig."

"Oh yes, please do," begged the Princess, turning to Tuck and Danner, "for I need the cheer."

Tuck looked into the pleading eyes of the Lady and could not refuse, and neither it seemed could Danner. And so, after a good stiff glog of mead, they most reluctantly stepped down upon the central floor and walked to the fore center.

King Aurion himself called for quiet, and a hush fell over the guests. Patrel plunked the strings, tuning the lute, and said under his breath to the other two, "Give it your best go." At their nods his fingers began dancing over the strings. And such a bright and lively tune sprang forth that it immediately set toes to tapping and fingers to rapping, and lustily the Warrows began to sing:

> *Oh—Fiddle-dee hi, fiddle-dee ho,*
> *Fiddle-dee hay ha hee.*
> *Wiggle-dee die, wiggle-dee doe,*
> *Wiggle-dee pig die dee.*
>
> *Once there was a very merry Man*
> *Who came to Boskledee.*
> *His coat was red and his horse was tan,*
> *And mittens, well he had three.*
>
> *He was so tall but his horse so small,*
> *His feet dragged on the ground.*
> *He didn't dismount when the steed was tired,*
> *He simply walked around.*

A great roar of laughter rose up from the assembly, and

here Tuck and Danner, silver- and black-armor clad, danced
a simple but rigorous to-and-fro jig to the beat of the tune,
occasionally linking arms to wildly circle oppositely.

> *Oh—ho ho ho, ha ha ha,*
> > *Higgle-dee hay hi hee.*
> *Har har har, ya ya ya,*
> > *Giggle-dee snig snag snee.*
>
> *He tumbled hand springs, wore seven rings,*
> > *Shot fireworks in the air.*
> *His pants were orange and his shoes bright green,*
> > *He cried, "Let's have a fair!"*
>
> *He strummed upon a six string-ed lute*
> > *And sang so merrily.*
> *His voice, it broke with a great loud croak,*
> > *And he laughed in happy glee.*

Again the warrior Captains howled in mirth and banged
the tables with their mead cups. Laurelin and Igon ran
down hand in hand, and they joined Danner and Tuck in
dancing the jig. To and fro, back and forth they danced,
bright smiles upon their faces. Blue, red, silver, and black,
all whirled and stepped to the notes played by gold. And
the assembly roared its vast approval.

> *Oh—Har har har, fa la la,*
> > *Cackle-dee ha ho hee.*
> *Ho ho ho, tra la la,*
> > *Giggle-dee tum ta tee.*
>
> *He disappeared with a flash and a bang*
> > *And maybe a puff of smoke.*
> *He left behind his clothes and his lute,*
> > *His steed, and a couple of jokes.*
>
> *And now there is in old Boskledee*
> > *Fireworks at the annual fair,*
> *Where we wear bright clothes and ride ponies*
> > *With gay songs filling the air.*

Oh—Tiddle tee tum, ho ho ho,
  Tra-la-la lay la lee.
Fiddle-dee fum, lo lo lo,
  Ha-ha-ha ho ha hee.

Oh—Fiddle-dee fum, lo lo lo,
  Ha-ha-ha ho ha hee.
Tiddle tee tum, ho ho ho,
  Tra-la-la lay la lee—Hey!

And with final *Hey!* Patrel twanged the lute and the fling stopped, the four dancers embracing and laughing in joy and panting with exertion. A great, wild cheering broke out, with whistling and cup banging and stomping and clapping. Marshal Vidron roared in laughter, while King Aurion banged his cup and Lord Gildor clapped. Laurelin and Igon, Danner and Tuck, and Patrel all bowed to one another and to the crowd, and Laurelin's eyes fairly danced with happiness.

But then:

Boom! Doom! The great doors of the Feast Hall boomed open, echoing through the chamber like the knelling of doom, and a begrimed warrior trod into the Hall, his left arm gashed and bleeding. Smiling countenances turned toward him, but gaiety fled before his unyielding pace. Silence clanged down like the stroke of an axe blade upon stone, and the only sound to be heard was the hard stride of the Man down the long floor. And as the soldier passed the Warrows and Laurelin and Igon, and strode toward the King, Tuck was whelmed by a dreadful foreboding, and it seemed as if he were rooted to the floor. All eyes were locked upon the warrior as he came unto the throne dais. He struck a clenched fist to his heart and knelt upon one knee before the King, and blood dripped upon the stone. And in the hanging quiet, all heard his words:

"Sire, on this dark Yule Eve, I bear thee tidings from my Lord Galen, though ill word it is: The Dimmendark now stalks this way, the Black Wall moves toward Challerain Keep. And in the Winter-night that follows, the Horde of ravers marches. The War with Modru has begun."

CHAPTER 5

The Dark Tide

A great uproar filled the Hall, and hands grasped futilely at weaponless girts, for all had come to the feast unarmed. Shouts of anger boiled up, and clenched fists struck tables in rage, and some tore at their hair. Tuck's heart thudded in his chest, and a cold chill raced through his veins, and from his confused wits one thought rose up above all: *It comes!*

At a sign from Aurion, a steward struck a great staff to the floor three times, and the knell of the gavel cut through the din. At last quiet returned to the Hall, and the King bade the warrior to speak on.

"Sire, I did but come from the Dimmendark five hours past," he continued. "Two of us were entrusted by my Lord Galen to bring this word. Three horses each had we, and all were ridden unto foundering. Yet I and my last steed were all that won through, for my comrade was Vulg slain along the way, and I am Vulg wounded."

"Modru's curs!" spat Aurion, his fists clenched in fury, and the scarlet patch upon his left eye seemed to flash anger. Shouting wrath filled the Hall.

"Oh my, your arm!" Distress was in Laurelin's voice, and she moved at last, rushing to the soldier's side. She gently took his arm and called out through the roar for a healer, sending a nearby page darting from the chamber after one.

Tuck's own paralysis was broken, and he joined Laurelin. Together they used the warrior's dagger to cut away his tattered sleeve, revealing a long, ugly gash. "This scratch was made at the very gates of the first wall," grunted the soldier, gratefully accepting a horn of mead from Patrel and quaffing it in one gulp. Danner refilled the cup from a pitcher. "Why, you are Waerlinga!" he exclaimed, seeing for the first time that he was attended by Wee Folk.

Again the gavelling of the steward's staff cut through the clamor, and slowly quiet was restored. "Your name, warrior," called Aurion, as Igon moved to stand beside his father.

"Haddon, Sire," answered the Man.

"Well done, Haddon! You have brought vital news, though dire it is. Say you this: How much time have we ere the Black Wall sweeps unto Challerain Keep?"

"Perhaps two days, three at most," answered Haddon, and a grim murmur ran throughout the assembly.

"Then we must make final our plans," Aurion called out to the gathering, and all fell silent. "It is now mid of night. First Yule steps into the Realm, and Princess Laurelin paces forward into her nineteenth year. Good times lay behind us, and better time yet lay ahead, but in betwixt will fall drear days. Modru's Horde now strikes south. Here at these walls they must be held. Go now unto your beds and rest, for we must be in the fullness of our strength to meet this foe." Aurion swept up a goblet from a nearby table and raised it on high. *"Hál!"* he cried in the ancient tongue of the North. *"Hēah Adoni cnāwen ūre weg!"* (Hail! High Adon knows our way!)

And the assembled raised their own horns and cups. *Hál! Aurion ūre Cyning!* (Hail Aurion our King!) And all drained their goblets to the bottom as through the doors returned the page with a sleepy healer in tow, nightcap still aperch his head. But all sleep fled from his eyes as he examined the wound.

"Vulg bite?" The healer's voice was startled. "Foul news. We must get this warrior to a cot. The fever has begun, and we need blankets, hot water, a poultice of gwynthyme, and . . ." His voice sank into mumbles as he rummaged through his healer's satchel. Laurelin sent pages scurrying to fetch the healer's needs.

With the healer and young buccen following, the Princess led the warrior through a postern behind the drapes in back of the throne. The door led to an alcove where there was a divan and fireplace and several chairs. Haddon's cloak and armor, jerkin and padding were removed, and he was made to lie down, though he protested that he was too grimy for the couch. A page bore hot water in, and the healer laved the wound as Laurelin spoke with Haddon.

"My Lord Galen, is he well?" she asked.

"Aye, my Lady," answered Haddon, pride in his voice. "He has the strength of two and the spirit of ten. And cunning he is, clever as a fox, for many a trap of his has the foe sprung to their woe."

"Does he say when he might return here to the Keep?" Laurelin filled a basin with water, exchanging it for the one now tinged red with blood.

"Nay, Princess." Haddon's brow now beaded with sweat. "He harasses the Horde's flanks, trying to turn their energies aside. Yet there are so many, and he now has less than a hundred in his ranks. We were sent to spy, not to thwart an army, yet I do not think he will flee back to the Keep." Laurelin's pale eyes were bleak as she heard this news.

The door opened and in strode Aurion, followed by Igon, Gildor, and Vidron. As Gildor drew the healer aside and spoke quietly with him, Aurion sat by the side of the couch.

"How many does Modru send against us?" asked the King, peering into Haddon's face, now flushed with fever.

"Sire, they are without number," answered Haddon, his voice weak and falling toward a whisper. A shudder of chills racked the scout's frame, but his low voice spoke on! "Sire . . . the Ghola . . . Ghola ride in their ranks."

"Guula!" cried Vidron, and his countenance was grim.

"Do you mean Ghûls?" asked Patrel.

"Aye, Waldan," answered the Hrosmarshal. "This foe is dreadful: Man-height, with lifeless black eyes and the blanched skin of the dead. Dire in combat, virtually unkillable, they take dreadful wounds without bleeding or falling. Lore has it that in but a few ways can they be slain: a fatal wound by a pure silver blade, wood driven through the heart, fire, beheading or dismemberment, and the Sun. Skilled with weapons they are, and cruel beyond measure. They ride to battle mounted upon Hèlsteeds, horselike but with cloven hooves and hairless tails." Vidron fell silent, stroking his silver beard and thinking deeply.

The healer came with a goblet containing a sleeping draught. "Sire, he must rest, else he will die. And we must sear the wound, for he will fall into foam-flecked madness otherwise. A poultice to draw the poison is needed, lest it run wild through his veins, if it does not do so even now."

As Tuck heard the healer's voice, his mind went back to the fright-filled night atop Rooks' Roost, the night Hob died from Vulg bite, and he realized at last that they had not had with them the means necessary to stay the young buccan's death; yet knowing this did not take the sting from behind Tuck's eyes.

The King nodded to the healer, and Haddon was held up to drink the potion. The warrior's eyes slowly glazed over, yet he roused long enough to beckon the King unto him. Aurion leant down to hear Haddon's faint whisper, listening closely. Then Haddon's eyes closed, and he said no more.

As Gildor withdrew a glowing dagger from the fire, Igon asked, "Sire, what said he?"

Wearily the King turned to them all. "He said, 'Rukha, Lokha, Ogrus.' "

There came a cry and the sound and smell of searing flesh as Gildor set the ruddy dagger to the Vulg wound, while the healer prepared a gwynthyme poultice, and Laurelin wept for Haddon's pain.

"Rūcks, Hlōks, and Ogrus?" asked Delber, voicing the question for all the Warrow company.

"And Ghûls, too," said Argo. "Don't forget the Ghûls."

"I knew it! I just knew it!" exclaimed Sandy. "That Black Wall stood out there like Doom, lurking on the horizon. You could feel it in the air, like a storm about to break. And now Modru comes at last."

All the company murmured in agreement, for each Warrow there had felt the menace crouched over the Land; and Tuck, Danner, and Patrel had come in the wee hours of the morning to tell them the dire news.

"Hold on, buccoes," said Patrel above the babble. When quiet returned, he spoke on. "Now I've told you about the Ghûls and their rattailed Hèlsteeds, just as Vidron described them to us, only he called 'em Guula while Gildor called 'em Ghûlka. But let me tell you what he and Gildor said about Rūcks, Hlōks, and Ogrus." Again a low murmur washed throughout the company until Patrel raised his hands for quiet.

"It seems that most of what we've been told in the past is correct," said Patrel in the hush. "The Rūck is a hand or three taller than we, and, unlike the corpse-white Ghûl, the Rūck is night dark. He's got bandy legs and skinny arms. His ears look like bat wings, and he's got the eye of a viper—yellow and slitty. Wide-mouthed he is, with gappy, pointed teeth. He's not got a lot of skill with weapons, but Gildor says he doesn't need much 'cause there's so many of 'em; they just swarm over you, conquering by their very numbers. Vidron calls 'em Rutcha and Goblins; Gildor calls 'em Rucha; but by any name, they're deadly."

Patrel paused and a hubbub rose up, and Dilby called out above the babble: "What do they fight with, Danner? Did Gildor say?"

"Ar, cudgels and hammers, mostly. Smashing weapons, he said," answered Danner. "The Ghûls use spears and tulwars; the Rūcks, smashing weapons, though some use bows with black-shafted arrows; Hlōks usually wield scimitars and maces; and the Ogrus fight mostly with great Warbars. All of them use other weapons, of course—whips, knives, strangling cords, scythes, flails, you name it—but in the main they stick with those I named first."

"Gildor says that the weapons with an edge or a point may be poisoned," added Tuck. A low growl rumbled through the company.

"Yar, a minor nick from one of those can do you in days later if not treated quickly," said Danner.

"What about the Hlōks," asked Argo, "and the Ogrus? What do they look like?"

"The Hlōk is Man-sized," answered Patrel, "like the Ghûl. Their looks are different, though, the Hlōk being more Ruck-like in appearance, darkish, viper eyes, bat-wing ears. His legs are straight, and his arms strong. Unlike their small look-alikes, the Hlōk is skilled with weapons, and clever, too. And cruel. There's not as many Hlōks as there are Rūcks, but the Hlōks command the Rūck squads, and in turn are commanded by the Ghûls."

"Who tells the Ogrus what to do?" asked Finley. "Ar, and what be they like?"

"As to who commands the Ogrus, Gildor didn't say," answered Patrel. "Whether it be Ghûls or Hlōks or someone else, he did not tell the which of it. But this he did say:

Trolls—that's what Gildor calls Ogrus—Trolls are huge, a giant Rūck some say, ten or twelve feet tall. They've got a stonelike hide, but scaled and greenish. Ordinary weapons don't usually cut Ogrus, and the only sure way to kill them is to drop a big rock on 'em, throw them off a cliff, or stab them with 'special' swords—that's what Gildor called them, 'special.' But I think he must mean 'magical,' though when I asked him about it, he didn't seem to know what I meant by the word 'magic.' "

"He did say that Ogrus sometimes could be slain by a stab in the eye, or groin, or mouth," added Tuck. "And, oh yes, fifty or more Dwarves have been known to band together in a Troll-squad and hew an Ogru down with axes, but at a frightful cost to the Dwarves."

"Hey," said Finley, "if ordinary weapons won't cut Ogrus, how come Dwarf axes work to slay them?"

"I don't know," answered Tuck. "Perhaps Dwarf axes are 'special' weapons."

"Nar," said Danner. "I think they just know where to chop."

"Anyhow, buccoes, that's all Gildor and Vidron told us," concluded Patrel. "All we have to do is wait and we'll see for ourselves, 'cause they're coming: Vulg, Rūck, Hlōk, Ogru, Ghûl: it's them we'll be fighting alongside the Men. Yet, that's a couple or more days in the future, and now we must gather some sleep, for our watch on the ramparts is but a few hours ahead, and our eyes need to be even sharper in the coming times."

And so they all took to their cots, but slumber was a long time coming to some, and others slept not at all. And they tossed and turned to no avail, occasionally rising up to see Tuck in a far corner scribing in his diary by candlelight.

The next morning a bleak grey dawn saw the Warrows come to the ramparts. North they looked, but the glowering skies were too sullen and the early light too blear to see the wall of Dimmendark. After the watch was set upon the bulwark, Delber and Sandy were left in charge while Tuck, Danner, and Patrel entered the castle to seek out the Princess. They went to bid her farewell, for this was the day she would leave. They took with them the clothes they had worn to her birthday feast, and also the armor, to return it. They found her in her chambers, taking one last look before departing.

"Oh pother!" she declared. "If ever you needed armor, now is the time, for War comes afoot."

"But my Lady," protested Patrel, "these hauberks are precious, heirlooms of the House of Aurion. We could not take them. They must be returned."

"Nay!" came the voice of the King as he stepped into Laurelin's parlor behind them. "The Princess speaks true. Armor is needed for my Kingsguards. Even now the leather-plate armor made for your company these past days is ready in my armories for your squads to don. But though I did not think of the Dwarf-made armor of my youth or that of my sons, Lady Laurelin remembered it. Now, too, she is right, yet not only because armor is needed, but also because you are the Captain and Lieutenants of the Wee Folk company, and my Men will find it easier to single out a Waerling in gold, silver, or black to relay my orders to. And so you will keep the mail corselets." He raised his hands to forestall their actions. "If you take issue with the gift, surely you cannot oppose me if we call it a loan. Keep the Dwarf-made armor, and, aye, the clothes, too, until I personally recall them. And if I never do so, then they are to remain in your hands, or in the possession of those you would trust. Gainsay me not in this, for it is my command." The Warrows bowed to the will of the King.

Laurelin smiled and her eyes were bright. "Oh, please do dress again as you were last night, for that was a happy time, and I would have you bid me farewell accoutered so."

Hence it was that in the grey morn the three Warrows were arrayed once more in armor and Elven cloaks, in steel helms and bright trews and soft jerkins—silveron and blue, gold and pale green, black and scarlet. 'Neath overcast skies they stood in the courtyard at the great west gate as wounded Haddon was gently placed in the first of the two wains standing on the cobbles. Prince Igon stood by his horse, Rust, with stern Captain Jarriel at his side holding the reins of a dun-colored steed. King Aurion and silver-bearded Vidron were there, too, along with Gildor the Elf Lord. Princess Laurelin came last of all.

"Advise Igon well, as you would me," said Aurion to Jarriel, and the Captain struck a clenched fist to his heart.

King Aurion then embraced his son. "Gather mine Host to me, my son, yet forget not your sword-oath to the Lady Laurelin." And Igon drew his sword and kissed the hilt and raised the blade unto the Princess. Laurelin smiled and inclined her head, accepting Igon's oath to see her safely to Stonehill.

Then the Lady Laurelin made her farewells: King Aurion she embraced and kissed upon the cheek, bidding him to whelm Modru and keep her Lord Galen safe. Of Lord Gildor she asked only that he serve the High King until the War was ended, and Gildor nodded, smiling. To Marshal Vidron she said nought but hugged him extra tight, for he had been like a father to her in this Land so far away from Riamon her home, and Tuck was amazed to see a glittering tear slide down the gruff warrior's cheek and into his silver beard. Captain Patrel she named minstrel of her court, and to Danner she smiled and called him her dancer. Last of all she turned to Tuck and kissed him, too, and whispered to him: "Someday I hope to meet your Merrilee of the silver locket, just as someday I would that you and my beloved Lord Galen could know one another, for I deem you would be boon companions. Keep safe, my Wee One."

And then Laurelin was escorted by Prince Igon to the last waggon, and she mounted up into it. At a sign from Aurion, the portcullises were raised and the great west gates opened. With a flip of reins and a call to the teams, the drivers slowly moved the wains forward and through the portal, the iron-rimmed wheels clattering upon the flagstones and cobbles, horses' hooves ringing, too. Igon followed behind upon Rust, who pranced and curvetted, eager to be under way, and Captain Jarriel upon the dun steed came after. Outside the gate they were joined by the escort, and slowly the waggons trundled down Mont Challerain, heading for the final caravan waiting below.

Behind stood Warrows, Men, and Elf, waving goodbye. Tuck's last sight of Laurelin was one of sorrow, for although he could see her returning the farewell, he also saw that she was weeping. And then with a clatter of gears and a grinding of metal, the portcullises lowered and the iron gates swung to, and Tuck stood staring at the dark iron long after the barrier clanged shut.

*   *   *

At last the three young buccen climbed up to the ramparts and stood long upon the south wall in the company of Danner's squad. They watched as the waggon train wended southward out through the first wall and into the foothills, driving toward the plains beyond. And they all had heavy hearts, for it seemed as if a brightness had gone from their lives, leaving behind cold bleak stone and grey iron and empty barren plains under drab leaden skies.

They were standing thus when Finley came. "Oh, hullo, there you are," he said. "I've found you at last. You'd better come, Cap'n Patrel, Tuck, Danner, come to the north rampart and look at Modru's Black Wall. It's growing."

"Growing?" barked Patrel. "This we must see."

Swiftly they strode along the castellated bulwark, coming soon to the north wall. Climbing upon the weapon shelf they looked through crenels northward. Tuck felt his heart lurch and the blood pound in his temples, for Modru's forbidding wall of Dimmendark now seemed half again as high as when last he had seen it.

"Summon Marshal Vidron," said Patrel, not taking his eyes from the growing darkness.

"It's been done, Cap'n," said Finley. "He's at the mid-wall gorge."

"Come then," Patrel bade Tuck and Danner, stepping down from the shelf and marching toward the mid of the bulwark. As they went to Vidron, King Aurion also came with Gildor, striding up the nearby bastion ramp. They came to the gorge, and again the young buccen mounted the shelf and looked at the far Black Wall.

At last Tuck asked, "Why is it growing?"

"It's not *growing,* Tuck," answered Danner, "it's coming *closer.*"

Of course! Tuck thought, surprised that he hadn't seen it for himself. *How stupid can I be? No wonder it looms larger: it's moving toward us. Haddon said it was coming, and it is!* His thoughts were interrupted by the King.

"Like a great dark tide, it comes, drowning all before it," said Aurion. "How much time do you deem we have, Marshal Vidron?"

"Two days, perhaps, but no more," answered the Man

from Valon, his hand stroking his silver beard. "Modru comes apace."

"Nay," said Gildor. "Not Modru: just his minions come, his Horde, but not him."

"*What?*" burst out Patrel. "Do you mean that he's not with them, that he doesn't lead his armies?"

"Oh, no, Wee One, he leads them aright, but by a hideous power, and he remains in his tower in Gron to do so," answered Gildor, his voice low.

Tuck shuddered, though he knew not from what. But Danner spat toward the north: "Modru, you cowardly toad, though you hide away now, someday you will yet face one of us, and in that battle you will lose!" Danner turned his back to the Dimmendark, leapt down from the weapon shelf, and marched angrily away to rejoin his squad along the south rampart.

Lord Gildor watched him go. "Ai, that one, he vents his fear in anger, though tell him not I said so. He will be a good one to stand beside in times of strife—if he can control his passion. Rare warriors like him I have seen in the past, though not of the Waerlinga: the more difficult the task, the greater is their grit to win through."

Tuck thought, *Gildor is right about Danner: the tougher a task, the more he strives. Grit, Gildor names it, though my dam called Danner "pugnacious," and my sire said he was "quarrelsome."*

"Aye," said Vidron, "I, too, have seen warriors who turn dread into rage, but at times the berserker comes upon them, and then they are awful to behold, for then they do nought but slay. Yet were this to happen unto one of the *Waldfolc,* he would not survive, for they are so small."

"Nay, Marshal Vidron," said King Aurion. "Were a Waerling to have the battle rage come upon him, to become a Slayer, I, too, think he would not survive—but not because he is so small: instead because he is what he is— a Waerling—and were he to become a Slayer, even in battle, he simply would not live beyond that time." A feeling of dire foreboding came over Tuck at these words, and he looked in the direction that Danner had gone.

All that morning, Captains and warriors came to the north rampart to watch the advance of the Dimmendark, and faces blenched to see the dreadful blackness stretching from horizon to horizon and stalking toward them. To the rampart, too, one at a time, came the young buccen of Danner's squad, now accoutered in their new corselets of leather plate, as were the Warrows of Tuck's squad. They watched the dark looming wall draw closer. Some made comments, but most simply stood without speaking and looked long before turning and going back to their posts.

"Ar, it looks like a great black wave," said Dilby as he stood beside Tuck.

"King Aurion said something like that, too, Dilbs," answered Tuck. "He called it a dark tide, though I think he meant Modru's Horde as well as the Dimmendark."

"Aurion Redeye can call 'em a dark tide if he wishes, but me, well, I think the Elves have the right of it when they call 'em *Spaunen,* though I would call them Modru's Spawn," Dilby averred. After a short pause, he spoke on. "I don't mind telling you, Tuck, seeing that Black Wall acomin', well, it makes me feel all squirmy inside."

Tuck threw Dilby a glance and then looked back at the blackness. "Me, too, Dilbs. Me, too."

Dilby clapped a hand to Tuck's shoulder. "Ar, squirmy or not, I hope it don't spoil our aim none," he said, and looked a moment more then stepped down from the shelf. "Ah, well, it's me for the south wall so as someone else can come here and see this black calamity."

"I'll go with you," said Tuck, jumping down beside Dilby. "I've watched Modru's canker long enough. Perhaps the view to the south will be more pleasant: perhaps Lady Laurelin's caravan is still in sight, though I would that it were gone far south days apast, for the Wall comes swiftly and the waggon train but plods."

To the south rampart they strode, where Tuck found Danner at the wall gazing south. Up beside him Tuck stepped and looked southward, too. "Oh, my!" gasped Tuck. "Have they gone no farther?" Out on the plains, seemingly but a short distance beyond the foothills of Mont Challerain, the caravan clearly could be seen, pulling up a long rise.

"They've been creeping like that all day," gritted Danner, grinding his teeth in frustration. "I keep telling myself that they're making good time, but deep inside I don't believe it. Look, you see that rise they go up now? Well that's the same one we galloped down on our last day toward the Keep. It took us a morning to arrive. It's taken the train about the same time to get from here to there. But, Tuck, I swear, their journey crawls slowly while ours trotted swiftly."

They stood and watched as the waggon train toiled up the slope. Tuck threw an arm over Danner's shoulders. "Were the waggons filled with strangers, mayhap the pace would seem right. Or if the Dimmendark came not this way, we would believe the caravan swift. Yet I think we see it move at a snail's pace because someone we care for rides in the last wain."

"Of course you're right," said Danner, "but knowing it does not help." The taller young buccan watched long moments more and then struck his fist to the cold grey stone. "Move faster, you slow-coaches, move faster!" he hissed through clenched teeth. Then, shrugging Tuck's arm from him, he turned and slumped down on the shelf and sat, letting his feet dangle from the ledge, his back to the cold stone merlon, refusing to look at the caravan.

Another half hour passed, then nearly an hour, and Patrel joined them. At last Tuck said, "There she goes, the last wain, over the hill." Danner scrambled to his feet, and the three of them watched as Laurelin's waggon slowly disappeared beyond the distant crest. And the white prairie lay empty before them.

Late in the day, Tuck and Patrel stood again at the north rampart as the Dimmendark inexorably drew closer. Often their eyes had intently scanned the edges of the Black Wall, but nought of note did they see as the 'Dark stalked south across the plain toward them. Tuck secretly hoped to see Lord Galen's troop ride forth upon the snow and come unto Challerain Keep, for he longed to meet this Prince who had won the heart of the Lady Laurelin. But no one came, and he, like Laurelin, began to fear that something had gone amiss. Yet Tuck told himself that Haddon the messenger had seen Lord Galen alive and well less than a day past. *Has it been such a short time?* he wondered. *Less than a day since we were having a grand birthday party? Ar, but it seems as if that happy time were years agone, and as if the dread of the coming Black Wall has been forever, instead of but a single dismal day.*

"Ai-oi!" Patrel's exclamation of puzzlement broke into Tuck's thoughts. "Look, Tuck, at the base of the 'Dark! What is it?"

Long did Tuck look, yet the distance and the failing light of the setting Sun through the overcast did not let him see clearly. "It looks like . . . like the snow is *boiling* all along the base of the Black Wall."

"Yar," agreed Patrel. "Boiling or swirling, I cannot say which."

"Swirling, I think, now that you've said it, Captain Patrel," confirmed Tuck. "But what would cause that? A wind, do you think?"

Patrel merely grunted, and the day faded into night, and they saw no more. At last the Warrows trooped wearily to their quarters as the Castle-ward changed.

The next morning the great Black Wall was less than ten miles distant and drawing closer. Each time Tuck looked at the looming darkness, his heart would thud anew, and he wondered at his courage: *Will I be strong enough when it o'ertops these ramparts, or will I run screaming?*

Now they could see that a wind blew wildly all along the Dimmendark front, as if the air were being violently shoved, plowed before the moving Black Wall. Like a tempest-driven ocean breaking upon an enormous black jetty, great boiling clouds of swirling snow were lofted high into the air. As to the 'Dark itself, the blackness rose from the plains, darkest near the ground, fading as it went up; yet high into the sky it reached before it could no longer be seen, perhaps a mile or more. And though the day was bright and the Sun shone golden, its light seemed *consumed* as it struck the Black Wall, as if swallowed by some dark monster.

Aurion, Gildor, Vidron, and the War-staff came often to the rampart, yet neither did their sight penetrate the churning snow or looming black, nor did aught emerge from the ebon wall.

The Sun stood at the zenith when at last the Dimmendark came upon Mont Challerain. Tuck stood braced upon the rampart and watched with dread as the Black Wall rushed forward. Before it the howling wind raced, and with it came the hurling snow. The Castle-ward was buffeted and battered by the shrieking gale on the rim of the Dimmendark. Tuck pulled the Elven cloak about his shoulders and the hood over his head, but still the swirling snow was driven into his squinting wind-watered eyes. The Sun began to grow dim as the dark tide swept on, as if a black night were swiftly falling, though it was yet high noon. Rapidly the sunlight failed as the Dimmendark engulfed the Keep: through dusk into darkness the day sped in but a trice, and night fell even though the Sun stood on high.

The shriek of the howling wind faded to but a distant murmur as the Black Wall swept on, and then even the murmur stilled. The lofted snow quietly drifted back down upon the ramparts and the ground. Tuck looked about in wide-eyed wonder. The Keep now lay in dark Winternight, and a bone-numbing chill stole upon the land. Above, the disk of the Sun could but faintly be seen, and then only by knowing exactly where to look. Yet a spectral light, a Shadowlight, shone out of the dark, as if from a bright Moon; but the source of the light seemed to be the very air itself, and not the Sun, the Moon, or the stars. Ebon shadows clotted around the feet of rock outjuts and seeped among the trees and hills, and vision was hard-pressed to peer into these pools of blackness. And even out where the land was more open, sight became lost in the Shadowlight, snubbed short by the spectral dark.

Tuck walked up and down the rampart, saying, "Steady, buccoes, steady." But whether he was trying to buck up his squad or was talking to himself, he did not know. Once more Tuck took up his position at the central bastion, and he stared out across the foothills. His eyes felt strange as he peered through the Dimmendark, as if the Shadowlight somehow contained a new color, perhaps a hue of deep violet, or beyond. Toward the open snowy plains he looked; he could see but a few miles through the ghostly 'Dark, yet still nought of any movement did he espy. And neither did Patrel, who joined Tuck in his vigil.

The awful cold crept into the very marrow of the bones, and Tuck sent his squad five at a time to their quarters to don their quilted down clothing. Patrel, who had gone, too, came bearing Tuck's togs, and Tuck quickly pulled the winter garb over his shivering frame.

"Trews and shiny armor are fine for birthday parties, but eiderdown is needed to withstand this cold Winternight," Tuck said as he slipped his jacket over the silveron mail and again affixed the Elven cloak 'round his shoulders, and cast the hood over his head. Slowly warmth returned to his body, and he and Patrel once more looked out upon the cold dark land.

At last the Warrows were relieved by the Men of the Castle-ward, though no one could tell when the Sun had set in the grim cold, for only near noon could the faint disk be seen, and it faded beyond sight as the orb fell toward the unseen horizon. Time now was measured in candle marks and by the water clocks and sand, and though it was now reckoned to be nighttime, neither Moon nor stars shone through the Dimmendark from the skies above. Yet still the harsh land below could be seen in the spectral Shadowlight.

After a troubled sleep, the Warrows arose to, as Danner put it, "A dawnless 'day,' if time in the Dimmendark can be measured in 'days,' that is—though Lord Gildor says that the *days* have now fled, and the *'Darkdays* are come upon us."

Dread filled the mess hall, and voices were grim and hushed. And after breaking their fast, once more the young buccen took station upon the walls of the Keep and gazed out upon the darkling land, out into the Shadowlight. Time wearily passed, and the stone of the walls grew bitter, for the cruel grasp of Winternight clutched full upon the hills and plains, and hoarfrost crept upon Challerain Keep, and ice rimed the battlements and glittered coldly.

King Aurion with Lord Gildor came once more unto the north rampart, riding caparisoned steeds into the bastion gorge below. Now they were armed and armored, with the King bearing a great sword at his belt and a spear in his hand. Lord Gildor had a lighter sword at his own girt, with an Elven long-knife to one side. They were clad in chain mail and capped with helms of steel. The King wore red and gold, Lord Gildor, Elven grey. The King's grey horse, Wildwind, and the Elf's white-stockinged chestnut, Fleetfoot, pranced and sidled as they came into the gorge, but stood quietly as the riders dismounted.

Up the ramp strode the two to join Tuck and Patrel, and Aurion stared out into the spectral dark, but little did he see in the ghostly werelight.

"How far see you, Lord Gildor?" asked the High King.

"To the fifth rise, no more," answered the Elf.

"Ai, that is a far sight in this icy shadow," said King Aurion. "Mine own one eye is accounted good among Men, yet I but see to the first, nay, the second rise. Perhaps a mile or two at most."

Aurion turned to Tuck and looked at the strange Warrow orbs, and even in the Shadowlight the young buccan's tilted eyes were bright and sapphire blue. "How far see you, Wee One?"

"Sire, I see north one hill further than Lord Gildor and even beyond a bit, out upon the plains, but after that I see nought but darkness," answered Tuck.

"Ai!" cried Gildor in wonderment. "Never before have the far-seeing Elven eyes been bested at sight. Yet here in this baffling shadow it happens. The vision of your strange eyes now proves to see beyond those of the First Folk in this Shadowlight. Yet, it is said among my kindred that the Waerlinga have talents not easily seen, and now I find it is true. Perhaps there is more to the tale of your Utruni eyes than I had thought true."

"Utruni eyes?" asked Tuck, puzzled. "Do you mean Giants?"

"Aye," answered Gildor. "It is believed among my Folk that the Wee Ones have in them something of each of the other Free Folk—of Elf, Dwarf, Man, and Utrun. In this case, even though the shape of Waerling eyes is the same as Elvenkind's, the hue is like that of the jewel-eyes of the Utruni."

"Jewel-eyes? The Giants had jewel-eyes?" blurted out Patrel.

"Yes," answered Gildor. "Great gems of eyes: ruby, emerald, opal, sapphire, amber, jade, and many other gemstones did their eyes resemble. Once I saw an Utrun with eyes of diamond."

"You *saw?* You *saw* an Utrun?" Tuck was astonished. "But I thought the Giants were no more."

"Nay, in that you are wrong." Gildor's own green eyes looked sad. "Though it has been many long seasons since I last saw Utruni, they exist still, but deep within the living stone of Mithgar, moving through the solid rock far below, toiling in their endless fashion to shape the Land. Aye, they live, but it is not likely that they will ever again help us surface dwellers in our petty struggles."

"Oi!" said Patrel, sharply. "I just remembered: there's an ancient Warrow legend that we are of the Giants."

"Ar, few would say they believe that hoary tale," said Tuck. "I mean, how could the smallest of Folk come forth from the largest?"

Gildor answered Tuck's question with a question of his own: "Who knows the way of Adon?" The Elf paused, then said: "Have I not said there seems to be in you something of each of the High Folk, even the Utruni? Mayhap that is why you see farther than Elves in this Shadow-light, for Utruni eyes are strange, too."

"And you say that we have eyes like theirs?" Patrel asked. "Gemstone eyes?"

"Nay, Captain Patrel, I say only that the hue of your eyes resembles theirs," answered Gildor. "The clear eyes of the Waerlinga are emerald green, or golden amber, or sapphire blue—three bright colors only, as you well know. Utruni eyes have many more hues, and seem to be the actual gemstones they resemble; moreover, they see by a different light than we, for it is told that they can peer a distance through solid stone, and that we are but insubstantial shadows to them. How they came to notice us in the Great War against Gyphon, only Adon knows, though fragments of lost legends have it that here, too, Waerlinga played some unknown but key role in gaining their aid."

"Are they as tall as I've heard?" asked Tuck.

"I know not what you have heard, but twelve to seventeen feet the grown ones reach in height," responded Gildor. "Yet wait, we could speak many days upon these strange Folk, and perhaps a time will come when we can talk at length about the Stone Giants, but now we must lay that aside and wrench our talk back to this War.

"King Aurion, I think we must turn the far-seeing eyes of the Wee Folk to our good. We know not how distant the eyes of the enemy forces can peer through this darkness sent by Modru, yet if the Waerlinga can see farther than the foe, then that will give us great vantage: advantage to set our forces beyond their vision and watch them come into our traps. Then we may strike swiftly and with deadly force, falling upon them out of the cover of their own dark myrk."

King Aurion struck a fist into his palm, and a fierce smile broke his frown. "Hail! At last a ray of hope. If you are right, Lord Gildor, if the Wee Folk can see farther than the eyes of the enemy, then they will prove to be the key to our tactics, for we shall place Waerling eyes throughout our forces and swoop down upon the Horde like hawks upon rabbits."

"Hsst!" Gildor suddenly held up a hand for silence, his head snapping up, and he listened intently. "A drum tolls." Swiftly Gildor drew sword from scabbard and held the weapon high, and *lo!* set within the blade was a rune-carved blood-red jewel, *and deep within the gem pulsed a ruby light!* "My sword Bale whispers that Evil comes," said the Elf, and he leapt to the wall and turned his head this way and that, trying to locate the drum sound. Tuck, too, as well as the others listened attentively, but they heard nought. "From the north it comes," said Gildor at last. Long moments fled, and all the while the faint glow grew within the scarlet jewel. Tuck knew that he looked upon one of the "special" Elven weapons forged long ago by the House of Aurinor. And the jewel-fire signalled that Evil came near, so they peered through the murk and listened, all eyes and ears.

"Hoy," breathed Patrel, "I hear it now."

So, too, did Aurion. And at last Tuck detected the faint pulse of a distant drum: *boom, boom, boom.* All about them on the walls, others, too, heard the regular throb: *boom, boom, boom.* Slowly, ever so slowly, the leaden pulse became louder. *Boom, boom, boom!* And Tuck's now-racing heart kept double time to the beat: *Boom! Boom! Boom!*

"So ho! Tuck!" A call from Finley sounded above the ominous pulse. "Look out beyond the hills!" *Boom! Boom!*

Tuck and Patrel peered intently to the north, and Tuck's heart leapt to his throat, and his blood surged in his ears. *Boom! Boom! Doom!*

"What is it?" cried Aurion Redeye, his own sight unable

to pierce the murk. "What see you?" Yet the Warrows did not immediately answer, waiting to be sure of their words ere speaking, and the beat of the drum came onward. *Boom! Doom! Doom!*

At last Patrel turned. "Modru's Horde," he said, his voice grim, a fell look in his viridian eyes. "Modru's Horde is come and their numbers are endless." *Doom! Boom! Doom!*

And out on the prairie vast arrays marched toward Challerain Keep, file after file emerging from the black Shadowlight, like a great flood of darkness pouring forth over the snowy plains, covering it with thousands upon thousands of Modru's ravers. Before them loped the evil black Vulgs, and within the ranks marched dark Rūcks and Hlōks. Upon Hèlsteeds amongst the Horde rode the corpse-white Ghûls. And they came to the pulse of a great War drum: *Doom! Doom! Doom!*

Into the foothills they came, flowing toward the Keep, and now Gildor's vision could see them, too, and his eyes glittered in the Shadowlight as he watched them pour forth, and now the ruby flame from Bale's blood-jewel flickered along the edge of the blade.

Doom! Doom! Doom!

King Aurion peered intently, and he struck the stone curtain in frustration. "Still I cannot see them. What are their numbers? The arrangement of their march? What kind of forces?"

Patrel spoke: "Thousands do I see. I cannot guess at their number, yet more come through the 'Dark behind. They are spread on a wide front, perhaps a mile or so. Most are what I take to be Rūcks, though among them stride the taller Hlōks, while one in a hundred are mounted Ghûls, and Vulgs range wide to fore and flank."

Aurion's face turned ashen to hear such dire figures, for his forces were meager compared to the Horde. "Is there aught else?"

"Nay, Sire," answered Patrel, "except that more march out from the 'Dark."

Doom! Boom! Doom! Boom!

The sound of drum was answered by a stirring call of Valonian horns, and Tuck looked down and saw the army of Challerain Keep march out to take up positions upon the hills below: pikemen to the fore with archers behind, foot soldiers with halberds and swords and axes came next, and mounted riders of Valon in back, with spears that would be couched for the charge through lanes when the enemy hove to.

"But Sire," protested Patrel, "they are too many and we too few to meet them in open battle. We have not one tenth their forces. It would be senseless sacrifice to set our handful 'gainst their Swarm."

"Pah!" grated Aurion. "Could I but see them, then would I know whether to strike hard or withdraw. Rather would I cleave into their ranks in fury than to fight like a cornered badger." He turned to Gildor.

"I think, Sire, that Captain Patrel is right," said the Elf as he sheathed burning Bale. But Aurion said nought in return, and Tuck's spirit wrenched in desperation as he watched the vast array inexorably march through the hills toward the King's forces. Yet Tuck, too, said nought, though his eyes brimmed with tears of distress.

Doom! Boom! Doom! Boom! Onward came the enemy. Vidron strode up the ramp and stood beside the King. At last the Horde hove into the range of Man-sight, and Aurion Redeye blenched to see the Swarm in all its numbers. With a groan, the High King signalled to Vidron, "Sound the withdrawal. They are too many to meet upon the field."

Vidron lifted his black-oxen horn to his lips, and an imperative call split the air: *Hahn, taa-roo! Hahn, taa-roo!* (Return! Return!) From the distant force below came a faint horn call. "Sire," rumbled Vidron, "Hagan questions the order."

Doom! Boom! Doom! Doom!

"Ah, Vidron, your Captains of Valon are brave, yet bravery alone is not enough to whelm that Horde. Only the numbers of mine own Host can even begin to challenge such a might, and they are yet far south." King Aurion looked weary. "We have no choice but to follow the Warcouncil's plan to defend the walls."

Hahn, taa-roo! Hahn, taa-roo! demanded Vidron's black horn. Slowly the meager army of Challerain Keep withdrew, coming at last through the first wall, and the gates clanged shut behind.

Boom! Boom! Doom! Doom! Onward came the Horde, a dark flood. Now the sharp Warrow eyes could see that among the Hlōks were those who lashed at the Rūcks with whips of thongs, driving them forward if any lagged or strayed in the slightest.

Boom! Doom! Boom! Still the vast Horde poured forth out of the blackness, and among the ranks were carried standards bearing Modru's sigil—a burning ring, scarlet on black, the sign of the Sun-Death. And where the standards were, there, too, rode Ghûls upon Hèlsteeds, pacing the Swarm forth. And they came until they were just beyond bow shot from the first wall, nor could mangonels fling missiles to reach their ranks.

With a hideous, chilling howl, like that of a Vulg, a Ghûl in fore center flung up his hand, tulwar raised high, and so signalled all the Ghûls. A harsh blat of Rūcken horns sounded, discordant and grating, and the ranks of the Horde split, like a vast flood cleaving around a great rock, curving east and west and south again. Once more the chilling Ghûlen howl rent the air, and as if released from a duty, the Vulgs left the Rūcken Horde and raced away to the south. Swiftly they ran, as if following the wave of Dimmendark engulfing the Lands afar. At last their black shapes were lost to Warrow sight, and the beasts passed beyond seeing, leaving the Horde and Keep far behind. And still the Swarm curved 'round the mount, at last to come together on the far side, beringing the walls.

And then the great drum pulsed loudly: DOOM! DOOM! DOOM! and fell silent.

The Horde ground to a halt and stood facing Challerain Keep, and the only sound was that of a thin chill wind gnawing through the merlons on the ramparts of the besieged mountain city.

An hour passed, and then another, and still the Horde stood fast, facing the Keep. On the ramparts the King paced back and forth, like a caged lion, and he would stop for long moments to stare down at the silent foe and then resume his pacing. At last he called Vidron and Gildor unto him, and they spoke softly. After a moment he summoned Patrel.

Tuck, nearby, heard the King's words: "Captain Patrel,

we must have sharp Waerling sight throughout the ranks of my forces, for only the strange jewel-eyes of your Folk have the vision to see afar through this myrk. And though it means a separation of kith from kith, friend from friend, and like from like, still I must ask that Waerlinga be at the right hand of as many of my Captains as are your numbers, save this: I would that you and your two Lieutenants remain with me and join my War-council, for I deem it will take all three of you to be our far-seeing eyes throughout the long days ahead."

Thus it was that the Warrow Company of the King was dispersed among the armies of Challerain Keep, and Tuck, Danner, and Patrel joined the War-council of the High King. Yet, as had been foreseen by the King himself, although the Wee Folk were honored by the special role given them by Aurion Redeye, still they were stricken by the sundering of their company. And Tuck was filled with the feeling that somehow he was abandoning the young buccen of his squad, or that he was being forsaken by them. Too, he felt guilty that he and Danner and Patrel would perhaps remain together while each of the other young buccen would be alone among strangers, the only consolation being that they were all still in Challerain Keep and would at times see one another.

Lord Gildor turned to Patrel. "Captain, if you will by my sharp-eyed comrade, then I'll teach you the harp while you show me the lute." Patrel's features split in a wide grin, and he inclined his head, accepting the Elf's offer.

King Aurion cocked his eye toward Marshal Vidron, who said, "Sire, it would please me if Sir Danner would peer through the blackness at my side." At the King's nod, Vidron strode off toward the south rampart to find Danner.

Thus it was that to Tuck fell the honor of being the far-seeing eyes of the High King. "Come, Wee One, walk with me while I take Wildwind back to the stables; you can lead Lord Gildor's Fleetfoot," said Aurion, and he and Tuck strode down to the horses while Patrel and Gildor remained behind upon the ramparts.

"Sire," a herald came breathless unto the King, "Lord Gildor sends word: something is afoot along the eastern flank."

"Sir Tuck!" called the King, and the young buccan popped out of the stall where his grey pony was stabled, a curry·comb in his hand. "Swift, to the east wall we go," barked Aurion, and Tuck spun and set aside the comb while snatching up his cloak. Legs churning, the Warrow had to run to catch the King, as Aurion strode rapidly out and across the courtyard. Up a ramp they went and to the mid-gorge of the east bulwark. There stood Gildor and Patrel, while Danner and Vidron came from the south.

"There," said Gildor, pointing.

Tuck looked, and a large force of Ghûls, Hlōks, and Rūcks could be seen to the east, marching southward. Far they were, just within Gildor's seeing, and no sound came unto the ramparts from their distant tramp. Like a sinister gliding shadow, they flowed through the werelight and across the land. All this Tuck described to Aurion while Vidron listened, for the force was beyond Man-sight.

Patrel said, "Sandy spotted them about an hour ago. Out of the north they came, and south they go, but where they march, I cannot say."

"Perhaps they march upon Weiunwood," said Danner. His fists were clenched.

"Or Stonehill." Aurion's voice was grim.

"Mayhap they have discovered that Arden Vale is an Elven strongholt," said Gildor, gripping the pommel of his long-knife. "Perhaps they will strike east for Talarin's hidden valley. Yet I think they would assault that gorge from the Grimwall. Aye, it's Weiunwood or Stonehill they march upon."

Yet wood, village, or valley, none knew where the force was bound; and Man, Elf, and Warrow stood as the buccen watched the distant Horde silently pass once more into the ominous 'Dark. And when none of the Warrows could any longer see it, Aurion sent heralds to call his War-council together. But as the King turned to go down into the castle, *Doom!* the mighty drum of the Horde sounded. *Doom!* Again came the pulse, and from the walls Tuck could see a great stir among the Rūcken ranks. His heart leapt to his mouth, and swiftly he nocked an arrow to his bow, his eyes never leaving the enemy. *Doom!*

"Pah! They break for camp," growled Vidron after a moment, "and not to charge the walls below." The Kingsgeneral sheathed his sword, and for the first time Tuck noted that he as well as Patrel, Danner, and Sandy had put arrow to string. But each one there upon the castle wall had readied a weapon of some sort at the boom of the great beat. Swords and poniards slid with metallic sounds back into sheaths, including Gildor's Bale. As Tuck returned arrow to quiver, he wondered if the others felt as foolish as he did, for even had the enemy charged, the fighting would not have been up here at the fifth wall, but instead down at the first wall, nearly a thousand feet below. *Doom!*

"Come," said Aurion, "let us to council." Down from the rampart they went, and into the Keep where pages went before, holding lanterns to show the way, for the pallid Shadowlight of the Dimmendark stole not into the castle. The King led them to a room where a great table stood in the center of the floor with massive chairs around, and maps and charts hung upon the walls. This was the War-council chambers, deep within the castle—but even here the slow beat of the Rūcken drum sounded, muffled and distant. *Doom!*

Other Men came: Hagan of Valon, young and strong and flaxen-haired; Medwyn of Pellar, grizzled and gnarled but with bright, alert eyes; Overn of Jugo, fat he was, with a great black beard and bushy eyebrows; Young Brill of Wellen, tall and slender, an air of detached inwardness, some said he was a berserker; and Gann of Riamon, taciturn and reserved, perhaps the best tactician there. A mixed lot they were, yet warriors all, and with Vidron and Gildor they formed the High King's War-council at Challerain Keep. Into this company came Tuck, Danner, and Patrel, and Tuck felt as out of place among these soldiers as would a child in a council of elders. *Doom!* All took seats 'round the table, including the young buccen, who found that they had to sit upon the chair arms to see and be seen over the flat expanse.

King Aurion spoke: "Warriors, we have fallen upon dire times." *Doom!* "The enemy numbers ten times our strength, and they surround our position: we are besieged. Too, others of Modru's forces move south, and we are helpless to stop them. Would that I knew where mine own Host stands, or when they will come. Even now the Legion may

be marching north, yet we know not, for Modru's curs way-
lay the messengers, and perhaps the muster has not yet
begun. But no word has come from the south, and with the
Horde 'round our walls, none shall come lest it be borne
by the Host itself.

"When last we met we chose two plans, each based upon
the strength of the enemy: in the first we would take to the
field and set our force 'gainst Modru's; in the second we
would defend these walls, and hold until the Legion arrives.
Well now the enemy is come, and his numbers would seem
to leave us little choice but to defend the ramparts, for we
are beringed by a mighty Horde, and, mark me, they will
attack." *Doom!*

"I have called you unto me to ask if there be aught we
can do but wait for the enemy to strike. Has any seen some
weakness in the Swarm we can turn to our vantage? Have
we any option but to ward the walls of Challerain Keep?
Advise me now, I listen."

No one spoke for long moments, and, reluctantly, Tuck
stood in his chair and was recognized. "I am sorry, Sire,
for being so stupid, but I have a question: Why has not the
enemy attacked? For what do they wait?"

The King looked to Lord Gildor, who said, "We know
not the mind of the Enemy in Gron, nor the full disposition
of his strength. Yet the Horde without surely awaits something." *Doom!* "I know not what, but something evil, of
that you can be certain." Lord Gildor fell silent, and Tuck
felt a chill in the very marrow of his bones.

"How long can we last? Food and drink, I mean,"
asked Patrel.

"Perhaps six months, no more," responded fat Overn, "if
we can repulse them from the bulwarks."

"Won't that be difficult?" interrupted Danner. "I mean,
our warriors will be spread thinly along the walls. It looks
as if they could break through anywhere."

"Yes, Sir Danner, you are right," answered Medwyn of
Pellar. "It will be difficult, especially on the lower walls. In
fact, those ramparts we expect to fall." *Doom!*

"*What?*" burst out Patrel. "You *expect* them to fall?"

"Indeed," answered Medwyn, "for the lower walls
stretch around the base of the mount and our numbers are
too few to defend their great length against such a vast

Horde. But the higher up the mount we come, the shorter it is around, and the less length we have to defend. Thus, as we fall back to successive ramparts, our strength effectively multiplies, for the perimeter of our defense grows smaller. Think of it this way: but a few sturdy warriors are needed to hold a narrow way—such as a bridge or a pass—for no matter how great is the enemy army, they can come at the defenders only a few at a time. Hence, a squad may defy a legion, just as we will defy the Horde—though we may have to fall back unto the last wall itself to do so." *Doom!*

Again Tuck's blood ran chill, and his mind was filled with visions of hordes of ravers swarming up and over the castle walls. *Doom!*

"But, Sire, I do not comprehend," said Patrel. "You expect to fight losing battles upon the lower walls, ever retreating higher until at last we defend only the castle, where perhaps our perimeter will be constricted enough to withstand this awful Horde. And for how long? Six months at most, for then our provisions expire. Sire, perhaps I do not understand the plan aright, for it seems to me that we but put our heads into a noose fashioned by the enemy, and he will draw it tight until we strangle." *Doom!*

"Nay, Captain Patrel," answered Aurion, "you understand the plan perfectly, for that is *exactly* our strategy, our road to victory."

"What?" burst out Danner. He leapt to his feet, his face livid, and shook off Tuck's hand, which reached out to restrain him. "A road to victory, you say? A path to destruction, I call it. I say let us cleave into their ranks and engage them in battle. If we are to die, let it be in full attack and not while trapped like cornered rats!"

Young Brill's eyes flashed hotly, and so, too, did Hagan's and Vidron's. These warriors seemed to agree with Danner, for this strategy suited their bold natures.

But Gann of Riamon quietly held the floor: "And what, Sir Danner, will such a move gain?"

"Why . . . why . . ." spluttered Danner, "we'll take many of the maggot-folk down with us. Die we will, but a mighty swatch we shall cleave among them." *Doom!*

"And then what?" Gann's voice was coldly measured.

"Then what, you ask? Then what?" Danner ground his teeth in fury. "Nothing! That's what! Nothing! We'll be dead, but so will many of the enemy. Yet we will have died a warrior's death, and not that of a trapped animal.''

"Precisely," said Gann, now standing, "and therein lies the flaw in your 'plan.' You would have us sally forth and do glorious battle with the Horde. Yet you yourself recognize that such a course leads but to Death's domain. Perhaps, though, we will be mighty and slay two or even three of them for each of us who falls. Yet, heed me: when we have all died your 'warrior's death'—each of us having taken our quota of the enemy down into the darkness with us—*there will still be a vast Horde left standing, a Horde now free to ravage southward,*" Gann's fist smashed to the table, *"crushing those in its path." Doom!*

Gann's eyes swept 'round the table, and it became clear to Tuck that the Man spoke to Vidron and Hagan and Young Brill as well as to Danner. "Attack? Nay, I say, for that path leads to a roving Horde free to savage the Land. Defend Challerain Keep? Aye, I say, for then we pin the Horde unto this place. And when the Host comes, 'tis the Spawn who will be trapped, and not we." Gann sat back down, and Danner's smoldering amber eyes refused to look into Gann's cold grey ones, for the Warrow could see the clear logic of the Man's argument. But still Danner seemed unwilling to accept Gann's strategy, for it went against his grain.

"Ah, Wee One," rumbled Hagan, his voice deep, "we in the War-council thought the Horde might be large, though we did not expect the vast number that came. We have argued this plan and others many times. I know how you feel, for I sense we are much alike in this, you and I. It galls the spirit to be ever on the defensive, ever in retreat. Attack! That is our solution to life's ills. Attack!''

Tuck was amazed at Hagan's keen insight into Danner's nature, for Tuck knew the Man was *right.* Danner *did* attack when faced with life's ills, be it fear, trouble, a different viewpoint, or any other adversity: when Danner was crossed, he attacked. Even when it led toward undesired ends, Danner still attacked. Why Tuck had not seen this about Danner before, he did not know, for it now seemed so obvious. It had taken two complete strangers—Gildor earlier and now Hagan—to show Tuck this truth about

Danner's nature, and Tuck did not think that either one of them would ever know just how clear his sight had been.

Tuck's thoughts were wrenched back to the problem at hand as Vidron spoke: "Aye. Gann's words ring true, and his strategy seems sound, for without moving we stop this Horde here in a place of great strength. We hold the high ground, and our defenses are mighty. But there are these problems with the plan: First, we may not be able to hold the walls 'gainst this might. Second, even if we do hold, our own Legion may not come soon enough or in enough strength to defeat this Horde. Third and last, Modru may have other Swarms raving across the Land that are the equal of or greater than that which we face: a smaller one passed to the east, as you well know. Three things I have named, and if one or more of these three are true, then this strategy is not best, though it may be too late to do aught else."

"Fie!" snorted Medwyn, starting to rise, but Aurion Red-eye held up a hand, and reluctantly the Man from Pellar sank back.

"Let us not again stir up that particular hornet's nest of plans and counterplans," said the King, "for we have been stung too many times by the barbs of argument from both sides. The balm of logic here does little good to soothe away the passion, for there are too many unknowns, and the best way is not clear.

"Instead, this I ask, for ye have all seen the numbers of our enemy, and they are mighty: Is there aught else we can do, now that we know what we face? Does another plan come to mind we have not already discarded?" The King slowly looked 'round the table, his eye resting upon each one there: Gildor, Vidron, Gann, Overn, Medwyn, Young Brill, Hagan, Patrel, Danner, and finally Tuck. Each shook his head no, and Tuck felt as if he had somehow failed when it came his turn to answer. *Doom!*

"Then this War-council is done." Aurion stood, but before leaving he turned to the Warrows. "Sir Tuck, move your belongings into my quarters, for I want you at my side should I need eyes to see through the Dimmendark. Captain Patrel, you'll stay in Lord Gildor's rooms, and Sir Danner, with Marshal Vidron. I return to the walls."

*   *   *

The three young buccen entered the barracks to find that they were the last to remove their things to other quarters. The hall was empty and silent, abandoned, somehow forlorn. Tuck scooped up his bedroll and pack and took a long look around, and no happy Warrow chatter fell upon his ears, nor did smiling young-buccen eyes look into his own. A great lonely feeling welled up through his being, and his sapphirine eyes brimmed with unlooked-for tears. Without speaking, he turned and trudged toward the barracks doors, and Danner and Patrel walked with him. And as the trio crossed the courtyard, they did not look back.

Tuck went alone to the King's quarters, bearing a lantern to light the way. He placed his belongings by a couch in the anteroom, selecting it as his sleeping cot. When he returned to the wall, Tuck found the King on the west end of the north rampart. Vidron and Danner were there, too, as well as Argo, now assigned to the Castle-ward company on duty. As Tuck came up the ramp he saw that all eyes were straining northward, and there was a stir of excitement.

"What's all the fuss?" Tuck asked, joining the others.

"Out there, Tuck, look," said Argo, pointing far to the northwest. "Nearly beyond seeing. I can't quite make it out. What is it?" *Doom!*

Tuck looked and at first saw nothing. He scanned intently, but still could see only the distant dark. Just as he was about to say he saw nought, a flicker caught his eyes, and at the very limit of his sight he saw . . . motion, but just of what he could not tell.

"Catch it out of the corner of your eye," said Danner, trying an old night-vision trick.

"I don't know," said Tuck after long moments, looking both sidelong and direct. "Perhaps . . . horses. A force upon horses, running swiftly."

"See!" crowed Argo. "I told you! That's what I think they are, too, Tuck, but Danner says no."

"Nar, I only said that it was too far to say," growled Danner. "Besides, it could just as well be Hèlsteeds as horses."

"Well, whatever it is, it's gone, lost in the Dimmendark."

King Aurion, again frustrated at not being able to penetrate the murk, cried, *"Rach!"* and struck the stone curtain with the edge of his fist. Then he mastered his ire and turned to Argo and said, "Pass the word among your Folk: search the very limits of the darkness for this and other sign. Mayhap some Waerling will see what we could not, and then we will know whether it is for good or evil." *Doom!*

When Tuck crawled wearily into his bed in the King's antechamber, the great Rūcken drum continued its leaden toll *(Doom!),* sounding the pulse of the waiting Horde—but what they waited for, Tuck could not say. His mind was awhirl with the day's events, and though exhausted, he did not see how he could sleep with the Keep surrounded by the enemy and a great drum throbbing. Yet in moments he was in deep slumber and did not awaken when at last Aurion passed through on his own weary way to bed. And all of that night Tuck's dreams were filled with fleeting glimpses of swift dark riders sliding in and out of distant shadows—but whether they were Men on horses or Ghûls upon Hèlsteeds, he could not tell. And somewhere a great heavy bell tolled a dreadful dirge: *Doom! Doom! Doom!*

Twice more before Tuck returned to the ramparts, movement was seen upon the edge of darkness at the very limit of Warrow vision—yet none could say what made it. These as well as other matters were brought to the attention of the King as he took his breakfast with Vidron, Gildor, and others of the War-council. Rage crossed the King's features when a messenger came bearing the news that the Rukha now plundered the barrow mounds along the north wall. "If, for nought else, they shall pay for this," he said grimly, and Tuck shuddered at the thought of the maggot-folk digging in the barrows and looting the tombs of dead Heroes and Nobles and of Othran the Seer.

To take his mind from the grave robbers, Tuck turned to Danner. "I dreamt last night of riders in the dark, but whether they were Men or Ghûls, I could not say."

"Ar, dreams didn't disturb me. I slept the sleep of the dead," answered Danner.

"I kept waking in the night," put in Patrel, "and, you know, every time I looked up, Gildor was sitting at his window seat, softly strumming his harp. When I asked, he said not to worry, that the sleep of Elves is 'different'—but just how, he did not say."

I wonder what he meant, 'different'?" Danner pondered, but before they could say on, it was time to go.

They rose and donned their outer winter garb and then strode through the halls and out upon the cobbles. When they came into the frigid air, Tuck was grateful for his snug eiderdown clothing, even though it hid his splendid silveron armor, for he thought that only a fool would exchange warmth for vanity.

As they went toward the ramparts, Danner said to Tuck, "I've been thinking about the pickle we're in. What it all boils down to is that the Horde still waits . . . for who or what, no one can say; and our own forces stand ready to defend the walls, falling back until we are trapped in this . . . stone tomb. I don't like it, Tuck, I don't like it at all, this waiting to be trapped. Instead, give me the freedom of the fens and fields and forests of the Seven Dells, and the Horde will rot before they conquer me there."

"I agree with you, Danner," said Tuck. "This waiting is awful. All we seem to do is wait, peering out over the enemy into the darkness beyond, rushing from this wall to that to see something—who knows what—flickering through the shadows, and all the while just waiting, waiting for the blow to fall. I feel thwarted, too, Danner, and trapped, and it's only been *one 'Darkday!* Lor, what are we going to do if they stand out there for weeks, or months? Go crackers, that's what. But let me point out one thing: we are not *waiting* to be trapped, we're *already* trapped. Now we have no choice but to follow Gann's strategy and hope it works. By staying here, we pin the Horde, too. And when the Host comes, the tables will be turned, for then it will be the Swarm who will be trapped."

"Only if the Host comes in enough force, and only if we can hold Challerain Keep," said Patrel. "As the King said, even his Host will be hard pressed to defeat this Horde. And as Vidron pointed out, should the Keep fall, the Horde will be free to strike southward." *Doom!*

On they went, and Tuck noted that ashes and cinders had been spread upon the paths and up the ramps and along the battlement ways, for the hoar-frost and ice made the footing treacherous. The cold was bitter, and hoods were pulled up and cloaks drawn tightly about to fend off the icy clutch.

At last they looked down upon the Horde, and it was vast and mighty *(Doom!)* and beringed the mount. Again Tuck felt a bodeful dread as he once more saw the great array. Yet the enemy had moved neither forward nor aback since he had last seen them; instead, they waited. *Doom! Doom!*

"Arg! That infernal drum!" cried Danner, his voice filled with ire. "If nought else comes of this, I'd like to stuff that Rūck drummer inside his own instrument and pound it to a fare-thee-well."

They all burst out laughing at Danner's words, especially Vidron, who found the thought of a Rutch trapped in a drum being whaled by a Waeran hilarious.

Their humor was interrupted by a cry from Patrel "Ai-oi! What's that? A fire. Something burns."

Far to the north, visible as yet but to Warrow eyes, a blaze burned. Even as they watched, the flames mounted upward and grew brighter, winging light through the Dimmendark. Higher leapt the fire. *Doom!*

"Look!" cried Tuck. "Around the blaze, riders race." Silhouetted by the flames, the Warrows could see a mounted force raging to and fro in battle, but who fought with whom, they could not say.

"Ai! Now I, too, see the fire," said Lord Gildor, "but not the riders." Bitterly the King and Vidron and other Men on the wall stared with their Man-sight to the north, as if willing their vision to pierce the murk. Yet they saw nought but shadow.

"What size the force?" barked Aurion. "Men or Ghola?"

"I cannot tell," replied Patrel, "for only fleeting silhouettes do we see."

Higher leapt the flames, and brighter. "It burns tall, like a tower," said Danner, "a tower where none stood before."

"Hola!" cried Vidron. "Now I, too, see the blaze—yet faintly, as a far-off candle in a dark fog."

"Or a dying coal from the hearth," breathed Aurion, who now at last could dimly see the fire.

"Hsst!" shushed Gildor. "Hearken below."

The blatting sound of Rūcken horn was mingled with the

harsh calls of Ghûls, and there was a great stir among the Horde. Tuck could see Ghûls springing upon the backs of Hèlsteeds and riding to the horn blares, gathering into a milling swarm. And then with a hideous cry, they raced away to the north, toward the swirling blaze.

"They ride as if to defend something, or to intercept a foe," said Vidron. "What of the other riders, the ones at the fire?"

"Gone," answered Patrel. "They're gone." *Doom!*

And Tuck realized that Patrel was right. For nought did he see but a far-off blaze threading upward in the distant shadow, and no longer did the fleeting silhouettes race past the flames. Tuck looked up at the King, who seemed lost in thought. And even as the Warrow watched, a flicker of understanding seemed to pass over Aurion Redeye's features, and he smacked a fist into the palm of his hand, and a gloating *"Hai!"* burst forth. Yet what his thoughts were, he did not say, but instead turned his gaze once more unto the dim red glow.

Below and racing north rode the Ghûls through the Winternight. Swift they were, passing through the foothills toward the prairie, and ere long they had ridden beyond Warrow vision into the Dimmendark, streaking toward a distant fire that shone like a solitary beacon through the blotting murk. Still the Warriors watched, and the flames grew dimmer, but at last the silhouettes of the Ghûls could be seen as they arrived at the waning blaze. *Doom!*

"I can no longer see it," growled Vidron, and the King, too, gnarled, for the fire now was too dim for Man-sight to detect. Yet the Warrows and Lord Gildor continued to watch the light fail. At last the Elf turned away, and not long after, the Warrows, for even their gem-hued eyes could see the fire no more.

"Well," asked Patrel, "what do you think it was?"

"Perhaps—" Gildor started to speak, but then: *"Hsst!* Something comes." Once more the Elf's hearing proved sharper than that of Man or Warrow, for they heard nought. Again Gildor leapt upon the wall and listened intently, turning his head this way and that. "I cannot say what it is, yet I sense that it's evil." *Doom!*

"There!" cried Danner, pointing. "Something looms in the dark."

"What is it?" Vidron's voice was grim. "What comes upon us?"

"Look there, in front!" cried Tuck. "Ogrus! They must be Ogrus!"

And out upon the plains came giant plodding Ogrus, hauling upon massive ropes. Behind them, on great creaking wheels turning upon protesting iron axles, they towed a mighty ram, and catapults, and giant siege towers.

"Ai!" cried Gildor upon hearing the news, "now we know what it is that the Horde awaits—the siege engines needed to assault the Keep. What an evil day this is." *Doom!*

King Aurion stared through the 'Dark, and though he now could hear the grinding wheels and turning axles, still he could see nought. "Sir Tuck, what see you now?"

"Teams of Ogrus still pull the engines toward us," answered Tuck. "In the fore is a great ram, and then three catapults come next. But behind are four . . . no, five tall towers, each high enough to o'ertop the walls. 'Round them all rides an escort of Ghûls." *Doom!*

The King's face was pale in the Shadowlight, yet the look in his eyes was more resolute than ever.

"Hey!" cried Danner. "That's what we must've seen burning out on the plains." At Tuck's blank look, Danner explained, exasperated that Tuck did not see it for himself. "The towers, Tuck, the towers. One of them must have been what we saw burning." Then a puzzled expression came over Danner's face. "But who would burn the tower? Surely not the Ogrus, for they would not torch their own engine of destruction."

"Lord Galen!" burst out Tuck, the pieces of the puzzle suddenly coming clear.

"Aye," said Aurion Redeye, a look of fierce pride upon his features. " 'Twas my son Galen and his company who did that deed, striking from the cover of the Enemy in Gron's own foul darkness, turning Modru's own vile cover 'gainst his lackeys, then melting away into the shadows ere the foe could strike back."

"Then it must have been Lord Galen and his Men we saw silhouetted by the flames of the burning tower," said

Tuck. "And, too, now I think that the glimpses we've had of distant riders slipping in and out of shadow at the limit of our vision also were of Lord Galen's band."

"Just so." Gildor nodded, for he had sensed that the shapes seen afar only by the Warrows were not foe, yet he had said nought.

"I wonder how many towers they burned beyond our seeing?" asked Tuck.

"We know not, yet I would that it had been five more," answered Patrel, inclining his head toward the five great towers creaking toward the keep.

The King called heralds to him and said, "The machines of the Enemy have come, and now his minions will assault the walls of the Keep. Go forth unto all of the companies and have them make ready their final preparations, for the Horde will not long wait." And as the messengers sped away, Aurion Redeye turned to the Warrows. "I am told you are archers without peer. Have you enough arrows for the coming days?" *Doom!*

"Sire," Captain Patrel answered, "many a bolt have we fletched, for the arrows of Men are too lengthy to suit our small bows—though we could use them in a pinch. Little else have we done both on watch and off, yet the numbers of the Horde are such as to make me wish we had ten times the quarrels."

"We simply shall have to make every one count," said Tuck, "for as my instructor, Old Barlow, would say, 'The arrow as strays might well'er been throwed away.' "

"Hmm," mused Gildor, "your instructor had the right of it."

"Sire!" exclaimed Vidron. "Look! Now I see them come from the darkness."

At last the siege engines lumbered into the view of Man, and Marshal Vidron shook his head in rue, for they were mighty, and cunningly wrought to protect those using them. Forward they creaked, axles squealing—ram, towers, catapults.

"Ai! What a vile bane is that ram!" cried Gildor, pointing at the great batter. Now they could see that it had a mighty iron head, shaped like a clenched fist, mounted on the end of a massive wooden beam. "It is called Whelm, and dark was the day it rent through the very gates of Lost

Duellin. I had thought it destroyed in the Great War, but now it seems that evil tokens have come upon us again." *Doom!*

Though Gildor seemed dismayed by the ram, it was the siege towers that frightened Tuck. Tall they were, and massive, clad with brass and iron. He did not see how Lord Galen's company could have set one afire. Yet inside was wood: platforms, a frame with stairs mounting up, ramps set to fall upon the besieged battlements—bridges for the foe to swarm across.

" 'Tis well that this castle is made of stone," said Vidron, "but I fear that the catapults will prove the undoing of the city below, for they are terrible machines and will fling fire. Much will burn to the ground." *Doom!*

Vidron's words made Tuck realize that they each had looked upon a different engine as being most dire: ram, tower, and trebuchet. Tuck wondered if Man, Elf, and Warrow—or other Folk for that matter—always viewed the selfsame scene through the eyes of their own People; or did each person instead see things through his own eyes? Tuck could not say, for he knew that individual Warrows saw a given event differently, yet he also suspected that each type of Folk shared a view common among their kind.

Slowly, the siege towers and catapults were drawn by the mighty Ogrus to places spaced 'round the mount, while the great ram, Whelm, was aimed at the north gate. The sound of the Rūcken drum pounded forth *(Doom! Boom! Doom!)* and the ranks of the Horde readied weapons: for the most part, cudgels and War-hammers and crescent scythes and great long dirks were brandished by the Rūcks. The Hlōks held flails and curved scimitars, wicked and sharp. The Ghûls, upon Hèlsteeds, couched barbed spears or bore fell tulwars. And great Troll Warbars were clutched in the massive hands of the Ogrus.

Yet the Horde did not attack. Instead, a blat of horns sounded, and a Ghûl and one other rode forth upon Hèlsteeds, while at their side loped a Rūck bearing the Sun-Death standard. Toward the north gate they paced.

"They come to parley," said Lord Gildor.

"Then I shall go forth to meet them," responded Aurion, turning to the ramp.

"But, Sire, I must protest!" cried Vidron. "There are two upon 'Steeds. It is a trap to lure you forth."

Aurion looked to Gildor, who in turn gazed long out upon the field with his sharp sight. "One is no Ghûlk," he said at last, "and he bears no weapon."

"Then he is Modru's messenger and speaks for the Evil One," said Aurion, "and the Ghol is his escort."

"Sire, let me go in thy stead." Vidron dropped to one knee and held the hilt of his sword forth to the King. "If not that, then at thy side."

"Nay, Hrosmarshal," answered Aurion Redeye. "Put thy sword away, until it is needed defending these walls. This I must do for myself, for I have been pent here too long—and I would have words with Modru's puppet."

"But, Sire, I beg thee, take one of us." Vidron's hand swept wide, gesturing to all the warriors upon the rampart.

Aurion turned. "I shall need sharp eyes at my side: Sir Tuck, you shall bear my colors." And as Vidron looked on in dismay, the King strode down from the wall with a wee Warrow running behind, legs churning to keep the pace.

And thus it was that Tuckerby Underbank was chosen to accompany the King; and he rushed to the stable and saddled his grey pony and rode down with Aurion, the young buccan bearing the High King's colors: a golden griffin rampant upon a scarlet field.

Down the mount they rode, passing through the gateways of the upper walls. To the north gate of the first wall they came at last, and King Aurion bade the Warrow to give over his bow and quiver of arrows to the gate guard—for standard bearers at parleys are honor-bound to carry no weapons, else treachery would be suspected.

A small side-postern was opened, and the two rode forth: Aurion upon grey Wildwind, prancing and curvetting, the horse's proud neck arched, hooves stepping high; and Tuck upon a small grey pony, plodding stolidly at the War-steed's side. And scarlet and gold flew from the staff held by the buccan. As they approached Modru's emissaries, Tuck's blood ran chill at the sight.

In the Rūck, Tuck saw what Gildor had described: a foe who was swart, skinny-armed, bandy-legged, with needle-teeth in a wide-gapped mouth, bat-winged ears, yellow viperous eyes—a hand or three taller than Warrows. Though repelled by the Rūck, Tuck felt no fear, yet the Sun-Death standard planted in the frozen snow gave the buccan pause.

But it was the Ghûl that set the Warrow's heart to pounding: Corpse-white he was, with flat dead-looking ebon eyes. Like a wound, a red mouth slashed across his pallid face, and his pale hands had long grasping fingers. Tall he was, Man-height, but no Man was this malignant being, clothed in black and astride a horselike creature.

As to the Hèlsteeds, Tuck was prepared for the cloven hooves, but when the great rat-tails lashed about, the buccan saw that they were *scaled;* and the eyes of the beasts bore *slitted* pupils. Yet neither Tuck nor his grey pony nor even Wildwind was prepared for the foetid maisma that the creatures exuded, a foulness that made Tuck gag and caused his pony and Aurion's horse to shy and skit. Only the firm hands of Warrow and King kept their mounts from bolting.

Last, Tuck's eye settled upon the third emissary: a Man, dark, as if from Hyree or Kistan. Yet he was strange, for spittle drooled from the corner of his mouth and his features were vapid, empty-eyed and slack-jawed, holding no spark of intelligence.

All this Tuck saw as they approached Modru's trio, standing midway between the Horde and the north gate. The Warrow and the King drew up facing the foul emissaries. The Ghûl looked from one to the other, his dead black eyes briefly locking upon Tuck's gemlike sapphire-blue ones, and dread coursed through Tuck's veins. The Ghûl escort then turned to Modru's messenger, and in a dreadful voice, *Like the dead would sound,* thought Tuck, the Ghûl spoke a word in the harsh, slobbering, foul Slûk speech: *"Gulgok!"*

The vacant features of the swart Man's face *writhed,* a malignant look of utter Evil *filled* his eyes, and his lips twisted into a cruel mocking snarl. With a cry, Tuck threw up his hand, and the King turned pale, for a great malevolence lashed out at them. And Tuck shuddered to hear the voice that followed, for it sounded like the hissing of pit adders.

"Aurion Redeye. I had not expected you," the voice gloated, and the evil eyes turned to Tuck and glittered. "This is even sweeter, for you draw mine other enemies into the trap with you." And Tuck felt the hackles on his neck rise, and his grip upon the staff showed white knuckles.

The vile stare turned back to the King. "Look around, you fool. With your feeble one eye see the might that has come to throw you down, and think not to oppose it. This great boon I offer you: lay down your arms, surrender now, and you shall be permitted to exist in slavery, serving me for the rest of your days. Think upon this with the wisdom you are reputed to have, for no second chance will be offered. But you must choose now, for time slips swiftly through your grasp. What will you have, slavery or death?" The sibilant voice fell silent, and scornful eyes leered from mocking face.

"Pah!" spat Aurion. "Say this to your vile Lord Modru: Aurion Redeye chooses freedom!"

A bone-chilling shriek of rage burst forth from the swart emissary, and malignant hatred blasted down upon Tuck like a vile living force. "Then, Redeye, you choose death!" screamed the voice, and the cruel mouth screeched a harsh command at the Ghûl and Rûck—"*Gluktu!*"—using the foul Slûk speech.

The Ghûl flung up a tulwar and spurred his Hèlsteed forward, while at the same time the Rûck tugged at his cloak, drew a bow from concealment, and fumbled at a black-shafted arrow to aim at the King.

"*Treachery!*" cried Tuck, clapping heels to his pony and riding at the Rûck, and out of the corner of his eye he saw King Aurion draw gleaming sword from scabbard and spur Wildwind forward. But then only the Rûck commanded Tuck's view, for the swart maggot had set his black arrow to string and was drawing aim upon the King, the barb dripping a vile ichor. Raising the standard, Tuck brought it crashing down upon the Rûck's head as the pony raced by, and the force of the blow was so great that the pole snapped in twain, leaving Tuck gripping a jagged shaft. The black arrow hissed wide of the mark as the Rûck fell dead—skull crushed, neck broken.

Tuck wheeled the pony around, and he heard and saw the clang of sword upon tulwar. And the Ghûl was skilled, for his blade slashed through Aurion's guard and skittered across the King's chain mail. But again, Tuck did not see more, for he rode his pony to come between the battling pair and the other emissary, placing himself in harm's way to fend off a charge by the third foe. Yet the Hèlsteed moved not, and Tuck looked up into the visage of this enemy, *but the eyes were vacant and the mouth slack and the face now void of wit.*

Clang! Chank! Sword and tulwar clashed. *Thunk!* The King's blade bit deeply, cleaving a great gash in the Ghûl, yet the foe did not bleed and fought on as if unwounded. *Ching! Thock!* Now the tulwar slashed across the King's forearm, and blood welled forth. *Chunk!* Again Aurion's sword rived, once more the Ghûl's flesh gaped, yet it was as if nought had happened.

"His mount!" cried Tuck, and Aurion's sword slashed through the throat of the Hèlsteed. Black gore spewed forth as the creature fell, flinging the Ghûl off. Tuck heard the snap of breaking bones, yet the Ghûl rose to his feet as if unharmed and slashed his tulwar up at Aurion, but the blow was caught by the King's blade. Now the Ghûl emitted a chilling howl, and like cries answered from the Horde. Hèlsteeds bearing Ghûls raced forth from the ranks. Tuck saw them hurtle out, and in desperation he clapped heels to his pony and charged at the Ghûl, couching the splintered flagstaff like a spear, as he had seen Igon do at practice. Forward raced the pony. With a hideous *Thuck!* the jagged shaft caught the Ghûl full in the back and punched through, the splintered end emerging from his chest, and the jolting impact hurled Tuck backward over the cantle and to the frozen ground as the pony ran on. Dazed, the Warrow could hear the King calling his name. He floundered to his feet, only to be jerked up off the ground and flung on his stomach in front of Aurion Redeye across Wildwind's withers.

Tuck could not catch his breath as the King's grey horse thundered for the north gate, and the pounding gallop caused Tuck to retch and lose his breakfast. Toward the portal they sped, with Ghûls in pursuit. But Wildwind was not to be headed, and he raced under a canopy of arrows shot from the walls at the pursuers. With howls of rage, the Ghûls sheered off the chase as Wildwind came to the side-postern and through, closely followed by Tuck's free-running pony.

*   *   *

"Killed 'em! Killed 'em both, he did!" cried Hogarth, the Gate Captain, a fierce grin splitting his face as he pulled Tuck from Wildwind's back and to the ground. But Tuck could not stand and fell forward to his knees, his arms clutched across his stomach, face down as he gasped for air. He found he was weeping. Aurion leapt down beside him.

"He's got the wind knocked out of him," said Aurion. "Stand back." And the King held the Warrow by the shoulders as the Wee One gasped and wept, while the Kingsmen upon the wall roared a mighty cheer.

At last Tuck got control of his breathing, and soon the weeping stopped, too. And the King said in a low voice that only the Waerling could hear, "Sir Tuck, you must mount up the wall so that all may see you. Heroes are needed in these dark times to rally the spirits of all of us."

"But, Sire, I am no hero," Tuck said.

The King looked at the Warrow in astonishment. "No hero, you say? Fie! Whether or not you feel like a hero, you are one, and we need you. So come, mount up to the parapet with me."

And so, up the ramp and to the battlements above the north gate went the King and Warrow, and all the Men shouted great praise. Tuck looked forth upon the field. Of the third emissary there was no sight, but out upon the snow, near the carcass of the Hèlsteed, lay a skull-crushed Rūck and a shaft-pierced Ghûl, slain by Tuck's own hand. Yet Tuck did not feel the pride that the shouting Men took in him; instead, a sickening horror filled his being. For although it is one thing to kill a snarling Vulg with arrow as he had done at Spindle Ford, it is quite another thing to slay beings that walk about upon two legs and wear clothes and speak a language. Too, it had been so utterly violent—smashing, crushing, jarring, stabbing. The sight of his victims brought only a bitter nausea upon him.

But another sight there upon the field overrode his horror and filled him with dread: *Oh, please let it not be an omen,* he thought, as there on the field, where the Rūck had planted it, stood the Sun-Death sigil of Modru, and below it, lying crumpled in the snow, was the broken scarlet-and-gold standard of Aurion.

*   *   *

Tuckerby shook his head to dispel the foreboding thoughts and realized that he was being spoken to.

"Lor! What a close chase," said Corby Platt, returning Tuck's bow and quiver to the Warrow hero. Corby was a young buccan formerly of Tuck's squad but now assigned to the north gate. And he gestured at the slain enemy. "That's two for the Bosky, Tuck, and one o' them was a *Ghûl!*"

"Wood through the heart," said Hogarth, "that's what slew the Ghol—impalement. And it's a good thing, too, for King Aurion had not the time to dismember it, for the other Ghola were riding hard upon you. Hoy! but it was a fine bit of lancery, Sir Tuck."

"It wasn't as if I *thought* to do it—to spear the Ghûl with wood, that is," said Tuck. "It's just that he was there and I had the shaft in my hand, and, well, it just *happened.*"

"Yet had you not acted, then it is we who would be crow bait, and not the other way around," said Aurion, placing a hand upon the shoulder of the Waerling. "You are a fine knight, Small One."

"But I was de-ponied!" exclaimed Tuck. "No knight am I."

"Ar, well," said Hogarth, "you just need to learn how to lean into your stirrups and clamp your thighs to your mount."

"No thank you! From now on I'll just stick to what I know." Tuck flourished his bow, and the Men upon the wall shouted another great cheer for the wee warrior. But this hail was cut short by the enemy: *Boom! Doom! Doom!* The great Rûcken drum took up a pounding beat, and harsh horns blatted.

"Sire, they move the trebuchets forward," called Hogarth.

"They begin the attack," said Aurion. "Signal our own catapults to prepare."

Rahn! Hogarth blew upon his oxen horn, and a signal flag was raised.

Out upon the field, Tuck could see the great Ogrus wheel forth one of the catapults. This one slowly approached the north gate. Word came from the east and west that the other two trebuchets were drawing toward the first wall, too. Behind came more Ogrus, towing waggons. As the

Trolls hauled the great engine into position, a sense of dread came upon Tuck, for he knew by Vidron's words earlier that these were terrible weapons.

"Lor, look where they stop," breathed Hogarth.

"What is it?" cried Tuck, alarmed but not knowing why.

"Our mangonels have not that range," answered Hogarth, pointing up the mount toward the King's own catapults between the first and second walls. "We cannot return their fire, for we cannot reach them." *Doom! Boom! Doom! Doom!* The Rūcken drum pounded on.

Through the pulsing drum beats, a distant clatter of gears sounded, and the throwing arm of the catapult was hauled down and loaded with a black sphere from one of the wagons. A Rūck with a torch set fire to the missile, and at a cry from a Hlōk, *Thuk! Whoosh!* the arm flew up, hurling a flaring pitch-and-sulphur ball sputtering through the sky and over the wall, to smash and explode upon one of the buildings. Fire splashed outward, and smoke rose up into the air. Warriors rushed to quench the blaze, but another burning ball burst nearby, and flames raged. Again and again the blazing missiles burst upon the city, crashing down upon the tile roofs and wooden walls, and flaming liquid splashed and dripped. Soldiers rushed thither and yon, trying to extinguish the fires, to beat out the flames. But the burning sulphur and pitch clung tenaciously to the blazing wood and ran in rivers of fire beyond reach, spreading in swift strokes. And where quenched, flames would burst forth anew as fire ran back to spring up again.

Missile after missile crashed down to add to the fires, and raging flames grew and fed upon the shops and houses lining the streets, and swept across the town. Away to the south and west rose the smoke of other fires as the great trebuchet there flung its hideous cargo of holocaust upon that part of Challerain Keep. And the third catapult of the enemy hurled fire upon the eastern flank of the city. *Thwok! Thock!* The fuming balls hurled forth, sailing down to blast apart. *Thock! Thack!* Time and again the enemy catapults sounded, hurtling a fiery rain upon the open Keep. All around the mount the flames raged wildly, springing from building to building and street to street, the fires from the north racing toward those raging forth from east and west. Black smoke billowed up and sent warriors reeling and coughing. The heat choked off breath, for the very air seared the lungs, and many collapsed. The fallen were borne forth from the inferno by their exhausted comrades, yet others perished, trapped in the fire storm.

Hours passed, and still the siege engines of Modru hurled sputtering Death, the *thwok!* of the great arms now unheard in the roar of the flames. The answering shots of the King's mangonels fell short, and the Men on the wall wept and raged in frustration, for the city burned and they could do nought to save it. Unchecked, the missiles crashed, and red and orange columns of roaring flames cast writhing shadows out into the Dimmendark. The works of centuries of man's existence upon Mont Challerain fell victim to the ravening fire. And Tuck recalled Vidron's words; and now the Warrow knew that these indeed were terrible machines, for the ancient city of Challerain Keep was being razed to the ground.

And thus the city burned, the great engines casting holocaust nearly unto the fourth wall. When it became apparent to the King that nought could be done to quench the raging flames, he ordered that the fires be let to run their course unchecked, for the warriors must needs save themselves for the coming battle. And so for two 'Darkdays they watched the burning of much they held to be precious and wept to see such destruction. The Horde beyond the walls jeered in revelment and brandished their weapons, but they made no move to assault the battlements. They knew that the fires sapped at the strength and spirit of the Kingsmen, and they waited for the moment when the defenders' will would be at its lowest ebb. And all through the burning, and finally unto the time that black char and ashes and thin tendrils of acrid smoke were all that remained where once stood a proud city, the great drum knelled: *Doom!*

The sharp ring of swift steps upon polished stone jolted Tuck awake. A lanthorn-bearing warrior of the Kingsguard strode hard past the Warrow's couch and into the King's chamber. Muzzy with sleep, Tuck sat up and rubbed his eyes, wanting nothing more than to fall again into exhausted slumber. But what he heard next jarred him fully awake.

"Sire," the warrior's voice was grim, "they stir as if to attack!"

Quickly, Tuck donned the underpadding and then the silveron armor, and he slipped into his boots and down overclothing. As he flung on his Elven cloak and took up his bow and quiver, the King strode out, girting his sword and helming himself.

"Come!" commanded Aurion, and he paced away, following the warrior with the lanthorn, while Tuck ran behind, clapping his simple steel cap upon his own head.

In the stables, as Tuck saddled his pony, Danner and Patrel came with Vidron and Gildor, but there was not time to say other than "Good fortune!" Then the King and Tuck mounted and hurriedly clattered out and across the courtyard.

Down through the charred ruins they rode, and by the twisting route they took, Tuck's grey was as quick as Aurion's Wildwind. Unto the north gate of the first wall the King and Warrow came, riding amid soldiery running toward the bulwark. Whence came these warriors, where quartered, Tuck did not know, for most of the buildings had burned. Yet here they were, streaming to the defense of the first wall, as Captains among them cried out orders. Yet above the shouts Tuck heard the blare of Rūcken horn and the beat of enemy drum: *Doom! Doom!* The advance had begun.

Mounting up to the battlement, the King looked grimly out upon the swarming Horde, and Tuck caught his breath to see them seething forward: Slowly they came, a black tide surging through the pallid Shadowlight and over the land. In the fore the great Troll-drawn siege tower trundled toward the wall, the giant wheels creaking, the Ogrus beneath an ironclad fire shield. To the rear came the Ghûls, riding to and fro behind the files of the Swarm. In boiling ranks came the Rūcks and Hlōks, and to Tuck's unpracticed eye they looked to be without number, stretching beyond his view in a great arc that encircled the mount entire. But Tuck's sight was drawn directly ahead, where aimed square at the north gate came the clenched iron fist of the great ram, Whelm.

With trembling hands, Tuck fumbled among his arrows,

ashamed that others might see his fright; yet if the High King or anyone else noticed aught, they did not speak of it.

"What lies beyond my vision?" asked Aurion, turning to Tuck.

The Warrow had to take a deep breath and let it out before he could speak. "Nothing, Sire, to the limit of my sight." And they turned to watch the advance.

Occasionally, lone arrows were loosed from the wall, gauging the Horde's range. At last a signal was given, and the mangonels of Challerain flung flaming missiles at the oncoming Swarm. The flaring trajectiles burst upon the ground before the advance, and great gouts of fire splattered and ran among the teeming Horde. Rūcks quailed back, but the snarling Hlōks amid them lashed with whips and drove them forward again.

Onward creaked the tower and great ram, now the targets of the King's catapults, yet the fire splashed without effect upon the brass and iron cladding. And forward they trundled.

With Tuck in his wake, Aurion Redeye strode up and down the battlement, saying words of encouragement to the defenders. As to the Warrows, scattered as they were among all of the King's companies, only a few were here along this part of the first wall. Yet to these Tuck said a few words of his own, wondering if they were as frightened as he, receiving grim smiles in return. *If Danner were here, he'd be yelling insults at the Rūcks,* thought Tuck, *and Patrel would know exactly what to tell the buccoes.* But those two Warrows had duties elsewhere, with Vidron and Gildor, repelling the attack east and west; hence Tuck alone was left with the task of bucking up the courage of the young buccen near the north gate.

Doom! Doom! Doom! Doom! Now the Horde was too close to the wall for the King's catapults to strike at them. Like maggots, the Swarm seethed and boiled onward, and scaling ladders were borne among them. Forward trundled the mighty ram, forward creaked the great tower. Now the massive Ogrus could be seen in all their awesome power, and Tuck caught his breath to look at them, for they were huge.

The King gave another signal, and hissing flights of arrows were loosed, streaking down upon the enemy.

Rūcks threw up shields to ward against the deadly shafts. Yet many found their marks, and Rūcks fell screaming. But the arrows pierced not the stone hides of the mighty Ōgrus, and the tower and ram came on.

Now Rūcken horns blatted, and the Horde cried out with an endless wordless yell. They broke for the wall, and their own black-shafted arrows hissed among the defenders; Men fell, pierced through. At last the howling running Swarm reached the first wall. Scaling ladders were flung up and mounted, while rope-bearing grapnels chanked upon the crenels and Rūcks swarmed up. Shouting Men sprang forward to dislodge the ladders and hooks, braving arrows to cast them down. The great tower trundled forward, now almost to the wall, and the ram came unto the north gate. *Boom! Boom!* The iron fist was driven upon the portal, and the iron gates shuddered under its mighty blows. Burning oil was loosed through the machicolations above to splash down upon the Ōgrus, but the fire shield fended the flaming liquid, splashing it aside. Calthrops, too, rained through the slots, yet Rūcks with besoms swept the dire spikes aside and Trolls stepped not upon them.

At last Tuck stood upon the weapons shelf, and through a crenel he took deadly aim, loosing bolt after bolt upon the enemy, driving the shafts down upon Rūcken archers; and he did not miss. *The arrow as strays might well'er been throwed away:* Old Barlo's words ran through Tuck's mind. And as he strung arrow and took aim and loosed each fatal quarrel, Tuck realized that he was deadly calm, his fright gone now that the waiting was over.

Finally the great tower came unto the wall, and a ramp thudded down upon the merlons. With hoarse shouts and grating snarls, swart Rūcks and Hlōks rushed upon it toward the battlements, swinging cudgels and scimitars, War-hammers and curved sickles. They were met by shouting Men with long pikes and gleaming swords, pole axes and brutal maces. Battle cries and oaths and death screams rent the air. Rūcks were slain and Hlōks, and Kingsmen, too, hurtling from the ramp and falling down the face of the bulwark. Here Aurion Redeye battled, his sword wreaking havoc among the enemy, raging fiercely, and no enemy had as yet set foot upon the stone of the wall.

Boom! Boom! whelmed ram upon gate, and Tuck's

arrows hissed true. Suddenly the Warrow's eye was caught
by a flicker of movement in the Dimmendark, and Tuck
looked up to see a force of horsemen, twenty strong, riding
at full gallop toward the wall. How they had gotten this
close without Tuck seeing them, he did not know. Yet here
they were and here they charged, and the horses were swift.
Those in front raced after one upon a jet-black steed, and
they bore clay pots tied with ropes, while in the rear sped
others, carrying flaming torches. Toward the tower they
streaked, and the Enemy knew not they came until they
thundered past, whirling the vessels overhead. Unto the
tower they clove, and the pots were hurled through the
open back to smash within the siege frame, and a clinging
dark liquid splashed upon the timbers and ran down the
wooden walls. The riders that raced behind flung their
burning brands after, and a great blaze *whooshed* up within
the tower. Wildfire flared, and Tuck shouted with fierce joy,
"Hai warriors!" Rūcks and Hlōks within screamed in the
agony of a fiery death, and some leapt forth flaming and
ran amok like living burning shrieking torches.

The Men on horses wheeled back through the ranks of
the enemy, but many fell to the black-shafted Rūck barbs.
Tuck rained bolt after bolt upon the foe, yet still the Rūcks
slew the horsemen, and Tuck wept to see them fall. Yet ten
or so broke free and raced toward the darkness, pursued by
Ghûls upon Hèlsteeds. Then Tuck could no longer watch,
for more scaling ladders thudded up against the wall.
Enemy archers slew Men, and the great ram whelmed:
Boom! Boom!

Tuck drew, aimed, and released, again and again, while
Men struggled and cursed and used long poles to push away
the ladders. Yet others hurled rocks and rained calthrops
and fire and arrows down upon the Horde. And all the
while the flames of the burning siege tower roared up into
the darkling sky.

Yet the numbers of the Horde were many while those
of the defenders were few, and here and there pockets of
Rūcks and Hlōks o'ertopped the wall and fierce battles
raged. And driven by the mighty Trolls, the great ram battered the gate: *Boom! Boom!* First one hinge shattered,
and then another gave way under the juddering iron fist of
Whelm. The outer gates began to buckle and sag, and word

came from elsewhere that the foe was pouring over the rampart.

"Withdraw!" commanded the King, and the order echoed up and down the line. Tuck followed Aurion down the ramp, where they mounted and rode among the defenders streaming back to the second wall. And the battle plan of Challerain Keep moved toward the next stage.

As they went, Tuck looked back to see jeering Rūcks and Hlōks clamber upon the stone bulwark, and the gates at last shattered under the mighty impact of Whelm. And pallid Ghûls upon Hèlsteeds rode through before the dark tide of the Horde to claim this first battle. And the Sun-Death standard of Modru was raised upon the wall above the sundered north gate.

"Upon a black steed, you say?" The King stood on the second wall and watched as the siege tower continued to flame, a fierce grin upon his face.

"Yes, Sire," answered Tuck, fletching another arrow. "Swift he was and all the Men brave, and he led them upon a horse darker than night, the color of jet."

"Hai! You have named it well, for Jet it was: no horse is blacker." Aurion smote fist into palm. "Ah me, would that I had seen it myself. It would have done my heart good to have witnessed that brave dash. But I was at swords, hewing foes upon the tower's ramp."

"Who rides the black?" asked Tuck, sighting down another shaft, believing he now knew the King's answer but awaiting Aurion's confirmation.

" 'Tis Galen rides Jet." Pride washed over the King's features. "No warrior can fight better."

So that was Lord Galen, thought Tuck. *My Lady Laurelin's Lord Galen.* Tuck's hand strayed to the silver locket at his throat, and for long moments he sat lost in quiet thought.

"See now, they lift Whelm over the first wall." The King's voice brought Tuck back to the present, and he stood and looked beyond the charred ruins of the lower city to see the massive Ogrus hauling upon thick ropes to raise the great ram over the first bulwark. The huge maul was too long to bring it through the twisting passageway of the north gate—or any other portal for that matter.

Tuck watched for a moment, then his eyes turned to the burning tower. "What about the other towers, Sire, will they be hauled across the wall, too?"

"Nay, Tuck, for they are too massive, even for the Troll Folk," answered the King. "And, too, the word has come that but one tower remains; all others are in flames, as is this one. They were set upon at one and the same time by Galen's band; my son divided his force to do so." Aurion's face turned grave. "They paid a high price to put them to the torch, for perhaps no more than forty Men escaped, all told, and even then they were pursued by Ghola. As to their fate, none here knows. Yet Galen is wily and will best them yet."

Tuck was glad to hear that the towers would no longer be a factor in the struggles to come, yet he fretted over the fate of the Men of Lord Galen. Tuck stepped down and again took up the shafts to work on, sitting with his back to the wall.

"You should rest now, Wee One," said Aurion, "for soon they will have Whelm reassembled and the battle for this wall will commence."

"Yes, Sire," answered Tuck, "but I must needs fletch a few more shafts first, for I spent nearly all my others, and, as I've said before, the arrows of Men are too long for Warrows, though in a pinch they would do."

As the King strode away, Tuck's fingers flew, and shaft after shaft was trimmed and fletched. Iron points were affixed, and the pile at his side grew. Back at the castle was a hoard of arrows feathered and tipped in past days by the Warrows. But Tuck knew that they would be needed later, and so he now made more. And he lost track of time in the crafting of bolts. Hence he did not know how long he had been working when he heard the distant *thwack!* of the enemy's trebuchet. Twice more it sounded, yet he did not look away from his work. But then he heard the anguished cries of Men, and at last he glanced up to see a grisly sight: the Rūcken Horde had decapitated the slain bodies of the fallen Men and dismembered them, and now the catapult flung the mutilated remains to rain down upon the defenders. *Thwack! Thwack!* Again and again the throwing arm of the great trebuchet swept upward, and weeping warriors stumbled through the char and ash of the

burned city to gather up all that was left of their slain
comrades, horribly disfigured, lidless eyes staring, lipless
mouths grinning in the rictus of death.

Tuck turned his face to the stone wall and wept the hopeless tears of a lost child, and still the catapult threw.

"Stand ready; they come." Aurion's voice was grim as
the Horde swept through the burned ruins of the lower city
and toward the second rampart. And the howl of Ghûls
sounded, and then the wordless shout of Rūcks and Hlōks.
Again Whelm creaked toward a gate—the north portal of
the second wall—and again the King and Tuck stood where
the ram came. Once more the Swarm drew within range of
arrow, but the defenders withheld their shafts, for they
knew that every shot had to count.

Slowly the iron ring of encircling foe squeezed shut, and
finally the Rūcken forces charged, ululating cries bursting
forth. From the crenellations arrows were loosed at last,
and the black shafts of Rūcks answered. Scaling ladders
slapped up against the wall, and grapnels bit the stone, and
foe mounted up. Men shoved with poles and chopped with
axes to send the scalers down, and Rūcks fell screaming to
land with sodden thuds upon the frozen stony ground.

Boom! Boom! Mighty Whelm rammed upon the portal.
A whoosh of burning oil gushed out under the gate, but
the flaming liquid was shunted aside by a barrier of iron
plates set in mud spread by Rūcks upon the cobbles before
the ram for just this purpose. And the Ogrus drove the
great iron fist again and again into the portal.

Here and there atop the wall Rūcks and Hlōks swarmed,
and sword met scimitar, pike drove at spear, hammers and
axes clashed, and the clangor of steel striking steel sounded
among War-cries and oaths and grunts and gasps of fierce
battle. The sound of Death screamed forth.

Grimly, Tuck loosed arrow after arrow, and where each
bolt flew Rūck fell dead, pierced through. The number of
those he had slain mounted; yet how many he slew, he did
not know, for he had not counted. But he had not missed
once, and now he had spent nearly sixty arrows—thirty-five
at the first wall. But he did not stop to think of this, for if
he had he would have been filled to gagging with sick horror. Instead, he nocked arrow, aimed, and loosed, nocked

arrow, aimed, and loosed—time after time, with machine-like precision. By the count of his victims, Tuck was by far the most effective warrior upon his part of the wall, this tiny Warrow, but a hand or so more than half the height of Man. Yet had more of the Wee Folk been present than a mere forty scattered thinly upon the battlements, the outcome of the struggle at this wall might well have been different. But more were not there, and soon the dark Rūcken tide swept over this rampart, too, and through the shattered gate, and the defenders withdrew unto the third bulwark.

Exhausted, Tuck slumped against the castle wall. He was weary beyond measure, for he had not slept over a span of two 'Darkdays. Four times the defenders had battled the Horde, and each time the Enemy had won, for their numbers were too many and the Kingsforce too few. Four gates lay shattered behind them, four walls had been o'ertopped. Thousands of Rūcks had fallen, yet tens of thousands remained. Each battle had been fierce, the fighting more intense upon succeeding walls, for General Gann's strategy was correct: the higher up the mount they had come, the less perimeter there was to defend, and the more concentrated became the King's forces. Yet whether they could hold out, they knew not, for the Kingsmen now numbered less than three thousand, and they faced a Horde ten times their strength. And now that Swarm stood before the last wall, Whelm's iron fist aimed at the west gate, and the defenders inside girded for a final assault.

Tuck had caught a brief glimpse of Danner, and later Patrel, and he was glad to see they still lived, for twelve of the Wee Folk had fallen, and he knew not who yet survived. They smiled wanly at one another, their features pinched by fatigue, but then they were swept apart again as the tides of War demanded.

Again came the blat of horns, once more the *Doom!* of drum; now the dark Horde strode forward: the fifth assault began. Tuck leaned wearily upon the merlon and watched grimly as they came, the wheels of Whelm rumbling on the cobbles as mighty Trolls pressed forth this bane. As before, the tactics of the Horde did not vary: slowly they advanced until they came into arrow range, then the Ghûls voiced howling cries, and shouting Rūcks and Hlōks, bearing scaling ladders and grapnels, charged through a hail of arrows, and the ram bore upon the gate.

Again ladders thudded against stone, and the hooks bit upon merlons and crenels. The air was filled with hissing death as arrow after arrow *thocked!* into flesh, and Rūck and Man fell dead or wounded. Tuck moved slowly along the wall, seeking out enemy archers, for they threw death at long range, and Tuck could stay their hand.

Boom! Boom! Whelm smashed against the west gate, iron fist pounding for entry upon the great iron door. But this time the Men had set an Ogru trap: the cobbles before the gate had been soaked with oil, and it was now set ablaze. *Whoosh!* Fire erupted upward and black smoke billowed as flames raged up under the fire shield canopy. The Trolls ran forth roaring in pain, slapping at the fire clinging to their scales, Whelm forgotten. And many stepped upon the calthrop spikes and howled in great agony and could but barely limp thereafter. Great boulders were flung down from the gate towers and fell upon the Ogrus, slaying three of the twelve-foot-high monsters and breaking the bones of two others.

In fury, the Ghûls rode forth upon their Hèlsteeds and lashed at the Ogrus, and they drove the creatures back to haul Whelm forth from the blaze. But the fire upon the ram was too fierce, the massive wooden driver burned with raging flames, and the Trolls could not come near. The ram was abandoned; no more would Whelm's iron fist knock for entry in this strife.

Atop the walls desperate battle raged. Man, Hlōk, Warrow, Rūck, and Elf: all strove weapon to weapon and hand to hand, fighting to the death, slashing, kicking, stabbing, gouging, hacking, smashing, biting, piercing, hurling one another from the battlements. War-cries and screams alike rent the air, as well as unheeded shouts of warning. There, too, was the skirl of steel upon steel, and the crunch of sundered bone, and the chang of iron striking stone, and the chop of blade into meat. Yet Tuck heard nought of it. For him there was only the sound of arrow loosed upon target; he paid little heed to the sounds of War. Nor did he see Young Brill rage past, swinging wide his great sword, cleaving a mighty swath, slaying Rūcks by the score, the battle madness upon him.

And at last the Horde was hurled back! For the first time their swarming failed to take the walls! With harsh blats of Rūcken horns, the Swarm withdrew down and away from the fifth bulwark.

And the defenders slumped down upon the castle battlements, exhausted beyond telling with this "victory." King Aurion called for a tally, and it showed that fewer than a thousand Men survived, and many of these were wounded, and only nineteen Warrows yet lived. Unto the west battlement the War-council was summoned. And among the Council, too, few survivors remained: Vidron, Gildor, and Young Brill yet lived; Gann, Medwyn, Hagan, and Overn had all fallen. Danner lived and so, too, did Patrel, though he was wounded in the hand.

"We cannot withstand the next assault," said Aurion. "They are too many and we too few. I ask for guidance, though our hope is scant."

Vidron spoke what was in his heart: "Sire, we cannot let you fall. Yet I deem there is but one course to prevent such an end: we must burst through Modru's ring of iron and leave the Keep behind. Aye, we had hoped to hold this fortress and pin the Horde here until the Host arrives, yet that hope has gone aglimmering, swallowed by the darkness. But though that plan has failed, there is yet a way to slow the enemy's march south: we need but adopt the tactics of Prince Galen: strike hard into a weakness and melt away into the shadow ere the enemy can strike back. But first we must break free of this trap ere we can bait the enemy."

Vidron fell silent and Aurion looked to his advisors, and they nodded in agreement with Vidron's words. The King turned back to his General. "Say on, Fieldmarshal."

"This is what I think we must do: when next the Horde begins to scale the walls, we must burst forth from the west gate, cleaving through their ranks, and hie down the mountain and out into the distant shadow upon the far plains." Vidron looked into each of their faces. "And this shall be the way of it: there are enough horses within these walls to mount the force needed for all of us to win through to the west stables, where the Men on foot can secure steeds of their own. Then with horses for all we will fly into the enemy's own darkness."

"But, Hrosmarshal," objected Young Brill, "we are not certain that any of the coursers at the west stable yet live. The foul Rukha may have slain them all in malice."

"Nay, Brill," answered Vidron, "the Rutcha will not kill them in malice. *Zlye pozhirately koneny!* They are vile eaters of horseflesh! and would save the steeds for that evil glut." Vidron's eyes flashed in anger, for there is a special bond between the Men of Valon and their steeds, and the thought of Rutcha rending horses brought rage into Vidron's heart.

Gildor spoke: "Whether or no the steeds live or are slain, there is little to choose from in this matter. Either we defend these walls one last time and die in the effort, or we attempt to break through the ring of *Rûpt*. If the horses at the west stable survive and we reach them, then some of us will live on to fight again. If the steeds are slain or if we do not reach them, then again we will die fighting, but many of the *Spaunen* will fall, too." Gildor fell silent, and all eyes turned to the King.

Aurion Redeye searched the features of each one there. "These then are the fates before us: to die upon the walls, to die at empty stables, or to win free upon horses. Of these three, only one lets us continue against Modru, and that is the fate we will seek. *Maeg Adoni laenan strengthu to ūre earms!*" (May Adon lend strength to our arms!) "Vidron, we will try your desperate plan."

Upon hearing these words, Tuck exhaled, discovering he had been holding his breath.

"Aye, it's a desperate plan, I know," answered Vidron, "but I see no other way to succeed. Upon the steeds stabled within these walls, those of us mounted must battle to hold back the Foul Folk, the Wrg, until all our comrades are horsed. Then we must fly, down the north slope through the sundered gates and away."

"Why the north slope?" asked Danner. "Why not down the south slope and straight away toward friendly Lands?"

"Because only the broken gates are certain to be open," answered Vidron. "The others may be closed and guarded. Yet you have given me pause to think more deeply. Should we get separated, we must choose a rendezvous. Where say you?"

"How about south to the Battle Downs?" offered Patrel. "Or even Stonehill."

"Aye!" agreed King Aurion. "Battle Downs first and then Stonehill, for that is the direction we must bear to gather allies."

"Wait a moment!" cried Tuck. "Warrows can't ride horses! But hold, our ponies are here in the castle stables, and they are swift—swifter than the maggot-folk on foot."

"But not swifter than Hèlsteeds," said Young Brill. "You'll have to ride horses, mounted behind warriors."

"Then you won't be able to fight," snapped Danner, "and neither will we."

"Let us at least ride our ponies down to the first wall," said Patrel. "Through the rubble they are as quick as horses. Then we will mount up behind Men on fleet steeds to be borne away when the fighting is done."

"Better still," said Aurion, "when we break out, it will be you, the Wee Folk, who race ahead and secure the stables while we stay the foe long enough for the Men on foot to come to you." The King looked about. "Is there aught else? Lord Gildor, you have spoken sagely but now seem troubled."

"Aye, King Aurion," said the Elf, "indeed I am troubled, but for nothing I can see, only for that which I feel. A dark foreboding casts a deep pall upon my spirit, yet I cannot say what this feeling augers. Only this: Beware, Aurion King, for past yon gate I sense a great Evil lurks, an Evil beyond the Horde at our door, and I deem it bodes ill for you."

A dread chill clutched at Tuck's heart upon hearing Gildor's words, for the Warrow, too, sensed that a fell fate awaited them. But except for a vague presentment, he could not pin down the cause of his unease.

"So be it," said Aurion. "Fortune now chooses our fate."

And so it was decided: Vidron's plan would be tried, for to do otherwise led only to death. The word was sent forth, and all the surviving defenders prepared for the escape, quietly withdrawing into the courtyard at the west gate. And as the forces of the King gathered, orders were passed among the ranks as the last-minute planning went on. Word was spread to " 'Ware the calthrops" and "Watch out for poisoned blades," as was other such advice, while they girded for the desperate chance.

All the horses in the castle stables had been bridled and saddled—perhaps a hundred steeds, no more—and warriors stood at their sides, Men of Valon for the most part, said to be the best riders in all the Realms. Other Men were afoot, filling the courtyard, holding their weapons ready for the bold charge. Among them came the Warrows, now but nineteen strong, each of them leading a pony. Other ponies wandered loose, mounts of slain young buccen, and they would run with the rest, adding to the enemy's confusion.

Outside the gate Whelm still blazed, but the flames that once raged upon the cobbles were now gone, for the oil had burned away. Downslope the vast Horde ringed the castle. Thus all stood for what seemed an eternity—the grim-faced warriors of the King within, the foul Rūcken Horde of Modru without.

At last the raucous blare of horns could be heard, as well as the *Doom!* of drum, and Men upon the battlements signalled that the enemy advance had begun. Warriors manned the west gate, ready to throw wide the portal. Men mounted up into saddles, and spears were couched in stirrup cups, a thicket of lances stirring to and fro. Now the horse column stood ready with King Aurion and Hrosmarshal Vidron at the point, and Lord Gildor, with Bale ablaze, just behind, Young Brill at his side. At the very back sat the Warrows astride their ponies, bows now strung with precious arrows, their quivers nearly empty. And Men upon foot fingered swords and pikes, though a few here and there bore axes and fewer yet held longbows. And all could hear the knell of the great drum as the Horde came forth: *Doom! Doom! Doom!*

Now came the howls of the Ghûls, followed by the harsh yells of Rūcks and Hlōks, and in his mind's eye Tuck could see the dark Horde running toward the walls. Black-shafted Rūcken arrows hissed through the air to shatter upon the stone merlons or to fly through the crenels atop the battlements. *Thock! Thud!* They heard the scaling ladders strike stone. *Clink! Chank!* Grapnels bit the castellations. Yet the King stayed his hand, watching the sentries in the gate towers. Tuck watched, too, waiting for the signal, and his heart was pounding. Crawling Rūcks swarmed up the ladder rungs and up the knotted ropes; swart fingers grasped over the lip of the battlements; and iron-helmed heads followed.

Now! At last the sign was given, and the sentries scrambled down as the gates were flung wide. And then with fierce cries the warriors swept forward, horses charging, spears lowered, ponies dashing after, Men sprinting and yelling, free ponies running madly in confusion. And as Tuck burst through the gate and past flaming Whelm, he looked to see startled Rūcken faces snarling, and then he was beyond them, his pony running full tilt downslope toward the distant stables.

Ahead of Tuck the column divided, horses wheeling right and left, curling back toward the flanks of the Men on foot. The Warrows charged straight ahead, galloping downhill, for it was their mission to secure the stables until those on foot arrived. Above the pounding sound of running ponies, Tuck could hear the enraged cries of the mounted Ghûls, but then his steed came again to a road, and he plunged along it and down the face of a craggy bluff, and all noise was drowned out but for the ring and clatter of hooves upon cobbles.

Below was another slope on which were the great western stables, and beyond them the land fell sharply unto the fourth wall. Now they thundered out and toward the stall barns and horse pens. As they ran, Tuck threw a fleeting glance back over his shoulder and saw that Men afoot were beginning to come down the road behind, and atop the butte, silhouetted against the Shadowlight sky, were the guarding warriors on horseback, wheeling about to meet the foe, some even now engaged in battle. Amid them Tuck could see the flash of Gildor's burning sword flaring red.

Tuck now looked ahead where lay the stables, and young buccen clapped heels to pony flanks, dashing cross-slope toward them. Some few horses could be seen in the outer pens, but carcasses could be seen there, too, and Tuck thought, *Oh, Lor, let there be live horses in the stalls!*

To the low horse barns they came, hauling the ponies up short and leaping to the snow. In pairs and triplets the Warrows spread out, running silently among the stables, jewel-eyes alert, arrows set to string, flitting through the Shadowlight to mew doors blackly ajar.

Through a portal leapt Tuck, with Wilrow swift upon his heels, dodging quickly around the door frame and ducking into deep shadow, eyes scanning darkened stalls, ready to slay lurking Spawn. Silence. Blackness. *Is nothing here?* Slowly they crept down the aisle. *Blam! Blam!* Two thunderous sounds shocked forth from the left, and Tuck's heart leapt to his throat as he dropped to one knee, his bow drawn to the full, arrow aimed into darkness where surged a frightened horse. In its fear it had lashed at the wall; now it backed into a corner and stood trembling. The steed's eyes rolled white in terror, and it heaved and snorted as if to blow its nostrils free of a dread odor. Slowly Tuck and Wilrow relaxed their aim and wondered at the creature's fear.

"Hst!" Wilrow motioned Tuck to him. He whispered, "There," and pointed into another stall. Tuck looked and then averted his eyes, for the sight was grisly—mangled remains of horse, scattered in sodden blood-soaked straw, with haunches rent from the carcass and gaping holes torn in the flesh, as if fangs and claws had ripped it asunder.

"Vidron was right," breathed Tuck to Wilrow. "This is Rūck work. They eat horseflesh. We must go on, and quickly. The Men will soon arrive."

Forward they pressed, passing down the row of stalls, some empty, most with frightened horses, and others reeking with the bloody carnage of mangled steeds partly consumed.

They had come nearly to the end of the barn when ahead they heard a hideous rending and tearing and a foul smacking of lips. And there, too, came a harsh laugh and the low sounds of grating words:

"Guk klur gog bleagh," came a guttural voice, speaking in the Slûk tongue, a foul speech common among the maggot-folk.

"Yar. Let them stupid grunts crack the High King's crib whilst we enjoys a bloody meal," came another voice, this one using a distorted form of the Common Tongue that Tuck could but barely recognize.

Again there was a rending sound and a smack of lips. Tuck and Wilrow slid forward to see two Rūcks hunkered down at the side of a slain horse, great gobbets of torn flesh clutched in their grasping hands, their blood-slathered faces buried in the dangling meat as they bit and chewed and gulped the raw flesh down their gullets, pausing only long enough to lap at the blood dripping from their fingers and running down their arms.

Th-thuun! Sssth-thok! Tuck's arrow struck the Rūck on the left, Wilrow's drove into the one on the right, and the maggot-folk were driven backwards, dead before they thudded into the wall and sprawled down lifeless.

As Wilrow stepped into the dark stall to make certain that the two were slain, a third Rūck leapt from behind a hay bin, where he had been squatting unseen. With a harsh cry he brought an iron cudgel smashing down upon Wilrow's helm, and the young buccan fell. Tuck shouted in rage and sprang forward and stabbed an arrow like a dagger into the Rūck's back. Spinning, the Rūck lashed out at Tuck, knocking the Warrow to the straw, and stepped forward snarling, cudgel raised; but then a look of surprise came upon his swart features, and he clawed at his back, trying to reach the shaft as he toppled dead at Tuck's side.

Tuck scrambled over to Wilrow's fallen form, but the young buccan was slain, too, killed by Rūck cudgel. And at that moment the Warrow heard the steps of running Men enter the stables and the shout of their voices. Sick at heart, Tuck closed Wilrow's golden eyes in final sleep and arranged his hands over his breast, and whispered, *"Thuna glath, Fral Wilrow"* (Go in peace, Friend Wilrow), speaking in the ancient Warrow Tongue. Then he stood and went to meet the Men, for the ruthless brunt of battle leaves no time to mourn the dead.

"Swift! Mount up! The King is hard-pressed!" Tuck heard a voice cry, and he ran through Men saddling and bridling horses and back outside unto his pony.

Tuck looked to the cobbled road along the face of the bluff. Halfway down, a fierce battle raged between the mounted Kingsmen and Ghûls upon Hèlsteed. As Tuck's sapphire eyes sought out the King, more Ghûls came to the top of the cliff and rode to the fray, while above on the lip, dark Rūcken forces hurled rocks upon the Men, and black-shafted arrows rained downward. Slowly the horsemen backed down, fighting for every inch yielded, and the King upon Wildwind was among the last to come. And the mêlée was furious, for they fought to the death; even as Tuck looked on, a Ghûl and Man, Hèlsteed and horse, locked in battle, plunged from the road and hurtled down. And boulders smashed among the Men from the cliffs above.

"Ya hoi! Ya hoi!" Tuck cried an ancient call to arms and sprang into the saddle and clapped his heels into his pony's flanks. As he raced back cross-slope he was joined by Danner and Patrel and other Warrows riding to the call.

They sped to the foot of the cliff and leapt to the snow. "The archers above!" cried Patrel. "The rock hurlers, too!" And the Warrows sped their deadly arrows toward the Rūcks upon the bluff above, taking careful aim, for the shot was a long one—eighty feet or more—and their shafts were few. Yet Patrel had directed their aim aright, for the black-shafted arrows and hurled rocks were taking a deadly toll among the Men, and Patrel knew that only the Warrows could slow the fatal rain from above.

Shaft after shaft hissed upward, and even at this distance they sped true. Rūcks quailed back from the cliff edge above the Men, and the fall of stone and arrow ebbed greatly. But snarling Hlōks lashed about with whips, and once more Rūcks came to the fore. They were joined by the Great Ogrus, who hurled huge boulders, and the deadly rain of rocks fell anew. Now the black arrows struck among the young buccen; some bolts found their marks, and Warrows fell. Tuck's arrows now were spent, but he scooped up the quiver of a slain comrade and sped six more quarrels into the enemy before these, too, were gone. He began plucking the black Rūck shafts from the earth, and these he winged into the foe. And then he was surrounded by thundering horses and yelling Men as those from the stables at last charged to the battle, and horns sounded their presence.

Now the Kingsmen upon the narrow cobbled road turned their steeds and sped down, for all the Men, the five hundred or so that yet survived, now were mounted, and the dash down the mount through the sundered gates could begin. Tuck sprang again into his saddle, and all the Warrows, now but twelve strong, sped their ponies to the north and down, down through a gauntlet of Rūcken archers; and four more of the Wee Folk were felled. Tuck and Danner

and Patrel yet lived, and together past the gauntlet and
through the broken north gate of the fourth wall and
among the char and rubble of the burned city they ran
along the steep twisting streets and down. And behind
came the Men on horses, and in back of them thundered
Ghûls on Hèlsteeds, overhauling riders from behind and
felling them with spears and tulwars as Men turned to make
a stand.

Veering down through the black spars of the burned ruin
they dashed, through the third gate and the second, and
ash flew up from the pounding hooves. Now they ran for
the first gate, the last before they would be free upon the
foothills and the plains beyond. Tuck thought, *Here we
must mount up behind Men, for the ponies will not be swift
enough once we leave the twisting path.* And then the north
gate of the first wall hove into view, and Tuck gasped in
dismay and hauled his pony up short; for there, massed
upon Hèlsteeds, stood row upon row of leering Ghûls.

Now the King rode up and checked Wildwind's gallop,
bringing the courser to a standstill. Even in his despair,
Tuck was glad to see that the King yet lived. Then came
Gildor and Vidron, and Young Brill, and three hundred
more, and all clattered to a stop, the steeds blowing plumes
of white breath into the cold air. And behind them the
pursuing Ghûls harshly reined up and jeered in victory—
for the Men were trapped.

At the gate, among the stark Ghûls, sat the vacant-eyed
emissary upon a Hèlsteed. Now he was led forth by a pallid
Ghûl to face the High King. Once again the messenger's
face *writhed,* and then Evil stared out upon the assembly.
Suddenly the jeers stopped, and Tuck heard Gildor gasp.
The Elf spurred Fleetfoot to the fore, and then he raised
Bale on high. Ruby fire blasted forth upon the blade, and
the Ghûls quailed back from its light. Yet the emissary
snarled a harsh command—*"Slath!"*—and now the lines
held firm.

Then the ghastly pit-adder voice hissed forth and carried
over the ruins: "You were given a choice, Aurion Redeye,
yet you spurned my mercy. You have sought to stand
against me and win, but the prize you have earned is
death!"

Young Brill began to shake, and spittle foamed upon his

mouth, and his eyes rolled white, then wide, as the battle madness seized him; and with an inarticulate cry of rage he spurred his horse forward, springing down the slope toward the emissary.

"Gluktu!" cried the ghastly voice, and the Ghûl at the messenger's side drove his Hèlsteed up, and Ghûl and Man raced at one another, and the sound of horse hoof and cloven hoof rang out upon the cobble. And Young Brill lashed his great sword out and down with unmatched fury. Sparks flew as blade met helm, and he clove the Ghûl from crown to crotch; yet the Ghûl had struck, too, and his tulwar chopped through Young Brill's neck; and they both fell dead unto the stone.

It was if a dam had burst, for Men and Ghûls alike vented cries of rage and spurred forward at one another to come together in a mighty clash of arms, and Tuck's pony was swept forth in the charge. Yet even as he surged forward, Tuck heard Danner shout in hatred, and an arrow hissed through the air to strike the emissary full in the forehead, crashing into the Man's brain and hurling him backward over the saddle and onto the frozen ground. And then Tuck was borne away, and all about him battle swirled and cries of death and fury filled the air. Tuck was without weapons, and he tried to ride toward the gate, but Ghûls there barred the way and fought with the King's forces. Tulwars and sabers skirled upon one another, and meaty chops sounded as blade met flesh. Only Gildor's sword, Bale, seemed to have effect, for where it slashed Ghûls fell, spewing black blood. But the swords of Men hacked into the pallid flesh, and great gashes opened; yet they bled not, and the Ghûls fought on unaffected, felling Men.

Beheading! Wood through the heart! Fire! Silver blade! Tuck's mind raged. *These are the ways to kill Ghûls. Not simple sword wounds or knife cuts. We stand no chance if we cannot flee.* Again he pressed through the mêlée, but still the gate was barred . . . yet wait! The Ghûlen force was turning, as if to meet a new foe. It *was* a new threat! For bursting through the ranks warding the north gate and scattering them asunder came a force of men, thirty strong, shouting and casting oil and torches upon the enemy. Flames sprang up and Ghûls howled, Hèlsteeds bolted, afire. And leading the Men was a grey-clad warrior upon a jet-black steed: Lord Galen!

"Now!" he cried. "The way is open!" and wheeled the black to meet Ghûl tulwar with steel sword.

Tuck spurred his pony forward, ducking a sweep of enemy iron. Through the gate he dashed, others speeding behind.

Danner also galloped into the passage, but a wild-running Hèlsteed slammed into his mount, and the young buccan was hurled to the cobbles, his pony fleeing from the stench of the beast. The Warrow scrambled to his feet. He heard a cry—*"Danner!"*—and looked back to see Patrel bearing down upon him, leaning out to catch him up. Danner reached high and grasped Patrel's hand, the wounded one, and swung up behind him, and they thundered out beyond the gate. Then others poured through behind.

When Tuck emerged outside the walls his steed ran but a short way north before the battle again caught up and swirled about him. Back he was pressed, and then forth, and he looked and saw . . . "My King! My King!" Aurion was besieged on all sides by Ghûls and Hèlsteeds. Wildwind reared and lashed out, belling challenges. Gildor spurred Fleetfoot toward the fray, Red Bale felling foe before him as he went.

Tuck, too, attempted to ride to the King, though the Warrow had no weapon. Yet Aurion Redeye was swept away by the combat, and Tuck's pony was buffeted by horse and Hèlsteed alike, and cursing Men and howling Ghûls drove him aside and to the edge of a ravine. And ere he could spur to the King, one of the foul, white, corpse-people slashed at Tuck with whistling blade, missing the Warrow but chopping into the pony's neck. The steed stumbled forward and fell slain, pitching with Tuck down into the blackness of the steep-sided ravine. Tuck was thrown free of the dead pony as down they tumbled, hurtling into scrub and rock, snow slithering behind. Then he struck his head and all consciousness left him, and the shout of battle above him went unheard.

When Tuck came to, he did not know how long it had been since he had fallen, yet now there were no sounds of combat. Instead, he could hear the distant yammering of

Rūcks, using the foul Slūk speech, coming along the ravine bottom, and from afar he could see the light of torches held high. He could hear another sound, too, nearer—hooves! *Ghûl!* he thought, floundering to his feet. *They search for survivors. Hide! I must hide!* Frantically his eyes sought concealment, yet nought did he see but the heap of his slain pony and his bow lying in the snow nearby. Snatching up the bow, he fled silently north along the ravine bottom, while behind came the sound of hooves and Rūcks.

Now the ravine narrowed and rose, and up Tuck ran, to come out into the Shadowlight. Around him were the rounded barrow mounds of Challerain Keep. He fled a short way among the grave mounds and came to a great tumbled ring of stone. *Orthran's Crypt!* his mind cried, and he ran to ring's center. There before him stood a low stone ruin; snow-laden brittle vines covered it. The door had been torn asunder and flung aside by plundering Rūcks. Inward Tuck fled, stumbling down three steps inside. There, in the center of a smooth marble floor, by the Shadowlight shining through the doorway, Tuck could see a tomb; it, too, had been defiled by the Foul Folk. The stone lid was cast off, and nearby urns and boxes had been smashed as if by War-hammer.

Outside, the sound of shouting Rūcks drew closer. Tuck's sapphirine eyes frantically searched the shadowed strewn rubble, but nought did he find to defend himself. *Yet wait! The tomb!* Quickly he stepped to the sarcophagus, sundered by the looters. The Shadowlight of the Dimmendark fell pale inward and illumed the bier. Lying in the dust of ages were the yellowed bones of the long-dead seer, smashed as if by Ruck cudgel, and vacant eyes stared from grinning skull into Tuck's own. Ancient remnants of sacerdotal raiments clung to the skeleton, and a plain but empty knife scabbard was girt at the waist. The fleshless arms were folded across ribs, as if in repose, but clutched in skeletal fingers were two weapons, one in each hand. Ceremonial they seemed, yet weapons naytheless: One was a Man's long-knife, gleaming and sharp though entombed ages agone, golden runes inlaid along silvery blade—unplundered by the defilers, for it was a blade of lost Atala and Rūcks could not abide its touch. But it was the other weapon that Tuck snatched to his bosom: an arrow, small and straight, dull red it was, and made of a strange light metal—yet it fit the Wee One's bow as if waiting ages to do so.

Now the shouting drew closer, and Tuck set shaft to string. *If they find me, at least one will die ere I do.* And Tuck slipped into the shadows behind the sarcophagus. There came a soft clatter of hooves, and the Shadowlight was blotted out as a form came through the entrance leading a steed. Ghûl! Tuck drew the metal shaft to the full, aiming at the dark figure, waiting for him to move into the spectral light, waiting to make certain of the shot.

Now the harsh voices grew loud as the Rūcks tramped past outside, and light flickered from the burning brands they bore, torches to search the darkness. Firelight guttered and shone into the crypt, and by its light Tuck centered his quivering aim, ready to loose hissing death into the shadows near the entrance. For there in the light Tuck could see a white hand gripping the hilt of a broken sword as the figure leaned forward to peer out at the passing Rūcks, and from his neck dangled a golden locket glittering in the receding torchlight, and behind him stood a jet-black steed.

CHAPTER 6

The Long Pursuit

"Lord Galen!" gasped Tuck, and the Man spun and crouched, holding out his shattered sword before him like a knife. Tuck turned his aim aside and down, letting the tension from his bow. "Lord Galen," he breathed, "I am a friend."

Long moments fled, and outside the Rūcks tramped away, their sounds growing faint. At last the Man spoke: "Friend, you say, yet you are Rukh-height. Can you prove this no trick of the Evil One?"

"Trick!" hissed Tuck in ire. "I am Tuckerby Underbank, a Warrow of the Boskydells, and no Rūck!" spat the young buccan, stepping forward into the pale Shadowlight, his sapphire-jewelled eyes flashing in anger.

"A *Waerling!*" Galen lowered the shard of his sword at last. "Forgive me, Sir Tuckerby, but these are suspicious times."

Jet, too, wondered at this small tomb-mate, and he shifted his stance and lowered his head and snuffled at the Wee One and seemed satisfied with the young buccan in spite of Tuck's anger.

"Oh, Lor!" cried Tuck, his mood shifting like quicksilver as he slumped to the floor, appalled.

"Sir Tuckerby, are you wounded?" The Prince swiftly knelt at the Warrow's side.

"Nay, Sire, not wounded," said the young buccan, a shaken look upon his face, his voice hushed, "but I just realized, I nearly shot you for a Ghûl."

"Ho, then, we are even," smiled Galen, "for I mistook you for a Rukh. Not the best of ways to start an acquaintance, I would say."

"Nay, Sire, not the best of ways." Tuck managed a weak grin, and then gestured at Jet. "Were it not for this black steed of yours, and the golden locket at your heart bearing a snippet of Laurelin's hair—"

"Laurelin!" Galen reached out and roughly grasped Tuck by the shoulders. "Is she safe?" The tension in Galen's voice fairly crackled the air.

Pain laced Tuck's voice as he spoke: "Sire, in the company of Prince Igon and Captain Jarriel and a mounted escort, she left the Keep bearing south in a waggon bound for Stonehill and beyond; that was one week agone, if my reckoning is right—one day ere the Dimmendark came upon Mont Challerain."

The Prince released Tuck's arms and stood, and the Warrow shrugged gingerly. "Forgive me, Sir Tuckerby," said Galen, wearily. "I meant no harm to you, and I have treated you rudely, yet this is the first word I've had of my love." Lord Galen extended his hand down, and Tuck took it and was raised to his feet. "I am fortunate to have met someone who could tell me of her," said Galen.

"Sire, more fortunate than you realize," answered Tuck, taking up his bow, "for had I not known your Lady, who told me of the locket you wear, and your sire, who spoke of your black horse, Jet, then surely you would have been pierced through with this arrow I found in yon bier." Tuck held out the bolt for Galen to see.

"Is that the only shaft you have?" asked the Prince. At Tuck's nod, Galen took up his shattered sword, blade snapped near the hilt. "Then we have not much to meet the foe with, you and I: a broken blade and a lone arrow."

"Nay, Lord Galen, there is another weapon here," said Tuck, stepping to the sarcophagus. "This bright edge." The young buccan drew forth the rune-marked blade from the long-dead grasp of Othran the Seer. In Tuck's hand it was long enough to be a Warrow's sword, but given over to Lord Galen, it became a Man's long-knife.

"Hai, but it has a sharp edge!" said Galen, testing it with his thumb. "These runes of power, I read them not, yet they look to be Atalain, the forgotten language of a drowned Realm. This, then, is an Atalar blade: these are renowned for their power to combat evil." He held the long-knife back out to Tuck.

"Nay, Lord Galen." Tuck refused to take it again. "Keep the blade, and take the sheath, too, that lies in the bier, for I know nothing of swords and would most likely end up cutting myself. This is my weapon, the bow. Besides, now we are each armed—though if I were given a choice, your steel would be longer and my quiver full."

Galen stepped to the shattered tomb and took up the plain scabbard at Othran's side. As the Prince girted himself, Tuck saw the resemblance Galen held to both Aurion, his sire, and Igon, his brother. In his middle twenties was Galen, with all the endurance and speed of youth matured into the fullness of strength. Tall he was, like his sire, six feet or an inch more. Dark brown was his hair, like that of Igon, and his eyes were steel-grey, too, though in the Shadowlight they seemed black. Grey quilted goose-down winter garments he wore, and his cloak was grey, too. A leather and steel helm was upon his head, and now a long-knife was at his waist. He tied his sword scabbard to Jet's saddle and turned to face Tuck and spoke: "Did you hear aught of plans where the Kingsmen gather?"

"The Battle Downs, and Stonehill after that," answered Tuck. A troubled frown came upon the Warrow's features. "Lord Galen, the King, is he safe? Did he win free? When last I saw him, he was beset. But I know nought of the battle's outcome, for I was thrown down into yon ravine."

The look upon Galen's face was grim to behold. "Sir Tuckerby, I know not the fate of my sire. We were sundered in the fight, and I saw him not again. Yet my heart is ever hopeful, though what I know bodes ill. They were too many, the Ghola. I was forced aside, and my sword was broken as it clove through Ghol helm. But ere I could take up another weapon, one from a slain hand, the remaining force of Men broke free; many were scattered, though most rode hard to the east. Yet my eyes saw not Wildwind, running with the King astride, though he could have been among the larger band. I turned Jet into the ravine, to wait until I, too, could ride away. But then the Rukha came searching, and I led Jet to the crypt, where now we stand. Yet as to my sire, I cannot say else."

Tuck's heart plummeted at this uncertain news. "Though I have been the King's far-seeing eyes but a short while, I love him well, for although he is a great leader, in many ways he is like unto my own sire."

"Far-seeing eyes?" Galen's look was puzzled. "There is

a tale here for the telling, yet you can speak of it as we ride south, for we must leave this place: Rukha abound, and may come again."

And so they peered out into the Shadowlight, and led Jet among the deserted barrow mounds. Mounting up, they rode forth quietly to the north and west, Warrow bestride horse behind the Man, armed with but a single arrow and a blade of Atala and nought else save their courage. In secret and by wending ways known unto Lord Galen, they slowly worked their way through the margins of the foothills and around Mont Challerain, turning west and finally south. Then, at last, away from the gutted, burned hulk of Challerain Keep they rode—Prince and Thornwalker—heading for the Battle Downs, leaving the sundered city behind.

"Hai, then, by my tally you with your small bow have slain seventy, eighty, or perhaps even more of the Yrm!" Lord Galen tilted his chair back from the table and gazed in wonder at his jewel-eyed companion. Flickering candlelight cast writhing shadows as Tuck mutely nodded, stricken by the very numbers. The Prince leaned forward and broke off another hunk of stale bread and ravenously bit into it.

They had ridden for hours, southward across the prairie, drifting westward, too, following alongside the Post Road. After reaching the plains, Tuck had ridden mounted before Galen, the Warrow's sharp sight ever on the alert for enemy movement. But they had seen no one, though Tuck once thought he had heard a distant cry above the hammer of Jet's hooves. Yet his searching eyes saw only rolling plains and dark thickets in the gloomy Shadowlight, and the call, if it was that, was not repeated as the black steed drove on. Swift was Jet, and strong, but even the best of coursers needs must rest and be fed and watered. At last they had come to an abandoned farmstead, and there they found grain and water and a stable with hay.

Tuck and Galen had entered the house. Small it was, with but two rooms—a kitchen and one other—and beds were in the loft above. Closing the shutters so that no light would shine out, they had lighted a candle and had found a scant store of food—stale bread, dried beans, a tin of tea, nought else. They had then kindled a small fire on the kitchen hearth and had set a pot of water to boil, from which tea had been brewed and the beans cooked. Now the travellers avidly consumed the meager meal as if it were a sumptuous banquet. And their talk was of the Winter War, as this struggle with Modru now was called.

"When Igon and I first came unto the Dimmendark, sent by Father to see what was this wall, we knew nought of what the darkness held. Outside it was a midsummer's day, and in the company of four Kingsmen we rode through the winds along the Black Wall and into the Shadowlight." Galen sopped up the last of his beans with a piece of bread. "Like riding into a winter night, it was, and snow lay upon the land and our eyes were filled with amaze. Back we rode into warm day, and Igon and I took the cloaks and jerkins and breeks from the Men of our escort, fairly stripping them bare ere we sent them home. Now, bundled against the cold, once more Igon and I pierced the Black Wall into the Winternight, this time determined to explore.

"Two 'Darkdays we rode within the black grasp and saw nought of any other living thing. But on the third 'Darkday, while riding through a twisting defile, we turned a corner, and there facing us stood a squad of startled Yrm. Without hesitation, Igon couched his lance and spitted a Rukh ere any could move even one step. Hai! But he will be a mighty warrior when he comes full into his years.

"It was a short fierce battle, Igon felling three Rukha in all, while I slew but one Rukh and one Lōkh. The other Yrm turned and ran, scrambling up the ravine walls and away; six or seven fled beyond our reach.

"Straightaway we rode to warn the King, for this was news of import: Rukha and Lōkha bestrode the land within the 'Dark. Not an hour after the battle, we came out through the Black Wall and the Sun rode high in the sky. Then we knew that in the Dimmendark, Adon's Ban ruled not, and the fell creatures of the night—Modru's minions— were free of the Covenant.

"Although my sire was ired at me for sending the Kingsmen back and taking Igon—'A mere lad!'—into what proved to be mortal danger, still the King was proud of what we had done and bade me to lead a force of warriors back into the Winternight to watch for sign of the gathering of Modru's Horde of old. A hundred Men came with me, yet Igon was not one of them, and bitter was his spirit, for he would ride at my side. Yet perhaps my sire was right in keeping him from the Dimmendark, for seventy of my Men had fallen ere the last battle with the Ghola at the Keep, and half or more of those remaining were slain in that final combat. And for what did all those who perished yield up their lives? Mayhap for nought, for Challerain Keep has fallen, and the Horde is now free to rave south." The Prince bitterly swirled the dregs of his drink in the bottom of his cup and then tossed the tea into the hearth, where it hissed and sputtered. "Ah me, but I am weary. Let us get some rest."

"You sleep, Lord Galen, I'll stand the first watch, for there is something I must do," said Tuck, taking his diary from his jerkin pocket.

"Ah, yes," Galen smiled, "the journal you spoke of. Perhaps some day I will ask you to scribe it into a Waerling history of the Winter War, some day when the fighting is done. But now, it's me for bed."

The Prince clambered up into the loft and fell asleep watching the Wee One's pencil slowly crawling through the candlelight and across a page in the diary, leaving a track of words behind it.

The next 'Darkday, south and west they pressed, taking with them the last of the bread and beans, as well as grain for Jet. Later they came upon another abandoned stead; this one was bestrewn with wreckage, as if a fight had occurred, and Tuck was reminded of the Vulg-shatter in Arlo and Willa Huggs' farmhouse along Two Fords Road in the Boskydells; it seemed so long ago, and yet it was just seven weeks past, when Hob and Tarpy were still alive, and Danner and Patrel, too. *Stop that!* Tuck angrily berated himself. *For all you know, Danner and Patrel yet live.*

In the wrack Galen found food—dried venison and some turnips.

Onward they rode for many hours, bearing ever south and west. Finally they stopped to camp in the lee of a thicket, huddled beside a small fire, its light shielded by brush.

Early after resuming their way, the margins of the Battle Downs hove first into Tuck's view and then into Galen's.

And they rode alongside the hills, going upon the Post Road now as it swung to the west. Miles passed under Jet's hooves, and Man and Warrow often dismounted and walked to rest the steed, feeding him grain when they took their own meal, as was their practice.

They had ridden some six hours, covering nearly twenty miles, when they rounded the flank of a hill and Tuck saw shapes ahead.

"Lord Galen, something stands upon the road," he quietly said.

Galen reined Jet to a stop. "Say on, Sir Tuck."

"It moves not, and appears to be . . . a waggon." Tuck peered intently. "I see no team, nor Folk of any kind."

"Mount behind me, Tuck, for we may meet the foe." At the Prince's command, Tuck swung to the rear of the cantle, removing his bow from across his shoulders and leaning out to see. Galen flicked the reins, and Jet stepped forward, moving at a walk. "Remember, Tuck," said Galen, "we will fight or flee if there be enemy. If we fight, you will slip straight back and drop to the ground and use that deadly bow of yours where it will do the most good. But recall, we have but a long-knife and a single arrow between us; thus it may be best to run. If we flee, hang on tightly, for Jet will veer and leap as he flies o'er the 'scape."

Along the road they went; now more waggons came into view, as Jet rounded the curve of the hill. Now Tuck could see that they were in disarray, some on the road, some off, and all were abandoned; many were burnt while others lay upon their sides.

Now Galen, too, could see them, and his voice was grim. "It's a waggon train." Tuck's heart pounded loudly in his ears.

Closer they drew, and other shapes could be seen lying in the snow—horses, Men . . . dead, felled. Tuck gasped, "Lord Galen! There! A slain Hèlsteed!"

Galen spurred Jet to a canter and swiftly closed the distance. They came unto the first of the bestrewn and burned wains. Dismounting, they walked among the slain, hacked by blades, pierced by spears, and frost and rime covered all.

"Lord Galen." Tuck's voice was filled with anguish, and he stood by a spear-pierced warrior, dead eyes staring up through icy glaze, broken shaft pointing at the darkling sky.

"Lord Galen, it is Captain Jarriel, and there lies your messenger, Haddon. Lord, this is the caravan of the Lady Laurelin!" And Tuck burst into tears.

Long they searched and much horror they saw as they moved up and down the grim train. Tuck's faltering steps carried him along in a benumbed state as he saw the savage slaughter that had occurred when the caravan had been overrun: Men were slain, and Women, too, as well as the oldsters; but worst of all were the children, some but babes in arms. Even the steeds were slaughtered, cut down in their very traces.

As to who had done the deed, there was no doubt, for Ghûls had been felled, as well as Hèlsteeds.

Yet neither the Lady Laurelin nor Prince Igon was found among the dead.

Galen had rearmed himself, taking up Jarriel's steel. And he filled Tuck's quiver with arrows found in one of the waggons. Now they stood at mid train, where a great track beat eastward through the snow.

"Five 'Darkdays agone," gritted Prince Galen, bale in his eyes, "and there lies their wake. East they fled from this butchery."

"But, Lord Galen," asked Tuck, "where is the Lady Laurelin, and Prince Igon?"

"I know not, Tuck," answered Galen, his eyes locked upon the Ghûlen track. "Igon may have won free with the Lady Laurelin and galloped south for Stonehill, for Rust is not among the slain steeds. Or they could, one or both, be captives of Modru's butchers." Galen struck a fist into palm and ground his teeth in rage. "Yet free or captive, the only trace lies there in the snow before us, and even though the trail is old we shall pursue these slayers. If they hold Laurelin or Igon, we will find a way to free them. And then there shall be another slaughter—only this time it will be the Ghola who fall."

Galen spun and headed for a waggon. "Come, Tuck, we must find provisions for a long pursuit, for they have a lead of five 'Darkdays upon us, and if they continue to run, the chase will be a lasting one." Galen wheeled and looked in the direction of the trail. "Yet we will follow these ravers, even unto Modru's Iron Tower if need be: this I swear as a Prince of the Realm!" Galen turned once more and made for the waggons.

Thus it was that in less than an hour the black horse thundered forth upon the eastward track of the Ghûls, saddlebags filled with grain for Jet and biscuits of crue waybread for Galen and Tuck. They bore no other food, for as Galen said, "We needs must make Jet's load a light one, for our chase may be long, and food such as venison or even beans carries more bulk and weight and less nourishment than these bland biscuits. Finding water for Jet will be our main concern, yet if we melt enough snow, then that, too, will be resolved."

East they went, following the swath in the snow made by the cloven hooves of many Hèlsteeds, the path curving to and fro among the Battle Downs but ever bearing eastward. Some hours Galen and Tuck rode, at times cantering, at times trotting, and occasionally walking, the Prince varying the gait of Jet but ever conserving the black steed's strength.

At last they stopped to camp in a sheltered dell. Jet was fed some grain as Tuck bolted down a crue biscuit. Although it tasted like nothing more than lightly seasoned flour, the Warrow's hunger disappeared, for as he said, "It certainly fills up the hollow spots."

"Fear not, Wee One, we'll not starve on this ration," said Galen, melting snow in a copper pan over the fire, chewing upon a biscuit of his own. "In fact, we may thrive on the diet, but this food will swiftly grow wearisome upon our tongues."

Soon Galen bedded down as Tuck took the first watch. And as the buccan melted snow for Jet, he trimmed the Man-sized arrows down in length to suit his Warrow bow. And when Galen awoke to take his turn, he found Tuck scribing in his diary.

Again they went upon the eastward track, moving through the Shadowlight of the Dimmendark, Tuck's jewel-hued eyes scanning to their limits. Yet nought did he see but the bleak 'scape of Winternight, and onward they pressed. And though he did not remark upon it, Tuck knew that this Darkday was Year's End day; tomorrow would be

Twelfth Yule, Merrilee's age-name birthday, the first day
of a new year—and Mithgar was in chaos.

The next 'Darkday, Year's Start Day, a snow began to fall,
and Galen raged at the darkling sky, for the Ghûlen track
before them began to fade 'neath the new fall. Eastward they
rode for many hours, and the snow swirled thickly. Now at
last they could no longer see the Ghûlen wake, yet Lord
Galen continued onward; but what track he followed or what
sign he used to guide him east, Tuck did not know. Yet the
young buccan sensed eastward they went, for Warrows are
wise in such matters.

Then before them, through the swirling snow, dark
shapes loomed. *Trees! Thickly wooded!* "Lord Galen, a forest lies ahead," said Tuck, his voice muffled by his hood
drawn tight.

"Aye, I see it," answered Galen, for in the thick snow
the Warrow's sight was no better than the Man's. "It is the
Weiunwood, I deem."

Weiunwood! An ancient homeland of the Warrows. Settled before the Boskydells. Steaded in the last days of the
Wanderjahre, near the end of the long journey of Home-
coming. Weiunwood, a shaggy forest in the Wilderland
north of Harth and south of Rian. Weiunwood, now stark
in winter dress.

"Slip behind me, Tuck," said Galen, "for we know not
what we may meet therein."

Into the barren woods they rode, and still the snow ed-
died down. Now Jet was slowed to a walk, picking his way
through the trees. They came among a stand of ancient
oaks and rode through into a glade. Across the open space
they went, but ere they entered the oaks again:

"Chelga!" came a sharp cry, and Tuck was astounded,
for it was a command in the ancient Warrow tongue and
meant "stand still and speak your name."

"Ellil!" (Friend!) cried Tuck, and urgently whispered,
"Stop Jet, Prince Galen, for we are under the eyes and
arrows of my kindred." And the black horse was reined to
a halt.

"Chelga!" came the command again, and Tuck slipped
over the tail of the steed and to the ground. He stepped
to the fore, casting back his hood, and called out, "I am

Tuckerby Underbank, Thornwalker of the Boskydells, and my companion is Prince Galen, son of High King Aurion."

"Welladay now! Why didn't ye say so in the first place?" came the voice from on high, and Tuck looked up to see a golden-eyed young buccan step out along one of the great limbs of an oak. In one hand he bore a bow, string nocked with arrow. "From the Bosky, are ye now? And ye, my Laird, is yer sire Redeye himself?"

Tuck nodded and Galen laughed, the first merry sound Tuck had heard in many a day.

"Well, then, I am called Baskin, and I come from the Westglade, south of here," said the young buccan. "Where be ye bound?"

"Sir Baskin," answered Galen, "we are on the track of a large force of Ghola. East they fled from a slaughter of innocents, perhaps with a hostage or two. They would have passed through here perhaps five 'Darkdays agone. Have you seen aught?"

"Nay, Laird Galen," responded Baskin. "But five 'Darkdays past we were locked in great struggle with Modru's Spawn. Whipped 'em, too, we did now, striking hard and melting back, and they couldn't get their grips on us. Three 'Darkdays we fought—the Warrows of Weiunwood, the Men of Stonehill, and the Elves from Arden—and a fine Alliance it is, for now the Spawn march east, lickin' their wounds, passin' us by.

"Yet as to the ones ye're chasin', they could have come here and none may know the better for they could have passed through unseen. Perhaps they joined the struggle, though I'm sure I can't say." Baskin paused in thought. "But wait, if perchance someone spied them then they would have sent word to Captain Arbagon. When my relief comes in an hour or so then I'll take ye to my squad's camp and get ye a guide to haul ye to the Captain."

And so they waited while snow fell to earth from the Dimmendark sky above. And while Baskin stood guard, both Tuck and Galen sat with their backs to the great oak and dozed, for they were weary. An hour passed and then another, and at last Baskin's relief came riding a small brown pony. Wide were the Warrow's emerald-green eyes to see Tuck and Galen, and he was but barely introduced—

Twillin was his name—before Baskin fetched his own hidden steed and led the strangers away.

"Aye, it's Captain Arbagon yer lookin' for, and he's to the east, followin' the progress of the nasty Spawn, makin' sure they're pullin' no tricks whilst they run away." The speaker was Lieutenant Pibb, leader of the squad assigned to keep watch in this area of the Weiunwood. "After ye've had yerselves a good rest, Baskin'll lead ye to him, and if anyone has reported sight of them that ye're after, then he'll have the word."

"Ye'll like Arbagon," said Baskin, "for a great buccan warrior is he. They call him Rūckslayer, now, for he slew many in battle. And once he even rode a horse to combat— one that was runnin' free, its own master felled. Arbagon got so mad, he got on that horse and rode it to the fight; and it was a real horse, too, and not a pony like Pudge there. Ah, ol' Arbagon must've been a terrible sight upon that great beastie."

Tuck looked at Jet tethered nearby and wondered how a small Warrow could ride in command of such a large creature.

With his stomach full of the first hot meal he'd had in more than a week, and with a Warrow squad standing guard close by, Tuck slept the sleep of the dead. Yet he did vaguely recall having a bodeful dream, one filled with visions of pursuit and dread—but whether he was chasing or being chased, he could not say.

Sometime during the hours they slept, the snow stopped. Yet the track of the Ghûls had long been hopelessly lost, and when Tuck awakened, his spirit was at a low ebb; for if Laurelin or Igon *had* been captured, Tuck did not see how they could be found, even with Arbagon's advice.

After breakfast, Baskin led them away through the winter forest, following unmarked Weiunwood trails. Tuck was again mounted before Galen upon Jet, for Pibb's squad had no ponies to spare for Tuck's use.

As they went they varied the pace of the steeds, at times dismounting and walking, for the trek to Arbagon's camp was a long one. During one of these walks, Baskin told them of the Battle of Weiunwood, at times his voice chanting like that of a skald's: "Three 'Darkdays we fought and had many battles, the first one bein' where the Elves led the Rūcks and the Hlōks headlong into a trap. Right into the gorge they ran, and we hurled rocks and boulders down upon them and set great logs to rolling, smashing them flat.

"But they were too many, and so we slipped away into the forest, Warrows leading Men and Elves alike. By the hidden pathways we went, brushing the snow behind to hide our tracks except where we wanted them to follow.

"In a great loop they chased us, to come runnin' out of the trees where they'd started. Oh, ye should've heard them howl in rage.

"Back into the 'Wood they ran, right into another trap, can ye believe? This time we fought with sword and pike and arrow, and a great slaughter befell the Rūckish Spawn.

"Out we drove them screamin', runnin' for their safety, for they didn't know how to fight among the trees, how to use them for shields and wards.

"And that was the end of the first 'Darkday.

"Now they licked their wounds for hours, but then the Ghûls came. Oh they howled in anger, made my blood chill to hear it.

"Once more into the woods they came, this time creeping forward in caution. Before them we faded like smoke, drawing them into deadfalls and staked pits, flying arrows at them from hiding, felling at a distance. Still they came on as we drew back.

"And that was the end of the second 'Darkday.

"At last, toward the great oak maze we led them, and into it they walked unsuspecting. Now their great force divided as they became confused, wandering among this wood.

"Split, they were, into several factions, and we came upon them one at a time, slaying one group, then falling upon another, till they ran forth shrieking in terror.

"Now the Ghûls became enraged, and to the woods they thundered in wild fury, upon Hèlsteeds swift and dark. A hundred raced in among the trees, where Men with long pikes lay in hiding. Now the pikemen leapt up to their feet, the lances braced well upon the ground. It was too late for the Ghûls to turn, and into the great spears they rode full tilt, impaling themselves upon the wood. Elves with bright swords sprang among the fallen; snick snack, they cut them into pieces. A hundred Ghûls had charged in fury; less than thirty fled in fear.

"And that was the end of the third 'Darkday.

"Toward the east they withdrew, marching for the Signal Mountains, skirting the Weiunwood, passing us by.

"Hundreds upon hundreds we had felled, but we escaped not unscathed, for many of our brethren had fallen—Men, Elves, and Warrows alike. And whether or no we can fight like that again, I know it not, for the tally of our slain was considerable.

"Yet this I say: Evil Modru will think twice before comin' at the Weiunwood again, for it'll cost him dear to conquer these glades."

With that, Baskin leapt upon his pony, while Tuck and Galen remounted Jet, and through the woods once more they rode. And Tuck could not but marvel at the victory won by the Alliance of Weiunwood.

Baskin's steed, Pudge, was quick through the woods, and they covered nearly thirty miles before making camp. And all the time they rode they saw neither Warrow, Man, nor Elf, though Tuck felt that they were safe, as if well watched by the shaggy Weiunwood itself.

Early after breaking camp, they rode into the site of the Weiunwood Alliance. Men, Elves, and Warrows were there, and all looked curiously at Tuck and Galen upon Jet as the black horse followed Baskin's pony to camp's center.

Arbagon Fenner, buccan, Captain of the Warrows, was at the main fire. Small he was, three inches short of Tuck's height, sapphire-eyed, brown-haired. When he learned of Lord Galen's identity, heralds were dispatched, and soon a rotund Man, Bockleman Brewster of Stonehill, arrived and knelt unto the Prince. Shortly thereafter came a tall Elf, Inarion by name, one of the Lian Guardians from Arden. These three—Arbagon, Bockleman, and Inarion—captained the Weiunwood Alliance.

"Well now, that's a bad piece of news that I never thought to hear," said Bockleman Brewster, wringing his hands in front as if wiping them upon the apron he customarily had worn as proprietor of the White Unicorn, the inn in Stonehill. "The Keep burnt and abandoned. What will Modru do next, I wonder?"

"Whatever it is, I'm thinkin' he'll steer clear of the Wei-unwood, after the drubbin' we've dealt him." Arbagon stood up to his full three-foot three-inch height and fetched another cup of tea for Tuck.

"Be not certain of that, Small One," said Inarion, softly, "for we are a thorn in Modru's side that he will want to pluck forth once he can bring his full weight to bear upon us. We met but a tithe of his strength, and then it was all we could do to fend them aside." The Elf turned to Tuck. "Those we met in battle must have been but a splinter of the Horde that brought down the Keep."

"Perhaps you fought that distant force we saw from afar marching to the south," said Tuck, harking back to the first 'Darkday the Horde had come to Challerain Keep.

"Well, splinter or Horde, they'll not root us out of these deep woods," responded Arbagon, "no matter how many they send against us."

"But, Arb," objected Bockleman, "they won't have to come in and get us. Modru'll just starve us out. You can't grow crops in Winternight, and that's a fact. All he has to do is wait till our food runs out, and then we're done for."

"Ye may be right, Bockleman," answered Arbagon, "and ye may be wrong. But, thinkin' like Modru, what's the good of conquerin' Mithgar if ye don't bag a bunch o' slaves to do yer biddin'? And how can ye keep a crop o' slaves if ye don't raise a crop o' food to nourish their bodies? I say this: Modru has some trick up his sleeve to banish the cold once he's brought Mithgar to its knees. Then we'll have crops aplenty to sustain us in our fight."

Inarion shook his head and smiled at Galen. "The debate goes on, and neither knows the mind of the Evil One. Bockleman is right, I think, in that Modru will take vile glee in starving many of us, warrior and innocent alike. As long as his power holds icy Winternight o'er the Land, crops will not grow, for there will be no spring nor summer, and no autumn harvest. Yet I think canny Arbagon has a strong point upon his side, too: Modru must have some plan for bending us all unto his will and tormenting us in the endless years of slavery thereafter; and this he cannot do if there is nought to keep us alive."

"Ar, you're right as rain about one thing, Lord Inarion: none of us knows the mind of Modru," said Bockleman. Then he turned to the Warrow Captain. "Arb, we don't need to inflict ourselves on our visitors." Now Bockleman turned his gaze upon Prince Galen. "Baskin tells us you and Master Tuck ride on a quest, m'Lord."

"Yes, Squire Brewster," answered Galen. "We follow a force of Ghola, perhaps one hundred strong. They butchered the folk of a waggon train upon the Post Road, on the north margins of the Battle Downs. The Ghola left the slaughter behind, their track beating east. This path in the snow we followed, but the storm of two 'Darkdays past has covered their wake, and we know not their destination. And my betrothed, Princess Laurelin, as well as my brother, Prince Igon, may be hostage of the ravers."

"Hostage?" Bockleman and Arbagon burst out together. Inarion shook his head in regret.

"Such a force did pass eastward," said the Elf, "on the first 'Darkday of battle with the *Spaunen*. We were just out on the plains, my company from Arden, horse-borne, ready to flee before the great force of *Rûpt*, to lure them into the trap we had set within the woods. From the west came the band of Ghûlka you name, to the east they went. Ah, but we did not think they may have had hostages among them, and so we did nought to stop them. Yet even as they went by, our plan was already in motion, and we were running south toward the forest, drawing the *Spaunen* behind." Inarion fell silent.

"Aye," continued Arbagon, "Warrow sentries elsewhere saw them, too. Our eyes followed them as they skirted east. When last we sighted them, five 'Darkdays past, they had swung a bit south as east they bore."

"What lies east and south?" asked Tuck. "What goal?"

Arbagon looked to Inarion, then said, "Many things: the Wilderness Hills, Drear Ford, Drearwood, Arden, all of Rhone, the Grimwall. *Pah!* I name but a small part of where they could be bound. Who knows their goal?"

Inarion pondered. "Drear Ford and Drearwood beyond, I would say. It was a fell place before the Purging. Perhaps they seek to make it a dread region as of old."

Arbagon pointed to a trail between two great pines. "Then that's the way to follow, for it runs through these woods to the Signal Mountains, and beyond them lies the open plain to Drear Ford on the River Caire."

"Hoy!" Bockleman interrupted, "didn't the north lookouts also tell of a lone rider on the same course, a 'Darkday or so behind?"

"Man or Ghol?" Lord Galen's voice was tense.

"That I cannot say," answered Arbagon. "Ghûl we thought, but Man it might have been."

Lord Galen turned to Tuck. "Sir Tuck, I must ride on, and soon. It would be better for you to stay with your kith in Weiunwood. Here you have food and shelter and companions to aid you, a safe haven. Whereas I ride after one hundred enemies, and—"

"Nay!" Tuck sprang to his feet, his denial vehement. "You cannot leave me behind, for I love Laurelin as a sister, and Igon as a brother. If they are captive, then you will need my bow." Tears welled in the young buccan's eyes. "Lord Galen, if you tell me that Jet cannot bear my weight, then I will take a pony and follow after. And if a pony I cannot have, then I will run on foot. But afoot or on pony, I will follow, even though I come days late. *Hlafor Galen, tuon nid legan mi hinda!*" (Lord Galen, do not leave me behind!) Tuck started to kneel to the Prince, but Galen raised him up ere he could do so.

"Nay, Tuck," answered Galen, "Jet can bear thy weight as well as mine. That is not why I would have thee stay. Tuck, I follow a hundred Ghola, to who knows what end? It will be dangerous beyond compare, and I would not have thee fare 'gainst such ill odds."

"I remind you, Lord Galen," Tuck held his bow on high, his voice grim, "I have slain more than eighty Rūcks with this. Know you another warrior who can say the same?"

"Eighty?" Arbagon's jewel-blue eyes went wide with wonder, and Bockleman put his hand to his mouth in astonishment.

"And I thought I had done well to slay eight," breathed Arbagon.

"And I nine," added Bockleman.

"Hai, Warrior!" cried Inarion, leaping to his feet and flashing his sword on high, then bowing to Tuck to the wonder of those nearby in the camp. Inarion then turned to the Prince. "Lord Galen, you forget one thing: you *must* take Sir Tuck, for you will need sharp Warrow eyes for vantage o'er the foe."

Before Inarion could say on, there was a great hubbub from the south, and into the camp an Elf on horseback thundered, hauling the steed short. "Alor Inarion!" cried the rider from the back of the rearing horse. "The *Spaunen* turn! South of here they attack the Weiunwood along the east flank, from the Signal Mountains!"

Horns sounded, and Man, Warrow, and Elf alike sprang to their feet. Pikes were hefted, and bows and swords sprang to hand. Ponies and horses were mounted, and quickly the force gathered to sprint southward to meet the enemy's thrust.

Inarion came leading a grey steed. "Prince Galen, come with us to fight the foe, or stay till we return. Then I and others will join you on your quest."

"Nay, Lord Inarion," answered Galen, "we cannot spare the time to stay, nor can you spend warriors upon a quest to follow Ghola who may hold no hostages at all. You will need all the strength at your command to repulse this foe that besets you now. And even more are at Challerain Keep, and they will march south to join their foul brethren, perhaps to fall upon this stronghold. Nay, I'll not wait, nor should you send warriors to aid. There shall come a time when we will stand shoulder to shoulder 'gainst Modru, but this is not the day." Galen drew his sword from scabbard and raised it on high. *"Poeir bē in thyne earms"* (Power be in thine arms!)

Inarion briefly clasped Galen's forearm and then leapt into the grey's saddle, and the horse reared, pawing at the air. "Should you need help, strike for Arden," called the Elf Lord, and he wheeled the horse to join a mounted troop of Elvenkind.

Arbagon Fenner came near upon a pony, and Baskin, too, rode nigh. "Good fortune!" cried the Warrow Captain, and Bockleman Brewster upon a horse hefted a pike in salute.

Lord Inarion turned one last time to Galen and Tuck, and the Elf scribed a rune in the air and called out, *"Fian nath dairia!"* (May your path be ever straight!)

And then there was another call of horns, and the frozen earth shuddered as hooves thundered forth. In moments the camp stood empty of all but Galen and Tuck and Jet, the black horse tossing his head in his desire to ride with the others to combat, as receding horn calls echoed among the ancient trees. Soon even these distant sounds faded into silence.

At last Galen turned to Tuck. "Come, Wee One, east south we go, with nought but slim hope that we will find the Gholen tracks again."

And so they mounted upon Jet, turning the black steed toward the far Drearwood, leaving behind the abandoned camp, silent now but for coals sputtering 'neath the quenching snow.

Hours they rode, passing among the hoary trees of eld Weiunwood, following the trail pointed out by Arbagon. At last the forest came to an end, and they rode into the chain of the ancient Signal Mountains, running south of Rian to Harth below, a range so timeworn by wind and water that it was but a set of lofty craggy hills. Atop the tallest of these tors were laid the beacon towers of old, now but tumbled ruins of stonework, remnants of a bygone era. From the towers had flared the balefires, signalling the march of War, back when Gyphon strove with Adon, four thousand years agone. Now, again, Mithgar was beset by an evil foe; indeed, Modru, the servant of Gyphon, once more harried a beleaguered world. But the beacon fires of old burned not: they did not signal the calamity now upon the Land. And even were the ancient fires kindled once again, the Dimmendark would muffle the call to muster, the black Shadowlight snuffing the warning cry ere it could be relayed on. Those thoughts Tuck scribed in his diary as he sat his watch by the small campblaze in the hills of the Signal Mountains.

Galen wakened Tuck to a bland breakfast of crue and water; now the Warrow knew what the Prince had meant when he had said that they would soon grow weary of the taste of the waybread. Still he ate it, thoughtfully chewing as he gazed through the Shadowlight at the flanks of the nearby tors. Jet, too, seemed tired of the unchanging grain of his diet, and Galen smiled at both of them.

"I know not which of you finds the taste of your food the more wearisome," said the Prince. "Yet it is all we'll see for many a day, and neither of you will have aught else to sustain you but this food and memories of sumptuous meals apast. So bite into your tasteless biscuit, Tuck, chew upon your constant grain, Jet, and dream of savory roasts and sweet clover."

Tuck growled, "Right now, I'd settle for the clover."

Lord Galen burst into broad laughter, and Tuck joined him. In a merry mood they broke camp and set forth upon their grim mission.

East they rode, veering south, coming through the Signal Mountains and out upon the snowy plains far north of the Wilderness Hills. All around them Shadowlight fell, and Tuck saw nought but bleak Winternight to the limits of his vision.

"Were Patrel here then we'd have a happy tune to help us on our way," said Tuck, and then his face darkened, a frown upon his features. "Oh, I do hope that he got away, and Danner, too, as well as the others from the Bosky. Not many of us made it to that last battle at the gate, you know—just eight—and I suspect, that even fewer escaped."

"I cannot say that I saw any Wee Folk mounted behind any in the force that broke free, nor did I note others scattering to the four winds," said Galen. "But I was engaged in battle and had no time to look about."

"Oh, Lor! I don't think I could take it if I were the only one to survive." Tuck's eyes brimmed with tears, and neither he nor Galen spoke for many miles.

At last, they again made camp, this time in a coppice upon a rolling hilltop, some fifty miles from Drear Ford.

Once more they continued eastward, the land falling gently toward the valley of the River Caire. Long they rode, down the sloping land, and when at last they made camp, they had not reached the river banks, stopping some fifteen miles shy. Tuck was impatient to be there, but they needs must save Jet's strength, for they knew not how long the chase would last. As yet they had seen no sign of the Ghûlen track, but Lord Galen said, "If they were bound for Drear Ford, then that is where we'll find their wake, for I deem the snowfall covered their tracks to the river, and perhaps some beyond. In any case, even had they passed nearby, leaving tracks for all to see, still we know not which way to turn to find them, north or south. And so, it is at the ford where lies our best hope to find their spoor and take up the pursuit once more."

Three hours after breaking camp, Tuck's eyes espied the trees of the border woodland along the banks of the River Caire.

"Look for a break in the tree line," said Galen, "for there will lie Drear Ford."

Long Tuck scanned as Jet cantered forth. "There! Far to the left," he said at last, pointing.

Down the fall of the land they rode, and now Galen's eyes could see the woodland as they bore north. Tuck continued to search the limits of his seeing for signs of life, yet nought moved upon the land but the black horse and his riders.

Suddenly, Galen reined Jet to a halt and sprang to the ground and knelt upon one knee. Tuck looked and leapt down, too, for there in the snow was the track of a lone steed, running in a line to the west and east.

"Pah! It is a track 'Darkdays old," said Galen, "so windworn that I cannot say whether it was made by horse or Hèlsteed, nor even whether it was ridden to the east or to the west, or if it was ridden at all. Were I to guess, I would deem it ran east, down toward the ford."

Tuck looked at the smooth shallow depressions and did not see how Galen chose east for the steed to be running.

Back upon Jet, they followed the track through the snow, coming at last to the ford. Here the approach to the river was low and gentle, but both upstream and down the banks fell steeply to the frozen river. Across the hard windswept surface went the black horse, hooves knelling upon the river ice, and Tuck could not help but remember the herald's steed at Spindle Ford, the slaying of the Vulg, and poor drowned Tarpy. And Tuck's heart thudded while Jet's hooves rang on the ice, a sense of relief washing over him when the horse reached the far shore.

Again Galen dismounted, gazing intently at the snow. The lone steed's track drifted leftward, east swinging slightly north. Long Galen looked, then grunted. "Here, Tuck, see the faint dimples in the snow? Widespread they are, and swing north, too. I think we see the track of the Ghola, and it was still snowing when they passed this way."

Again Jet paced forward, and every mile east the wake grew more pronounced. Now the lone steed's track they had followed could be pointed out no longer, for it was lost among the spoor of the others. Yet even though that trace was lost, Tuck's heart soared, for again they were on the track of the Ghûls.

"The trees of another forest lie ahead, Lord Galen," said Tuck, peering through the Dimmendark, "and the Ghûlen spoor runs into it."

"It is Drearwood, Tuck," answered Lord Galen. "We will camp there when we come to it."

Camp in Drearwood? Tuck felt a vague sense of foreboding at the thought of staying in this dread wood, for in days of old this dark-forested hill country was a region most dire. Hearthtales abounded of lone travellers or small bands who had passed into the dark woods never to be seen again. And stories came of large caravans and groups of armed warriors who had beaten off grim monsters half seen in the night, and many had lost their lives to the grisly creatures. This Land had been shunned by all except those who had no choice but to cross it, or by those adventurers who sought fame, most of whom did not live to grasp their glory. Yet seventy years past there had been the Great Purging of the 'Wood by the Lian Guardians, and no fell creatures had been seen in the area since. But now that the Shadowlight pressed darkly upon the Land, Tuck wondered if Modru had caused the dire monsters to return.

Now they came among the trees, and Galen stopped to camp. All that night during Tuck's watch, the slightest sound caused him to jerk up from his diary and peer this way and that for sign of danger. But in spite of his foreboding, when it came his turn to sleep, he immediately fell into a deep, dreamless slumber.

It seemed to Tuck that he had no more than put his head down ere the Prince was shaking him by the shoulder.

"Come, Tuck, we must away," said Galen, fetching the Warrow a biscuit and handing him one of the leathern water bottles.

Stumpily, his joints creaking, Tuck hunkered down by the fire and ate his crue while watching Jet at his grain. "Hmph!" grunted the buccan, "not enough warmth, drink, food, or rest. And we are surrounded on all sides by a wood reputed to be full of monsters." Then his mouth turned up in a wry smile. "Ah, but this is the life, eh Jet?"

The black horse rolled his eyes at the Warrow and tossed his head, and Tuck and Galen burst out in laughter. And while Tuck bundled the blankets and quenched the campfire with snow, Galen removed Jet's feed-bag and saddled the steed. The blanket rolls were tied behind the cantle, and then the warriors mounted up, and once more the long chase resumed.

Into Drearwood the track led, and among the dark trees went the three—Warrow, Man, and horse. Tuck now rode behind the Prince, for here the buccan's sight was no better than Galen's, and in these close quarters there could come an unexpected need to fight.

Now the Ghûlen wake turned straight to the east, and as they went it came sharp and clear; for here the wind did not reach, and no new snow had fallen since the Hèlsteeds had trod this way.

On they went, through the grim woods, and the Shadowlight fell dim among the clutching branches. Hours they rode, and at times walked, ever following the eastward trek. At last they came into the open, leaving the trees behind.

Ten miles or more they travelled across a great clearing where the trees grew not, and Tuck now rode on Jet's withers. Then ahead the Warrow again saw a line of trees as they came once more to the Drearwood.

"Lord Galen! Something lies in the snow ahead." Tuck strained to see what it was, but he could not discern its form. "Nought else is there near, only a crumpled bundle on the ground, just at the edge of the woods."

Jet was spurred forward, and his canter swiftly closed the distance. Now Galen's sight saw it, too. "A body, I think."

Now they came to it, and Tuck could see that the Prince was right. Galen reined Jet to a halt, and Tuck sprang down, his heart racing, and ran to the form lying face down in the snow. Tuck dropped to his knees and reached forth with trembling hands, reaching across and taking hold of a shoulder, fearful of what he would see, and he rolled the body toward him, the face coming into view.

"Waugh!" he cried, scrambling backwards, *for he was staring into the dead black eyes of one of the corpse-people.*

"He's dead, Tuck, the Ghol is dead, yet he is unmarked by weapon." Galen stood and looked at the Warrow. "How he was slain, I cannot say."

"Lor, but he gave me a fright," said Tuck. "My heart is still pounding at a gallop. I don't know what I expected, but it certainly was no Ghûl." Tuck looked down at the pallid flesh and the blood-red slash of a mouth, and he shuddered. "Why is he here? What was he doing?" asked the Warrow, but the Man shook his head and said nought.

Now Lord Galen examined the tracks leading east. Just beyond the tree line he found the ashened remains of a burnt-out fire, and all around the blanket of snow was beaten down.

"Here they made camp," said Galen, and he took up a charred limb from the dead fire and held it to his nose. *"Rach!"* he cursed, flinging the wood aside. "Tuck, we have not gained more than one 'Darkday upon them, if that, for this fire is four or even five 'Darkdays old." Galen strode away a few paces and stood long in thought. At last he turned to Tuck. "If we but had more steeds, then we could ride apace. Yet here we must make camp, too, for Jet alone cannot run forever. He is not made of iron as was Durgan's fabled steed. Even so, Jet has borne us nearly four hundred miles these past twelve 'Darkdays, from Challerain Keep to this dismal place, and he may need to go four hundred more ere we are done with this chase."

And so they made camp; but ere Lord Galen settled down for his rest, he took up his sword and strode past the trees and out to where the Ghûl lay. When he came back, his sword was black with gore. "I have made certain that he is dead beyond recall," said Galen, and Tuck shuddered but understood.

East they rode, soon emerging from the woods, and the track began swinging northward. "They are striking for the

mountains," said Galen, "but whether the Rigga, the Grimwall, or the Gronfangs, I cannot say, for north they come
together, north those three dread ranges join. There, too,
is the frozen Grūwen Pass, known to the Elves as Kregyn,
and it leads down into the Land of Gron, Modru's Realm
of old."

Onward they paced, and the miles glided by 'neath Jet's
steady hooves. The land began to rise around them, for
they were coming into the fringes of the foothills of the
unseen mountain range ahead.

Eleven leagues they rode—thirty-three miles—before
they again stopped to make camp, this time in a sparse
coppice set against the granite side of a craggy loom running north and south beyond seeing.

Lord Galen was asleep and Tuck sat scribing in his diary
when the Warrow looked up from his journal to see two
Elves standing across the fire from him, bright swords
gleaming in the flickering light.

"Wha—" cried the Warrow, springing to his feet, and the
sound of his call brought Lord Galen up, sword in hand.

"Kest!" (Stop!) barked one of the strangers, holding his
blade at guard, but Galen had seen that they were Elves
and lowered the tip of his sword to the snow. "Take warning," spoke the Elf, "you are under the arrows of the
Lian."

"But wait!" cried Tuck, stepping closer to the firelight.
"We are friends!"

"Waerling!" gasped the second Elf, astonished.

Their stances relaxed a bit, yet still they did not lower
their swords. "Your names and your mission."

Lord Galen spoke: "My companion is Sir Tuckerby Underbank, Waerling of the Boskydells, Land of the
Thornwall. He is a Thornwalker and a Rukh slayer and
serves in the Company of High King Aurion, and now rides
with me as my trusted companion. We are on the track of
a band of foul Ghola, slayers of innocents ten 'Darkdays
past."

"And your name?" One Elf had now lowered his sword.

"I am Galen, son of Aurion," said the Prince, softly.

"Hai!" The Elves now sheathed their blades, and one
turned and signalled to the crags above. "I am Duorn and
this is Tillaron, and we were sent to slay you if you served

the Evil One, or to fetch you if you be friends, for you are camped upon our very doorstep."

"But . . . how . . . I did not hear you approach," stammered Tuck, then his voice turned to self-disgust: "Hmph! This rock would make a better sentry than I."

"Blame not yourself, Wee One," said Tillaron, "for at times we can move as softly as even the Waerlinga." And his tilted eyes twinkled as Tuck's rueful laugh sounded quietly among the crags.

"If you are to fetch us, then who sent you, and where are we to go?" Lord Galen asked.

"Captain Elaria sent us," answered Duorn, "and as to where we will go, why, to Arden Vale."

"Arden?" blurted Tuck. "That's where Lord Inarion bade us seek help if aught was needed. Lord Gildor spoke of it, too. But I thought Arden lay to the south, down near the Crossland Road."

"Aye, it is in the south, Wee One," answered Tillaron, "yet Arden reaches far north, too, and is but a few steps from here—less than a league to shelter and warm food."

And so they broke camp, scattering the fire, quenching the embers with snow. Then toward the craggy bluff they went on foot, Galen leading Jet. Straight at the sheer stone they strode, and Tuck wondered at their course. Through close-set pines they pressed, and into a hidden cleft in the rock. Jet's hooves rang upon rock as into an arched granite cavern they were led, hands outstretched before them, for they could see nought in the dark. "Trail your hand along the wall on your left," Duorn's voice came, echoing softly, "and fear not for your toes or your crown, for the floor is smooth and the ceiling high. Five hundred paces we will go in the dark, for a light might be seen by unfriendly eyes."

It was nearly nine hundred paces by Tuck's count ere they came out of the tunnel, yet he had expected it to be so, for his stride could not match that of the tall Lian. When they emerged into the Shadowlight, Tuck could see a deep craggy gorge lying before him, a gorge lined by tall pines growing thickly in the soil that lay on either side of the river below, now frozen in the winter cold.

A steep narrow path fell down the gorge wall to come among the pines. And Tuck could see several long low buildings nestled in the trees below.

Along the path they went, and as they strode down they heard the horn of a sentry signalling the arrival of strangers into the gorge. Down the path and among the pines they went, to come at last to the central shelter. An Elf took Jet and led him away as Tuck and Galen were ushered inside. Vivid colors and warmth and the smell of food assaulted Tuck's senses as they entered the great hall, lambent with yellow lamps glowing in cressets and fires burning on the hearths. Bright Elves turned as the strangers entered, and silence reigned as the Elven leader stood to greet them, his consort at his side.

Tuck and Galen doffed their cloaks; their quilted goose-down outer clothing was shed, too. And there before the assembly came two bright warriors, Tuck's armor silveron and Galen's bright red. And Galen looked at the Warrow "Princeling" and smiled a broad grin, receiving a smile in return, for neither had seen the other in aught but bulky down, and now they both looked the part of warriors.

And as they strode to the dais, Elves murmured in amaze, for visits to Arden by Men were rare, but here come among them was a jewel-eyed Waerling.

"My Lord Talarin," said Duorn in a voice all could hear, "I bring you Prince Galen, son of Aurion King, and Sir Tuckerby Underbank, Waerling of the Boskydells."

Talarin bowed, a tall slim figure with golden hair and green eyes, dressed in soft grey. He turned to his consort. "Prince Galen, Sir Tuckerby, this is the fair Rael."

Tuck raised his eyes, and his heart was filled with wonder, for here was a beauty like unto that of the Lady Laurelin. Fair was Rael, and graceful, too, yet where Laurelin's hair was wheaten and her eyes pale grey, Rael's locks were golden and her eyes deep blue. Dressed in green, she was, with her hair bound in ribbons. And she smiled down at Tuck, and his sapphire eyes sparkled.

"You must eat and drink and spend some days with us," said the Elfess, "and rest from your journey."

"Ah, my Lady, much as we would like, we cannot," responded Galen. "Yes, tonight, perhaps, we will eat and drink and be warm, and rest under your guard—"

"And take a bath, too, please," interrupted Tuck, his head bobbing.

"Aye, and bathe, too, if we may," continued Galen, smiling. "But on the morrow we must leave at haste, for we are on the track of Ghola, and north we ride."

"On the track of Ghûlka?" exclaimed Talarin. "Prince Galen, ere you set at our board, there is someone you must see, for it may bear upon your mission. Follow me."

Talarin strode quickly down the length of the hall and out the doors and across the snow with Galen and Tuck in his wake. As they crossed toward another building, Tuck heard the sentry's horn announcing another arrival, and he looked up at the gorge wall to see a horse bearing an Elf clattering swiftly down the distant path.

But Tuck's attention was drawn to Lord Talarin's words: "He was found three 'Darkdays past," Talarin said as they walked, "lying in the snow, wounded and fevered, cut upon the brow, perhaps by poisoned blade. He would have frozen had my patrol not happened upon him. His horse had bore him toward the entrance to the gorge, and he was not far away. But he had fallen from the saddle and lay among the rocks—for how long, I cannot say—and he was nearly dead.

"But he, too, mumbled of Ghûlka, and now at times he rages, fevered. Even so, he might bear you news, though he has not awakened."

Into the building Talarin led them, and down a central hall of doorways. Tuck's heart was racing, and a great sense of foreboding filled his being. Ahead, a door opened, and an Elven healer stepped into the corridor. "Alor, Talarin," the Elf greeted the Lian leader.

"How fares the youth?" asked Talarin.

"His face is flush with heat, yet I deem the fever has begun to break, for he is at times no longer racked with chills, and he will waken soon." The Elf's eyes slid over Tuck and Galen, wonder in his gaze, but he spoke on to Talarin: "Yet he has been near death, and trembles with weakness. His strength will not return for a fortnight or two, and then only if the herbs the Dara Rael used can throw off the poison of the *Rûpt* blade."

"I would that Lord Galen sees him, for it may bear upon the Prince's quest," said Lord Talarin, and the healer stepped aside, opening the door.

With Tuck's pulse thudding in his ears, into the candlelit

room they quietly stepped. There in a bed lay a young
Man, his face to the wall, and he was weeping.

Galen spoke softly to him, anguish in his voice: "Igon."

And as Tuck's hopes crashed down around his heart,
Prince Igon turned his face to that of his brother. "Galen,
oh, Galen," he wept, "they've got Laurelin."

Tuck sat numbly on a bench against the wall as Lord
Galen held Igon to him, and tears streamed down the faces
of all three. Yet the look upon Galen's visage was grim to
behold. The candles cast a soft yellow glow over the room,
and Lord Talarin stood by the door, his eyes glittering in
the light. But then Galen gently lowered Igon unto the bed
and called for the healer, for the youth's fever had flared
again, and the young Prince had swooned.

As the healer stepped to the bedside, there came the
muffled steps of someone striding hard down the hall, and
Talarin stepped into the corridor. Tuck heard the faint
sound of hushed voices, muted by the door, and then into
the room came Talarin, and another Elf was with him,
dressed in stained riding garb. Tuck looked up. *"Lord
Gildor!"*

Galen turned his bleak face to Lord Gildor's, and the
Elf gripped something tight in his fist.

"I come bearing woeful news, Galen King." Lord Gildor
held out his hand, closed upon a token, and Galen reached
forth to take what was offered—a scarlet eye-patch. "Aurion Redeye is dead."

Tuck sat stunned. He could not seem to get enough air
to breathe, and he no longer could see through his tears.

Galen spoke at last: "My sire is slain, and my betrothed
is taken captive, and my brother lies wounded by poisoned
blade. And Modru's dark tide drowns the Land. These are
evil days for Mithgar, and evil choices am I given."

"Galen King," said Lord Gildor next, "for all of Mithgar,
you must ride south to lead the Host against vile Modru's
Horde."

"North! Ride north!" Igon cried, starting up from a fevered dream, his wild eyes unseeing. "Save the Lady
Laurelin!"

BOOK TWO

Shadows of Doom

"The days have now fled, and the 'Darkdays are come upon us."
—Gildor Goldbranch
December 22, 4E2018

CHAPTER 1

Captive!

Nearly two days ere the Dimmendark came unto Challerain Keep, the Lady Laurelin was borne away south in the last caravan. Slowly, the wagon trundled down from the mount, and the Princess wept silently while her chaperon, Saril, eldest handmatron, chattered about inconsequential trivialities and complained about the discomfort of the wain. What the Princess needed at this moment was to be held and soothed and to have her hair stroked, although even this would not heal a heart in despair, for only time could serve that end. Yet Saril appeared unaware of the weeping damosel's needs, seeming not to sense the quiet anguish of the maiden as she looked with tear-blind eyes out through the open flap and back at the passing hill country—though the handmatron did give over a linen kerchief to the Princess when Laurelin could not find her own.

Onward the wain groaned, last in the line of a hundred waggons, along the south-bearing Post Road. Down through the foothills they wended, and out upon the snowy plains. At last Laurelin's weeping subsided, yet now she knelt upon blankets at the tailboard and looked ever backward toward the Keep and did not speak.

Time passed, and slow miles rolled by to the flap of the canvas cover, the creak and jingle of singletrees and harness, the plod of horse hooves, an occasional command of the driver, and above all the grind of axle and iron-rimmed wheels turning upon the frozen snow.

In midafternoon the train pulled up a long hill, snowy slopes to either side. Laurelin's gaze held still to the north, toward the distant fortress. Finally, her wain topped the crest and started down the far side, and Challerain Keep could be seen no more.

"Oh, Saril, I'm afraid I've made a sodden mess of your

kerchief," said Laurelin, turning to her companion and holding forth the crumpled linen for the other to see.

"La, my Lady, worry not," said Saril, reaching forth and taking the cloth. "Oh, my! It *is* wet, isn't it? Why, there must be enough tears in here to last several years." She held it out and away, a thumb and forefinger grasping one corner. "We'd best spread this out; else the cold will freeze it into a lump hard as a rock."

"Well, then, perhaps we just should let it freeze that way," replied Laurelin, attempting a smile. "Then it can be used as a missile in some warrior's sling and flung at Modru."

At the mention of the Enemy in Gron, Saril made a swift gesture with her hand, as if scribing a rune in the air to ward off the presence of the Evil One. "My Lady, I think it best not to mention that name, for I hear that even the speaking of it draws his vileness down upon the speaker as surely as iron is drawn to lodestone."

"Oh, Saril," chided Laurelin, "now 'tis my turn to say 'La!' for what could he want with Women and children, or the oldsters and the lame?"

"I don't know, my Lady," answered Saril, her matronly features apprehensive, glancing over her shoulder as if someone may have been creeping up from behind, "yet mine own eyes have seen the lodestone reach out with an invisible hand to snatch the iron, and so I know that is true; thuswise there's no reason to believe that the other isn't just as true, too."

"Oh, Saril," responded Laurelin, "just because the one is so, it doesn't mean that the other follows."

"Maybe not, my Lady," answered Saril after a bit, "but just the same, I would not tempt him."

They spoke no more of it, but Saril's words seemed to hang like a silent echo in the thoughts of Laurelin the rest of the day.

Just at sunset, camp was made some twenty-two miles south of Mont Challerain. Although the train had paused several times along the way to tend the horses and stretch the legs and see to other needs, still it was not the same as being out of the waggons and encamped for the night. And now that the train had stopped for the eventide, Laurelin walked the full length of the caravan and back, some two miles in all, speaking to oldsters and young alike, buoying up spirits, and she passed Prince Igon doing the same.

When at last the Princess returned to the fire by her waggon, Saril had prepared a stew over the small blaze. Wounded Haddon sat on a log near the warmth, eating, his arm in a sling but his appetite ravenous, though his features were pale and drawn.

"My Lady," he said, startled by the Princess's sudden appearance from the darkness, struggling to gain his feet, but Laurelin bade him to sit.

"And now, Warrior Haddon," said the Princess, taking up a bowl of stew and a cup of tea and seating herself beside the soldier, "speak to me of my Lord Galen, for I would hear of him."

And long into the night, Haddon told of the forays, skirmishes, and scouting missions that Galen's One Hundred carried forth in the bitter Winternight to the north. And as the warrior spoke, Lord Igon came to the fire to take a meal, and so, too, did Captain Jarriel, ever present at the side of the Prince. Igon's eye sparkled in the firelight as he heard tell of the probing in the Dimmendark to find Modru's Horde:

"Along the Argent Hills we rode, and to the Rigga Mountains," said Haddon, his eyes lost in memory, "but nought did we find: Modru's myrk hid all. North we turned, toward the Boreal Sea, and at last our search bore fruit— though bitter it was—for a vast Horde we found, and it moved south along that dire range, coming down the western margins of the Rigga. From dark clefts and deep holts within those grim crags they came swarming, and their ranks swelled as they marched.

"Vulgs were with them, running their flanks, and we could not raid, for those dark beasts would sense us from afar and give the enemy warning ere we could close with the Spawn. King Aurion named them aright: Modru's curs." Haddon paused as Saril, whose eyes were wide from listening to the tale, refilled the warrior's teacup.

"Messengers were sent to Challerain," continued Haddon, "to tell the King of the Horde."

"None arrived," said Igon grimly, shaking his head.

"Then they were cut down ere they could do so, my

Prince," responded Haddon, and he held forth his sling-bound arm: "As the Vulgs slew Boeder, and nearly me, they must have hauled down those sent to carry word to the Keep."

"Prince Igon tells me you spoke of Ghola," said Captain Jarriel.

"Aye," answered the warrior, eyes deep in craggy face lost in reflection. "Ghola there are, and upon Hèlsteed. Many were the times they pursued us, but Lord Galen always gave them the slip, e'en in the snow. Wily is the Prince, clever as a fox. We would wait till 'twas right to strike, when there were no Vulgs about, and when some o' the Spawn would be separated from the Horde. Oh, then we'd lash into those pockets like bolts from Adon's Hammer. Back we'd jump, with Hèlsteeds after, but Lord Galen's black steed would fly to the north and us right behind. Onto the trampled snow we'd ride, our tracks mingling with and lost within the wide wake of the very Horde we'd struck. Along this beaten swath we'd run a ways, soon to slip aside to hide among crags or bracken or hills, and watch the Ghola race by while we were concealed by the very Enemy's own dark myrk."

"Say you that their sight is no better than ours?" Prince Igon seemed surprised. "I had thought that all night-spawn could see well in the dark."

"I don't know how well they can see in ordinary dark, but Lord Galen says that the Shadowlight baffles their eyes as well as ours." Haddon drank the last of his tea. "This I do know: Mine own sight never reached beyond two miles in the Dimmendark, and at that distance I could see but vaguely: the movement of the Horde, many Ghola racing upon Hèlsteeds, and at times a mountain flank: only these could I see from afar. Even things nearby in that shadowy glow held little detail for me; color is lost beyond a few paces." Prince Igon nodded his understanding, for he, too, had spent time in the Winternight.

"I hear that Elven eyes see beyond those of all mortals," said Laurelin. "Perhaps their sight pierces even the shadow of the Dimmendark."

"Mayhap, my Lady," responded Haddon, "yet strange eyes indeed would it take to see afar in that myrk."

Strange eyes. An unbidden image sprang into Laurelin's

thoughts, for suddenly she pictured Tuck's wide sapphirine gaze looking into her own, and she wondered about the jewel-eyes of Warrows.

The dawn found the horses being harnessed to the waggons by some, while others ate the last of their breakfasts. Laurelin aided the healer in putting salve and a fresh bandage on Haddon's slashed arm, and the healer pronounced him fit enough to lay his sling aside, "if you treat it gingerly. We cauterized it that night, you know, with a red-hot blade to sear out the poison, or at least to hold off its effects till the Sun rose. It's the burn we're ministering to now, and the healing of the gash, for daylight and Adon's Ban have destroyed the Vulg venom."

Soon all was in readiness, and at the calls of the escort's horns the train got under way once more, continuing on its southerly course along the Post Road, away from Challerain Keep and toward the Battle Downs and Stonehill and beyond.

All day the waggons jostled and jounced over the icy way, and Laurelin found the brief hourly stops a welcome relief from the juddering, swaying wain.

She saw little of Igon, for he along with Captain Jarriel rode at the fore of the train to be first to receive word from the far-ranging horse-borne forward scouts of the caravan escort.

But Saril kept the Princess company, and they whiled away the afternoon hours in conversation, though in the morning they had played *zhon,* a tarot of omens gamed often at court. Yet instead, of the pleasant time at cards she had expected, the more they played, the more uneasy Laurelin became; and even though the suit of Suns was filled with nought but bright portents, still her eyes sought only the four of Swords and the Dark Queen, her heart lurching at the turn of each card. At last she bade Saril to lay aside the deck, for Laurelin had lost the joy of the game.

In midafternoon of the next day, as was her wont, Laurelin sat at the rear of the wain peering out through the canvas flap and back at the passing countryside, and rolling hills began to rise up from the prairie as the caravan approached the northernmost margins of the Battle Downs. Many pleasant miles had passed by when suddenly her eye caught the movement of a running horse, and she heard the sound of a horn: it was the rear scout, riding hard to overtake the train. Soon he thundered past, urgent horn ablare, snow flinging from the steed's pounding hooves as he flew southwest toward the lead waggons, and Laurelin's heart thudded in her breast and she wondered at his haste.

Time passed, and again the Princess heard the tattoo of hooves; horses beat past: Igon, Captain Jarriel, and the scout raced north, their cloaks streaming behind as they flew back along the caravan's track. They veered from the Post Road and galloped to the top of a hillock where they reined to a stop. Long they sat without moving, looking to the north, back in the direction of Challerain Keep, now far beyond the horizon. Laurelin gazed at their dark silhouettes shadowed against the afternoon sky, and once more her heart raced, and she felt a deep foreboding. And there was something about the way the trio sat, and then she realized: *How like the ancient wood carvings of the Three Harbingers of Gelvin's Doom they look;* and a grim pall fell upon her breast, for that was a tale most dire.

At last Igon and Jarriel turned and plunged back down the snowy slopes, leaving the rear scout behind upon the hill. The horses cantered toward the slow-moving train, overtaking it swiftly. Jarriel rode on to the fore as Igon drew Rust up to the tailgate of Laurelin's wain. She threw wide the flap and raised her voice above the rumble of axles and wheels: "What is it? What see you to the north?"

"It is the Black Wall, my Lady," said Igon grimly. "It moves south steadily. I deem Challerain Keep to have been engulfed by the Dimmendark, nigh yesternoon, I ween; most assuredly it now lies deep within the grasp of bitter Winternight. Yet the Wall has come on apace, and if nought changes its course, it will o'ertake this train on the morrow.

"Tonight, you and I must go among the folk and prepare them for this black curse, for it will scourge their spirits and sap the fire in their hearts." Igon reined Rust back and to the side, calling, "I must away to set the escort plans." And the great roan plunged forward at Igon's urging.

Laurelin's heart was filled with dread by this news, and

she despaired for those left behind at the Keep: Aurion, Vidron, Gildor, the Warrows, especially Tuck, all of the warriors, and, somewhere, Galen. And the Princess wondered who would comfort her own heart, her own spirit, when the darkness came. And she turned to look at Saril and saw that the matron wept and shook with dread, for she had heard all that Igon said. Laurelin drew Saril unto her and soothed her as a lost child. And Laurelin knew that none would comfort a Princess, for it is common knowledge that royalty feels not the fears nor anguishes of the ordinary folk.

That night, Laurelin's uneasy slumber was filled with desperate dreams of being trapped.

The next day at dawn the Black Wall was plain for all to see, jutting upward on the horizon, seeming to grow taller as it drew closer. Children cried and clung to their mothers, and faces bore stricken looks as the 'Dark stalked southward.

Swiftly camp was broken, and the caravan once more took up the long trek, moving slowly upon the Post Road as it swung westerly along the Battle Downs. And Saril wept because now the road did not run south and away from the approaching Wall. And sweeping toward them out of the north like a great dark wave came the murk of the Evil One, flowing nearer with every passing moment.

Slowly the Sun rose into the sky, climbing toward the zenith, but its golden rays did not stay the advance of the darkness as the morning passed and noon drew nigh; yet so, too, did the evil dark tide, now rearing up into the sky perhaps a mile or more: a great, looming, vile Black Wall. Before it, a boiling cloud of snow swirled, and there came the rumble of wind churning along the base of the dark rampart.

Horses began to shy and skit, and from the wains there rose the cries of children, the sobbing of Women, and the moans of old Men.

Grimly, Laurelin watched the blackness come, her features pale and her lips clamped in a tight line; but her gaze was steady and she flinched not as the Wall drove down upon her. Behind her in the waggon, Saril knelt over double with her face buried in her hands, moaning and rocking in distressed fear, a huddled ball of dread as the 'Dark plowed onward.

Now the train was engulfed in a blinding, driven blizzard, and firm hands were needed to rein rearing horses to as the shrieking white howled about them.

The Sun's light began to fail, swiftly growing dimmer as the 'Dark swept on, fading into black Shadowlight, spectral and glowing.

Then the wave was past, and the wind yowl slowly fell into muteness; the billowing snow began drifting back unto the ground. The caravan now stood in the full Dimmendark, and the grasp of bitter Winternight reached forth to clutch this land. A dread silence fell across the plains and into the Battle Downs, broken only by the solitary wails of those frightened beyond the limits of their courage.

Twenty miles the waggon train went that day, ten in the sunlight, ten in the 'Dark. Camp was made and meals prepared, but the people were without stomach and little food was taken. Laurelin forced herself to eat a full meal, but Saril only picked at her food, her eyes red from weeping. On the other hand, Haddon's appetite seemed unaffected by the Shadowlight, but then he had spent many 'Darkdays within its glow as a member of Galen's One Hundred, and he ate readily; but his look was grim and wary, for he knew that where fell the Dimmendark, so, too, went creatures of evil.

Igon and Jarriel came to the fire to take their own meal.

Captain Jarriel looked thoughtful as he ate, and soon he broached his concern, his speech that of court parlance: "My Lady, on the morrow I propose to the wain to train center whither thou will be safer."

"How so, Captain?" Laurelin asked.

"Here at train's end thy wain is greatly exposed," answered Jarriel, setting aside his cup, "manifestly open to attack by hostile foe. I would move thee to where it is more difficult to single thee out, to a place more easily defended."

"But then, Captain," responded the Princess, "someone else would be last and exposed. I cannot ask another to take my place."

"Oh, but you must," moaned Saril, her eyes wide with

fear, her hands wringing. "Please, let us move to train center. We'll be safe there."

Laurelin looked with pity upon her frightened handmatron. "Saril, no place is safe from the Evil One: not train's end, center, nor fore. I chose this position to be closer to my beloved Lord Galen, and that reason still holds true."

For a moment no one spoke and the only sounds were the crackle of the fire and the whimpering of Saril. Then rough-hewn Haddon spoke: "My Princess, the Lady Saril is right, but for the wrong reasons, and so, too, is Captain Jarriel. You must move to train center, e'en though it may be no safer from the Enemy in Gron than any other space in this train, nor more easily protected either. Nay, I stand with you on those two reasons, yet still I think that you must move, for something else compels:

"Did you watch the people tonight as you bestrode the length of the caravan? I did, and this is what I saw: Grim were their looks and fell were their spirits ere you went among them. Yet many of the most frightened mustered a wan smile when you came through the Shadowlight. Oh, they be still frightened, yet not as much as before. And that is why you must ride at train center. For you are the gentle heart and bright spirit of the people, and at their heart you should go, as near to as many as you may be; and though you cannot ride in each one's waggon, amid all waggons you can ride. Then all may know that you are among them, and not remote and distant at train's end."

Now Haddon's voice took on the courtly manner: "I will take thy present place at the last of the caravan, but thou must take thy true place amid thine own."

Haddon fell silent, his rush of words at an end. He was a warrior and not of the court, yet no courtier could have spoken more eloquently.

Laurelin looked into the flames of the fire, and tears clung to her lashes, and none said aught. At last she turned to Captain Jarriel and gave a curt nod, for she could not trust her voice, and Jarriel sighed in relief and relaxed, while Saril began rushing about, collecting and stowing things as if the move were to occur instantaneously.

Igon turned to Haddon: "Ai-oi, Warrior Haddon, I must have thee by my side when next we need make treaty with another nation, for thy rough exterior doth conceal a golden tongue."

Laurelin's silver laugh rang out above the campfire, and Igon, Haddon, and Jarriel joined in her mirth, as Saril stood gaping at the merriment, wondering what anyone could possibly find humorous in this dreadful 'Dark.

But then a warrior of the escort came riding to the fire, leaning down to speak with Captain Jarriel: "Sir, Vulgs lope by in the distant shadow, running south as if to o'ertake the moving edge of the Black Wall. Yet it is thought that some turned back, racing along the track whence they came. If so, what it portends, I cannot say."

Jarriel sprang up and mounted his nearby steed, and Igon vaulted astride Rust, and they rode away from the mealfire and toward the fore of the train, and with them went the messenger.

Laurelin and Haddon sat for long moments more, and little was said by either, the only sound being that of Saril, now sitting in the waggon and muttering in fear as she peered out through the flap of the wain and into the shadowed land nearby.

Laurelin's sleep was broken by the sounds of the camp stirring to wakefulness.

"Come, Saril," said the Princess, shaking her handmatron by the shoulder, " 'tis time to break our fast, for we shall soon be under way."

Saril groaned, not fully awake: "Is it dawn, my Lady?"

"Nay, Saril," answered Laurelin, "there'll be no dawn this 'Darkday, nor perhaps for many to come."

Saril blenched, and would have hidden 'neath her blanket but Laurelin would not allow it and bade her instead to dress, inwardly despairing of Saril ever gaining a measure of courage to face the Dimmendark.

Soon they descended from the wain to make tea over the rekindled campblaze, tea to take with their otherwise cold morning meal. Bergil, their driver, harnessed the horses and hitched them to the waggon. Then he came to the fire.

"Ar, my Lady," said Bergil, shuffling his feet in the snow as if to wipe them clean ere stepping through some imaginary door, acutely aware that he was speaking to the Princess instead of to Saril as usual. "When we're done wi' the eatin', I'm to drive us to the middle o' the train. Them was Cap'n Jarriel's direct orders, miss: 'to the middle o' the train,' he said, he did."

At Laurelin's nod, relief washed over Bergil's weathered features, for it was not every day that coachmen dealt face to face with royalty—footmen, now, well that was a different matter altogether, for they often directly helps Lords and Ladies alike, but then footmen are trained to do so, e'en though they answers to the driver.

Bergil took his tea and a portion of the bread and cold venison and hunkered down opposite the fire to eat with the Ladies instead of joining some of his fellow drivers at another fire as he normally did, for they soon would be moving to train center and Bergil had not the time. Haddon, too, came from the next waggon to join them. They sat and ate with little converse, looking out into the spectral 'scape of the surrounding Dimmendark.

No sooner, it seemed, had they finished their meal than through the Shadowlight came riding Igon and Jarriel.

"My Lady Laurelin," asked Igon, "be thou ready to move forward?"

"Yes, Lord Igon." Laurelin stood and smiled down at Haddon, gesturing him to remain seated. "Another takes place at train's end."

Igon turned to Jarriel. "Let it be so. Sound the ready."

Jarriel raised a horn to his lips and blew a rising call that echoed down the line of wains and out into the surrounding countryside. *Aroo!* (Prepare!) And from the land nearby came answering cries: *Ahn!* (Ready!) *Ahn! Ahn!* From fore, aft, and north came the answers.

Jarriel waited, yet no call came from the south, from the Battle Downs, dark hills to the leftward of the train. Again he sounded the call, and again all answered but the south guard.

"Sire, something is amiss," said Jarriel to Igon, a grim look upon his face. "The south hillguard answers not. Perhaps . . ."

"Hsst!" shushed Igon, holding up his hand, and in the quiet that followed they could hear the pounding of running hooves—many hooves—hammering upon the hard frozen ground to the south.

"Sound assembly!" Igon shouted, flashing bright sword from scabbard.

Jarriel raised horn to lips: *Ahn! Hahn!* the imperative call split the air as the drum of hooves grew louder. *Ahn! Hahn! Ahn! Hahn!*

And then, bursting through the spectral shadows clutching the sinister hills to the south, erupted the enemy: Ghola upon thundering Hèlsteeds, striking down upon the standing train with shattering violence: cruel barbed spears driven by running Death, slashing tulwars cleaving into innocent flesh, slaughter racing upon cloven hooves, shocking into and through and over Women and children, oldsters and the lame, the ill and wounded, the sundering blades and impaling shafts riving a great bloody swath through the unprepared caravan. Some stood stunned and were cut down like cattle at butcher. Yet others turned to flee and were slain while running: thus did Saril die, clambering to hide in the waggon.

A running Hèlsteed struck Laurelin a glancing blow, and she was whelmed back against the side of the wain, to pitch forward, smashing face down to the ground, her cheek pressed against the snow, her arms scrabbling futilely as she desperately tried to rise while at the same time trying to breathe, but she was unable to, for all the wind had been slammed from her lungs.

Captain Jarriel crashed dead unto the ground beside her, his chest pierced through by a broken-shafted spear. Laurelin tried to reach out to him but could not, for she had no control of her limbs and she could not breathe, and dark motes swirled before her eyes and her sight dimmed.

But at last she drew in a great ragged sob of air, and her lungs began pumping in harsh gasps while tears ran down her face. She heard herself moaning but could not stop.

Crying in anguish, she rose to her hands and knees and looked up to see Haddon lashing with a burning brand at a Ghol on Hèlsteed. And the vile creature's dead black eyes stared from the corpse-white flesh as he slashed the tulwar through Haddon's throat, and the warrior fell slain beside the body of dead Bergil.

Horses in harness plunged wildly and screamed in terror, for the stench of Hèlsteeds was among them. Some ran amok, bolting toward the plains and hills, only to have the wains overturn and throw the horses' legs from under them, or drag them to a halt.

Amid the milling confusion, a knot of warriors fought: Prince Igon upon Rust had rallied a band unto him. The young Lord's sword hacked and chopped ceaselessly, and others laid about with their steel glaives.

Laurelin saw a Hèlsteed stumble, dropping to the snow, throat gushing black. Yet the pallid Ghol rider rolled free and sprang up to impale a young warrior upon his barbed spear.

Then Igon saw the Princess on hands and knees where she'd been hammered to the ground. "Laurelin!" he cried, and spurred Rust toward her, driving into the foe. But a Ghol on Hèlsteed rode to bar his way, and rage distorted Igon's features beyond recognition. *Shang! Chang!* Sword and tulwar clashed together amid a shower of sparks. *Chank!* The Ghol's blade was shivered into shards; and as the Ghol threw up his arm to ward the blow—*Shunk!*—Igon's steel drove completely through the Ghol's wrist and pallid neck: riven hand and severed head flew wide, while chalky corpse-body toppled into the snow.

Once more Igon drove Rust toward Laurelin, crying out her name, but again Ghola blocked the way, this time attacking in concert. Three, then four, fell upon the youth, and he was hard-pressed; yet Igon's blade hewed into the enemy, driven by fury and desperate strength. Another Ghol fell dead, his skull cloven in twain, and Igon's voice cried out, "For the Lady! For the Lady Laurelin!"

A Ghol on Hèlsteed crashed into Rust, and the great red horse was staggered, yet he kept his War-trained footing and wheeled about for Igon to meet the Gholen foe. Igon's blade swung in a wide arc, driven so hard it hummed; and the sharp steel clove through Gholen armor and sinews, and chopped deep into bone, where it lodged. Furiously, Igon wrenched at the blade, but just as he hauled it free, an enemy tulwar smashed down and sundered his helm, and blood splashed crimson over the youth's face as he crashed to the ground to move no more.

Laurelin saw Igon fall and staggered to her feet at last. "Igon! Igon!" The words were rent from her throat in horror, but the Prince moved not, his blood welling to run in scarlet rivulets and fall adrip to the snow. Screaming in rage she snatched up dead Jarriel's dagger and hurled herself into the mêlée, poniard clutched in her fist, and with a hoarse cry of hatred she plunged the blade to the hilt into the back of the Ghol on foot. Unaffected by the steel lodged deep in his ribcage, the Ghol turned from the battle and smashed her aside with the sweeping haft of his spear.

Laurelin was dashed to the ground, her arm shattered by the blow, the Princess so battered she could no longer stand. And she sat and wept as the Gholen ravers smote the survivors.

Now all the soldiers were slain, and the foe turned to easier game, their swords riving, and the snow ran red with blood. Ghols stalked among the waggons, their dead black eyes looking for the innocent and defenseless, and where they strode, none was spared: no Woman, no child, no oldster, none. Even the struggling horses were slain, trapped in their traces, and some waggons were set afire.

And Laurelin sat in the snow and wept at the horror and waited for them to come and cut her throat.

Another waited also, but this one in anger and defiance: it was Rust! The great roan stood above Igon's fallen form, teeth bared and hooves lashing out at passing Ghola, the War-horse defending his master as he had been trained.

Laurelin saw the horse and exulted, for the Ghola gave it wide berth. Yet one hefted a spear, preparing to hurl it at the steed. *"Jagga, Rust! Jagga!"* (Hide, Rust! Hide!) Laurelin screamed, the cry torn from the depths of her anguish. The roan whirled and looked at the Princess. *"Jagga!"* came the command again.

Rust sprang forward just as the spear was flung, and the haft glanced off the roan's withers as he thundered forth for the nearby hills hurtling past Laurelin as he fled for the Battle Downs, obeying the War command to hide.

Ghola on Hèlsteeds spurred after him, but the great red horse ran swiftly before them, and the gap widened. "Ya, Rust! Run!" cried Laurelin, "Run!" The words were hurled after the fleeing steed, and Rust ran as if his feet were winged. And Laurelin watched him fly into the Dimmendark, to disappear into the Shadowlight grasping the hills. "Run," she whispered after him, but he was gone.

A corpse-white Ghol bearing a barbed spear stalked up to Laurelin, his red gash of a mouth writhing in anger, his dead black eyes staring soullessly down. Laurelin glared up at him, unable to stand, cradling her broken arm with the other. Her eyes blazed with hatred, and she jerked her head in the direction Rust had flown. "That's one of us you won't get, *Spaunen!*" she spat defiantly, her pale eyes boring triumphantly into his dead black ones.

The Ghol raised his spear, both hands on the shaft, preparing to plunge it through her breast. Laurelin's teeth ground in fury, her eyes flared up at him with unflinching wrath. Back drew the spear for the final thrust.

"Slath!" lashed out a command from behind her, the hissing voice hideous, and Laurelin felt as if vipers slithered over her spine. The Ghol lowered the shaft, and the Princess turned her head to see a Man upon Hèlsteed. A Naudron he was, one of the folk that roam the northern barrens hunting seal and whale and the antlered beasts of the tundra. Yet when Laurelin looked beyond his yellow-copper skin and into his dark eyes, utter Evil stared malignantly back at her.

"Where is the other, the youth?" The hiss of puff adders filled the air.

"Ghun." The Ghol's voice was dull, flat.

"I said to spare the two of them!" the sibilant voice cried. "But you give me only the Princess." The evil eyes turned upon Laurelin, and she felt as if her skin were crawling, and she wanted to run and hide from this being. Yet she stared back at him and blenched not. "Where is puling Igon?" hissed the serpent voice.

Laurelin's spirit almost broke then, for Igon lay in the snow not twenty feet away. Yet she made no sign.

"Nabba thek!" spat the order, and Ghola dismounted and began moving slowly among the slaughtered, catching the barbs of their spears in the clothing and flesh of the slain, turning them face up, dead eyes staring, mouths agape.

Laurelin looked on in horror. "Leave them alone, *Spaunen!*" she cried. "Leave them alone!" And then her voice lost its strength, sinking to a whisper: "Leave them alone." Still the cruel barbs jabbed and hauled as the faces of the slain were inspected. Laurelin turned to the Naudron and cried, "He's dead! Igon is dead!" Uncontrollable sobbing racked her frame as the horror of the brutal slaughter overwhelmed her at last.

"Dead?" The Naudron's voice was filled with rage. "I commanded that he be spared! All in this party will suffer for disobeying." Evil glared out at the Ghola, yet still they stalked among the dead.

"Slath!" the puff adder voice commanded. *"Garja ush!"* The Ghola turned from their grisly task, and two came and dragged Laurelin to her feet, the broken bones grinding in her right forearm. Blackness swirled, and the Princess felt her mind falling down a dark tunnel.

Laurelin became aware that icy hands clutched her, and a burning liquid was forced down her throat. Coughing and sputtering, she tried to fend away the leather flask, and agonizing pain jagged through her right arm, jerking her full awake. Ghola held her. Her right arm from wrist to shoulder was swathed by heavy bindings over a rude splint bent at the elbow. Again the liquid was forced upon her, its fire burning inside her chest and stomach and running into her limbs. She struck away the flask and turned her face aside. Yet once more the Ghola forced the burning drink upon her, roughly grasping her head and wrenching her face upright, pouring until she gagged, spraying the vile liquid wide.

"Ush!" Again Laurelin was hauled to her feet, and she stood weakly, shuddering, swaying. *"Rul durg!"* And the chill hands of the corpse-people rent the clothing from Laurelin till she stood naked before the Naudron. He sat upon the Hèlsteed and his evil eyes gloated. Laurelin felt a great horror and loathing, and the cold was numbing, yet she stood defiantly. Quilted Rukken clothing was flung at her feet, and fleece-lined boots. Ghola forced her to don the garb: filthy it was, and mite-infested, and overlarge upon her, but it was warm. During the dressing the only sound she made was a gasp through clenched teeth as the right sleeve of the jacket was slit from wrist to shoulder and forced onto her, then roughly wrapped over and bound to the splinted arm.

The Naudron's voice spat and hissed commands in the foul Slûk tongue too rapidly for Laurelin to make out individual words from the guttural, slobbering drool-speech.

Then the evil eyes turned upon her as her arm was jerked into a sling. A Hèlsteed was brought forth and Laurelin was hauled astride the hideous beast, and its foul odor was nearly enough to make her retch.

"Now you will be brought to my strongholt," hissed the voice, "where I have a purpose for you to serve."

"Never," said Laurelin, her voice gritting forth. "Never will I serve you. You set yourself on too high a seat."

"I shall remind you of your words, Princess, when it is time for the throne of Mithgar to be mine." Malevolence crawled over the Naudron's gloating features.

"There is one, nay, there are many in Challerain Keep who will thwart that aspiration, *Spaunen!*" Laurelin's voice snapped.

"Pah! Challerain Keep!" the Naudron's voice sneered. "Even now that pile of hovels is aflame, set to the torch by my engines of destruction. Challerain will burn to the ground ere this 'Darkday ends, and there is nothing that Aurion Redeye with his puny force can do to prevent it: nothing! And the fire will sap his will; the strength of his Men will fall into the ashes of its destruction. Then will I strike: my Horde to whelm the gates, to scale the walls, to slay the fools trapped inside."

Laurelin's blood ran chill to hear such words, yet she betrayed no sign of fear, and she said nought.

"We waste time," he hissed, then cried a command to the force of Ghola now arrayed behind: *"Urb schla! Drek!"* Then once more he addressed Laurelin: "We shall speak again, Princess."

And even as Laurelin looked on, the Naudron's features writhed and then fell lax, and the malignant glare was utterly gone, replaced by a witless, vacant, slack-jawed look.

A Ghol rode to take the reins of the Naudron's Hèlsteed to lead the beast, while another took up Laurelin's, and at a sharp bark the Gholen column rode forth, heading east.

Behind, amid strewn and burning waggons and butchered steeds, lay the slaughtered: babes and mothers, the lame, Women, oldsters, soldiers, and youths, sprawled upon blood-soaked snow, some with their unseeing eyes staring at the track of the Gholen column as it disappeared into the Dimmendark; and nought was said by any, for the dead speak not.

* * *

Thirty grinding miles the Ghola rode through the Winternight, through the icy Shadowlight grasping the northern hills of the Battle Downs; and the jolting of the Hèlsteed drove shattering agony up Laurelin's arm. At times she nearly swooned, yet still the pounding went on. Her features became gaunt, drawn into haggard lines of pain, and she could no longer hold herself erect. That she did not collapse was perhaps due to the burning liquid forced upon her, for she did not fall, though how not she could not say. And the cruel miles hammered on. At last the column stopped to make camp. Laurelin was hauled down from her mount and she could not stand. She sat in the snow and dully stared as the Ghola took the vacant-eyed Naudron from his 'Steed.

Once more she was forced to drink the burning liquid, and then given a meal. She numbly ate the stale dark bread and thin gruel but touched not the unknown meat. And she sat revulsed, watching the Foul Folk tear voraciously at their own food, all, that is, but the vacuous Naudron, who chewed and slavered with dull-witted sluggishness upon the runny porridge spoon-fed to him by a Ghol.

And as she sat in this camp of ravers, her desperate thought was, *Galen, oh, Galen, where are you?*

Laurelin was kicked awake and given the flask of fiery liquid. Her battered body shrieked with pain: arm in torment, joints aflame, muscles knotted in agony. This time she drank from the flask without being forced, for the vile fluid dulled the harrowing rack.

Once more the Ghola prepared to go on, and Laurelin was given no privacy to take care of her needs. And she felt utterly degraded by the dead black eyes.

On through the Dimmendark they rode, beating steadily eastward, still within the northern margins of the Battle Downs. This time they covered nearly thirty-five miles before making camp.

Laurelin could but barely move when they stopped at last, for the unremitting pain in her arm had grown, thoroughly sapping her energy; and her legs, buttocks, back, and even her feet were tormented beyond telling from the pounding Hèlsteed ride.

Dully, she took her meal, eating without thinking. But

then a cold chill fell upon her heart, and without knowing how she knew, Laurelin suddenly became aware that the Evil once more looked upon her: she turned and saw that it was so, for malignancy again glared forth from the Naudron's face.

"Challerain is burned to the ground," gloated the voice. "The first and second walls have fallen to Whelmram and my Horde. Aurion Redeye and his pitiful few retreat up the mount, trapped like rabbits before the serpent."

Dread thudded within Laurelin's breast, yet rage burned there, too. "Why say you this?" she demanded. "Think you that these things you say will cause me fear on your spoken word alone?"

But the Naudron answered not, for now his eyes were blank.

Racked with agony, the stabbing pain pulsing in her arm, Laurelin wondered how long she could endure. Yet she gave no outward sign of her torment, as once more the column bore east, and her mind sought ways she might escape, yet none were forthcoming.

Three leagues they rode, then four, passing through the Shadowlight toward the eastern reaches of the Battle Downs north of Weiunwood. Twelve miles they rode ere an uneasy stirring rippled down the column. Laurelin craned her neck, and ahead, just within the limit of her vision, she saw . . . *Elves! Elves on horses!* Her heart leapt with hope. *Rescue!* But wait: they were not coming this way. Instead, they rode swiftly toward a line of trees to the south; and behind, running on foot, pursued a great force of Yrm in close chase, their harsh yells drifting over the snow, "Wait!" cried Laurelin, but her voice was lost amid the gleeful howls of the Gholen column, gloating to see Elves flee into Weiunwood with Rukha and Lākha in full cry.

As the Elves disappeared into the winter forest, Laurelin's heart fell into despair and tears rilled down her face. Yet inwardly she raged at herself: *Give them not the satisfaction,* she thought, *not the satisfaction,* and she sat up straight in Hèlsteed saddle and fought to stifle her weeping ere any Ghol could see. And she watched as the first of the yelling Rukha and Lōkha now rushed headlong into the 'Wood, and hundreds upon hundreds of others poured after.

The Gholen column continued eastward, swinging slightly north to pass behind the force of Yrm invading Weiunwood. As they rode, ahead Laurelin could see another band of Ghola sitting still upon Hèlsteed, watching the force disappear into the trees.

The two Gholen columns met and merged, and spoke with flat, dull voices, sounding bereft of life except when one or several would emit bone-chilling howls. Some came to inspect Laurelin, their dead black eyes fixed upon her, and she stared defiantly back at them.

The new force of Ghola numbered nearly one hundred strong, and Laurelin saw that among this band, too, rode a Man: black he was, as if from the Land of Chabba south across the Avagon Sea. And then Laurelin saw that his eyes were vacant, and drool ebbed down his chin, just like the Naudron's. And, also like the Naudron, the Chabbain, too, was led by a Ghol. It was as if neither Man bore any wit or will.

Yet even as she looked, the black face filled with malice, and Evil stared out at her. "The third wall of Challerain Keep now has fallen, as will the last two," hissed the Chabbain; and Laurelin's hand flew to her lips and she gasped in dread, *for it was the same viperous voice she'd heard issue forth from the Naudron's mouth!* But then the ebon face went slack, the eyes emptied out, the Evil was gone. And Laurelin spun to look at the Naudron and saw the same vacant stare. And she shuddered, for now she knew with whom she dealt.

Onward went the column with Laurelin, resuming the trek to the east. And as they rode forth, the Princess looked back at the stationary band of Ghola waiting near the fringes of the Weiunwood. And her eyes were drawn one last time to the Man from Chabba, his dark skin standing out amid the pasty pallidness of the Ghola like a slug among maggots. Shuddering, she turned her gaze to the fore and did not look back again.

Another four leagues they rode before emerging at last from the Battle Downs, and they made camp two leagues beyond upon the open plains. And as Laurelin spooned thin gruel to her mouth with her left hand, her broken arm throbbed in its sling; and pulsing with that pain, her mind kept echoing the hissing words: *"The third wall of Challerain Keep now has fallen, as will the last two."*

The next 'Darkday, the fifth since Laurelin's capture, the Gholen column crossed the plains to camp within sight of a northeast arm of the Weiunwood. Still their track bore eastward, and they had ridden thirty or so miles each of those five 'Darkdays. Yet the Hèlsteeds were not spent, for although they were not as fleet as a good horse, their endurance was greater.

Nay, it was not the tiring of the Hèlsteeds that determined where the column would camp, nor was it the amount of pain that Laurelin could withstand. It was instead the limits of the Naudron that paced the force of Ghola, though how the corpse-people could tell that the vacant-eyed Man needed rest, Laurelin could not say. Yet she did not care how it was done, for she was weary beyond measure when the camp was set.

She had just fallen into exhausted slumber when a Ghol kicked her awake. Opposite the campfire, Evil looked upon her. "The Keep has fallen and is now mine," hissed the puff adder voice. "Your brave Aurion Redeye has fled. And though I now have no eyes to see, I think none shall escape."

Laurelin's pale gaze locked with that of the dark-eyed Naudron's. *"Zūo Hēlan widar iu!"* (To Hèl with you!) she gritted in the old high language of Riamon, and lay back down to sleep, as evil laughter hissed in her ears. But though she lay with her eyes closed, her mind would not let go: *"The Keep has fallen . . . Redeye has fled . . . None shall escape."*

The next trek took Laurelin beyond the margins of the Weiunwood and into the low-set craggy tors of the Signal Mountains. And just ere they stopped to camp, the Naudron's blank eyes suddenly glared with Evil. "They seek to defy me!" the voice shrilly screamed, no longer a sibilant hiss. Laurelin snapped around to see rage upon the features of the Man of the Naud. "The fools of mine Hèlborne Reavers raced straight into their trap! But this ragtag Alliance of Elves, Men, and jewel-eyed runts shall not bar me from conquest. Weiunwood shall fall by my hand!''

Now the voice sank into viperous sibilation: *"Thuggon oog. Laug glog racktu!"* At these festering Slûk words, nearly half of the Ghola turned southwest along the Signal Mountains, while the rest continued to bear eastward, taking Laurelin with them.

As they divided, the voice hissed at the Princess, "They go to replace those impaled upon the wood. Think not to gloat over this minor setback, for the final victory shall be mine!"

But Laurelin's eyes bore into his, and she smiled fiercely.

Three 'Darkdays later, snow was falling down through the Dimmendark when Laurelin awakened, and their trek began in flakes swirling thickly. The past two 'Darkdays had been spent out upon the open plains, bearing south of east from the Signal Mountains, crossing the land north of the Wilderness Hills. And each of those days had been filled with dull ache for Laurelin, and her mind seemed to haze in and out of awareness: at times her thoughts were preternaturally sharp, at other times sluggish beyond her understanding. Yet she fought to show no sign of weakness and to let no sound of pain pass her thin-drawn lips.

Once more their journey carried them southward, and they had gone nearly ten miles when they came to a high-bluffed river. South they ranged along the wall to come to a low place where there was a frozen ford. Through the swirling snow and across the ice they went, cloven hooves ringing on the surface. As they came to the far side, the snow began to slacken, yet Laurelin knew that their tracks had been covered, and anyone following would have lost the trail. But perhaps this vague feeling that someone came after was only a girlish dream, and whether or not the snow covered their wake, it did not matter.

As they rode into the land beyond the ford, the column turned, slightly north of east, and Laurelin noted a strange run of excitement ripple through the Ghola. But she knew not what it portended.

Onward they went, the snow diminishing as they rode, finally to stop altogether. They came in among dark trees, and Laurelin felt a deep foreboding—from what, she could not say. It was in these woods that they made camp.

As Laurelin was drifting off to an aching sleep, a thought came unbidden to her mind: *It is Last Yule, Year's Start Day, Merrilee's birthday. Where are you now, Sir Tuck?*

Once more the trek resumed, and still the Ghola acted strangely: their flat voices arguing among themselves, their heads turning this way and that as they rode through a wood dismal, a wood from which darkness seemed to flow beyond that of the Shadowlight. And the Ghola appeared to revel in this miasma of dimness and vague dread.

Miles they went among the trees, at last to break into the open: a great clearing. Across the treeless expanse they rode, ten miles or more, to come once again unto the wood. At its very edge they made camp, and still the Ghola spoke, as if the dead debated what course to follow.

And as the campfire was lighted, without warning the evil voice hissed forth: "Why are we here? Why have you not turned north for the pass?"

The dead black eyes turned to the Naudron, and Laurelin sensed fear running among the Ghola, though she knew not why.

"Ah, I see," the sibilant whisper came, "you thought to make the Drearwood into a place of dread as of old."

Drearwood! Of course! That's were we are! thought Laurelin. *And the pass he spoke of is Grūwen Pass.* Then her heart plummeted, and she felt as if she had been struck in the stomach, and her spirit cried out in despair: *Oh, Adon! They bear me to Gron, to Modru himself!* Agony lanced up her arm.

Her thoughts were broken by a shrill scream: "Did I not say that *my* plans come first? Which of you has guided us here instead of toward the pass?"

Black eyes turned briefly toward one of the Ghola standing in the open snow, and his flat voice spoke: *"Glu shtom!"*

"You would stay?" hissed the sibilant voice at him. "You say you would stay?" Now the voice rose in a scream and shrieked, "Then stay!" And for the first time Laurelin saw the Naudron move when the Evil was present: he raised his arm and reached toward the Ghol and his hand made a clutching, squeezing motion, and the Ghol fell, flopping face down into the snow, dead.

The Naudron's arm dropped limply back to his side, the Evil flickering weakly in his eyes: "Thus to all who obey not my will. *Nabbu gla oth.*"

North and east the column rode, passing through five or so miles of Drearwood before coming into the open. Twenty more miles they went, the land rising steadily; and although she could not see afar through the murk of the Dimmendark, Laurelin had been raised in Dael in the ring of the Rimmen Mountains, and she knew that the slant of the land around her bespoke of tall peaks ahead.

They came to a high-faced bluff stretching out beside them, and the Ghola spurred up the pace as they rode alongside the cliff, as if to pass by this place as quickly as possible. Seven more miles they rode at this swift gait along the wall, and the agony jolted and jabbed through Laurelin like hot, lancing flames. And deep breaths hissed through her clenched teeth, but no groans escaped her lips.

Then they were beyond the long butte and the pace slackened, and they came into a stone-walled valley, yet still they did not stop, but rode eighteen miles more, until at last they reached the beginning rise of Grūwen Pass, and mountains loomed upward into the Dimmendark.

Fifty miles they had ridden, and Laurelin knew not when they stopped. Rough hands dragged her down from her mount, and she could not stand, but lay gasping in the snow where they dropped her. Inside her mind she shrieked in agony, but no sound of pain did she make.

Grūwen Pass was nearly thirty-five miles in length, and northward through the long slot the Gholen column rode. Great buttresses of ice-clad stone mounted up perpendicular cliffs into the Shadowlight, and rime glistened along their path. Bitter was the cold of the Winternight, and the irony-grey stone looked black in its light. Hard-frozen snow lay packed in shadowed crannies, and the echoing ring of cloven hooves juddered down the tall rocks.

When they stopped at last to camp, Laurelin was chilled to the marrow, and she could not seem to stop shuddering with the cold. Once more a Ghol brought her the leather flask, and he bruised her lips as she drank, for her left hand was too numb to hold the bottle. Yet the vile, fiery liquid brought a measure of warmth to her veins, and the campblaze made from wood they had borne with them and the hot gruel warmed her even more.

They had ridden the full length of the Pass—the slot where the Rigga Mountains met those of the Grimwall and the Gronfangs. And now the column had come down into the wastes of Gron—Modru's Realm of old—and Laurelin despaired, for this Land was dire.

From the edge of the pass, down the length of Grūwen Vale they rode the next 'Darkday, the stone of the valley dropping toward the plains of Gron below. Nothing seemed to grow in this land: no trees, no brush, no grass, no moss—not even lichen clung to the rock. Only ice and stone and snow could be seen about them, and sharp-edged darkness where the Shadowlight fell not.

They camped three leagues beyond the mouth of the vale, out upon the desolate plains of Gron. Though her arm throbbed dreadfully, that was not what caused Laurelin concern: it was instead that now that she was in Gron, a great bitterness clutched at her heart, and she was distressed by its sting.

Two 'Darkdays they rode north through the Winternight across a barren wasteland, and still no sign of life did they see. Laurelin knew that off to the left rose the Rigga Mountains, and to the right the Gronfangs. But they were too distant to see in the Dimmendark, though were the Sun to shine they could have been seen far over the plains. But there was no Sun, only cold Shadowlight, and Laurelin could have wept.

On neither day was there wood for a campfire, but dead tundra moss made a feeble flame, and Laurelin ate cold gruel for her meals.

At the end of the third 'Darkday upon the plains, the Ghola made camp along the southern edge of the Gwasp, a great swamp squatting in the angle of Gron. This sump was reputed to have midges beyond number and mire beyond depth in the summer, yet now it stood frozen in Winternight, looking to all like a lifeless morass. It was said that in days of yore Agron's entire army had disappeared within the sucking environs; but Agron's unknown fate merely added to the dire legends of the Gwasp, for it *always* had been a place of dread.

All the next 'Darkday they rode along the Gwasp's eastern flank, crossing frozen rills and seeps feeding the great bog, once passing across the ice of a river that descended down from the unseen Gronfangs. When they finally reached the far northern flank of the Great Swamp, they again made camp.

As she ate, Laurelin looked upon the vacant-eyed Naudron. It had been eight 'Darkdays since he had last spoken, and then it was to slay a Ghol; twelve days since he had last spoken to her; thirteen days since she had last said aught, and that was to tell the Evil to go to Hèl; sixteen days since she had been captured: sixteen 'Darkdays since she had last heard a friendly voice; twenty-one days since she had last been happy: at her nineteenth birthday party. When Laurelin slept at last, tears ran silently down her cheeks.

They crossed another frozen river and rode north. Some six hours later they passed close by tall black crags to their left as the column rode through Claw Gap and onto the flats known as Claw Moor, a high, desolate land.

Upon the Moor they rode, going some eighteen miles farther before making camp.

Once more Laurelin was kicked awake; once more the column rode north. Now their pace grew swifter, for they neared their goal. Agony jarred through Laurelin's arm with every stride the Hèlsteed took. They had ridden for hours, and her pain-dulled mind no longer held coherent thoughts. But, unbent, she sat in the saddle, straight as an iron rod, a rod now tempered in the very forge of Hèl. Miles had passed beneath the cloven hooves, nearly thirty-five this 'Darkday alone, nearly six hundred twenty since her capture eighteen 'Darkdays past.

Groggily, she saw black mountains loom up ahead, and in the face of the rock was clutched the towers of a dark fortress. Massive stone tiers buttressed turreted walls, and one central tower stood above all. Laurelin struggled with what she was seeing and suddenly snapped awake, and fear coursed through her, for now she realized that she gazed upon Modru's stronghold: the dreaded Iron Tower.

Across an iron drawbridge above a rocky chasm the column clattered, riding past a great, scaled Troll guarding the gate. Raucous horns blatted, and Lōkha screamed harsh orders as the Hèlsteeds came on, and Rukha leapt forward to winch up an iron portcullis with a great rattle of gears.

Into a stone courtyard the Gholen force rode, and Rukha ran forth snarling and elbowing one another, jostling for position to see and jeer at the prisoner.

To the central Iron Tower they rode and stopped before a great studded door. Laurelin was dragged down from her mount and led up steps to the portal. A leering Rukh hauled it open, and the Princess was shoved stumbling inside. And but one Ghol came after, and the great door boomed shut: *Doom!*

A torchlit hall stood before her. A Rukh thrall scuttled down the passage toward Laurelin and the Ghol and motioned for them to follow, croaking, "Uuh! Uuh!" for he had no tongue.

He led her along the cold black granite hall to another massive door warded by two Lôkha, who cringed away from the approaching Ghol. Fearfully, the tongueless Rukh raised the iron knocker and let it fall on the metal door-plate, once—*tok!*—the sound muffled, as if swallowed by the pools of gloom clustered in the angles of the stone hallway. Then slowly, cautiously, the Rukh opened the heavy portal and stood back for Laurelin to pass through. With a hard shove from behind, the Ghol thrust her into the chamber, the door to ponderously swing shut behind and slam to with a thunderous *Boom!*

The great room she stumbled into was lighted by flickering, cresseted torches, and at one end dark wood burned in a gaping stone fireplace, casting writhing shadows throughout the gloom-clutched chamber, though what little heat and light it gave off was swallowed by the chill silence within; heavy wall-hangings and massive furniture burdened the room. But none of this did Laurelin see. Instead her eyes were drawn toward a great *clot* of blackness sitting on a throne on an ebon-dark dais. And the shadows seemed to stream inward to gather unto the throne and coalesce thereon, until they formed a black-cloaked, black-clad figure. And then the figure stood and stepped down from the dais and stood before her, his arms folded across his chest. A Man he seemed, for Man-height he was, yet an immense, vile aura of malignancy exuded from his very being. As to his face, it could not be seen, for he was masked with a hideous iron-beaked helm, like the snouted face of a gargoyle of legend. But from the visor, eyes of evil stared: the same evil eyes she had seen upon the face of the Naudron, the same vileness that had looked forth from the eyes of the Chabbain. Yet no distant puppet was this baneful figure; instead, it seemed the quintessence of utter Evil.

And then the maleficent reptilian voice hissed out at her: "Welcome to my Iron Tower, Princess Laurelin. Though we have spoken many times, we meet face to face at last. *Ssss,* I am Modru."

Malignancy washed through the room, and Laurelin reeled under the impact. A woeful bale, a crushing desolation, reached out to clutch at her spirit, and her heart fell to the nadir of despair.

He stepped forward, and, although inwardly she shrank back, outwardly she did not flinch. And he took her by the hand as he drew her into the room. She wanted to scream in horror, for his very touch made her feel *violated,* as if his essence invaded her and made her unclean, polluted by a hideous corruption.

"Ah, my dear, why do I feel you shrink from me?" his sibilant voice hissed.

"If you feel me shrink from your hand," her clear voice answered, "it is because you are foul to the touch and vile to the eye: an abomination."

"*I?*" His voice rose in anger, and rage burned in the malignant eyes behind the hideous iron mask. "*I?* You say *I* am foul to the touch, vile to the eye?" Jerking her roughly after, he strode to a black-velvet-covered panel and wrenched her before it; and he stood to one side and ripped away the black cloth. It had covered a great mirror. "Behold, O Beautiful Princess, what an abomination truly is!"

Laurelin gasped at the apparition reflected in the glass: a grimy, gaunt, filthy drudge with a broken arm in a soiled sling stood before her, dressed in foul, stained, quilted, Rukken clothing; she stank of Hèlsteed and of human waste; and there were dark rings under the sunken eyes set deep in her grime-streaked face and dirty, tangled, lice-ridden hair matted down on her unclean head.

Long this haggard wretch stared at herself in the full-length mirror, and then she turned and spat in Modru's face.

CHAPTER 2

Grimwall

Tuck looked from Talarin to Gildor to Galen to Igon, the young Prince now asleep, his face flush with the dregs of fever. *South to Pellar or north to Gron? Which way to turn? Rescue the Princess or lead the Host against Modru's minions?* In despair, Tuck put his face in his hands, and tears welled from his sapphirine eyes.

Galen held the red eye-patch in his hands, smoothing out the scarlet tiecords.

"I took the patch so that the *Rûpt* would not defile Aurion King's body," said Gildor.

Galen nodded without speaking or looking up.

Long moments passed, and Igon's breathing lost its ragged edge. "His fever is gone," said the Elven healer. "He has cast off the poison from the enemy blade at last. When he awakens, he will be weak but his mind will be clear; yet it will take a fortnight or more for his full strength to return, and he will bear a scar for the rest of his days."

Galen now turned from his brother and looked up into the face of Talarin: "We are four, perhaps five 'Darkdays behind the band of Ghola fleeing north with the Lady Laurelin. I deem they fly toward Modru's strongholt. Where think you that they would be now?"

Talarin turned to Gildor, and Tuck looked and saw that these two Elves were much alike. "In other times you and your brother Vanidor have been upon the angle of Gron," said Talarin, "even unto Claw Moor and the Iron Tower itself. What say you?"

Gildor thought but a moment. "If they are five true days to the north, then they have come to the Gwasp; if but four instead, then they are one ride short of that morass, Galen King. And in three or four 'Darkdays at most, they will come to the Enemy's fortress."

Galen's voice was bleak: "You confirm my thoughts, Lord Gildor. This, then, is my dilemma: ere we can overtake the Ghola, Laurelin will be locked in Modru's strongholt, and nothing short of a great army—the Host—will e'er break down those dire doors; and even the Host would be hard-pressed to do so. In any event, foul Modru may maim or even slay the Lady ere the Host can throw down his Tower."

"Slay the Lady?" Tuck gasped, jumping to his feet.

"Her life is as nothing to him," answered Gildor.

"Hold, my son," said Talarin, raising a hand in thought. "What you say is true, yet Modru has gone to great lengths to bring her to him. Perhaps he has a purpose for her."

"Purpose?" cried Tuck.

"Aye," answered Talarin. "Hostage perhaps . . . or worse."

"Worse?" Tuck's voice dropped to a desperate whisper. "Something . . . we must do . . . something."

Galen spoke, setting forth the seed of a perilous plan: "Perhaps a few can succeed where an army would fail. It can be no more than a hand of people: to gain the walls of Modru's holt, to slip unseen within, and to draw her free."

No one spoke for moments, then Gildor broke the silence: "Galen King, such a plan might prevail, though I think it unlikely, for the Iron Tower is a mighty fortress. Yet you have spoken of only half of your quandary: the plight of the Lady Laurelin. The other horn of this dilemma is even sharper: the Realm is beset, for Winternight and Modru's *Spaunen* rave down the Land, and the Host must be led to stop them."

"But Lord Gildor," responded Galen, anguish in his voice, "Pellar lies more than one thousand miles to the south. To journey there and return with the Host will take weeks, months!"

Again long moments fled in silence, and Igon stirred, then opened his eyes. Clear they were now, not wild, and in the yellow lamplight he saw those around him.

"Galen"—Igon's voice was thready, weak—"know you of Laurelin?" At Galen's nod, tears welled in Igon's eyes, and he squeezed them shut, the drops to run down his cheeks. "I did not succeed," he whispered. "I did not succeed. I failed in my sword-oath to see her to safety. And now she is in the Enemy's clutch." The Prince fell silent.

Time stretched, and just as Tuck thought that Igon had gone back to sleep: "They were so many, the Ghola, and they cut us down as if we were but sheep led to the slaughter. I was felled, and knew nought thereafter. Next I remember, Rust stood over me, nudging with his muzzle; how he was spared, I cannot say. So cold, I was so cold, yet I managed to start a fire from a coal still red in the ashes of a smoldering wain."

Again the Prince fell silent a long while, mustering his strength to continue: "Their track was a 'Darkday old, yet I took food and grain and followed. I remember not much of that chase, though it did snow once, and I recall despairing I'd ever find their tracks—yet Rust knew, he knew, and bore me on: Drearwood, perhaps.

"Dead Ghol next to the forest: was he real?

"North from there . . .

"I remember nothing more, Galen, nothing more." Igon's voice had fallen to a faint whisper. "Grūwen Pass . . . Gron . . . Modru Kinstealer . . ." The Prince sank again into unconsciousness, the effort spent to eke out his report exhausting his feeble strength.

The healer turned to Galen: "I do not know where he found the will to speak, for his life ebbs dangerously low. You must leave ere he wakes again, for it drains him beyond his limits to give over his words to you."

"Galen King," said Talarin, "you must eat and bathe and rest, and renew your own strength, for on the morrow you must choose the course you will follow."

As Tuck drifted to sleep, in his mind Talarin's words echoed again and again: *"On the morrow you must choose . . . On the morrow . . ."*

Tuck awakened once to see Galen standing at a window looking out into the Shadowlight: in his hand he held a scarlet eye-patch; at his throat was a golden locket.

Their clothing had been washed clean and dried before a fire as the two slept. Now Tuck and Galen dressed, yet the thoughts of neither dwelled upon the freshness of his garb.

At last Tuck broke the silence: "Sire, perhaps it is not my place to speak, and the words I am about to say are like to choke me unto death, yet still I must say them, be they right or wrong.

"The Lady Laurelin I hold dear; she stands near the center of my heart, next to my own Merrilee. And I would follow my heart unto the very Iron Tower itself, to batter down the gates or to creep in stealth to win her free. And I will shout with joy if that is the course you choose."

Tears began to stream down Tuck's face. "Yet my head and not my heart tells me that the grasp of Modru strangles the Realm, and a King is needed to lead the Host, to hurl back the Horde, to rescue the Land. And you are King now, none other.

"I think a squad must enter Gron and perhaps even attempt to penetrate the Iron Tower, to bring forth the Lady Laurelin. Yet neither you nor I should ride north with that squad: her fate must be put in the hands of others, for you must go south to lead the Host, and I"—Tuck's voice now broke—"I must go with you to be your eyes."

Tuck turned to the window and looked forth into the Shadowlight, but his vision swam with tears and he saw nought. His voice was now low, and he spoke haltingly: "When we stood at the slaughtered waggon train, you swore an oath as a Prince of the Realm to run these kinstealers unto the ground. But you swore that oath as a Prince; yet again I say, now you are King . . . and a higher duty here calls, and you are honor-bound to answer . . . no matter what your heart cries out to do. Even though it will take . . . weeks . . . months . . . still our course should be south . . . to Pellar . . . to the Host. You must crush Modru Kinstealer, at the last, but crush his Horde ere then, for it lays waste to the Land.

"This, also, I know: were the . . . were the Lady Laurelin able to say, she, too, would urge you south, to save the Realm, for you are King."

Tuck fell silent, his face to the window, and Galen said nought.

There came a knock at the door, and the Elf Lords Talarin and Gildor entered. Talarin spoke: "Galen King, the time has come to choose."

Galen's voice was grim, barely above a whisper. "South. We ride south. For I am King."

A dreadful pall fell upon the hearts of those in the room, and Tuck wept bitter tears.

Long moments fled, then Gildor stepped to Galen's side: "When last I saw your Lady Laurelin," said Gildor, "she bade me to stand by the King and advise him, and I gave my pledge. Now you are King, Galen, and if you will have me in your company, I would ride south with you, for I would not break my word to that young damosel."

Galen simply nodded.

At last they walked down from the guest quarters and joined the Lady Rael seated at a large table. Upon hearing that Gildor would fare with Galen, Rael smiled. "It has ever been so that the High King has accepted one of the Lian Guardians unto his service," said the Elfess, and she reached out to clasp Talarin's and Gildor's hands. "It pleases me that you accept our son, as did Aurion, your father."

Gildor is Talarin's son! thought Tuck, somewhat astonished, looking from one to the other. *No wonder they favor.* Then Tuck's eye glanced from Rael to Gildor: *Yet there is something of Rael in him, too.*

Food was served and they broke their fast. And while they ate, they were joined by another, one who looked to be Gildor's twin. Tuck stared in amazement from one to the other, yet, but for their clothes, he could not tell them apart.

The stranger smiled at the Warrow's confusion, and winked.

"Ah," said Talarin, looking up, "Vanidor." The Lian Lord turned to his guests. "Galen King, Sir Tuck, this is my other son, Vanidor; he is but three 'Darkdays back from abandoned Lianion, the First Land, the domain also known as Rell. He can tell you of the regions to the south, toward your goal of Pellar."

Vanidor bowed to Galen and Tuck, then sat and took a bowl of *dele,* a type of porridge, but like none other Tuck had ever tasted, for it was delicious.

"Lianion falls into darkness," said Vanidor. "Modru's myrk hides all: down the Grimwall it has stalked, reaching nearly unto the Quadran when last I saw, some fifteen 'Darkdays past.

"Your mission is to Pellar, and so you must fare south through Lianion, but not upon the Old Rell Way, for that is the route of the *Rûpt:* Ruch, Lok, Ghûlk, Vulg. They, too, march south along the Grimwall, following the tide of the Dimmendark."

"Crestan Pass, it is near," said Galen. "Can we not take the Crossland Road up and the Landover down to come to the Argon? If unfrozen, we could ride that river south along the marches of Riamon and Valon to Pellar."

"The River Argon is frozen, Galen King," answered Vanidor, "in the north, that is, perhaps unto Bellon Falls. Even so, you could not cross the Grimwall at Crestan Pass, for it is winter, and the cold is too bitter at those heights. Too, the approaches are held by the *Spaunen*. Nay, your first chance to pass over the Grimwall will be perhaps at Quadran Pass—if it is not snowed in or held also."

"If Quadran Pass is blocked by winter or foe," said Gildor, "then Gûnar Slot will be our next chance, then through Gûnarring Gap to Valon and along Pendwyr Road to Pellar."

"Can the enemy be that far south?" asked Tuck, remembering the maps of the War-council.

"Perhaps; perhaps not," answered Vanidor. "Their goal could be the Quadran, for under those four mountains lies Drimmen-deeve, where rules the Dread! And if the Dimmendark sets that creature free, then Darda Galion will be their target."

At Vanidor's pronouncement, grim looks came upon the visages of Talarin, Gildor, and Rael, for dearly did they love Darda Galion, Land of the Silverlarks, Land where grew the twilight Eld Trees, home now of the Lian. And for a Gargon to be free to rave into that faer sylva would be a dire prospect indeed.

"This, then, is my advice," said Vanidor: "Go south through Arden Vale to come to Lianion. Follow parallel to the Old Rell Way and not upon it, for there go *Spaunen*. You can try to cross the Grimwall at Quadran Pass, and if the way is free, you can fare south through Darda Galion where our Lian kindred will aid you on your way.

"Should the Quadran Pass be held by the foe, or if it is closed by winter snow, then you must turn south once more for Gûnar Slot, or even Ralo Pass beyond, and then to the Gûnarring Gap and on to far Pellar. Because I know not the mind of the Enemy in Gron, none of these ways over the Grimwall may be open, and how you will ultimately come to Caer Pendwyr I cannot say, yet there you must go, and those are the choices before you."

Galen nodded his understanding, but it was Talarin who spoke next: "Galen King, if I thought it would help, I would send an Elven warrior escort with you. But I think that evil eyes would follow a large force and set a trap, where but two or three might slip south undetected.

"This, too, I say: Aurion King was a beloved friend and we share your loss. And we know you journey southward when your heart cries out, *North*. And though my son has not told you, last night we held counsel and debated our course should you choose north, or south. You have chosen south, and this is now our plan: Vanidor, Duorn, and two you have not met—Flandrena and Varion—will slip into Gron. By stealth they will approach the Iron Tower, and if there be any a way to rescue your Lady Laurelin, they will do so. Else, they will bring word of Modru's forces at his stronghold, so that when the time does come at last, we will know something of the Enemy's strength and disposition. This we will do while you muster the Host."

Galen said nought, but there stood tears in his eyes, and he gripped Vanidor's hand.

"Prince Igon is awake, Galen King," said the healer. "Pray, tax him not."

Galen and Tuck stepped through the door. While Tuck stood at the portal, Galen stepped to the bedside. Igon smiled wanly, the youth pale in the yellow lamplight. Galen spoke: "We now go south, my brother, to gather the Host."

"South? But no!" Igon protested, his voice weak and atremble. "Laurelin is north!" Then he seemed to see the Waerling for the first time. "Sir Tuck, why are you here? Challerain Keep . . . Father . . ." There was a silence, and then Igon asked, "Are you King now, Galen?" At Galen's nod the young Prince wept. "Then it was not a fevered dream as I had hoped. Father is dead." He turned his face to the wall.

The healer made motions to Galen, and the new King took his brother's hand and held it in his own two. "We must go now, Igon. The Horde must be stopped."

Galen loosed Igon's hand and gently stroked the young Prince's hair, then stepped to the door where stood Tuck. Igon turned his face to them. "I understand, Galen. I understand. You are King, and the Host is south." And as Galen and Tuck passed through the door, behind they could hear Igon's quiet weeping.

Now it came time for the parting, and Tuck and Galen stood in the company of Elves. And neither the Dimmendark nor the solemnity of the occasion could dim the fair brightness of the Lian. Beautiful Rael stood with Talarin and at their side was Vanidor. As they stood, three rode up: Duorn, Flandrena, and Varion. With Vanidor they would issue into Gron and attempt to reach the Iron Tower itself. Assembled there, too, were other Elves: warriors in the main: Lian Guardians.

Gildor, Galen, and Tuck stood before Talarin; and the warrior leader of Arden Vale turned and held out his hand, and Rael the Elfess came to stand at her Elf Lord's side. "Galen King," said Talarin, "ere I bid you and your comrades farewell, I would have my Lady Rael speak, for her words often bear portents."

The gentle voice of the graceful consort fell softly upon their ears: "Galen King, the way before you is arduous, for the Land is fraught with dire peril. Along your path will lie great danger, yet unbidden aid will be found there, too, just as you and others before you found our aid here at the Hidden Stand. Now you and your small companion go forth with my son, and you take all of our blessings with you. Yet hearken: even as you three fare south, four others will bear north." Now Vanidor and his three companions came to stand before golden Rael, too. "And so both of my sons—Gildor Goldbranch and Vanidor Silverbranch—as well as all of us are caught up in events of Modru's making.

"And that is what Evil does: forces us all down dark

pathways we otherwise would not have trod. By choice we would not have stepped out upon these courses, yet little or no choice are we given, and our energies are turned aside, turned away from the creation of good and toward the destruction of Evil. Make no mistake, Evil must be crushed, not only to eliminate the suffering Evil causes, but also to atone for the good lost. But if for no other reason, Evil must be destroyed so that we can once more guide our own destinies.

"Until that time, the fates of us all are intertwined, yet the fortune of one weighs heavily upon me. Ever have there been soothsayers in my lineage, and auguries come unannounced at times. Yet this sooth has long been upon me, since the flaming Dragon Star fell, but now seems to be the time to speak it:

> *"Neither of two Evils must thy strike claim;*
> *Instead smite the Darkness between the same."*

At these words Tuck's heart pounded unexpectedly, but he did not know why, and he did not understand the message. And Tuck looked to see that the others were just as puzzled as he by Rael's rede, yet what she said next only added to the mystery: "I know not what it means nor to whom its portent bodes."

Rael moved to the wayfarers and pressed the hand of each, kissing Gildor and Vanidor upon the cheek. And when she stood before Galen, she said, "We will tend young Igon until he has the strength to join you. Hence, fret not upon his state as you fare south, for that would be needless worry." Then she stepped back to Talarin's side and spoke no more, though her eyes were bright.

Now Talarin spoke: "Galen King, should your course be through Darda Galion, bear our greetings to our Lian kindred; they will help you on your way. Unlike Arden Vale, their Realm is wide and their strength is great. Yet this, too, I will say: though my warrior band in Arden is small, still Modru's minions give the Lian wide berth, for they fear us. Yet though the Dimmendark does not grasp this vale as much as it cloaks it, if the *Spaunen* are left unchecked, there will come a time when they will fall upon us, both here and in Darda Galion; and we, too, will drown beneath that dark tide. But ere then, with good fortune, you shall guide the force to shatter Modru's black dreams of power. And now this last: when you need us, we will be at your side."

Now all the wayfarers mounted up, and Tuck was boosted astride the packhorse to sit before the supplies strapped to a cradle cinched to its back.

Galen upon Jet turned to Vanidor and the three Elven comrades who were to steal into Gron. "My heart goes with you to the holt of Modru Kinstealer. May fortune smile upon you."

Then Galen faced Talarin and Rael and the Elven gathering, and he raised his hand. "Dark days lie behind us, and darker days loom ahead, yet, by my troth, one day the Evil in Gron shall be overthrown and the bright Sun shall shine again down into this deep-cloven vale."

Galen flashed his sword from its scabbard and to the sky and cried to all: *"Cepān wyllan, Lian; wir gān bringan thē Sunna!"* (Keep well, Lian; we go to bring the Sun!)

Gildor, too, raised his sword, as did Vanidor. *"Cianin taegi!"* (Shining days!) cried Gildor. *"Cianin taegi!"* answered Vanidor, and a great shout rang up from all.

And as the sound echoed through the pines, Galen, Gildor, and Tuck started south while Vanidor, Duorn, Flandrena, and Varion set off for the north.

And Tuck on the packhorse being led by Gildor on Fleetfoot spoke quietly under his breath: "May the fair face of Fortune smile upon us all."

South they rode—Gildor, Galen, and Tuck—alongside the frozen Tumble River running through the deep cleft of the vale. Pines covered the valley floor, and craggy stone palisades could be seen rising steeply up into the Shadowlight. Narrow was the vale, at times pinching down to widths less than a furlong from wall to wall, and in these places the river spanned the full vale width. In these narrow gaps, pathways could be seen carven upon the faces of the stone bluffs, but the trio shunned these icy ways, choosing instead to go upon the frozen surface of the river below.

Long they rode down the vale, yet when at last they stopped to make camp, still they were between the high stone walls, for Arden Vale was lengthy. Some thirty-five

miles they had ridden south, and Gildor said that perhaps
fifteen miles more lay ahead ere they would leave the
gorge.

Their supper consisted of Lian wayfarer's food: dried
fruit and vegetables, hot tea, and, much to Tuck's delight,
mian, a delicious Elven waybread made of oats and honey
and several kinds of nuts. "Sure beats crue all hollow," said
the Warrow, taking another bite and savoring it.

Tuck prepared to bed down, for he was weary and had
the midwatch and so needed sleep. But ere doing so, he
reclined against a log by the small campfire and wrote in
his diary. Nearby, Galen sat with his back to a tree and
gazed at the red eye-patch in his hand.

"Lord Gildor, speak to me of the last hours of my father." Galen's voice was low, nearly a whisper.

Gildor looked upon the Man and then spoke: "When
there we stood upon the final parapet of Challerain Keep
and chose that last desperate course—to break through the
Rûpt ring and win free—I felt a deep foreboding, and this
I said to thy sire: 'Beware, Aurion King, for beyond yon
gate I sense a great Evil lurks, an Evil beyond the Horde
at our door, and I deem it bodes ill for you.' Little did I
know that at the north gate of the first wall would we be
met by Ghûlka led by Modru."

"Modru?" cried Tuck, sitting bolt upright with a start.

"Aye, Modru," answered Gildor. "It was he who taunted
the King before the sundered gates."

"But that was a Man!" exclaimed Tuck. "The Man from
Hyree! Modru's emissary!"

" 'Twas Evil Modru who spoke at the north gate," answered Gildor, but ere he could say more, Tuck interrupted.

"Then Danner slew him." Tuck's fist smacked into palm.
"Danner's arrow struck him full in the forehead, crashing
into his brain; he was dead even as he pitched backward
off his Hèlsteed."

"Nay, Wee One," answered Gildor, holding up a hand
to forestall Tuck's protests. "It was only one of Modru's
puppets that was slain. Did I not say that Modru uses hideous powers to command his Horde? This, then, is one of
them: though the Evil One sits afar in his Iron Tower, still
he can look out upon distant scenes through the eyes of

his emissaries, listen through their ears, speak through their mouths, and at times slay through their hands. None knows how far he can reach out to *possess* his pawns, but his power is great. Yet perhaps it diminishes with distance.

"Nay, it was not the Evil One himself slain by Danner's arrow, though I think Modru felt the unexpected blow. Yet, at the most, Danner's bolt has but delayed Modru's plans: for Danner slew the puppet, and now Modru has lost his eyes and ears, his mouth and hands at Challerain Keep— though another pawn by now must have been sent to take the place of the one slain, for Modru will not long allow the Horde to sit idle at the mount."

Tuck shuddered at the thought of the Evil One *possessing* another; and now the Warrow understood why the emissary's slack face writhed and became evil when Aurion and Tuck came to parley: *It was Modru "taking over."* And Tuck thought he knew, too, why the emissary did not join in that treacherous fight upon the parley field: *If the hideous power diminishes with distance, it just might be that Modru back in Gron could not control the Hyranan well enough to engage in combat upon the fields of distant Challerain.*

Tuck's speculations were interrupted by Gildor speaking: "Galen King, thy sire won through the north gate after you and your band broke the Ghûlka ring. Yet he was sorely beset, and had taken many wounds. But still he fought with the strength of many. At the last he was surrounded, and pierced through by Ghûlken spear. Even with the lance in him, he slew two more foe ere he fell forward to Wild-wind's back."

Gildor drew both his sword and long-knife and thrust them out before him. Each held a blade-jewel, one blood-red, the other ocean-blue, and they glinted in the firelight. "Even with these two blades, Bale and Bane, still I could not win to his side in time to save him. Yet the scarlet fire of Bale and the cobalt blaze of Bane drove the Ghûlka back, for they fear these weapons forged long ago in Lost Duellin, forged to battle evils such as they. When they fled, I caught up Wildwind's reins and rode free of the mêlée.

"On a nearby slope, I eased Aurion King to the ground. He said but one thing ere he died: 'Tell Galen . . . Igon . . . I chose freedom.' Then he was gone. What he meant, I do not know."

Tuck sat with tears in his eyes. "I know the pith of his words," said the Warrow. "When the emissary . . . when Modru met us on the field to parley, he offered to spare the King's life in return for the surrender of all of us into slavery. But the King said, 'Pah! Say this to your vile Lord Modru: Aurion Redeye chooses freedom!' "

For long moments no word was said, and the only sound was the crackle of the fire. At last, Gildor stirred. "I cut loose the eye-patch so that none would know him or defile his body, and so that Modru would not know that Aurion King had been slain. Then I laid his sword beside him and composed his hands over his breast, and remounted Fleetfoot to return to the fray.

"But Vidron at the head of a band had broken free and raced eastward. Catching up Wildwind's reins, I followed.

"East we ran through the foothills, with Ghûlka hard on our trail. But Hèlsteed has not the speed of horse, and we finally escaped their clutch.

"Far to the east through the Dimmendark we had fled, unto the Signal Mountains, but now we circled southward, heading for the rendezvous to join with any others who might have broken free. Our course swung just to the north of the Weiunwood, and while Vidron bore on west and south, riding for the Battle Downs and Stonehill beyond, I turned aside into the forest to seek tidings from the Weiunwood Alliance and to bear them the news of the downfall of Challerain Keep and of the death of Aurion. There I discovered from one of my kindred that you and Tuck had passed through on the trail of the kinstealers.

"I asked that word be sent to Vidron in Stonehill, and I left Wildwind in the care of my kith, a Lian recovering from a battle wound, and came after you, one 'Darkday behind your track when I started, though I had nearly overtaken you by the time we came to Arden."

Tuck spoke: "Have you any news of other Warrows? Did any win free? Danner, Patrel, any?"

"I know not, Wee One, for none were with us. The last I saw of any Waerling ere I came to Weiunwood was 'Darkdays past, when we all broke through the sundered north gate." Gildor's eyes glittered in the firelight.

Tuck's heart fell at this news, for he still hoped that others of his kindred had escaped the ruins of Challerain Keep.

Again long moments fled. Finally, Galen returned the red patch to his breast pocket. "You say you spoke with a wounded Lian at the Weiunwood," said Galen. "Many went off to battle with *Spaunen* when last we were there. Did he say aught of the outcome?"

"Nay," answered Gildor, "for he knew it not. Yet that explains the empty campsite I came to on the eastern edge of the 'Wood: they had gone to War and I was a full 'Dark-day behind then. I know nought of that battle, for I but followed you."

Little was said after that, and Tuck bedded down and went to sleep. But when his turn at watch came, he spent the time scribing in his journal, recording Gildor's words.

After an uneasy rest, they broke camp and continued southward through Arden Gorge. High stone canyon walls loomed up to either side, at times near, but at other times two or three miles distant, beyond the limits of Galen's vision in the Shadowlight. Tuck again rode upon the pack-horse, trailing behind Gildor as the trio wended through the pines along the frozen river.

Some fourteen miles south they went, enwrapped in snowy silence, saying little or nothing, and Tuck's mind fell into a state where he was at one with the woods: moving among the evergreens and watching the trees go by, thinking no thoughts of substance, attuned only to the canyon forest.

Gildor's voice fell unexpectedly upon his ears, breaking into his state of accord: "We are less than a mile from the end of Arden Vale," said the Elf. "Around the bend we will come to the camp of my kindred standing Arden-ward. We shall take a meal with them under the shelter of the Lone Eld Tree."

"Lone Eld Tree?" asked Tuck, trying to remember what he'd heard about these legendary forest giants. "Aren't they the ones said to *gather* the twilight and *hold* it if Elves dwell nearby?" At Gildor's nod, Tuck was surprised: "But I thought that was just a myth."

Gildor laughed. "Then, Wee Waerling, if they are myths, you had better not let this Eld Tree know it, for it might vanish, and so might the entire forest of Darda Galion."

Tuck smiled at Gildor's reply and wondered at his own ignorance as onward they went.

The river curved 'round a bend, and now a distant roar of falling water could be heard as they rode through the pines. Gildor pointed ahead, and there Tuck could see that the gorge squeezed to a narrow cleft that seemed to be filled with a white mist streaming up into the Winternight sky. Gildor pointed again, and Tuck's eyes fell upon an enormous tree, pinelike but with broad leaves and not needles; and even in the Shadowlight, the Warrow could see that the leaves were dusky, as if unaffected by the Dimmendark but shining with a soft twilight of their own.

"Lor, what a giant!" exclaimed Tuck, his tilted eyes wide at the sight of a tree looming hundreds of feet into the air. "Are there other Eld Trees in Arden?"

"No. Just this one. That is why we call it the Lone Eld Tree," answered Gildor. "It was brought here from Darda Galion by my sire when it was but a seedling and planted in the rich soil of Arden Gorge soon after this hidden vale was first discovered by my people."

"Planted by your sire? By Talarin? But this giant must be thousands of years old . . ." Tuck's mind boggled to think of the age of Elves.

Galen spoke: "That tree is the symbol of the Warder of the Northern Regions of Rell, now Lord Talarin. That sigil has been nobly borne into battle many times 'gainst dark forces: green tree 'pon field of grey. Such a flag hangs in the Gathering Hall of Caer Pendwyr, and another at Challerain Keep."

"No more at Challerain Keep, I fear, Galen King," said Gildor, "for Modru's Horde will have rent it down as well as the other flags of the Alliance."

No more was said as they spurred toward the Elven camp under the branches of the Lone Eld Tree.

"Aye, the approach to Crestan Pass is held by the *Rûpt*," said Jandrel, Captain of the Arden-ward, "and the Ghûlka, Modru's Reavers, patrol the Old Rell Way. Somewhere south a Horde marches along the abandoned road. Down out of the Grimwall north of the Pass they came, three 'Darkdays past. Where the *Spaunen* are bound, I cannot say, yet they march apace. Perhaps they strike for Quadran Pass and Drimmendeeve, or Darda Galion beyond."

"We ride for Quadran Pass," said Galen, pouring himself another cup of tea from the pot hanging on the fire irons above the small campblaze. "If we can cross the Grimwall there, we will warn the Lian in the Larkenwald of this Horde as we pass through on our way to Pellar."

"Be wary," said Jandrel, "for not only are there Ghûlka and Rucha and Loka with the Horde, but Vulgs, too. Give them wide berth, for Modru's evil scouts will smell you out should you come near."

"Scouts?" asked Tuck. "Vulgs are scouts?"

"Aye, Master Waerling," answered Jandrel, "scouts. It has ever been so that Vulgs do Modru's bidding, and at times he uses them on vile missions where their speed, stealth, or savagery suits his ends. But for the most part, he uses them to ward the flanks of his Hordes, or to spy out the Lands that he intends to invade."

"Spy out Lands . . . but they were in the Bosky!" cried Tuck, leaping to his feet, the sense of tranquility he had felt under the branches of the Eld Tree completely shattered. "They're going to invade the Bosky! I've got to get back! They must be warned! Merrilee . . ." Tuck took several running steps toward the horses, but then jerked to a stop as if arrow-pierced and slowly turned toward his comrades, falling to his knees in the snow and burying his face in his hands.

In six swift strides Galen knelt by the Warrow. "Tuck, if you must return to the Boskydells, you are free to go, though how you will get there, I cannot say."

"I can't go. I can't go," whispered Tuck. "There are no ponies; even if there were, I'd be too late. And you need my eyes."

Flowing under the ice, the swift-running Tumble River emerged from the last walls of Arden Gorge and fell down a precipice in a wide cataract. Swirling vapors rose up and obscured the view of the cloven vale, and where the mist settled unto the frigid rock, strange, twisting shapes of ice formed.

Behind the roar of water the trio went upon a hidden icy road, the stone clad in thick sheets of frozen mist: here was the secret entrance into the hidden valley—an entrance concealed by the fall of water. At last, they emerged from behind the cataract and twined through crags to come at last to the wolds of Rell.

The horses were spurred to a canter, and south they ran, and Tuck looked back toward Arden Gorge, back at the final cleft where the high, sheer stone walls split out of the earth, but the perpetual white mist veiled all beyond Arden Falls: neither pine forests nor stone walls were visible through the mist—not even the Lone Eld Tree could be seen.

Yet Tuck's bitter thoughts were not on the hidden valley; instead, he fretted over the Vulg scouts spying out the Boskydells, foreshadowing an invasion. And he recalled Galen's words spoken only two 'Darkdays past: *"These are evil days for Mithgar, and evil choices am I given."* Now more than ever, Tuck realized the truth of Rael's words: *"Evil . . . forces us all down dark pathways we otherwise would not have trod."* And Tuck thought, *Even when I would choose to fight a great evil elsewhere, no choice am I given, for if King Galen does not reach Pellar, then a greater evil will fall upon the world . . . Oh, Merrilee, my love . . .*

Tuck turned his face away from the vale, for he could no longer see it.

Less than one mile south the Tumble turned westward while the trio bore on; and just after, they passed over the Crossland Road, the main east-west pike reaching far overland from the distant Ryngar Arm of the Weston Ocean to the nearby Grimwall Mountains. Although this tradeway was extensive, most commerce in this part of Mithgar flowed on the watercourse of the Isleborne River, or came by road from south and west. Beyond the Crossland Road they went, south through the folds of the land, another fifteen miles before they made camp.

Tuck stood at the edge of the thicket, peering to the west, his jewel-eyed vision limited by the Dimmendark. Gildor came and stood beside him.

"West some twenty miles or so lies the Tumble River," said the Elf. "Beyond Arden Ford is the Drearwood, and beyond that the River Caire. Yet I know your thoughts roam far to the west: beyond Rhone and Harth and to your Land of the Thorns, a fortnight away by swift steed.

"Tuck, the Vulgs have roamed your homeland at the Evil One's command, and this I think is the why of it: Once before, all of Mithgar faced this Foe, and he was overthrown at the last. In his defeat it was your Folk who played the key role, and Modru has not forgotten; that is why he sends his minions against your Land. I would that it were not so, for the Boskydell is a gentle Realm of peace, ill fitted for a War against Modru's *Spaunen*.

"Yet hearken: *no* Land is well suited to War. And I have seen your kindred in battle. There is surprising grit to be found in your Folk.

"And though you would be in your beloved Bosky, there are those who will stand in your stead. Trust in them to choose the correct course, just as you have chosen rightly."

Gildor turned and walked back to the small shielded fire, and Tuck said nought. But soon he came and took supper, and afterward he slept well.

Although Elves pay little heed to hours and days and even weeks, seeming to note only the passing of the seasons, still they know at all times where stand the Sun, Moon, and stars. And even the murk of the Dimmendark changed not this power of theirs. And though at times the dim disk of the Sun vaguely could be seen as it passed through the zenith, still it was Gildor who kept track of time's flow for the trio.

Three more 'Darkdays they bore southward, riding parallel to and ten or so miles west of the Old Rell Way, an abandoned trade route, long fallen into ruin. The land they passed through was rough, high moor with sparse trees, there being barren thickets or lone giants clutching with empty winter branches at the Dimmendark sky. In the folds of the land grew brush and brambles, and cold winter snow covered all. Yet across the upland they went, bearing ever southward.

Five 'Darkdays past they had left the Elvenholt in the northernmost reaches of Arden Vale, narly fifty-five leagues behind. Eleven leagues a 'Darkday they rode, more or less, thirty-three miles each leg, for haste was needed in these dire times. Yet though they had pressed long and

hard, neither Jet nor Fleetfoot nor the packhorse seemed
to be tiring, and Tuck wondered at their endurance.

The sixth 'Darkday they turned at last to the Old Rell
Way, for now they had to follow its course through the wide
gap in a westward spur of the Grimwall Mountains standing
across the way.

Tuck sat astride Jet's withers before Galen, for the road
was fraught with peril and the Waerling's eyes were needed
up front to ward the way rather than "in back lolling on a pack
animal," as Galen smilingly put it. Yet though Galen had
smiled, they were come to a dangerous pass, and if Spawn
roamed it, the way would be filled with risk.

Southward they went, through rising hill country, ten miles
before coming to the Old Rell Way where it first entered
the wide gap. No enemy did they see, though the snow was
beaten down in a wide track made by many feet tramping.

"This wake is fresh, perhaps a 'Darkday old, made by an
army moving south," said Galen, remounting Jet.

"The Swarm Jandrel spoke of," said Gildor. "Keep a sharp
eye, Tuck, for they are before us."

Into the gap they went and beyond, riding another two
leagues; and the land began to fall, the close hills spreading
out, while the route they followed swung southeastward,
rounding the side chain and heading for the Quadran
through mounting hill country.

"Well, my Wee One," said Galen, "it appears that the
danger is past, for the land opens up and we can leave this
abandoned road once more. Though there be a Horde before us, we will travel beside its course, this time to the
east, I think." Then he turned to Gildor: "We must go
swifter and 'round the Spawn ere we come to Quadran
Pass, for we would not want them to get there first." Galen
reined Jet to a halt. "Tuck, you may once more ride at
your ease upon the cargo."

Smiling, Tuck swung his leg over to leap to the ground.
One last time he swept his sapphirine gaze to the limits of
his vision, and far to the south . . .

Quickly, he threw his leg back over Jet. "Hola! Galen
King, something afar: down the Old Rell Way in the flats
below. Take me closer."

Jet was spurred forward, Gildor following upon Fleet-foot, leading the packhorse. Swiftly they cantered along the abandoned road to bring Tuck's eyes into range. And as they went, Tuck strained his vision to its uttermost limits, and soon he gave a groan, for there before him down in the flats nearly five miles distant, a dark Rūcken Horde boiled southeastward, force-marching down the Old Rell Way. No sound reached up to Tuck's ears from the Swarm, the distance lending the illusion of a vast army moving along in eerie silence.

"Galen King, it is the Horde," gritted Tuck. "We must leave this road and swing around them."

To the east of the Way they slipped aside, riding once more across the open moors. And as they went, the land began to rise, for they were bordering upon the foothills of the Grimwall. An hour they rode, and then another, Tuck's eyes keeping the Swarm just in view as the trio passed behind thickets and hills to the east of the *Spaunen*.

"We have drawn even with them now," said Tuck grimly as Jet at a walk bore him from behind the flank of a hill and his jewel-hued vision saw the foe once more.

"How many are there?" asked Galen, for his own eyes could not see them.

"I know not," answered Tuck, "but they flow as a dark flood perhaps three miles in length. How like a plague of ravenous vermin they seem, swarming forth to ravage the Land."

"It is well that this Realm has been long abandoned, then," said Gildor, riding beside them, "else this blight would have struck down many an innocent victim."

"Are there Vulgs?" Galen's thoughts turned to the dire scouts of Modru.

"Yes," answered Tuck, seeking and finding the sinister dark shapes gliding o'er the land. "They roam the Horde's fringes, but I see none more than a mile from the Swarm."

"Keep your eyes set for them," said Galen, "for if they scent us, they will bring the Ghola."

Once more they spurred up the pace, and Jet and Fleet-foot bore them southeastward and the packhorse cantered behind. An hour they rode at a varying gait, for they must needs husband the strength of the steeds, and at the end of that time Tuck could no longer see the Horde behind.

"On the morrow we must risk the road once more," said Galen, "for our pace will be swifter upon its abandoned bed than through this rough hill country."

"But, Sire, won't the Vulgs smell us out if we run along a course they will soon follow upon?" protested Tuck.

"That is a danger, Wee One," answered Galen, "yet we cannot make haste through this broken land unless we soon take to the Old Rell Way; it begins its long run up to the Quadran, and ravines and bluffs will bar our route if we are not upon the Way. And haste is needed, for not only must we hie for Pellar, we must also try to warn the Larkenwald of the Horde behind us. There is this, too: if we start up to Quadran Pass and find we cannot cross through—because of snow or Spawn—then we will be forced to retrace our steps, coming back down before turning south for Gûnar Slot. And we must not meet up with this Horde on that narrow road down from the heights.

"Aye, Tuck, you are right to think of the Vulgs, and we will not rejoin the Old Rell Way until we are far ahead of here. Perhaps they will not scent a 'Darkday-old trail. But we must at last come again to the Way to gain greater speed, for not to do so poses a greater risk."

Through the hills they wended, bearing southeastward, and the land grew rougher as they went. And as Galen had said, ravines and bluffs began to bar their way. And as if the Fates had conspired perversely, ramparts and fissures slowly began to force the trio south, back toward the Old Rell Way. *Too soon!* thought Tuck. *Too soon! We go where the Vulgs will scent us!* Yet there was nought they could do to change their course as they turned through stone and rounded thickets and rode along the faces of low-walled, sheer bluffs.

"I deem we must now strike for the Way and make a run for it," said Galen grimly, "for where we ride now, the Vulgs will cut our trail." And so they turned and deliberately pressed toward the abandoned road, coming down through the ruptured land.

As they came along a twisting valley, suddenly Gildor kicked Fleetfoot forward and grabbed Jet's bridle, bringing the horses to a halt.

"Hsst!" he said. "Listen!" And the Elf pointed ahead toward a bend.

Both Tuck and Galen strained their hearing, and above the blowing of the steeds they could faintly hear the skirl of steel upon steel, the clash of combat, the clangor of a duel.

At a motion from Galen, Tuck mounted behind the Man just as a pony bearing supplies scaddled around the bend and bolted past them, his eyes rolled white with terror, his hooves beating a frantic tattoo upon the stony ground.

Tuck gripped his bow and pulled an arrow from his quiver: it was the red shaft from Othran's Tomb. Quickly he replaced it and took another, stringing it to his bow.

Galen drew his sword and Gildor had Bale in hand, its blood-red blade-jewel streaming scarlet fire along the weapon's edge, silently shouting, *Evil is near!*

At a nod from Galen, forward they went, the steeds at a walk, nearing the bend. Tuck's heart thudded as he prepared for fight or flight, for they knew not what lay ahead. *Ching! Clang!* came the sounds, louder.

Slowly they rounded the bend, to come upon a scene of great carnage. Rūcks there were, lying dead, slain Hlōks, too, cleft by great gaping wounds. *Chank! Dlang!* Ponies were slaughtered, some still kicking in their death throes. But Tuck's eye was drawn elsewhere, for here and there other warrior Folk lay: *Dwarves!*

Dwarves slain by scimitar and cudgel!

Dwarven axes asplash with black Rūck grume bloodily attested to the deaths of the *Spaunen,* just as red-washed Rūcken blades spoke of the Dwarven dead. *Chank! Shang!*

At last the trio came full 'round the bend; from the road-bed of the Old Rell Way the ring of steel upon steel hammered forth. *Dhank! Chang!* It was a Dwarf! And a Hlōk! And they fought to the death: the last two survivors of a gory slaughter, the last two. And they fought on in a bloody battleground, awash with the ichor of the slain.

Tuck leapt down and drew his arrow to the full, aiming at the Hlōk, waiting for a safe shot.

"No!" shouted the Dwarf, hate-filled eyes never leaving his foe. "He is mine!"

The Hlōk's eyes darted toward the trio, and he snarled in rage and leapt toward the Dwarf. *Clank! Dring!*

Galen's grim voice spoke above the ring of steel: "Hold your arrow, Tuck. He has the right."

It was axe against scimitar, but an axe wielded in a manner that Tuck had never imagined. The Dwarf grasped the oaken helve with a two-handed grip: right hand high near the blade, left hand low near the haft butt. And he used the haft to parry scimitar blows; and stabbed forward with the cruel axe beak, and shifted his grip to strike with fury, lashing out the double-bitted blade in sweeping blows, driven by the power of broad Dwarven shoulders.

Yet the Hlōk was skilled, too, and stood a full head taller than his foe. His reach with the scimitar was considerably longer, and the hack and thrust of his broad, curved blade was swift and deadly. And the edge of his weapon was smeared with a black substance, but whether it was poison, Tuck could not say.

Clang! Chank! cried the tortured steel, as blade met blade, and the Dwarf was pressed back, and Tuck readied his bow. But then with a hoarse shout, the Dwarf vented the ancient battle cry of his Folk, *"Châkka shok! Châkka cor!"* (Dwarven axes! Dwarven might!) and attacked in fury. The Hlōk desperately hacked downward—a mighty blow—but the curved blade chopped into the soft brass strip embedded the length of the axe helve, inlaid there for just that purpose. Swiftly, the Dwarf whipped the helve left, thrusting the edge-caught scimitar aside, then jabbed forward the steel axe-beak, taking the Hlōk in the chest, the iron fang bursting through the Hlōk's scale mail and spearing into his heart. And ere the dead Hlōk could fall unto the ground, the Dwarf whipped the axe back and swung a chopping blow, the bit cleaving through the Hlōk's temple, and bile filled Tuck's throat to see it.

And as the foe fell dead to the snow, the Dwarf stepped back and raised his axe and cried: *"Châkka shok! Châkka cor!"*

Sheathing his sword, Galen dismounted, and so did Gildor, and with Tuck they strode unto the Dwarf, the sole survivor of the nearly two hundred forty combatants slain there that 'Darkday. And he stood among the dead—*as if he owns this bloody battleground,* thought Tuck—and warily watched as the trio came nigh, his gore-splashed axe gripped in gnarled hands.

Dwarf he was, dressed in earth-colored quilted mountain

gear; linked rings of black-iron chain mail could be seen under his open jacket. He stood perhaps four and a half feet tall, and brown locks fell to his shoulders from his plain steel helm. His eyes were deep brown, nearly black, and a forked beard reached to his chest. His shoulders were half again as wide as a Man's.

"That's close enough," he growled, wary of the strangers, raising his axe to the ready, "close enough till I know more of you. I was here first, yet still will I give you my name: I am Brega, Bekki's son. What be you hight?"

It was Lord Gildor who answered: "The Waerling is Sir Tuckerby Underbank from the Land of the Thorns, from the Boskydels." Tuck bowed to the Dwarf and received a stiff bow in return, yet wonder shone in Brega's eye.

"I am Gildor, Lian Guardian, seed of Talarin and son of Rael, of old from Darda Galion but now of Arden." Gildor bowed, and Brega returned the courtesy, his axe now resting with its beak down to the ancient pave.

"And this is Galen King, son of slain Aurion King, now High Ruler of all Mithgar."

Brega's face blenched to hear this news. "Aurion Redeye is dead?" he blurted, and at Gildor's nod: "What ill news you bear." And then Brega made a sweeping bow to Galen.

"King Galen," said the Dwarf, "it was in answer to the summons from your sire that I and the comrades I captain marched north." Brega swept his hand in a wide gesture over the battlefield, and then seemed to realize for the first time that he stood alone. Shock registered upon his features, and without another word he stepped to a cloak lying in the snow and fixed it around his shoulders and cast the hood over his head, in deep mourning.

"Galen King," said Tuck, pointing northwestward along the Old Rell Way, "the Horde: they heave into my view."

Back along the abandoned road the dark Spawn boiled southerly, swarming toward the four.

"Horde?" barked Brega, his face enshadowed within his hood.

"Aye," said Galen, "south they come, a dark tide bound toward the Quadran, but whither they go, we cannot say. This band your warriors slew was perhaps the vanguard of the Horde that comes behind."

"How know you this?" Brega's voice was harsh as he

peered to the northwest. "I can see no Foul Folk, no Grg, through this cursed blackness."

"The Waerling sees them," said Gildor, "for his jewel-hued eyes pierce further through this myrk than those of other Folk."

Brega stepped close to Tuck and looked into the Warrow's wide, tilted, sapphirine gaze. "Utruni eyes," grunted the Dwarf. "I believe you now, Waeran."

"Then let us mount up and get south," urged Tuck, glancing north.

South came the Horde.

"But my dead kindred," protested Brega. "Are we to leave them lying here upon the open battlefield? Stone or fire, that is the way of the Châkka. If they are not laid to rest in stone, or burned on a fitting pyre, their shades will wander an extra age before a rebirthing can occur."

"We have not the time for a proper burial, Warrior Brega," said Tuck, "for the press of Modru's Spawn will not permit it."

"Aye, you are right, Waeran. It is not the time for mourning or burial." Brega cast back his hood, and retrieved a pack from the snow and shouldered it. Then he looked over the field of carnage. "They were fine comrades, the forty Châkka I strode beside, and mighty were their axes."

"Forty?" Galen's voice was filled with amazement. "Do you say that but forty Dwarven warriors slew all of these foe? There must be two hundred *Spaunen* here. Hai! mighty *were* their axes."

Still the Horde marched onward, drawing closer.

Galen mounted Jet and drew Tuck up before him. Gildor, too, vaulted to the back of Fleetfoot, and held a hand out to Brega: "Mount up behind, Warrior Brega."

Brega looked up at Fleetfoot looming above him, and the Dwarf's face blenched. Quickly he backed away, holding his hands before him, palms out. "No, Gildor Elf, I shall ride a pony, and not upon the back of such a great beast."

Exasperation filled Gildor's voice: "Drimm Brega, you have no choice!" Gildor's gesture swept the field. "All of the ponies are slain or have fled. You must mount my horse. It is not as if you will be commanding Fleetfoot, for

I will do that deed. You will sit behind, nothing more, while we fare south."

"But I do have a choice." Brega's voice flared with ire at Gildor's tone, and his eyes smoldered. "I can stand here athwart the road and meet with the Horde. My axe will drink more blood of the Squam ere this 'Darkday is done." Brega unshouldered his weapon and turned to face the north.

Southward swarmed the Horde, their hard stride bearing them toward the four.

"Up behind me, you stubborn fool!" commanded Gildor. "The *Spaunen* have hove into *my* sight now, and we have not the time nor patience to argue with a stiff-necked, horse-fearing Drimm!"

With a snarl, Brega spun around to face Gildor and hefted his axe.

"Wait!" cried Tuck, "let us not fight amongst ourselves. We are allies! Warrior Brega, the maggot-folk will just slay you from afar by black-shafted arrow, and you will have died for nought. Come with us and you will be able to avenge your brethren, as I will be able to avenge mine."

Brega lowered his axe.

Then Galen spoke: "Warrior Brega, I need your strength and skill by my side. Our journey south is fraught with peril and I must reach the Host. With you in our company our chances improve. I ask you in the name of all Mithgar to join us."

The Dwarf looked at the High King, and then to Tuck, and his eyes strayed to his slain kindred. To the shadowed north he looked, where beyond his sight the Horde boiled southward. Last of all he looked at Gildor's outstretched hand, and with a growl Brega slung his axe down his back by its carrying thong and reached up to grasp the Elf's grip, stepping into the stirrup and swinging up onto Fleetfoot's back behind Lord Gildor. And Tuck's sharp ears heard the Dwarf exclaim, *"Durek, varak an!"* (Durek, forgive me!)

And as they spurred forward through the Shadowlight, Tuck looked back at the Horde and gasped, for they were but a league distant, and the Vulgs that loped before them had drawn even closer.

Southeasterly along the Old Rell Way ran Jet, with Fleetfoot alongside, the packhorse in tow. Swiftly, ·the gap between horses and Horde widened, and soon Tuck could no longer see them. Galen dropped back the pace, and they went single file once more.

"Fear not, Tuck," said Galen in a low voice, "they saw us not, for I did not see them. And though I did not say this before Brega, when the *Spaunen* come to the scene of the battle, they will stop to loot and mutilate and search for survivors, and perhaps make camp. And now our south-ward track mingles with that made by the Dwarves going north, and so the Vulgs will not single out our passage, confusing our spoor with that of Brega's force.

"We shall ride another ten miles or so and then make our camp. The Swarm will not come that far, for we have covered more than thirty miles to here, and since we did not see sign of where last the Horde camped, it must have been back beyond the gap. Even Rukha and Lōkha will not march forty miles a leg.

"No, I think that they will camp back at the slaugh-terground and squabble over the loot of the slain." Galen fell silent, and the horses cantered on.

The four made camp in a barren thicket well up and off the road. And as they took travelers' rations, Brega told his tale, and Galen's face became grim, for the news from Pellar was dire:

"There's War, bloody War to the south. The Rovers of Kistan, the Lakh from Hyree, through Vancha and Tugal they came marching, across Hoven and Jugo, and over the Avagon Sea in ships.

"Pellar was unprepared, and was struck to the knees, nearly a killing blow. But Valon rallied, and the outlying muster sounded. Even now the struggle goes on.

"Word was sent north to High King Aurion, yet no mes-sages returned. Then we learned that the Hyranee held Gûnarring Gap and the heralds had been felled.

"Word came, too, from far Riamon that a fearful dark-ness had fallen upon the Grimwall and now swept south.

"At last a rider from Challerain Keep won through. How? I cannot say, but he bore word of Modru's Horde in the north.

"We could send but a token of the Red Hills Châkka to aid at the north Keep, for the rest stood against the Jihad.

"I was chosen to captain the forty, and by pony we marched north. Up through Valon we went, staying east of the Gûnarring Gap, for it was and perhaps still is held by the foe. North we went instead, some fifty miles up from the Gap, for there lies an ancient secret way across the Gûnarring, known to Châkka as the Walkover.

"By this route we came, crossing into Gûnar, and then north again. Up through Gûnar Slot we went, and when we came to the River Hâth, there we found this foul darkness. Agog we were, but through the blinding snow we pressed, across Hâth Ford and into the Dimmendark beyond: and it was like walking into a deep phosphor cave, this Shadowlight.

"Through the Winternight we marched, along the west flank of the Grimwall: we were making for Rhone Ford, the Stone-arches Bridge, and finally for the Signal Mountains and Challerain Keep at their end.

"A long trip would it have been, for we had already been on the march nearly thirty days and expected to tramp twenty more; but the vanguard of the Horde fell upon us. All were slain but me." Brega fell silent and once more cast his hood over his head.

"Ai, this is foul news indeed," said Gildor, "but it explains much: why our messages did not get through and why no word came from the south, for Gûnarring Gap is held by the foe. It also explains why the Host has not come north, for it wars against the enemy from the south."

"The War, Brega, what news?" asked Galen, his voice grim, his eyes cold.

"Sire, I know not how it fares now," replied Brega, "for a month has fled since last I knew. Pellar reeled under the onslaught, but the horsemen from Valon came and drove them back a ways. The battles seesawed like a teeter-totter, but more enemy came in ships. At the time I marched north, the scales seemed tipped against us, and our prospects seemed dire."

No one spoke for a moment, then Tuck called down from atop the rock where he sat watch: "You used a word I do not know, Brega: 'Jihad.' What is a Jihad?"

"It is a great Jihad they fight," answered Brega. "A Holy War. *They are convinced that Gyphon will return and cast Adon down.*"

Gildor's face turned ashen. "How can it be?" he gasped. "The Great Evil is banished beyond the Spheres. He cannot return."

Brega merely shrugged his shoulders.

" 'How can it be?' you ask," said Galen, his voice bitter. "Lord Gildor, I shall answer your question with one of my own." He gestured at the Dimmendark. "How can *this* be, I ask, that Adon's Covenant is broken by the Winternight? What dark force, what eater of light, rules the Sun such that it cannot pierce this shadowy clutch? And if this can be—that Adon's Covenant is broken after four thousand years—then perhaps Gyphon can indeed return."

"Ai," cried Gildor, "if that could happen, then the world would be cast down into a pit so cruel that Hèl itself would appear as a paradise in its stead."

No word was said by any for a long while, and dread pounded through Tuck's veins, for although Tuck knew little of Gyphon, the effect upon Gildor had driven terror like a cruel spike into the Warrow's heart.

At last Galen spoke: "We must get some rest, for tomorrow we ride to the foot of Quadran Pass, and the next 'Darkday we attempt to cross over."

"I'll watch," said Tuck from his perch, "for the Horde is behind us and my eyes are needed now. Besides, I don't think I can sleep."

"Nay, Waerling," countered Gildor. "You are weary, I can see it, and during these next few 'Darkdays your vision will be most critical. You rest and I will watch, for my eyes, though not equal to yours in this myrk, are more than a match for the *Rûpt*. And the sleep of Elves is different from that of mortals, for I can rest and watch at one and the same time, though not forever—even Elves need sound sleep on occasion—yet many days can I keep the vigil ere that comes to pass."

And so all bedded down but Gildor, and he sat upon the high stone and kept the watch, resting his mind in gentle memories while his eyes warded them all.

But it was a long time ere Tuck fell asleep, for still his heart pounded with apprehension, and his thoughts had returned to that long-past day that Danner had told of Gyphon's downfall, and had spoken the last words the Great Evil had uttered, and the words echoed through Tuck's mind: *"Even now I have set into motion events you cannot stop. I shall return! I shall conquer! I shall rule!"*

When they broke camp, once more Brega seemed reluctant to mount up behind Gildor on Fleetfoot, and Tuck wondered how such a fierce warrior as the Dwarf could be so *daunted* by the thought of riding a horse. Yet Brega gritted his teeth and bestrode the steed.

With a hand up from Galen, Tuck swung onto Jet's withers, and once more they rode southeastward.

Up through the foothills they went, the land rising around them as they made for the Quadran: four great mountains of the Grimwall: Greytower, Loftcrag, Grimspire, and the mightiest of all, Stormhelm. Beneath these four peaks was delved Drimmen-deeve, ancient Dwarven homeland, now abandoned by them and fallen into dread, for therein dwelled a horror: a Gargon: Modru's Dread: an evil Vûlk: servant of Gron in the Great War of the Ban. And as Vanidor's words had suggested to the trio ere they set out from Arden Vale, the Dimmendark may have set this vile monster free from its exile under the Quadran and loosed it to reave within the Shadowlight. A hideous ally to Modru's Horde would it be, for the Gargon is a fear caster: armies would break and run before its dread power, or the soldiers would be paralyzed with terror, frozen like unto stone itself, and easy prey.

And toward the domain of this horror the four rode, for they thought to cross through the Quadran Pass and warn the Lian in Darda Galion of the Horde marching behind them.

Twenty miles south they rode, up through the rising foothills. Then the abandoned road divided: the Old Rell Way continued south along the western flanks of the Grimwall; the other path turned left and east and climbed up into the mountains, for it was the road over the Quadran Pass.

This left-hand way they followed, going some fifteen miles more before making camp. Thirty-five miles they had ridden that leg, and they were weary.

They supped on wayfarer's rations: tea, mian, and chewy cubes of a salted meat said by Brega to come from cod prepared by the fishermen of Leut and brought to Jugo in trading fleets of Arbalin.

"What is it that you do, Waeran?" asked Brega as Tuck sat near the small shielded fire, drinking tea and making notes.

Tuck looked up from his diary. "I scribe the day's events, Brega." The Warrow held up the booklet. "It is my journal."

Brega cocked his head to one side but said nought, so Tuck read his final sentence aloud: "Tomorrow we try Quadran Pass, up the flank of Stormhelm. Perhaps we will cross if it is free of snow or Rūcks or the Dread said to dwell in Drimmen-deeve."

Brega grunted, and stroked his forked beard. "Stormhelm. Drimmen-deeve. Your tongue is a mixture of Man and Elf, but I do not hear words of the Châkka."

"Châkka?" Now Tuck tilted his head, questioning.

"Châkka: the name Dwarves call themselves," said Galen.

"We name them Drimma," came Gildor's voice from his lookout.

"Then Drimmen-deeve means . . ." Tuck groped.

"Dwarven-delvings," supplied Galen.

"Aye," grumbled Brega, "Drimmen-deeve to Elf, Black Hole to Man, but its true name is Kraggen-cor. Yet no matter what it is called, it is the ancient Châkkaholt delved under the Quadran"—Brega shook his head in regret—"though the Châkka no longer dwell there." Now the Dwarf leapt to his feet and paced in agitation, a dark look upon his face, his eyes smoldering in ire. "Four times have we been bested by a foe beyond our limits: twice by Dragons, once by a Ghath—a Gargon—and the other time I shall not speak of. In Kraggen-cor it was the Ghath.

"Glorious were our days spent in that mighty Realm: mining ores, gems, and precious starsilver—what you call silveron. There, too, were our unmatched forges where were crafted tools and weapons and worthy things. And our homes were filled with happiness and industry. But the old tales say a silveron shaft was driven on a course of little promise; why, I do not know. Some say it was Modru's will that set our way, for our digging set free the evil Ghath, Modru's Dread, from a chamber he had been trapped in since the Great War of the Ban."

"The Lost Prison," said Gildor, then fell silent.

"Prison you name it"—Brega looked up at the Elf and smote a clenched fist into an open palm—"and prison it was, until that fatal day the Ghath burst from his lair and through the end of the shaft wall and slew many Châkka.

"In vain we tried to slay it, but it overmastered my Folk, and in the end we fled: out through the Dusken Door and out through the Daūn Gate, west and east of the Grimwall, for the corridors of Kraggen-cor reach from one side of the Mountains to the other."

Brega slumped down upon a log, and his fierce manner evaporated, replaced by a dark, somber mood. "More than one thousand years have passed since last the Châkka dwelt in Kraggen-cor, and still we yearn for its mighty halls. Yet although many have dreamt of living in those chambers, none have gone back but Braggi's squad, for Braggi led a raid to slay the Ghath: the Doomed Raid of Braggi, for none of that band were ever seen again.

"Some say that Kraggen-cor will be ours once more when Deathbreaker Durek is reborn. Then again will we dwell there: under Uchan, Ghatan, Aggarath, and Rávenor—Mountains you name Greytower, Loftcrag, Grimspire, and Stormhelm. And we will make it into a mighty realm as of old. When, I cannot say, for none knows when Khana Durek will return."

Morose, Brega fell silent, and nought was said for long moments while Tuck scribbled in his journal. "Lord Gildor, what names do the Elves give to the Quadran?" Tuck asked.

"In the Sylva tongue they are named Gralon, Chagor, Aevor, and Coron," answered Gildor, naming them in the same order as did Brega.

Again Tuck scribed, then said, "Brega, something puzzles me: When you spoke of the eld days, you said, '*our* forges, *our* homes, *our* digging, *we* fled.' But those days are a thousand years past. Surely *you* were not there."

"Perhaps I was, Waeran. Perhaps I was," answered Brega. The Dwarf fell silent, and just as Tuck thought he would learn no more, Brega spoke on: "Châkka believe that each spirit is reborn many times. And so, every Châk now alive, or those yet to be born, perhaps at one time walked the chambers of mighty Kraggen-cor."

Again long moments passed without speech, then Gildor

broke the silence: "Once in my youth I strode through the halls of Drimmen-deeve, a journey I have long remembered, for the Black Deeves are mighty indeed."

"You have walked in Kgraggen-cor?" Brega was astonished.

Gildor nodded. "It was a trade mission from Lianion to Darda Galion, and the way across the Quadran Pass was blocked by winter snow. Through Drimmen-deeve we were allowed to pass, from Dusk-Door to Dawn-Gate, though we paid a stiff toll to do so, I recall. Yet the toll was less than the cost of faring south through Gûnar and north again through Valon. That was in the days when there was much trade between Trellinath, Harth, Gûnar, Lianion, and Drimmen-deeve."

Brega rocked back and looked long up at Gildor. "Lord Gildor," said the Dwarf at last, "if this Winter War ever comes to an end, you and I must have a long talk. Priceless knowledge of Kraggen-cor has been lost to my people, and you can tell us much."

Little else was said ere they bedded down while Gildor once more kept the watch. But though he was weary, Tuck found it difficult to fall asleep, for names whirled through his mind: *Kraggen-cor, Drimmen-deeve, Black Hole; Châkka, Drimma, Dwarves; Gargon, Modru's Dread, Lost Prison; Dusk-Door, Dawn-Gate, Grimwall; Quadran, Quadran Pass* . . .

It was this last name, Quadran Pass, that surfaced in Tuck's thoughts over and again, for none of the four comrades knew whether Rūcks or snow or the Gargon barred the way, or if they could get through. But on the morrow they would attempt to cross it, and Tuck fell asleep wondering what the morrow would bring.

As they broke camp, Galen set out their strategy: "Tuck, you will ride behind me, for the way before us is narrow and twisting, and so my eyes will serve during most of this passage, though where needed you will peer around me. We shall go first, Gildor with Brega to follow, leading the packhorse. Keep sword, axe, and arrow to hand.

"Should we come to snow blocking the way, we must turn and swiftly come back down, for a Horde force-marches behind us, and we must not become entrapped upon this mountain flank.

"Yet should the way be held by the Yrm, then we will try to slay them—if their force is small. In that case, Tuck, your bow may become all-important in striking down a sentry in silence and from a distance.

"If a larger force holds the way, we may try to burst through and flee down the far side. Yet, too, we may simply turn back without alerting them and come this way once more, again at haste to elude the Horde now at our heels.

"Should the Dread hold the way, we will know it by the terror in our hearts, and turn back ere we come unto him, for he is a foe we cannot face.

"And if we do not cross, then we will make south for Gûnar Slot and hope it is free of the enemy, as it was when Brega came north.

"But if neither snow nor Spawn nor the Gargon block the Quadran Pass, then we will make our way down the Quadran Run to the Pitch below, then east turning south for Darda Galion to warn them of the coming Horde.

"Is there aught that any would add to the plan?" Galen peered into the face of each.

How like his sire is Galen, thought Tuck, his mind returning to the War-council at Challerain Keep.

Brega spoke: "It will be a cold crossing, for not only is it winter, but this evil Winternight clutches the heights above. Were this the Crestan Pass, I think we would not survive; but it is the Quadran Pass, and it does not reach to the same heights. Yet we must be swift, else we'll not move again until a spring thaw." Brega turned and in vain his sight tried to pierce the Dimmendark to see the way upward. "It may be many a year ere a spring comes again unto this Land, for Modru intends to grasp it forever."

"Not if I can help it, Dwarf Brega," said Galen, his grey eyes resolute. "If it be in my power, these mountains shall once more feel the warm kiss of the Sun."

Gildor mounted Fleetfoot with Brega after, and Tuck swung up behind Galen. But just ere they spurred forward, Brega called, "King Galen, I have this moment remembered an eld Châkka tale: there is the story of a secret High Gate somewhere upon Rávenor's flank, a gate that opens into Quadran Pass, a gate that leads down into the halls of Kraggencor. It may be a fable, it may be true; but if this legend is so, and if the Ghath or Squam hold it, then they may issue

out of it to assail us. Fact or fiction, I know nought else of
this High Gate."

Galen paused and then said, "High Gate or no, still we
must try," and spurred forward.

Up the slope of Quadran Road they pressed, Jet first,
with Fleetfoot and the packhorse following. A league they
went, and beyond, the way rising before them, and now
Tuck's eyes could see mighty mountain flanks soaring upward into the Dimmendark. To his left was Stormhelm and
to the right Grimspire, two of the four peaks of the Quadran. The Road itself was carven along Stormhelm's flank,
and buttresses and groins of rust-red granite vaulted in
massive tiers up Stormhelm's side, or fell away sheer, dropping down to meet the looming ramparts of dark Grimspire. Sheets of ice glazed the lofty pinnacles, and the
Shadowlight glow glittered in the hoarfrost, giving the tall
rocks a phosphorescent luminance. And up the twisting
walls of the Quadran Road shuddered the echoes of knelling hooves as Man, Dwarf, Elf, and Warrow rode up
through the Winternight.

Through defiles they rode, and upon ridges where crests
had been carven flat and the shoulders of the road pitched
steeply down to either side. Yet always upward the comrades went. In places they dismounted and led the horses
to give them respite from bearing riders, but they walked
a quickstep, for time was not their ally.

Miles passed—ten, fifteen, and more—and with each mile
the air grew thinner and colder, and hoods were drawn
over heads and cloaks were wrapped tightly around.

At last the path started down: Tuck could see it falling
below them, down Stormhelm's eastern flank.

"Sire, the twisting way before us drops," said Tuck in
jubilance. "I do believe that we have crested the brow of
Quadran Pass."

Galen's voice came muffled by his cloak: "No guards as
yet. But stranger still, no great depth of winter snow, only
this shallow fall, and that hardly on the road."

Down they rode, with Tuck in deep thought. At last he
spoke: "They say Modru is the Master of the Cold. Perhaps
it is he who has kept the deep snow from these ways.
But why?"

"You have it!" exclaimed Galen. "Without snow, his

Horde can cross this gap to fall upon the Larkenwald. Now more than ever we must warn the Lian."

On they rode, descending along Quadran Run, as the eastern way was called. Beside the road fell a stream—also named the Quadran Run—now frozen in Winternight's icy clutch. They passed along ridges and through defiles and around tall spires as they descended, heading for the unseen Pitch below, a sloping valley hemmed by the four mountains of the Quadran.

Tuck leaned out to see the way, but for the most part stone walls and tall rocks blocked the view. Yet at times he could glimpse through the juts and spires to see the Run below.

It was at one of these places: "Hold, Sire!" Tuck urgently whispered, and slipped off the back of Jet. The Warrow ran to a slot between two tall rocks and peered intently downward. Galen dismounted and came after.

"Ghûls," said Tuck, his voice bitter. "Twenty or thirty. Perhaps three miles downslope. They come this way riding Hèlsteeds."

"*Rach!*" swore Galen. "See you any place to hide?"

"Nay, Sire," Tuck answered after but a moment. "The way ahead is open ridge."

Galen's voice shook with frustration. "Then we must turn back ere they see us."

"But we've come such a long way!" cried Tuck.

"We have no choice!" spat Galen, then more gently: "Ah, Tuck, we have no choice."

Galen turned to Gildor and Brega astride standing Fleetfoot. "We must turn back: Ghola come this way."

Ire flashed in Brega's eye, and he unslung his axe and raised it on high. "Have we come all this way just to suffer the thwart of Modru's lackeys?"

"How many, Galen King?" asked Gildor.

"A score or more, says Tuck," answered Galen, remounting Jet and hoisting the Warrow up after.

Gildor turned to the Dwarf, saying, "Sling thy axe, Drimm Brega, for even thy vaunted prowess is overmatched by twenty of the corpse-folk."

Brega ground his teeth in rage, yet slung his axe as they started back the way they had come.

As they rode swiftly back up the Run, Tuck asked above

the clack of hooves, "Sire, the Ghûls, why come they this way? Where have they been?"

"I know not," answered Galen over his shoulder. "Mayhap they are an advance party that came from the Horde down the far slope, and they return from the margins of the Larkenwald—returning to the Swarm to report what their foray has revealed."

The Horde! Tuck's heart pounded. *I had forgotten! And now we ride toward them!*

Back to the crest of the Pass they ran along the twisting Quadran Run, and they started down the western way, the way they had just toiled up. Tuck's eyes searched ever downward for sign of the Horde, glimpsing the way below as it shuttered by through slots among the rocks, at times getting long looks when they crossed open ridges. Always, too, he scanned for places to slip aside, to hide and let the Ghûls pass; yet there were no crevices nor canyons into which they could ride: the Quadran Road twisted down the flank of Stormhelm with no places to step from its stricture.

Down through the steep-walled defiles they went apace, coming ever lower on the margins of the mountain. Three hours they had ridden, and now the road began to level out as they came toward the flats.

"Sire, the Horde! I see it!" cried Tuck.

Boiling up through the foothills came the dark Swarm, and before it loped black Vulgs. Tuck threw a glance back the way they had come. Just at the limit of his jewel-hued vision along an open ridge rode the Ghûls. *Trapped!* Tuck's mind shouted. *A Swarm before us and Ghûls behind us!*

"When can we leave this road?" Galen's voice cut through Tuck's dismay.

"Wha—what?" Tuck found his tongue.

"When can we leave this road?" Galen repeated, his voice crackling with tension.

Tuck's eyes swept along the way ahead. "A mile or so!" he cried, his heart leaping with hope. "We can leave the way to the left, just where a ridge comes to a defile. We can ride up onto a plateau above. There is no path, yet we can escape the road!"

"I see it," declared Galen, urging Jet to greater speed. The black steed leapt forward and Fleetfoot sprang after, with the packhorse running behind.

Down the way they ran. Before them came the Rûcken Horde; behind them rode the Ghûls. Swiftly the comrades galloped out upon the ridge, thundering across, then bore up and left, off the road, up onto the plateau.

Galen immediately reined to a halt, throwing up a hand, stopping Lord Gildor. "Brega! Your axe!" Galen barked. "Cut bracken! Sweep our tracks from the snow!"

Brega leapt down and cut a winter-dried bush with his axe and ran back down to the rocky road. With great sweeping arcs, he obliterated their tracks, backing as he went. A hundred feet or more he came, nearing the horses, and at Galen's terse call, he dropped the bush and re-mounted Fleetfoot, and the horses leapt forth. South they bolted, away from the Quadran Road, through a blasted land, rough and boulder-strewn. And as they raced, Tuck looked back over his shoulder to see the Ghûls on Hèlsteeds cantering down one of the ridges toward the Horde force-marching upward.

When they had run two miles from the Quadran Road, Galen reined Jet to a walk, and Gildor slowed Fleetfoot and the packhorse, too, the lathered steeds blowing white from their nostrils, their lungs pumping.

"Ai, but that was close," called Gildor, whose eyes had also seen.

"We've slipped their trap," gloated Brega. But then his voice caught in his throat, and he stabbed a finger forward and rage flashed over his face. *"Kruk!"*

Tuck's head snapped 'round in the direction Brega pointed, and there in the Shadowlight padding out from behind a huge dark boulder trotted a black Vulg, one of the scouts of the Horde. The horses snorted and shied, the pack animal rearing in panic, trying to break free, but Brega held firm to the lead line. The dark Vulg's baleful yellow eyes glared at the four, and writhing jaws snarled. Then this evil outrunner raised his slavering muzzle to the Winternight sky and loosed a yawling cry. Again the black brute voiced a wrawl to the Swarm, a cry answered in kind by bone-chilling howls from other Vulgs, and Ghûls, too.

Tuck leapt down from skitting Jet and set an arrow to his bow and let fly as the Vulg gave vent to another ululating yowl, a cry that was chopped off in mid-howl as the true-sped arrow struck the black beast in the throat and it fell dead. Tuck spun to see Ghûls on Hèlsteeds burst over the ridge and up onto the plateau, snow flying from cloven hooves as they came in answer to the howling summons. Hurtling alongside raced black Vulgs, muzzles to the ground.

Tuck leapt to Jet's flank. "Quick, Sire, they come now on our track: Ghûls and Vulgs. They know we are here."

Galen hauled the Warrow up and spurred Jet forward, with Fleetfoot and the packhorse galloping after. And Tuck despaired, for he knew not how far they could fly, for the hard-running horses already were weary.

South they fled, across a snow-covered, broken land, south along a plateau caught between the looming flank of dark Grimspire to the east and a small mountain to the west: Redguard. And running on their trail behind came Ghûls on Hèlsteeds, and Vulgs with their snouts to the track.

Southward hammered the great black Jet with Fleetfoot's white stockings flashing after. Last of all scaddled the packhorse in tow, fleeing in panic from the chill Vulg howls. How long they had run, Tuck did not know, but slowly they gained ground on their pursuers, twisting through great rocks and spires, running across long, flat stretches.

Five or six miles they galloped, and gradually drew away. But then Tuck's heart plunged in despair, for Galen harshly reined Jet to a skidding halt on the brink of a great cliff falling sheer before them.

"Tuck!" barked Galen as Fleetfoot thundered up. "Use your eyes! Look for a way down!"

Tuck leapt to the snow and flung himself belly-down on the verge of the bluff, looking over the edge and down. He scanned left then right. *There! Just to the right and running past below!* "Sire! A long sloping path down the plumb face! Fifty paces westward!" Tuck started to stand, then groaned as he leapt to his feet. "Sire, ahead two miles or three, I think I see the brink of another drop like this one."

"Mount up, Tuck. We have no choice." Galen extended his hand, hauling Tuck up behind. "We'll plunge down that one when we get there, not before."

They spurred to the sloping path and turned and started down, and as they went below the level of the rim, Tuck's last sight of the upper plateau showed running Vulgs and Hèlsteeds.

The way down before them was narrow and icy, with sheer, frost-clad stone looming on the left and open space plunging perpendicularly to the right. Slowly, Jet picked his way down the treacherous course, and Tuck could hear Fleetfoot and the packhorse stepping behind. Tuck glanced down the fall but once, then kept his eyes firmly fixed upon Galen's back. The Warrow could feel Jet's hooves slip along the ice, and each time the steed lurched, so did Tuck's heart, pounding in fear. The descent seemed to drag on without end as slowly they crept downward. And above, back upon the plateau, loping Vulgs and Ghûls on Hèlsteeds came.

At last Jet reached the bottom of the cliff, coming out upon another plateau, with the other horses right behind, and once more they ran to the south. And as they hammered away, Tuck flung a glance back to see the great stone massif jutting upward; nearby, a great black vertical crack was riven in its face, and west of the cleft, silhouetted against the spectral Shadowlight sky, came Modru's creatures. And when the Ghûls saw the horses fleeing southward below, they set up a wild howling, for now they knew they pursued but four riders. One Ghûls howl rose above the others, and they turned and made for the icy path, to work their way down after the quarry.

Swiftly south the four rode, the gap widening between hunters and hunted, for the Ghûls were slowed by the descent. Two miles south the horses ran, to come to another sheer drop. This time there was no sloping path.

"Sire! East! There seems to be a canyon that I can see coming out through the face below." Tuck leapt to his feet. "Perhaps it is a way down." Once more Galen pulled him back upon Jet.

East they ran, to come to a canyon at their feet so narrow that Tuck thought a horse could perhaps leap its width. They could not see its bottom, but it did breach the face of the massif that thwarted them.

Back to the north they ran, back toward the Ghûls, the horses racing along the rim of the cleft, seeking to find its entrance.

At last they came to where the narrow split emerged upon the plateau. A path led into the dark cranny.

"In we go!" cried Galen. "Else we are trapped along the rim wall."

"Hold!" Brega called. "I have a lantern. Follow us. I will light the way."

Tuck could see that the Ghûls had just reached the base of the distant cliff, and Vulgs loped across the flats.

Brega fumbled in his pack and drew forth a crystal-and-brass lantern, throwing the shutter wide; and without a flame being kindled at all, a blue-green phosphorescent light leapt forth. "Go!" Brega barked at Gildor, and Fleet-foot sprang forward into the dark slot, with Jet following the packhorse.

Down a narrow, twisting corridor they went, Brega's high-held lantern casting swaying, pendulous shadows among the rocks and boulders, and blue-green light glinted and bounced amid the great icicles hanging down from the ragged, shadowed stone overhead. The sound of blowing horses and the clatter of hooves reverberated along the broken walls and echoed back from dark holes boring away, their ends beyond seeing.

Tuck felt the black walls looming above him, and it seemed as if he could nearly reach out and touch the sides, spanning the width. He looked upward, and high above was a swatch of dim Shadowlight, jagging in a thin line, marking the rim of the narrow crevice they followed.

Downward they went, ever deeper, twisting along a tortuous path, at times scraping against the ice-clad rock, Gildor leading, Galen following, Brega's lantern showing the way.

At last Tuck's eyes saw a great vertical cleft filled with spectral Winternight glow, and he breathed a sigh of relief, for they had come to the end.

Out of the crack they rode, out into a broken hill country. "South we go, bearing west," called Galen as Brega shuttered the lantern and returned it to his pack. "We strike for the Old Rell Way. And if ever we elude the curs at our heels, we'll make for Gûnar Slot."

And on they ran, black Vulgs following the scent, Ghûls on Hèlsteeds after.

Fifteen more miles they went, south verging west, and the mounts were near to spent, for each was bearing double and the chase was long, with little or no respite. And behind them the hills blocked Tuck's view, and he could no longer see the pursuers; hence, he did not know the length of their lead.

"Galen King," called Gildor, "Fleetfoot begins to falter. We must do something to throw the Ghûlka off our track."

Galen signed that he had heard but did not otherwise reply, riding onward instead.

At last they came out of the hills to see the Old Rell Way before them, and they rode along its abandoned bed, finally coming to a fork: to the left was a cloven vale; to the right the road bore on southward. Here Galen reined Jet to a halt, and Gildor stopped Fleetfoot and the pack-horse, and the steeds stood lathered and trembling.

"Tuck, Lord Gildor, retrieve your knapsacks from the packhorse," said Galen. "Fill them with provisions. Get grain sacks, too, for Jet and Fleetfoot.

"Brega, again use your axe to chop brush: three large bushes. I have one way we may escape."

While Brega cut the winter-dried brushwood, Galen, Gildor, and Tuck took provisions from the packhorse. Then, while Brega filled his own knapsack, Galen tied the brush close behind the two riding mounts by loops of rope, each horse with a large bush set to drag close upon its heels.

To the packhorse, though, he broke off and fastened a brushy limb above the pack cradle. Then, temporarily shedding his outerwear, he removed his sweat-soaked jerkin and tied it to a long rope so that it would trail along in the snow behind the animal.

"Lord Gildor, take up Jet's reins as well as Fleetfoot's," said Galen. "Hold them firmly; keep them calm. Here I turn the packhorse eastward into the valley. Brega, grasp his reins now. Tuck, your flint and steel: set some touch-wood glowing. I am going to set this brushwood on his back afire."

"But, Sire," protested Tuck, "he will burn."

"Nay, Tuck, the cradle will protect him, though he will not think so," answered Galen. "He will bolt east into the vale, spreading my scent after, while we fare south, the brush we drag behind obscuring our tracks. Let us hope the Vulgs are fooled."

Tuck struck steel to flint, setting touchwood glowing,

thinking, *Poor beast; yet we have little choice, and perhaps he, too, will escape the Vulgs in the end.* The Warrow handed the small tin of glowing shavings to Galen, who held it to the brush and blew it aflame. As the tinder-dry branch burst into flame, Jet and Fleetfoot pulled back, but Gildor held them firmly by the bit-straps. The packhorse, too, plunged and reared, and as the flame roared up, Brega loosed the reins and stepped aside as Galen cried, "Hai!" and slapped the horse on the rump.

Screaming in fear, the animal fled in panic, running full tilt to escape the flame riding the cradle on its back, and trailing in the snow behind was Galen's sweat-soaked jerkin. *But the horse wheeled and bolted south instead of running east!*

"*Rach!*" spat Galen.

"Sire, he drags your scent along our course!" cried Tuck, dismayed.

"Stupid horse," growled Brega. "Now it is *we* who are left with the eastern way. Let us ride into the valley and hide until the danger is past."

At the mention of danger, Tuck turned his sapphirine gaze back toward the foothills. "We must go quickly," he said bitterly, "for again I can see the foe coming along our track."

East they bore, into the valley, the brush dragging in the snow behind, obscuring their tracks. The slopes of the vale rose up around them, looming higher the farther east they went, till they rode in a deep-riven valley far below a distant rim. The floor of the vale curved this way and that, and the road they followed ran along the edge of a winding ravine, shallow and rocky and without water or ice, though a dusting of snow covered the dry streambed.

As they rode, Tuck saw Galen glance at the gentle slopes rising to either side, where the vale canted up finally to meet a wall that loomed sheer. Suddenly, Galen smote his forehead with a palm.

"Sire?" called the Warrow above the weary beat of hooves.

"Tuck, don't you see?" called Galen back. "We are trapped. We should have ridden west out onto the open land and not east into this sheer-walled cleft, for here we cannot get out. And now it is too late to turn back. The packhorse should have bolted this way and not us, and I was distracted when he ran south, a lapse that may cost us our lives." Galen's voice was bitter.

"But, Sire, they will follow the scent of your shirt and not our scrubbed track," responded Tuck, though a shiver ran through him.

"Let us hope, Tuck," answered Galen. "Let us hope."

Tuck looked back along the twisting way, but he could no longer see the entrance to the valley, and he desperately hoped that their trick had deceived the Vulgs and Ghûls, and prayed that their wake was clear of those evil creatures.

On they rode eastward without speaking, and the only sounds made were the ragged thud of overweary hooves, the labored gasps of pumping lungs, and the scraggle of brush hauled behind.

How long they had fled, Tuck was not certain, yet both Jet and Fleetfoot had borne double to the limits of their endurance, and they were near to foundering.

Galen reined to a halt and dismounted, signing for Tuck to do the same. As the Warrow dropped to the snow, Fleetfoot stumbled to a halt behind, and Gildor and Brega leapt down, too.

Galen began walking east leading Jet, the horse trembling with each step, his breathing tortured, his flanks foamed with lather, and Tuck could have cried over the steed's agony. The Warrow looked back at Fleetfoot following, and Gildor's horse, too, had been ridden to his uttermost limits.

Of their pursuers Tuck could see nought, but the way behind curved beyond seeing, and whether the Ghûls followed false trail or true, he could not say.

Galen looked at the valley around him, a puzzled frown upon his features. "Tuck, there is something strangely familiar about this vale: the road, the ravine to our right, the sheer rim. It is as if I should know it, though I have never been here, but from childhood a haunting memory gnaws, though I know not what it is."

They rounded a curve and stopped, for less than a mile before them was the head of the vale: a high stone cliff jumped up perpendicular from the valley floor; the spur of road they followed cut upward along the face of the bluff, to disappear over its top. Also carved in the stone of the face was a steep stairway leading up beyond the rim, up a pinnacle standing high above the bluff, up to a sentinel stand atop the spire overlooking the valley. And beyond the rampart and dwarfing it, looming out and arching over, was a great massif of Grimspire Mountain rising up into the Dimmendark.

Gildor and Brega came to their side. Brega spoke, his voice hushed: "It is as we suspected: this is Ragad Vale."

"Ai! Of course!" Galen slapped a palm to his forehead. "The Valley of the Door!"

"Valley of the Door?" Tuck asked. "What door?"

"Dusk-Door," answered Gildor. "The western entrance into Drimmen-deeve. Atop that bluff and carven in the wall of the Great Loom of Aevor stands the Dusk-Door: shut now for nearly five hundred years, though it stood open for five hundred before that, left ajar by the Drimma as they fled from the Dread, loosed at last from the Lost Prison and stalking through their domain."

"I must see it now that I am here," said Brega.

Forward they started, following the abandoned road, and while they went, Brega spoke: "There on that pinnacle is the Sentinel Stand, where Châkka warders of old stood watching o'er the vale. Down the bluff, water once fell in a graceful falls—Sentinel Falls—fed by the Duskrill, the stream said to have carven this very valley.

"This road we follow is the Rell Spur, a tradeway of old, abandoned when the Gargon came to rule Kraggen-cor.

"If the tales be true, the Dusken Door itself stands within a great portico against the Loom, on a marble courtyard surrounded by a moat with drawbridge.

"Long have my eyes wanted to see this Land, yet I had hoped it would be when the Châkka came to make of it a mighty Realm as of old, and not as a fugitive fleeing vile foe."

"The Dusk-Door," said Galen, "it is told in the old tales that it opened by word alone. Is that true?"

"Aye," answered Brega, "if the word be spoken by a Châk whose hand presses upon the Door—at least Châkka lore would have it so."

"The Lian say that the Wizard Grevan helped in its crafting," said Gildor.

"With Gatemaster Valki he made it," said Brega.

"Do you know the lore words that cause it to open?" asked Tuck, his great tilted eyes wide with wonder.

"Aye, they are with me," answered Brega, "for my grandsire was a Gatemaster, and he taught them to me. But I followed the trade of my own sire, Bekki, and chose to be a warrior instead. Yet, even though I know the lore, I would not open that Door for all the starsilver in Kraggen-cor, for behind it dwells the Ghath."

Leading the steeds, they came to where the road turned up the face of the bluff, the way free of snow. They stopped long enough to discard the brush they had dragged behind the horses, for it was no longer needed. The comrades then started upward, both horses quivering at each step with the effort of mounting up the slope.

"The steeds are spent," said Galen, his voice filled with regret. "What evil fortune, for until they have rested long— a week or more—feeding upon grain and pure water to restore their strength, we cannot ride."

"But then, how will we fare south?" asked Tuck.

Brega gave a terse answer: "Walk."

"No, I mean our plans to hie to the Host and lead them against Modru will be delayed greatly," protested Tuck, "just as our plans to warn the Lian in Larkenwald of the marching Horde are dashed. How can we recover from this ill fortune that has befallen us?"

"I know not," said Galen, wear in his manner.

Gildor spoke: "Wee One, our plans to warn Darda Galion and to fare swiftly south may be dashed, as you say, yet though we do not know our course, still we must strive and not abandon hope."

All fell silent as they trudged onward.

Up the slope of the road along the bluff they went, at last topping the rise. Above them, hovering over, was the great natural hemidome of the Loomwall, and within its cavernous embrace lay a long, thin black lakelet, no more than three furlongs across, and, from the north end where they stood, Tuck saw that it ran nearly two and a half miles to the south. The lake was made by a dam of great stones wedged in a wall across the ravine atop the Stair Falls. The Rell Spur they followed disappeared into the ebon waters.

"This black tarn should not be here!" cried Brega.

"It is the Dark Mere," said Gildor, "and the Lian tell that something evil dwells within. What, I cannot say, but stay wide of its shore."

"Ai-oi! Here's a riddle!" exclaimed Galen. "Why is not this lake frozen?"

Tuck realized that Galen had indeed pointed out an enigma: except for a narrow rim of thin ice embracing the shoulders here and there, the black waters of the Dark Mere undulated torpidly, *As if pulsing with evil,* thought Tuck.

"Perhaps it is not frozen because it is sheltered by the Loom," said Brega, eyeing the great vault of stone above.

"Perhaps it is not frozen because Modru does not want it to be," responded Gildor. "Just as the Quadran Pass held no snow, this Dark Mere, too, escapes the clutch of deep Winternight. Mayhap it does not suit Modru's purposes to have it otherwise, and he *is* Master of the Cold."

"What purpose could he have to keep this lakelet free of ice?" growled Brega, but none could give him the answer.

"It is so *black,*" said Tuck.

"Even were there sunlight, it would look so," said Gildor. "Some say it is because it lies under the black granite of the Loomwall above; others say it is because the Dark Mere is evil."

Tuck looked up at the Great Loom arching cavern-like hundreds of feet overhead. Then his eyes roamed the distant shoreline. "So ho! Over there against the Loom I see tall white columns holding up a great roof."

"It is the portico of the Dusk-Door," said Brega, his eyes following Tuck's pointing finger. "Lying before it should be a marble courtyard, bounded by the Dusk-Moat fed by the Duskrill. Yet they are flooded by this Dark Mere. But see, there endures the ancient drawbridge, standing open above where the moat should have been. There, too, is the Rell Spur, where it runs along the base of the Loom. But all else is drowned in blackness." Brega's voice was filled with rage over the desecration of the environs by the Dark Mere.

"Perhaps—" Galen started to say, but his words were interrupted by a long, chilling, Vulg howl echoing up Ragad Vale. Jet and Fleetfoot jerked their weary heads up, and their ears stood listening.

"Vulgs!" cried Brega. "In the Vale!"

Tuck's heart pounded, he spun and looked down the valley, but he could see nought 'round its curves. "The Sentinel Stand!" he cried, and ran for the stone steps some two furlongs to the south.

Huffing with effort, up the steps he scrambled to the top of the spire, and he could see past the curves and down the valley before him: Ghûls with torches rode slowly toward the head of the Vale, searching out the crevices and shadows where fugitives might hide, while Vulgs with their snouts to the snow slow-stepped along the faint scent-trail obscured by the dragged brush.

Back down the steps Tuck scuttled, down to the others, now waiting below. "Ghûls! Vulgs, too! They comb the Vale, seeking where we hide. They are spread wide, blocking the width of the valley."

"Yet we cannot burst past them," gritted Galen, "for Jet and Fleetfoot can bear no more."

"If we can get across the old moat," said Brega, "we can hide on the portico."

"But the drawbridge is up!" cried Tuck. "We cannot float through the air!"

"Do not abandon hope until we look," said Gildor, his voice sharp.

"Aye," added Galen, "cross no bridge until it stands before you; burn no bridge if you would go back."

"Let's go, then," chafed Tuck, "though I fear we will have burned all of our bridges behind us when we come to the one before."

North they ran, drawing the horses behind, around the end of the Mere, crossing through a shallow, muck-bottomed seep. Now the stone of the Loom arched above them, and Tuck felt as if he could almost hear the weight of the rock groaning overhead.

South they turned and swiftly they went alongside the dark granite wall, perhaps a half mile before coming to a sundered causeway where the Rell Spur emerged from the black waters of the Dark Mere. The pave of the Spur was riven with age, and they wended through the upheaved rocks south toward the portico, the Loom to their left and the Mere to their right but a few paces away.

Three furlongs more they pressed, coming at last to a

great drawbridge made of massive wooden timbers. Out upon the span they strode, their steps ringing hollowly, and the waters of the Dark Mere lapped less than a yard below. But they had to stop short, for the bascule was up, and open water undulated before them.

And from Ragad Vale came the howl of a Vulg.

"When the Châkka fled Kraggen-cor, the span was left down," growled Brega. "Now it is up."

Gildor began stripping his outer garments, handing over Bale sword and Bane long-knife to Tuck. "It was raised by *Rûpt*," said the Elf. "If we survive, I will tell you the tale. But now I will swim to the far side and try to lower the bascule."

"But the ropes are made untrustworthy by age," protested Brega.

"I do not see we have a choice," said Gildor, now clothed only in breeks.

Incongruously, Tuck thought, *He goes without armor!* for no mail nor plate had the Elf taken off, not even a steel helm.

"Take care," said Tuck, sensing danger, though he knew not why.

With a flat dive, Gildor plunged into the frigid dark waters. Swiftly he stroked across the gap, no more than twenty yards wide. But as he clambered up a stone pier and onto the far span, a great swirl twisted in the water at his feet, as if something huge had passed near under the black surface, and Tuck gasped in fear; but the waves and ripples quickly died away, and the undulate surface pulsed slowly again.

Gildor grasped hold of the ancient halyards controlling the bascule, and they were stiff with age. Looking up, he shook them, and dust flew from the pulley blocks atop the anchor posts. Then with a grimace of effort, the Elf hauled against the lines. And with the pulleys squealing in protest and the great bridge axle groaning, slowly the bascule began canting down from vertical.

"Once we're across; we'll pull it back up," said Brega. "Then if the foe finds us, still they will not be able to get at us unless they swim." Brega thumbed his axe. "Easy prey."

Slowly, down tilted the protesting span, descending

toward the mooring pier. Halfway it had come, and just as Tuck was beginning to breathe easier, with a dull snap, the ancient rope haul broke. Squealing and groaning, the massive bascule rushed down faster and faster to slam to with a thunderous, juddering *BOOM!* that rolled forth from the hemidome of the Great Loom to reverberate down the length of Ragad Vale:

BOOM! Boom! boom! boom . . . oom . . .

As the dinning echoes crashed along the walls of the valley, Galen shouted, "Swift!" and bolted across the span hauling the frightened horses behind, with Brega and Tuck running after.

And from the Vale came shuddering howls of Vulgs and Ghûls, now in full cry.

Over the downed bascule ran the trio, Brega last, for he had paused to scoop up Gildor's pack and clothing.

"Can the haul be repaired?" Galen's question shot forth, directed at Gildor, but the Elf handed the frayed end of the rope to Brega, taking his clothes in return.

The Dwarf looked at the ancient halyard fiber and then up to the pulley blocks chained to the anchor posts. "Nay, King Galen, not in time."

"Sire!" cried Tuck, pointing.

Along the Rell Spur over the lip of the butte loped black Vulgs, their snouts to the ground. The lead Vulg turned, making for the spire of the Sentinel Stand, following the scent of their prey.

"The Ghûls can't be far behind." Tuck's voice trembled and his heart pounded.

Brega hefted his axe. "Shall we fend the bridge or the portico, King Galen?"

"The portico, I think," said Galen, his voice grim but steady. "They cannot bring the Hèlsteeds to bear down upon us between the great stone columns."

Gildor tugged his last boot on and leapt to his feet fully dressed. Tuck handed over the sword, Bale, but as Gildor buckled on the blade, he said to the Waerling, "Keep Bane as your own weapon, Tuck, for the long-knife will be as a sword to you, and in this fight there will come a time when your arrows will be spent, or the quarters will be too close for bow, and then you will need a blade."

"But I know nothing of swordplay, Lord Gildor," protested Tuck, yet the Elf would hear nought of his argument, and the Waerling girted Bane to his waist and drew the long-knife from its sheath. Blue were-light burst forth from Bane's blade-jewel and ran a bright cobalt flame down the sharp edges.

"Bane's light speaks of evil nearby," said Gildor. "Yet the Vulgs are still distant, and the Ghûlka farther yet, and the blade should not glow with this intensity." Gildor drew Bale, and its red light, too, was flame-bright; and the Elf frowned in concentration: "They both whisper that evil is nearer."

At Gildor's words, Tuck's eye was drawn irresistibly to the black waters of the Dark Mere.

"Ar, we can't stand here all day puzzling over the fine points of Elven blades," growled Brega. "Let us to the portico to make our stand, and though we may not survive, this will be a battle the bards will sing of if word of it comes their way."

Tuck and Gildor sheathed the blades and the four comrades ran to the great portico, drawing the horses behind, following along the Loomwall. Through fluted columns they went, to come upon a great semicircular stone slab held within the half ring of pillars around. Above, a great carven edifice was supported. As they discarded their packs, Tuck looked out upon the dark waters covering the sunken courtyard where stood the clawing hulk of an enormous tree, drowned, dead for ages, yet still anchored upright. Black water lapped at the steps rising up from the unseen flooded court.

"They come," said Gildor softly, pointing back toward the far side of the lake.

Torch-bearing Ghûls on Hèlsteeds burst over the rim of the bluff and cast about, questing for the fugitives. The Vulg pack loped north from the Sentinel Stand, still on the scent. The Ghûlen leader howled at the dark brutes, and growls from the beasts answered him.

Along the north bank of the Dark Mere the Vulgs raced, on the wake of the hunted, and the hammer of cloven Hèlsteed hooves shocked along the Loomwall as the Ghûls plunged after.

Around the north end of the lake they came, and the

four comrades looked on grimly. Brega grasped his double-bitted axe in the Dwarven two-handed battle-grip, and Gildor drew Red Bale, while Galen held Jarriel's gleaming steel in his right hand and in his left the rune-marked silvery Atalar Blade from the tomb of Othran the Seer. Tuck readied his bow and stepped to a pillar, taking a stand where his arrows would fly unhindered.

Now the Ghûls turned southward, riding along the Loom, plunging straight toward the sundered causeway and, beyond, the bridge and portico.

Yet, of a sudden the Ghûlen leader howled and savagely reined his Hèlsteed to a halt, and behind, the other Hèlsteeds were cruelly checked.

"What's this?" growled Brega, stepping forward for a better look.

The Ghûls had ridden to the causeway but no further, and now they milled in seeming confusion, as if unwilling to ride its length to get at the four. Some called glottal commands at the Vulgs, and the black beasts stopped, too, and turned and slunk back to sit on their haunches, tongues lolling over slavering, fanged jaws, but they came no closer. Ghûls dismounted.

"What's this?" growled Brega again. "Can they be afraid of us? We are but four while they are thirty."

The four comrades looked long at the Ghûls and Vulgs, yet no clue came as to what halted their charge.

"I know not why they stopped," said Gildor, "but as long as they stand there athwart our path, we are trapped here."

"No we are not, Lord Gildor," Tuck spoke up. "We can always go through the Dusk-Door."

"The Dusk-Door!" exclaimed Galen. "I had forgotten! Tuck is right! We *can* escape the Ghola!"

"Out of the crucible and into the forge your plan would lead us!" cried Brega. "Do you forget, King Galen, that the Ghath rules Kraggen-cor?"

"Nay, Brega," answered Galen, "I forget it not, but this I propose: We will enter the Dusk-Door and close it behind, and the Ghola will think we seek to make our way under the Grimwall and out the Dawn-Gate. Yet we will wait to see if they leave; if so, then back out we go and south to Gûnarring Gap."

"But what if they don't leave?" blurted Tuck. "Then what?"

"Then we are no worse off than we are now," answered Gildor.

"But, I mean, why can't we do as Galen King has suggested?" asked Tuck. "Why *can't* we go under the Grimwall?"

"You know not what you ask, Wee One," answered Gildor. "Better would it be to face a hundred Ghûlka than but one Gargon. Were it just the *Rûpt* that dwell in Drimmen-deeve that we had to win past, then I would counsel that we try it; but it is their master I would not face. Nay, if we use the Door it will be to deceive the Ghûlka, and not to tread through the Black Deeves."

"Well, then, where *is* the Door anyway?" asked Tuck, his eyes searching the blank stone of the Loom. "Though I cannot see it, it must be here somewhere."

"There," said Brega, pointing, yet still Tuck saw nought but frowning rock. "There where the pave is worn leading up to it," Brega continued. "It is closed and cannot be seen, though when the Châkka abandoned Kraggen-cor, we left it ajar."

"*Spaunen* closed it," said Gildor, "five hundred years after the Drimma fled. But that, too, is a long tale to be told later, for now we are concerned with Galen King's plan."

"I like not this plan," growled Brega, "this game of cat and mouse, for it is one where we chance the Ghath; yet I have none better."

"Are we agreed then?" asked Galen, and at each one's nod: "Then let it be done."

Brega slung his axe across his back by its carrying thong and stepped to the Loom and placed his hands firmly upon the blank stone; and he muttered low, guttural words. And springing forth from where his hands pressed, *as if it grew from the Dwarf's very fingers,* there spread outward upon the dark granite a silver tracery that shone brightly in the shadow. And as it grew it took form. *And suddenly there was the Door!*—its outline shimmering on the smooth stone.

Sensing something amiss, Tuck glanced up at Gildor, and the Lian was pale and trembling. Sweat beaded on his brow. Only Tuck seemed to note it, and he asked the Elf, "What is wrong, Lord Gildor?"

"I know not, Tuck," answered the Lian warrior, "but something terribly evil . . . afar . . ."

Brega stepped back and unslung his axe. "Ready your weapons," Brega said, his voice hoarse, and Gildor and Galen gripped their blades while Tuck hastily shouldered his bow and drew the long-knife. Bale's red light blended with Bane's blue, while Galen held gleaming steel and the blade of Atala.

Brega turned back to the Door and placed a hand within the one glowing rune-circle, and he called out the Wizard word of opening: *"Gaard!"*

The glowing Wizard-metal tracery flared up brightly, and then, *as if being drawn back into Brega's hand,* all the lines, sigils, and glyphs began to retract, fading in sparkles as they withdrew, until once again the dark granite was blank and stern. And Brega stepped back away. And slowly the stone seemed to split in twain as two great doors appeared and silently swung outward to come to rest against the Great Loom. A dark opening yawned before them, and they could see the beginnings of the West Hall receding into darkness; to the right a steep stairwell mounted up into the black shadows.

Tuck's heart was pounding furiously as he stared into the empty silence yawning before them, and his knuckles were white upon blue-flaming Bane's hilt.

And from behind came shattering screams!

The four whirled to see great, slimy tentacles writhing out of the black water, grasping the struggling, screaming horses, drawing them toward the foul waters.

"Kraken!" cried Galen.

"Madûk!" shouted Brega.

"Fleetfoot!" Gildor sprang forward, Bale blazing, but ere he could bring the sword to bear: *"Vanidor!"* he cried, and dropped to his knees as if stunned, his face in his hands, Bale falling from his nerveless fingers, the blade ringing upon the stone. *"Vanidor!"* Again he cried his brother's name in anguish, and a ropy tendril whipped around the stricken Elf and drew him toward the Dark Mere. Galen leapt forward and brought his sword down upon the great arm, but the blade did not cut. Once more Galen hacked down to no avail. Then he chopped the rune-marked Atalar long-knife into the tentacle, and the silvery weapon from Othran's barrow cut a great gash in the Kraken's flesh where the sword blade had been turned back.

Gildor was flung aside unconscious as the wounded tentacle was jerked back into the black waters. The screaming horses, too, were savagely wrenched under the ebon surface, and other arms boiled forth to rage and whip and grasp at the four.

Brega leapt forward to pull stunned Gildor back, while Tuck scooped up the red-blazing Elven blade and darted for the portal.

"The packs!" cried Galen, catching up one and then another while Brega hauled Gildor through the Dusk-Door.

Tuck dashed back, dodging through whipping arms, and grabbed up the other two packs, but he was slapped down by a glancing blow as he tried again for the portal. Scrambling and scuttling, he scurried toward the Door on all fours, packs, bow, Bane, and Bale in his possession. Galen came behind and boosted the Warrow to his feet, and they stumbled forward through the portal and into the West Hall.

The enraged Monster lashed at them, and pounded at the Door with a great stone, and wrenched at the gates. The great dead tree was rent from the Mere and hammered at the portal, its limbs to shatter in the lashing; and deadly, jagged, flying bolts of wood hurtled into the chamber, to scud across the floor or to smash to shivers upon the stone. And great tentacles twined around the pillars and wrenched back and forth.

"The chain! The chain!" cried Brega, leaping to a great iron chain dangling down from the darkness above. "We must close the gates, else they will be rent from their hinges!"

Tuck and Galen leapt forward, and the three hauled upon the great iron links trying to close the Dusk-Door, but the strength of the raging Kraken opposed them and was too much to overcome. And writhing tentacles whipped and groped within the portal to seek them out.

Into this nest of snakes Brega leapt and slapped his hand

against one of the great hinges and cried, *"Gaard!"* leaping back to avoid the Monster's clutch. And slowly, the shuddering doors began to grind shut, responding to the Wizard word, and all the while, the creature hammered at the gates and struggled to rend them open, yet still they slowly groaned toward one another. And as the protesting gates swung to, Brega's last sight through the portal was of the creature wrenching at one of the great columns of the edifice, grinding it away from its base. And then the gates swung to and Brega saw no more.

The Kraken loosed the Door just as it closed—*Boom!*—and the four were shut in the pitch blackness of dark Drimmen-deeve.

"My pack," Brega panted. "Where is my pack?" Tuck heard him fumbling in the darkness. "The lantern. We need light," muttered the Dwarf.

Tuck took his flint and steel from his jerkin and struck a spark. In the flash he saw the other three, frozen by the brief glint.

"Again," said Brega.

Once more Tuck struck steel to flint, and again and again. Each time the spark showed a different frozen scene as Brega made for his knapsack.

The soft blue-green phosphorescent glow bathed the four as Brega unshuttered his lantern. Gildor was now sitting up, his features white and drawn as if he were in pain or grief.

A loud crashing rumble sounded through the Door.

"Wha—?" cried Tuck.

"The edifice," answered Brega. "The Madûk in its fury has torn down the columns. It has collapsed."

Boom! Boom! Boom! A thunderous whelming sounded.

"The Hèlarms hurls stone at the Door in rage now," said Gildor, "for you have thwarted him, cheated him of his victims."

"Brega, can you try to open the doors again?" Galen looked grim. *Boom! Boom!*

"Aye, King Galen, *but why?* There is a mad Monster waiting to crush us on the other side." Brega was dumbfounded by Galen's request. *Boom! Boom! Boom!*

"Because we may be trapped, Brega," answered Galen. "And Modru's Dread dwells in our prison."

Brega's face blenched, and grimly he went to the Door. *Boom! Boom!* Once more he put his hand to one of the strange, massive hinges and muttered words, and after a moment he cried, *"Gaard!"* But nought seemed to happen, though Brega held his hand to the portal and said, "It trembles, but whether from trying to open or from the fearful pounding, I cannot say. The hinges now may be broken or the Door may be blocked, but it opens not." *Boom! Boom! Boom!* Once more Brega placed his hand on the hinge. *"Gaard!"* he barked, revoking the command to open.

"Did I not say, 'I do not like this plan'? And now we are trapped. We cannot get out." Brega's voice was bitter. "We cannot get out." *Boom! Boom!*

"Except perhaps through the Dawn-Gate," Galen said grimly.

"But that is on the other side of the Grimwall!" cried Brega. "And I do not know the way."

"Gildor has strode it," said Tuck.

"That was long ago, and but once," answered Gildor, holding a hand to his chest and breathing slowly. But Tuck could sense that the Elf suffered a distress beyond that of punished ribs, and the Warrow wondered at Gildor crying out his twin brother's name, *"Vanidor!"*

Boom!

"Yet we have no other choice," said Galen. "We now must try to pierce the length of the Black Hole and escape through the Dawn-Gate, for the Dusk-Door is closed to us. And we must be out and away ere the Ghola can ride over the Quadran Pass and carry word of us to the Gargon, else that evil Vûlk will seek us out." *Boom! Boom!*

"What you say is true," said Gildor, groaning to his feet and retrieving Bane and Red Bale from under the packs where Tuck had dropped them. Handing the blazing long-knife to the buccan, the Elf sheathed his own scarlet-flaming sword, saying, "We must attempt to go through, and quickly. In this we have no choice." *Boom!*

And so the four shouldered their packs, and, after some thought, Gildor led them up the stairs, Brega at his side holding high the lamp, with Tuck and Galen coming after.

Into Black Drimmen-deeve they strode, into the halls of the Dread, while behind them knelling down the ebon corridors the enraged pounding went on: *Boom! Boom! Boom!*

CHAPTER 3

The Struggles

Out through the sundered north gate of Challerain Keep fled the pony bearing double, past struggling Men and Ghûls, beyond screaming horses and grunting Hèlsteeds, away from the ring and skirl of steel upon steel and the howls of ravers and the cries of death. And Danner clasped Patrel tightly around the waist as west they galloped under the shadow of the first wall, turning across the foregate flats and bolting up and into the foothills.

On the slopes of a low hill they stopped and watched the battle boil out of the gate, raging in fury. Clots of struggling Men broke free only to be engaged again, and many fell dead unto the snow.

"Have you any arrows?" asked Patrel.

"None," answered Danner. "I spent my last when I slew Snake-Voice."

"Weaponless, we cannot rejoin the combat"—Patrel's voice was grim—"for then we would be a hindrance rather than a help."

They dismounted and looked down upon the seething battle: Patrel squatted before the pony, his gaze intent; Danner stood and glared, clenching and unclenching his fists.

This way and that the fighting raged, a swirling chaotic mêlée of riving swords and thrusting spears along the edge of a ravine. Helms were sundered and mail was pierced, and cries rang out through the air. Men fell dead, and Ghûls, too, and now and then a Warrow. Horses ran free, unchecked by their fallen riders, and at times ponies fled alone.

And Danner stomped back and forth in the snow, his teeth grinding in fury, his smoldering amber eyes never looking away, while Patrel squatted impassively, his viridian gaze glinting.

Suddenly Patrel sprang to his feet. "The King!" he cried, pointing to where combat swirled around gray Wildwind.

Aurion Redeye was surrounded and he smote mightily with his sword. Ghûls fell dead, skulls cloven, beheaded, yet others pressed inward, one to hurl a lance that pierced the King through. Still Aurion hewed and smote, and two more foe fell slain. Into the clot charged the Elf Lord Gildor, his blazing red sword slashing, a flaming blue long-knife fending tulwar strikes. To Aurion's side he rived a path, and the Ghûls quailed back before the werelight of the two Elven blades. For a moment they faced the foe— warrior Elf and spear-pierced King confronting raver Ghûls—and neither side moved; but then Aurion slumped forward upon the back of Wildwind, and the howling Ghûls turned and spurred away.

Danner stood stock still, his face gone cold, his eyes auric ice, while Patrel now paced in fury, green fire in his gaze. And then they both stood without moving as they watched Lord Gildor ride away from the battleground leading Wildwind; when he was clear of the mêlée, the Elf dismounted and lowered Aurion to the ground and after a moment composed the King's hands across his breast and laid his sword beside him.

"Aurion Redeye is dead," said Danner, his voice flat and emotionless, while Patrel turned his face away, his emerald eyes full of tears.

"Hai, look!" called Danner. "Vidron breaks away!"

Patrel turned to see a force of Men burst free at last, led by silver-bearded Vidron: horses running east, Ghûls in hot pursuit. Gildor, too, spurred forth, Wildwind in tow, swing-ing wide to pass outside the pursuing Ghûls, Fleetfoot's swift strides racing around and beyond the Hèlsteeds' hammering pace.

Rūcks and Hlōks boiled out of the north gate, as well as an Ogru or two, and began looting the bodies of the slain. Ghûls, too, there were, standing athwart the path taken by the fleeing Men.

"They block our way," gritted Danner. "Now we cannot follow without a detour."

"The rendezvous is at the Battle Downs," said Patrel. "We'll circle west and go down the Post Road."

Again they mounted Patrel's pie-faced pony, Danner behind, and made their way into the Shadowlight covering the foothills clutched unto Mont Challerain.

"Did you see aught of other Warrows who broke free?" asked Patrel.

"No," grunted Danner. "Neither afoot nor on pony nor astride horse behind Man."

"Only eight of us made it to the north gate," said Patrel. "And I saw two, no . . . three, fall after that, though I am not sure who they were. Sandy, perhaps, but who else I cannot say."

"Tuck?" Danner's voice nearly choked.

"I don't know, Danner," answered Patrel. "It could have been Tuck, but I just can't say. Listen, Danner, we've got to face the fact that we may be the last of the Company of the King. No one else may have survived."

They rode in silence for a while. "We'll find out at the rendezvous whether or not any other Thornwalkers came through," said Danner at last.

Onward they went, winding through the slopes.

"Look!" cried Patrel, pointing. Ahead in the vale before them stood a white pony, saddled and bridled—one of those ridden by the Warrows.

"Go easy," said Danner, "for he still may be spooked by the battle, or the stench of Hèlsteeds."

Slowly they rode down to the small steed, and Patrel's pie-faced pony whickered, and the white came trotting, as if glad to see another pony, and the Warrows, too.

Danner dismounted and, cooing, took up the reins, inspecting the white for battle wounds. "She's unscathed," said the buccan after a pause, then: "Looks like Teddy's pony, though it could be Sandy's white."

"No more, Danner, no more," responded Patrel. "Whoever had her before, she's now yours to ride."

Danner mounted and on they went, swinging southward now, edging through the hills.

Twenty miles they rode before making camp in a thicket on a rolling slope upon the plains south of Mont Challerain. Crue they had in their saddlebags, but no grain for the steeds. Danner dug under the snow and found quantities

of prairie grass, still nourishing to the ponies, for Modru's
early winter had preserved it.

At last they rebandaged Patrel's wounded hand, the left
one, cut shallowly by an enemy blade at the battle for the
fourth wall. "Let us hope that edge was not poisoned,"
grunted Danner.

Patrel took the first watch and Danner bedded down in
the cold; they had made no fire, for they were yet too near
the enemy.

Danner had not slept long when he was awakened by
Patrel: "A rider bears south out upon the plains to the west
of us."

They stood at the edge of the thicket and watched as the
far black steed hammered past through the Shadowlight, a
mile or so to the west.

"Hoy!" exclaimed Danner. "I think that's a horse, not a
Hèlsteed. And look, mounted before! Is that another rider?
A Warrow?"

Danner sprang forth from the thicket. "Hiyo!" he cried,
waving his arms, but the distant courser hammered on, and
ere he could call out again: "Danner!" barked Patrel. "Hail
not! For even if it is a horse, and I think you are right, still
we know not what other ears may hear your shout—and
we are without weapons."

Reluctantly, Danner held his call, for Patrel was right;
and they watched the black steed drive onward into the
Dimmendark, to disappear at last in the distant Shadowlight.

South they bore, two more 'Darkdays, heading for the
Battle Downs, though neither knew just where they should
ride, for as Patrel put it: "The Battle Downs is a wide place,
easily fifty miles broad and more than a hundred long. An
army could be lost in there. How we'll find the remnants
of the force from the Keep, I cannot say, yet they'll need
our eyes to guide them if no other Warrows have escaped
at their side."

"We'll go on to Stonehill, then," said Danner. "That was
the next rendezvous point."

And so southward they rode.

*   *   *

The next 'Darkday, as they broke camp, Patrel said, "If my reckoning is correct, it is the last day of December, Year's End Day. Tomorrow is Twelfth Yule."

"Ar, I don't think we'll be doing any celebrating tonight," responded Danner, "even though the old year dies and the new one begins." Danner looked about. "Never in my wildest dreams did I ever envision spending a Year's End Day like this: weary, hungry, half frozen, and fleeing weaponless from a teeming foe through a dismal murk sent by an evil power living in an iron tower in the Wastes of Gron."

Patrel finished cinching the saddle on his pony and turned to Danner. "Tell me, Danner," said the diminutive buccan, "what are you going to do next year when things *really* get bad?"

Flabbergasted, his mouth agape, Danner stared at Patrel. Then gales of laughter burst forth long and hard, Patrel whooping and shrieking, Danner doubled over holding his sides, his shouting guffaws ringing out across the plains. The ponies turned their heads back toward the whooping Warrows and cocked an eye and an ear, and this set Danner to laughing even harder, and he pointed and fell backwards in the snow, while Patrel looked and dropped to his knees, tears running down his face.

Long they laughed, gales bursting out anew, and Danner walked on his knees through the snow and threw his arms about Patrel and hugged him and laughed. At last, wiping their eyes with the heels of their hands, they both stood and mounted up and headed southward once more. Each rode with a great smile on his face and now and again would explode into a fit of giggles or great belly laughs to be joined by the other; and weary and hungry and half frozen, they fled weaponless from a teeming foe through a dismal murk sent by an evil power in an iron tower in the Wastes of Gron—and they laughed.

They had ridden nearly ten miles along the Post Road, wending along the northern margins of the Battle Downs, when they came upon the ravaged waggon train, and the carnage appalled them.

"This is Laurelin's caravan," grated Danner, his fists clenched knuckle-white as they strode past the victims.

Down one side of the train they went and back up the other, searching for survivors, but there were only the frozen corpses of the slain.

"Oi! Look here," said Patrel, kneeling in the snow. "A wide track beats east, cloven hooves: Hèlsteeds."

"Ghûls!" spat Danner, and then as if to confirm it, they saw the slain body of one of the corpse-people, head cloven in twain by sword. "How old is the track?"

"That I cannot judge," answered Patrel. "At least five 'Darkdays, perhaps seven or more."

"Wait," said Danner, "this train left the Keep on First Yule and this is Eleventh Yule. They couldn't have gotten here before late Fourth Yule even if they raced south, nor would they have dallied to pass here after Seventh Yule."

"That would make it six 'Darkdays old, then," said Patrel, "give or take a day."

On they pressed, back along the train, looking into the wains and at the faces of the slain.

"She's missing," gritted Danner. "Prince Igon too."

"Either they got away or are hostage," responded Patrel. "If they escaped, they've most likely headed south; if hostage . . ." Patrel pointed east along the Ghûlen wake.

Danner angrily smacked fist into palm. "Ponies can't catch Hèlsteeds." His voice was filled with frustration.

"Even if they could," said Patrel, "the Ghûls have got an insurmountable lead on us, and who knows where they're bound? Besides, we know not whether Laurelin or Igon are hostage. Perhaps they escaped."

Danner stood in brooding thought. Without warning, he shouted out a wordless cry of wrath. "Ar, what evil choices!" he spat, and then visibly tried to gather in his emotions. At last he grated, "You are right, Patrel, they ride Hèlsteeds, not ponies, and a six-day lead could as well be sixty for all we could do to catch them, whether or not the two are captive. Let us press on for Stonehill; when we tell this tale, Vidron or Gildor will lead fleet horses in pursuit of the Ghûls if need be—if there is still a chance, though I think it will have gone aglimmering."

Patrel nodded. "Let us find some arrows, and grain, and perhaps other supplies from this whelmed caravan. Then will we push for Stonehill."

An hour later, west they went following along the Post Road, leaving the butchered waggon train behind.

That night, angled far off the road, they sat trimming arrows by a small shielded campfire, the first one they had made since leaving Challerain Keep, and Patrel looked up to see tears aglisten in Danner's amber eyes. Danner stared into the fire, unseeing, his voice breaking: "She called me her dancer, you know."

The Post Road swung south again as it rounded the Battle Downs, and down it the ponies went, Patrel on the piebald, Danner on the white, and all about them the Shadowlight streamed.

"This road certainly looks different now than when we first fared north," said Patrel.

Danner merely grunted, and the ponies plodded on as snow began to fall. "Welcome to the new year," growled Danner, looking upward into the Dimmendark at the eddying flakes. Then he looked at Patrel: "Welcome to the new year, Paddy, for it's Last Yule. And remember: this is the year our troubles *really* begin." And they managed wan smiles at one another.

On the night of the sixth 'Darkday since leaving Challerain Keep, they camped on a slope to the east of where the Upland Way met the Post Road.

Danner stood looking down at that junction, and as Patrel brought him a cup of hot tea, the smaller Warrow said, "To think, Danner, it was but four weeks past that we came across Spindle Ford and out of the Bosky and up that road."

"Four weeks?" Danner sipped his tea, his eyes never leaving the road. "Seems like years instead of weeks. At least I feel years older."

Patrel threw a hand onto Danner's shoulder. "Perhaps you *are* years older, Danner; perhaps we all are."

Four 'Darkdays later, they rode onto a causeway over a dike and through gates flung wide in a high guard wall and into the village of Stonehill. Around them a hundred or so stone houses mounted up the slopes of the coomb, a great swale hollowed into the side of the large hill to the north and east. The ponies' hooves rang hollowly upon the cobbles and echoed back from the closed and shuttered houses, and no movement at all could be seen on the empty village streets.

"It looks abandoned," said Patrel, unshouldering his bow and setting arrow to string.

Danner said nought as he, too, readied his weapon, his eyes sweeping the dark doorways and closed-up windows. A thin wind sprang up, gnawing around corners, sending tiny twisting streamers of snow scurrying amongst the pave-stones.

On through the vacant streets they went, coming at last to Stonehill's one hostel, its signpost squeaking in the chill wind.

"If anyone's here, they'll be at the inn," said Danner, squinting up at the sign displaying the likeness of a white unicorn rampant on a field of red, bearing the words: *The White Unicorn, Bockleman Brewster, Prop.*

Stonehill was a village on the western fringes of the sparsely settled Wilderland, a village situated at the junction of the east-west Crossland Road and the Post Road running north and south. It was a trading center for farmers, woods dwellers, and travelers. The White Unicorn, with its many rooms, usually had a wayfarer or two as well as a nearby settler staying overnight. But occasionally there would be some "real" strangers, such as King's-soldiers from the Keep heading south, or a company of traveling Dwarves; in which case the local folk would be sure to drop in to the Unicorn's common room for a pint or two and a look at the strangers and to hear the news from far away, and there'd be much singing and merriment.

But when Danner and Patrel unlatched the door and stepped in, only silence greeted them, for the inn was cold and dark and the hearths were without fire.

Patrel shivered in the empty chill as Danner found the stub of a candle and managed to get it lit.

"I wonder where all the people have got to?" asked Patrel as they moved across the common room, past the longtable and benches and through the small tables and chairs.

"South, I should think," answered Danner, spying a lamp and using the candle to light it.

"Or to Weiunwood," said Patrel, answering his own question. "The fit and hale have gone to Weiunwood to fight the Spawn."

"What now, Paddy?" Danner turned to Patrel, the lamp casting a yellow glow upon both buccens' features. "Where do we wait for Vidron and Gildor and the rest that broke free?"

"Right here, Danner," answered Patrel, his hand sweeping in a wide gesture. "The best inn in town."

Danner looked about into the chill, empty darkness surrounding him and smiled. "And you said that this was going to be a bad year."

Patrel smiled back, his green eyes atwinkle, then said, "Why don't you look for something for us to eat while I get the ponies into the stables and out of sight."

They found another lamp and lit it, and Patrel took it with him to stable the mounts while Danner found the kitchen and rummaged through the pantry.

When Patrel returned, Danner had started a small fire and had set a small kettle to boil, and a pungent odor was redolent in the room.

"Smells good," said Patrel, rubbing his hands briskly. "What is it?"

"Leeks," answered Danner.

"Leeks? Lor, Danner, I *hate* leeks." Patrel made a sour face.

"Hate 'em or not, Paddy," responded Danner, "that's our meal, unless you prefer crue."

Danner set a pot on for tea while Patrel glowered at the leafy leeks bubbling in the kettle. Slumping down in a chair, Patrel said, "You'd think in an inn as big as this one there'd be something to eat besides leeks."

"It looks like they took everything with them, everything but the leeks," said Danner.

"See, I *told* you they were no good," shot back Patrel, then he burst out laughing. "It *is* the worst of years if I've got to eat boiled leeks."

Danner roared.

"I say, they weren't so bad after all," said Patrel, sopping up the last of the leeks with a piece of crue and popping it into his mouth.

"Maybe you've just not been hungry before," said Danner. "I mean, you had three helpings." ·

"Perhaps you're right, Danner," answered Patrel, chewing thoughtfully. "Perhaps I've not ever been hungry before. Of course, I've never before eaten crue as a ·steady diet for days on end. On the other hand, I suppose it wasn't too bad finding the leeks; it could have been worse, you know."

"What do you mean, 'worse'?" asked Danner.

"Well, for one thing," answered Patrel, making a face and shuddering, "it could have been oatmeal."

The rest of the 'Darkday, Danner paced the floor like a caged animal, frequently stepping out onto the porch and scanning for sign of Vidron or Gildor or any other survivor of Challerain Keep.

"Ar, I feel trapped, Paddy," said Danner, returning from one of his excursions outside. "You know, we're not at all certain that anyone else escaped. The Ghûls were in hot pursuit. What if no one else got away?"

"If that's the case," responded Patrel, his eyes grim, "then no one will come."

"Oh, no," said Danner, "someone will come all right: Spawn will come. Remember, there's a great Horde at Challerain Keep, and they'll march right through Stonehill on their way south. And we don't want to be here when they arrive."

"You're right, Danner," answered Patrel. "But, the maggot-folk won't be here very soon. They'll pick over the corpse of Challerain Keep first. But you're right: sooner or later they *will* march through Stonehill."

Patrel fell into brooding thought, not stirring or turning his gaze from the fire when Danner stalked back to the door and outside. When the buccan strode in once more, Patrel looked up. "This is the way I see it, Danner," said the smaller Warrow, "horses are faster than ponies, and the Men should have been here by now unless they were driven far afield."

"Or slain," interrupted Danner.

"Yes—or slain," continued Patrel. "In either case we cannot spend too long waiting, for we do not know when

Ghûls, Vulgs, or any of the Spawn will get here. But they *will* come.

"This, too, we know: Warrows see farther through this dismal murk than Men or Elves—who can say, perhaps we see through the Shadowlight better than any other Folk. The Realm needs our eyes, Danner, but you and I are not enough: more Thornwalkers are wanted than just us two.

"Here is what I propose: Let us remain here the rest of this 'Darkday and tomorrow. If neither Vidron nor Gildor nor others come, then the day after, we will leave Stonehill for the Bosky. We will go to Captain Alver and tell him what we know. Then we will form a Thornwalker company to fare south to Pellar, a company to join the Host and see for them: to be their eyes, to be their scouts, to watch the movements of the foe, and to give the edge in battle to the King's Legions."

Patrel gripped Danner's forearm and looked him in the eye. "None other than Warrows can do this thing, Danner. What say you?"

A wide grin split Danner's face. "Hai! I like this plan of yours. Even should Vidron or others come, still one of us must return to the Bosky and gather more Thornwalkers." Then the smile evaporated, replaced by a dark look. "Modru has much to answer for."

They heated water and took baths and washed their clothes, hanging them by the fire for drying. And they slept in beds!

All the next 'Darkday they kept watch for sign of survivors from the Keep, riding up the coomb to the hilltop to watch, but nought did they see of Men from Challerain, though they did note several Warrow burrows high up the swale, but they were vacant like all the other homes in Stonehill.

"Some of Toby Holder's kith, perhaps," said Danner, remembering that Toby frequently made trips to trade with the Stonehillers, and the Holders always did claim they'd come from near the Weiunwood originally.

They cooked more leeks, and Patrel managed to find a small wedge of cheese overlooked by the Brewsters when they'd gone to Weiunwood—"Just enough cheese for a bite

apiece," said Patrel—but they savored it as if it were priceless ambrosia, and spent the rest of the 'Darkday recounting the feast on Laurelin's birthday eve.

The next 'Darkday they rode once more to the hilltop
and looked long but saw nought of survivors, and so went
back to the inn and extinguished the fire and gathered
their things.

"If I had a copper penny or two," said Danner, casting
a last look around, "I'd leave it for Bockleman Brewster
to pay for the bath and the washing of clothes and the loan
of the bed I slept in."

"The bath alone was worth a silver," said Patrel.

"Even a gold," replied Danner.

"Come on, Danner, let's get out of here before we owe
Bockleman a chest of jewels," Patrel laughed, and out the
door they strode, latching it behind.

They went to the stables and put grain in their saddlebags for the ponies, and then rode down the vacant streets
and out through the west gate. And as they crossed the
causeway out to join the Crossland Road, they did not see
or hear Hrosmarshal Vidron at the head of a weary band
of grimy horsemen ride forth from the twsiting hills and
in through the eastern gates of Stonehill, into that now
empty town.

South and west went the Crossland Road, swinging below
the southern reaches of the Battle Downs, heading for
Edgewood and, beyond, the Boskydells. Along this way
rode the buccen, camping first along the hills and next
within the forest.

On the third 'Darkday, through the winter trees of Edgewood they sighted the great Thornwall, and came unto the
thorn tunnel leading into the Bosky. They took up torches
and lit one, riding into the barrier, and their eyes brimmed
with glittering tears, for they had come home.

At last they emerged from the Thornwall, coming to a
wooden span set upon stone piers—the bridge over the
River Spindle. Of the four main ways into the Bosky, this
was the only bridge, the other three ways being fords: Spin-

dle Ford, Wenden Ford, and Tine Ford. But, as is the manner of Warrows in many things, the bridge was simply called "the bridge."

"Hey," said Danner, perplexed as they came out of the thorn barrier and onto the span, "there are no guards, no Thornwalkers."

Patrel, too, cast looks about, concerned, yet he said nought. Beyond the bridge he could see where again the barrier grew, and once more a black tunnel bored onward: two miles had they come within the thorny way to reach the bridge, and nearly three more miles beyond would they go before escaping the Thornwall. Across the span the ponies trotted, their hooves drumming on the great planks and timbers. Below, the frozen Spindle shone pearl grey in the Shadowlight. Soon they crossed the bridge and once more entered the gloom, their guttering torch casting a writhing light upon the great tangle of razor-sharp spikes clawing outward.

In all, nearly two hours they rode within the barrier, to emerge as the last of their torches burned low. And no Beyonder Guard greeted them as they came into the Bosky, only the cold Shadowlight of the Dimmendark.

"What do you think it means, Danner: the 'Guard gone, the way open, the camp deserted?" Patrel's voice was grim as his viridian eyes swept the countryside for sign of life but found none.

"I think it means something foul is afoot," grated Danner, leaning down and jabbing the torch into the snow, quenching the flame. "Let's go; we've got to get to someone who can tell us what's going on."

West they rode, into the Bosky, following the Crossland Road, faring through rolling farmland, now fallow in Winternight's grip. West they rode for nearly three more hours, covering some nine miles, coming to the village of Greenfields. As they approached the hamlet, they could see no lights, as if the village was deserted.

"Hoy, Danner, look!" barked Patrel. "Some of the homes are burned."

Setting arrows to bows, they spurred forward, swiftly coming in among the houses, into the town. Doors stood ajar, windows were broken, and some buildings were charred ruins. The streets were empty; no life could be seen anywhere.

Eyes alert, to the Commons they rode.

"Paddy, by the fire gong . . ." Danner's voice was grim, and Patrel looked to see the frozen corpse of a buccan, barbed lance standing forth from his back. "Ghûlen spear!" spat Danner. "Ghûls are in the Bosky!"

Patrel's face blenched to hear such dire news, and he surveyed the grim evidence. "He was ringing the gong when the Spawn got him. Perhaps his warning saved others. Let's search further."

Through the small hamlet they rode, dismounting now and again to search houses. And they found more slain: dammen, buccen, younglings, wee babes, granthers, grandams.

In one house twelve slain were found: eleven children and a young damman. Danner ran out into the street shouting in rage: "Modru! Skut! Swine! Coward! Where are you, you butcher?" And he fell to his knees and dropped his bow and pounded the frozen earth with his fist, and his voice sank into dark gutturals, and no word could be understood though words he spoke.

At last Patrel got Danner to his feet and mounted upon the white pony and led him to the west edge of town where stood the Happy Otter Inn, and they bedded down in the hayloft of the inn stable.

And it was late in the dark Winternight when Patrel started up from a deep, dreamless sleep to hear the pounding of hooves thundering past. He glanced at Danner lying in the hay; and Danner did not awaken, though the buccan tossed restlessly and moaned.

Taking up his bow, Patrel crept down from the loft and out into the Dimmendark. In the distant Shadowlight he saw a force of fifty or sixty riders hammering away to the west along the Crossland Road, but whether they were Men on horses, or Ghûls on Hèlsteeds, he could not say, as the sound of the drumming hooves faded beyond hearing and the riders disappeared into the far Winternight.

The next 'Darkday they continued west along the Crossland Road, riding through Raffin and Tillok and coming to Willowdell, and these hamlets, too, were deserted, buildings burned, Warrows slain. And all 'Darkday Danner said no word, though his lips were pressed into a thin white line, and his knuckles clenched tightly upon the pony reins.

They stopped at the edge of Willowdell, staying in an abandoned barn, for neither buccan could bear to sleep in a house of one of the victims.

"Rood," said Patrel. "We're going to Rood. Thornwalker headquarters are in Rood; perhaps we can find Captain Alver there—or the Chief Constable of the Bosky if Thornwalkers aren't about."

"What if they're all destroyed?" Danner spoke his first words in more than a 'Darkday, and his voice was bleak.

"All destroyed?" Patrel turned to his comrade.

"All the villages, all the towns," said Danner.

Patrel blenched at this dire thought, and Danner began saddling the white pony.

"I'm going to Woody Hollow, Paddy," said Danner. "It's only eleven or twelve miles from here. We'll go to Rood after—if there's a need to—but I can't pass this close without going to the Hollow. Are you coming?"

Patrel nodded, for he knew how he would feel were they but eleven miles from the woods where he had been raised.

Mounting up, once more they went west along the Crossland Road, riding some six miles before turning northwest up Byroad Lane, the way to Budgens and, beyond, to Woody Hollow.

They had ridden nearly three more miles and were just coming past flanking trees and into Budgens when Danner shouted, "Look! Fires! Woody Hollow is on fire!" and clapped his heels into the white's flanks, crying, "Yah!"

Patrel spurred after him, and as he rode, his green eyes saw flames raging in Woody Hollow, some two miles distant.

Through Budgens galloped the ponies, then westward along Woody Hollow Road, skittering on the ice over Rill Ford across the Southrill. Danner turned north, racing along the East Footway and across the frozen Dingle-rill with Patrel plunging after, flying past the Rillstones and up the north bank and into Woody Hollow proper. They turned west and rode toward the Commons.

Upslope and down, fires raged as homes burned. And the buccen could see dark shapes silhouetted against the flames: Ghûls on Hèlsteeds! *Modru's Reavers were in the Hollow!*

Danner and Patrel hauled their ponies to a halt and leapt down, setting arrows to bowstrings. Flitting among the boles of trees, they moved silently toward the reavers now milling in the Commons. But as the buccen worked their way toward the foe, the Ghûls vented howling cries and spurred Hèlsteeds southward, galloping out and across the bridge and down the Westway Trace, leaving Woody Hollow aflame behind them.

Danner ran shouting a few steps after them, and both he and Patrel sent their arrows winging, but the Ghûls were beyond their range, and the bolts fell futilely in the distant snow.

And as they watched the reavers ride away, they heard a shrill voice cry " 'Ware!" and the hammer of cloven hooves behind. The buccen spun to see a charging Hèlsteed bearing down upon them, and a grinning Ghûl with a blood-splashed tulwar raised to cleave once, twice more.

Sssthock! An arrow flew from the Shadowlighted trees behind, passing over Patrel's shoulder to pierce the charging Ghûl's breast, and the pale white corpse-foe fell asprawl to the snow, slain, while the Hèlsteed ran on.

"Wha—?" cried Danner, and spun again, to see who his rescuer was.

A small form bearing a bow stepped from behind a tree and came forward, sapphire-blue eyes locked in hatred and loathing and horror upon the slain Ghûl.

Danner looked at the grimy, disheveled young damman before him. "Merrilee!" he cried in disbelief. "Merrilee Holt!"

"Danner! Oh, Danner!" Merrilee ran sobbing to the young buccan and clung to him as if she were lost.

"He's dead, all right," said Patrel, standing up from the slain Ghûl. "But I don't know why. I must've feathered ten to no avail back at the Keep."

"Wood through the heart," said Danner above Merrilee's head as he held her to him. "Merrilee's bolt hit him square in the heart." Danner spoke down to the weeping damman: "Anywhere else, Merrilee, and we'd've been the deaders, and not him."

"Lor, you're right," breathed Patrel, looking at the shaft

standing forth from the Ghûl's chest. "Wood through the heart! Stakes and spears I thought of, yes, but not of arrows." Patrel then grinned fiercely and clenched one of his own bolts in a fist and raised it to the sky. "Hai! Now we've got a way to fight them!"

"They killed my dam and sire, Danner." Merrilee's voice was muffled, then she pushed back and turned from the buccan and wiped her eyes and nose in the crook of her sleeve and looked down at the dead Ghûl, hatred in her gaze.

"Bringo and Bessie, dead?" Danner's voice was hushed.

"Tuck's parents, too," said Merrilee, her eyes again brimming with tears, but once more she brushed them aside.

"Tuck's parents, too?" burst out Danner. "How?"

"We came to get the last of the ponies at Dad's stable," answered Merrilee, "to take them up to the Dinglewood, where most folks have got to. Tulip and my dam wanted to get their herbs and medicines, and so they came, too.

"While we were down at the stables, my sire and I, the Ghûls came. Dad shoved me into a feed bin and shut the lid. And they came in . . . and just . . . killed him." Merrilee burst into tears. Danner put an arm around her shoulders, his own eyes glistening. Patrel managed to find a kerchief and gave it to her.

After a moment, she continued: "They set the place on fire when they left. I couldn't get to Dad, and I ran out the back way and up across the Pony Field, crying, and through the woods of Hollow End to warn Mother and the Underbanks. But I was too late.

"The Ghûls had Tulip, dragging her by the hair. Burt came running, and the only thing he had to fight them with was his mason's hammer. But he broke the arm of one of them before they killed him. And they speared Tulip, too, as she tore free and ran to Burt. And then they were both dead."

Merrilee's voice rushed on as she relived the horror of those dire moments: "The Ghûls threw a torch into The Root, setting the burrow aflame. And they rode down and across End Field.

"I ran to our burrow, and Mother was lying dead on the walkway: hacked by blade, savagely murdered.

"I went in and got my bow—the one Tuck gave me—

but I could find only one arrow." Merrilee gestured at the shaft standing full from the slain Ghûl's chest.

"I came down to the Commons, to kill at least one of the butchers before they got me. But they rode away, all except that one. Where he was lurking, I do not know. But as he galloped to catch the other murderers, he was going to cut you down, like they did Dad and Mom, and the Underbanks. So I shot him."

"It's a good thing, too, Merrilee, else we'd be dead," said Patrel. "We foolishly loosed our bolts at the Ghûls beyond our range, and we had nothing in hand to stop this one."

" 'The arrow as strays might weller been throwed away,' " said Danner, quoting old Barlo. "One of Tuck's favorite sayings."

At the mention of Tuck's name, Merrilee looked out through the trees, then up at Danner. "Tuck. Where's Tuck?" Anxiety filled her voice.

Danner groped for words, but none came.

"We don't know, Merrilee," said Patrel. "The last we saw of him was at Challerain Keep."

"Challerain Keep? But I thought you were at Ford Spindle!" Merrilee's eyes were wide.

"Didn't the word get back? Didn't Tuck's letter come to you?" Danner asked, and at the shake of her head: "Skut!" he spat.

"We knew some buccen had gone to the Keep, but not who." Merrilee's voice was low. "Tell me of Tuck."

"The last we saw, he was alive at the sundered north gate of Challerain," said Patrel, "when we broke free of the Horde. But we were separated in the midst of that fight, and we know nought of his fate after that."

Merrilee said nothing for a moment, then: "Did any other Warrows win free?"

Patrel spread his hands palms up. "We just don't know."

"Merrilee," Danner's voice was taut, "my folks, are they all right?"

Now it was Merrilee who knew not: "I cannot say, Danner. In the rush of the evacuation—when we left Woody Hollow—there seemed to be nothing but confusion: people running hither and yon, some heading north, others south, some vowing to stay. But your parents, Danner, I didn't see them; I know not their fate."

Danner's jaw muscles jumped as he gritted his teeth. Then he spun to Patrel. "Look, Paddy, we've got to stop the Ghûls in the Bosky, and Merrilee's shown us the way: wood through the heart. We've got to get up to the Dingle-wood and get folks organized; then we can strike back at the Modru's Reavers."

"We need Thornwalkers, present or past," said Patrel, "folk who are good with bow and arrow."

"I'm good with bow and arrow." Merrilee's voice was low.

"Wha—what?" Patrel was nonplussed.

"I said, I am good with bow and arrow," answered Merrilee, speaking up.

"I heard you the first time," said Patrel. "What I meant to say is, you're a damman."

"What does that have to do with anything?" snapped Merrilee, snatching her bow up from the snow.

"Why, everything. I mean, you're a damman." Patrel seemed to be groping for words.

"You said that before; it didn't make any better sense then either," shot back Merrilee, her eyes aflash. "Look, Tuck taught me how to shoot and shoot well. He's not here, and may never come, so I'll stand in his stead, though I cannot take his place. But even were he here, still would I join you, for skill is needed and I have it: my arrows fly true, and for that you should be glad, for the proof lies at your feet: the arrow in that reaver's heart is no accident; it struck exactly where I aimed—nowhere else—otherwise you would be dead." A dark look fell upon Merrilee's features and her voice sank low. "They've slain my sire and my dam, and the Underbanks, and countless others, perhaps Tuck, too. And for that they must pay . . . they must pay."

Danner looked at her soot-streaked, tear-stained face and then up in the direction of the Pony Field and beyond, where he knew that Bringo and Bessie and the Underbanks lay murdered. Then his gaze swung in the direction of his own home, and lastly his eye fell upon the slain Ghûl. "She's right, you know. What has her being a damman got to do with anything?"

Patrel sputtered and fumed and several times started to speak but did not, and at last reluctantly gave a stiff nod of his head, and when Merrilee threw her arms around him and hugged him, over her shoulder he cocked an eye at Danner as if to say, "See! I *told* you she was a damman!"

Merrilee stepped back. "I've seen you before," she said to Patrel, "but I don't know your name."

"Patrel Rushlock, from the narrow treeland east of Midwood," said the diminutive buccan.

"Paddy was our Captain at the Keep," said Danner.

"I remember now: I saw you the day Tuck left. On the Commons. You guided Tuck, Hob, Tarpy, and Danner north." At Patrel's nod, Merrilee said, "I'm Merrilee Holt."

"I know," said Patrel. "Tuck spoke of you often."

"Look, we can't stand here the rest of the Winter War," grumbled Danner. "We've got to get up to the Dinglewood and start fighting back. Let's go."

Up through the Hollow from the Commons the three went, swinging by Danner's stone house, but there was no clue as to the fate of Hanlo and Glory Bramblethorn, Danner's parents. Onward the trio went.

The stables burned furiously.

"Bringo would have been proud to know that his damsel saved two from certain death, Merrilee," said Danner.

Merrilee did not reply, and they went past the blazing barn and into the Pony Field behind. There they rounded up eleven ponies and continued on up the coomb.

Gently, they wrapped the bodies of Burt and Tulip Underbank and Merrilee's dam in soft blankets and tied them over the backs of three ponies. "We'll take them up to the Dinglewood and bury them in a peaceful glade," said Danner, his arms about Merrilee as she wept anew.

"They'll pay," she whispered fiercely. "They'll pay."

Merrilee led them to a camp of Warrows in a wide glen west of where the North Trace entered the Dinglewood. When the trio rode in leading a string of ponies, there was a scattering of cheers that quickly fell into subdued silence as the three bodies were seen draped over three of the steeds.

Buccen were dispatched to dig graves, and Danner and Patrel and Merrilee went to speak with the camp elders. A circle of Warrows formed 'round them to listen to their words.

"We return from Mont Challerain and bear woeful tidings: the Keep has fallen to Modru's Horde, and High King Aurion is slain." The onlookers moaned to hear Patrel speak such news, for they loved their good King Redeye, though none there had ever seen him. Patrel waited for the hubbub to dwindle, then spoke on: "Of the forty-three buccen serving upon the walls at the Battle of the Keep, I know of only two who survived: Danner Bramblethorn and myself." Again there was a stir among the onlookers, and Patrel held his hand up for silence. "Others may have won free, but no more than a handful, for only eight of us lived to fight the last battle, and I saw three more fall there."

"What of the King's Host in the south?" asked an elder. "Did they not come? Do they not take the field against Modru's Hordes?"

"We know not where the Host is," answered Patrel, "but they did not come to Challerain. Why? I cannot say, for no word of them came either. And the Keep fell to Modru's Swarm.

"From that ruin, Danner and I fared south, along the Post Road to Stonehill; and from Stonehill we came west, across the bridge and into the Bosky. And much evil have we seen. In the Bosky alone, Greenfields, Raffin, Tillok, and Willowdell all lie in ruins, and there has been much death at the hands of Modru's Reavers. And now Woody Hollow burns—"

Woody Hollow? Burns? Shouts interrupted Patrel, and some turned to go, to ride to their homes. *"Hold!"* thundered Danner, leaping to his feet. "Stop where you are!" Warrows paused and quiet returned. "There's nought you can do now," Danner said, his voice sharp. "What's burned has burned, and what hasn't still stands. There's no need to go running off willy-nilly into the spears of the Ghûls." Danner sat back down on the log, motioning Patrel to continue.

But ere he could do so: "Captain Patrel, do you bring us no good news?" asked one of the elders, and there was a general murmur among council and spectators alike.

"Yes! I bring the best of news," said Patrel fiercely. "We know how Warrows may slay the Ghûls." Amidst a hubbub Patrel held up an arrow. "Wood through the heart. This wood. Arrow wood. And none is better at casting these quarrels than the Warrow." A general murmur rose up among the Wee Folk, and Patrel held up a hand. "Think it no easy task, for the Ghûl's heart must be struck fair and square, else the bolt will have no effect."

Then he turned to the elders. "This is what I propose: Send riders—messengers—to other camps, to speak with free Warrows everywhere. Tell them how to slay the Ghûls. Have all those who live nearby and who are skilled archers come together at some common place, a place well out of the paths that the Ghûls ride." Patrel looked to Danner for suggestions.

"Whitby's barn east of Budgens," proposed Danner. "It is in a vale nearly hidden by woods, yet it will serve as a large meeting hall all know of."

"So be it," declared Patrel. "Whitby's barn it is. There we shall gather together a company to hurl the Ghûls forth from these Boskydells.

"Let the heralds carry forth this word, too: Warrow eyes see further through this murk than those of Men and even those of Elves. And it may be that our eyes see further than those of the enemy. If so, then we will have another advantage over the foe, for by keeping a sharp watch we will be able to slip aside when they come nigh if needs dictate, or to lay a trap at other times. So send the word to post wards, to cover any tracks so that the reavers may not follow sign of Warrow in the snow, and to use Warrow woods-trickery to foil their designs. And if there is no other choice, and you are cornered when you do not expect it, aim for the heart.

"Now let the messengers ride to spread the word, to call upon Warrows everywhere to form companies of archers to defend their districts, and to summon those in this region who are skilled to meet at Whitby's barn, for on the morrow we begin to *fight back!*"

Patrel fell silent, and for a moment none spoke, then an elder, Mayor Geront Gabben, stood. "Hip, hip, hooray!" he cried, and was joined by the fired-up townsfolk: *Hip, hip, hooray! Hip, hip, hooray! Hip, hip, hooray!* Thrice the shout rang forth. And then Warrows rushed thither and yon; hasty plans were made as to who would ride where and who would stand guard. Messengers were reminded that some skilled archers would be needed to ward the camps, but that others were to form into companies to fight the Ghûls. And since most skilled archers either were now or had at times been Thornwalkers, the formation of companies would come easily.

In the midst of the bustle, a youngling came to Merrilee to say that the graves were ready. With Danner and Patrel at her side, Merrilee went to the glade where stood three fresh mounds; and as the three slain were laid to rest and Merrilee wept, Patrel's clear voice sang throughout the glen:

> "In Winter's glade now cold and bare
> Your 'ternal rest begins.
> There'll be a day Spring fills the air
> In fields and woods and fens.
>
> Then Summer's touch will grace us all
> And bring forth Nature's Tide.
> The Harvesting will come this Fall
> As leaves fall by your side.
>
> And Winter's cold will come again
> As Seasons swing full 'round.
> Goodbye my loves, till we are laid
> In this most hallowed ground."

Merrilee, Danner, and Patrel each crumbled a handful of earth into each grave, and then Bessie Holt, Burt Underbank and Tulip Underbank were covered to become one with the Land.

There was a buzz of buccen voices in Whitby's great barn when Danner and Patrel and Merrilee stepped inside. And in the yellow lamplight they saw nearly one hundred Warrows, each armed with a bow. Buccen seemed to be everywhere: in the loft and stalls, upon bales of hay and feed bins, standing in the main aisle and on barrels—from every nook and cranny curious Warrow faces peered out.

Danner and Patrel and Merrilee wormed their way through the crowd to barn-center where stood a makeshift platform, and onto this the trio climbed. A hush fell upon the assembly as Patrel held up his hands for silence. It was warm in the bar, so he and Danner and Merrilee shed their outer jackets, and a surprised hum rose up among the buccen, for there before them stood two helmed warriors in armor, and a damman. Neither Danner nor Patrel had thought of the impact such a sight would have upon the assembly, for little did they realize just how splendid they looked: Danner in black armor, Patrel in gold. And just what was a damman doing here anyhow?

Again Patrel held his hands up for silence, and once more a hush fell over the assembly. Danner and Merrilee sat down cross-legged upon the platform, and Patrel spoke, recounting the fall of Challerain Keep, the death of Aurion, the bravery of the Warrows that had been slain, the sights that he and Danner had seen on their journey to Woody Hollow. Groans of dismay and cries of rage greeted his words, and often Patrel had to pause until the hubbub died down.

Then he spoke of the slaying of the Ghûl by Merrilee's bolt, and of the hope this boded for the Warrows. He also spoke of the Warrow's ability to see farther through the Dimmendark than others, and the advantage this could give to the Wee Folk.

"This, then, is what I hope to do: to lure Ghûls into traps of our devising, to slay them with well-placed bolts, to drive Modru's Reavers from the Land." Patrel gestured at Merrilee and Danner. "We three here have sworn to do this thing, and I think you all have come here prepared to join us. What say you?"

There was a great shout that rattled the rafters, for the buccen at last could see a way to combat the corpse-people.

Yet one buccan stood to be recognized: Luth Chuker from Willowdell. "Ar, what you say makes plenty of sense, Captain Patrel. All but one thing, that is."

"What's that, Luth?" asked Patrel.

"Uh, well, no offense, miss, but we can't be expected to have this damman in our company," said Luth. Some in the assembly said, *Hear, hear.*

"And why is that, Luth?" asked Patrel.

"Why, she's a *damman!*" exclaimed Luth. "Don't take me wrong, I mean, my wife and my dammsel are both dammen, but . . ."

"But what, Luth?" Patrel didn't let up, for he had slogged through this same morass and knew that the issue needed to be dealt with in the open, and now.

"We just don't let our dammen fight, that's what," said Luth, and here and there, murmurs of agreement were heard.

"Would you rather that they die without a struggle?" Patrel's words were harsh. "Like those in Greenfields, Raffin, Tillok?"

Luth now squirmed, and some in the assembly argued with their neighbors.

"Listen, each of you!" cried Patrel above the babble. "Of all the archers here, including me, and including Danner, Merrilee is the only one I know of who has actually slain a Ghûl. Can any of you say the same? I cannot."

Again arguments broke out, and once more Patrel called for quiet, but now he was angry, green fire in his eyes. "Merrilee saved my stupid skin once with her skill, and until you earn it, I trust her and Danner above all others here!"

Patrel's statement brought forth an uproar from the assembly, and many shouted in ire. But Merrilee, too, was spluttering angry, for she had listened to the buccen argue about her fate *as if she weren't even present to speak for herself.* And she started to spring to her feet, but Danner put a hand on her shoulder and held her down as he stood. Again the assembly fell quiet, for most knew of Danner's extraordinary skill as an archer.

"Captain Patrel is right," said the black-armored buccan, "none else can boast of slaying a Ghûl. But this, too, I would say: Merrilee hit the Ghûl square in the heart, the only place where an arrow would slay him, *and he was on the back of a Hèlsteed running full tilt!* Think you now: would you bar such an archer from our company? And think deeply, *for the skill she has already mastered is the skill you must match!*" Danner paused. "If there are no more objections"—quiet filled the barn—"then let us get on with the planning of this War." Danner resumed his seat, and Merrilee squeezed his hand, her cobalt eyes shining brightly.

Because most of the buccen there knew each other, at least by reputation, and since all had been Thornwalkers

in their young-buccen days, squads were quickly formed
and Lieutenants selected. There was never any question
that they would serve under Captain Patrel Rushlock and
that Captain Danner Bramblethorn was to be second in
command. The damman, Merrilee Holt, was the hard one
to fit in, for she had not the Thornwalker training. At the
last, it was decided that she would serve on Captain Patrel's
staff, till her experience could catch up to the others.

Now all the Lieutenants gathered 'round the table, sitting
on barrels for chairs, and Patrel, Danner, and Merrilee
stepped down to join them. The other buccen in the barn
fell silent and strained their ears to hear what was said by
the eight: Captains Patrel and Danner; Lieutenants Orbin
Theed, Norv Odger, Dinby Hatch, Alvy Willoby, and Luth
Chuker who, in spite of his objections to Merrilee, was
eagerly selected as a Lieutenant, for such was his reputation
as a Thornwalker; and lastly at the table stood the damman,
Merrilee Holt, looking small and meek among the warrior
buccen. And as they held council, planning the course of
the War, other Warrows continued to arrive at Whitby's
barn, coming to answer the summons.

Patrel spoke: "Does any here know of the Ghûlen
movements?"

"Aye," said Norv Odger, "at least I think I do. They
roam the Bosky roads: the Crossland Road, the Tineway,
and Two Fords Road, for certain. And if that pattern holds,
then they're on the Southpike, the Wenden Way, West
Spur, the Upland Way—all of the Bosky roads, reaving the
towns as they go."

"They may be reaving the towns for now," said Merrilee,
"but soon they'll begin laying waste to farms, and to homes
in the woods and fens. No bothy, no cot, no flet, no burrow
will be safe from the Spawn." A murmur of agreement
rippled through the barn at the damman's bitter words.

"How did they get into the Bosky?" asked Danner.
"How did they penetrate the Thornwall, get past the Beyonder Guard?"

None at the table knew the answer to Danner's question,
but one of the newcomers to the barn asked to speak, and
Patrel signified so, asking his name.

"I'm Danby Rigg from Dinburg. I was up near Northdune when word came that Ghûls were in the Bosky. It

was said that they came in through the Thornwall at the old abandoned Northwood tunnel."

"But that only goes partway through the 'Wall," interrupted Orbin, slapping his hand to the table.

"Aye," said Danby, "but let me finish. They came through that way as far as it went, to come to the headwaters of the Spindle River. Then they rode down that frozen waterway: the ice is thick and easily will bear their weight, for now it is solid all the way to the bottom, I hear. They rode to the Inner-break at the fork ten miles west of Spindle Ford. Up over the granite they went; then they were in the Bosky."

An uproar greeted Danby's words, for this was news to them all. The old Northwood tunnel had been abandoned years past, and Warrow grangers had set about encouraging the Spindlethorn to fill in the southern half, and it had grown shut. But the northern half of the tunnel had been left to grow closed on its own, and, without help from Warrows, Spindlethorn grows notoriously slowly. The old north barricades had been left shut, but they could have been moved with effort by Modru's agents. The Inner-break was a great breech in the Thornwall on the south bank of the Spindle where a massive slope of granite hove up through the soil, the great stone slab reaching nearly five miles into the Bosky. And the Spindle River was frozen this year, an event that had never before happened in living Warrow memory.

Patrel asked for silence, and it quickly came, and Merrilee said, "Hai! Then that's how the Vulgs first came to the Bosky, too: through the northern half of the Northwood tunnel, down the frozen Spindle, then up over the Inner-break." Once more agreement rippled through the buccen at the slight damman's words.

Danner spoke: "All right, so we know how the Ghûls got in and how the Vulgs first came. But now the problem is how to drive Modru's Reavers out. Where do we start?"

No one spoke for a moment, then Norv Odger said, "Each 'Darkday so far, a squad of Ghûls has patrolled the Crossland Road between Willowdell and Brackenboro. It may have been this bunch that set the torches to those two towns."

"Woody Hollow, too," said Merrilee, her voice low.

"Aye, Woody Hollow, too," continued Norv. "There are perhaps twenty, twenty-five of the reavers. They could be our target, but it's a goodly sized gang."

Danner looked about. "I gauge that there are now nearly one hundred twenty-five of us, what with the latecomers. That seems to be good enough odds to me: five of us for each Ghûl and Hèlsteed."

"Yes, good odds," said Patrel, "but remember, the Ghûls won't be sitting targets; and they'll use tulwar, spear, and Hèlsteed to balance the exchange."

Patrel suspended the planning a moment to form another squad from the newcomers and to select a Lieutenant to command it: Regin Burk, a farmer from near the Mid Ford. And during this pause Merrilee sat with her hands steepled before her, deep in thought. Regin joined the council and looked at Merrilee in surprise, but said nought.

"All right," said Patrel, "if this band of reavers is to be our first target, how shall we go about it?"

No one spoke, and silence drummed loudly upon the ear. At last, Merrilee cleared her throat, and Patrel cocked an eye at her, and she said, "I know little of War, and so know nought of strategy, tactics, or battle. I do know how to use bow and arrow, and I know much about ponies. Yet something you said, Patrel, caused me to think. Your words were, 'the Ghûls won't be sitting targets.' But what if they were? Sitting targets, that is. Our task would be immeasurably eased." A murmur washed over the listening buccen, but quickly stilled as Merrilee continued. "These, then, are my thoughts: Let us lure the Ghûls into a high-walled trap and shut the door behind. Then slay them in their pen." Once more a murmur started to swell, but Merrilee raised her voice sharply, and silence fell again. "*Yet!* I can hear some say, *there is no high-walled trap nearby.* But if you say that, then you are wrong. For there *is* a trap, and it is called Budgens—the hamlet of Budgens. Hear now my plan: A band of Warrows on pony will be seen by the Ghûls. Fleeing in panic, the poor Warrows will gallop up Byroad Lane for the village of Budgens. Yet even though the Warrows have a small lead—perhaps but a mile or so— reavers know that ponies cannot outrun Hèlsteeds, and they give swift chase. Into Budgens run the foolish Warrows, down the central street, now the Ghûls right after.

But *lo!* as the Spawn charge through Budgens, the Warrows have vanished; instead, there is a barricade across the road and it bursts into flame. The Ghûls turn, and behind is another waggon-borne flaming barricade, now also shut. And the gaps between the buildings cannot be broached, for they, too, are filled. Then Warrows spring up from rooftop concealment and arrows pierce Spawn hearts, for now it is the hunters who have become the hunted, as the Warrows war upon the reavers."

Merrilee fell silent, and quiet filled the barn—a stillness so deep that the hush drummed heavily upon the ears. Then the silence was shattered by a great, wild cheering that shook the walls of Whitby's barn, and broad grins split faces and Patrel grabbed Merrilee and fiercely hugged her to him, calling in her ear above the shouts and applause, "So you are the one who knows nothing of strategy, tactics, or battle? Would that I were so ignorant." And tears glistened in Merrilee's eyes as Danner smiled and squeezed her hand, saying, "Your vow against the reavers will be kept, Merrilee, for with this plan, they *will* pay."

Much was debated ere all the final details of Merrilee's plan were hammered out, and in this the damman proved to ask canny questions and to point out many particulars of value. And when all was said and done, the last detail decided upon, Luth Chuker looked across the table at Merrilee and said, "Damman, I was wrong. Will you forgive me?" And Merrilee smiled and inclined her head, and Luth grinned in return.

Patrel called for silence, then said, "This 'Darkday is done; our plans are laid. Tomorrow we prepare our trap in Budgens, and the next 'Darkday, if the Ghûls are willing, we spring it shut upon the Spawn. But ere we go to take our rest, I would hear a few words from the chief architect of our design: Merrilee Holt."

Again applause and cheering broke out, and Merrilee was stunned, for although it was one thing to tell others of an idea she had, it is altogether a different thing to give a *speech* to a company of warriors. Danner leaned over and whispered in her ear, "Just say what is in your heart." And then two buccen boosted her up onto the table.

She stood and slowly turned, looking at all of the Warrow faces, all of the Thornwalkers with their bows, eager to take the War to Modru's Reavers, eager to avenge their lost loved ones. And sadness fell upon her heart, but so, too, did fierce pride.

And then she spoke in a clear voice, and all heard her words: "Let the word go forth here and now from this place of liberty that no longer will Warrows flee in fear before Modru's Reavers. The Evil in Gron has chosen the wrong Land to try to crush under his iron tread, for sharp thorn will meet his heel and we will wound him deeply. We did not choose this War, but now that it is visited upon us, not only will we fight to survive, we will fight to *win*. Let it be said now and for all the days hereafter that on this day the struggle began, and Evil met its match."

Amid thunderous cheering, Merrilee stood down from the table, and she saw that some wept openly.

"They're no longer calling it the Winter War, Merrilee," said Danner. "Now they name it after what you said in your speech: the Struggles."

Before Merrilee could reply, Patrel strode into the barn. "Well, the trap in Budgens is set. Tomorrow is the 'Darkday we spring it. And, concealed, we watched the Ghûlen squad ride along the Crossland Road on their patrol. There are twenty-seven of them. The odds are good, maybe now even better. How have things gone here?"

"More Thornwalkers, past and present, have arrived. Our ranks have swelled to double their numbers. There's nearly two hundred fifty now, and more trickle in all the time," said Danner. "Lor! Tomorrow in Budgens the air will be solid with arrows. Why don't we leave some buccen behind?"

"No," objected Merrilee. "It will be important that all share in tomorrow. Victory, we think, but perhaps defeat. Yet Win or lose, all should be there."

"Tell me, damman, what could possibly go wrong tomorrow?" Luth looked up from the arrows he fletched.

"If I knew, Luth," answered Merrilee, "then it wouldn't happen."

"Well," said Luth, "nothing will go wrong tomorrow. You've just got a case of battle-eve jitters."

"I hope you're right, Luth," responded Merrilee, "for I'm not sure I could stand it if things go wrong."

Danner laughed and changed the subject: "Ah, Paddy, you should've seen it when some of the newcomers objected to a damman in the company. Luth set 'em down, he did."

Luth smiled penitently, but there was an ireful glare in his eye: "Them skuts! Oh, pardon, Merrilee, but they make me angry still."

Patrel laughed, too. "Luth, there's nothing worse than a reformed malefactor, one who has seen the error of his ways. I know, for I am one, too."

Luth stood and smiled again, and handed Merrilee the arrows. "Here you are, damman, arrows fletched to fit your draw. Wing them well and true, for on the morrow we snap a trap shut upon a squad of reavers."

. And as Luth took to his bed, and so too did Danner and Patrel, Merrilee sat and gazed at the arrows and searched for a flaw in her plan.

Nearly three hundred Warrows had mustered when the company rode west through the Shadowlight to Budgens. Buccen took station upon rooftops and behind barricades. A band of twenty upon ponies was dispatched southward down Byroad Lane; they were the decoy, whose job it was to draw the Ghûls into the trap.

Merrilee and Patrel took station upon the roof of the Blue Bull, Budgens' one inn. Across the street upon the smithery Merrilee could see Danner, and she waved before taking her place of concealment. All Warrows slipped out of sight, though some kept watch upon the south where could be seen the pony squad standing now on Byroad Lane near the Crossland Road.

And the wait began . . .

Minutes seemed like hours, and hours dragged by like days. And still the wait went on and the Ghûls did not come. Merrilee fidgeted and checked her arrows again and again, while Patrel hummed a soft tune under his breath, and others spoke quietly and waited; but the Ghûlen squad came not. Time trudged by on halting feet: plodding, lagging, dragging. And Merrilee knew then what her plan did not take into account: "We know not if the Ghûls will even come," she said to Patrel, "for we control not their ranks, their numbers."

And still the wait went on . . .

And Merrilee thought: *All this work will have gone for nought.*

And time dragged past . . .

"Here they come, Captain," said the lookout. "Oh, Lor!"

At the sentry's exclamation, Merrilee peeped over the edge of the roof, looking south through the Dimmendark toward the junction of the Crossland Road and Byroad Lane. Her eyes immediately saw the pony squad; and beyond, coming into view from behind the hills flanking the Crossland Road, cantered dark Hèlsteeds bearing Ghûls. And Merrilee's heart lurched, *for there were fully one hundred of Modru's Reavers and not a mere squad of twenty-seven.* But it was too late to change the plan, for the buccen on Byroad Lane wheeled their ponies and bolted for Budgens, and howling Ghûls plunged in pursuit.

Down the road they thundered, racing for the village, the Hèlsteeds overhauling the ponies at an alarming rate. Merrilee clenched her fist and beat upon the roof. "Ride, buccen, ride! Ride for your lives!" she whispered fiercely, fervently hoping that she had correctly gauged the speed of pony against Hèlsteed.

Now the spears of the racing Ghûls were lowered, as they made ready to lance the fleeing Warrows verging on the fringe of Budgens.

The lead Ghûl howled a command, and a score raced to the left, riding for the gap between Budgens and the Rillmere, striking to head off any Warrows who might flee that way. *These twenty reavers would be outside the trap!*

Merrilee glanced across the street to see Danner take two squads of buccen, to disappear beyond her vision as they leapt to the ground in back of the smithery.

And then the ponies bearing Warrows thundered past down the street, and behind raced the Ghûls on Hèlsteeds, howling in victory now, for they were closing upon their quarry.

Through the far barricade the ponies scaddled, and the gap in the wall closed as a brush-bearing waggon rolled into the slot. Flames sprang up as torches fired the wood splashed with lamp oil. The racing Hèlsteeds squealed in pain and skidded to a halt as the Ghûls, sensing a trap, hauled hard upon reins, wheeling 'round to ride back south. But there, too, a barricade rolled to, and flames burst forth.

The trap slammed shut.

But twenty Ghûls were outside.

Patrel stood and set to his lips the Horn of the Reach— the silver bugle given to him by Marshal Vidron on the day they first met—and a silver call split the air, its notes belling wide across the countryside, and everywhere that Warrows heard it, a burst of hope sprang full in their hearts. Below in the streets of Budgens, Ghûls quailed from the sound and Hèlsteeds reared in fear. Warrows stood upon the roof-tops and at Patrel's second pure clarion call, a storm of arrows whistled through the air to rain death upon the Ghûls.

Merrilee stood straight as a wand, her bow nocked with arrow, and Tuck's voice spoke softly in her mind: *"Inhale full. Exhale half. Draw to your anchor point. Center your aim. Loose."* Again and again she sped arrows down into the Ghûls, and over and over Tuck whispered in her memory. And where she aimed, arrows flew, piercing Ghûl breast and heart. It did not matter that all about her ap-peared to be confusion and that the streets were a churning mass below, that Hèlsteeds reared and spears were flung at buccen and cries of death rent the air; all that mattered were Tuck's words: *"Inhale full. Exhale half. Draw to your anchor point. Center your aim. Loose."* And feathered Death sped from her bow.

Yet the Ghûls were savage reavers, and they threw spears to pierce Warrows. Ghûls dismounted, some quilled with arrows, and they clambered up porch posts to reach the rooftops where their tulwars clove ere these reavers were felled by arrows loosed in close quarters, or by buc-cen-wielded wooden lances made for just this purpose.

Merrilee did not note the Ghûl that came upon her roof, but Patrel felled it by an arrow through the heart.

The Ghûlen number dwindled in the streets below. But there came an uproar from the northern barricade, as the score of Ghûls outside the trap fought to tear it open. And the barricade was breached. Surviving Ghûls in the street

spurred for the gap to escape this fanged nest. Warrows
upon the rooftops ran leaping from roof to roof, loosing
arrows at the fleeing Ghûls below. The two squads com-
mandeered by Danner fell upon the twenty foe outside,
and arrows thudded into corpse-flesh. The Ghûls wheeled
about, and Hèlsteeds bore down upon the Warrows on
foot. Spears slew some while tulwars clove others. Yet the
buccen stood their ground and carefully aimed, and arrows
burst through Ghûl hearts. Danner's two squads were
joined by those who had ridden the decoy ponies, and these
buccen slammed the barricade shut again before most of
the Ghûls in the street could race free, and only four or
five of those trapped had managed to flee through the gap.
Then the decoy buccen turned upon the Spawn outside,
and Death hissed into the once-proud Ghûlen ranks, and
but three won free of these barb-spitting Warrows, and
those three fled in fear.

In the trap, none survived.

And when the Warrows saw that the Battle of Budgens
had ended, a cheering broke forth and there were calls for
Merrilee. But she turned to Patrel and clung to him sobbing, and he looked to the others as if to say: "Well, she's
a damman, you know."

Ninety-seven Ghûls had been felled: six by spears upon
the rooftops, the rest by arrows through the heart. It was
a smashing victory by all accounts, but a victory purchased
at a dear price:

Nineteen Warrows had been killed, and thirty others
wounded, some by tulwar, some by spear; some of the
wounded would never fight again, but most would heal to
carry on.

Word of the Battle of Budgens spread across the Seven
Dells like wildfire, igniting Warrow spirits, for the first of
the Struggles had gone to the Bosky, and the Wee Folk
now knew that the Ghûls could be beaten. Word spread,
too, about the "Damman Thornwalker," but most thought
it just a rumor.

And in the Northwood, Southwood, and the hills around
Weevin, Thornwalkers came together to fight for liberty.
In the Updunes, the Claydunes, and the Eastwood, traps
were laid and Ghûls slain. And in Bigfen, Littlefen, and

the Cliffs to the west, Warrows smiled, for they had been fighting all along and knew the Ghûls were vulnerable, though the count of Ghûlen dead at Budgens surprised even them.

Back at Whitby's barn, the council of Lieutenants sat in session with Captain Patrel, Captain Danner, and damman Merrilee. Patrel spoke: "We are all agreed then: though we know not how to do it, we must take the fight now to the Ghûls: we must devastate their strongholt in the ruins of Brackenboro."

Merrilee looked 'round the table, and a chill sense of foreboding shivered up her spine.

CHAPTER 4

Myrkenstone

Spittle ran down Modru's hideous iron mask, and his eyes blazed with rage. With a backhanded sweep, his black-gauntleted fist crashed into the side of Laurelin's face, and she was smashed to the floor. *"Khakt!"* Modru's spitting cry brought the mute Rukh scuttling into the room. The Rukh's glance darted thither and yon, and he scurried to the mirror and drew the black cloth over the glass. Then he ran to bob and grovel before Modru.

"Shuul!" hissed Modru, and the mute sprang out the door. The black-cloaked figure turned back to Laurelin. "Perhaps your manners will improve after a rest in your quarters," he said, then sibilant laughter hissed forth.

The mute Rukh came scuttling back, and with him were two Lōkha.

"Shabba Dūl!" spat Modru, and the Lōkha jerked Laurelin to her feet and shoved her from the room.

Along the central hall they took her, till they came to a heavy, studded door. One Lōkh hauled forth a ring of keys and rattled one into the lock, while the other took up a brand and lighted it. The portal creaked open and musty air seeped forth. Through the door they led her, the guttering torch held high, and Laurelin saw that they were in a stairwell with steep steps twisting downward into blackness. Down they went, the Princess hugging leftward against the wall adrip with slime, for there was no bannister to the right. Down they went: one flight, two, more; she lost count of the steps. At last, they came to a landing with a rusted iron door, and even though the steps pitched on downward into the blackness below, the Lōkh with the keys stopped, clattering one into the padlock.

Venting oaths, he struggled to turn the key; then with a grating sound, at last the tumblers gave way. The Lōkh hammered on the lock and the shackle opened. He pried the hasp back and then, jerking, inched open the portal until they could squeeze through.

Beyond was a narrow, tortuous passage canting down. Iron-grilled gates were spaced along this twisting way, but they yielded to the keys, and downward the Lōkha took Laurelin. At last they emerged in a foul chamber, littered with filth and splintered bones, the marrow tongued out. The twisting passage could be seen to continue on, exiting out the far end of the chamber. An iron-barred cell with filthy straw on the floor was to the left. And into this foul cage Laurelin was pushed.

Clang! slammed the door.

Clack! shut the lock.

And then the Lōkha turned and stamped away.

And they took the light with them.

Laurelin could hear their foul voices in slobbering speech and raucous laughter as they went back up the way they had come, and the clash of the iron-grilled gates slamming to behind them, and the rusty screech of the iron door as it was forced shut again. And then she was alone in the blackness.

Her good hand stretched out before her, Laurelin slowly stepped forward until she came up against the bars of the cell. Now she turned right and, occasionally touching the bars for guidance, once more stepped slowly until again she came up against a wall, this one made of stone. Again she turned right and paced in the utter blackness, counting as she went.

Laurelin's cell was fifteen paces wide and ten paces deep. Three walls were slimy stone, one wall iron bars. Rotted straw littered the floor. Along the back wall was a small stone pier that Laurelin sat upon as if it were a bench, her back to the wall, her feet drawn up. And for the first time since her capture, alone and in the pitch dark, she pressed her forehead against her drawn-up knees and quietly wept.

Laurelin awakened to hear the distant screech of protesting iron and the clang of gates being opened, and the glow of a flaming torch grew as someone came down the twisting passage. It was her Lōkh jailor. The torchlight was painful to Laurelin's eyes, and she shadowed her face with an out-held hand, blinking back watery tears. The Lōkh set two buckets upon the floor just outside her cell door, then turned and went back the way he had come, slamming the gates behind, shutting the iron door.

Bright afterimages slashing through her eyes, Laurelin fumbled her way to the cage bars, reaching through until she found a bucket. It contained water, and she drank thirstily using the cup found in the bucket bottom; and though the water tasted of sulphur, to her it was sweet. Still on her knees in the sour straw, she groped about and found the other wooden pail. She reached in and discovered a coarse hunk of stale bread. Cradling the chunk in her broken arm, once more she groped into the bucket and snatched her arm back with a hiss of air sucked in through clenched teeth, for something wet with small claws had scuttled across her hand.

Laurelin sat on the stone pier and ate the coarse bread, listening to a far-off drip of water tinking slowly, the sound echoing through the pitch blackness.

The Princess did not know how long she had slept nor what had awakened her. She sat upon the stone pier and listened intently to the dark. Something had *changed,* yet she knew not what, but her heart raced and fear coursed through her veins. She pressed back against the stone wall behind her and held her breath, trying to sense whatever it was she could not see. And gradually she became convinced that in the blackness a huge creature stood pressed up against her cage and reached long arms through the bars trying to grasp her. She drew up her legs and feet and made herself as small as possible, trying to avoid the clutch, and she thought of the splintered bones littering the floor outside the cell. Her throat was dry and she was athirst, but she did not drink, for the water bucket stood where also stood terror.

When next she heard the jailor coming, Laurelin waited until the nearing light faintly illumed the corridor, showing it empty, and she ran to the bars and stood. Again the torchlight was painful, but she squinted and turned her face aside. The moment the Lōkh set the buckets down, Laurelin snatched the cup from bucket bottom and drank greedily: two cups, three, four. She forced the water down while the Lōkh sneered at her snorting, *"Schtuga!"* Laurelin snatched up the bread and two turnips from the other pail, leaving the meat behind, cradling the food with her splinted arm as she dipped up another cup of water and went back to the stone pier. The Lōkh took up the first two wooden pails, leaving the latest behind, and, laughing harshly, he stalked away up the twisting passage.

And Laurelin sat with her back pressed against the stone and her feet drawn up, a full cup of water beside her as she ate the turnips and bread. And she thought, *Now, monster of the dark, if you are truly there, my food and drink are here with me and not sitting at your feet.*

Over the next few "days," Laurelin lived along the back wall of the cell, spending much of her time on the stone pier, but frequently pacing to one corner or the other for exercise and other needs. And whenever the jailor came, she would step to the bars as soon as the light coming down the twisting passage showed the corridor clear, waiting to force down water and to snatch up her food ere the Lōkh's torch was gone again.

On many occasions Laurelin sensed the sinister presence before her cell, and then she would stay upon the pier. But at other times the corridor seemed empty, and then would she pace the back wall.

Although she had no certain way of telling time, she believed that the Lōkh visited but once each "day," bringing food and water. She kept count of these "days" by using her thumbnail to scribe a notch in the wood of her splint where a stub stuck out beyond her bandage.

She had marked five such notches when she heard the sounds of the doors rattling open and saw the glow of a torch reflecting down the passage. But it had not yet been a "day" since the jailor had last come to her cage. Yet the light came onward, and from her position next to the bars, Laurelin saw two Lōkh enter the corridor.

With a clack of keys, one Lōkh unlocked her cell, and she was shoved out. Blinking from the light, once more

Laurelin trod through the twisting passage, and along the stairwell, this time going upward instead of down.

Up the steps they went, and now Laurelin counted: eight flights they climbed before coming to the door at the top. The Princess was trembling when they reached the central hall, for she had been weakened by her captivity.

Yet the Lōkha turned and led her through an adjacent door, and they climbed more stairs, finally coming to a large, empty stone floor, and more steps spiraled upward into darkness, twisting up inside Modru's Iron Tower. Ascending the dark stairwell, one Lōkh before and the other after, Laurelin once again clung to the wall beside her, for here, too, there was no bannister to keep her from falling.

Up they went, past narrow window-slits looking out into the Dimmendark, up flight after flight, Laurelin's breath coming in harsh gasps. And just as she would have collapsed, the Lōkha stopped to rest, for they, also, were winded. Laurelin slumped to the landing and leaned her head against the cold wall and panted.

Sooner than she was ready, the Lōkha got to their feet and snarled at her, and once more the tortuous ascent began. Four more flights they took her, at last to come to an ironbound door with a brazen knocker that the lead Lōkh let rise and fall once.

After a moment, the door was opened by a Rukh, this one made mute also. Laurelin was led into the great chamber atop the Iron Tower. Round it was and nearly sixty feet in diameter, and full of dark shadows. Yet along the walls dimly could be seen scroll-cluttered tables littered with prisms, alembics and astrolabes, charts and geometrical figures cast in metal, vials of chemicals, and other strange devices and books of lore.

Here, too, were instruments of torture: a brazier with hot irons, shackles, a rack, and other hideous implements.

But the thing that drew Laurelin's eye stood on a massive pedestal in the center of the room; yet her gaze was baffled by what she saw atop the platform: it looked like a great irregular *blot;* not so much black it was, but rather it seemed to be an *absence* of light that held her gaze. It had the shape and size of a ponderous irregular stone: huge, seven feet long, four high, four wide. And it sat massy and jagged, like a great dark *gape* sucking light into its bottomless black maw.

The Lōkha led Laurelin around this *thing* and to a chain affixed to an iron post, and cuffed her good hand in the iron bracelet. And as they stomped out, Laurelin tore her gaze from the black blotch and looked elsewhere and gasped, for there, wrists shackled to the wall, head slumped forward, was an Elf!

"Lord Gildor!" Laurelin cried.

Slowly the Elf lifted his head and looked at her; his face was badly battered. Long he gazed, then said at last, "Nay, lady, I am Vanidor, Gildor's twin."

Sibilant laughter hissed forth from the dark shadows: "So, it is Lord Vanidor, is it?"

Laurelin spun about to see dark Modru step out of the blackness.

"Lord Vanidor, fifth in line to the Lian Crown," said the Evil. One. "Perhaps, my dear, he should take your place, for although you stand next to the throne of the High King, he bears the blood of the *Dolh*." Then Modru paused and spread his hands. "But alas, the noble blood of a royal damosel suits my needs even more so than that of a high Lian, for you are of Mithgar and he is not."

"Royal damosel?" Vanidor looked again at Laurelin.

"Yes!" Modru's voice gloated as he grasped the Princess by her matted hair and twisted her face into the torchlight. "Here is the prize you seek, fool!"

Sunken-cheeked and hollow-eyed, the left side of her face purple with bruise, covered with sour rot from the cell, her clothes and the bandage of her splinted arm unspeakably filthy, Laurelin was displayed to Vanidor, and it was long ere the Elf spoke, and then it was but to say, "I am sorry, my Lady."

"Faugh! Sorry?" hissed Modru, but then his eyes flashed triumph through the iron-snouted visor. "Yes, I see. Sorry. But more than you know. You would have rescued this maiden—if you could have found her, and recognized her, and if you had not been captured. But she would not have been an easy prize to snatch, even had you managed to elude the guards in the courtyard, for she has been keeping company with one of my . . . aides. And *he* would not have spared those who came to steal his . . . pretty. Oh, worry not, my dear, for he has been instructed to be . . . gentle."

Modru spun and faced Vanidor, and his voice lashed out harshly: "How many of you came on this fool's errand?"

Vanidor said nought.

"Surely more than three," spat Modru.

"Ask them," said the Elf.

"You know they are dead, fool Vanidor," hissed Modru, "and so I now ask you. And you will tell me also how you breached my walls."

Again Vanidor did not speak.

Modru signed to the mute Rukh: *"Vhuul!"* The Rukh scuttled out the door and away, while Modru walked to the massive pedestal and gloated at the ponderous black maw: "I'll give you but a moment to reflect upon your reticence, oaf, and then if you will not give me the answers I seek, I will extract them from you."

At these words Laurelin's heart plummeted, and she looked into Vanidor's green eyes, and her own grey ones brimmed with tears. But Vanidor said nothing.

"Perhaps I should persuade you to speak by dealing with the Princess while you watch," Modru's cold voice suggested. "But, no, I need her unblemished."

The door opened and in scuttled the Rukh, and stooping through the portal behind came a great cave Troll. Twelve feet tall he was, with glaring red eyes and tusks that protruded through his lips. Greenish was his skin, and *scaled,* like armor plate. Black leather breeks he wore, and nothing else. Into the room he shambled, stooping over, his massive arms hanging down. Steering wide of the *blot* on the pedestal, he came before Modru, his brutish face leering at Laurelin.

Her heart thudded heavily, and she had barely the will to stare back without blenching.

"Dolh schluu gogger!" commanded Modru in the foul Slûk tongue. And the Ogru turned and grasped one of Vanidor's arms while the Rukh unlocked the wrist shackles. Then the Elf was hauled to the rack and his feet and wrists were locked again. The great Ogru-Troll sat hunkered beside the rack, one arm hugging his knees in anticipation, a massive hand upon the turn-wheel, a dull-witted leer upon his face.

At a sign from Modru, the Ogru slowly turned the wheel: *Clack! Clack! Clack! Clack!* the wooden rachet clattered as the wrist cuffs pulled upward. *Clack! Clack! Clack!* Now all of the slack was gone from the ropes and Vanidor's arms and legs were pulled straight. Here the Troll stopped, his mouth gaping wide, his thick tongue running over his yellow teeth.

"How many came with you?" hissed Modru.

Vanidor said nought.

Clack!

"I ask you again, fool: were there more than three of you?" Modru faced Laurelin, and she said nothing, her lips pressed in a grim line.

Clack!

"Tell me this, oaf: what were the names of your slain companions?" Modru faced Vanidor, the Elf's body taut.

"Tell him, Lord Vanidor!" cried Laurelin in anguish. "It cannot hurt, for they are dead!"

"Duorn and Varion," said Vanidor, speaking at last.

"Ahh, the dolt *does* have a tongue," hissed Modru. "Duorn and Varion, eh? And what of other companions: did they, too, have names?"

Again Vanidor clamped his lips shut.

The Troll grinned in glee.

Clack!

"You might as well speak, fool," sissed Modru, "for your silence will not stay my Master's return."

"Your Master?" Vanidor's question jerked out through clenched teeth. Sweat beaded upon the Elf's brow and trickled down his face.

"Gyphon!" Modru's voice lashed out in exultation.

"Gyphon?" gasped Vanidor. "But He is beyond the Spheres."

"At the moment, yes," crowed Modru, "but on the Darkest Day the Myrkenstone will open the way.

"But we dally, fool. Name me names."

Silence.

Clack!

A groan escaped Vanidor's lips, and Laurelin wept silently.

"Myrkenstone?" Vanidor's breath shuddered in and out.

Modru gloated at him and paused as if debating whether to share a secret. "Why not? You'll not tell this tale to others.'' The Evil One strode to the *blotch* on the pedestal. "Here, fool, is the great Myrkenstone. Sent on its way by my Master four millennia agone. Long was its journey, but it came at last, five years past. Did not my Master say unto Adon: *'Even now I have set into motion events you cannot stop.'* Did He not say so?''

Modru strode back to Vanidor. "Your companions, dolt, their names.''

The Elf bit his lip till blood came, but spoke not.

Clack!

Vanidor was in agony, his shoulders separated from their sockets, his hips and spine pulled near their limits. His ribs stood stark upon his heaving chest.

"Why, my Lord Vanidor,'' sneered Modru, "you look puzzled by my tale of the Myrkenstone. Whence came this thing, you ask? From the sky, fool! What you simpletons name the Dragon Star, that was Gyphon's sending: a great flaming comet whose only purpose was to bear the Myrkenstone to me, to plunge to Mithgar in dark, blazing glory, the 'Stone plummeting to fall at my retreat in the Barrens. Why think you I dwelled there *lo* these many years? Out of fear? Nay! Say instead out of anticipation.

"Now yield me the names of your comrades.''

Only Laurelin's sobs answered him.

Spittle drooled from the corner of the Troll's mouth.

Clack!

Vanidor's wrists bled, and his ankles were disjoint. Wordless sounds came from his throat.

"Think you that it was an accident of nature?'' Modru's viperous voice asked. "Nay, 'twas my Master's doing! And a great weapon it is. How deem you the Dimmendark is made? What's that? You cannot say? Then I shall have to tell you: by the Myrkenstone, fool! It *eats* the cursed sunlight, sending Shadowlight in its stead. And with it I control the reach of Winternight, to the woe of the world. But when my Master comes, I and my minions will be set free from the Sunbane, then nought will stop our rule.''

Modru's clenched fist smote the rack, and he loomed darkly over the Elf. "Names, fool, names,'' spat Modru.

"Oh, my Lord Vanidor, speak!'' cried Laurelin. "Please speak!''

Cries were wrested from Vanidor, but he said no name.

The great Ogru's lips smacked wetly.

Clack!

"Ride, Flandrena, ride!" Vanidor's cry was rent from his screaming throat.

"Flandrena?" hissed Modru. "Is that one of your companions?"

Vanidor's hoarse shrieks filled the tower, and Laurelin jerked at her chain and wrenched back and forth and cried in great gasping sobs and tried to reach the Elf.

Clack!

"Gildor!" Vanidor's tortured scream shattered through the tower, and then was no more, for the Lian warrior was dead.

Laurelin fell to her knees, her arms clutched across her stomach, and she doubled over, rocking back and forth in torment, great sobs racking her frame. Yet she was driven so deeply into grief and horror that no sounds issued from her throat. And she was but vaguely aware of Lōkha unshackling her from the iron post and leading her back down the twisting stairwell; for the torturous murder of Vanidor Silverbranch had pushed Laurelin beyond her uttermost limits. And as she stumbled blindly down the steps, behind her sissed Modru's sibilant laughter.

She was taken down to a main corridor, but the Lōkha did not force her back to the dark cell. Instead, she was given over to two scuttling Rukha who led her into a richly appointed room.

" 'Unblemished,' he said," croaked one Rukh.

"But, *sss,* the arm, the arm," hissed the other.

"The drink'll heal that, you stupid gob," snarled the first, "after we bind it."

Ungently, the two Rukha stripped the foul clothing from the Princess, hauling her this way and that. And when she was naked, they used iron shears to cut the wrappings holding the splint in place. And all the while they worked, Laurelin sobbed quietly, tears smearing through the grime on her face.

At last the injured arm was bared, and although the bone had already begun to knit—for it had been twenty-three days since it had been broken—still the Rukha set Laurelin's break in a binding made by dipping long, wide strips of cloth in a liquescent paste and wrapping them 'round her arm where they quickly dried. When the two were done, the stiffened wrap went from above her bent elbow to below her wrist.

And they poured the hot burning drink down her throat, the same fiery liquid forced upon her by the Ghola on the long ride to Modru's Iron Tower.

They took her into another room and sat her in a hot bath, and with harsh soaps and rough hands they scrubbed her hair and scoured the filth from her face and elsewhere. And Laurelin paid but little heed to their unfeeling ministrations.

That night she slept in a bed, but her dreams were of the Iron Tower, and she woke up screaming, *"Vanidor!"* And, weeping, she fell back into exhausted sleep.

And in her dreams, a golden-haired Elfess came to her and soothed her.

And then a sad-eyed Elf stood before her. *Are you Vanidor? Are you Gildor?* But he said nought, smiling gently.

Lastly, she had a vision of her Lord Galen, and he stood in a dark place and held her locket at his throat.

When she awakened, she found she was weeping, and her mind kept returning to those unbearable moments in the tower: unspeakably cruel, ruthless moments that endlessly repeated in her thoughts.

The mute Rukh brought her food, yet she touched it not, and sat abed watching the fire in the chimney with unseeing eyes: grieving. All 'Darkday she sat thus, cold horror clutching her heart; for what the slaughter of a waggon train had failed to do, what eighteen 'Darkdays at the hands of the Ghola had failed to do, and what five "days" locked in a filthy, lightless cell had failed to do, being forced to watch helplessly the torture-murder of Vanidor had at last done: it had driven her spirit into a dark realm of no hope.

That night, again Laurelin dreamed of the golden-haired Lady. And this time the Elfess planted a seed in black soil. A green shoot emerged and swiftly blossomed into a beautiful flower. Just as swiftly, the flower withered and died. And a wind blew, carrying the shriveled leaves and petals swirling up and away, but also bearing silken fluffs floating upon the breeze. And the Elfess reached up and caught one of the fluffs and held it for Laurelin to see. And *lo!* it was a seed.

Laurelin awakened, and sat in the flickering firelight and pondered the fair Lady's message, and the Princess at last thought she knew its import: *From Life comes Death, from Death comes Life, a never-ending circle.*

And in that moment, aided by a golden-haired Elfess she had never met, Laurelin's spirit began to heal.

CHAPTER 5

Drimmen-Deeve

Up the long staircase they climbed, Brega and Gildor first with the lantern, Tuck and Galen after. And from below pounded thunder as the maddened Kraken hammered upon the Door: *Boom! Boom!*

At the top of the steps they paused, catching their breath.

"Two hundred treads," said Brega, and turned to Gildor. "It is odd that a trade route would start with such an obstacle as a two-hundred-step rise."

"Nevertheless, Drimm Brega," answered Gildor, "this is the way I came. Mayhap heavy goods are borne by train a different way, perhaps out through a level passage from the chamber below; yet when we trod under the Grimwall through Drimmen-deeve those many years past, this is the way we were led."

Brega merely grunted.

Boom! Boom! Boom!

"Let us move on," said Brega, "else the Madûk may jar loose the hidden linchpins to bring these passages down upon us."

Onward they went, along a high, curving corridor, passages and fissures alike boring blackly off to either side. The floor was level and covered with a fine layer of rock dust, and no tracks could be seen in it except those they left in their wake.

Boom. Boom. Behind, the Kraken raged on, the rolling echoes fading with distance as the four strode forth: *boom . . . boom . . . oom . . .* until finally they could hear the savage hammering no more.

The floor had begun to slope downward, and still corridors and crevices radiated outward, away from the passageway the comrades followed. But Gildor stayed in the main tunnel and did not turn aside.

Down they went, deeper under the dark granite of Grim-spire Mountain, and their pace was swift. Four miles, five miles, and more, they marched away from the Door, their hard stride carrying them onward. For as Galen put it: "We must be away from this Black Maze ere the Ghola can bear word to the Gargon that intruders now walk his Realm."

But each one of the four was weary, exhausted by the long pursuit ere they had set foot into Black Drimmen-deeve, and so, when they came into an enormous, long hall, nearly four hundred yards in length, perhaps eighty yards wide, set, according to Brega, some seven miles from the Door, Gildor called a halt.

"We must rest and eat, and let me study the ways before us," said the Lian warrior, waving a hand at the four major portals gaping blackly into the chamber, "for I must choose the proper path out."

Grateful for the chance to rest, Tuck slumped to the floor in the middle of the hall. He fished around in his pack and gave a biscuit of mian to Galen while keeping one for himself. They sat in the shadows in the center of the chamber and watched as Gildor and Brega made the rounds of the exits, peering down each and discussing the paths that they saw. At last the Elf and Dwarf came and sat beside the Man and Warrow and took food for themselves.

Brega wolfed down his ration, yet Gildor but barely touched his food, seeming pensive, troubled.

"Elf Gildor," said Brega, sipping from his canteen, "be there water along this path of ours?"

"Yes, if I step it out true," answered Gildor. "Water aplenty for the drinking, sweet and pure when I came so long ago."

"Elf Gildor," Brega spoke again, "while we rest ere we go on, you said you would speak of some events of long ago, after the Châkka abandoned Kraggen-cor. How came the drawbridge to be up? The Door to be closed? The Black Mere to be made?"

"Ah, yes," said Gildor, "I did promise you that tale. Hear me, then, for this is what I know: When the Dread broke free of the Lost Prison, the Drimma fled Drimmen-deeve, and some Elves fled Darda Galion, for such is the Gargon's horror. Drimma fled east and west, turning north and south; so, too, did the Elves that ran, or they rode the Twilight Ride.

"With the Drimma gone, Rucha and Loka began to gather in the Black Deeves, coming to serve the Gargon in his dread-filled Realm. Many were the skirmishes with the *Spaunen,* and the Lian set watch upon the portals: Dusk-Door, Dawn-Gate.

"The *Rûpt,* too, set wards at these entrances, though why they guarded this place, it is not known; yet guard it the *Spaunen* did. Perhaps they feared the Lian Guardians would enter, yet even the Lian cannot withstand Gargoni: it was but through the power of the Wizards of the Black Mountain of Xian that these dread creatures were held at bay during the Great War of the Ban. And had there been more Gargoni, even the Wizards would have failed.

"Yet the *Spaunen* guarded the Door, though none else would enter, and the Lian watched patiently as the seasons passed into one another and the years flowed by.

"Then came a time five centuries past when two great Trolls came each night and quarried stone, building a dam across the Duskrill. A year they labored, until it was done at last. No longer did the Duskrill tumble down the linn in a graceful waterfall; instead, the water was trapped behind the Troll-dam. And the Black Mere—the Dark Mere— grew swiftly and soon filled all the swale up under the Loomwall.

"Another time passed: one more year, I think. And then in the dark of night a mighty Dragon came winging."

"Dragon!" burst out Tuck.

"Aye, Dragon," answered Gildor, nodding.

"Then the old tales are true," responded Tuck. "Dragons are real and not just fabulous creatures of legend, not just hearthtale fables."

"Aye, Tuck," confirmed Gildor. "Dragons are real: Fire-drakes and Cold-drakes both. Once, all Dragons gushed flame, but those who aided Gyphon in the Great War were bereft of their fire and became Cold-drakes; and they suffer the Ban, for the Sun slays them, though they die not the *Withering Death:* their Dragon-scaled hides spare them that. Even so, Cold-drakes are awesome enemies, and their spew is terrible: though it flames not, still it dissolves rock and base metal—even silver corrodes under that dire drip, and the spume chars flesh without fire."

"Then where are they, the Fire-drakes and Cold-drakes?" asked Tuck. "I mean, if Dragons are real, why don't people see them around?"

"They sleep, Tuck," answered Gildor. "For a thousand years they hide away in lairs in the remote high mountains only to awaken and ravage the Land, bellowing their brazen calls. Five hundred years agone they took to their lairs to sleep; five hundred years hence they will awaken, and they will be hungry, and begin a two-millennia rampage ere they sleep again. They are dire creatures all, especially the Renegades and Cold-drakes, for they are not bound by the pledge."

Tuck frowned. "Renegades? Pledge?"

"Long past," said Gildor, "in the First Era of Mithgar, Drakes came unto Black Mountain bearing a great token—the Dragonstone. In return for the Mages pledging to hide the stone away forever and to leave its secrets unlearned and to ward it from all who would do otherwise, most of the Dragons pledged to limit their raids to that needed for sustenance—a cow, a horse, or other such now and again. Too, they pledged to refrain from mixing in the affairs of other folk, unless these folk first meddled in the affairs of Dragons, in which case they are free to take just retribution. They also pledged to not plunder—but for sustenance—unless they were first plundered by others. They also pledged to not seek treasures owned, though abandoned treasures were and are fair game.

"Some of the Drakes refused to be bound by the pledge, just as some of the Mages also refused to be bound by their part of the bargain, and these are Renegades all."

"Evil will be the day when Dragons wake," said Brega, grimly, "for they are the bane of all Folk, especially, as you say, Lord Gildor, the Renegades and the Cold-drakes. The Châkka have often suffered from these dire creatures: Dragons would plunder our treasuries and hoard our hard-won wealth." Brega turned to Gildor. "But the Dragon that came through the night to the Dusk-Door, was it a Cold-drake, like Sleeth?"

"Aye, like Sleeth but not Sleeth, for that Orm had already been slain by Elgo," answered Gildor. At the mention of Elgo's name, Brega's eyes flashed with ire, and he seemed about to speak, but Gildor went on: "When the great creature winged south from the Northern Wastes, at first we thought it was mighty Ebonskaith himself, but then we saw that instead it was Skail of the Barrens. And he bore a great burden—*a writhing* burden—something evil and alive, and he dropped it in the Black Mere."

"The Kraken," said Galen.

"The Madûk," echoed Brega.

"Aye," answered Gildor, nodding, "though then we did not know what it was, today, five hundred years later, we four have discovered to our woe it was a Hèlarms."

"Hèlarms?" Again Tuck bore a puzzled look. "Whence came this creature?"

"I deem it most likely that Skail bore it here from the Great Maelstrom off the Seabane Island in the Boreal Sea, for that is a haunt of these creatures, hauling ships down into the great whirlpool, there where the Gronfang Mountains plunge into the brine," answered Gildor. "Yet it could have come from other places as well: It is told that fell monsters from beyond the borders of time inhabit the deeps—not only the great ocean abysses, but also the cold, dark lakes: the Grimmere, Nordlake, and others. And the waters rushing in blackness 'neath the Land—the lightless undermountain torrents, the rivers carving stone, the bottomless black pools—they, too, are said to hold dire creatures, and are better left undisturbed."

Tuck shuddered and gazed about into the shadows mustered near as Gildor spoke on: "Skail dropped the burden into the Black Mere and then winged north, anxious to be safe in his lair ere the Sun arose. And with this Monster now in the waters, when daybreak came, the Lian warriors saw that the drawbridge was up and the Dusk-Door closed; the *Rûpt* no longer stood watch at this portal."

"There was no need," said Galen, "for the Krakenward now guarded this entrance."

"Aye," answered Gildor, "and now we know why the Ghûlka attacked us not: they feared the Hèlarms."

Again Tuck shuddered. "What a vile Monster: lurking in black waters, waiting to snatch innocent victims."

No one spoke for a moment, and then Galen quietly said, "I loved Jet."

"And I Fleetfoot," Gildor added.

Again no one spoke for long moments, and tears glimmered in Tuck's eyes. Even Brega seemed stricken by the deaths of the horses who had striven to their uttermost limits only to be cruelly slain by a hideous creature, for Brega said, his voice husky, "No two steeds could have given more."

At last Galen stood, saying, "Be there ought else, Gildor? We must press on."

"Only this, Galen King," said Gildor, rising to his feet also, "the Monster was put here at the behest of Modru, on this you can mark my words, for none else would do such a vile thing. Hearken unto this, too: the power of the Evil in Gron must be vast to cause a Dragon to bear a Hèlarms from the Great Maelstrom to here, and to cause a Hèlarms to suffer being borne."

"Perhaps," said Brega, shouldering his pack, "there is something to the legend that Dragons mate with Madûks."

"What?" burst out Tuck. "Dragons mate with Krakens?"

" 'Tis but a legend," answered Brega, "yet it is also true that no female Dragons are known to the Châkka." Brega cocked an eye at Gildor, who merely shrugged and agreed that no female Dragons were known to the Elves either.

Once more they set out upon their journey, striding to reach the Dawn-Gate ere they could be detected. And the deeper they strode into Drimmen-deeve, the more uneasy Tuck became, yet he knew not why.

The corridor that Gildor chose continued to slant downward, and less than a mile from the "Long Hall," as Brega called it, they came to a wide fissure in the floor, nearly eight feet across; the passage continued on the other side. And from the black depths of the crack came a hideous *sucking* sound.

"Ah," said Gildor, "now I know we follow the path I trod long ago, for this *slurping* crevice I remember well. Yet there was a wooden span when we crossed it."

"What makes the suck?" asked Tuck, peering down into the blackness but seeing nought, then pulling back. "It sounds as if some hideous creature lies below, trying to draw us into its maw." Tuck's thoughts were upon Gildor's words about monsters living in deep, dark places.

Brega listened. "A whirl of water, I think. Had this place a name, Elf Gildor, when you last were here?"

Gildor shook his head, and Tuck said, "Then I name it the Drawing Dark, for it seems to want to pull us down into its lost depths. A slurking whirl of water it may be, but a sucking maw it sounds."

"Think you that you can leap this, Tuck?" asked Galen.

Tuck eyed the distance, the jump a long one for a three-and-a-half-foot-tall Warrow. "Aye," said the Wee One, "though I'd rather have a bridge."

"Here, Waeran," said Brega, setting down the lantern and his pack and uncoiling a rope, "remove your pack and tie this to your waist, then throw the loose end to me; I will anchor you if you fall short."

With three running strides, Brega sprang across. Tuck threw the Dwarf the coil of rope, one end tied to the Warrow's waist. When Brega had looped it over his shoulders and had taken a firm grip, he nodded to the buccan.

Tuck took one last look at the black gap, trying to banish the thought of being sucked down into a monstrous maw, and ran and leapt with all his might. He cleared the gap by a good two feet.

The packs and lantern were tossed across, then Gildor and lastly Galen leapt the fissure, and they strode onward, leaving the hideous suck of the Drawing Dark behind.

Deeper under the dark granite of Grimspire they strode, the path ever pitching downward, corridors and branchings splitting outward from the passage they trod, unexpected cracks yawning in the floor, though none the width of the Drawing Dark. And the farther they went, the more Tuck's heart pounded in vague apprehension.

"It is the Dread, Tuck," said Gildor, noting the perspiration beaded upon the Waerling's lip. "We stride toward him now, and the fear will grow."

Onward they went through the shadowy maze, coming to a great oval chamber—"Eleven miles from the Door," said Brega. This hall, too, was enormous: nearly three hundred yards in extent, two hundred at its widest. Straight across the floor they strode, out the far side.

Still the passage pitched downward, and Tuck was most weary, his steps beginning to lag. Long had this "day" been, for it had begun many hours past with the attempt to cross Quadran Pass.

"When next we come to a chamber, we will rest," said Galen, "for worn-out legs will not bear us swiftly if fleetness ever becomes our need."

But they tramped four more miles through the black tunnels, downward past splits and forks and joinings, before coming to another chamber, this one also huge. Brega held high the lantern and Gildor smiled in relief and pointed. "This, too, I remember, for here is where we stopped to take water."

Tuck peered past Gildor to see a chamber nearly round, two hundred yards across. And by the phosphorescent glow of the Dwarven lantern he could see a low stone bridge crossing above a clear stream that emerged from the wall to the left and rushed through a wide channel cutting across the west end of the chamber to disappear under the wall to the south. Several low stone parapets beringed the room.

"This is called Bottom Chamber," said Brega. "Châkka lore speaks of this bridge o'er the drinking stream. Sweet has been this water in all the Châkka days."

"Sweet, too, was the Duskrill ere the Dark Mere came to be," said Gildor. "But now that water has been spoiled by the Hèlarms, and it is foul to the taste and touch. Let us hope the drinking stream remains safe and pure."

Across the carven arch they went, stopping long enough at the far side to stoop and test and then drink deeply and refill their leather water bottles with the cold, clean, crystalline liquid.

They sat with their backs to one of the stone parapets and took a meal. And as they ate, apprehension coursed through Tuck's veins; the fear had grown, for they had strode four miles nearer to the Dread.

They had but finished their rations when Gildor softly spoke: "Galen King, I bear woeful news. I could not speak of it before; my grief was too great. Yet now I must say this while I can: I fear the mission to rescue the Lady Laurelin has failed, for Vanidor is dead."

"Vanidor . . ." Tuck blurted; then: "How know you this, Lord Gildor?"

"The place where he stood in my heart is now empty." Gildor looked away, silent for a moment, then spoke on, his voice but a whisper: "I felt his final pain. I heard his last cry. Evil slew him."

Gildor rose up and walked into the shadows. And now all the company knew why the Elf had fallen to his knees, whelmed, crying *"Vanidor!"* in that dire instant when the Krakenward had struck.

After a moment Galen, too, arose and went into the shadows, following Gildor's steps. And they stood and spoke softly, but what they said, Tuck did not know as tears slid down his face.

And Brega sat with his hood cast over his head.

Again Gildor stood guard while the others slept; and the sad eyes of the Elf watched the faint ruby flicker running along Bale's edges, the sword whispering of evil afar.

After but six hours' respite, once more they took up the trek.

From the Bottom Chamber they took a southeasterly exit that curved away to the east as they followed the course of the corridor. Now the floor rose upward as they tramped on, and still crevices and tunnels bore away to left and right.

Three miles they marched, and Gildor stopped where a large corridor came in from the south. He stood unsure and spoke with Brega, but the lore of the Dwarf was of little or no help. They stepped southward along this large corridor to enter a great side hall, and Gildor shook his head and led them back out to follow the eastward way instead.

Still the passage sloped upward and curved unto the north, and along this section there were no side tunnels nor crevices cleaving away.

Three more miles they strode, to be confronted by four passages: the left way was wide and straight and sloped downward; the right-hand passage, too, was wide, only it bore on upward; the two middle ways were twisting and narrow, one bearing up, the other down. To the immediate left a stone door stood open.

"Ach! I cannot remember," said Gildor, looking at the four ways before him.

"No matter which of the four you choose," said Brega, "they all lead into Rávenor."

"Stormhelm?" asked Tuck. "But I thought we walked beneath the stone of Grimspire."

"Look, Waeran, and see," pointed Brega. "Here is the black granite of Aggarath, while there is the rudden stone of Rávenor. Yes, here we leave the dark rock of what you call 'Grimspire' to trod the rust red of 'Stormhelm.' "

In spite of the growing feeling of disquiet as they had trod eastward, still Tuck's heart gave a leap of hope. "Isn't the Dawn-Gate upon the flanks of Stormhelm?" At Brega's nod: "Then we have come to the mountain that holds our gateway eastward."

"Ah, but Friend Tuck," said Brega, "though we have come twenty-one miles under the rock of Aggarath, still we must stride twenty-five or thirty miles more beneath the red stone of Rávenor ere we can walk in the open again."

Tuck's heart fell to hear these distances, and plummeted even further when Gildor said, "Twenty-five or thirty miles if I can find the way, but much longer if I cannot."

Galen spoke: "Let us rest and take some food while you try to recall the way, Lord Gildor."

At the Elf's nod, Brega led them through the open stone door into a small chamber no more than twenty feet square, with a low ceiling—the first small room they had seen in Drimmen-deeve.

"Oi!" exclaimed Brega, holding up the lantern.

Centered in the room, a great chain dangled down through a narrow, grate-covered square shaft set in the ceiling and passed through a like grate placed in the floor, the huge links appearing out of the constricting blackness above and disappearing into the darkness of the strait shaft below.

Brega examined the iron-barred grille set in the floor. " 'Ware. This grate is loose, though at one time it was anchored firmly in the stone."

Tuck looked at the small chamber in puzzlement, and at the narrow shaft piercing the room, the massive chain, and the grids covering the openings above and below. "What is it for, Brega, the shaft and the chain? And why the iron bars?"

The Dwarf merely shrugged. "I know not its purpose,

Friend Tuck. Air shafts, window shafts, shafts to mine ores, well shafts for water, holes to raise and lower things: these I understand. Yet this construction is beyond my knowledge, though other Châkka could, no doubt, explain its purpose. As to the bars, all I can guess is that they are set there to keep something in."

"Or to keep something out," added Gildor.

"Is this the Lost Prison?" Tuck's heart skipped a beat.

"Nay, Tuck," said Gildor, gesturing at the stone door and iron bars. "Such a flimsy construction would not hold even a determined Ruch, much less thwart the power of an evil Vûlk."

Brega bristled. "Elf, this room was crafted by Châkka; you exaggerate when you say it could not hold an Ukh . . . though you speak true of the Ghath."

At the naming of the Dread, Tuck's heart again raced loudly in his ears.

"I stand corrected, Drimm Brega, and I apologize for my errant mouth." Gildor bowed to the Dwarf, and Brega inclined his head in return.

They sat and took a bit of mian and water, and Gildor pondered the question of the four corridors: "This I think: Neither of the two middle corridors should be our path, for I know that long ago I trod not their narrow, twisting ways. But as to the far left or right, I cannot say which one we should follow."

"Does your lore speak aught of this fourfold split, Brega?" asked Galen.

"Nay, King Galen," answered the Dwarf.

"Then, Lord Gildor," said Galen, "you must choose one of the two ways and hope we come to something that you recognize."

Suddenly, a great wash of dread inundated Tuck's heart, and he gasped in terror. Galen, Gildor, and Brega also blenched. Just as suddenly, the fear was gone, leaving racing hearts behind.

"He knows!" cried Gildor, leaping to his feet. "The Dread knows we are in his domain and casts about, questing for the spark of us."

"The Ghola," spat Galen, "they've borne the word to him."

"We must get out!" cried Brega. "We must get out before he finds us!" In haste the Dwarf shouldered his pack and stepped to the door, holding high the lantern as the others scrambled after.

And they stood before the four passages. "Which way, Lord Gildor?" asked Galen. "We cannot delay. You must choose."

"Then let it be the leftmost," answered Gildor, "for the way is widest."

And down the sloping corridor they hastened, matching Tuck's stride, for the Warrow was smallest and so he set the pace.

And Gildor withdrew flickering Red Bale from its scabbard and bore the sword in the open, its werelight to warn the four should *Spaunen* come near.

A half mile they went through the smooth-walled carven tunnel, but *lo!* Gildor's steps began to slow as if he were reluctant to press onward, yet Bale's scarlet blade-jewel glinted but lightly.

Another furlong they paced, and then the Elf stopped, and so, too, did the companions, Brega pattering on but a few more steps. "We must go no further this way," gritted Gildor, his face white.

"But the path is wide and smooth," growled Brega, pointing to the open passage before them.

"We walk toward a foul place," responded Gildor. "It has the stench of a great viper pit, though no vipers in it dwell."

Now Tuck sniffed, and a faint reek of adders hung on the air. "What is it, Lord Gildor? What makes this foetor?"

"I know not for certain, Tuck," answered the Elf, "yet when I strode the battlefields of the War of the Ban, it clung where Gargoni had been."

They retraced their steps to the corridors at the Grate Room, and this time they took the right-hand passage. And as they stepped upon its upward-sloping floor, again the pounding fear swept across them and away, leaving Tuck trembling, his legs weakened.

"He searches." Gildor's voice was tight, and he spoke to faces drawn grim.

Up the passage they strode, Tuck's legs continuing to set the pace as they marched through a delved corridor, the stone arching above them. Swiftly along the carven tunnel they went, but slowly its character changed: the walls became rougher, less worked by Dwarven tools. And then a small crack appeared along the floor and swiftly widened to become a chasm to their left, yawning black and bottomless; the floor they strode along narrowed, becoming a broad shelf lipping the fissure; and then the shelf constricted to a narrow ledge, and they sidled for scores of feet along the wall, the gulf yawning below them. At last they came once more to a wide floor, and Tuck sighed in relief as he stepped onto the broad stone.

At that moment dread fear again shocked through the four as the Gargon tried to sense them, his questing power coursing through the stone halls of Black Drimmen-deeve.

Upward sloped the way, and wide cracks appeared in the floor, and Tuck had to leap over three-and four-foot-wide crevices: long jumps for one who was only three and a half feet tall.

But finally the floor smoothed out, and once more they strode through an arched tunnel, and after three hours of walking, leaping, and sidling—going some six miles in all—they came to a great round chamber, and Tuck asked for a short rest.

Tuck sat and massaged his legs, yet his heart was filled with dire foreboding, for they had come six miles closer to the Dread. To distract his own mind Tuck said, "Well, now I have gone from being a Thornwalker to being a Deevewalker."

"Ai, you have named us, Tuck," said Gildor, "and if our tale is ever told, they will call us the Walkers of the Deeves."

"Ar!" growled Brega. "Deevewalkers we are. But of us four, only *I* have long dreamed of striding the corridors of Kraggen-cor, and now it is so, yet I would have it otherwise. For I come not marching in triumph, but instead slink through furtively. And if I live to tell of this journey to my kindred, this is what I will say: I have walked in Kraggen-cor, a bygone Realm of might; but its light is gone, and dread now stalks the halls."

Again the pounding fear washed over them, stronger now than before, and all four leapt to their feet as if to fly; then it passed onward, and Tuck unclenched his fists.

They made a circuit of the round chamber, and Gildor

spoke with Brega; and the eastward way was chosen, for
its path was broad and worn by the travel of many feet.
Forward they strode and the floor was smooth and level.

"Is there aught the Gargon fears?" puffed Tuck, stepping
along swiftly upon his Warrow legs.

"Nought that I know of," answered Gildor, "else we
would use it against him."

"He fears the Sun," said Galen, striding at Tuck's side,
"and perhaps he fears the power of Modru, yet neither of
these are at our beck to stave off the Horror."

"What about Wizards?" asked Tuck. "Lord Gildor, you
spoke of them as fending Gargons in the Ban War."

"The Mages of Xian have not been seen since that time,"
responded Gildor, "except perhaps by Elyn and Thork in
the Quest of Black Mountain: it is said they found the
Wizardholt."

Onward they strode, the lantern casting swaying shadows
along the hall, its light revealing passages and arched openings to the side.

"Is there aught that Modru fears?" asked Tuck, still
keeping the pace for all.

"The Sun," answered Galen, "and Gyphon."

"Too, it is said that Modru loathes mirrors," added
Gildor.

"Mirrors?" grunted Brega, surprised.

"I think he sees something of his true soul cast back
from the glass," answered Gildor. "And it is told that he
cannot abide his reflection in a pure silver mirror, for then
his image is stripped of all disguise and stands revealed
before him; yet it is also said that those who have seen
Modru's reflection in an argent speculum are driven foam-
ing mad forever."

The passage they followed curved to the northward, and
their hard stride bore them along its wide level floor. They
had come nearly two miles from the Round Chamber, as
Brega had dubbed it, when Gildor held up a hand. *"Hsst!"*
he whispered sharply. "I hear ironshod feet; and look: Bale
speaks of evil. Shutter the lamp, Brega."

Quickly, Brega snapped the hood down upon the lantern,
and they stood in the dark hall listening. Ahead, they could
hear the clatter of scaled armor and the tread of many feet
slapping upon the stone. And the light of burning brands

could be seen bobbing in the distance, growing brighter as a force of many came toward them. And Tuck's heart hammered in fear.

"The Drēad sends Rukha and Lōkha searching these halls for us," said Galen, his voice grim.

Brega raised the hood of the lantern a crack and searched for an exit to bolt through. "This way," he whispered, and they entered a narrow corridor bearing eastward.

The hall they followed was but lightly worked and had the look of a natural cavern. And there were occasional splits and fissures in the floor; most could be stepped over, but at times Tuck would have to spring across, though none of the others did, being taller than the Warrow.

They strode a mile and stopped to listen, and Gildor's sharp senses told them some of the *Spaunen* followed down the corridor behind.

Onward the four continued, and the further east they went, the more finished the passageway became. Gildor kept a sharp eye on Bale's blade-jewel; yet the red glimmer told that the evil was yet distant, though each step they took caused the fear to increase, for still they strode toward the Gargon.

Again, pounding dread swept across them, causing Tuck to gasp. And when it was past, on eastward they went.

At last they came unto a broad hall and cautiously peered in, looking for the flame of Rūcken torches: the hall stood dark and empty. Brega threw the lamp shutter wide, and they saw by its glow that the chamber was enormous: nearly four hundred yards long, two hundred across. The four had come in through the west side.

"Ai!" said Gildor softly. "I remember this place, though then it was that we came in through the far north portal. Yes, and now our path lies there to the east."

"How far, Lord Gildor, how far to the Dawn-Gate?" asked Galen as they strode across the chamber.

"Perhaps fifteen miles, perhaps twenty," answered Gildor, "I cannot say for certain." Gildor spoke to Brega: "Drimm Brega, how far have we come?"

"Two and thirty miles from the Dusken Door," answered the Dwarf with a certainty that brooked no dispute.

"Then, if I can find the way," responded Gildor, "we

are more likely to be fifteen miles than twenty from the distant exit."

Out through an eastern portal they went, and entered a lightly delved corridor: though the floor was smooth, the walls and ceiling were but little worked by Dwarven tools and had a rough look. The floor sloped up and the corridor curved this way and that, once turning in a great long spiral upward. There were many side fissures cleaving off into the darkness, their ends beyond seeing.

"If I am right," said Brega, excitement rising in his voice, "Châkka lore calls this the Upward Way. It is part of the trade road through Kraggen-cor and runs from the Broad Hall to the Great Chamber of the Sixth Rise. That must have been the Broad Hall we just left. And though I know not the way, we indeed stride toward the eastern portal, for the spoken lore tells that the Great Chamber is just under two miles from the Daūn Gate."

Up they went, their hopes rising, but so, too, rose their fear, for they strode ever toward the Dread.

"Hsst!" Again Gildor shushed the others and Brega shuttered the lantern. Red Bale's flame grew, and the clatter of Rūcks came toward them.

They slipped aside into a crevice, hiding deep in its dark recesses. Bale was sheathed so that its ruby light would not give them away, and they waited.

Now they could hear voices, speaking in the foul Slûk tongue, and louder came the tramp of feet and the rattle of arms. Torchlight grew, and passed the mouth of the crevice. And Tuck's pulse hammered in his ears. *And one of the Rūcks stepped in to search the fissure, his burning brand held aloft!*

Deep in the dark at the back of the crack and as yet unseen by the Rūck, Tuck reached for an arrow, but ere he could string it to bow, the lash of the dire Dread swept across them all, and a wail of fear rose up from the Rūcks, and the one coming along the crevice shrieked and dropped the brand and covered his ears in terror. And then the surging horror was past, and the Rūck snatched up the torch and ran back to join the others, abandoning his search of this fissure.

A snarling Hlōk amongst the Rūcks flailed about with a whip and drove them back to their hunt. But they had moved beyond the crevice hiding the four and so found them not, as onward tramped the foul squad, ferreting out the other fissures as they went, their torchlight fading in the distance.

"The Dread has foiled his own search," whispered Tuck, his hands still trembling. "Yet it surprises me that his power whelms the Rūcks, too."

"To his fear casting none are immune," said Gildor, "perhaps not even Modru himself."

"Let us go ere other Squam come this way," insisted Brega.

Gildor withdrew Bale and the blade-jewel's light faded as they watched, for the Rūcken squad had moved on, passing beyond seeing. Swiftly, back out of the crevice the four stepped and to the east, and soon they came to another huge cavern, and great square-cut stone blocks were scattered across the floor.

Brega pointed at one of the cubes. "I name this the Rest Chamber, for I think the Waeran's wee legs grow weary, and we can rest among these stone seats, and hide among them should searchers come."

"Good advice, Warrior Brega," said Galen, sitting upon the floor with his back to stone, "for on our next leg I deem we must be prepared for swiftness, and rest is needed."

And so, with Red Bale standing silent sentry, they sat in the Rest Chamber and took mian and water, and their hearts pounded in fear.

According to Brega's measure, they had marched thirty-nine miles since leaving the Dusk-Door, and had taken but six hours' sleep in the Bottom Chamber and no more than an hour's rest at their other stops. Drained, they sat in the Rest Chamber for perhaps another hour, gathering strength for the final dash to the Dawn-Gate, estimated by Lord Gildor to be less than ten miles eastward.

Once more an intense lash of fear brought them to their feet ere it swept on, leaving them standing in grim alarm.

"Aie," moaned Brega, "we must get out."

"Let us go now," said Gildor, taking up Bale, "for to wait invites disaster."

"Tuck?" questioned Galen, and at the buccan's nod, eastward they went upon weary legs.

Upward the passage led, rising gently, curving leftward then right again. Bale's blade-jewel flickered a faint ruby, the glimmer slowly growing, warning of a distant danger coming closer as the four strode on. Quickly they marched between vertical walls and under an arched roof. Along the way, deep-carven runes were etched in the walls, but the Deevewalkers took no time to read the ancient messages. Long they strode, nearly two hours, and no side entrances nor exits did they see; neither were there crevices, only smooth carven walls. And the roadway continued to curve gently upward, turning left once more and again rightward.

At last they came to a huge cavern, its ends lost beyond seeing in black emptiness. Bale now cried that evil lurked near, and their hearts pounded in dread, but no sign of any foe did they see.

"Quick, across the floor and out the passage to the east," said Gildor, "for evil is coming."

They strode great strides upon the stone, and Tuck trotted, setting the pace. Two hundred yards, three hundred, and more they went, and still the blank emptiness stretched out before them.

"This is the Great Chamber of the Sixth Rise," panted Brega. "We are less than two miles from the Daūn Gate."

"Hsst!" shushed Gildor, sheathing Bale. "Look ahead. Lights. Someone comes. Shutter the lantern, Brega."

Tuck could see torchlight reflected from a portal far to the east.

"South, too," hissed Galen, pointing to lights coming up a passage that way also.

"To the north a passage stands dark." Brega's voice was low and urgent.

"North it is!" barked Galen, and they bolted across the stone floor, Brega's lantern hood now but barely cracked, the faint light showing them the way.

No sooner had they entered the north passage than from the east and south, Rūcks and Hlōks beyond count boiled into the Great Chamber.

"It is the Horde," said Galen, his voice weary as he peered out at the distant tide of Spawn flooding into the Great Chamber. "They have come at last across the Quadran Pass and into the Black Hole to join the Gargon."

"Ai, and the Horror will use the Deeves as a black fortress and launch War against Darda Galion, and the *Spaunen* will be his army." Gildor's words fell grim.

"But first the Squam will search for us," snapped Brega, "and if we would escape to warn the Larkenwald, let us fly now."

North they fled, nearly two furlongs ere coming to a broken door upon the right. The corridor stretched on before them, turning to the left in the distance, but they could see torchlight reflected around its curve.

"Quick, in here!" cried Brega, and they bolted through the damaged door.

They came into another great chamber, narrow but lengthy, and with a low ceiling. One hundred paces long it was and only twelve wide, and an exit could be seen at the far eastern end.

But supporting the ceiling mid way was a massive arch, and great runes of power were carven into its stone.

And as they started across the floor for the distant exit, Tuck's eye fell upon signs of an ancient battle: broken weapons, shattered armor, the skulls and bones of long-dead combatants.

And smeared upon the walls in a black ichor now dried were the Dwarven runes: ᛏᚠᚱᚢᛑᛑᛁ

Brega looked, too. "Braggi!" he cried. "That is Braggi's rune, written with the blood of Squam. He came to slay the Ghath but was nevermore seen." On they strode without pause, passing now among the remains of the battle-slain. Dwarf armor there was, and the plate of Spawn, as well as shattered axes, broken scimitars, War hammers; and cudgels.

Brega cast his hood over his head as they hurried onward. "Here in the Hall of the Gravenarch, Braggi made his stand. But the signs tell the tale that the Ghath came and slew Braggi and his raiders as they stood frozen."

Tuck shuddered, his gaze darting into the far reaches of the hall, his glance seeking to avoid the mute evidence from that long-ago time when the Gargon stalked down the length of a fear-rooted Dwarven column, the monster slaying as it went—and when the hideous creature had come to the last Dwarf, Braggi and his valiant raiders were no more.

Across the floor swiftly the four strode for the eastern portal, coming to the rune-marked Gravenarch. Just as they passed below it, the surging fear of the Dread pounded through their veins, *yet this time it did not sweep on past them but stayed locked upon their hammering hearts, and terror arrested their steps.*

"He has found us!" gasped Gildor. "He comes, and is near!"

Tuck's lungs were heaving, yet he could not seem to get enough to breathe, and his limbs were nearly beyond his control, for he could but barely move.

Brega clutched his arms across his chest and air hissed in through clenched teeth; his face turned upward and his hood fell back from his head. His eyes widened. "The arch," his voice jerked out. "The keystone . . . like a linchpin . . . cut off pursuit."

Dread pulsed through them as Brega forced himself to stoop and grasp a broken War hammer. "Lift me up," he gritted. "Lift me . . . when I smite it, drop me . . . run . . . the ceiling will collapse."

"But you may be killed!" Tuck's words seemed muffled in the waves of fear.

Now Brega's rage crested above the numbing dread. "Lift, by Adon, I command it!"

Galen and Gildor hoisted the Dwarf, and he stood upon their shoulders as they braced him, his left hand upon the stone of the arch, the War hammer in his right. Tuck stood behind them, and only the Warrow's eyes were upon the portal where stood the broken door. And it seemed as if he could hear massive steps stalking through the terror, ponderous feet of stone pacing toward the door. And just as something dreadful loomed forth through the shadows: *"Yah!"* cried Brega, and swung the hammer with all the might of his powerful shoulders. *Crack!* The maul shattered through the keystone of the Gravenarch, and with a great rumble the vault above gave way. Gildor, Galen, and Brega tumbled backward, scrambling as stone fell 'round them. And Brega grabbed up Tuck and ran, for only the Warrow had glimpsed the shadow-wrapped Gargon, and the buccan could not cause his legs to move.

East they dashed for the door, just ahead of the ceiling crashing unto the floor behind them, filling the chamber with shattered stone. And as they raced through the portal and down a flight of steps, the roof gave way completely in one great roar, blocking all pursuit.

And waves of numbing dread beat through the stone and whelmed at them, and Tuck thought his heart would burst, yet now the Warrow could move again under his own power, and down a narrow hall they struggled while behind them endless horror ravened.

"Down," gasped Brega, "we've got to get down to the Mustering Chamber of the First Neath—the War Hall—for there is the drawbridge over the Great Dēop. And we must pass over it to come to the Daūn Gate. At least the lore says so."

"Ai, Drimm Brega, we crossed the Great Deep by drawbridge," answered Lord Gildor, his voice thin with fear, "though we came not this way, but instead passed down long steps to come to an enormous chamber: your War Hall."

"We are here upon the Fifth Rise," gritted Brega, his face blenched, for the power of the Dread was now locked onto their hammering hearts. "Six flights we must go down to reach the War Hall."

Passing by a tunnel on the left, east they reeled, curving south, down another flight of steps. "Fourth Rise," Brega grated as southward the narrow passage led. They passed one more tunnel to the left and kept on straight and down another staircase. "Third Rise," said Brega, and still the fear coursed through them and they knew the Gargon pursued by a different route. The tunnel they entered bore east and west, and to the east they fled, their legs seeming nearly too cumbersome to control. Another flight of stairs; "Second Rise," came Brega's trembling voice.

Tuck and his companions were weary beyond measure and the hideous fear sapped at their will, yet onward they fled, for to stop meant certain destruction. North and south the passage now went, and rightward they turned, southward, and once more steep steps pitched downward. "First Rise," Brega counted, and beyond a footway leading west the tunnel curved east.

On they faltered in abject fear, the dread power lashing after, and then came once more to stone steps down; "Gate

Level," Brega croaked at the bottom, and still they staggered on.

Again the passage arced to the south, and, as before, they ignored another tunnel on the left, for the ways they chose bore down, south, and east, and all other paths were rejected.

One more long flight of steps they stumbled down, and *lo!* they came into a great dark hall. And they tottered outward into the chamber, and still the terror whelmed their hearts, and they could barely carry forth.

"Ai, a Dragon Pillar," gasped Brega, pointing to a huge delved column carven to resemble a great Dragon coiling up an enormous fluted shaft. "This is the War Hall of the First Neath. To the east will be the bridge over the Great Dēop."

Leftward they reeled, their legs trembling with fear and barely under their control. Now along the lip of a deep abyss they staggered, to come to a great wooden span springing across the chasm. And *behold!* the bascule was down, the bridge unguarded!

"Great was the Gargon's pride," Galen's voice grated, "for he ne'er thought we would reach this place, else he would have posted a Swarm here to greet us."

They passed among barrels of pitch and oil and past rope-bound bundles of torches used by the maggotfolk to light their way through the black halls of Drimmen-deeve; and they came to the bridge at the edge of the Great Deep, a huge fissure that yawned blackly at their feet, jagging out of the darkness on their left, disappearing beyond the ebon shadows to their right, as much as a hundred feet wide where Tuck could see, pinching down to fifty where stood the bridge. And sheer sides dropped into bottomless depths below.

And as they stepped upon the span: "Hold!" cried Galen. "If we fell this bridge, then pursuit will be cut off."

"How?" Tuck's heart hammered, and every fiber in his being cried out, *Run, fool, run!* yet he knew Galen was right. "How do we fell the bridge?"

"Fire!" Galen's voice was hoarse. "With fire!"

No sooner were the words out of Galen's mouth than Brega, spurred by hope, sprang to a barrel of pitch and rolled it out upon the span, smashing the wooden keg open with his axe. Gildor, too, as well as Galen, rolled great casks out to Brega, and these the Dwarf smashed open as well, the pitch flowing viscidly over the wooden span.

"A torch, Tuck!" cried Galen as he pressed back for another keg.

And the buccan drew blue-flaming Bane and cut the binding on a stack of torches, and he ran across the span while Brega crashed open two more kegs of the oily pitch.

Standing at the eastern end of the bridge, Tuck struck steel to flint and lighted the torch. And now Gildor, Galen, and Brega came, and Tuck gave the burning brand to the Elf, saying, "You led us through, Lord Gildor; now cut off our pursuers."

The Lian Guardian hefted the torch to throw it, and Horror stepped forth out of the shadows at the far end of the span and fixed them with its unendurable gaze.

The Dread had come to slay them.

Tuck fell to his knees, engulfed in unbearable terror, and he was not at all aware that the shrill, piercing screams filling the air were rent from his own throat.

Thdd! Thdd! Onward came the grey, stonelike creature, scaled like a serpent, but walking upright upon two legs, a malevolent, evil parody of a huge reptilian Man.

Gildor stood paralyzed, transfixed in limitless horror, his eyes fastened inextricably upon a vision beyond seeing.

Thdd! Thdd! The ponderous Mandrak stalked forward, eight feet tall, taloned hands and feet, glittering rows of fangs in a lizard-snouted face.

Beads of sweat stood forth upon Galen's brow, and his entire being quivered with an effort beyond all measure. And slowly he raised up the tip of his sword until it was pointed level at the Gargon, but then he froze, unable to do more, for the Dread's gaze flicked upon him and the hideous power bereft him of his will.

Thdd! Thdd! Now the evil Gargon stalked past Tuck, the shrill-screaming Warrow beneath his contempt. And the stench of vipers reeked upon the air.

And as the Gargon passed him, the buccan was no longer under the direct gaze of Modru's Dread, and in that moment Tuck's horror-filled eyes saw Bane's blue light blazing up wildly, the weapon still in his grasp; and shrieking in unending shock, with fear beyond comprehension racking through his very substance, Tuck desperately lashed out with all the terror-driven force of his being, spastically hewing the Elven long-knife into the sinews of the Gargon's leg—*Thkk!* Keen beyond reckoning, the elden blade of Duellin rived through reptilian scales and chopped deeply into the creature's massive shank, and a blinding blast of cobalt flame burst forth from the blade-jewel.

With a brazen roar of pain, the Gargon began to turn, reaching for Tuck, the massive talons set to rend the shrilling Warrow to shreds.

Yet the Dread's eyes now had left Galen, and the Man plunged Jarriel's sword straight and deep into the Gargon's gut—*Shkk!*—the blade shattering at the hilt as the hideous creature bellowed again and glared directly into Galen's eyes, blasting him with a dread so deep that it would burst a Man's heart. And Galen was hurled back by the horrendous power.

But at that moment came a tumbling glitter as Brega's axe flashed end over end through the air to strike the creature full in the forehead—*Chnk!*—and the roaring monster staggered hindward upon the span.

And Gildor threw the torch upon the pitch-drenched wood, and with a great *Phoom!* flames exploded upward, and Brega snatched Tuck forth from the bridge as the fire blasted outward.

And they dragged stunned Galen away from the whooshing blaze, for the Man had been whelmed by the Gargon's dreadful burst of power.

And upon the bridge the Gargon bellowed brazen roars, engulfed in raging flame, an axe cloven deep in his skull, a shivered sword plunged through his gut.

In the War Hall behind, there came the sounds of running feet as Rūcks and Hlōks poured out of corridors and into the great chamber. They ran among the fourfold rows of Dragon Pillars to come to the far edge of the bottomless Great Deep. And Tuck could hear them crying, *Glâr! Glâr!* (Fire! Fire!)

And then great waves of unbearable dread blasted outward, and *Spaunen* fell groveling upon the floor of the War Hall and shrieked in terror, while Gildor, Brega, and Tuck gasped for air and dropped to their knees, transfixed like unto stone statues.

And the dreadful crests of racking horror seemed to course through them forever.

But then the Gargon collapsed and lay in the whirling flames of the burning span, and of a sudden the harrowing dread was gone.

"Quickly," gasped Gildor, recovering first, "we must bear Galen King beyond arrow flight."

And so, weak with passing fear, they dragged the stunned Man up a flight of steps and to the outbound passage. And while Gildor worked to revive Galen, Tuck and Brega stood guard, one with an Elven long-knife, the other with Gildor's sword, the red-jeweled blade seeming awkward in the Dwarf's gnarled hand—a hand better suited to wield an axe.

"Ai, look at the vastness of the Mustering Chamber, Tuck," said Brega, in awe, as the flames roared upward. "It must be a mile to the far end, and half that wide."

And Tuck looked past the Rūcks and Hlōks running hither and thither, and by the light of the burning bridge he saw the rows of Dragon Pillars marching off into the distance past great fissures in the floor, and he knew that Brega gauged true.

At last Galen regained consciousness, yet he was weak, shaken, his face pale, drawn, and deep within his eyes lurked a haunted look, for he had been whelmed by a Gargon's fear-blast, a blast that would have destroyed Galen; but he had been saved in the nick of time by Brega's well-thrown axe. Even so, Galen nearly had been slain, and he could not rise to his feet. And thus, they waited on the stone landing above the broad steps leading down toward the shelf of the abyss while strength and will slowly ebbed back into the Dread-hammered King. And long they watched the flames until the burning span collapsed, plummeting into the Great Deep, carrying the charred corpse of the slain Gargon down into the bottomless depths.

And when the drawbridge plunged, the four Deevewalkers stood and made their way eastward, Galen on faltering feet, supported by sturdy Brega. Along a corridor they went two furlongs, up a gentle slope, up from the First Neath unto the Gate Level. Now they came to the East

Hall and crossed its wide floor to pass beyond the broken portals of the Dawn-Gate and out from under the mountain, out into the open at last.

Before them in the Shadowlight of the Dimmendark stood the sloping valley called the Pitch leading down out of the Quadran. And out upon this cambered vale the four went, heading east, soon to bear south, for distant Darda Galion, to bring to the Lian word of the Horde in Drimmen-deeve and to tell them the remarkable news of the Gargon's death.

It had taken all four to slay the Horror, and it was by mere happenstance that they had succeeded. Yet among these four heroes there was one who had struck the first spark, for as Galen King said, his voice strained, halting— for the impact of the Gargon was still upon him— "When . . . when we stood frozen . . . lost beyond all hope, Tuck, yours was the blow that released us . . . yours was the strike that told."

CHAPTER 6

Shadows of Doom

Tuck's jewel-hued eyes swept to the limits of his vision through the Shadowlight lying across the 'scape of the cambered valley held in the lap of the Quadran, and no enemy was in sight. And down from the Dawn-Gate on weary legs trudged the four Deevewalkers: Tuck and Gildor first, Galen and Brega coming after. Down out of Drimmendeeve they trod, down onto the old abandoned tradeway that ran south a short way ere swinging easterly to follow the slope of the Pitch as it slowly fell toward the mouth of the Quadran, perhaps twenty-five miles distant.

And as they wearily paced down the steps and onto the ancient pave, Brega gravely said, "All my days were filled with a yearning to come unto Kraggen-cor, yet now I am glad to leave it behind."

Onward they plodded, Galen no longer leaning upon Brega. The four were exhausted beyond telling, yet they had to get well away from the vicinity of the Gate, for as Galen pointed out, "Ghola were not among the Yrm in the Black Hole. I deem they ride this Dimmendark somewhere. But they will return unto Drimmen-deeve, and we must be gone long ere then."

And so they trudged down the old trade road, southward along the shore of the Quadmere, a lakelet less than a mile from the Dawn-Gate. Normally, the clear tarn was fed by the high melt of Stormhelm flowing pure down Quadran Run; but both the Run and 'Mere were now frozen by the Winternight cold. And as the lagging steps of the four carried them alongside the iced-over water, Tuck could hear a far-off low rumble of . . . *what?* . . . but his mind was too weary to grasp an answer.

Along the high-bluffed western shore of the Quadmere they plodded, down past a snow-dusted, runecarven

Realmstone marking the ancient boundary where began the Dwarven Kingdom of Drimmen-deeve.

Southeastward down the Pitch they went, now following the course of the Quadrill, a river running down from the Grimwall to come eventually to the Argon River far to the east.

They trudged without speaking ten miles or so, weary unto their very bones, leaving the Dawn-Gate and Drimmen-deeve behind, the mysterious rumble fading as they went, and at last they made camp in the whin and pine along the slopes of the Pitch. And though they were exhausted unto numbness, still they took turns at watch in spite of Gildor's protest that he alone should stand the ward. And each in his turn fought off sleep by walking slow rounds circling the camp. No fire was kindled and the cold was bitter; even so, dressed as they were in quilted down and enwrapped in cloaks, they slept the sleep of the dead.

Twelve hours or so they remained in the pines, all sleeping except for the one on watch; and red-gemmed Bale stood ward with each sentry, the blade-jewel whispering only of distant evil. But at last Gildor, who stood the final watch, awakened the others, for he knew that still they were too near the Deeves to be safe and could remain no longer.

"We must press onward," said the Elf, "for when the Ghûlka return to the caverns, they will be swift on our trail." Gildor gestured to the barren, windswept pavestones of the old trade road below, its course for the most part free of snow. "The *Rûpt* will soon discover that this is the way we follow, for no tracks will they find crossing the land.

"But beyond our immediate danger, Galen King, I sense a doom lying in the days ahead, but what it is I cannot say. Yet I feel we must go forth swiftly, for ever since the Hèlarms struck, I have felt an urgent need to press on, else I think all will fail and Modru will have his way."

At these dire words the four took a quick meal of mian and water. But ere they set out, Brega borrowed the Elven long-knife from Tuck, using Bane to fashion a wooden cudgel of yew as a weapon, while Galen plied the Atalar Blade to cut a quarterstaff of pine for himself to bear. The work was done swiftly, for Bane's edge was keen beyond reckoning, and the blade of Atala hewed sharply, too.

"There," grunted Brega, hefting the wooden club as he gave over the Elven knife to Tuck, "this suits me better than that toothpick of yours, Waeran."

"Oh, not mine," answered Tuck, preparing to unbuckle the worn black leather sheath to return the long-knife to Gildor. "It was just borrowed for the jaunt through Drimmen-deeve."

But Lord Gildor would have none of this return of the blade. "Wee One, keep Bane. You have earned this weapon. Had you not been bearing it, we all would have fallen to the Gargon. It is now yours."

Tuck was astounded, for Bane was a "special" weapon, and like most Warrows he knew little or nothing of swords. "In my hands it is but wasted!" he protested.

"Nay," said Gildor. "In your hands it was used well for the first time since its forging. I deem it was made for you."

Thus it was that when the four strode down from the pines and back to the road, each now was armed: Brega bore a blunt wooden cudgel; Galen carried a quarterstaff and an Atalar long-knife; Gildor wore Bale strapped to his side; and Tuck bore bow and arrows, with Bane, the Elven long-knife, girted at his waist, the blue-jeweled blade a sword to Warrow hands. And they went apace, for Gildor's dire words pushed them forth.

Although each had slept but nine hours or so—standing three hours at watch—still they were rested somewhat, and the pall of fatigue that had smothered them was gone. And now their stride was firm and their eyes clear, except for Galen's, for a faint haggard look still lingered deep within his gaze: the afterclap of the Gargon's blast. Even so, he along with the others searched to the limits of their vision, but Modru's myrk still hid the distant 'scape. Yet in spite of the Dimmendark, Tuck reveled in the *openness* of the land before him, and though the air was icy with Winternight cold, he listened to *distant* sounds instead of close echoes from confining cavern walls. And there was a slow susurration of free-moving air, a silence of open space.

"Brega," asked Tuck, "when we came down the steps of

the Dawn-Gate, I could hear a faint rumble off in the distance. Now it is gone. Can you say what it was?"

"Aye," grunted Brega, "the Vorvor. Tucked in a great fold of Stone on Ghatan's flank is the Vorvor: a mighty whirlpool of water where a great underground river bursts from the side of Ghatan to thunder around the walls of the canyon and disappear down under the Mountains once more. There it was that the Wars with the Grg began, for jeering Ukhs and japing Hrōks cast Durek—first King of my Folk—into its ravening depths." Anger crossed Brega's features and fire smoldered in his eyes at the thought of the sneering Squam, but with visible effort he mastered his passion and continued the tale: "And First Durek was sucked down under the stone by the rage, yet somehow he survived, and he became the first Châk to stride the undelved halls of Kraggen-cor, for that is where the suck drew him. And it is told that he came out from under the Mountains at the place where Daūn Gate was later delved, yet how he crossed the Great Dēop it is not known, though some say it was the Utruni who helped him."

"Utruni?" Wonder filled Tuck's voice.

"Aye, Utruni," answered Brega, "for it is said the Stone Giants respect the work of the Châkka, for we strengthen the living stone. And the Utruni detest the Grg, for though the Squam live under the Mountains, too, they befoul the very rock itself and destroy the precious works of the ageless Underland."

"But how could the Utruni aid Durek?" asked Tuck. "I mean, the Great Deep is at least fifty feet wide, and who knows where its bottom lies—if it even has a bottom—so how could they help?"

"Utruni have a special power over stone," answered Brega. "They are able to pass through rock that they fissure with their very hands *and then seal shut behind as they move on.*" Tuck gasped, and Gildor nodded confirming Brega's words. Brega spoke on: "With this gift, they could aid anyone trapped as Durek was."

Tuck pondered upon this tale of Durek as the four strode southeasterly, following alongside the Quadrill as it led down the Pitch toward the unseen exit from the Quadran.

"Brega, when first we met, you said I had Utruni eyes," said Tuck. "How so?"

"I meant only that your eyes perhaps resemble theirs, Waeran," answered Brega. "It is said Utruni eyes are great crystal spheres, or are gems. And they see by a different light than we, for they can look through solid stone itself. And your eyes, Waeran, see by a different light, too, for how else could your vision pierce this myrk?"

Tuck strode along in silence and deep thought.

The Dwarf's statement had echoed what the Elves had said earlier. Yet Tuck had listened to Brega with great interest, for, just as were the Giants, Dwarves, too, are stone dwellers, and somehow that lent credence to Brega's words.

South and east they strode, down the Pitch, called Baralan by the Dwarves, and named Falanith by the Elves; but by any name it was the great tilt of land hemmed in by the four mountains of the Quadran: Stormhelm, Grimspire, Loftcrag, and Greytower. And as they went, Tuck noted a curious thing: "Hoy, Brega, can you see the stone above yon slopes?" Brega shook his head, no, and Tuck spoke on: "It is almost white. We came from the red granite of Stormhelm, past the black of Grimspire. Now I see the granite of another mountain and it is pale grey."

"That is Uchan, what you call Greytower and the Elves named Gralon," answered Brega. "Now the only Mountain of the Quadran you have not seen is Ghatan, and its stone is blue-tinged. Rust, ebon, azure, gris: these are the colors of the four great Mountains, and under each, different ores, different treasures, lie."

Down along the old tradeway they strode, between the Quadrill and Greytower, and their pace was hard. Some twelve hours they tramped in all, and their path swung south around the flank of the mountain as they came at last down off the Pitch and out of the mouth of the Quadran. Finally, they stopped to make camp and rest, again hidden in a grove of low pine. They had marched some twenty-five miles and were too weary to stride on.

When they took up the trek again, their course bore due south as they strode for Darda Galion. Still the frozen Quadrill ran upon their left while to their right rose the steep eastern ramparts of lofty Greytower. And the farther south they trod, the less they saw of the ancient pave they followed, for in places the stones lay half buried, while elsewhere they had sunk beyond seeing into the loam of the land alongside the riverbank.

Some nine hours they strode, faring ever southward. They stopped but once for a meal and a short rest, and then moved on quickly, for Lord Gildor felt a vague sense of foreboding, as if distant pursuit came upon their heels, drawing nearer with every step they took. Yet, as they marched, the scarlet blade-jewel of Red Bale was examined often, but no glimmer of warning flashed in its depths.

Another hour they walked, and Tuck's eyes searched to their limits, scanning for foe, friend, or aught else, yet nought did he see but sparse trees and sloping land falling southward along the Quadrill.

But then: "Hoy, ahead," said Tuck. "Something looms, barring our way. I cannot say what. Perhaps a mountain."

"There should be no Mountain before us," growled Brega. Gildor nodded in agreement with the Dwarf's words.

"How far?" asked Galen.

"At the bound of my vision," answered Tuck. "Perhaps five miles at most."

Onward they strode, Tuck's gaze seeking to see what stood across their way. Another mile they went. "Ai!" exclaimed the Warrow. "It is a storm. Snow flies."

"Ha!" barked Brega. "I *knew* it was no Mountain."

"The flakes are dark in this Shadowlight," responded Tuck, "and the snow looks like a stone-grey *wall* from here, for it seems neither to advance nor retreat."

Onward they pressed, and the wind began to rise as they came toward the fringes of the stillstorm. Soon they walked in a moan of air, and scattered flakes swirled about them.

"Hsst!" warned Gildor, casting his hood from his head. "Listen!"

Tuck, too, pushed his cloak hood back and strained his ears, yet he heard nought but the sobbing wind.

"I thought . . ." Gildor began; then: *"There!"* And all four heard the drifting howl of distant Vulg.

Once more Gildor drew Red Bale from scabbard, and the Elf sucked a hiss of air through clenched teeth, for a crimson fire glowed in the blade-gem. "They come," said the Lian warrior grimly.

"Kruk!" spat Brega upon seeing the jewel's gleam, while

Tuck stared long and hard to the north, back along the way they had come.

Again there came the shuddering howl of Vulg.

Through the scant wind-borne flakes Tuck's eyes scanned. "I see them now: a great force: Ghûls on Hèlsteeds: fifty or more. Swift they run on our track."

"Wee One," said Gildor, "I see no place to hide. Is there any?"

"Lord Gildor," interjected Galen, "you forget, they have Vulgs with them: Vulgs to follow our scent. E'en were there a place to hide, still Modru's curs would find us. Instead, we must seek a site we can defend." Galen hefted his quarterstaff and turned to the Warrow. "Tuck, look for a stand where neither Vulg nor Hèlsteed nor Ghûl can come at us easily: a narrow lieu or a place up high: close-set rocks or trees, or a tor."

Again Tuck scanned the Dimmendark. "None, Sire. The trees are sparse and the land is nought but a long slope—"

Once more there came the feral howl of Vulg.

Brega hefted his cudgel and set his feet wide. "Then we make our stand here on the bank of the Quadrill," gritted the Dwarf.

"Nay, Warrior Brega," barked Galen, "not here."

"Then where, King Galen?" Brega's voice was sharp with exasperation. "The Waeran said that there is no site to defend, and we cannot hide from Vulgs. This bank, then, is as good a place as any to make our last stand, for they cannot come at our backs if we choose to fight here."

"Debate me not, Warrior Brega; there is no time," snapped Galen. "For there is a way we might lose the *Spaunen:* the storm! If it thickens ahead, if it rages, and if we can come unto its fury ere the Spawn can catch us, the wind and snow will cover our track and hide us. Let us forth—quickly!"

Galen the Fox! cried Tuck's mind as the buccan ran southward.

And behind careered hurtling Vulgs and hammering Hèlsteeds, swiftly closing the gap.

From the fringes and toward the heart of the tempest sped the four—seeking its blast—and the farther south they ran, the greater was the storm's turmoil; yet behind raced the Spawn, their pounding strides drumming over the land at a headlong pace, rapidly gaining upon their distant quarry.

On ran the four, and the wind howl rose and the snow thickened, flying darkly in the Shadowlight. Tuck threw desperate glances over his shoulder through the grey swirl, and his heart lurched to see how swiftly the Spawn came.

Now the Vulgs gave vent to juddering howls, and Ghûls answered them, for although they had not yet seen their prey, the spoor was growing fresher as they rapidly overhauled the hunted.

Tuck's lungs pumped in harsh gasps as he ran on, his legs pounding over the frozen ground. And all about him groaned the dark-laden wind, whistling flakes stinging his face as he plunged deeper into the storm.

Yet the howl of the Vulgs and Ghûls rose above the cry of the wind, for the Spawn at last spotted the fleeing game, and exultation filled their ululating yawls.

Headlong into the thickening snow rushed Tuck, the rising shriek of the driven wind drowning out all noise but his own racking breath, and now he could no longer see his companions in the black swirling blast. He threw a look over his shoulder, only to trip and fall sprawling flat upon his face. And as he struggled up to his hands and knees, a Hèlsteed thundered past, for the spear-bearing Ghûl upon its back did not see the fallen Warrow.

Tuck sprang to his feet and ran on, and he was unable to see more than a pace or two in the shrieking dark howl. Yet vague black shapes hurtled by, and the buccan knew that it was but a matter of time ere he would be spotted. Even so, onward he ran.

Now the fury of the driving storm about him somehow altered: still the raging blast screamed and blinding snow hurtled through the air, yet the blizzard was *brighter:* less black, more grey. Did the storm weaken, the snow diminish? Nay, for yet he could see no farther than a pace or two and did not know where either friend or foe went in the blinding clutch, as on he plunged.

Once again he fell, and as he rose up, the wind around him seemed to pause, and a dark shape loomed out of the blast twenty yards behind and stalked toward him: a leering Ghûl upon Hèlsteed. And the corpse-foe lowered his barbed spear and charged as Tuck fumbled for his bow and arrow. The buccan stood no chance, for the Hèlsteed was too swift. Death came on cloven hooves.

The spear dipped to pierce the Warrow, and Tuck sprang aside, rolling in the snow; the Hèlsteed hammered past, and *lo!* Tuck was unscathed, for inexplicably the Ghûl had not shifted his aim to strike the dodging Warrow; yet something was amiss with the corpse-foe, for the Hèlsteed ran on another twenty yards and then *collapsed,* and the foe did not rise up from the snow.

Tuck drew blue-flaming Bane and ran to the downed enemy, the Warrow girding himself to strike off the Ghûl's head; yet, as he came near, the corpse-foe twitched convulsively, fingers scrabbling, face grimacing, and then the Ghûl began to *wither, shriveling* even as Tuck looked on, the snow blowing whitely, the wind shrieking. And as Tuck's horror-stricken eyes watched, the reaver's body began to *buckle* and *fold in upon itself,* and collapse into ashen ruin to be whipped at by the howling blast. Shuddering in revulsion, the young buccan pressed on into the blinding whiteness.

The shriek rose until Tuck could but barely think, yet he stumbled onward. Forward he struggled, within a ravening white wall, but at last he passed through the worst of it and the sound began to diminish, the wind still ripping at him, but its force lessening as he struggled on.

And then he seemed to stumble out of a wall of white and into the arms of his comrades.

And overhead the Sun shone brightly.

And Tuck then knew that they were no longer in the Dimmendark, and the Warrow burst into tears.

South they went, another ten miles or so, away from the shrieking wind and blinding snow that raged along the flank of the hideous Black Wall; and they left the dread 'Dark behind. And all the while they walked, Tuck reveled in the sensations of vision: bright daylight, high blue sky, distant winter forests and mountains. And his heart was filled near to bursting with gladness, for there was the *Sun!* And Tuck marveled at how his own shadow matched him stride for stride and grew longer as the Sun rode toward the evening. And he was amazed that the day seemed so bright.

And his talk was full of wonder: "Is the Sun a flame eternal?" he asked. "Will it one day die? The sky is so blue; whence comes its color?"

To most of his questions his comrades could but shake their heads and smile and answer, "Only Adon knows."

Even though the Sun was still in the sky, they made camp on a small tor overlooking the Quadrill, a tor easily defended, for although they had passed beyond the Black Wall, night would still fall and Spawn could rove. Yet the comrades were weary beyond measure, for they had walked long since their last camp and could not press any further.

Exhausted, Tuck sat in the waning sunlight, his back to a rock as he took a meal with the others. The buccan's wayworn gaze strayed back along the direction whence they had come; and he still could see the distant Black Wall standing across the valley and reaching up into the Grimwall Mountains like some great, dark, stationary monster poised to strike. With a shudder the Warrow wrenched his eyes away, only to catch the gaze of the Lian Elf.

"Lord Gildor," asked Tuck, "though we now stand in the light of day—and I would not have it otherwise—still I wonder, why has the Dimmendark stopped? I mean, why does it stand there just to the north, halted, not moving?"

"Bear in mind, Tuck," replied Gildor, "the myrk stood for days, weeks, in the Argent Hills north of Challerain Keep even while the Dimmendark marched down the Grimwall to engulf Arden Vale and rush on toward the Lands to the south. And as you know, later Modru caused the Winternight to sweep from the Argent Hills down through Rian to swallow Mont Challerain, and the Weiunwood, and beyond. Hence, the Evil One can cause the myrk to stand still in places while elsewhere he presses it forth to smother the land."

Gildor paused, his own eyes following the towering flank of the Wall, then he spoke on: "As to your question: I know not why the Black Wall has stopped where it has. Perhaps it stands at the limit of Modru's power, though I doubt it, for I think he intends to use the Horde in Drimmen-deeve to attack Darda Galion, and he will need the myrk to do so. Hence, I deem he but pauses, biding his time till all is set, and then once more the Wall will sweep forth at his bidding. Yet I cannot say for certain that my thoughts are true, for I know not the mind of the Evil One."

Brega bit off a chew of mian and growled, "Mayhap he leaves this Land undarkened for the Lakh of Hyree to invade, or the Kistanee Rovers."

"Perhaps," responded Gildor, "and perhaps not. Yet no matter the which of it, whether Lakh, Rovers, or Horde, whether Modru bides his time or is at the limit of his power, here the Wall lurks while we must not. We *must* press on, yet we cannot do so without rest. Let us bed down and permit the eventide to renew our spent energies."

Tuck finished his meal in silence and watched as the Sun slipped down between the crags of the Grimwall; and though he tried to scribe in his diary, he was too exhausted to do so and fell asleep ere dusk.

Sometime in the night Tuck startled awake, and the blackness was so deep that his heart lurched, for he thought that he was somehow back in the Dimmendark. But then he saw the Bright Veil spangled across the heavens, and the silvery stars overhead, and the fingernail-thin crescent of a last-quarter Moon that rode wan in the sky; and Tuck sighed in contentment and slipped back into slumber. And none of his companions awakened him for a turn at watch, for the Warrow had tramped more than thirty-five miles that day alone—a grueling journey for one so small.

As the four took breakfast the next morning, Tuck watched with tears in his eyes as the Sun rose through the dawn. And again he marveled at how bright was the day and how dark had been the night, so different from the foul Shadowlight of Winternight. Sun, Moon, stars, sky: what wonders to behold! And Tuck was not the only one entranced by the sight of the Sun, for Galen, Gildor, and Brega stood as if spellbound and watched the golden orb rise over the rim of Mithgar to shine down upon the Land.

South they strode, down the wending valley of the Quadrill, the land about them richly filled with the subtle shades of winter—drab to any but those who had just come from the long 'Darkdays of Shadowlight.

Tuck's eyes swept out across this wondrous 'scape; Up the slopes to the west reared the Grimwall Mountains, marching out of the north and onward to the south their mighty peaks capped in snow. Beyond the valley slopes to the east, and hence unseen by the four, a rolling upland wold fell toward the distant Rothro River and beyond to the Argon. At their backs, to the north, loomed the now distant vile Black Wall of the Dimmendark. And as they rounded a bend, ahead far to the south Tuck saw . . .

"Hola! Lord Gildor, to the fore," said the Warrow. "What is that? I cannot make it out."

"Hai!" answered the Lian warrior. "Here in the day of Adon's Sun, once again Elven eyes prove to see farther than those of all other Folk. It is the margin of Darda Galion, Tuck, the Land of the Silverlarks. Your Waerling eyes look upon the beginnings of the great forest of Eld Trees—the Realm you call the Larkenwald."

Larkenwald, thought Tuck, his mind envisioning the maps of the War-council. Larkenwald: an Elven Land running from the Grimwall on the west to the Argon River in the east, and from the wold to the north to the Great Escarpment along the south where began the Land of Valon. Larkenwald, also called Darda Galion: a Land of trees, a Land of rivers—the Rothro, the Quadrill, the Cellener, and the Nith, and all of their tributaries, their sparkling waters to course through the forest to flow at last into the broad rush of the mighty Argon.

South they tramped toward the distant forest, and as they went, Tuck heard the sound of running water, and he looked to see dark, gurgling pools in the ice of the Quadrill where the grip of the cold had been broken and water tumbled past. And unbidden, the Warrow's thoughts slipped back to the night at Ford Spindle when the Kingsherald's horse had crashed through a stream such as this, and the Man and Tarpy had drowned.

Wrenching his mind from this dark path, Tuck studied the Eld Trees as the four comrades neared the forest: mighty were these great-girthed sylvan giants, soaring into the sky, their leaves a dusky green, for Elven Folk lived among the mammoth boles and so the trees *gathered* the twilight.

"Lor," breathed Tuck. "The trees . . . how tall are they?"

Gildor smiled. "It is said that if their heights could be stepped out, one hundred fifty Lian strides it would take for each; yet I know of one old fellow deep in the woods at least two hundred paces tall."

Tuck looked at the Elf's stride—a yard or so when stepping out a measure—and the Warrow gasped.

"Ah, Wee One, but these are not as great as the ones in Adonar, whence these trees came as seedlings long ago, borne hence by my ancestors, and planted in this Land of many rivers."

A forest from Adonar! Borne here as seedlings! Yet now they are giants! Tuck's mind boggled at the scale of the work undertaken by the Elves to plant an entire forest of Eld Trees here in the Middle Plane: the span of time needed was staggering.

At last they came among the massive trunks towering upward, the dusky leaves interlaced overhead, the land below fallen into a soft twilight though the Sun stood on high.

"Kèst!" barked a voice, the speaker hidden.

"Stop," said Gildor, and the comrades halted. *"Vio Gildor!"* (I am Goldbranch!) called the Lian.

Tuck gasped, for of a sudden they were surrounded by a company of grey-clad Elven warriors seeming to take shape from the very twilight shadows of the Eldwood itself. Some bore bows, others gleaming swords, but striding to the fore came a Lian bearing a black spear.

"Tuon," said Gildor, recognizing the flaxen-haired spear wielder.

Tuon smiled at Gildor, yet he did not ground the butt of his spear to the earth; instead, he held the ebon weapon at guard, his wary gaze scanning Lord Gildor's companions, his eyes showing surprise as he looked upon the Waerling. "Ah, Tuon," said Gildor, raising his voice so that all could hear, "set aside Black Galgor, for these are trusted companions."

Tuon's grip shifted upon the weapon and the black spear swung aside. "These are chary times, Alor Gildor, for the Enemy in Gron reaches forth with his mailed fist to grasp the Land. Yet though I would not gainsay thy words, still I would know thy comrades' names."

"Nay, Tuon," answered Gildor, "though I intend no

slight, I will hold fast their names, for such are the deeds of these warriors that Coron Eiron should be the first to hear their names and listen to the tale of their valor. Yet this I will tell: Drimm, Waerling, Man, Lian: these past days we four have strode through the halls of Drimmen-deeve! We have pierced its lightless maze from the Dusk-Door to the Dawn-Gate! *Hai!* We are the Walkers of the Deeves!"

Cries of amazement rose up from the Elves of Tuon's company, and eyes flew wide in wonderment; the Elf Captain stepped back a pace, startled, and his mouth groped for words, yet Gildor held up a hand. "Nay, Tuon, it is to the Coron I would first speak my words, for the marvel of our news must be borne to Eiron's ears before all. Yet if you must name these three, call them Axe-thrower, Bane-wielder, and Shatter-sword." Gildor gestured in turn to Brega, Tuck, and Galen. "And you may name me Torch-flinger.

"But other news—dire news—I bear, and you of the March-ward need know it first: A mighty Horde of *Spaunen* now camp in Black Drimmen-deeve—ten thousand or more *Rûpt*, I deem. Yet I do not think they will strike south for many days or weeks to come, for their ranks are presently in disarray, and the Black Wall as yet stands still and moves no closer to Darda Galion. Yet you must be ever vigilant, for the *Spaunen* writhe in Drimmen-deeve like maggots in a carcass." Gildor fell silent, and a murmur of consternation swept through the Elven ranks.

"Ai, Alor Gildor, that *is* news of dire import!" cried Tuon. "That a mighty swarm of *Spaunen* teems in the Quadran means we must stand on high alert along the margins of the Eld Trees, for Drimmen-deeve lies at our very doorstep. Even so, should the *Rûpt* march, many Lian will be needed to hurl them back; yet most are in the north, as you will learn from Coron Eiron. He himself is but recently returned from Riamon, and you are fortunate to find him here." Tuon then gazed upon the comrades, and questions battered at his lips, yet he did not speak them, but instead inclined his head toward Gildor, accepting the Elf Lord's will to tell the Deevewalker tale first to Eiron, Coron of all the Lian in Mithgar. Yet Tuon was canny, and this he said: "Though you tell of the Horde, Alor, you say nought of the Horror, and I deem your silence speaks loudly to those who can hear its voice. Yet we will abide by your wishes and probe not for names and deeds; forsooth, your story must be mighty if you have strode through the Black Deeves.

"But come, we will share a meal. And there are horses to bear you to a cache of boats along the Quadrill, where the ice reaches not and the river flows free, though it sits low along the banks, for the cold locks much of the water to the north." With soundless hand signals Tuon gestured to the Lian of the March-ward troop; and as the Bearer of the Black Spear spun on his heel and led the comrades toward his campsite, the remainder of his company faded noiselessly into the lofty silence of the Eld Tree forest.

Once more Gildor and Galen rode horses, and Brega was mounted behind the Elf while Tuck sat in back of the Man. And they swiftly cantered among the mighty Eld Trees along the south bank of the Quadrill. Before them rode Theril, Lian warrior assigned by Tuon to lead them to the boats.

Through the soft twilight of the great trees wended their trail, the hoofbeats of the horses muffled by the moss underfoot, and what little sound they made was lost in the dim galleries under the dusky interlace high overhead.

Tuck marveled at the massive trees, and he saw that Gildor had spoken truly, for the giants towered hundreds of feet into the air; and the girth of each bole was many paces around. Tuck knew, too, that the wood of the Eld Tree was precious—prized above all others—for none of these giants had ever been felled by any of the Free Folk, though some had been hacked down in malice by *Rûpt;* and Elves still spoke bitterly of the Felling of the Nine. But the Elven vengeance had been swift and utterly without mercy, and chilling examples were made of the axe wielders, and their remains were displayed to *Spaunen* in their mountain haunts in Mithgar; and never again was an Eld Tree hewn in Darda Galion. Yet at times a harvest of sorts was made in the forest, for occasionally lightning or a great wind sweeping o'er the wide plains of Valon would cause branches to fall; and these would be collected by the Lian storm-gleaners and the wood cherished, each branch studied long ere the carver's tools would touch the grain. And gentle Elven hands made treasures dear of this precious wood.

And through this soaring timber cantered three swift horses, two bearing double following a third. Several hours they rode thus, coming at last to the curve of a high bank along the Quadrill where the long moss hung down to the water. Here Theril reined to a halt and dismounted, as did the comrades. And eve was falling upon the twilight Land.

"Here you will make camp, Alor Gildor," said Theril, "and on the morrow ride a boat down the Quadrill to where it is joined by the River Cellener. Just past, upon the south bank, you will find another March-ward camp, where there will be horses to bear you to Woods'-heart, to Coron Eiron."

"Boat?" grunted Brega. "I see none. Must we weave one from moss?"

"Hai, Axe-thrower!" laughed Theril. "Weave one? Nay! Yet from the moss you *will* draw one forth!" And the Lian guide leapt down the bank of the Quadrill and drew aside the dangling bry, and *lo!* concealed under a broad stone overhang a dozen Elven boats rode silently at tether, each slender craft nearly six paces in length, with tapered bow and stern; and spruce ribs curved from wale to wale, giving each craft a rounded bottom.

Brega's laugh barked above the sound of the river, and he looked upon the boats with appreciation, for Brega was a rarity among the Dwarven Folk: he could both swim *and* ply small wherries such as these, even though these shells were paddled, not rowed.

On the other hand, Tuck, although he swam well, knew little or nothing of boats, and he looked askance at the round-bottomed craft and wondered why they did not just roll over and sink.

After camp was made, and a meal taken, once more Theril mounted his steed and caught up the reins of the other two horses. "Alor, I go now to rejoin the March-ward. Is there word you would have me bear?"

Gildor looked to the others, and Galen spoke: "Just this, Theril: The Lady Rael of Arden said that aid unbidden would come along the way of our destiny. Tell Tuon and your comrades that Rael's words were indeed true: first we came upon the Axe-thrower, and then upon your company. Say, too, that the High King ever will have an open hand to the March-ward of the Larkenwald."

Galen fell silent and Theril looked keenly at the Man. "You must be close, indeed, to the High King to know his mind that well, Shatter-sword. There is a tale here that I am eager to hear. Yet I will bear your message to my company, and should any of us ever meet the High King face to face, we will say this: 'I have met with Shatter-sword, a Man of noble bearing, and though at the time I knew not his name, rank, or deeds, I am proud to have helped him and his comrades: Axe-thrower, Bane-wielder, and Torch-flinger.' "

Theril saluted each in turn and, crying *"Hai!"* wheeled his horse and thundered off into the twilit forest, the other two mounts in tow. And Tuck cried after the fleeing steeds, "Fare you well, Lian Theril, and all your comrades, too!"

The next morning found the four in an Elven boat upon the swift-flowing Quadrill. Brega knelt in the stern, his powerful shoulders driving a hand-held paddle while Gildor in the bow stroked, too. Tuck sat on a mid-thwart, aft of the Elf, with Galen behind the Warrow. Galen also plied an oar, and only Tuck was without one; yet the Warrow knew that for him to try to row would merely hinder the others. And so he sat and watched the mossy banks swiftly pass by in the twilight woods, and he marveled at the difference between the soft shadows of this dimly lit land and the harsh blackness of the Dimmendark.

All day they traveled thus, occasionally shooting through rapids where the water foamed white and tumbled loudly among rocks, and here Brega, Galen, and Gildor would stroke swift and strong while Tuck held on tightly. At other times the water flowed placidly between low, ferny banks or high stone walls, and the hush of the soaring Eldwood stole over Tuck and he nodded in doze and lost track of the hours in the timeless twilight.

Easterly they traveled throughout the day, stopping but a time or two, and as evening fell once more, they came to the inflow of the Cellener. And just past the mouth of this river they espied the light of a March-ward campfire set back in the woods on the south bank of the Quadrill.

*   *   *

The next daybreak found them bearing southeastward, once more riding double on borrowed horses. This time they had no guide, for Gildor knew the way to Wood's-heart, some twenty miles distant.

Swift were the steeds, and in midmorn the four comrades were passed through a picket of Lian warders and came at last to dwellings nestled among the giant Eld Trees: they were come to Wood's-heart, the Elvenholt central to the great forest of Darda Galion.

Gildor led them toward a large, low building in the midst of the others; and as the four approached, Elves stopped to watch this strange assortment of Man, Drimm, Waerling, and Lian ride by. At last the comrades came to the Coron-hall, and warders asked their names while other attendants took their steeds.

"Vio Gildor," replied Lord Gildor. *"Vio ivon Arden."* (I am come from Arden.) "My companions I will name to Coron Eiron, and to his consort Faeon."

At mention of the Elfess Faeon, troubled looks passed across the faces of the warders. "Alor Gildor," said the Captain of the Door-ward, "you may pass and speak to the Coron; yet you will find his spirits low, but it is for him to tell you why. I can only hope that you bear news that will lift him from his doldrums."

"Hai!" cried Gildor. "That I can guarantee, for we bear the best of tidings! Delay us no longer; let us pass!"

And into the great hall they strode, yet it was glum and but barely lighted. And at the far end of the long floor, sitting upon a throne among the shadows, was a weary Elf: Eiron, the High Coron of all the Lian in Mithgar.

Across the floor strode the comrades, to come to the steps at the foot of the dais. Eiron lifted his hand from his brow and gazed at the four, his eyes widening in surprise at sight of Man, Drimm, and Waerling. "Alor Gildor," he said at last, turning to the Elf, his quiet voice filled with sadness.

"Coron Eiron," spake Gildor, bowing slightly, "these are my comrades: Drimm Brega of the Red Hills, mighty warrior, *Rûpt* killer, arch breaker, axe thrower; Waerling Tuckerby Underbank, Thornwalker of the Boskydells, arrow caster, *Spaunen* slayer, Bane wielder." Gildor paused, and both Tuck and Brega bowed to the Elven King, who inclined his head in return. Then Gildor spoke on: "And Coron, though I present him last, this Man, too, is a warrior without peer: Horde harrier, Ghûlk slayer, sword shatterer, son of Aurion King now dead . . . Coron Eiron, this is Galen King, now High King of Mithgar."

These last words brought Eiron to his feet, and he bowed low to Galen, who bowed in turn to the Elven Coron.

"Ah, but this is woeful news you bring me, for Aurion and I had nought but goodwill toward one another and I am saddened to learn of his death," said Eiron. "Let us all sit and talk and break bread together, and tell me your tale, for I glean among Alor Gildor's words that you bear tidings of import, yet I hope that some of your news is good, for I am grieved in my heart and would cherish fair word."

Gildor's face broke out in a great smile, and he flashed Red Bale from its scabbard and thrust it toward the sky and cried, "*Coron Eiron, va Draedan sa nond!*" (King Eiron, the Gargon is dead!)

Coron Eiron staggered backward, the hind of his knees striking the throne, and he abruptly dropped to the seat. *"Nond? Va Draedan sa nond?"* Eiron could not believe his ears.

"Ai! It is so!" crowed Gildor, slamming Bale home in its scabbard. "We four slew it five days past in the dark halls of Drimmen-deeve: Tuck slashed it with Bane, thus breaking its dread gaze; Galen King shattered a sword deep within its gut, freeing Drimm Brega; Brega hurled the axe that clove into its skull, setting me loose; and I cast the torch that engulfed it in an inferno; and the flames at last slew it. And it was dead ere the pyre in the end collapsed and fell into the Great Deep of Drimmen-deeve, carrying the charred corpse of the Gargon unto the bottomless depths."

Eiron's face flushed with gladness, and the Elven King leapt to his feet and called a page unto him. "Light the lamps! Kindle the fires! Prepare for a feast! And send me Havor!" And no sooner had the attendant scurried from them than a Lian warrior—Havor, Captain of the Doorward—strode to the summons of his Coron. And Eiron commanded, "Let the word go forth unto all corners of

Darda Galion and to the Lands beyond: to the Greatwood and Darda Erynian, to Riamon and Valon, to the Lian now in the north, and to the Host in the south: *Va Draedan sa nond!* Slain by these four: Drimm Brega of the Red Hills; Tuckerby Underbank, Waerling of the Land of the Thorns; Alor Gildor, Lian of Arden; and Galen King, High King of Mithgar!"

Havor's eyes flew wide, for the Horror in Drimmendeeve had long ruled the Quadran, and fear of its dread power had caused Dwarf and Man and even Elf to flee from these regions. Yet though many Elves took flight to Adonar, others of the Lian remained behind in Darda Galion, vowing to stay in Mithgar and continue their guardianship. Even so, the faint pulse of the Fear to the north ran like a thread through their lives; and only the Sun held the Horror at bay, for at night it stalked the sloping valley known to the Elves as Falanith and to Man as the Pitch; but at dawn the Gargon would return to the Black Deeves, for Adon's Ban ruled its kind. And none but Braggi and his raiders had e'er challenged the Dread, and they had not succeeded: for never had a Gargon been slain without the aid of a Wizard, and these mages were gone from the sight of all, though where they went none knew. Yet here were four who had killed with their own hands one of the terrible Gargoni—perhaps the last of its kind. The Dread of Drimmen-deeve was dead! Havor raised a clenched fist and cried, *"Hál, valagalana!"* (Hail, valiant warriors!) and the Captain rushed from the hall to start the remarkable news to spreading, while Eiron led his guests to warm hearths and baths and restful quarters where he could hear their tale in full.

Great joy spread throughout the Elvenholt, and heralds on swift horses raced forth across the Land. And everywhere the word went, celebrating began, for long had the yoke of dread fettered their hearts; and when they heard the glad tidings, all knew the tale to be true, for they listened to their inner beings, and the exhalation of fear no longer whispered forth from Black Drimmen-deeve: the Horror was dead.

And in the guest quarters the four heroes rested and

spoke quietly with Eiron. Yet not only did they tell him their tale, they learned much from the Coron in return.

"Ay, Galen King," said Eiron, "there is seesaw strife to the south, for the Lakh of Hyree and the Rovers of Kistan muster in endless numbers, and all the Hosts of Hoven and Jugo, and of Pellar and Valon are hard pressed. The Drimma of the Red Hills join the strife, yet the Alliance is woefully outnumbered."

"What of the Lian?" asked Galen. "What of the Men of Riamon?"

"We fight in the north," answered Eiron. "The Evil in Gron sends his Hordes through Jallor Pass and the Crestan, and they come down from secret doors hidden high in the flanks of the Grimwall. My Lian join with the Dylvana—Elves of Darda Erynian and the Greatwood—as well as with the Drimma of Mineholt North, the Men of Riamon, and the Baeron Men. We fight in the fastness above Delon and in the Rimmen Mountains and in the Land of Aven. Yet we have battled as far south as Eryn Ford and the ruins of Caer Lindor. And everywhere we are hard pressed, for Modru's Swarms are mighty and they assail in great strength.

"Hearken, Galen King: I do not wish to cast doubt upon your mission, but surely you now see that your plan to gather the Host and march north to battle *Rûpt* must be abandoned; you cannot come unto the north with your Legions and leave the south undefended, for the Evil One's clutch is everywhere.

"Aye. North, south, east, west—all around—like the coils of a great serpent, Modru's minions seek to crush us. And now you bring me news of a Horde teeming in the Quadran. Yet the force of Lian Guardians presently husbanded in Darda Galion is but a remnant which I had come to gather to lead back to join their brethren in the northern battles. But now I will not do so, for I would not leave this Land undefended in the face of the threat of the Swarm in Drimmen-deeve, even though alone the remaining Marchward could not press back the foe should the Dimmendark sweep south and the *Spaunen* come.

"I curse the day that the Evil in Gron became master of this foul darkness that blots the land, for with it he defies Adon's Ban and looses holocaust down upon us.

"Yet even where the darkness falls not, still Modru works his evil, for the Hyrania and Kistania assail the south, believing that this War is but a prelude to Gyphon's coming. Yet, that cannot be, for the *Vani-lērihha* have not yet returned and the Dawn Sword remains lost."

"*Vani-lērihha?* Dawn Sword?" Tuck's Warrowish curiosity was piqued. "What do you mean, Coron Eiron?"

"The *Vani-lērihha* are the Silverlarks, Tuck," answered the Elven King. "Ere the Sundering, these argent songbirds dwelled in Darda Galion high among the Eld Trees, and their melodies of the twilight caroled beauty throughout the Land. Yet after the Sundering, the *Vani-lērihha* disappeared, and we knew not where they went. A thousand years passed, and the forest stood empty of their song and was the poorer for it. And we had come to believe that they were gone forever; but then the Lady Rael in Arden divined a sooth of baleful portent:

> '*Bright Silverlarks and Silver Sword,*
> *Borne hence upon the Dawn,*
> *Return to earth; Elves girt thyselves*
> *To struggle for the One.*
>
> *Death's wind shall blow, and crushing Woe*
> *Will hammer down the Land.*
> *Not grief, not tears, not High Adon*
> *Shall stay Great Evil's hand.*'

The Silverlarks of her words we know, and we think that the Silver Sword of the rede is the Dawn Sword—the great weapon said to have the power to slay the High Vûlk, Gyphon Himself. But the Dawn Sword disappeared in the region of Dalgor March during the Great War, and until Rael's portent we thought that it was lost or that Gyphon had contrived to take it, for He fears it. Yet now we think it to be in Adonar, for how else could it be 'borne hence upon the Dawn'? For the same reason, we think the *Vani-lērihha* to be in Adonar, too, though we still are not certain. And both Silverlarks and Silver Sword will return to Mithgar some direful dawn yet to come, to the woe of the world." Eiron fell silent.

After a moment Brega grunted. "The Châkka, too, have

baleful sooths as yet unfulfilled, and we dread the day their words fall true. Yet, come, think you not that this prophecy of yours is being fulfilled even now? For we *struggle; Death's wind blows. Woe hammers the Land.* Many of the portents fit."

"Nay, Drimm Brega," answered Eiron. "This prophecy looks yet to come, for there are no Silverlarks in the Land, and the Dawn Sword—the token of power—has not returned to fulfill its destiny."

" 'Token of power'?" asked Tuck. "Just what is a 'token of power,' and what do you mean, 'fulfill its destiny'?"

Again Eiron turned to the Waerling. "As to what is a token of power, they are at times hard to recognize, while at other times known to all. And they can be for Good or Ill: Whelmram is a token of power for Evil—a feartoken—for it has crashed through many a gate for the *Spaunen.* So, too, was Gelvin's Doom, an evil device in the end. Those for Good are sometimes known: one was the Kammerling; too, there is Bale, and Bane, and perhaps Black Galgor: these would appear to fit the mold. Others are unknown until they fulfill their destiny, and beforehand seem to hold no power at all: jewels, poniards, rings, a trinket. Not all are as blatant as Galen King's rune-marked Atalar Blade that hewed the Hèlarms as foretold."

"Foretold?" burst out Tuck in surprise.

"Aye, foretold," answered Eiron, "for it was I who long ago translated the writing on Othran's tomb:

> 'Loose not the Red Quarrel
> Ere appointed dark time.
> Blade shall brave vile Warder
> From the deep, black slime.'

I knew not what the words meant when I deciphered them, yet it seems certain that the blade Galen King bears is a token of power meant to strike the Warder from the deep, black slime, for that was its foretold destiny. Just as Bane, Jarriel's sword, and Brega's axe, along with a Ruchen torch, were meant to combine to slay the *Draedan.*"

"But what if we had not succeeded?" asked Tuck. "What then of the destiny?"

Eiron signed for Alor Gildor to answer the Waerling.

"Tokens of power seem to have ways of fulfilling their own destiny," answered Gildor. "Had we been felled ere reaching Drimmen-deeve, still would the Atalar Blade have sought out the Hèlarms; still would Bane have come against the Gargon: but it would have been by other hands, not ours. Some tokens would seem to have more than one destiny: Gelvin's Doom; the Green Stone of Xian. Perhaps Bane or the Atalar Blade are not yet done with their ordained work; heed me, it may be that their greatest deeds lie ahead, as I think Red Bale's work is yet to be done.

"Aye, Tuck, tokens of power are mysterious things, perhaps guided by Adon from afar. Yet none can say for certain which things are tokens, and we can only guess at best; if a thing was made in Xian, or forged in Lost Duellin, then it would seem to have a better chance of bearing a destiny; yet many have come from elsewhere, and none can say which are the tokens until their destinies come to pass."

At this moment a page came to Eiron, and the Coron announced that the feast was ready.

And as they strode to the Coron-hall, Tuck was lost in deep thought: *If the Lian are right, then it would seem that we all are driven to fulfill the destinies of these "tokens of power." What then does it matter that we strive to reach our own ends? For whether or no we wish it, we are compelled by hidden sway . . . Or is it that the paths of the tokens and their bearers happen to be going in the same direction? Perhaps I choose the token for it suits my aims, and the token chooses me for the selfsame reason.*

They came into the Coron-hall, and it was full of brightness, for Elven lamps glowed fulgently, and fires were in the hearths, and bright Lian filled the hall. And Eiron led them to the throne dais and they mounted up the steps: Brega clad in black-iron mail, Tuck in silveron, Galen in scarlet, and Gildor without any armor at all. Eiron raised his voice so that all could hear: *"Ealle hál va Deevestrīdena, slēanra a va Draedan!"* (All hail the Deevewalkers, slayers of the Gargon!)

And thrice a great, glad shout burst forth from the gathered Lian: *Hál! . . . Hál! . . . Hál!*

And then the guests were led to a full board, and the feast of thanksgiving began. Yet Gildor's eyes swept the assembly, as if seeking a face not there. At last he turned to Eiron. "Coron Eiron, I see not my sister Faeon, bright Mistress of Darda Galion."

Now anguish filled Eiron's features. "Faeon has ridden the Twilight Ride," said the Coron. "Seven days past."

Gildor fell back stricken, disbelief upon his face. "But the Sundering! None has made the Dawn Ride since."

"Alor Gildor, just as you did, Faeon, too, felt Vanidor's death cry, and she was distraught. She has ridden the Twilight Ride to Adonar, to ask the High One Himself to intercede and stop the Evil in Gron." Eiron's hands were trembling in distress.

"But Adon has said—nay, pledged—that He will not directly act in Mithgar." Gildor's voice was filled with woe. "Yet still she went to plead with Him? Did Faeon not consider that the way back is closed: sundered?"

"She knew it all too well, Gildor . . . all too well," answered Eiron. "She knew that not until the time of the Silverlarks and the Silver Sword will the Dawn Ride be made again, and then perhaps but by His messenger. Yet she thought perhaps this once . . ." Eiron drew a long, shuddering breath. "Vanidor's death drove her thus."

Gildor rose and walked to a fireplace and stood long gazing into the flames. Eiron, too, left the table, and his footsteps carried him to a window where he looked out into the Eld Trees and spoke to no one.

"Now we know what grieves Eiron," said Galen after a moment. "His consort Faeon is gone from Mithgar, never to return."

"I do not understand, Galen King," said Tuck. "Where has she gone? And why can she not return?"

"She has ridden the Twilight Ride to Adonar, Wee One," answered Galen, and at the buccan's puzzled look, Galen spoke on: "Tuck, this is the way it was told to me long ago. In the First Days, when the Spheres were made, among the three Planes were divided the worlds: the Hōhgarda, the Mittegarda, and the Untargarda. And days without number passed. And it came to pass that Adon and others of the High Ones began to dwell in Adonar in the Upper Plane, but whence came the High Ones, it is not told. Again days beyond reckoning fled by, but then, in the Lower Plane, in the bleak underland of Neddra, Yrm sprang forth from the sere land—some say by Gyphon's hand. And then only the Mittegarda lay fallow, empty of Folk. But at last, Man, Dwarf, Warrow, and others moved across the face of the world, but how we, the youngest, came to be—by whose hand—it is not known, though some say Adon set us here, while others claim it was His daughter, Elwydd, and yet others say that each of the Folk was made by a different hand. Regardless, now the three Planes each held dwellers.

"In those ancient days, the ways between the Planes were open, and those who knew how could pass from one Plane to the other.

"And in that dim time, Gyphon—the High Vûlk—ruled in the Untargarda; but His rule was by the sufferance of Adon, and Gyphon was greatly galled, for He coveted power over all things.

"And Gyphon thought to rule the whole of creation, and so He sent His emissaries to Mithgar to sway those living here away from Adon and unto Him; for if Gyphon could gain control of the Middle Plane, the fulcrum, then like the balance of a great teeter-totter, the Forces of Power would shift to Him, and Adon would be cast down.

"And many of the Middle Plane came to believe in Gyphon's vile promises, and thus followed His ways. But others had clearer sight and saw him as the Great Deceiver, and rejected His rule.

"And Gyphon ranted, and sent Hordes of his Spawn from Neddra into Mithgar, for if He could not persuade those who dwelt here to follow Him, He would use force.

"Adon was enraged, and He sundered the way between the Untargarda and the Mittegarda, so that no more *Spaunen* could pass through. And Adon called Gyphon to task, and humbled Him. And Gyphon groveled before the High One and foreswore His ambitions.

"Hence there was at that time no War, but myriads of the Foul Folk now dwelt in Mithgar, and much grievous harm has come of that.

"Yet although Gyphon had sworn loyalty to Adon, still He harbored a lust for power in His black heart. And He yet ruled the Untargarda; could He gain control in but one other Plane—the Hōhgarda or the Mittegarda—then He would rule all.

"His lust seethed long Eras, and at last He set a plan in

motion, for in Mithgar He had a mighty servant: Modru! Gyphon launched an attack upon Adonar, and at the same time, Modru struck at all of Mithgar; thus, the Great War of the Ban began.

"But Gyphon's true plan was to thrust across the High World and come unto the Middle Plane Himself, to conquer the lesser beings at struggle here, for none here could withstand the power of the High Vûlk. But ere He could do so, Adon sundered the High and Middle Planes one from the other, just as He had sundered the ways to the Low Plane Eras before. By cutting Adonar off from Mithgar, Adon barred Gyphon from coming to conquer.

"Still, the War was fought upon all three Planes, but the crucial outcome was to be in the Middle Plane, where the struggle here in Mithgar raged between the Grand Alliance and Modru and his minions. And as you know, Modru lost. Hence, the Great Evil did not conquer here. But had the way not been sundered by Adon, the outcome would have been different.

"Yet even in the Sundering, Adon was merciful: for though none can now come from Adonar to Mithgar, still the opposite way—the way from Mithgar to Adonar—remains open.

"You see, for Eras the Elven Folk of Adonar had been passing back and forth between the Hōhgarda and the Mittegarda, for though they love Mithgar well, Elves are a Folk of the High Plane: Starsholm in Adonar is their true home. Yet many would dwell here, for in the Mittegarda they find their skills are much needed. But the Hōhgarda— the High Worlds call at them, too, for there they can rest and be at peace and develop new skills. And though I do not know it for certain, still I think that only in Adonar can they have children, for legend says that no Elven child has ever been born on Mithgar, yet in past Eras striplings were known to come to the Mittegarda with other Elves on the Dawn Ride. But though they dwell here, still they are of the High Plane, and Adon would have His Elves come home; thus, they can yet take the Twilight Ride."

"Twilight Ride . . . Dawn Ride," interrupted Tuck. "These things I know nought of. What are they?"

"They were the ways between Adonar and Mithgar, Tuck, but only Elves could follow the paths, and not Man,

Warrow, Dwarf, or for that matter any other Folk." Galen took a drink of wela, a heady Elven mead, and then continued. "Somehow, at twilight, the way between the Planes is open, and an Elf astride a horse can ride from here to Adonar. And, ere the Sundering, the way from Adonar to Mithgar could be ridden at dawn: *'Go upon the twilight, return upon the dawn'*: it is an ancient Elven benediction. But now only the Twilight Ride can be made, and then only by the Elven Folk."

Brega, who had been listening as intently as Tuck, made a rumbling sound deep in his throat. "Eerie is this Twilight Ride, for in my youth I saw it from afar: Elf astride a horse, riding in the woods below, the steed walking through the forest as if guided in a pattern. My ears may have played me tricks, yet I think I heard singing, or perhaps it was chanting; I cannot say. Dusk seemed to gather around them as they flickered among the trees, Elf and horse going from one to another. They passed behind an oak, and did not come out the other side. I rubbed my eyes, but it was no trick of vision. Quickly I ran down the slope, for darkness was falling swiftly. I found the steed's tracks there by the tree, and they faded away as if the horse and Elf had turned into smoke. I cast about for other sign, but night fell, and starlight is too dim to track by. I hurried on my way and said nought to any, for I would not have had others sneer at me behind my back." Brega quaffed his wela. "This is the first I've told of it."

Tuck was silent for a long moment, lost in Galen's and Brega's words. At last he said, "Well, then, if I understand it correctly, the Twilight Ride is a one-way ride, and Elves who go to Adonar can never come back, for the path from there to here has been sundered and none have ridden the Dawn Ride since." At Galen's nod Tuck looked with sad eyes upon Eiron and Gildor, for Eiron's consort, Gildor's sister, Faeon, had ridden the Twilight Ride to plead with Adon for succor. Yet Adon had never directly intervened in Mithgar in all the Eras past, and He had pledged never to do so. Even so, Rael's rede about the Silverlarks and the Silver Sword *"Borne hence upon the Dawn"* would seem to say that the way would be opened again; but when . . . no one could say. And Tuck's mind conjured up a vision of an Elven warrior astride a horse appearing like a wraith from the early morning mist and bearing a silver sword to be given to another to wield against the Great Evil. The Warrow shook his head to clear it of this image.

"Perhaps that's why the Silverlarks are gone," mused Tuck; and at Galen's and Brega's puzzled looks, the buccan elaborated: "If the Silverlarks could fly the Twilight Path, then they've gotten to Adonar and can't get back." Both Brega and Galen nodded in surprise at the Warrow's canny remark and wondered why they had not thought of it that way.

Soon Lord Gildor and then Eiron returned to the feast board, but the conversation at the table of honor all but dwindled to nought. And even though they sat at a great banquet of thanksgiving, and smiled when toasted by the gay revelers, the hearts of the Deevewalkers were heavy, for a pall of sadness weighted them down.

Tuck yawned deeply, his eyes owlish, for he was weary. Even so, he paid close heed to what was being said, for he and Galen and Brega now sat in council with Eiron. In the distance, strains of music sounded as the feast continued, but the comrades had retired to discuss the ways before them, and Eiron had joined them to yield up his advice.

Long had they talked, and now Galen set forth their choices: "These, then, are the two courses deemed best: To bear south on horseback across the plains of Valon toward Pellar; and along that path in the Land of Valon is the city of Vanar, some eighty to ninety leagues hence, and it would be our first goal, for there would we find Vanadurin to lead us to the Legions; but if the Host fights in Pellar, then we needs must ride ninety leagues beyond Vanar just to come to the crossing into that southern Land.

"Our other choice is to continue by boat, going down the River Nith to the Argon, and thence southward to Pellar; this way is more uncertain, and perhaps more dangerous, for we may not come unto those who will aid us until we reach the Argon Ferry along the Pendwyr Road, and then it may not be aid we find, for that crossing perhaps is held by the enemy. But even if it is in friendly hands, still it lies some three hundred leagues distant by the great eastward arc of the river route."

Galen paused in long thought, then said: "We will go by

river, for although it is longer and more uncertain, still it is swifter, for the Nith and the Argon need no rest and run their courses day and night. And if we eat and sleep in the boat, stopping only as needs dictate, then we can reach the Argon Ferry in a sevenday or less; whereas by horseback across Valon, unless we press the steeds unmercifully, we cannot arrive at the Ferry in less than a tenday—more likely it will take a fortnight if we rest the mounts. Nay, the river is best for those who must fly south in haste."

And so it was decided: by Elven boat to Argon Ferry would the comrades go, for horses tire, but the river does not.

The next morning a great retinue set out from Woodsheart bearing south: Coron Eiron and an escort of Lian Guardians accompanied Galen, Gildor, Brega, and Tuck as they headed for a cache of boats upon the River Nith.

Once more Tuck was mounted behind Galen astride a cantering horse, and the buccan gazed with weary eyes at the passing Eld Tree forest. The Warrow had not slept out all the sleep that was in him, for the discussion as to how to proceed had lasted long into the night, and they had risen early to be on their way. And among the great boles they went swiftly, for a feeling of dire urgency pressed upon them all, especially upon Lord Gildor, who still sensed a *doom* lying in the days ahead, but what it was he could not say.

At the fleet pace they rode, in an hour or so they came to a glade upon the banks of the River Nith, and the purl of its swift-flowing waters murmured through the twilit wood.

The horses were reined to a halt, and all the company dismounted. One Elf leapt down the bank and drew forth an Elven boat from another hidden cache.

Eiron looked upon the craft, then said: "This boat will bear you to the turn above Vanil Falls. On the south shore beneath the Leaning Stone you will secrete it. Down the Great Escarpment by the Long Stair you will come to the Cauldron, and in the willow roots you will find another craft. Stay along the south shore until you pass mighty Bellon and are upon the Argon proper."

The four nodded at Eiron's words, for he but repeated

what he had said the night before as they had planned the journey south.

Their replenished knapsacks were laded in the craft, and now the comrades prepared to embark. Yet ere the four stepped into the Elven boat, Eiron bade them stay but a moment more, and he summoned a Lian unto him. And the warrior came bearing a long tray, and it was covered by a golden cloth. The Coron turned to the Deevewalkers, and though his voice was soft, all in the glade could hear him: "*Va Draedan sa nond,* slain by you four heroes. It was a deed beyond our wildest hopes, for the Horror was an evil dread power drove even the bravest mad with fear. Yet in the end you prevailed where none else had succeeded. But, although Modru's Dread has been felled, the vast power of the Evil in Gron still assails the Land, and so your mission must go forth, and on the waters of the Nith you will leave us; for though we would have you stay, we know that now is not the time for you to rest from your labors. Yet we would not have you depart without being fully armed. Drimm Brega, you lost your axe, and Galen King, your sword: the one clove into the skull of the Dread, the other shivered asunder in his gut; both now lie in the unplumbed depths of the Great Deep. But from the armories of Darda Galion, by mine own hand I have chosen these blades for you to bear as your own." Eiron folded back the golden cloth, and there upon the tray were two gleaming weapons: an Elven sword of silvery brightness and a black-helved axe of steel. Runes of power were etched in each blade, their messages wrought in ebon glyphs. Eiron gave the sword over to Galen, and the axe to Brega.

The Dwarf examined the weapon with a keen eye as if appraising its workmanship. And then with a cry—"*Hai!*"—he leapt out into the open glade and clove the air with the double-bitted blade; and driven by his broad Dwarven shoulders, the weapon *whooshed,* and glittered in the twilight. Then, laughing, he threw it up flashing, and caught it again by its black helve. And the assembled Elves *oohed* and *ahhed* to see the Drimm's power and skill. "*Hai!*" cried Brega again; then: "Squam beware, for this axe fits my hand as if made for it!"

Galen, too, hefted his gleaming blade, feeling the balance

of the weapon and noting the trueness of its edge. "I have shattered two swords in the War: one at the gates of Challerain Keep, the other at the bridge in Drimmen-deeve. Yet I deem this blade I now hold shall never be broken in combat."

Eiron smiled, then said: "They were forged long ago in Lost Duellin. The runes speak in ancient tongue and whisper deeply to the metal, telling of the keenness of edge, of the strength of blade, of the firmness of grip of hilt and haft, and of the power to smite. And each weapon is named by its runes: your axe, Drimm Brega, in the Sylva Tongue is called Eborane, which means Dark Reaver; and your blade, Galen King, is named Talarn, which means Steel-heart."

Brega held up his axe. "Elves may call this axe Eborane, and Man, Dark Reaver, but its true name—its Châkka name—is Drakkalan!" (Dark Shedder!)

Eiron turned back to the tray and took up a black scabbard and belt, each scribed with scarlet-and-gold tracery, and he gave them over to King Galen. And Galen slid Steel-heart into the sheath and girted the weapon to his waist. Then he stepped to the boat and untied his old scabbard from his pack, giving the empty sheath over to the Coron, saying, "Perhaps, Eiron, you can find a suitable weapon for this sword holder; it has served Mithgar well, for it bore the blade that shattered deep within the bowels of the Gargon."

With honor the Lian Coron received the scabbard and carefully laid it on the tray. Then he took up four Elven-wrought cloak clasps: gold they were, and sun-burst-shaped, and set with a jet stone. And one by one he fastened the jeweled clasps to the collars of the four. "By these tokens all will come to know you as the Four Who Strode the Deeves—the Dread Slayers—and they will welcome you to their hearths and sing of your deeds 'round the fires."

Now the Coron stepped back from the four and bowed deeply, and so, too, did all the Elven warriors of the retinue. And the Deevewalkers bowed in return, and Galen spoke for the four of them: "Coron, in haste we came and in haste we go, for our mission is urgent. Yet a day will come when we can linger awhile, and then would I stride long in the twilight vaults of the Larkenwald. But now we fare south to find mine Host; yet what else we shall discover, it is not known, though this I say: When Modru is at last cast down—his foul darkness to yield to the light—long will it be remembered that Elf, Dwarf, Waerling, and Man joined axes and swords, arrows and spears, and hands, to throw down Evil. And long will the bond between our Folk endure." Galen flashed Steel-heart unto the air. *"Hál ūre allience! Hál ūre bōnd!"* (Hail our alliance! Hail our bond!)

A great shout rose up from the Lian warriors, and they brandished gleaming swords and spears as the four comrades stepped into the boat and cast away from shore. And as Brega, Galen, and Gildor took up the paddles to prepare for swift journey, the retinue of Elven Guardians mounted their steeds and lined the bank. And as with one voice they cried, *Hál, valagalana!* and wheeled as a company and rode swiftly away to the north to disappear among the great boles of the soaring Eld Trees.

And the Elven boat was plied to midstream, where the fleet current of the River Nith rapidly bore the four comrades easterly, toward the distant waters of the mighty Argon, along the road of their destiny.

Hastily the River Nith hurried apace toward its ending, and the boat rushed down its course. Still, it was some ninety miles whence they had embarked down to Vanil Falls, and the Sun would set ere the four could come to their landing. Hence, they would make camp at sunset, for to approach the high cataract in the dark of a new Moon was too dangerous a thing to do; this last fact Tuck recorded in his diary, along with the statement that Gildor greatly begrudged the delay, for the unknown pressing doom felt by the Elf had grown stronger with each passing day. Yet, delay or not, still they would make camp when the light failed, else they chanced being carried over the falls if they missed their landing at the Leaning Stone.

And so all day the nimble craft coursed through the leaping water, and in turn Brega, Gildor, and Galen sat in the stern and guided the boat, while Tuck sat gazing at the shoreline and into the great woods marching off into dusky dimness, or watching the clear water churn. At times the Warrow would scribe in his diary, and at other times he

would doze—such was the case when they made their final
landing, for the grounding of the bow jarred the napping
buccan awake.

Stiffly, they stumped along the shoreline, Brega gathering
scrub for a campblaze, Tuck setting a fire-ring of stone,
Gildor and Galen beaching the boat. Soon the fire was
kindled by Tuck's flint and steel, and they took a short
meal. Little was said ere they bedded down, for they were
made weary by the long boat ride. And as Tuck took his
turn at watch, he wondered how they would fare when they
reached the Argon, for then they would stay in the boat—
except for brief stops—until they reached the Argon Ferry
at Pendwyr Road, making no camps for nearly a week; the
thought of the confinement made the Warrow's legs ache.

Tuck was awakened just ere dawn by Lord Gildor, who
paced restlessly, anxious to set forth. "If we leave now,
we'll reach the Leaning Stone just after daybreak," said the
Lian. And so they took a quick breakfast as they broke
camp, and embarked downriver just as the eastern sky
began to pale.

Now the Elven boat sliced swiftly through the plashy
tumble as the River Nith drew narrower and ran more
quickly down toward the eastern dawnlight. Two miles they
went, then two more, and the river swung northeasterly;
and through the dusky Eld Tree leaves where the dawn
could be seen, Tuck watched the sky change from grey to
pearl to pink to blue; and low through the massive boles
now and then the Warrow could glimpse the flaming orange
rim of the Sun as it brightly limned the horizon. In the
distance Tuck could hear growing the faintest of rumbles
grumbling above the splash of rushing water.

"Yon is the Leaning Stone!" cried Gildor, pointing.
"Strike for the south shore!" And Galen stroked strongly,
following Gildor's lead; but at the stern it was Brega whose
massive shoulders swiftly impelled the craft into a safe
eddy, bringing the boat into the shadow of a great rock
shaped like a huge monolithic column that stood atilt in
the water, leaning against the high stone bank. At Gildor's
instruction Brega guided the boat into the cavity between
the huge stone and the high bank. And in the dimness their
craft slid to berth alongside one other slender Elven wherry

at tether. Disembarking and tying up their own craft, the four girted their weapons and shouldered their packs and followed a rocky path up out of the shadow and onto the high bank.

A mile or so eastward they marched, alongside the river, to come at last to the Great Escarpment, a sheer thousand-foot-high cliff over which the River Nith leapt wildly at Vanil Falls to plunge without hindrance straight down into a vast churn of water named the Cauldron.

Tuck stood in awe upon the edge of the sheer drop. Far could his eyes see, far across the land below, and in the morning light his vision followed this massive flank; and some seven miles to the east he descried another cataract, an enormous cascade plunging down the face of the Great Escarpment to thunder into the Cauldron: it was mighty Bellon, the falls marking where the great Argon River plummeted down the vast wall. Eastward, beyond the Cauldron, the Argon continued, flowing at the foot of the Escarpment marching off beyond the horizon.

"Lor!" breathed Tuck. "When the Ghûls chased us south from Quadran Pass, I thought the cliff we came down *then* was a great drop, yet this wall makes that seem but a short step by comparison. How high is this cliff, and how far does it stretch? Do you know?"

"Aye, Tuck," answered Lord Gildor. "In places it is two hundred fathoms from top to bottom, though far to the east it dwindles down to meet the riverbank. Here at your feet it drops one thousand feet sheer. As to its length: eastward it comes twisting behind us, some two hundred miles from the Grimwall to the Argon there before us; on eastward beyond the Argon, another two hundred miles it reaches, curving at last southeasterly alongside part of the Greatwood. On this side of the Argon the escarpment marks the boundary between Darda Galion and Valon: up here to the north it is the Land of the Lian; down there to the south, the Realm of the Harlingar."

"How do we get down?" asked Tuck.

"By the Long Stair . . . there," answered Gildor, pointing.

Tuck could see a narrow, steep path with many switchbacks pitching down the face of the cliff alongside the silvery cascade of Vanil Falls.

By this way the four descended in single file: Gildor first, Brega last, and Tuck before Galen. Long was the descent, and they made frequent stops to rest, for they found that climbing down a long, steep slope was nearly as difficult as climbing up. And all the way down Tuck pressed against the cliff, for the drop was sheer and frightening. And as they came down, the roar of the water of the Nith plunging into the Cauldron became louder and louder, and they had to shout into one another's ears to be heard; but finally all converse became impossible as they neared the bottom, a half mile south of where Vanil Falls thundered into the churn. And rainbows played in the great swirls of mist.

At last they reached the banks of the Cauldron, and in the roar Gildor led them to a grove of willows and pointed out a hidden Elven craft. Quickly they embarked, and by hand signals Gildor directed them along the southern shoreline of the churning water, their powerful strokes driving the boat through the swirling eddies and across the tugging backwash.

A mile or so they went, and again they could hear loud speech as the roar of the Vanil cascade receded behind them. But ahead Tuck could now hear the rumble of Bellon Falls, though it was still some six miles distant.

Swiftly they paddled, all but Tuck, and the banks of the Cauldron sped by. A mile, then two they swept, hugging the south shore, and the water became choppy and full of swirls, and once again they could not hear to speak. Another mile passed, and then one more, and the endless yell of Bellon hammered at Tuck and shook his small frame. Here the Cauldron began twisting the boat this way and that, but the skill of the three paddlers kept the craft on course. Another mile they went, and now they were at their closest approach to mighty Bellon, thundering some three miles to the north across the Cauldron; yet the towering curve of the sheer stone of the Great Escarpment hurled the shout of the mighty cataract out upon them, and its whelming roar rattled Tuck's every bone and jarred his teeth, and his very thoughts were lost in the thunderous blast. Now it was all that the three could do to keep the craft driving straight, for here the chop and churn was great; yet on they pressed, past Bellon.

And as they went by, Tuck squinted and blinked with

watery eyes at the great cascade: more than a mile wide, it was, and a thousand feet high; yet where Vanil had fallen silvery, Bellon was tinged pale jade.

East they went, slowly passing beyond the great falls; but it was long ere the roar began to diminish, and still they fought the Cauldron's churn. On they pressed, and the shout lessened, and the chop quelled; and at last the boat passed out of the swirls and eddies, for now they came to where the Argon gathered itself up once more to flow toward the distant Avagon Sea. And as the craft slipped out of the Cauldron and into the laminar flow, Tuck knew that now began their long trip down the Argon to the ferry.

Behind them, Bellon roared on, but by raising their voices, again the comrades could talk.

"In the Châkka speech we call that great cataract Ctor," called Brega. "In the Common Tongue that means Shouter. But though it is called Ctor, never did I dream that its voice was so great."

"Bellon shouts louder still to the Argon merchants," spoke up Galen, "for these River Drummers come even closer to its yell. They portage their trade goods up the Over Stair—there upon the Great Escarpment—coming within a mile of the bellow. They are said to stuff beeswax in their ears to keep from going deaf."

Tuck looked to where Galen pointed, and winding up the face of the escarpment just to the east of Bellon was another path, a portage—the Over Stair—a trade road considerably broader than the narrow path they had descended back at Vanil Falls. But even though the Over Stair was wider than the Long Stair, still Tuck would not have traded routes, for he could not imagine being closer to Bellon than they had been; and he could fancy his mother saying, *"Why, it just might rattle a body apart!"*

Now began the journey down the Great Argon River. East they went, alongside the Great Escarpment, rearing a thousand feet upward on their left; to their right lay the grassy plains of the North Reach of Valon, and before them was the wide, swift-flowing Argon, the great river of Mithgar. The way ahead would curve over hundreds of miles from east to south and then back southwesterly; their far goal was Pendwyr Road at the Argon Ferry, some seven hundred fifty miles away as the river flowed. And there they hoped to find the crossing in friendly hands, and steeds and guides to lead them to the Host.

All day they rode the river, stopping but once, briefly, on the south shore at sunset. But as soon as their needs were taken care of, again they launched their craft and pulled out into the swift current in mid-river, Tuck now helping, for earlier Brega had used Bane to trim down a paddle to fit the Warrow and had shown the young buccan how to ply it in the straight bow stroke.

Dusk deepened into dark night and stars glittered brightly in the black firmament, while the shadowy orb of an old Moon clasped in the silvery arms of a thin crescent of a new Moon sank low to the west. And Brega seemed spellbound by the spangled heavens, and pointed to one of the brightest glints standing high in the east.

"Have you the name for that one, Lord Gildor?" The Dwarf's voice was filled with a reverence for the celestial beacons.

"The Lian call it Cianin Andele: Shining Nomad," answered Gildor, "for it is one of the five wandering stars; but at times it pauses, and then steps backward, only to pause again and continue forth upon its cyclical journey. Why, I cannot say, though hearthtales speak of a lost shoe."

Brega grunted, then said, "Châkka lore tells that there are many wanderers, some too faint to see. Five are known, including that one, and it is brightest. We name it Jarak: Courser."

"Is it the brightest star of all?" asked Tuck, looking at the blaze.

"Aye," answered Brega.

"Nay," said Gildor at nearly the same time.

Tuck looked from one to the other in the dark, but nought could he read in their shadowed features. "Which is it," he asked, "the aye or the nay?"

"Both answers are right," responded Gildor, "for although Cianin Andele is usually brightest, at times others grow brighter; in elden days, for a brief time the blaze of the Ban Star surpassed all, though it is now gone."

"Ban Star?" Tuck's voice was filled with curiosity.

"Aye, Wee One," answered Gildor, "when Adon set His Ban upon the *Rûpt*, the blaze of a new star lighted the heavens, a star where none had been before, growing so bright that it nearly rivaled the Sun: not only did the star o'erwhelm the late night sky; it could be seen in the early morning, too. So dazzling it grew that it was hard to look at, nearly blinding, for it hurt the eye. Many long nights did it shine—the Ban Star—growing brighter, but fading at last until it was gone, and once more that place in the night sky stood black and empty. And by this token Adon set His Ban upon those who had aided Gyphon in the Great War."

"Lor! A bright new star," breathed Tuck. "And one that disappeared, too. It must have been quite a sight, perhaps as wondrous as the Dragon Star."

At mention of the Dragon Star, an unseen look of puzzlement came over Gildor's features, as if he were searching for an elusive memory.

Brega pointed to the silvery crescent of the setting Moon. "I deem the most wondrous thing is when the Moon eats the Sun, biting into one side only to spit it out the other."

Again Lord Gildor seemed to cast back in his mind for a lost thought.

"When will that be?" asked Tuck.

Brega shrugged. "Elf Gildor knows, perhaps."

Tuck turned to the Lian. "Know you, Lord Gildor? Know you when the Moon will next eat the Sun?"

Gildor thought but a moment, and then answered, and none questioned his knowledge, for the Elven Folk know of the movements of the Sun, Moon, and stars. "*Aro!* Why, in but twenty-eight days will it happen, Tuck. Yet here the Moon will not swallow all of the Sun; but north, in Rian and Gron and upon the Steppes of Jord, the Moon will completely consume the Sun, taking it in whole and keeping it for many long minutes ere yielding it up again."

"Lor!" exclaimed Tuck once more. "When that happens, there in the Dimmendark, there in the Wastes of Gron, it will be the darkest day ever."

"Aye, Tuck, the darkest . . ." Suddenly Lord Gildor fell silent, for at last his mind grasped the elusive memory—a hidden memory buried deep within the grief and shock of Vanidor's death—and he drew in a long, shuddering breath; then his voice came quiet: "Galen King, we must fare to the Host with all the haste we can muster, for an unknown doom is set to fall. What it is, I cannot say, but still it comes. For when Vanidor reached out with his death cry, he called my name; and in that fearful moment, a dire rede was thrust upon me:

> 'The Darkest Day,
> The Greatest Evil . . .'

Vanidor died giving warning, but I judge his message incomplete, for I sense there was something more—about the Dragon Star, and the Dimmendark—but what it was, I know not, for my brother's flame was quenched by Death."

Gildor fell silent, and nought was said for long moments, and though Tuck could not see the Lian's face, he knew the Elf was weeping, and the buccan's own tears ran freely.

Then Gildor's soft voice spoke once more: "Now I think Vanidor's rede speaks to the day when the Moon will eat the Sun, for Tuck's words ring true: in Gron it *will be* the Darkest Day; and then will come the Greatest Evil."

Again Gildor fell silent, and none else spoke for a span of time. And the Elven craft was borne along the Argon River; the low bordering banks crouched blackly nearly a mile to either side. And to the north the Great Escarpment reared high and shone darkly in the glittering starlight.

At last Galen spoke: "And you say that the Sun Death is but two fortnights hence?"

At Galen's words Tuck shuddered, for to his mind came the image of Modru's standard: a burning ring, scarlet on black: the Sun Death. And the Warrow's memory returned to that 'Darkday upon the field before the north gate of Challerain Keep when the Sun-Death sigil of Modru stood above the broken scarlet-and-gold standard of Aurion.

Gildor's answer broke into Tuck's thoughts. "Aye, Galen King. In four weeks, when the Sun stands at the zenith, then will its light be eclipsed, then will it be the Darkest Day."

"Then will the Greatest Evil come," rumbled Brega. "Perhaps the Hyranee and Kistanee have the right of it: mayhap Vanidor's warning was of the Great Evil, of Gyphon, returning to cast Adon down."

Tuck's heart plummeted to hear Brega's words, and Gildor's breath hissed in through clenched teeth, for what the Dwarf said had the knell of truth.

"Warrior Brega, you may be right," said Galen. "In any case we will follow Lord Gildor's advice and fare to the Host as swiftly as we can, though how we can thwart Modru on the Darkest Day, I cannot now say, for we know in truth not what Vanidor's rede means. But if we are to go swiftly, we must add our own speed to that of the river; we will take turns: two paddle while two rest—four hours and four—till we come to our goal."

"Tuck and I will take the first turn," Brega volunteered.

Tuck was surprised at Brega's choice to pair up with him, for the buccan knew that he lacked the skill and strength to match that of his comrades, especially that of Brega. But Tuck also realized Brega's power alone was nearly the equal of Galen's and Gildor's combined, and so the team of Dwarf and Warrow should match that of Man and Elf.

"Take the bow, Tuck," called Brega. "I will take the stern. King Galen, Elf Gildor, we will awaken you in four hours."

And so it was that while Galen and Gildor bedded down, Brega and Tuck began plying oars to the waters of the mighty Argon, and the Elven boat sprang forth swiftly upon the current. And the race for the Argon Ferry began.

Long, grueling hours of punishing toil followed one upon the other as Dwarf and Warrow, then Lian and Man, plied the Elven boat down the long course of the mighty Argon. Four hours of wearying labor were followed by four hours of restless slumber; and each time it seemed to Tuck that no sooner had he gotten to sleep than it was time to paddle again—and the exhausting grind seemed endless. They would waken from sleep and take a meal of mian and then begin anew their arduous toil; and the Warrow wondered if their food would last, for the Elven waybread was being consumed avidly to keep up their flagging strength.

And they tried every trick they knew to ease their labor: they sought the swiftest channels, and quartered the craft slightly in the current to gain greater aid from the flow of the river, but the banks passed by at what seemed to Tuck to be a maddeningly slow rate; they rubbed oil from the boat-kit onto their hands to ease the chafing, yet still the paddles caused painful blisters; they rested ten minutes of every hour to renew their waning energy, but slowly it ebbed from them anyway; they stopped perhaps a half an hour of a morning and evening to stretch and take care of other needs, yet muscles became sore and stiff and knotted from the confinement. But, weary and sore, cramped and blistered, down the Argon they struck for their goal.

Mid of night the first eventide found them passing an unnamed isle in the river. Beyond the trees of the river-border forest the Great Escarpment hove up in the north-east, while west and south past the island and over the river and on the far side of the fringing trees lay the wide Realm of Valon. Now Galen and Gildor were awakened to take their turn while Brega and Tuck cast themselves into the bottom of the craft to clutch at sleep. Yet it seemed no sooner had he lain down than Tuck had to groan awake to take his turn again, and still the stars shone forth.

And as Tuck and Brega plied down the river, dawn came, and they could see through the bordering trees that the Great Escarpment had begun to dwindle, the cliff tapering down as the land fell to the south and east. And the sky slowly changed, heralding the arrival of the Sun. The golden orb at last rose up over the Greatwood to the east; this mighty forest reached from the River Rissanin in the far northwest to the Glave Hills in the remote southeast—a forest stretching some six or seven hundred miles in all. And the trees stood grey and barren in their winter dress.

They grounded the craft on the western shore and took their morning break standing on the soil of Valon.

Once more they took up the journey, and Tuck and Brega slept while Galen and Gildor pressed downstream, and the Sun stood at the zenith when Tuck's turn came again.

That evening, ere sunset, they stopped once more for a shore break, and the Warrow jotted brief notes in his diary. Then it came time to drive on, and Tuck wondered if they would have the energy to reach the Argon Ferry.

And as they embarked, Gildor said, "The coming weather looks foul. We may be in for winter rain or snow."

Tuck looked all around, but the late afternoon skies seemed clear, though some thin clouds laddered the high blue.

Brega watched the Warrow cast about, then grunted, "Look to the west for the coming skies and to the east for those that have gone."

Here the river-border trees were sparse, and Tuck looked out over the plains of Valon, and low upon the horizon stood a dark bank of clouds that the Sun had fallen partly behind.

That night a cold rain drizzled across the land, and Tuck was miserable as he and Brega paddled, but he was even more miserable when he tried to sleep.

The rain stopped just as they landed for their morning break on the north spit of an island in mid-river, and instead of continuing to bail, they beached the boat and turned it upside down, draining the last of the rainwater from the shell. As Galen and Brega uprighted the boat again, Tuck's vision scanned to the horizons: As far as the eye could see, the sky stood bleak and leaden. To the east stood the Glave Hills, marking the end of the Greatwood and the beginning of Pellar. Still to the west lay Valon; yet they had come many miles around its borders: they had started some four hundred fifty miles upriver, traveling east along the North Reach of Valon; slowly the Argon swung in a great arc, from east to southeast to south, and the North Reach became the East Reach; ahead the Argon would continue to curve, to flow southwest between the margins of the South Reach of Valon and the Kingdom of Pellar, where, some three hundred fifty miles ahead, lay the Argon Ferry; since leaving the Cauldron, they had come more than halfway to their goal, yet it was still far downriver.

Once more they embarked upon the Argon, and a cold westerly wind sprang up, quartering across their bow. And Brega cursed, for the thin gust would slow their progress.

At the eleven o'clock of night, the wind started to fall, and the stars began to come out, bright and cold, as the skies slowly cleared.

The morning break of their fourth day upon the Argon found the travelers weak of shank, for the long hours of confinement in the craft had taken their toll. Yet they did not spend overlong upon the Pellarian shore of the river, for as Galen said, "Were we to have many more days of this ceaseless travel, then would we spend a day on shore, resting. But this should be our final Sun in the narrow craft: we should reach the Argon Ferry this eve."

Brega grunted, and patted the outwale of the boat. "This is the finest craft I have ever mastered, yet I will be glad to leave her behind—else the stretch will ne'er return to my legs."

Though Brega seemed casual to think they would soon leave the boat, Tuck's heart thudded to hear Galen's words, for they did not know what awaited them at the Argon Ferry: would they be met by friend or foe?

Once more they set out upon the river, now flowing wider and more slowly, wending between long, gentle curves. South and west lay Pellar; north and east was the South Reach of Valon. Overhead, the vault was blue, and the Sun rose to warm the morning sky. The air was calm, though the headway of the boat caused Tuck's hair to riffle. And the dip, pull, and return of Galen's and Gildor's paddle strokes soon lulled the weary Warrow into exhausted slumber.

At the end of the rest period of the late afternoon grounding, ere they launched the boat, Galen said, "Now will we all stay awake, for the ferry lies but two or three hours ahead. We must approach it with caution—all eyes alert—for it controls the Pendwyr Road crossing, and hence has value to friend and foe alike. There we may find our allies, or the Host; yet there, too, could be the Hyrania or Kistania: Modru's minions."

Again they embarked, and now all four paddled: Gildor in the bow, with Tuck then Galen aft, and Brega in the stern, where power and skill would be most demanded to turn and dart should the need arise.

One hour passed, then another, and the Sun set and darkness fell, and the banks of the Argon slid blackly past. One more hour went by, and—*hsst!*—lights could be seen ahead: on either shore, and in mid-river: it was the ferry!

"King Galen, Tuck, quietly ship aboard your paddles," whispered Brega. "Elf Gildor, make all return strokes under water; we need no drip or splash to give us away."

Cautiously, Galen and Tuck brought their paddles inboard, but kept them at hand should they be needed. Tuck also took up his bow and set arrow to string, knowing that he would be more effective defending them than paddling should they have to flee.

Now they could hear the distant shouts of Men and the jingle of armor echoing o'er the water, for a great crossing was under way; but whether the words spoken were in the Common Tongue, or in the speech of the Southerlings, they could not tell.

Along the shadow of the western shore slipped the Elven craft, Brega and Gildor plying their paddles such that they did not withdraw them on the return stroke, instead reaching forward with the blade cutting edgeways underwater before turning square for the thrusting stroke; neither drip nor splash betrayed them.

Yet the first-quarter Moon was still in the sky, and through a gap in the bordering trees its silvery rays shone down aslant upon them; and just as Tuck wished they were back in the deep shadows of the banks ahead: *"Hold!"* barked a voice from upon high. *"Who be down there in that boat, friends of the King, or scum of Modru?"*

Tuck whirled, and upon the bank above them sat a row of flaxen-haired, mail-clad, horse-mounted warriors, their steel helms adorned with raven's wings and horsehair gauds; and they held bent bows in their firm grips, the poised arrows drawn, set to hurl death down upon the four.

"Hál, Vanadurin!" cried Galen. "We are friends!"

Tuck slumped back against a boat thwart, the arrow of his own bow slipping from his fingers. Relief flooded throughout his being, for the Harlingar—the Riders of Valon—had discovered them. They were in friendly hands.

Yet the bows of the horsemen relaxed not, and again the voice barked, "If you be friends of the King, ground that boat and disembark!"

Brega and Gildor swiftly stroked to a landing, and the four beached the craft and scrambled up the bank to stand beringed by the Riders of the Valanreach.

"'Ware!" said the Captain of the riders. "Come no closer, for two of you are squatty—the belikes of Rutcha— though howso you come to be here far from the 'Dark, I cannot say."

Brega brought his axe Drakkalan to hand, and ere any

other could speak: "Squatty? Rutch?" he flared, anger in his voice. "I am no Ukh! And if you would be separated from your head, say so again."

"A Dwarf," growled the Captain. "I should have known. But what of the other? No Dwarf is he. Do you bring a child into this War-torn Land?"

Before Tuck could say aught, Galen stepped forward and said, to the wonderment of the Harlingar, "Captain, I am Galen, son of King Aurion, and these are my comrades: Warrior Brega, Dwarf of the Red Hills; Elf Lord Gildor, Lian Guardian of Arden Vale; Waerling Tuckerby Underbank, Thornwalker of the Boskydells."

The Captain of the Reach Riders signaled his Men, and bows were relaxed and arrows lowered, for now they could see in the moonlight that it was not foe they faced; on the contrary, if the words spoken were true, then not only was it a Man, Elf, and Dwarf that stood before them, but also one of the legendary *Waldfolc*.

"Captain," said Galen, "any could make the claim to be the son of Aurion as I have, yet take me to your commander and I will prove my words. And I bear news of import."

And so it was that on command two of the Harlingar sprang down and took to the boat, giving over their steeds to Galen and Gildor. And the Man and the Elf vaulted to the backs of the coursers, and Tuck and Brega mounted up behind. And they rode at a gallop unto the camp of the Vanadurin on the west bank of the Argon.

"You have shown me the scarlet eye-patch and bespoken your tale, and I am prone to believe you, if for nought else than you have an Elf and a Waldan at your side." Brega *hmpphed!* at the Valonian Marshal's words. "And of course, a Dwarf, too," smiled the Man, continuing. "Yet I would not be the commander I am if I did not verify words spoken to me when the means were at hand. And one crosses the ferry even now who can support you: he is Reggian, Steward of Pendwyr when the court is away at Challerain Keep."

The speaker was Marshal Ubrik of Valon. He was a Man in his middle years, yet he was hale of limb and bright of eye. Dressed in a corselet of chain mail was he, with a fleece-clad torso. Dark breeks and soft leathern boots he wore. His hair was the color of dark honey, streaked with silver. His face was clean-shaven, and his eyes were blue.

The four sat in the tent of the Valonian Marshal, where they'd been led, while outside, the crossing of an army in retreat from the east bank to the west went on. And time passed in silence as they waited for Kingssteward Reggian.

At last came the steps of an escort, and into the tent strode a silver-haired warrior, his face lined with worry.

"Reggian," said Galen softly.

The elder warrior turned to Galen and exclaimed, "My Prince!" and knelt upon one knee, his helm under one arm.

"Nay, Reggian, I am a Prince no longer," replied Galen. "My sire is dead."

"King Aurion, dead?" Reggian's eyes went wide. "Aie! What dire news!" Then the warrior knelt on both knees, and now Ubrik, too, went to one knee. "King Galen," said Reggian, "my sword is yours to command, though as Steward you may want to replace me, for Caer Pendwyr has fallen to Modru, and his minions now march across Pellar."

Long into the night spoke Galen and his comrades to Reggian and Ubrik. And the news of the War in the south was as dire as that in the north. The Rovers of Kistan had sailed into Hile Bay and landed a great force of Hyrania upon the isle of Caer Pendwyr. Long had that fortress withstood the assault, yet at last it had fallen. The Caer Host had withdrawn up Pendwyr Road, going northwest to the Fian Dunes. Again long battles ensued with the Lakh of Hyree, but the numbers of the foe were too great, and now the Pellarians withdrew across the Argon.

To the west, Hoven had fallen into the enemy's hands, but the foe had been stopped in the Brin Downs, the border between Hoven and Jugo.

To the northwest, Gûnarring Gap was held by an army of the Hyrani who had marched covertly and swiftly at the War's start to capture it ere any knew of Modru's plan. But even now the Vanadurin fought to break the hold on that vital passage.

"What of the Châkka?" asked Brega. "Where do the Folk of the Red Hills fight?"

"In the Brin Downs," answered Ubrik. "Without them, Jugo by now would have fallen, too."

"What of the fleet of Arbalin?" asked Galen.

"They lie up in Thell Cove in secret and make ready to strike at the Rovers," answered Reggian. "If they can pin them in at Hile Bay—even though the Arbalina are outnumbered—they can prevent the Kistani Fleet from being used again. But the Arbalina need perhaps three weeks, perhaps four, to be ready to strike."

"Pah!" cried Brega. "In four weeks—nay, less—the Darkest Day will have come. And then, mayhap, it will be too late."

Ubrik and Reggian shook their heads, for they had been told of Vanidor's Death Rede, and it was dire.

"Modru's grasp squeezes us tightly," said Reggian. "Like that of a—"

"Snake!" cried Brega, leaping to his feet. "That is what Eiron of the Larkenwald said. And list, for this I say: Modru is but Gyphon's servant, and perhaps the Great Evil does prepare to return upon the Darkest Day. And to that end the coils of Modru's minions draw tighter and tighter around us, like those of a great serpent crushing his victim. But this, too, I know: cut the head from a snake and the body dies—thrashing to be sure, and it can cause great damage, yet still it dies." Brega brandished his axe Drakkalan. "Let us go after Modru! Let us strike the head from this serpent!" Drakkalan chopped down through the air, thunking into a fire log, and chips flew.

"But, Dwarf Brega!" cried Reggian. "Gron and the Iron Tower are far to the north, some thirteen or fourteen hundred miles as the horse runs. We can't get an army there ere the coming of the next new Moon!"

"The Harlingar could be there ere then," said Ubrik after a moment. "The horses would be well-nigh spent, yet we could come unto that far land—unto Modru's fortress— ere the Darkest Day."

"You can make it only if you can get through Gûnarring Gap," said Gildor. "And that is held by the enemy."

"Perhaps; perhaps not," answered Ubrik. "Even now the Vanadurin wage War to free it."

"What about the Walkover?" asked Tuck. "The way

known but to the Dwarves. Can we go through it and by-pass the Gap?"

"Nay, Tuck," answered Brega. "For along that secret way lies a long, low tunnel fit only for Dwarves and ponies. Even a Man would have to stoop. A horse would never get through. Nay, it is Gûnarring Gap or nought."

"But can we fight Modru himself?" asked Tuck.

It was Gildor who answered: "Nay, Tuck, we cannot. But have we any other choice?"

And so after much debate it was decided that Ubrik, Galen, Gildor, Brega, and Tuck would ride for Gûnarring Gap. Extra horses would be taken, and mounts switched off to spare the steeds on the long dash. New horses would be obtained from the garrison at the north end of the Red Hills, and the race for the Gap would go on. If the Gap was free, then the Vanadurin there would be mustered to ride to Gron—to ride to the Iron Tower. And, although they did not think they could defeat Modru, still, if they could storm his strongholt and upset his plans—perhaps even preventing the return of Gyphon, if that was indeed his scheme—then their bold strike would have been worth it, although they all might die.

Reggian would continue to command the allies in the south, for the Steward had fought with cunning and bold-ness even though at the moment he was in retreat; for as King Galen had said over the Steward's protests: "The War is not over until the last battle. Hark back to the legends of the Great War of the Ban: the Allies, then too, were hard pressed, yet in the end they won. Reggian, none could have done more than you, and many less. You are Steward . . . now be Steward."

And the silver-haired warrior stood tall and struck a clenched fist to his heart.

At dawn, Galen, Gildor, Tuck, Brega, and Ubrik pre-pared to set out for Gûnarring Gap. Ten horses had they: five were to be ridden while the other five would trail be-hind on long tethers—remounts to share the task of bearing the riders north. The stirrups on two of the coursers had been shortened for Dwarf and Warrow, and the two were hoisted up astradle their own steeds; yet neither Tuck nor

Brega commanded their mounts—instead, they grasped the high fore-cantle and held on tightly while Galen and Gildor led them forth. And Brega's knuckles were white with the strength of his grip, for once again he was mounted upon a *horse!*

Without a word Galen saluted Reggian, and so did they all, and then the sprint for Gûnarring Gap began.

Northwest along Pendwyr Road ran the horses, five bearing weight, five running unburdened; their gait was at the varied pace of a Valanreach long-ride, and the miles hammered away beneath their hooves. All day they ran thus: the riders switching mounts every two hours, pausing now and again to stretch their legs and feed the horses some grain or to take water from the streams flowing down from the distant Red Hills.

Long they rode into the late night, and when they stopped at last, it was nearly mid of night. And they had covered some one hundred twenty miles. Yet ere the riders cast themselves to the ground to sleep the horses were rubbed down and given grain and drink.

At dawn the next day, once more they set forth upon Pendwyr Road. Tuck was weary nearly beyond measure, and he wondered whether the horses could hold the pace; yet the steeds bore up well, for even though they ran swift and far, still half of the time they carried no burden. It was the riders who felt the brunt of the journey, for four of them had spent days confined in a boat, and the fifth was weary from hard-fought battles.

Yet on they strove, northwest along Pendwyr Road. Now they ran alongside the lower slopes of the Red Hills, homeland of Brega: Tall they were, standing to the left, mountains rather than hills; they sprang up near the Argon and reached some two hundred miles northwest ere dwindling back into the prairie. Valon stood on one flank, Jugo on the other. And the stone of the chain was a rudden shade, like the red stone of Stormhelm. Fir and pine mounted up the slopes, and high, stark massifs sprang up frowning. Occasionally, Tuck could see what might be a dark gape opening into the mountains, into the Dwarven shafts and halls below; here dwelled many of Brega's kith, and here was made the finest steel in all the Realms.

Just after night had fallen, they came unto the Harlingar garrison at the north end of the hills. In spite of the fact that the post was nearly deserted—for the soldiers had ridden to War—in less than an hour the comrades were on their way again, riding five new horses for the Gap, with five more running behind.

Dawn of the next day found them once more coursing north, and Tuck was so sore he thought he would cry out at every thud of hoof; yet he did not, and on they ran.

Now they raced across the open plains between Jugo and Valon, the West Reach to their right, the North of Jugo to their left. Miles of flat grassland rolled away as far as the eye could see: this was the treasure of Valon, yellowed in winter dress; but come green spring, no sweeter grazing could be found for the fiery steeds of Mithgar.

Across this prairie all day they rode and far into the night. And when they stopped to camp, a spur of the Gûnarring stood to their left.

As the Sun rose, once more the five set off for their goal, now but fifty miles northward. And as they rode, Tuck could see the southeast rim of the Gûnarring, a great loop of mountains encircling the abandoned Kingdom of Gûnar, the ring a part of the Grimwall. Three well-known ways led into Gûnar: the Gap between Valon and Gûnar; Ralo Pass climbing over the Grimwall from South Trellinath into the Land; and Gûnar Slot, cleaving deeply through the Grimwall, from Lianion into Gûnar. Finally, there was the secret Dwarven way—the Walkover—a narrow pass across the Gûnarring, up from Vaon and down into the empty Realm.

And toward the Gap the five rode at the ground-devouring pace of a Valanreach long-ride.

An hour passed and then another, and the mountains of the Gûnarring stood stark upon the left and marched away in a long line stretching out before the riders. Another hour passed, and they stopped long enough to change the saddles over to the remounts, then struck to the north once more.

Now the mountains began to dwindle, sinking toward the Gap. Far ahead, Tuck could see a great column of black smoke rising into the morning sky, but he could not see what caused it, for it lay yet some twenty miles to the north.

Onward they rode, and the Sun mounted up through the sky. At last they could see a great movement of horses and Men on the plains before them, and they came to a mounted squad of Harlingar standing watch athwart Pendwyr Road. The five reined to a halt before the readied spears, and Ubrik paced his steed forward.

"Reachmarshal Ubrik!" cried one of the mounted warriors.

"Hál, Borel!" hailed Ubrik. "What news?"

"The best!" answered Borel. "Victory! The Hyrania are whelmed! The Gap is ours!"

"Hail!" shouted Brega, and the comrades looked one to the other, fierce grins upon their countenances, for the Gap now was in the hands of the Allies, and their plan to assail Modru's fortress perhaps could go forth.

"And King Aranor: how fares he?" Ubrik's voice was tense, for well he loved his warrior King.

"Hai roi! He fought like a daemon, and took a cut or two; yet he is well, though his arm will be in a sling for some days to come." Borel couched his spear in a stirrup cup and so did his squadmates.

"Your tidings are sweet to my ears," said Ubrik, "and I would like nothing more than to hear the tale from your lips, yet we cannot stay. We would pass your ward, Borel, for we have urgent business with King Aranor."

In response to Ubrik's words Borel signaled his squad and reined to one side. And the five were permitted to ride onward. And as they passed, Tuck heard some exclaim in wonder, for never before had any seen a Dwarf astride a horse, and they now saw that Tuck was a pointed-eared, jewel-eyed Waldan! *And lo! an Elf rides among them, too! Strange companions portend uncommon events.*

Forth rode the five, and less than four miles before them stood the Gûnarring Gap. Now they came among the carnage of a great battle: broken armor and cloven helms, shattered weapons, slain horses and Men: some were blond-haired Harlingar, more were swarthy Hyrania; yet whether the skin was dark or light, still they were dead: pierced by spear and arrow, slashed by saber and tulwar, broken by hammer and mace. Tuck tried not to look at the slaughtered Men, yet they were everywhere.

They passed by several squads of captured Hyrania, guarded by Vanadurin, and the prisoners moved among the slain and gathered them for burial or burning: the slain of Valon were laid to rest in great mounds covered by grassy turves, while the Hyrania were burned on a vast pyre of logs from which the great column of black smoke rose skyward.

"Why do they honor the dead of Hyree and not the slain of Valon?" growled Brega to Tuck. "Fire lifts up the spirits of valiant warriors slain, just as clean stone purifies them. But root-tangled sod traps their shades, and they are a long time escaping the dark, worm-laden soil."

"Perhaps they think as my Folk do, Brega," answered Tuck. "The earth sustains us while we are alive, and we return to it after death. But fire, stone, soil, or even the sea, it matters not, for it is the way of our living that is testament to our spirits, and perhaps the way that we die; and the way of our burial means little, for what we have been is gone, though our spirits may live on in the hearts of others . . . for a little while, at least."

Brega listened to Tuck's words, then shook his head but said no more.

At last they came to the encampment of the Vanadurin and rode to the pavilion in the center. And the green-and-white colors of Valon flew above the tent, for here was quartered King Aranor.

A guard took them into the King's presence, and Aranor, white-haired but hale, stood cursing as a healer changed a bloody bandage on the King's sword arm.

"Rach, Dagnall, take care with that poultice; I would have this arm next year, too!" King Aranor looked up as the five entered, and his eyes widened. "Hola, Ubrik, I thought you south." Now Aranor's sight took in Ubrik's traveling companions. "Hoy! Man, Elf, Dwarf, and—by the very bones of Sleeth—a Waldan! There is a tale here for the telling. And do my eyes deceive me, or is it truly you, Prince Galen?"

Quiet fell in the tent—Galen's voice, at last silent, his tale told—and Aranor again wiped an eye with the sleeve of his left arm.

"Your news saddens me, King Galen," said Aranor.
"Aurion and I trained at arms together, and hunted far
afield in our youth. He was as close to me as a brother.

"And the rest of your tale bears good news, and bad.
The fall of Challerain Keep whelms me, yet I am buoyed
by the fighters of Weiunwood. The Dread of the Black
Hole is slain, and for that my heart sings, yet this cursed
Dimmendark I do not like. And the north is beset by Mo-
dru's Hordes.

"But here in the south we, too, reel under the blows of
servants of the Enemy in Gron. They seem without number, and ultimately we must fall back before them.

"Yet Vanidor's warning bears dire portent, and you propose to storm the Iron Tower itself. I think your plan cannot succeed, yet this I say unto you: Galen, you are High
King of all Mithgar, and my heart and soul are pledged to
serve you. You ask for Warriors of the Reach to go with
you unto the frozen wastes of Gron, for none else can reach
the holt of the Kinstealer ere the fall of the Darkest Day.

"Galen King, here at Gûnarring Gap there are perhaps
but five thousand Vanadurin who are War-ready and hale;
the others are wounded, such as I, and would merely slow
you. Five thousand are but a pittance to take against the
Iron Tower, yet they are yours to command as you would.

"This, only, I ask of you: do not cast their lives in vain."
Aranor fell silent, and there were tears in both his and
Galen's eyes.

Long moments passed, for Galen did not trust his voice
to speak without breaking, but at last he said, "We ride on
the morrow's dawn."

Horns sounded and the muster went forth. Captains were
called and plans were made. King Galen would command,
and Ubrik would ride in the stead of King Aranor, for the
King's wounds kept him in Valon. On the morrow would
they begin the long-ride: some nine hundred miles away
lay their goal, and they would have but twenty or so days
to reach it. Such a ride had never before been made in the
long history of the Harlingar, yet they were confident that
it could be done.

And as Tuck scribed in his diary that night, he wondered
at their fate. And as he ungirted Bane from his waist to lie

down to sleep, he wondered, too, whether any among them
bore a token of power for Good: *Bane? Bale? Steel-heart?
Dark Reaver? Are any of these weapons tokens whose destinies are rushing toward fulfillment? Or is some other unknown token being borne unsuspectingly toward Gron? And
if so, will it stand up to the feartokens of the Enemy?* Tuck
fell asleep, his questions unanswered.

Dawn found the Riders of Valon drawn up in ranks as
King Galen, King Aranor, and Reachmarshal Ubrik rode
forth to pass by them. Somewhere Aranor had found a flag
of Pellar, and two standard-bearers followed the Kings: one
bearing the colors of Valon: white horse rearing on a field
of green; the other bearing the standard of Pellar: golden
griffin rampant upon a scarlet field. And the Vanadurin sat
in rows on their mounts as the High King of Mithgar passed
before them, his armor glinting crimson in the rising Sun.

Now at last the review was done, and King Aranor, his
arm in a sling, sat ahorse and looked stern, for he and
Galen, had said their farewells earlier. And Galen turned
to give the order to begin the long-ride, but ere he could
do so, a Valonian black-oxen horn sounded from afar, and
a stir went through the ranks.

Ubrik turned to Galen, and Tuck's heart thudded at the
Valanreach Marshal's words: "King Galen, hold your command, for we may yet need to fight another battle for the
Gûnarring Gap. An army approaches from the northwest—
down the Ralo Road. Yet whether they be friend or foe, I
cannot say."

Ubrik barked a command in Valur, the ancient War
tongue of Valon, and horns sounded, and the files of the
Vanadurin wheeled and formed to face into Gûnar, lances
and sabers at the ready.

And Tuck turned his eyes to the road through the Gap;
in the distance he saw a churning dark mass of hundreds
upon hundreds of hard-running steeds, their pounding
hooves hammering to strike the land as they bore an unknown force thundering down upon the Gap.

"They attack!" cried Ubrik. "Hál Vanadurin! Draw the
sabers! Lower the lances! Sound the horns! Ride to War!"
And with the black-oxen horns of Valon blowing wildly,
the Vanadurin spurred forward and gathered speed and
hurtled toward the oncoming mass of charging warriors.

BOOK THREE

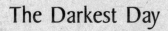

The Darkest Day

". . . it is the way of our living that is testament to our spirits, and perhaps the way we die . . ."

—Tuckerby Underbank
February 1, 4E2019

CHAPTER 1

The Gathering

It was the 'Darkday following the Battle of Budgens, and at Whitby's barn a breathless buccan scout flung himself down from his lathered blowing pony and dashed into the huge byre.

"Cap'n Patrel!" he cried. "The Ghûls! The Ghûls have burnt Budgens!"

"Wha—?" Patrel's eyes jerked up from the map lying on the rough table before the council, and he spun toward the scout as the rushing buccan skidded to a halt before him. "What did you say, Arcy? Did you say Budgens?"

"Yar, Cap'n Patrel, Budgens!" blurted Arcy, red-faced, gesturing wildly. "The Ghûls, they came—a great drove of them—lookin' for Warrows. And when they didn't find any, they put the whole town to the torch!"

Luth's clenched fist slammed down to the planking, and Merrilee's hand flew to her mouth, her eyes wide. Bitter looks fell upon the faces of some Lieutenants, while others ground their teeth in rage.

"They seek revenge for what we did to them," said Patrel, his voice grim. "Woe to the Warrow who falls into their hands, for death will come slowly, but agony swift."

Orbin leapt to his feet and paced in agitation. "We've got to root them out of the Seven Dells before the Bosky is destroyed! For even should we win this War, it will go hard on the survivors, and harder still if there is no place to live, no shelter!"

"Argh!" gnashed Norv, the muscles in his jaw jumping. "I say we've got to kill 'em all, or at least enough of 'em to drive 'em out, else none of us will survive, shelter or no!" Shouts of agreement rose up.

"Calm down, all of you!" barked Patrel, facing the council. Then he turned once more to the scout. "After torching Budgens, Arcy, which way did they ride?"

"South, Cap'n," replied Arcy, "back toward the Crossland Road."

Luth growled. "They've probably got back to Brackenboro. How about the patrol, Arcy, the one we sent to the ruins?"

"Ar, Lieutenant Luth, they were gone on before the Ghûls came, so Cap'n Danner and his scouts weren't delayed any," answered the buccan.

At mention of the scouting party sent to the ruins of Brackenboro, Merrilee's face took on a frown, for Danner had gone with four others south through the Dimmendark to come among the hills surrounding that devastated place to spy out the movements of the Ghûls. Merrilee was beset by doubt, for it was a dangerous mission—a mission of her own devising.

"Well," said Patrel, vexed, "until Danner gets back, we'll do nothing."

Over the next two 'Darkdays, Patrel paced the barn floor and gritted his teeth and flung himself busily into fletching arrows and often rode through the Shadowlight to the top of Whitby's Hill to look for Danner; but of the Woody Hollow buccan and his quartet of scouts, there was no sign. And when Patrel would come back to the barn and faintly shake his head no to Merrilee, both of their spirits would fall.

The damman, too, spent long hours staring through the Dimmendark for sign of Danner's band; yet, like Patrel, Merrilee would come dejected back to the Warrow headquarters and throw herself into busywork.

And secretly in both their hearts they wondered if something had gone awry: Perhaps Danner and the others had been wounded or slain . . . or worse yet, captured by the vile maggot-folk. But of these covert fears they said nought to one another, although each knew the hidden dreads harbored in the bosom of the other.

Yet late on the third 'Darkday, Danner and his squad came unannounced unto the barn. Danner was filled near to bursting with glad news, and he grabbed Merrilee up and hugged her and dizzily spun her around and set her down awhirl, and then he slapped Patrel on the back.

"Paddy! Merrilee! I saw my dad! He's alive! He says my mom is fine, too! He and she and a great many other Warrows have got to the Eastwood—folks from Bryn and Midwood, Thimble and Willowdell, and some from Budgens and Woody Hollow . . . and Brackenboro, too. They're all making it into a stronghold, like Gildor told that the Weiunwood is. Dad's helping organize the resistance—got his own company of archers: Hanlo's Reya, they call themselves in the old tongue—Hanlo's Foxes. They haven't fought yet, but they'll join with us at Brackenboro when we strike."

And Danner and his scouts were drawn inside and given a warm meal and hot tea, and tears of happiness glistened in Merrilee's eyes, for the squad was safe.

"Down along the Southrill we went, till we came to the hills around Brackenboro." Danner paused long enough to fill his pipe with leaf and light it, leaning back to blow a smoke ring or two. "When the town was due west of us, into the downs we went, cautious as field mice slipping past the weasel.

"Imagine our surprise, then, when before we could reach sight of the ruins, another band of Warrows came like smoke out of the bracken to ask us who we were and what was our mission.

"When I gave 'em our names and told 'em our purpose, they said to follow them, they'd show us what we were up against. Seems that they, too, were spying on the Ghûls in Brackenboro. Those eight buccen had all lived in the 'Boro before the Dimmendark and the reavers came. But they had fled to the Eastwood and had formed companies, and had come back to scout out the Ghûls, for the Eastwooders are thinking of attack, too.

"Now we came to the hills directly surrounding Brackenboro, and we all slipped down from our ponies and stealthily crept on foot to the crests overlooking the town.

"It's a ruin, Paddy: all burnt down, but for a few buildings. And Ghûls swarm all around, and sweep in and out like a plague of locusts that comes and goes. There are a thousand or so of them—"

"A thousand!" interrupted Luth. "But we've only got

three hundred, four hundred Warrows! We can't take on nearly three times our number!"

"Aye, Luth," answered Danner, "you are right. And that's exactly what I thought at first. But I don't think it'll come to that. You see, all one thousand of the Ghûls aren't always at Brackenboro at the same time. While we were there, companies of them rode in and out, and at times there were as many as eight, nine hundred. *But at other times there were as few as one hundred.*"

As few as one hundred, thought Merrilee. *Just days ago, one hundred Ghûls would have seemed an invincible force, yet now we think once more to attack five score of these monstrous reavers, as we did in Budgens. But this time they will not be caught in a high-walled trap.*

Merrilee's attention was tugged back to the council as Danner spoke on: "And so we lay belly-down on the back-slopes of the ridgetops and watched the Ghûls come and go all that 'Darkday. And as we watched, the Eastwooders spoke of the burning of the 'Boro, and how they and other Warrows had come to the woods, though they'd left many dead behind.

"And they told how they formed companies out of six hundred or so archers, and set about preparing to defend the Eastwood. But one of their Captains, back in the 'Wood, had said as how they ought not only to defend, but also ought to attack if a way could be found to kill Ghûls. And, 'Oh, by the way,' said one of the Eastwooders as we lay there on the ridgetop, 'your name is Bramblethorn . . . Are you any kin to that Captain? Hanlo is his name, Hanlo Bramblethorn.'

"Lor! I could have grabbed up that Eastwooder and kissed him right there on the spot, but the Ghûls below might have disapproved if they had seen us, and so I just lay there looking down at a ruined town teeming with relentless enemies, and I couldn't stop grinning for joy.

"I had sent some of the buccoes around to the south and some to the north, and when they finally reported back, we compared with each other what we'd seen that 'Darkday, and with what the Eastwooders had seen on other 'Days.

"And we decided then and there that the only way we can attack the enemy is by joining our two forces and falling upon Brackenboro when the Ghûlen numbers are at a low ebb. We can bring perhaps nine, ten hundred archers to bear, and if the enemy is at a hundred or so, then we can whelm them, even though they won't be penned up like they were in Budgens."

A murmur of agreement rippled through the Lieutenants.

"What do the Eastwooders say?" asked Patrel.

"They're for it," answered Danner. "We rode from Brackenboro deep into the Eastwood, and the next 'Darkday we met with their Captains and Lieutenants. That's when I saw my sire. Lor! You should have seen him start when he clapped eyes on me. Almost crushed me in a bear hug, he did. But I think his ribs creaked a bit, too.

"In council, I told them of the way to slay Ghûls, and what we'd done at Budgens. They'd heard none of it before, and it was glad news to them, for now they knew that they had a way to fight. I also told them about Challerain Keep, and that King Aurion was dead. These dire tidings only stiffened their resolve.

"Paddy, they want us to bring all our company down into the Eastwood, to join with them and lay assaults upon Brackenboro until the enemy is driven out—out of that town, out of all towns, out of the Dells, out of the Bosky."

Danner paused, then said, "My sire put his finger on it: 'There's a loose Horde up at the Keep, now,' he said, 'and soon they'll be marching south, I ween. We've got to have these Ghûls out of the Boskydells and the Thornring stoppered up tight before Modru's Swarm comes knocking on our doors; for if they come before we can shut them out, nothing will survive. All will die. Modru will see to it. The forests will be hewn down and the trees left to rot where they lie; fields will be plowed and salted; the wells, streams, lakes, and rivers, poisoned; animals, both wild and tame, will be slaughtered; and Warrows, put to the death or let slowly starve in bondage. This doom must not befall the Dells!' " Danner's countenance was drained of blood, his lips compressed in a thin line. "My sire is right. We have much to do and little time to do it in. We must strike the Ghûls, and strike now!"

The next 'Darkday, the entire company—three hundred sixty-two buccen and one damman—rode south by covert ways into the Eastwood, where they joined with the Warrows waiting there. Long did they lay out their plans, with Captains Patrel and Danner joining the four Eastwood Captains in a great council of Lieutenants. And when the plans were laid, the last question was asked by Neddy Finch, a Lieutenant from Midwood: "The only thing left to decide is when we strike, so I asks it: When?"

Hanlo Bramblethorn spoke up: "You all know how I feel in this matter—the sooner we strike, the better. Yet though my Reya are ready now, we'd best get some rest, for the fight may be long and hard, and the pursuit merciless. But this I do say, not a 'Darkday should pass without action against the Ghûls. Hence, I say we fight on the morrow." And the chestnut-haired, amber-eyed buccan sat down. Merrilee's heart hammered in her bosom, but when the vote came, she added her *aye* to all the others.

They rode from the barren Eastwood, crossing first the Southrill and then the trace running north and south, and they came at last among the Brackenboro Hills. They were six companies strong: fifty-four squads, one thousand eighty-six Warrows, armed with nought but bow and arrow to go up against the spears and tulwars and Hèlsteeds of the Ghûls.

Among the Warrow companies rode the guides from Brackenboro, buccen familiar with the hills and vales around the town. And they led the squads behind the ridges and through the downs until the 'Boro was beringed by the Warrow warriors.

Long did they wait, hidden on the hillsides, and they watched as companies of Ghûls on Hèlsteeds rode along the Boro Spur, coming and going to their evil ends.

Now the Warrows crept unseen down through the bracken—unto the very edges of the ruins—and once more they waited, this time for the signal.

Ghûls rode in and Ghûls rode out, and yet still too many stayed among the ruins. Merrilee's heart hammered loudly in her ears, and she despaired that the odds would ever tumble in the Warrows' favor. And every moment that passed increased the chances of discovery. But at last more reavers seemed to be riding out than rode in, and the numbers of the remaining Ghûls began to dwindle.

The Warrow strategy was simplicity itself: When the

Ghûl numbers had diminished favorably, the archers would strike fast and hard, and if they overwhelmed the Ghûls remaining in Brackenboro, then the archers would lie in ambush along the Boro Spur and slay the Ghûlen companies as they each in turn came back from their foul missions. Should the odds shift in the Ghûls' favor, then the Warrows would retreat through the Shadowlight, first to the hills and then to Eastwood, covering their tracks in the snow, losing the foe in the Dimmendark. Yet though their overall scheme was simple, still they had planned their movements and signals down to the finest possible detail, with alternative plans should events turn in other ways. And now approached the moment to see if their stratagems would succeed or fall.

The numbers of Ghûls had fallen below five hundred; and still the Warrows watched. And Merrilee's heart raced, for two more Ghûlen companies prepared to set forth; and she knew that when they were gone, the signal would sound and the attack would begin. Once again she checked her arrows. She bore two full quivers, and nearby lay bundled sheaves of extra quarrels.

Now the Hèlsteeds' hooves thundered as the two companies of Ghûls set forth upon the Boro Spur, swinging west then north to join the Crossland Road. And Time seemed to step on quickened feet.

At last the companies passed beyond seeing behind the downs, but still the signal was not sounded, for the Warrows waited until the Ghûls were beyond hearing. It would not do to have the reavers hear the call to battle, or the sounds of combat.

Time passed, and Patrel kept watch upon the hill northwest of Brackenboro, and so did nearly all the Warrows; for upon that hill a lookout was posted, and he would signal when the Ghûls were beyond seeing.

At last the hooded lantern flashed—just once—and all then knew the battle was only a tick of time away.

And arrows nocked strings . . .

And hearts thudded . . .

And eyes sought out the nearest Ghûls, the nearest targets . . .

And breaths were drawn in . . .

And time seemed frozen.

*   *   *

And Patrel raised the silver Horn of the Reach—the Horn of Valon—to his lips, and a clarion call split the air: a call to arms, a call to War, a call to attack: *Ta, tahn! Ta, tahn! Ta, tahn!* Even as the silver notes pealed forth, a sleet of arrows hissed through the air to strike home. Warrows were up and running and setting new bolts to string, then stopping to loose the quarrels ere dashing forth once more.

Again and again the silver call belled forth, and everywhere brave hearts were lifted and bold spirits surged. Yet the Ghûls quailed to hear such notes, and Hèlsteeds reared in fright.

Hails of arrows thudded into corpse-flesh, and foe fell slain, pierced through the heart. But Ghûls rallied and mounted beasts and spurred forth upon the Wee Folk. Barbed spears and curved tulwars pierced and hacked, and some Warrows were caught unaware and slain by point, edge, and hoof, for the Hèlsteeds were trained to trample enemy underfoot. Yet though Warrows died, still the flying quarrels rained into the Ghûls.

Merrilee nocked arrow after arrow, her eyes and aim following charging Ghûl, and Tuck whispered in her mind as she methodically loosed bolt upon bolt. And where she aimed, reaver fell.

But Danner was magnificent, for his amber eyes were everywhere his arrows could reach, and he dropped Ghûls left and right. Along with a select few, Danner's was the chore to spot Ghûls coming at Warrows unknowing, and to slay the foe ere they could rend death. And only one buccan in Danner's sector fell by Ghûlen hand, and that was by a flung spear.

And almost as soon as it had begun, the battle was ended. The Ghûls had stood little chance, for the odds were five to one against them. And the Warrows had cast death from afar and did not stand to fight, but instead slipped aside as elusive as the shadows in and out of which they faded. The Warrows had been victorious, but not all the Ghûls had died, for a score or so had fled on Hèlsteeds, some down the Boro Spur, others up through the hills.

A scattered cheering broke out among the Warrow ranks but was silenced quickly, for only this skirmish had been won and not the Battle of Brackenboro, not the War of the Boskydells: the Struggles went on. And squads were assembled to trot swiftly down the Spur to set up ambush for the returning Ghûlen companies, likely now to be on alert, for the escaped foe would warn them.

The six Warrow companies lay in Shadowlighted ambuscade along the Boro Spur—three on the north side, three on the south—and this was their plan: once the returning Ghûls were deep within the trap, the companies would catch them in a deadly cross fire. And when the Ghûls were slain, if need be the companies would move up the road away from the slaughter and lay in ambush again.

But though that was their plan, no Ghûl had yet fallen victim, for none had yet returned. Long had the Warrows waited; and all about them a westerly breeze rustled through the winter-dried bracken.

"They've never stayed away this long before," said Rollo Breed, one of the Brackenboro scouts. "By now the 'Boro should be full of them again."

"Ar. Those that escaped have warned them off," gritted Hanlo. "Like as not, they'll be coming in force and we'll have to melt away before them."

Patrel looked to the hilltop with the sentinel on it and fretted, for no signal had come from the lookout that Ghûls were on the way: green meant that the returning force was small and could be ambushed, whereas red would mean retreat.

On a premonition, Patrel said, "Rollo, head up to the hilltop. Make certain that nothing untoward has befallen Chubb. I just now recall that one or two escaping Ghûls rode that way."

Rollo ran through the stirring bracken and sprang upon the back of his pony. And as the buccan spurred up the snowy hill, Danner grunted, "Good idea." They watched the scout as he disappeared among the winter-dried fern brakes.

Long they peered, both along the road and up the hill. Yet nought did they see. Then Hanlo raised his hand and barked, "Hist! I hear . . . something." And before any could say aught, the elder Bramblethorn dropped to the ground and laid his ear to the earth. "Hooves! Many hooves! Like thunder they come!" he cried.

At that moment Rollo and his pony burst back through the bracken. "Cap'n! The Ghûls! The Ghûls are coming!" Rollo leapt down at Patrel's side, breathless words tumbling past one another in the scout's urgency to get them all out. "Chubb is dead, slain by Ghûl spear, and a dead reaver lies nearby, but I found the tracks of *two* Hèlsteeds. Chubb got one Ghûl, but the other got him. Chubb's lamps were shattered, so I couldn't signal you when I saw the Ghûls down on the Boro Spur. Ghûls come on Hèlsteeds: hundreds . . . and fast. And three miles or so behind comes another bunch: *five, six times as many*. We've got to get away! Now! They are too many!"

"Too late!" spat Hanlo, setting an arrow to string. "Here they come!" And bursting 'round a bend in the Boro Spur hammered five hundred Hèlsteeds, howling Ghûls on their backs, Ghûls yawling for revenge.

Patrel glanced at Danner for his advice, but that young buccan, just like his sire Hanlo, set arrow to bow, preparing for battle.

"Wait!" cried Merrilee. "Rollo is right! We can't stand and fight them! They are too many, and an even greater force follows these! Signal the retreat, Patrel, and most of us will live to fight again!"

Patrel looked sharply at Merrilee and then at the charging Ghûls, now less than a half mile away, the Hèlsteeds' driving pace rapidly closing the distance.

Withdraw! Withdraw! Withdraw! The silent hand signal flashed up and down the Warrow ranks on either side of the road, as Patrel gave the order to retreat. And buccen began to slip quietly back into the Shadowlighted fern brakes, moving with the legendary stealth of the Wee Folk.

But then the foetid scent of the charging Hèlsteeds was borne by the wind unto Rollo's pony, being led through the brake, and the small steed plunged and reared and screamed in fear at this foul stink. The animal jerked the reins from Rollo's hand and bolted in fright through the bracken and onto the road, fleeing eastward down the Spur.

At sight of the stampeding pony, the Ghûls harshly checked their 'Steeds to churn about while some stalked forward, their dull, flat, dead black eyes trying to pierce the rustling bracken alongside the Spur; it had not occurred to the Ghûls that an ambush could have lain along their path, for they had thought instead that their foe now occupied the ruins of Brackenboro.

A Ghûl in the fore uttered harsh barks and howls, and the Hèlsteed force split in twain: half rode into the bracken to the left, half to the right. And now they were alert and wary, their spears lowered at the ready, tulwars in hand. The Hèlsteeds breasted through the rattling fern brakes, surging, lunging apace, while before them—as yet unseen— the Warrows faded back among the shadows.

Yet Hèlsteed is swifter than Warrow on foot, and suddenly there came a Ghûl yawl, cut short in mid howl by swift arrow; even so, fleeting Warrows on the north side of the Boro Spur had been discovered, and at nearly the same time Hèlsteeds stumbled across pockets of Warrows on the south side, too. Chilling yowls split the air, and there came the raucous blats of Rūckish horns, answered by the hiss of deadly quarrels as Warrows paused to loose arrows at the questing foe ere fading onward through the bracken.

Now the Ghûls knew their enemy, but despite the fact that the corpse-foe had been whelmed in Brackenboro, they as yet held the Wee Folk in contempt, and charged the Hèlsteeds through the winter-dried fern brakes. *Swish! Swash!* rattled the bracken at the passage of the Hèlspawn, while hidden Warrows fled among the shielding growth.

But the balance between the reavers and the archers began to shift, for the close-set bracken was a two-edged sword: not only did it shield the Wee Folk, but it also hid the Ghûls, and Warrows could not see to loose their arrows. And Ghûls burst forth upon buccen, and spears dipped to take their toll, or slashing tulwars rived redly, and Warrows were trampled under cloven hooves. Thus did Regin Burk die, and Alvy Willoby, and Neddy Finch, and many others, for now the spear and blade and driving 'Steed were favored in the shock of sudden onslaught, and Warrows fell by the tens and twenties as they fled through the brakes and up the hill slopes.

Danner and Patrel and Merrilee ran among the bracken, and to right and left Hèlsteeds crashed by unseen. Now and again the trio would glimpse other Warrows flitting through the Shadowlight, but for the most part they saw no one else, though howls of Ghûls and blat of horns and grunts of Hèlsteeds and hammer of cloven hooves were all about them, as well as the grim cry of Death.

Merrilee's breath came in harsh gasps as she dodged among the brittle ferns with Danner and Patrel at her side, and racing blood pounded in her ears. North and up over the hills they had tried to flee, but always it seemed they heard Ghûls that way, and so they were driven east, back toward the ruins of Brackenboro. And Merrilee felt as if she were being *herded* by cruel hounds. East they went, and east some more, flying before blind pursuit. At last, after endless running, they were driven from the rattling brakes to come in among the charred spars of the ravaged 'Boro, and they fled along streets littered with the corpses of Ghûls the Warrows had slain earlier. They heard the clatter of cloven hooves sounding on the cobbles around the corner ahead, and the trio crouched in hiding amid tumbled rubble alongside a blackened wall.

"We've got to get out of here," panted Danner. "The Ghûls'll come, some already are here, and we've got to be away before then."

Patrel squinted at the hills above, his breath blowing in and out. "Our ponies are yon, beyond the near downs, yet Ghûls hunt the slopes between there and here. Perhaps we can—"

Patrel's words were chopped short by a hideous howl as a Ghûl on Hèlsteed rounded the broken wall and saw the trio.

Thuun . . . shthock! Danner's loosed arrow struck the reaver in the breast, and the foe pitched dead from the saddle. But a lifeless foot was stirrup-caught, and the Hèlsteed grunted and squealed in terror at this dragging thing and plunged away bucking. Yet though the Ghûl was dead, his last howl had brought others running, and three more Spawn on Hèlsteeds galloped around the corner, cloven hooves ringing on the cobblestones.

Ssthack! Sssthok! Thock! Flying death hissed through the air to fell two of the reavers. The third hauled his Hèlsteed back and over too sharply, and the creature crashed to the icy cobbles. And as the Ghûl rose to his feet, *Th-th-thock!* three arrows slammed into him, any one of which would have slain him, and he fell slaughtered as his 'Steed scrambled up and bolted.

But now the three Warrows heard the hammer of more
cloven hooves upon the pave, and other Ghûls burst 'round
the edge.

Taa-tahn! Taa-tahn! The silver call of the Horn of Valon
split the air as Patrel set the rune-marked bugle to his lips
and blew. And the Ghûls checked their Hèlsteeds and
quailed back from the pure, bell-like call, for the notes
drove fear deep into the corpse-foe. Danner and Merrilee
loosed hissing death upon the milling Ghûls, and two fell
slain while the remaining five spurred forward, howling in
anger.

Calmly, Merrilee continued to pluck arrows from her
quiver and set them to bow, and her bolts flew at the oncoming foe. Danner's quarrels, too, and now Patrel's sissed
in deadly flight through the air. And the Ghûls charged at
the Warrows, barbed lances lowered to spit these three;
cloven hooves rang on the cobble as on the Hèlsteeds came.

But bolts sped true to pierce Ghûl breast and heart, and
corpse-foe fell slain. 'Steeds veered wide, no longer commanded. Four Ghûls came on . . . now three . . . now two;
and as the pair thundered down upon the Warrows, Danner, Patrel, and Merrilee leapt aside among the rubble, falling and rolling as the hooves hammered past. The barbed
spears missed the dodging targets, though a point pierced
Patrel's jacket to skitter and glance along the golden armor
underneath. Danner sprang up cursing and felled one more
Ghûl as the two reavers raced away. The lone survivor
veered his Hèlsteed, and Merrilee's arrow thudded into the
Ghûl's side and did not pierce his heart.

Now the Hèlsteed passed beyond arrow range, and the
Ghûl spun his mount and checked it. He plucked the of-
fending arrow from below his ribs and flung it away, and
then he raised a brazen horn to his lips and blatted a call
of assembly. Blares of nearby Rūckish horns clamantly answered from the surrounding ruins.

Calmly Danner began laying out arrows before him upon
a fallen spar, where the quarrels would be within easy
reach. "They've got us cornered, Paddy, Merrilee, and
they'll come in numbers too great to overcome, yet we'll
take as many down with us as we can."

Harsh blares and brazen blats drew nearer, and there
was the clatter of cloven hooves upon the cobble pave.

Now two, then eight more corpse-folk rode into sight to join the surviving Ghûl at the north end of the street. Wrawling horn blasts came from the south, as distant Ghûls hove into view, and calls from east and west sounded, too.

Merrilee set her quiver before her and put arrow to string. Her jaw was set at a grim angle, and her breathing was deep and measured. There was no hint of fear in her clear, sapphire-blue gaze.

Patrel took up the Horn of the Reach. "I'll sound it one last time. Then we'll give 'em a battle that bards would tell of ages from now if any but knew."

And amid the blats and blares of the brazen *Spaunen* horns, a pure silver clarion cry rose up into the sky and across the land as three Warrows—two buccen and a dam-man—prepared to fight a last battle, prepared to fight and die.

And as the call of the Horn of the Reach pealed across the land, the blatting blares of the Rūckish brass fell silent, though in the distance it seemed that other horns sounded, too, as the silver echoes rang from the hills. The Ghûls paused a time, and peered uneasily about.

But at last the chief Ghûl among them raised his face to the darkling sky and howled a chilling cry. And from the west—from around the corner of the standing wall—there came the sounds of driving hooves upon the stones of Brackenboro and blasts upon belling horns.

"They're coming!" cried Patrel, facing toward the corner, his bow drawn to the full, death set to fly.

Now the hooves drummed louder—a thunder to the ear—and the pealing of horns rang clear. Then the first of many riders hove past the wall and into view:

Men upon horses!

"No!" cried Danner, knocking Patrel's arm up, sending the arrow flying skyward over the silver-bearded horse-man's head. *"It's Vidron!"*

And thundering upon coursers charging through the streets of Brackenboro came a full one thousand Men: warriors bearing the blue-and-white colors of Wellen, warriors sounding the horn calls of that western Land, warriors led by Kingsgeneral Vidron, Hrosmarshal of Valon. Squads and companies hurtled among the ruins of Brackenboro, and swords rived and lances pierced. The deadly Ghûls were utterly overwhelmed as shafts burst through their hearts and blades clove their heads from their bodies.

Amid the clash and clangor of battle, and while the hooves of steeds hammered past, and as the peals of horns split the air and lifted spirits, three Warrows—two buccen and a damman—danced about and shouted deliriously and hugged each other and cried.

"Arn, Captain Patrel, when I heard that silver horn— Elgo's horn of Sleeth's hoard—I knew 'twas you in desperate straits!" A wide grin split Fieldmarshal Vidron's face as he sat on a crate by the burnt-out wall where he'd come riding to find them. The reunion was like that of a grand uncle and his favorite nephews. And when Merrilee was introduced, the eyes of the veteran warrior widened in amaze. And he bowed to the damman, yet by his hearty manner he put her at her ease. Now they all sat in converse. "And so, to save your scalawag necks, I ordered the charge into Brackenboro, and no company of Guula are going to withstand a thousand horse-borne Wellenan warriors."

"But General Vidron," Merrilee quietly protested, "these are not all the Ghûls: another four hundred or so ride the downs and bracken, searching for our kindred. Warrows are now hard-pressed by the corpse-folk: The Ghûls hunt them like reya, like hounds after foxes."

"Aye, we know, lass," responded Vidron, beaming at the damman. "Some of your lads stopped us on the road and told us. Two thousand more of the Wellenen hunt the foul Wrg even now; list, you'll hear their horns." From the hills—north, south, and east—intermittently sounded the calls of the horns of Wellen.

"Two thousand more?" Patrel's eyes flew wide. "How came you by this army, Fieldmarshal? And in the Bosky, at that!"

"Why, lad, I went to Wellen and got them," answered Vidron. "And as to why, let me say this: When we broke free of the Guula at the north gate of Challerain Keep, we rode in a long arc to come at last to Stonehill—"

"Stonehill!" burst out Danner. "But we—Paddy and I— we were in Stonehill, waiting . . . three days."

"Two and a half," interjected Patrel.

"Two and a half days, then," continued Danner, "and no one came."

"When?" asked Vidron.

"Let me see," said Danner, reckoning the day while Patrel counted on his fingers. "I make it exactly two weeks past when we arrived there, early in the 'Darkday. The rest of the 'Day we stayed . . . all the next, too. Finally we left early on the third 'Darkday. And if my reckoning is right, that would make it the eighth of January." Patrel nodded in confirmation.

"Why, then," responded Vidron, "your path to Stonehill was swifter than mine." Then the Man's eyes widened in surprise. "Hola! If you left early on the eighth, you must have ridden out of one gate just as we rode in another!"

Danner and Patrel looked at one another and then at Vidron, and all three realized how close they had come to meeting together in Stonehill. And each realized, too, that the difference of but a moment in a person's life can alter the course of events forever. Why, perhaps if the Warrows had met with Vidron, the Battle of Budgens would not have occurred, or Vidron's journey to Wellen might not have taken place. Yet perhaps these things would have happened in any case, with the outcomes altered—in major or minor aspects—or . . .

Merrilee's question broke into the thoughts of the three. "General Vidron, did any Warrows ride from Challerain Keep with you? Perhaps Tuck . . ." Her voice trailed off, her eyes anxious.

"Ah, but no, lass," answered Vidron, shaking his head sadly. "When we broke free, not a Waldan was among us."

Merrilee looked away from the Hrosmarshal, and her shoulders sagged in despair. Silence reigned among the four for long moments, though the hills cast occasional horn calls to their ears, and the clatter of hooves rattled on the cobblestones of Brackenboro.

At last Vidron cleared his throat and spoke: "Of the five thousand defenders at Challerain Keep, I had thought that only sixty-three of us survived that last battle—sixty-two Men and one Elf, Lord Gildor. But now I find that Danner and Patrel cheated Death, too, bringing the tally up to sixty-five. And so there is yet hope—though slim it is—that others also survived the ordeal and live on . . . perhaps your Tuck." Vidron reached out and drew Merrilee next to him. The young damman sat with the Man and leaned her head against the warrior's side, and tears trickled down her face, yet she made no sound.

After a long pause Vidron picked up the thread of his tale: "On the second 'Darkday after we rode into Stonehill, a horseman came from the south. An ex-soldier he was, named Jarek. His cottage is in the Alnawood in Gûnar. His tale was chilling, though it explains much. Yet it leaves as many questions behind as it answers.

"It seems that Jarek was on his way to Valon, only to find that the Gûnarring Gap had been seized by a force of swarthy warriors—perhaps from the south: Chabba, Hurn, Hyree, or Kistan, he did not know the which of it. Ai! But Fortune favored him, turning her smiling face his way, and he was not discovered by the foe.

"And Jarek turned north, riding for Challerain Keep, bearing the word to Aurion . . . or if not to the High King, then to the Kingsmen.

"Across Ralo Pass he came and down into the Riverwood. Near the ruins of Luren, at the ford across the River Isleborne, he came through the Black Wall and into the cursed Dimmendark.

"Again Fortune favored him, for no Spawn did he meet while riding through the Shadowlight up along the Post Road, though at the bridge spanning the Bog River, he did hear the distant howling of 'Wolves,' though I deem it was Vulgs instead.

"At last Jarek came to Stonehill, and there he found us—the pitiful remnants of Aurion's northern might. And he told me his tale.

"Ai, but it was dire news, for I then knew why no word came from the south, and why the Host did not come to Challerain Keep: They fight an invading army in the south . . . likely our ancient enemies from Hyree or Kistan or both—for, ages past, they were in league with Modru, during the Great War."

"But that means the Host will not come," protested Patrel. "At least not for a while. Who, then, will fight the Horde? Who will keep them from the Bosky?"

"The Thornwall will thwart the Horde," said Danner, "if

we can get it stoppered up again. But we've got to slay the Ghûls, too, or drive 'em out."

"We must slay them." Merrilee's voice was low.

"Vengeance?" asked Vidron.

"Nay," answered Merrilee, "though to some vengeance would taste sweet. No, not revenge, but instead this: We must close the Thornwall now, to keep the Horde out. And the Ghûls must be slain, to keep them from opening it up again, as they did before at Spindle Ford, and the bridge, and perhaps at the other crossings, too. There is this, too: I think Modru uses the Ghûls to reave us, to keep our minds on them and not on the Barrier. Till now he has succeeded, and if the 'Wall is left open, then his Swarm will march in and raze the Boskydells, as Hanlo so aptly foresaw. Hence, we must close the Thornring ere they come."

"You are right, Merrilee," said Patrel. "Even though by closing the Thornwall, we shut the Ghûls in with us, it must be done . . . and that means we will have to slay the reavers rather than drive them out. For to leave the Thornring open invites Modru's Horde to enter, though why they have not already come, I cannot say."

"Perhaps they still loot Challerain Keep," said Danner.

"Nay," spoke up Vidron, "for Modru would not allow petty spoils to disturb his careful plans. Nay, it is something else that delays his hand. Perhaps the Warlord of the Horde was slain in that last battle, and they await a new tyrant to drive them on."

"Hey! The emissary!" exclaimed Patrel. "The one Danner slew at the north gate. Perhaps he was the Warlord you speak of. Mayhap your arrow, Danner, has stayed their hand thus far."

"Be that as it may, it won't stop 'em: If they don't already have a Warlord, Modru will just send another," responded Danner. "Merrilee's right: We've got to plug up the Thornwall now. And then we'll set about killing the Ghûls."

"Ah, but your tactics must change," Vidron said. "The Guula will be wary, now, and no longer fall easy prey to ambuscades. That's why I will leave half of the Wellenan horsemen here in the Boskydells to aid you. The rest I take to Gûnarring Gap to try to break the enemy's hold there."

"The Gap?" said Patrel. "You go to the Gap?"

"Aye," answered Vidron. "When Jarek brought me the news of the enemy at that pass, I knew then that my mission would be to break their hold. I took my Men from Stonehill and we headed for Wellen, but Jarek I sent on to the Weiunwood to bear the news unto the Alliance and to Lord Gildor."

"Lord Gildor?" asked Patrel. "Wasn't he with you?"

"Nay, lad," answered Vidron. "Gildor had turned aside earlier as we went north of the 'Wood. I went on to the Battle Downs and then south to Stonehill to keep the rendezvous, while he went to seek tidings from his kin, Inarion, and to bear to the Weiunwooders the sad news of the fall of Challerain Keep and of the death of King Aurion."

"We saw Aurion slain," said Danner, his voice low. "He fought well and bravely, but there were just too many Ghûls."

"He was a great King and a valiant warrior," responded Vidron, "and his keen sword and royal hand will be sorely missed in the days ahead. If Galen survived, he is King now, and if not him, then young Igon."

"But wait!" cried Patrel. "Do you not know?" Then the buccan smote his forehead. "Ach, how could you? Laurelin's waggon train was Ghûl-slaughtered. All were slain but for Igon and the Princess, and they either escaped or were captured and borne east; at least that's the way it looked to Danner and me when we came upon the wrack, six or seven days after the Ghûls fell upon that ill-fated train."

Vidron's face blenched at this dire news. "When was this, and where?" he gritted.

"It was on the Post Road where it swings west above the Battle Downs," answered Patrel. "And, as to when, I would guess the Ghûls attacked the train on Fifth Yule, perhaps—nearly two fortnights past."

"*Rach!*" Vidron struck a clenched fist into open palm and sprang to his feet in agitation. "That explains the mystery, then, as to why Jarek saw no waggon train bearing south along either Ralo Road or the Post Road as he came north with the news of the Gûnarring Gap. Ai, but he saw no riders either, and so the Ghûls may indeed have Laurelin and Igon, though it is by no means certain."

Like a caged beast, Vidron paced in silence; but then he abruptly sat down once more. "Ah, but my heart cries out to do something—to go after the Prince and Princess . . . but where? They could be nearly anywhere! And their trail has grown cold beyond following. *Garn!*" He fell silent again, then at last said, "When we get to Gûnarring Gap, the foe will pay for this foul deed." And there was a fell look in the warrior's eyes.

At that moment a horse-borne warrior wearing one of the blue-and-white helms of Wellen clattered up. "Sire, the Men begin to return, and Wee Folk come at their side," said the warrior. "The Ghûls are slain or scattered and at the moment are no threat."

"Hai!" exclaimed Vidron. "Now if these *Waldfolc* can but get the Thornwall plugged, then with the help of the Wellenan warriors who remain behind, this Land will be made safe again."

And as the herald wheeled his steed and cantered off, Danner and Patrel and Merrilee looked at one another in astonishment and then fierce joy. For, less than two hours past, they were plunged into despair fleeing a dreadful foe—knowing that the fate of the Bosky was perhaps teetering on the brink of doom—but now, with the arrival of the Men of Wellen, their fortunes had entirely reversed.

Vidron beamed down upon them, and his hearty voice said, "I think my promise to your Thornwalker Captain Alver has been kept."

"Captain Alver?" burst out Patrel. "Do you know Captain Alver? And what promise?"

"Aye, lad," answered Vidron. "Alver and I met when I rode through the Boskydells on my way from Stonehill to Wellen."

"You rode through the Bosky? Why, of course, you *had* to. Down the Crossland Road?" At Vidron's nod, Patrel exclaimed, "Then *that's* who it was! It was you and your sixty-odd Men who thundered past in the Shadowlight while Danner and I bedded down in the loft of the stable of the Happy Otter Inn at Greenfields. *Again* we just missed you!"

"The fortunes of War turn on small moments," replied Vidron. "That we missed each other in Stonehill and then again in your Greenfields may have had little to do with this War, but on the other hand may have altered its course beyond measure. And we will never know what would have been had we met in either place."

"If you'd met in Stonehill," said Merrilee, "I think all of you would have ridden in pursuit of the Ghûls who perhaps stole Princess Laurelin and Prince Igon, and the Warrows of the Bosky would not have dealt with the Ghûls as we did. How else we might have faced them—in what other fashion—is beyond our knowing. But that did not happen, you did not meet, and so it was Danner and Patrel who rallied us in our time of need, and you, General Vidron, who rescued us when all hope seemed lost."

"Lass, you and I, we are right about one thing: we will never know," answered Vidron. "And if Captain Alver had not given me and my Men food and shelter as we rode toward Wellen, then I would not have heard of the Guulen strongholt here in the ruins of Brackenboro, hence I would not have brought the Wellenen to fall upon them. But, my chance meeting with Alver near your village of Rood changed all that, and I *did* hear of the strongholt, and we *did* fall upon it just as soon as I returned with the Men of the eastern garrison of Wellen. And it was only the happenstance of keeping my promise to your Captain Alver to purge this place of the Guula that we were here at all to hear the Horn of Elgo blowing in distress, calling us to the attack. A long string of slim chance led us here, and a longer string may lie before us. In any case, on the morrow I will take half the Wellenen and make for the Gûnarring Gap. And thus will I see what my improbable string of chance will lead me to henceforward."

"Improbable or not," said Patrel, "I am glad your path led you here . . . and in the nick of time at that, else we three would be the deaders and not the Ghûls."

"Hoy, look!" exclaimed Danner. "Here comes Luth and some others."

"There's your dad, Danner," said Merrilee, pointing. "I am so happy for you."

And as Danner ran down the street to meet his sire, tens and twenties of Warrows came into the village of Brackenboro, some on foot, some on ponies, and here and there amidst them rode the warriors of Wellen. And some of the Warrows wept, for they were from Brackenboro, and it was

Rollo who said it best for them all: "The 'Boro may lie in charred ruins, its buildings burnt and sundered, but, by Adon, it is our home, and now it is free again."

Men began to drag the corpses of the Ghûls to a nearby ravine to burn in a great fire made there, and billowing smoke rose into the Shadowlight where it was lost in the blot above. The bodies of the slain Men and Warrows were recovered, and there began the raising of a great common burial mound on the bracken-covered hillside. And warriors large and small alike wept to see their comrades laid in the earth.

Men and Warrows continued to straggle in, and camp was made outside the ruins. And a council of Captains and Lieutenants was held and tallies taken to judge the losses: Of the nearly one thousand Ghûls, four hundred twenty-one dead were counted, two hundred seventeen of which had been felled by Warrow bolts. Of the three thousand Men, ninety-two were known to be slain, though another one hundred twenty-three were missing; some were known to be yet on Ghûlen track, while others could be lying dead or wounded. Of the one thousand eighty-six Warrows, one hundred fourteen were known to be dead, and nearly three hundred were missing, though Hanlo and others believed that most of these were alive and cautiously making their way back to the Eastwood rendezvous points.

Parties were sent out to scour the hills, and to sound the trumpets to assemble. Warrows were dispatched to the Eastwood rendezvous locations and to the camps to spread the word of the victory.

And in the council, plans were made to leave half the Wellenen in the Boskydells under the command of Captain Stohl. Warrows would join forces with Men to run the surviving Ghûls to earth, for the reavers would yet be a formidable force in the Boskydells should they reassemble. Plans also were made to plug the Thornwall at Wenden, Spindle, and Tine fords, and to stopper the way across the bridge over the Spindle River, and to close off the old abandoned Northwood tunnel, for there was still the Horde to keep out of the Bosky should the Spawn march from Challerain Keep.

Then the council turned its thoughts to the freeing of

Gûnarring Gap. And it soon became obvious that Vidron could use the sight of the Wee Folk to see for him in the Dimmendark. Danner and Patrel looked at one another, and Danner nodded to Patrel's unvoiced question, but ere he could say aught, Merrilee spoke up:

"Kingsgeneral Vidron, you will need Warrow eyes to see for you in the Shadowlight. Were my Tuck here, he would go with you; but he is not, and I will go in his stead. Yet you must take more than my eyes alone, for should I be slain, still you will need the Warrow sight. I deem ten of us will be enough, and I see that Danner and Patrel would go with you also. That leaves us but seven more to choose, and so I ask my kindred: Would any of you come with us?"

There was a great uproar among the Warrows, as some cried *No! You are needed here!* while others leapt up to join the quest south. Luth Chuker smiled to himself, for he alone seemed to appreciate Merrilee's canny maneuver: By speaking first as she had done, it was she who had set forth the terms of Vidron's need, and she had gauged it well, for ten Warrows spaced the length of a two-mile-long horse column would more than fill Vidron's requirements; and by speaking first, Merrilee had established her *right* to go with Vidron, though some might have said it was no place for a damman had she merely volunteered to go after another had set forth the identical plan; but as it was, none questioned her *right* to go, they only questioned whether or not she—as well as Danner and Patrel—would be more valuable in the Boskydells than in Vidron's strike force. And so, while Luth sat back and smiled, some Warrows argued over the merits of losing these three to Vidron, while others argued over their own right to fill the last seven open slots.

Finally, it was Hanlo who "set them all straight," for, when he at last held the floor, in an uncharacteristically quiet voice he turned to his bucco and asked, "Would you go on this mission, son?" At Danner's nod, Hanlo said, "Captain Rushlock, who would you appoint in your stead?"

"Luth," answered Patrel, "Luth Chuker."

"Damman Thornwalker Merrilee Holt," asked Hanlo, and by this very statement he established for all time the recognition that Merrilee was indeed a full-fledged Thornwalker, damman or no, "who would you take with you?"

"Two more from the Company of Whitby's barn, and five from the Eastwood Company," answered Merrilee. "That's five from each, even-handed."

"Then make your choices," said Hanlo, "for in this entire matter we would not gainsay you. General Vidron deserves the best, and you *are* the best."

Hanlo sat down again, and none raised his voice in protest. Now it could be seen where Danner got his air of command: Like sire like bucco, they always say, and in this case the saying was true.

And so it was that Merrilee, Danner, Patrel, Teddy Proudhand, and Arch Hockley—all from Whitby's barn—and Rollo Breed, Dink Weller, Harven Culp, Dill Thorven, and Burt Arboran—from Eastwood—were selected to go with Vidron's force to free Gûnarring Gap, or if not to free it, then to harass the enemy until reinforcements came from Wellen. For even now the muster went forth in that Land, and a portion of the levy was to come south if needed.

At last Fieldmarshal Vidron stood. "We can plan no more here this 'Darkday, for we have come to the limits of speculation. Let us now take to our beds, for on the morrow we must set forth on our missions. But ere we adjourn, this I say: Long shall the bards and tale-tellers speak of the alliance of *Waldfolc* and Men, and their words will be glorious, and their sagas full of valor, for we do battle with the forces of darkness and evil, and we shall prevail!"

A great cheer broke forth from the assembled council, and spirits were aflame. Though none knew what the morrow would bring, still they were filled with confidence and faith, and they were *proud,* for on this day they indeed had met the evil foe, and they *had* prevailed.

Early the next 'Darkday, Vidron set forth with fifteen hundred Men and ten Warrows, the Warrows mounted upon lightly loaded packhorses, for ponies would not be able to match the pace of a Valanreach long-ride.

As they rode forth from the ruins of Brackenboro, those remaining behind—Men and Warrows both—stood along the streets and gave them a rousing cheer to send them on. And, in turn, those departing cheered the ones who remained behind to sweep the Bosky clean of Spawn and to plug shut the Thornwall. And so, shouting goodbyes and good fortune, Vidron's force wended eastward through the downs to turn southerly along the margins of the Eastwood as they followed the South Trace, making for the Tineway, which they would then follow southeastward and out of the Boskydells at Tine Ford.

All 'Darkday they travelled thus at the varying pace of a Valanreach long-ride. And they saw no sign of friend or foe, for the land seemed deserted. At last they came to the Tineway, some twenty miles east of Thimble.

Now they swung along the tradeway, heading east and south for Tine Ford. But they rode no more than ten miles down the Tineway, for they had come some fifty-two miles that 'Darkday alone.·

The Warrows were weary, and, soon after their meal, all but the one on watch quickly fell asleep; for they were not used to the rigors of a Valanreach long-ride, and they welcomed the comfort of their bedrolls spread upon the hard, frozen ground.

The next 'Darkday was much the same as the previous one, the unremitting miles of cold 'scape passing by as hooves hammered at a canter and fast trot, and clipped at a slow trot, and clopped at a walk, as Vidron varied the pace to save the steeds, stopping now and again to feed and water the horses and to stretch legs and take care of other needs. But even while the mounts were eating grain from nosebags, at times the Men would walk forward leading the steeds, bearing ever toward their goal.

It was late when they made camp at the road junction where the Wendenway met the Tineway. They had come to Downdell. The next 'Darkday would see them leave the Bosky.

Mid of the third 'Darkday, the two-mile-long column came to the Thornwall at Tine Ford. But *lo!* this crossing was guarded by Thornwalkers. As their Captain Willinby said, "Yar, they came lots, but we just hid out in the Thornring itself, and when the Ghûls were gone, back we went on guard, putting the thorn plugs back in place. Finally I guess they got tired of unplugging the tunnel, 'cause they've not come in a while."

Danner and Patrel shook their heads in admiration at the pragmatic persistence of this dogged Downdell company, and they thought that if the other Thornwalker companies had only used this tactic, then the other ways into the Boskydells would now be Thornguarded, too.

Little did they know that even as they rode out through the thorn tunnel and across the frozen Spindle River at Tine Ford and beyond the thorn barrier and into Harth, far to the north the vanguard of the Horde from Challerain Keep was at that very moment marching down the abandoned Northwood tunnel and into the Northdell of the Bosky. And some ten leagues behind, swarming across the southern plains of Rian, came the seething Horde, marching to the beat of a great Rūcken drum: *Boom! Doom! Boom! Doom!*

Late that same 'Darkday the Wellenan column made camp where the Tineway met the Post Road, some one hundred twenty miles south of Stonehill and the Battle Downs.

The next 'Darkday Vidron's force turned southeastward along the Post Road, riding through the bleak Winternight. Down through the southern reaches of Harth they rode, and the ground-eating pace of the Valanreach long-ride hammered away at the iron-hard, snow-covered 'scape, and miles of frozen land faded behind them.

Seventeen or so leagues a day they rode—fifty or more miles a leg—and the Warrows were glad each time camp was made, for they were weary of riding. In the beginning their muscles had protested mightily each 'Darkday, especially when they arose to break their fast. Yet each 'Day they had become more inured to the rigors of the long-ride, and the Warrows now suffered only an occasional twinge.

The horses, too, settled in to the long hours of travel, the varying pace conserving their strength. And all the riders, including the Warrows, saw to it that the steeds were frequently fed grain and given enough to drink and rubbed down each 'Night ere the warriors saw to their own comfort.

*   *   *

Late on the second 'Darkday upon the Post Road, the column made camp deep within the western margins of the Riverwood, a great forest stretching out many miles to either side of the Isleborne River and growing along its length for fifty leagues or more. And some miles ahead, at the heart of the Riverwood and upon the banks of the Isleborne, stood the ruins of Luren, once a great trade city, but destroyed in elden times: first devastated by the terrible Dark Plague that swept all of Mithgar and slew nearly one out of three; then, years later, ruined by a great fire—and this time Luren was abandoned. Both the plague and the fire were said to be sendings of Modru.

The next 'Darkday the column rode through the ruins; but the wind had begun to howl, and flying snow obscured their vision, and so they saw nought of the remains. But even had the wind not been blowing and the snow not flying and their cloak hoods not drawn tightly over their heads, still Luren had fallen into such utter decay that little would have been seen of the former great city in any event.

They crossed the frozen Isleborne at Luren Ford, and Vidron's force turned southward along Ralo Road; this was the road that would bear them across the Grimwall through Ralo Pass and then down through Gûnar to the Gûnarring Gap.

But the Warrows were not thinking of their route, for the shrieking wind doubled its fury and the fling of snow lashed at them; and they ducked their heads and were glad that the packhorses they rode were being led on tethers behind riders who seemed to know where they were bound.

And the howl tore at them, and white snow flew and spun, raging past. Yet the column pressed on into the blast . . . and suddenly they were come out of the Dimmendark and out of the flying snow and into overcast daylight.

And glad yells sounded above the howl of the wind along the Black Wall.

When Merrilee was led forth upon her packhorse out of the Dimmendark, waiting for her were Danner and Patrel, joyous smiles upon their beaming faces, eyes brimming; and the damman looked at the blear light of a dismal day and, overwhelmed, she burst into tears.

The rest of the day they rode southward through the winter Riverwood, and there was much singing along the horse-borne column, even though the overcast skies darkened as a brewing storm drew nigh. For Man and Warrow alike were filled near to bursting with the joy of the *day,* and they reveled in Adon's light; even the horses seemed glad to see the daytide.

That evening they made camp still in the Riverwood, and a miserable driving sleet lashed at them. Even so, the joy of day persisted. Folk would glance up from the ground and look through the frigid ice-rain at one another, and great smiles would burst forth upon their faces as they shuddered and shivered in the blast.

When dawn came it fell through grey skies onto a frozen, ice-laden land, and a chill wind blew from the west along the great arch of the Grimwall and over the Riverwood. But even though the coming day promised to be bleak and of little comfort, still all the column broke their fast in high spirits, for it was *dawn* they witnessed, the first they'd seen in more than a month, the first since the Shadowlight of the Dimmendark had swept down from the icy Wastes of Gron to grasp the northlands in the frigid clutch of Winternight.

That day they rode down through the southern reaches of the Riverwood, and as they rode the leaden cast of the sky began to lighten. By midday great swatches of blue sky slashed overhead, riving the clouds to the wonder and delight of the south-bearing soldiers. And just as they rode from the last of the Riverwood, the Sun broke through, and a great jubilant cry rose up to greet it.

Up through the foothills of the Grimwall they rode, up toward the mountains standing before them; warrior songs of the road spontaneously burst forth from their lips as the cavalcade pounded over the crystalline 'scape toward the Ralo Pass ahead.

In early afternoon they came to the rise of the gap, and Vidron called a halt, for the pass was fully fifty miles through. And although here the Grimwall could be crossed at this time of year, night would fall ere they had gone halfway, and he did not want to camp upon the icy heights.

But on the morrow they would make the crossing in a single day, to come down into the abandoned Land of Gûnar and thenceforward across its open plains to come to their goal: the enemy-held Gûnarring Gap.

The Sun of the next day found the column deep in the icy channel of Ralo Pass, southbound over the Grimwall, and the breaths of horses and Men and Warrows alike gushed forth in white plumes and rose into the bitter-cold mountain air. To either side of the wide col sheer rock buttresses glared icily down upon the passing warriors, and the ringing echoes of driven hooves shocked and shattered among the frozen crags.

And the Sun had set and darkness had fallen when they came at last down out of the pass and into the southern foothills. At last they were come into Gûnar.

Over the next four days, Vidron dropped back the pace but sent horseborne scouts ranging to the flanks and fore, and across the plains the fifteen hundred riders went.

At night they camped, but burned no fires, for they did not want to be revealed to unfriendly eyes.

On the fourth day into Gûnar, the scouts went forth with special caution, alert for sight of the enemy, for late on this day they would come nearly to the mouth of the Gûnar-ring Gap.

At midday the Ralo Road came to the sparse forest northwest of the Gap, and onward pressed the column. Southeast they rode, and the Sun fell towards dusk. And the closer to the Gap the cavalcade drew, the more dense became the woods to the west of the road. In midafternoon they passed the junction where the Gap Road came south from Gûnar Slot and joined the Ralo Road, and on pressed the warriors. Just ere sunset, the column turned aside to ride in among the trees; here they would make camp concealed from any who might pass along Ralo Road.

Scouts now were sent forth to ride the last few miles to the Gap, there to spy out the strength of those warding it.

And it was late in the night when they returned, and their news was dismal. "Marshal Vidron," reported the chief among the scouts, a Wellenan named Brūd, "there are many warriors guarding the Gap—five or six thousand, I ween. Hundreds of campfires we saw, and here and there were huge fires—special fires—but what they were for, we could not get near enough to tell. Yet we did creep close enough to make certain that it was no ruse of the enemy, that warriors surely were at each pyre—and indeed they were there, for we saw them from afar. But pickets rode Moon-lit perimeters, and had we come closer, they would have discovered us. Yet we counted the fires—more than five hundred in all—and we judged from that count the number of warriors. Too, they have horses—many, many horses. Perhaps it is a cavalry we looked upon, though we cannot be certain, for the bulk of the herd was beyond the Gap, moving like a great black shadow out upon the winter grass of Valon. Nought else have I to report, Hrosmarshal Vidron." Brūd fell silent and looked to the scouts that had gone with him, but they said nought.

Vidron turned to his advisors, Wellenan and Warrow alike, seated in council. "Our course is clear then: we must use tactics that will allow our force of fifteen hundred to defeat an army of five or six thousand."

Vidron paused, and before any could say aught, Patrel spoke: "Strike and flee."

"Hai!" exclaimed Vidron, the light of the quarter Moon shining pale upon his silver beard and white teeth. "My thoughts exactly. Harass them as the Horde was harried by Galen, now King if he yet lives. But, lad, you spoke first. Say on."

"Kingsgeneral," said Patrel in a clear voice, looking to Vidron, "I deem that the Wellenen can strike hard and unexpectedly and withdraw in haste ere the enemy can group to give chase. Even if the foe sends pursuit, most of them will be left behind to hold the Gap. Hence, only a token will give chase, if any. We can regroup in these woods to assail the pursuers, should they come. If I am wrong and a great number follows, then we will fade away without engaging them.

"But it will take more than one assault to vanquish the foemen, and it is to the second strike and the third and all thereafter that we must give extra caution, for the enemy will be on guard and wary. Here the quarrels of the Warrow bows will be most valuable, for we are the Wee Folk and can move as quietly as the falling leaf. And our arrows will be used to strike down their sentinels in silence, to breach their warding ring and let the Wellenen through to lash forth without warning.

"That is the gist of my thought, Fieldmarshal Vidron. It is the only way that I think fifteen hundred can prevail over six thousand." Patrel fell silent. And Merrilee, seated next to Vidron, nodded to herself in agreement with the buccan's strategy.

Vidron rocked back, a look of admiration upon his face. "Ho, Waldan, but I am glad you are not my enemy, for your battle plans are most formidable."

"Perhaps, Fieldmarshal," responded Patrel. "Yet I am not the tactician of this group of Warrows. Merrilee Holt holds that place."

"Hai, lass!" cried Vidron, slapping a hand to his leg in pleasure and hugging the damman over to him with one arm. And the air whooshed from Merrilee's lungs and her tilted blue eyes flew wide in his fierce embrace. Then Vidron released her, and as she struggled back to an upright sitting position, he spoke on: "Tactician or not, Captain Patrel, your plan is sound, and your thoughts match mine. We will follow that course, at least until more Men muster in Wellen and join us.

"Yet there is much we must speak on to flesh out the tactics of this stroke, for all must go smoothly. We must set forth the order of the companies, the direction of the strike and withdrawal, the horn signals to be used, and much else. Yet, I would fall upon the enemy at the morrow's dawning, for then we will come out of the shadows of the pass as a catamount striking from dark crags." Vidron turned to his Captains. "What say you? How shall we carry forth with this plan?"

Thus it was that the detailed plans were made to strike the foe in the Gûnarring Gap and then to withdraw unto the woods. In this first strike the Warrows would play no role, for the enemy expected no attack and their guard would be sparse and lax. Hence, along with a few herdsmen to watch over the packhorses, the ten Wee Ones would take shelter in the forest to the west of Ralo Road. But in subsequent strikes, Warrows would lead the way.

The council met until after mid of night, but at last the plans were set and the orders relayed. In the dawn the Wellenen would foray against the force in Gûnarring Gap.

It was yet dark when the column set forth from the woods and went upon the Ralo Road to the southeast: dark shapes in the waning starlit night, moving out of the trees and toward the Gap ahead. And the Warrows stood at the fringe of the woods and watched the raiders bear off. When the last one had ridden by, the Wee Folk turned to go in among the trees, and behind them the sound of hooves faded southerly as the skies greyed in the east.

Vidron rode at the head of the force, and after him came the full of his strength, save those few left in the woods. And the Hrosmarshal's eyes strove to pierce the gloom of the foredawn and see through the enshadowed Gap to the warders at the far side.

Into the slot rode the fifteen hundred, lances and sabers at the ready. And the skies lightened to the east as they rode onward in the cloaking dark of the Gap.

When the Sun lipped the rim of the world, a mile or so ahead the warriors could see where the Gap came to an end. And there the Ralo Road split in twain: Bearing left-ward and to the east ran the Reach Road, passing hundreds of miles across the plains of Valon to come at last to Vanar, the city in the center of that Land where King Aranor had his throne; rightward went Pendwyr Road, reaching southeastward all the way to Caer Pendwyr, nearly three hundred leagues away, where dwelt the High Kings of Mithgar.

But Vidron's eyes were not upon the junction of the roads nor beyond to the Land of his home. Instead he looked where stood a great cavalry, warriors mounted upon horses as if for some ceremony. And although their flags were unfurled, no wind blew, and so he could not see their sigil to say if they were from Hyree, Kistan, or some other Realm. And their numbers were very great, and Vidron knew that his strike would have to be lightning quick and swiftly withdrawn, for to stay and fight would mean defeat. Even as the outriding scouts fell back to join the oncoming ranks, the Hrosmarshal gave a silent hand signal that passed back along the column, and the Wellenen spread wide in attack formation. At another signal they lowered their lances and began a trot forward. And the long line of warriors moved as one great military unit.

Onward they went, and now Vidron signalled once more, and the horses broke into a canter. The Fieldmarshal's eyes swept left and right along the formation and then to the force ahead, and those warders had not yet seen the oncoming Wellenen, for they stood in ranks with their backs to the Gap.

Vidron raised his black-oxen horn to his lips, and when the long file burst forth from the shadows of Gûnarring Gap, he blew a mighty blast that echoed up and down the line as the horns of Wellen took up the call. And they raced forth at a headlong run, deadly spears leveled to strike: Death flying upon thundering hooves.

Now Vidron couched his spear and urged his racing steed to greater speed. Yet even as he flew over the ground, his eyes were locked upon the horsemen in the closing distance. And Vidron gasped in dismay, for with great precision they wheeled about and swiftly spread wide to meet the oncoming Wellenen, *and began a charge of their own!*

And Vidron knew that his force would not survive the shock of their clash.

CHAPTER 2

Encounter at Gûnarring Gap

Tuck, Galen, Gildor, Brega and Aranor looked to see the unknown force charging out of the shadows of the Gûnarring Gap. Ubrik barked a command in Valur, the ancient War-tongue of Valon, and horns sounded, and the files of the Vanadurin wheeled and swiftly formed to face into Gûnar, lances and sabers at the ready.

Galen flashed Steel-heart from its scabbard, and Gildor drew Bale, and as Ubrik cried another command, the High King and the Elf Lord spurred forth with the Harlingar and to the fore of the answering charge.

King Aranor cursed his wounded arm but caught up a spear in his off hand and thundered after.

Tuck and Brega standing upon the ground, looked at one another, and then the Dwarf took Drakkalan in hand and growled, "Come on, Tuck."

And the Dwarf and Warrow ran on foot after the horse-borne warriors, Brega bearing his black-hafted axe, Tuck his arrows and bow.

And now the buccan could hear the horns of Valon blowing wildly as the riders raced toward one another, spears lowered for the death-dealing clash.

But *lo!* bugles sounded in the oncoming force, and the file veered left! *They were sheering off the attack!* And now the horns of Valon sounded, too! *And the charge of the Vanadurin turned aside, also!*

Spears were raised and sabers lowered as the two forces swerved oppositely. Trumpets blew and were answered by black-oxen horns, and then the armies rode together to mingle.

Tuck and Brega ran toward the now-milling warriors, and the Warrow could see the standard borne by the others: white falcon upon blue field—*the flag of Wellen!*

464

And as Tuck dodged among the seething tide of shifting horses and stamping hooves and worked his way toward the center of the mass, he heard the familiar hearty laughter of a silver-bearded Hrosmarshal and looked up to see Vidron clasping Galen's hand.

CHAPTER 3

The Valanreach Long-ride

Now the mighty cavalcade thundered northwest through the Gûnarring Gap, six thousand five hundred strong, for Vidron's fifteen hundred Wellenen had joined the five thousand Harlingar; and among the column and near its head rode a Warrow and a Dwarf upon stirrup-shortened saddles, each of their steeds led on a long tether by a warrior riding before them, and the strength of the Dwarf's grip upon the fore cantle made his knuckles white. Wellenen, Vanadurin, Warrow, and Dwarf: they all rode in the Legion of King Galen, and their goal was the cruel Iron Tower in the Wastes of Gron.

They rode into Gûnar. First they would gather Vidron's packhorses from the woods west of the Ralo Road, and then they would swing north to begin the long-ride to Claw Moor. The Hrosmarshal had smiled mysteriously at Tuck but had said nought other than he had a "special gift" awaiting the buccan back in the forest by the road, though what this surprise might be, Tuck could not imagine.

And they rode along the margin of the woods, the Wellen horns pealing the calls of assembly, the sounds ringing among the trees.

At last the calls were answered, and Tuck could see the shapes of horses and Men moving through the forest to come to the verge of the road. And then his sapphirine eyes saw smaller shapes: *Warrows!*

Now the column halted, and, his heart pounding, Tuck leapt down and trotted toward his kith. And *lo!* he saw among them one taller than the rest: *Danner!*

"Danner!" he yelled, running now, nearly stumbling in his haste, "Danner!"

Warrows turned at Tuck's call. *There was Patrel, too!*

But another figure broke forth from the Warrow ranks

and ran toward the oncoming buccan. "Tuck! Oh, Tuck!" she called his name, and he saw that it was *Merrilee!* And then she was hugging him and kissing him, and Danner and Patrel were pounding him on the back in jubilation, and unabashed tears streamed down all of their faces, while smiling Vidron sat upon his steed and looked down at them as he wiped the tears from his own eyes, too.

What are you doing here? How did you escape the Ghûls at Challerain Keep? Did you know that Aurion is slain and Galen is now King? Are these others from the Bosky? Questions flew back and forth, but no answers.

At last Tuck threw up his hands. "Wait!" he cried. "We've a long trip ahead of us and plenty of time to tell our tales and hear the stories of the others. Just let me ask this: Dammia I know not why you are here, nor how you came unto this place, but you must have come lately from the Bosky. What news is there of Woody Hollow? And how fare my sire and dam?"

At his question Merrilee's face fell, and new tears brimmed her eyes. She took Tuck by the hand and led him away from the others. And Danner and Patrel watched from afar as she stood and spoke softly to her buccaran, telling him of the last hours of Tulip and Burt, and of the burial in the glade in the Dinglewood. When she was finished, she wept and stroked his hair and clasped him to her as he held on tightly and cried.

Horns and bugles blew the calls to mount up, and though he wept still, Tuck went to his horse and was lifted to the saddle, for the press of War yields no time to grieve. And once more the column started forth while horse-borne scouts scattered to the fore, flank, and rear.

Lord Gildor glanced up at the Sun standing near the zenith and spurred forward to ride alongside Galen. "Galen King, the Iron Tower lies nearly three hundred leagues to the north as the horse runs. And exactly twenty days from this very hour will come the Darkest Day: The Moon will eat the Sun, and Gron will stand in the utter blackness of the 'Darkday. We cannot delay, for though I do not know how we may upset the Evil One's plans, we must do so ere that darkest moment comes." Gildor fell silent.

"I do not plan to tarry, Lord Gildor," responded Galen. "Yet our horses must last long enough to get us there, and the Wellenen have already come some eight hundred miles at the pace of a Valanreach long-ride. Their steeds may not endure unto Gron and the Iron Tower." Galen held up a hand to forestall the protests coming to Lord Gildor's lips. "Aye, Goldbranch, I know. And if need be, we will ride on without the army Vidron brought from afar. Yet I would rather have their strength with me when we assail the Kin-stealer's holt than leave them behind in our wake."

Gildor inclined his head and then dropped back to ride alongside Brega, but what they spoke about is not told.

North the cavalcade turned, north along the Gap Road, heading toward Gûnar Slot, that great cleft through the Grimwall where the mountains changed course, running away westerly on one side of the Slot, curving to the north on the other.

It was after sunset when they made camp in the margins of sparse woods to either side of the Gap Road. The Warrows gathered about their own campfire, and Tuck held hands with Merrilee as he exchanged his story with Danner and Patrel and the damman, while the other buccen listened and commented and added to the story of the Struggles. And occasionally Tuck would glance in his diary to recall a point or date. And all the Warrows *oohed* and *ahhed* when Tuck told of the harrowing pursuit of the Ghûls that led to the Dusk-Door, and their flight from the Krakenward, and the slaying of the Gargon.

But as he listened to the tale of the Struggles—of the reaving of the Bosky, and of Merrilee's rescue of Danner and Patrel, and of the battles of Budgens and Brack-enboro—Tuck's face would now and then cloud over. Tears would well from his eyes, and he would walk away to stand weeping in the darkness with Merrilee at his side. And when he returned to the fire, the tale would go on, taking up where it had left off as if it had not stopped at all.

And even while they talked and hoped fervently that the Thornwall had been closed up tight, the Horde raged across the Boskydells—ravaging, pillaging, slaughtering—while Warrows fled before them.

*   *   *

Three more days the cavalcade hammered to the north, and at last they reached the Gûnar Slot, camping near the woods at its mouth. And during these same three days, Tuck slowly recovered his good spirits, though a look of sadness would sometimes haunt his eyes. But then, whether he was staring into a campfire or the night, or whether he was riding during the day, Tuck would look up to see Merrilee gazing at him, and he would lose himself in her warm smile and grin foolishly back at her.

The next day they rode into the vast cleft, ranging in breadth from seven miles at its narrowest to seventeen at its widest. And the walls of the mountains to either side rose sheer, as if cloven by a great axe. Trees lined the floor for many miles, though long stretches of barren stone frowned at the riders from one side or the other. The Gap Road ran for nearly seventy-five miles through the Gûnar Slot, and so the Legion camped in the great notch that night.

The following day they pressed onward, coming out the north end of the Slot near the noontide and swinging slightly west for the ford on the River Hâth. And Brega grumbled that it seemed he was getting nowhere, for this was the very same route he had followed some five weeks past.

That night they camped just south of Hâth Ford, where the Gap Road came to the Old Rell Way. Before them stood the hideous Black Wall, the wind and snow rumbling along the great ebon flank of the Dimmendark. On the morrow they would enter once more into the cruel Winternight, and the hearts of all the warriors of the Legion fell because of it. And many sat up late into the night and watched the silvery full Moon and the glittering stars wheel overhead, for they knew it would be a long time ere any saw them again.

And Tuck and Merrilee sat with arms about each other and gazed at the Moon and whispered gentle things, and the argent orb sailed through the spangled night and shone its silver rays down upon them.

But Lord Gildor looked at the Moon with another thought—a dire thought—in mind; for he knew that just under fifteen days hence, the gentle Moon would consume the fiery Sun, and the Darkest Day would come unto Gron, to the woe of all Mithgar.

In the morning they passed through the howling wind and driving snow to enter the spectral Shadowlight, and Warrow eyes took over the chore of scouting. And all that 'Darkday they fared northerly along the Old Rell Way.

At mid of 'Darkday the Legion passed by the mouth of the Valley of the Door, and Tuck pointed out to Merrilee the vale where stood the Dusk-Door carven in the Grimspire, unseen in the Dimmendark. And Merrilee shuddered, for she knew that in the distant Shadowlight in a black mere dwelled the monstrous Krakenward.

On the second 'Darkday the cavalcade continued north and passed by the road leading up to Quadran Pass, and onward up the Old Rell Way they went. Soon they came to the place where Brega's Dwarven company had battled the vanguard of the Horde. And as they rode by, Tuck gasped in shock, and Merrilee turned her eyes down and away and did not look up again through her tears of distress; but Brega looked upon the Warground and his frame shook with rage, for the Horde that had come later had mutilated the slain Dwarves: Hands and arms and feet and legs had been sundered from the bodies, and heads stood on poles driven into crevices in the frozen ground, and dead eyes stared from maimed faces at the passing Legion; and the Spawn had committed other unspeakably foul acts of butchery that turned the stomachs of many a staunch warrior. And as the column rode past, Brega raised his face to the Dimmendark and cried out in anguish, *"Châkka djalk aggar theck!"* and cast his hood over his head and said no more. And what his words meant—what oath of vengeance or cry of sorrow he had uttered—none could say.

In the following 'Darkdays the horses of the Wellenen began to weaken, for they had come an enormous distance these past twenty-five days: more than one thousand miles in all, from Wellen across the Boskydells and down to Gûnarring Gap; then north through the Gûnar Slot and past the Quadran; and all of it at the pace of a Valanreach long-ride, which, although it got the most distance from a steed at the least cost to the horse, nevertheless took its toll in the long run. Each 'Darkday the Legion rode north was one more 'Day of nearly fifty miles of travel, and the Wellenan horses began to flag as the cavalcade rode through the spur of the Grimwall that stood across the Old Rell Way and turned aside to make for Rhone Ford across the frozen Tumble River. Galen King had chosen to leave the ancient Rell tradeway, for, as Gildor reminded him, it was the route used by *Spaunen* to travel to and from the region of the Crestan Pass along the western side of the Grimwall. And although the Legion had seen no signs of the foe, still it would not do to meet up with a southbound Horde. And so the column rode for the ford leading into the Rhone and crossed into that Land ere making camp.

The following 'Darkday they swung wide around a dense winter-bared forest growing along the western side of the River Tumble and then pressed back northward and east to come at last to the southern margins of Drearwood, where once more the Legion made camp. And now the talk around the campfires was whether or not the Wellenen would continue on, for their steeds were clearly showing the fatigue of the long journey they had made.

But on the 'Darkday next, once again the entire cavalcade bore onward. Up the narrow plain between the Drearwood and the River Tumble they went, at last to camp just north of the Crossland Road where it crossed the Tumble at Arden Ford. Galen spent a lengthy time inspecting the horses of Wellen, and there was a brooding look upon his face when he took to his bed for sleep.

And Tuck sat by the campfire and scribed in his diary, his sapphire gaze often straying to his dammia who was sleeping nearby. And out on the perimeter—alongside Men—stood two Warrows at watch, their tilted Utruni eyes scanning the spectral Dimmendark.

The following 'Darkday saw the Legion ride alongside the high Arden Bluff. Beyond the stone massif lay the hidden Arden Vale, and Tuck wondered what the Lian were doing. And he told Merrilee about the food and baths and clean clothing he and Galen had enjoyed in the Hidden

Refuge. Merrilee Holt thought back and realized that she had not had a bath in nearly four weeks, since three days after the Battle of Budgens—and that one had been but a quick laving from a basin, hastily done in a stall in Whitby's barn, and not a proper bath at all. And Merrilee longed to be in a real tub full of warm soapy water, and her eyes stung with tears.

That 'Night they camped at the northern reaches of the Drearwood. They had come only thirty-two miles that 'Darkday, for the horses of Wellen could no longer hold the pace.

"They are nearly played out," said Vidron. "Oh, some can go onward—in fact they all can—but no longer at the pace of a Valanreach long-ride. King Galen, I am troubled, for the Wellenen are nearly a quarter of your Legion. I would not have you face the Enemy in Gron at less than full strength. This I advise: drop the pace back to eight leagues a day—say at most twenty-five miles, no more—then we will ride with you all the way to the Iron Tower, and thence you will arrive at full strength."

"At full strength, yea," spoke up Lord Gildor, "but far too late. For the Darkest Day will arrive less than nine days hence. Let the Wellenen come, Galen King, but at their own pace, for they may be needed in the times ahead. Yet we must fly onward, and leave them behind, for the Moon is a clock that none of us can stay. We have no other choice."

Galen looked up from the flames of the campfire, but what he would have said is lost forever, for at that moment a horseman rode up. "Sire!" called the rider. "The Waldan at the north watch reports a small party on horses riding towards us! He says they are Elves!"

It was Lord Talarin! And he came with an escort of six Lian. And at his side, astride Rust, came Igon! And when the Prince saw Galen's fire, he spurred the great roan forward and came at a gallop before the others, the steed's strides devouring the distance. With a glad shout—"Hai, Igon!"—Galen leapt to his feet as Rust pounded forward, at last to thunder to a halt, and the Prince sprang down; and the two brothers embraced. And the youth of fifteen summers looked hale once more, for under the Elves' ministrations he had recovered his strength.

Galen spoke: "My brother, your eye is clear and your grip firm, and for that I am most grateful. No doubt you have been hacking some training manikin to shreds with your sword, or puncturing it with spear."

Igon laughed. "You are right, elder brother. I *have* tattered Lord Talarin's devices to a fare-thee-well. Yet those times are at an end now that you are here, for I propose to join you and go against the *Spaunen*."

A troubled look crossed Galen's face. "Igon, I ride into grave danger. I would not have both of Aurion's heirs fall to the Enemy in Gron in a single battle should the tide turn against us. Together, we can both be felled at one and the same time; apart, Modru has to come at us twice and win both times ere we are foredone. I would that you stay somewhere safe."

"Brother of mine," replied Igon, "you seek the same solution as did our sire." A fleeting look of pain crossed both their faces at mention of slain Aurion, yet Igon continued: "But heed! He sought to send me away south to safe haven, yet I was nearly killed by Ghol sword stroke; it was only the smiling face of Fortune that spared me.

"My meaning is this, Galen, King: Nowhere in Mithgar is safe today, for the enemy is everywhere. You would have me seek refuge in Arden instead of face the foe at your side, yet Arden itself is on the brink. And so, I ask this boon: to go at your side. But ere you say yea or nay, listen first to the words of Lord Talarin, for he bears tidings of import, and perhaps they will influence your decision."

The King nodded his acceptance of Prince Igon's terms and turned to watch Lord Talarin and the escort ride up. "Hál, Warder of the Northern Reaches of Rell!" called Galen.

"Hál, Galen King!" cried Talarin as he reached the fire and leapt down from his steed and bowed. At the High King's nod, acknowledging the Elf Lord's courtesy, Talarin's eyes sought his son, Gildor, and the two Lian smiled each upon the other. And Talarin clapped a hand to Tuck's shoulder. "Hai, but we meet again, Waerling."

And among the Elves now moving into the light of the Kingsfire came a Lian whom Tuck recognized: Inarion! It was Lord Inarion from the Weiunwood!

But then came an even greater shock to Tuck, for now

there stepped from among the Elves . . . *Flandrena!* Flandrena, who had ridden into Gron with Vanidor and Duorn and Varion! And now he was here! And both Gildor and Galen were shaken, too, on seeing the Lian warrior. But neither said aught, for Inarion was speaking, and he held on a long tether a grey horse; and tears sprang to the Warrow's eyes, for it was Wildwind, slain King Aurion's steed.

"Galen King, I have brought you the horse of your sire, though that was not my purpose when I took him from the Weiunwood, for I did not expect to find you on the bounds of Arden. Yet he is a swift steed, and my urgency was great, for I rode in haste to the Hidden Refuge to bear dire news, and I had vital need for a fleet remount to aid my own Wingfoot. But now I give Wildwind over from my keep into yours: from Sire to Son, from King to King, goes this noble steed. Care for him well, for he is a horse befitting the High King of all Mithgar." Inarion handed the reins of Wildwind to Galen and bowed.

Galen took the horse and stroked Wildwind's muzzle, and the glitter of the fire shone brightly in the King's eyes. And Wildwind looked upon Galen and then lowered his head as if in obeisance, but then quickly raised it and whickered.

"We shall get along well, old fellow, you and I," said Galen, his voice husky with emotion. "But now you are wanting some grain, no doubt, and perhaps the company of other steeds. But most of all, I suspect, you would like to gambol in a sunny meadow, or graze quietly under the Moon and stars. Perhaps one day. Perhaps . . ."

At a gesture from the King an attendant came and took the steed, and Galen led all of Talarin's party to council around the Kingsfire. As soon as all were seated in a great circle, Talarin turned to Galen. "Word came to me by swift riders of your yester camp at Arden Ford, and the sentinels atop the long Arden Bluff have signalled of your progress along your course. Yet why you come this way, I cannot say, and I would ask that you quench my curiosity."

"We ride for the Iron Tower in Gron," responded Galen, and Talarin's eyes flew wide at this news.

Talarin turned to Inarion. "Ai! This may explain your tidings, Alor Inarion."

Then Talarin turned once more to Galen. "There is much

we have to speak upon, Galen King, fell news from the west. But I am troubled by your course, for you have less than seven thousand in your Legion, or so my scouts say. Yet to attack Gron—the Iron Tower—seven *times* seven thousand seems hardly enough to breach those walls."

"We have no choice, Father," said Gildor. "Vanidor . . ." Talarin's face clouded with grief.

"Vanidor called my name at his dying," Gildor continued. "And he thrust this rede upon me:

> 'The Darkest Day,
> The Greatest Evil . . .'

And though we know not for certain what it means, these are our thoughts: The Darkest Day . . . will be when the Moon eats the Sun over Gron less than nine days hence; the Greatest Evil . . . is Gyphon." Talarin gasped, and grim looks fell upon his Elven escort. Gildor spoke on: "We think Vanidor warned that Modru plans something most vile on the Darkest Day."

"So *this* is the rede Rael felt pass her by!" declared Talarin. "And dire it is if you have guessed its meaning. Yet, how can it be? Gyphon is beyond the Spheres!"

"Yet the Hyrania and Kistania believe that the Great Evil shall return," responded Gildor. "And we must attack the Iron Tower and turn Modru's energies aside ere he can, somehow, *release* Gyphon."

"Then why have you not brought more warriors?" asked Talarin.

"Even as we speak, Lord Talarin," answered Galen, "the Lakh of Hyree and the Rovers of Kistan stagger the Realm in the south. They have cast down Hoven and Pellar, and now the struggle to whelm Jugo and Valon goes on. All the Hosts are needed in those battles, and even then their numbers may not be sufficient. This Legion, made up of Vanadurin and Wellenen, is all that I could bring and still hope to reach the Iron Tower ere the Darkest Day."

"But I do not think seven thousand enough to cast it down," responded Talarin. "What say you, Flandrena?"

"Can seven thousand cast down the Iron Tower? That I do not know, Alor Talarin," answered the slim Elf after some thought. "For even were there not swarms of *Rûpt* upon its walls, still it is a deadly fortress, and to breach it is a task perhaps beyond doing."

"How know you this?" growled Brega.

"I was there, Drimm," replied Flandrena, his eyes glittering in the firelight, his voice sinking low. "With Vanidor, Duorn, and Varion, I was there."

None said aught for long moments, then Gildor spoke: "Say on, Flandrena for I would hear of my brother."

Tuck put his arm about Merrilee and drew her to him as Flandrena told his tale:

"Six 'Darkdays and some, we rode north from Arden—swift across the Wastes of Gron—and at times we had to turn aside from the path to avoid the patrols of the Evil One. Yet at last we came unto Claw Moor, and thence to Modru's dark bastion.

"Long we lay and watched the ones within, counting the *Spaunen* numbers, gauging their considerable strength. Modru has held back perhaps eight thousand *Rûpt* to ward his Iron Tower. Too, we watched the wall patrols, and crept around the perimeters of the chasm that berings the holt while looking for a way to enter, for it was in all our minds to clamber o'er those palisades and rescue Princess Laurelin.

"But the crevasse is deep with sheer walls, and the iron drawbridge is Troll-guarded. Yet we continued our search. At last Duorn saw a thin crevice on the far side of the chasm, running from floor to rim. And Varion deemed we could climb it . . . as well as one corner of the fortress wall.

"Yet Vanidor said that one of us would have to bear word of the count of Modru's strength back to Arden, for then if the mission to rescue the Princess failed, all would not be lost.

"As Captain, Vanidor chose to try the walls, and Varion he asked to go with him, for Varion was the most skilled at climbing. That left Duorn and me to decide between us who would get to go with them and who would ride south. But we both argued to try the bastion, and so Vanidor plucked two dry blades of grass and held them out for us to choose. I pulled the short blade and lost—hence, I would bear the word back to Arden, while those three would breach the walls.

"We said our farewells, and when last I saw them, they

started down a rope toward rift's bottom. I went back to where the horses were concealed and mounted my steed and rode southward for Arden.

"Many miles I had ridden, yet still I was on Claw Moor when I felt Vanidor's cry: *'Ride, Flandrena, ride!'* was his desperate last command . . . *'Ride, Flandrena, ride . . .'*" Flandrena's voice sank to a whisper, and his eyes stared deeply into the fire. Tears welled in Tuck's eyes, and Merrilee gripped his hand tightly, her own eyes misting over. And Brega sat with his hood cast over his head.

At last Flandrena continued. "Vanidor had given me his last command, yet I nearly turned back. But his call echoed and rang in my mind, and I could not refuse it. And so, weeping in rage and anguish, I spurred forth, for I knew then that the mission to rescue Princess Laurelin had failed and that I alone would carry to Arden word of Modru's strength.

"Swiftmane ran as he had never run before, and the leagues fell away beneath his hooves. He would have run until his heart burst, if I had asked it—but I did not. Still it was not four full 'Darkdays ere we came into the Hidden Vale.

"That is my tale, Alor Gildor; that is my tale, Galen King. But it is a story as yet unfinished, for I would return to Gron with you and avenge my lost comrades. How? I cannot say, for the fortress is formidable, and even though it is defended by less than a full Horde, still it will be hard to break . . . perhaps impossible. Yet I would go with you to try." Flandrena's Elven eyes held a steely glint.

"If your Lord will give you leave, I welcome your sword in my Legion," said Galen, and Talarin inclined his head in assent.

"My King," Vidron spoke, "you have gained one warrior, but you are about to lose fifteen hundred: The horses of Wellen cannot hold the pace. Perhaps the Lian of Arden Vale can provide us with mounts."

Galen turned to Talarin, and the Elf spoke: "Galen King, ere I answer your unvoiced request, first you must hear the news Alor Inarion carries, for I think it will bear heavily upon what we decide in this council."

All eyes turned to Inarion, and the Elf Lord spoke: "Six 'Darkdays past, the Horde sent by Modru to whelm the

Weiunwood broke off their attack against the Alliance and began force-marching eastward along the Crossland Road. Forty miles a 'Day they raced—"

"Forty miles a day!" burst out Vidron. "But they are on foot! At least the Drōkha and Rutcha go afoot. Do the Guula ride with them, or do they come ahead?"

"The Ghûlka ride with the *Spaunen* and drive them unmercifully eastward," answered Inarion, "yet none knows why, though we had guessed that they strike for Arden Vale to cast down the Hidden Refuge. But now another reason has come to mind: perhaps they thought to intercept your Legion, Galen King."

"Six 'Darkdays past, you say, they began their march . . . ai, I deem it was then that we had just come into the Dimmendark at Hâth Ford," reflected Galen. "Yet how Modru could have known of this—"

"Spies!" spat Brega. "His spies must watch the roads inward."

"But then how did the Horde in Stonehill know of this?" asked Patrel.

"His emissaries," answered Tuck, and Lord Gildor nodded. Patrel shuddered, for Tuck had told him and Danner and Merrilee of Modru's hideous power to *possess* another. "But why the Horde in Stonehill?" asked Tuck. "I mean, why not the one in Drimmen-deeve? All they would have had to do was march over Quadran Pass and stand athwart the Old Rell Way. Surely Modru would have chosen them to intercept us."

"Mayhap they are still trapped in Kraggen-cor," proposed Brega. "Mayhap they cannot cross the Great Dēop, for the bridge is felled."

Talarin looked curiously at the Drimm, for here was a tale the Lian of Arden had not heard. But before the Elf could ask aught, Galen said, "I deem it was the Evil One's agent we slew in the Black Hole, yet whether this severed Modru's command of that Horde, I cannot say."

"What about the Horde in Challerain Keep?" asked Danner. "Do they march this way, too?"

A look of pain crossed Inarion's features. "I am sorry, Wee Ones, to bear you evil tidings, but the Horde of Challerain Keep has gone into your Land of the Thorns."

What! Danner and Patrel and Tuck all leapt to their feet, and Merrilee buried her face in her hands.

"In the Bosky? The Horde is in the Bosky?" demanded Danner, his fists clenched, his entire body quivering in rage, his words guttural and but barely understandable.

"I am afraid it is so." Inarion's eyes were filled with deep sadness. "Three weeks past."

"Three weeks?" Tuck's legs gave way under him, and he slumped down by Merrilee. Then he saw for the first time that she wept. Tuck reached out and put his arms around her and drew her close.

Patrel smacked a clenched fist into open palm. "Danner, we've got to go back. We never should have left. They need us more than ever now."

Danner's lips were white, and he gave a short jerky nod, but then Merrilee looked up through her tears and cried, "No! That's not the way! West to the Bosky is not the way!" Her sharp cry split through the shell of rage engulfing Danner, and, blinking, he looked down at her. Patrel, too, turned toward her. "North!" she spat. "Our way lies north!" Then her voice became deadly calm. "In Gron dwells the source of the evil. Brega has the right of it: the best way to kill a snake is to cut off its head. And that's where we are going, to snare the viper in its nest.

"Why do you think he sends his Horde to intercept us? He is frightened! That's why! We give him good cause to fear us, though we know not why. Perhaps he simply fears that we will upset his careful plans, as Lord Gildor has suggested is our mission's purpose. But whatever the reasons—whatever are Modru's fears—we should act to make the most of them. And so I for one say we strike north unto the very Iron Tower itself. Let us go forth and slay this serpent." Merrilee fell silent, and Lord Talarin, as well as King Galen and many others, looked upon the damman in wonder, for, unlike Patrel and Danner, they had never before heard a female speak as would a warrior. And first Patrel and then Danner reluctantly bowed to the wisdom of her words, and the two buccen grudgingly sat back down.

But Vidron voiced a doubt he held: "Perhaps you are right, lass. Perhaps Modru *does* fear us and sends a Horde to intercept us ere we can gain Gron. Yet there are other explanations, too: The Spawn may be marching upon

Arden Vale, as Inarion first guessed; they may have some
other target in mind, perhaps even beyond the Grimwall;
*or they may be seeking to trap us in Gron, to fall upon us
from behind as we attack the Iron Tower.*"

"But then, Hrosmarshal Vidron," said Galen, "Modru
would need to know that we head for Gron. How could he
have knowledge of our goal?"

"He is evil and suspicious, Galen King," answered
Gildor. "I think the bringing of the Legion into the north
surprised him, for he did not expect his grasp on the Gûnarring Gap to be broken, nor any of the southern defenders
to come north in any event . . . at least not as long as the
Hyrania and Kistania assail the Realm. There is this, too:
Where else would we be bound if not for Gron? Modru
asks himself that question, and the answer he finds is not
to his liking, I deem, and so he acts in haste to prevent the
upset of his plans."

Gildor fell silent, and Talarin, whose eyes had widened
at mention of the hold on the Gûnarring Gap, seemed
about to speak. Yet he held his silence, and it was Galen
who spoke: "Lord Inarion, where is the Horde now? And
what is their strength?"

"Five 'Darkdays past, I took Wildwind and Wingfoot
from the Weiunwood and rode to intercept the Horde,"
responded Inarion. "I came upon the *Rûpt* at Beacontor,
where they rested, and I stayed beyond the range of their
vision and watched them and counted them. I deem their
ranks to be ten thousand strong. And I waited to see if this
march of theirs was a feint or not . . . waiting to see if
they would bear onward, or would turn upon Weiunwood
once more.

"The next 'Darkday they pressed forth again, tramping
east along the Crossland Road. At the end of that 'Day, I
knew it was no ruse. They were truly bound eastward, and
sought not to attack the Weiunwood by surprise maneuver.

"I left them encamped in the land north of the Wilder
River, and I hied up through the Wilderness Hills to Drear
Ford and across Rhone to Arden, riding apace to warn the
Hidden Refuge. And so I saw the *Rûpt* not again, but if
they have kept up their quickstep along the Crossland
Road, they are now camped along that pike midway
through the Drearwood."

Vidron gasped. "That is but two 'Darkdays' march behind us at the hard stride they set!"

"Aye," said Ubrik, "but at the pace of a Valanreach long-ride, we shall slowly draw away from them."

"But the Wellenan horses!" exclaimed Vidron. "They cannot keep the pace! They have at best but one or two more hard rides left in them, and then they will need long rest. Now more than ever, Lord Talarin, we need fresh steeds. Can you supply them?"

"Not enough to mount fifteen hundred warriors," answered Talarin, "nor even a third of that count. The Lian of Arden are far flung on forays against the *Spaunen:* along the Old Rell Way, and in the approaches to the Crestan Pass. Even now the recall order goes swiftly forth, and Lian will come at speed back unto the vale to defend it if the Horde seeks to attack the Refuge. But were they all here now, their steeds would not number enough to give you relief."

Vidron turned to Galen in anguish. "Sire, the Wellenen then cannot keep the pace. They will come, but late . . . perhaps too late to aid you in your time of need."

"Hrosmarshal Vidron, my time of need is now," said Galen, "and my needs are changed by this Horde at our backs. I would not have them fall upon us from behind as we assault the Iron Tower." Galen paused and looked the Kingsgeneral straight in the eye. "I have a most fearful duty to thrust upon you, for only you have the Valonian battle skills to be able to lead the Men of Wellen and do what I need done: I would have you take the Wellenen and stop this Horde for as many 'Darkdays as you can hold them."

Tuck's eyes flew wide. "But, Galen King," he protested, "there are ten thousand of the maggot-folk and but fifteen hundred Wellenen!"

"That I know full well, Wee One," acknowledged Galen. "But the Horde is two 'Darkdays behind us now, and when our Valanreach longride comes to the Iron Tower, they will be a full four 'Days' march in arrears. And each 'Darkday of additional delay that Vidron can win for us will be one more 'Day we can assault the Tower ere we must turn our energies aside to meet a foe falling upon us from behind."

Galen turned to Vidron. "Hrosmarshal, this is the plan I propose: Set the Wellenen athwart Grūwen Pass; it is strait and the Yrm will have great difficulty bringing their numbers to bear upon you. You will be a barrier of iron that they will find hard to sunder."

"Aye, Sire," responded the Kingsgeneral, "your plan is sound, yet the horses are all but spent." Vidron clenched a fist and smote his palm. "But by the very bones of Sleeth, we *will* bar the way of the Horde!"

At mention of the Dragon's name, Brega growled low in his throat, but he held his tongue.

Talarin spoke: "Galen King, not long past I pledged to you in the name of the Lian of Arden Vale that when you need us we will be at your side. This then *is* the hour of your need, and we *are* at your side. My Guardians and I shall aid Kingsgeneral Vidron in holding Kregyn—Grūwen Pass—to buy you time at the Iron Tower. Our horses will be fresh and our arms stout."

Galen's eyes glittered in the firelight, and his heart was filled with emotion, and he could not speak; but Vidron leapt to his feet and flashed his sword to the darkling sky and cried in the ancient War-tongue of Valon: *"Hál, Deva Talarin! Vanada al tro da halka"!* (Hail, Elf Talarin! Together we shall be mighty!)

Talarin raised his hand in salute and smiled, and then he turned to one of the Lian. "Feron, hie to the hidden entrance and down into the Refuge. Gather the returning Guardians and have them prepare to come forth and join in the blockade of Kregyn. The scouts along Arden Bluff will track the *Rûpt*. Come forth with all my strength when this Horde is a 'Darkday's march south of the pass."

Feron leapt up to go, but Talarin held up a hand and called, "Wait!" And when Feron turned once more to him, Talarin said, "This, too, I think should be done, Feron: Seek out the Lady Rael. Tell her of Vanidor's rede:

> 'The Darkest Day,
> The Greatest Evil . . .'

Perhaps she will divine the meaning of his warning, for she is versed in such things."

Of course! Tuck thought. *The Lady Rael should be told the rede and her counsel sought. Perhaps she can shed some light upon this darkness.*

Talarin nodded to Feron, and then the Lian herald was gone.

And as the drum of the hooves of Feron's horse faded to the north, Prince Igon turned to Galen and spoke: "Galen King, now I ask that you grant my boon: I would fight at your side. And as you have known, and heard again in this council tonight, no place is safe from the Evil in Gron: not Arden, not Rian, not Pellar; neither Harth, nor Rell, nor Rhone; not Hoven, Jugo, Valon, Gûnar, or Riamon; not even the Land of the Wee Folk. Aye, it is to Gron you go, yet Gron is no more dangerous than elsewhere, for the foe is everywhere—if not now, then he soon will be.

"You have said it would be better if we were apart, for then Modru will have to strike twice and succeed both times to end the House of Aurion, and that is true. But heed me! If you have guessed aright, then the Darkest Day will bring the Greatest Evil less than nine 'Darkdays hence. And if that Evil is Gyphon, then the House of Aurion is ended then and there, for no mortal can withstand Gyphon—nor can the Elves.

"And so this I say: if we are to be defeated, my brother, let it be as we stand shoulder to shoulder; but if, on the other hand, we are to win, then let that victory come as we stand shoulder to shoulder, too." Igon fell silent.

Galen thought long, staring at the fire, and at last he looked up and nodded his assent. Igon let out a sharp cry— *"Hai!"*—and leapt to his feet in joy, as all the council smiled at this youth-warrior verging into manhood. Abruptly Igon sat back down again, his face drawn into solemnity, but it was a solemnity often broken by an inward smile.

And Talarin turned to Galen. "Now, Galen King, you must tell me your tale, for I have many times wondered this 'Night at the path that has brought your footsteps nearly full circle to my door."

Galen looked to Gildor and nodded, and Gildor turned to Talarin and said, "First, Father, this I must say: *Va Draedan sa nond . . .*"

*   *   *

After the council ended, Tuck lay wearily down to sleep. But his mind churned with chaotic thoughts: *The Horde is in the Bosky. Ai! What foul news! And Danner and Patrel feel as I do: They would run the hundreds of miles on foot, if necessary, to go back and help, whether or not it would do any good. Yet, I did not like the look that came over Danner—his rage was awful to behold; it may be his undoing one day.*

But what if we have guessed right about the Darkest Day, the Greatest Evil? Then Gyphon will somehow come and it will be the end of the world as we know it. And if that is true, then whether or not Vidron delays the Horde behind us will not matter, for Modru and Gyphon will cloak Mithgar in an evil wrap that will smother all that was once good. Does that mean that Vidron's stand in Grūwen Pass is all for nought? Perhaps. But what if we have guessed wrong, and the Darkest Day does not come? Then Vidron's stand will buy us more time to assault the Iron Tower. Yet, if we cannot throw it down, or if Modru's power is too great . . .

Tuck fell into a restless dream-filled sleep: dreams of years of no summer, no crops, starvation, famine—the babies, oh the babies, swollen bellies—plague, cruel slavery, death. And he would start awake to escape the nightmares, and then fall back asleep exhausted. And nearby, Merrilee moaned in her own dark dreams.

At the breaking of camp the next 'Darkday, Danner, Patrel, Merrilee, and the other Warrows that had been mounted upon the packhorses from Wellen were placed instead upon steeds from Valon—packhorses whose loads of food and grain had become light with the long-ride. And once more Galen's cavalcade set forth, the five thousand Harlingar leaving Vidron and the Wellenen to come after. And Tuck felt as if they were somehow abandoning or being abandoned by the silver-bearded Hrosmarshal and his warriors. Yet north rode the Vanadurin, the Thornwalkers in their company—as well as two Elves and a Dwarf.

Three hours later the column came upon the Lady Rael and her escort of Lian Guardians as they stood beside the Legion's route where it swung close to the concealed entrance into the Hidden Stand of Arden Vale. Galen and much of his War-council turned to the side to speak to Rael, as the long line of horse-borne soldiers passed.

And Rael's eyes widened at the sight of Merrilee in this company of warriors. As for Merrilee, she had never seen anyone or anything quite as beautiful as golden Rael, and the damman felt awkward in the presence of Rael's Elven grace. Yet Rael took her by the hand, and all reserves between them melted.

"Galen King," said Rael, inclining her head in courtesy as Galen stepped down from Wildwind and bowed.

"My Lady Rael," Galen spoke with regard. "Though I would stir up no painful memories, still I must ask: Know you what Vanidor's rede means?"

"Nay, Galen King," answered Rael, her eyes filled with ache and sorrow. "Had Vanidor Silverbranch called my name at the last, then his final message would have been thrust upon me and not Gildor Goldbranch. Yet, although I would have spared my eldest that blow, still I think I would know no more than I do now. I can add nought to your interpretations. The Darkest Day comes on the eighth 'Darkday hence—if that is its meaning. And the Greatest Evil is indeed Gyphon, the High Vûlk."

As they rode away, Tuck looked back and waved at Talarin and Rael as the sad-eyed Elves stood and watched the Legion press onward. And somewhere behind—beyond Tuck's vision—riding at a slower pace came Hrosmarshal Vidron of Valon and the Wellenen, while even farther away marched the pursuing Horde.

All that 'Darkday the Legion rode, passing swiftly over the frozen stony ground at the pace of a Valanreach longride. And slowly the slopes around them rose as they came into the approaches of Grüwen Pass where the land veered upward to meet the Rigga Mountains.

Up through the rising canyon they rode, toward the rift through the mountains, and the ice-clad walls glinted darkly in the Shadowlight.

Into the notch they went, cloaked in the frigid Winternight. And as the air grew thinner, the steeds labored, yet the pace did not slacken, for they could not camp at these heights.

Onward they pressed, up through the frozen stone of Grūwen Pass cracking in the hoarfrost and rime. Now the floor of the col became more or less level, and they rode steadily northeastward through the blacklimned crags. Hours passed, and the notch swung northerly and began sloping downward. On they went, the ring of hooves knelling back at them from the sheer walls.

At last they came down through the Dimmendark and into the Land of Gron. And the horses and riders were weary, for they had ridden nearly sixty miles that 'Darkday alone—a long 'Day, even for a Valanreach longride.

And after he had tended to his steed and taken a meal, Tuck spoke briefly with Merrilee and others, and recorded a bit in his journal, ere falling into exhausted slumber.

Over the next three 'Darkdays the Legion rode north across the barren Wastes of Gron. King Galen had slackened the pace a bit to allow the horses to recover from the long trek through Grūwen Col, and at the end of the third 'Darkday they camped near the southern edge of the frozen Gwasp. A raw wind blew down upon them from the Gronfangs off to the east as they sat around cheerless peat fires and shivered in the blast.

"Hey!" exclaimed Danner. "I just thought of something. If Modru is the Master of the Cold, why hasn't . . . why *doesn't* he just summon up a blizzard and stop us here and now? He could freeze us solid, us being out in the open— no shelter, no firewood. Is it that he cannot control the cold? Is that just an old dammen's tale?"

Merrilee shot Danner a squint-eyed look and responded. "Perhaps, Danner, it is instead just an old *buccen's* tale, generated by an overdose of ale down at the One-Eyed Crow."

"Ar, Merrilee, you know what I mean," squirmed Danner.

"And you know what I mean, too, loud buccan," shot back Merrilee.

"Hold on now," soothed Tuck. "We are all tired and cold and cross. Let us not to argue amongst ourselves out of sheer weariness."

"Danner's got a good point, though," spoke up wee Patrel. "I mean about Modru being the Master of the Cold, and all. Why *doesn't* he just bury us with a blizzard? Or is his reputation false?"

"Modru has the power, all right," spoke up slim Flandrena. "He *is* Master of the Cold. And he *could* bring a blizzard down upon us, for that is his most terrible weapon. Yet why he does not use it now, I cannot say. Perhaps it requires all of his power to do so, and he is saving his energy for some other reason . . . mayhap saving it for the Darkest Day."

At Flandrena's words, Tuck felt a deep foreboding race through his veins, and he shivered with its dire portent; and he glanced up to see a dark look in Merrilee's eyes, too.

"Well," yawned Danner, "I don't know either, but I am just too tired to stay awake and dwell upon it any longer." And the buccan spread out his bedroll and prepared to sleep. And as if that were a signal to the others, they too crawled into their blankets.

But ere Tuck fell into slumber, long ululating howls shuddered through the Winternight as Modru's curs wailed in the Wastes of Gron, and a cold chill ran up the buccan's spine.

And far away to the south, at the mouth of Grūwen Pass, Vidron, Talarin, the Wellenen, and the Lian Guardians all watched as the Swarm of *Spaunen* marched northward toward them, northward up the approach to the col: ten thousand Wrg marching upon two thousand defenders.

The next 'Darkday saw the Legion ride across the wastes to the north end of the Gwasp, where they made camp.

And once again the juddering howls of Vulgs called through the Shadowlight, other cries sounding to the northward and beyond, as if yawling messages were being relayed to the north, to the dark fortress of Modru.

And to the south at Grūwen Pass, that same 'Darkday had seen the Horde launch four attacks upon the Men and Elves, and four times Vidron's Host had hurled the *Spaunen* back. But each time, like a great battering ram, the Horde had smashed into the defenders, and each time the Alliance of Wellen and Arden had been driven reeling backwards, deeper into the pass.

Another 'Darkday passed, and the wayworn Legion rode through Claw Gap and onto Claw Moor, driving northward toward Modru's stronghold. No enemy barred their way or sought to strike at them, though Modru's curs—Modru's spies—hounded their flanks and yawled shuddering messages across the moor. The Legion at last made camp and rested in the mid of the high frozen land. On the morrow they would reach their goal.

And at Grūwen Pass, thrice more on this 'Darkday the Spawn sought to break through Vidron's Host. And thrice more the spent horses and exhausted Men and worn Elves rallied to hold the gap shut to the *Rûpt*. And the count of the slain mounted as the hammer of the Wrg smashed into the anvil of the Allies, driving them another eight miles deeper into the pass.

It was noon, the only time of 'Day that the faint disk of the Sun could be seen through the Dimmendark, and then but barely and only by knowing exactly where to look in the Winternight. And now the dim orb stood shadowy vague at its brumal zenith. High King Galen, son of Aurion, sat astride Wildwind and looked high in the southern sky at the dimly seen circle, while behind him sat unmoving the five thousand warriors of his Legion. And as he looked at the shadow-faint disk, Galen knew that in just two more 'Darkdays, at this very hour, the unseen Moon would eat the Sun, and the Darkest Day would come, and the Greatest Evil.

And Galen dropped his gaze to the east and looked at the dark fortress standing before him. Massive it was, and formidable, and beringed by a deep crevasse plummeting into ebon depths below. The great iron bridge was drawn up 'gainst sheer walls of black stone blocks rising up to towering battlements. And in the center, from atop the highest tower, flew the Sun-Death standard, a scarlet ring of fire upon a field of black. And now more than ever the Sun-Death sigil seemed to hold dire portent. Galen took a deep breath, and his eyes swept the ramparts for some sign of weakness, some place of entrance, some chink by which this bastion could be cast down. For the Legion stood now before their goal: They had come at last to Modru Kinstealer's holt. They had come at last to the dreaded Iron Tower.

CHAPTER 4

The Iron Tower

The 'Darkdays following Vanidor's torture-murder had been 'Days of anguish for Princess Laurelin. Yet whenever her mind stumbled into the black memories of those endless moments in Modru's chamber high in the tower—moments filled with hissing questions, and the *Clack!* of a Troll-driven rack wheel, and raw screams of agony—whenever Laurelin's mind returned to that hideous time, visions of a golden Elfess guided the Princess past the pain and horror and into a quiet domain of mourning. Laurelin grieved, but no longer did her wits fall stunned; nor did her heart plunge into an icy pall, and no longer did her soul flee through an unending labyrinth of despair. Instead she wept for the lost promise of Vanidor, and through her tears, her spirit began to heal. And even though she remained in the clutch of the Enemy, his will had not broken hers. And slowly she returned from that place of no hope to come back into the realm of reality, and she began to take note of her surroundings.

The chamber in which Laurelin was held was along a main corridor of the Iron Tower, and through the massive door she could at times hear fragments of snarling conversations of Yrm passing in the hallway as they went to and fro on their vile errands. Often they would be speaking in the Slûk tongue, and the Princess could not understand this foul, slobbering, guttural speech; at other times, though, a debased form of the Common Tongue would be used, and then she could piece together some of what was said. Yet she learned little from their talk, for most of it consisted of cursing and threats and insults aimed at one another.

The foul Rukh that grudgingly brought her food and drink and tended her fire was no source of information either, for he had no tongue and did not speak except to snarl at her. And when he came to do his chores, he was ever leering and prowling about, and his eyes followed her every movement. And whenever his small figure scuttled in through the door, Laurelin was repelled by the loathsome creature and took pains to ignore him.

Even so, the Princess did learn something of the course of the War—from the Evil One himself.

Not forty-eight hours following Vanidor's death, Modru's enraged shrieks echoed throughout the tower, and slapping footfalls of fleeing lackeys could be heard scrambling along the hallway past Laurelin's room. And the small filthy Rukh that served the Princess came scuttling in through the door, slamming it shut behind.

Hissing a tongueless snarl at Laurelin, the Rukh pressed his ear to the portal and listened intently. Modru's shrill cries of wrath rang in the corridor; yet abruptly the Evil One's stridor fell silent.

Now the Rukh listened even more intently to the ominous hush beyond the heavy panel, but he could hear nought.

Suddenly the door burst open, sending the mute asprawl, and Modru stalked into the chamber, his eyes glaring in rage through his hideous iron mask.

To the Princess he strode, and she stood defiant before him. The mute Rukh fled the room, limping and gibbering in fear.

"They will pay! They will pay!" Modru's wrath lashed out at her. Then his voice fell to the hiss of a poison-laden viper. "I will find them out—these four—when I am Master of all Mithgar, and they will suffer endless days at my hands. I will make them eternally regret that they strode through the *Dubh* caverns. They will forever rue the day that they slew my Negus of Terror."

Laurelin knew not of what event Modru spoke, nor what were the *Dubh* caverns, nor who or what a Negus of Terror was; but it was plain that four unknown heroes had thwarted some vile plan of the Evil One. And the Princess smiled in triumph at Modru.

The Evil One snarled and loomed above her and raised a black-gauntleted fist to strike, yet Laurelin did not flinch or cower before him. And just as it seemed his clench would crash down upon her, Modru hissed unto himself, "Unblemished," and he spun in rage upon his heel and strode from the room, his black cloak billowing behind.

In the long 'Darkdays that followed, Modru came often to gloat—his viperous mouthings, his sibilant whisperings, filling the room with malignancy as he boasted of his victories in Pellar, in Hoven, in Aven, and especially in the Realm of Riamon, where Laurelin's father, King Dorn, ruled: "Your dotard of a sire falls back before my power in the Rimmen Mountains. Dael soon will be mine. I think I shall make of it a great bonfire, and I will let King Shallowpate Dorn witness the burning . . . from a seat in the midst of the pyre!"

Though Laurelin knew he told her these things to break her spirit, still she listened carefully, for amid his sibilant puff-adder hissings was news of the War: news of the *Dubh*—the Dwarves—trapped in Mineholt North, "where they think to defy *me!—sstha!*—the foul-beards will be grovelling at my feet ere long, begging for mercy, but I will chain them to their forges, where they will eat and sleep and toil, and their hammers and anvils and sweat will serve Gron ever after"; news of the Baeron—the woodsmen of the Great Greenhall—fighting in the fastness of the Grimwall Mountains above Delon, struggling to close the secret Rukken doors upon the mountain slopes, "drooling imbeciles who will forever regret that they strove against *me—sss*—when they are in fetters, I think I shall have them carve new doors and new chambers in the flanks of the Grimwall, for I hear that they walk tall beneath the open skies and through the forests, and so stooping grinding labor in the dark labyrinths under the mountains seems a most . . . fitting task"; and news of the *Dolh*—the Elves—with their bright swords and swift steeds, "stinking lordlings—*sssth*—who shall not escape *my* wrath, for even Adonar will not be a haven when I am victorious. And I will drag them kicking and screaming back into Mithgar, and I will sit and watch while they hew down to lie in rot each and every one of those obscene trees of theirs. And then I shall bring the *Dolh* north and see if they can . . . *sss* . . . dig through the muck and find the bottom of the Gwasp."

Hissing and gurgling, Modru's vile gloating seemed endless. Yet it was not among his boastings that Laurelin gleaned tidings that kept alive the spark of hope within her heart; it was instead in his moments of rage as some fortune went 'gainst him that the Princess found faint glimmers of promise.

Two 'Darkdays after he had last burst into her chamber prison—raving that his Negus of Terror had been slain—again Modru's wrath rang throughout the tower, this 'Day twice. And when next he came with his sibilant whisperings, Laurelin found among his mutterings and threats indications that the four heroes had somehow escaped his grasp. Modru also hissed a vile pledge to torture and starve the "runtish scum" that had twice ambushed his reavers.

Inwardly the Princess smiled, for here were two more things that buoyed her spirit. Yet whether the four heroes were in any way associated with the "scum" and the ambushing of Modru's Reavers, she could not say.

Four 'Darkdays later Laurelin found out who the "runtish scum" were, for Modru came to gloat and hiss, saying that the Horde that had destroyed Challerain Keep was "even now marching through the ring of thorns and into the Land of the Runts."

And Laurelin's heart wrenched, and in her mind rose the faces of Tuck and Danner and Patrel, and her soul cried out to these gentle Folk of the Boskydells.

And when Modru left the chamber, Laurelin sat by the fire and wept.

It was in this time that Laurelin began to think upon escape, and she carefully examined her plight:

There were but two possible ways to leave the chamber: There was the door, but it opened out into a hallway heavily trafficked by the Spawn; further, the door was kept shut by a great brass bolt on the outside. And there was a single narrow window overlooking a courtyard, but the window was barred and was some twenty-five feet above the rough cobbles.

Neither way seemed to hold much promise of her escaping. And too, if she *could* get out, what then? How to avoid the teeming Yrm to slip across the courtyard? How to get beyond the walls and drawbridge? How to cross the Wastes of Gron? Horses? Nay, for the *Spaunen* rode Hèlsteeds. And although she had ridden one of these vile beasts to the Iron Tower, it had been led by a Ghol, and Laurelin was not certain that a Hèlsteed would permit a human to guide it. And what about food? And clothing, too, must be considered, for the garments provided by the mute Rukh were not suitable for travel o'er the Wastes in the bitter Winternight cold.

Laurelin did not know the resolutions to these considerations or to the others that came to her mind; yet, in spite of her broken arm, she began working to loosen a bar from the sill of the window, chipping with a fireplace tool at the mortar, praying that the heavy drapes would muffle the sound of her work . . . praying, too, that neither Modru nor the Rukh would come upon her unawares. And grain by grain, chip by chip, the mortar slowly, infinitesimally, began to yield.

Five more 'Darkdays passed, and Laurelin continued to chip at the mortar in which the bar was embedded, stopping whenever she heard the doorbolt *thunk!* back as the Rukh or Modru came. And they would find her prodding the fire with the iron.

Such was the case when Modru came to gloat on the fifth 'Day, and she stirred the blaze and then set the iron aside as Modru's hissings began. Among his reptilian mouthings, Laurelin gleaned that a battle between the Vanadurin and the Hyrania had begun.

The next 'Darkday, Laurelin managed to free the lower end of the bar, and she started chipping away at the upper end. And while she worked, she began to think upon how to twist or braid a rope out of cloth so that she could lower herself to the courtyard below.

Again Modru came and boasted. And Laurelin came to know that the fighting still raged between the Vanadurin and the Hyrania, and that it was at Gûnarring Gap. And the Evil One crowed at how clever he had been to seize the Gap at the War's outset.

Still his malignant hissings went on, and he spoke of many things. Laurelin was repelled to hear of the future he planned for Mithgar, but she gave no outward sign of her revulsion.

And as Modru prepared to leave her chamber—his malevolent gloating done—the Princess spoke to him for only the second time since arriving at the Iron Tower:

"Vile One, Yrm may thrive on fire-smoke and confinement, yet I would walk in the fresh air." Laurelin stood and spoke with the air of command of a royal Princess, yet inside she was wound tense as a spring, for she *needed* Modru to grant this request. Her only knowledge of the fortress was made up of chaotic memories from that time twenty-one 'Darkdays past when she had been led captive into the hold. Yet if she were ever to escape, she would need to know more of the arrangement of the strongholt ere attempting flight.

Modru's maleficent eyes glared at her through his iron-beaked mask. "*Ssstha!* Perhaps instead I will fling you back into my dungeons." And as Laurelin's heart plummeted to hear those words . . . "But then, *sss,* your health *is* a consideration." Modru spun on his heel and left.

An hour or so later the bolt slid back, and the filthy Rukh hobbled in bearing quilted Rukken garments, and boots, and a cloak. He flung them all in a pile in the center of the room and limped out.

The garb was crawling with vermin, yet Laurelin clasped it to her breast. Her heart pounded with glad excitement, for here was the clothing necessary for her survival in the Winternight cold while she crossed the Wastes of Gron.

And she washed the garments with the harsh soap provided for her bath and hung them before the fire to dry.

The next 'Darkday two iron-helmed Lōkha came and snarled at her to get dressed for her outdoor stroll. And as they walked the Lōkha spoke in a debased form of the Common Tongue, but their talk was of a revenge they planned upon one of their own kind and so Laurelin paid them little heed; instead her eyes sought ways she might escape.

The escort took the Princess across the rough cobbles toward the soaring battlements, and everywhere she looked was filth. Yammering Yrm snarled at one another and quarreled. Dark squatty Rukha, swart Lōkha and dead-white

Ghola swarmed within the walls. A great iron portcullis barred the way to the drawbridge, and it was Troll-guarded.

As she mounted up the ramps to the bastion parapets, the Princess saw the stables where the Hèlsteeds were kept, just inside the gate. And there, too, stood a Troll guard—a leering Ogru dressed in nought but black leather breeks in spite of the cold—and Laurelin's heart leapt with shock upon seeing the foul hulking creature, for it was the same Troll that had slain Vanidor on the rack. Her heart pounded with rage and loathing as the Lōkha led her up to the ramparts.

They walked along the battlements, and Laurelin deliberately shoved the vile image of the Elf-slaying Ogru from her mind and looked down through the Shadowlight at the great fissure that split the stone to encircle the fortress with a deep chasm.

She thought upon all that he had seen, and her heart plummeted, for she knew that she could not get out unless she could somehow pass undetected across teeming courtyards to take a Troll-guarded Hèlsteed and ride through a barred portcullis past its hulking warder and across an iron drawbridge above a black chasm.

When she returned to her chamber, the Princess took up the fire iron and chipped at the mortar holding the upper end of the bar, and tears ran down her face as she toiled in what she now believed to be a hopeless cause.

Again Modru's enraged screams resounded throughout the tower, and once more the bolt shot back and the small filthy form of the mute Rukh scuttled through the door, slamming it behind.

But this time the Evil One did not come, and after a long while the Rukh hobbled out.

The next 'Darkday Modru ranted, now promising to lay waste to the Land of Valon: "No horse, no rider, no filth of a Harlingar, nothing—not even the smallest blade of grass—shall escape my wrath!" And Laurelin then knew that at the Gûnarring Gap the Hyrania had suffered defeat at the hands of the Riders of Valon, and her heart sang.

*   *   *

Six more 'Darkdays passed, and Modru's maleficent boastings hissed unremittingly, and there was nought to buoy Laurelin's spirit. But on the seventh 'Day:

"Fools! They enter *my* darkness now," spat the Evil One. "And though my minions in the *Dubh* caverns are not yet able to come at them, I have broken off my attack against the Weiunwood and sent my Horde marching east along the Crossland Road to intercept this paltry Legion. These riders will rue the 'Day that they set forth to come against *me.*"

Laurelin knew not where this Legion was from nor where it was headed, yet she hoped with all her being that Modru's plans would be foiled.

On the next 'Darkday the window bar came loose. Laurelin took it from the casement and saw with relief that she could now squeeze her slight form through the resulting gap. Carefully she set the bar back into the sill so that all would appear normal to the casual eye.

Now she turned her mind and hands to the manufacture of a cloth-strip rope, and she set about acquiring more food for her journey across Gron: "Yrm, your evil lord wants me in perfect health," she couched her voice in hauteur and imperiously demanded of the mute Rukh, "yet how can I become hale when you bring me not enough provender to feed a sparrow? Shall I speak to your master of your neglect?"

The foul Rukh snarled at her, but each meal he brought thereafter held extra bread and more vegetables—turnips, potatoes, and the like.

And Laurelin began concealing food in a pillowcase she planned to use as a knapsack.

Each 'Darkday she plaited more of her escape rope, carefully tearing strips of her bedding sheets and twisting and tying and braiding the cloth, praying that it would hold her weight.

And each 'Darkday her Lōkken escort would take her to the battlements for her "fresh air." And still her eyes did not see and her mind could not imagine how she might escape.

*   *   *

But still she toiled onward.

And a week of 'Darkdays passed.

And on the seventh 'Darkday they came to remove the wrap from Laurelin's arm. It had been eight weeks and three 'Days since the time of her capture, when her arm had been broken, and a month since it had been lapped in the stiff binding. And while the nervous Rûkha worked, peeling away the layers of plastered cloth, Modru looked on and seethed in rage at events miles from the Tower:

"*Tsssth!* I would set a blizzard down upon this ragtag Legion that has come through Grûwen Pass and into Gron," sissed the Evil One, "a blizzard they would not survive. But I am forced to conserve my energies for the coming Darkest Day . . . Careful, fools! I would not have her arm broken again!"

A Legion in Gron? Laurelin's heart leapt with hope, but she gave no outward sign and instead watched the plastered cloth come loose. Laurelin was as anxious to see her arm as Modru seemed, for she knew she would need it to be strong and healthy for her climb down the rope when the time of her escape came.

At last the wrapping was off. Her right arm was thin, and the skin was scaly and sloughed off in large flakes. She could not straighten her elbow. And her muscles felt . . . stiff . . . fibrous.

"*Sssath!*" spat Modru, his vile eyes glaring malignantly through the hideous iron mask. "One week till the Sun-Death. That's all the time you have. You will carry a weight to straighten the limb. And you will flex the arm to strengthen it. And you will clean the skin, and treat it with oils. You will do this for hours each 'Day. And if you lag in your progress, *ssss,* I will have it done for you. For in one week will come that Darkest Day I have waited four thousand years to see. And you, my Princess, at that time must be . . . presentable."

Long grueling 'Days of pain and effort followed as Laurelin stressed and flexed and worked her arm, striving to straighten her elbow and bend it full, and to stretch the muscles and strengthen them. Slowly the arm began to respond as the tissues lost their fibrous feel and started to take on the tone and flexure of healthy sinews. She worked hard at restoring her arm not because Modru had so bade her; instead she did this so as to be able to climb down a rope and escape.

She did not know what Modru's long-awaited Darkest Day would bring, nor her role in it; yet she feared it, for she knew that it had something to do with Gyphon's return, and she planned to fly ere then. But her arm was terribly weak, and whether she would be able to manage the climb in but a few more days was questionable. Yet she worked with a single-minded determination.

And Modru came each 'Darkday to check her progress and sissed at her to work harder; yet he did not set his lackeys upon her to force her arm beyond its limits.

And each 'Darkday he hissed news of the War: "My Vulpen scouts slink upon their four legs and stay hidden in the scrub and track the ragtag Legion as they ride across Gron. *Ssss.* It seems as if these *fools* come to assault the Iron Tower itself! And the howls of my Vulpen report that this paltry Legion is but five thousand strong. *Fa!* Five thousand, where *fifty* thousand would fail! *Imbeciles!* Little do they know that my Horde marches upon their trail."

"Fools!" spat Modru the following 'Darkday. "Do they hope to stop me? Ten thousand of *my* minions against but two thousand or so of them? I shall batter through Grūwen Pass in less than a 'Day! Then once again will my Horde come after the ragtags."

The next 'Darkday, Modru did not come, and so the Princess learned nought of the conduct of the War. But the following 'Day she listened to the guttural slobberings of her Lōkken escort as she walked upon the battlements, for they spoke first of Modru, then of fighting in the south:

"He's in a foul mood, they say," said one guard.

"Har! When ain't he?" barked the other.

"Ar, you stupid gob," snarled the first, "I mean *worse* than a foul mood. I won't cross his path if I see him comin'."

"They say somethin's wrong at Grūwen. The Horde's been stopped by Men . . . and, *sss,* Elves," said the second

Lōkh. "And more Men camp on Claw Moor . . . a Legion, they say . . . comin' here!"

On Claw Moor! Laurelin's spirit leapt with hope, yet plummeted again when she thought of the impossibility of throwing down this mighty fortress.

The Lōkha said little else of interest as they led her back to her chamber, but Modru was there to inspect her arm. And what he said caused her heart to cry out to the Men coming toward the Iron Tower.

"*Ssss,* I will show these fools who come to my dark citadel. From Aven and from your Riamon, through the Jallor Pass to Jord, and thence by secret ways through the Gronfangs, my reavers come. And this puling ragtag Legion that now camps upon the moor . . . *tssah!* My Hèlsteed cavalry will soon slam the Gap shut behind them and fall upon them from the rear."

That 'Night, Laurelin sat in deep thought. Through all of Modru's hissings and rantings she had striven to strengthen her arm. And slowly it had improved. Soon, she felt, she could attempt her escape. But still she did not see how to accomplish it. And her daily walks out to the walls and around the battlements and then back to her chamber did nought to shed light on how she should set about fleeing.

And though she did not know who made up this "ragtag" Legion, her heart leapt with hope to hear that they came toward the Iron Tower and plunged in despair to hear that a great force of Ghola was now gathering to fall upon them from behind.

Yet she thought that if the Legion *did* come, then perhaps they would provide the diversion needed for her own escape. And it seemed as if indeed they were coming to the Iron Tower, and soon, for now they camped upon Claw Moor itself, and the moor led to the very gates of Modru's fortress.

The next 'Darkday the Princess was taken for her walk, and great turmoil filled the courtyards as Rukken horns blatted and Yrm rushed thither and yon, bearing weapons up to the battlements.

And when Laurelin strode up the ramparts and looked out through the crenellations, out through the Shadowlight, out upon the moor, there before her she saw arrayed a great force of horsemen, a forest of spears stirring to and fro.

And she gasped, and her heart hammered wildly, and her spirit soared up to the sky, and joy flooded her being.

For there flew the white and green of Valon . . .

And the scarlet and gold of Pellar . . .

And in the fore stood proudly the grey steed Wildwind, yet upon his back sat not High King Aurion, but instead a Man clad in scarlet armor—*the scarlet armor of . . . Lord Galen!*

Her beloved had come at last!

Laurelin caught her breath and tears filled her eyes, and she would have called out, but the Princess knew that the Legion was too far away to understand her words. Yet her heart cried out for her somehow to warn her Lord Galen that Ghola in force were even now riding from Jord into Gron to come to the Tower and fall upon the Legion from the rear. But she must not let the Lōkken escort know what she would shout, else when the warriors *did* come nigh enough to hear, she would not be permitted upon the walls.

Since she saw no way to give the warning, she held her tongue and brushed aside her tears as the Lōkha marched her along the ramparts. And all about her Yrm rushed to their stations and made ready their weapons: cauldrons of hot oil; sinuous bows and black-shafted arrows; scimitars, tulwars, dirks; hammers, cudgels, bludgeons, iron bars. Above the gate, with a harsh clatter of gears, Lōkha wound taut a great crank-bow, and they laid a spear-length iron-pointed shaft in the launch groove and pivoted the weapon upon its pedestal and aimed it at the Legion.

But Laurelin did not see this writhing turmoil atop the ramparts; her eyes were locked upon the figure of her beloved. She could not seem to see enough of him, and her gaze drank in his distant form, and her heart sang, for he had come at last. And as she was marched along the walls, she looked long at him. But at last she tore her eyes from the scarlet-clad figure upon the grey horse and turned her gaze to scan among the warriors of the Legion, searching for others she knew. And with a rush her heart leapt to her throat, for there was a horse she knew could be not any but Rust, and upon his back sat . . . Prince Igon! *Yet, how could this be?* With her very own eyes she had seen him slain at the waggon train! And she herself had given the command for Rust to flee. Yet here they were—and Igon was *Alive!*—and they stood before the gates of the Iron Tower.

She shook her head as if to clear it of phantoms, yet the Prince remained solid and real. And then she knew that, somehow, Igon had survived the cut of the Ghol tulwar that had cloven through the youth's steel helm and smashed him down.

Again her eyes scanned the fore of the Legion, and there was one she took to be Lord Gildor, yet she was not certain, for the Elf was not astride Fleetfoot.

There, too, were the small forms of—*Waerlinga!* But whether Sir Tuck, or Sir Danner, or Captain Patrel was among them, she did not see, for at that moment she was marched down from the walls and back to her chamber.

When the door was slammed shut and bolted, the Princess sat and tried to assemble her chaotic thoughts. At last much of Modru's disjoint hissings became clear in her mind: *This* was the Legion that had ridden north through the Dimmendark—a Legion from Valon, a Legion led by her beloved Lord Galen. Perhaps this was the same Legion that had defeated the Hyrania at the Gûnarring Gap. If so, then they had come north through Grûwen Pass and had left a rear guard behind to stave off a pursuing Horde. Yet, how came Lord Galen to be at the head of this force? And upon Wildwind? Where was Aurion King?

Fa! The answers to none of these questions mattered now. Instead, all that mattered was that she must warn Galen of the force of Ghola gathering to attack him.

And she had to warn Galen that Modru planned some great vileness in but two days, for that was when the Evil One's Darkest Day would arrive.

Laurelin began to pace the floor in agitation, for now more than ever she knew that she had to escape . . . Yet how? Although she could climb through the window and down, and perhaps win her way across the courtyard, still, how could she pass the walls? And how could she cross the ravine? Until she had an answer, did she dare attempt aught? For if she were caught in an unsuccessful try, Modru would lock her in other quarters—quarters with no windows, no bars, no hope of escape.

Moaning in distress, Laurelin jerked bolt upright in her bed, her eyes flying wide as she shocked awake from a hideous dream of terror and bondage. Her heart pounded frantically, and her entangled bedding was knotted and twisted about her and was wet with perspiration. Fragments of her nightmare clung to her mind like wisps of chill mist. Yet all she could remember of the dream was a great sucking maw of blackness coming to swallow her whole, and she could not flee, and behind her *Spaunen* had jeered and thrummed some monstrous instrument of torture.

As the Princess struggled free of the bedclothes, *Thuunn!* she heard the deep twanging sound of her nightmare, and it was followed by the raucous japing of Spawn.

For a moment Laurelin's dream terror struck at her heart; but she knew that what she heard now was real and not some phantom of sleep. She padded from her bed to the window, stepping behind the heavy drapes and peering out through the Shadowlight.

Thruum! There it was again! And amid the howling jeers of the *Spaunen,* the Princess could hear a harsh clatter of gears. Although she could not see it from her window, Laurelin knew that the great crank-bow on the battlements above the gate was being wound taut by Lōkha, soon to hurl another iron-pointed spear at the Legion.

Laurelin's eyes drifted to the courtyard below, and she gasped in dismay, for there, directly under her window, a pair of Lōkha stood watching as Rukken lackeys parcelled out gobbets of stringy meat and bowls of cold gruel to squads of Yrm coming from the walls. And to one side stood one of the corpse-foe—a Ghol watching o'er all. And even as she looked, he turned his dead black soulless eyes to her window, and his red gash of a mouth split in an evil grin, his rows of pointed teeth gleaming yellow in the Shadowlight.

Thuunn!

Tears welled in Laurelin's eyes, and she turned from the window and made her way back to the bed. And her heart despaired, for even though she did not know how she could have gotten past the ramparts and beyond the ravine, still she had thought that escape somehow might have been possible. Yet now she could not even climb down from her window, for that way led directly into the clutch of the *Spaunen* below.

That 'Darkday no Lōkken escort came to march her around the walls. Neither did Modru come. And the Princess knew that they prepared for War.

And all 'Day long Laurelin frequently checked the window, but the Yrm feeding station remained below. Her mind raced, yet no plan came to light as to how she could even escape her room, much less reach the ranks of the Legion.

And throughout the 'Day the deep-pitched *Thuunn!* of the spear-hurling crank-bow thrummed upon the wall.

The next 'Darkday, Laurelin paced her chamber as would a caged animal. Her mind screamed at her to *do something!* Yet just as loudly her thoughts cried, *What? What can I do?* She was dressed in her quilted Rukken garb, and she was ready to fly . . . but Yrm stood below her window, and the door to her chamber was bolted.

And this was the 'Day Modru had raved about: this was the Darkest Day.

Time lagged as moments turned into long spans of minutes, and the minutes dragged into hours, and the 'Day slowly seeped toward the time of the Sun-Death.

Laurelin frequently trod to her window, and yet nothing changed; and her heart despaired, and she felt as if something foul—something evil—was drawing nigh. But what it was, she did not know.

Now it was nearly mid of 'Darkday, and once more she strode to the window. And as she stood looking, a great hubbub broke out atop the walls. She could hear the harsh blats of Rukken horns. And there came the clash and clangor of weapons, and hoarse snarls and shouts, and she could see Yrm running upon the ramparts in the direction of the unseen gate.

And in the courtyard below, with harsh cries the Spawn beneath her window snatched up their weapons and rushed toward the uproar.

Now was her chance!

Quickly Laurelin donned her cloak and removed the window bar, setting the thick iron rod aside. She tied the cloth rope to a remaining bar and cast the braided line out the window, her knapsack tied to the distant end of the braid, where it dropped to within a few feet of the stone cobbles below.

As she tugged on the rope, testing the strength of her knot, she heard the enraged screams of Modru ringing throughout the tower, and there sounded the slap of feet running past her door.

There was a moment of silence, and then *Thunk!* the bolt on her door shot back, and although she could not see, she heard scrabbling footsteps hobble in and the door slam shut behind. There were the hash gasps of labored breathing, *and then the limping steps and blowing breath came straight toward the window!*

Behind the heavy drapes, her heart hammering, Laurelin silently took up the loose iron bar and raised it on high, girding herself to bring it crashing down upon the intruder's head in a killing blow, and then make good her escape.

CHAPTER 5

The Darkest Day

Astride Wildwind, King Galen turned his steel-grey eyes from the faint disk standing at its zenith in the southerly sky and looked eastward toward the Iron Tower. The dark battlements rose upward in the Shadowlight, the black fortress looming balefully in the Dimmendark. And in the forescape and curving beyond seeing 'round the stark walls, a black chasm gaped.

To Galen's left, Brega stood upon the frozen ground, his dark gaze surveying the bastion; the Dwarf stroked his forked beard and muttered under his breath. Upon Galen's right Lord Gildor sat ahorse, his own sight still locked upon the pale circle, wan in the darkling sky. And behind the King, drawn up in long files, sabers unsheathed and spears stirring to and fro, was mounted the High King's Legion.

"In but two 'Days comes the Sun-Death, Galen King," said the Elf, turning his eyes away from the faint glow and to the ramparts.

Galen merely grunted, his sight searching the stone of the dark citadel, seeking a weak chink through which the Legion could strike. And somewhere in the Kinstealer's holt his beloved Princess Laurelin was captive—if she still lived.

And in a rank immediately behind the King, the Warrows talked among themselves:

"Hoy, Tuck," exclaimed Danner, his voice low, "look at the central tower—the tall one."

"I see it, Danner. I see it." Tuck's voice was grim, for he too saw that all about the top of the spire a dark nimbus streamed. "Lord Gildor," called the buccan, "see you that black halo around the tallest tower?"

The Lian warrior shifted his gaze to the pinnacle. "Nay, Tuck, I do not. Your Waerling sight alone descries it."

"Perhaps in that tower lies some hideous device of the Evil One," speculated Patrel, his viridian eyes watching the fluxing blackness enshrouding the spire.

"Mayhap the heart of the Dimmendark lies in that pinnacle," suggested Merrilee after a moment. At her ominous words Tuck's heart hammered within his breast, for with his sapphirine gaze he saw the awful darkness pulsating forth. And in that moment Tuck knew that from this tower emanated not only the Shadowlight of the Dimmendark, but all of the evil that now beset Mithgar. The buccan shuddered at this thought, but said nought as all stared at the looming fortress.

Long moments they sat upon their steeds in silence and peered at the dark citadel, and then at last King Galen spoke: "Sound the call to make camp, and summon the scouts to me. Set the wards and pass the word to be ever vigilant, for we know not what Modru plans."

Ubrik raised his black-oxen horn to his lips and split the air with resonant calls, and the mounted ranks of the Legion broke for camp. And Galen once more donned his quilted jacket, for the High King had shown his colors and his armor to the enemy in challenge, but the foe had not deigned to answer.

Camp was made out upon the moor to the north and west of the drawbridge road; scouts were dispatched to encircle the dark citadel, to seek ways the Legion might enter into the fortress, and to spy out the paths by which the foe might issue forth to fall upon the Host.

Hours passed, and one by one the riders returned with the word that the ravine ringed all, that Wrg patrols paced the far side, and that atop the battlements Spawn warders jeered from afar. And the riders reported that there seemed to be no means of ingress or egress to or from the strongholt other than over the drawbridge and through the gate.

Now the Warrows set forth with the scouts, for it was suggested that in the Dimmendark their jewel-hued eyes might see fine detail of the fortress that Men's eyes saw not. Gildor and Flandrena went also, their Elvensight to probe the bastion. So, too, went Brega mounted behind

Flandrena upon Swiftmane, for, as the Dwarf said, "Châkka eyes will gaze upon these defences as well."

Long they searched while the weary Legion slept within a ring of warders, and the hours fell away. Yet these scouts, too—Men, Warrows, two Elves and a Dwarf—came at last to King Galen to report no success in their quest.

Thus did the 'Darkday pass.

Thuun! Tuck was awakened by a deep thrumming sound. He sat up in his blankets and rubbed sleep from his eyes and looked up to see Merrilee standing and gazing toward the dark fortress. Tuck, too, got to his feet; he stepped to her side and put an arm about her, and she leaned her head upon his shoulder without taking her eyes from the distant battlements.

"What is it, my dammia?" asked Tuck, peering toward the walls.

"I know not, Tuck," she answered. "I was awakened by . . . a sound."

Thuunn!

"There! There it is again!" exclaimed the damman. "And look!" She pointed.

Both Warrows saw a great shaft soar upward through the Shadowlight to arc down toward the Legion.

"Wha—what can hurl a spear like that?" breathed Tuck as he watched the flight of the shaft.

From behind them came the answer to Tuck's question: "The Wrg have a great crank-bow mounted above the gate." Marshal Ubrik stepped beside the Warrows, his eyes, too, following the flight of the spear.

The shaft lanced into the earth amid warriors scrambling to get out of the way, and the far-off gibes of Spawn jeered out from the walls and onto the moor.

Thrumm! The ballista hurled forth another spear to arc through the Shadowlight and strike among the Legion, and once more the hoots of the maggot-folk fleered from the battlements.

Feartoken, thought Tuck. *This is another feartoken of the Evil One.*

Yet Ubrik said, "Worry not here about this weapon, for where we now stand the shafts are easily avoided. The Spawn but use the crank-bow to harass us. It amuses them to see us jump. Only if we have to cross the drawbridge will it make a difference, and then it will fell warrior and steed alike. That is its purpose—to ward the bridge—and then it becomes a mighty weapon; then it is a most dread device."

· *Thuumm!*

All that early 'Darkday the strum of the crankbow sounded, but none of the warriors had yet been struck by the spears, for, as Ubrik had said, here the shafts were easily avoided. Yet as the 'Day crept forward, tempers began to fray, for the enemy hurled insults as well as spears, and the Legion did not strike back.

And as the noontide came, the faint glow of the pale disk began to show dimly—a glow that would last for but a quarter hour or less as the enfeebled darkling Sun rode past zenith in the Winternight sky.

Thumn!

Lord Gildor turned his eyes from the dimly seen disk. "Galen King, we must do something soon, for at this time on the morrow the Darkest Day will come."

Galen nodded and spoke: "Lord Gildor, it is in my mind that we must strike at the right time, a time that will upset Modru's plan. If we try too soon and fail, then our effort will have gone for nought. And if we wait too long, then no endeavor will succeed. Aye, we must strike at a time that will give us the best chance to distract the Evil One. Then, whether or no we succeed or fail to overthrow the fortress, still we may cause his plan to fall into ruin.

"Yet, you are right: We must do something soon. I deem now is the time to gather the War-council together to discuss Flandrena's plan." Galen turned and spoke to Fieldmarshal Ubrik: "Call the council unto me. Let us begin this War."

Tuck and Merrilee came last to the War-council, joining the circle already seated, taking their places between Danner and Patrel. Tuck's eyes swept 'round the ring—a ring of Men, Elves, Warrows, and a Dwarf. High King Galen sat before all, his visage stern. To his right was Prince Igon and then Marshal Ubrik and four more grim warriors of Valon. To Galen's left came two Elves and then the four

Warrows. And opposite Galen and completing the circle sat Brega, his Dwarven axe, Drakkalan, held across his lap in a two-handed grip.

Galen spoke: "You have all seen the quandary of Modru Kinstealer's holt: High are the ramparts and well warded by *Spaunen*. These walls *alone* would be difficult to o'ertop even had we the siege towers to do so; yet we do not, and no forest lies nearby to yield the timber for their construction. But e'en were a woodland nigh, still we could not surmount the walls by normal dint, for a mighty chasm rings the fortress entire—a chasm that has never yet been crossed by siege engine. Over this ravine is but one road into the holt, and that way passes across a drawbridge, a span now held tight 'gainst the bulwarks.

"This, then, is our problem: How do we bring the Legion to bear upon the Yrm within? How can we cross the chasm and top the walls and throw this dark citadel down?"

Galen let his questions hang upon the still air for a moment. Then he nodded to Flandrena, and the slim Elf's soft voice broke the silence: "Galen King, as you have said, there is no means at hand to build the mighty siege engines needed to span the gulf and top the walls. Yet even if there were the means, still we have not the time to construct them ere the Darkest Day arrives. Hence I deem we have no choice but to try this plan: While the Legion provides a diversion, a small force must go in secret to scale first the ravine and then the walls of Modru's fortress, as Vanidor, Duorn, and Varion did. And then this squad must gain the drawbridge winch and lower the bascule while raising the portcullis. And when this is done, elements of the Legion can charge across the span and into the courtyards within and engage the Horde until the Host entire arrives.

"Aye, it is a simple plan, but it is the only one I deem can succeed in the allotted time. Yet the plan is fraught with danger, for much has changed since Vanidor, Duorn, and Varion scaled the walls: Now *Rûpt* patrols walk the ravine at the base of the ramparts. Now *Spaunen* teem upon the bulwarks. And the route taken by my brethren up the chasm side no longer can be used, for now there is a station along the lip of the ravine near the crevice they climbed—a station used by the *Rûpt* as a reporting place for their chasm patrols.

"Still the crevasse can be climbed; yester 'Darkday Drimm Brega and I searched for another way up that far chasm side, and his eyes found one."

Flandrena held out his hand toward Brega, and the Dwarf stood to speak, still holding Drakkalan in a two-handed grip.

"King Galen, like all the Châkka well do I know stone." Brega's rough voice held a note of pride. "And among my Folk I am accounted a good climber. Yet this I say unto you: that ravine has been worked by Grg pick to thwart easy access up the sides, for it is mattock-smoothed for most of its length. The place where Vanidor and his comrades climbed was one of the few places where the rift wall can be scaled, and that is only because the cleft fissures most deeply, and for the Grg to have smoothed it would have undermined the battlements.

"Yet, given time, any section of the ravine could be scaled, using rocknails and jams and rings and rope. But we have not the time for a slow climb, and even if we did, the sounds of our hammers would bring the Squam running. Nay, what we must do is mount up swift and silent, and there is but one place to do so: 'round on the eastern side of the fortress, where an outjut clambers from bottom to rim.

"But the stone at that place is layered, and subject to crumbling under stress. And so the climb will be danger-ous—not only because of the Grg patrols and Squam upon the battlements, but also because the stone may give way and carry the climbers to their deaths.

"This then is what I propose: I will take a small squad up that ravine side, for I have the skills to lead that climb. But those who come with me must be, first of all, good climbers and, second, light of weight, so as not to stress the stone. Lastly, they must be of a stature to pass for Ůkh, Hrōk, or Khōl, for we must still climb the battlements and then march as a Grg squad along the ramparts and to the distant gate."

Amid a murmur among the War-council, Brega sat back down crosslegged and laid Drakkalan across his lap.

"Drimm Brega," Lord Gildor spoke up, "what weight can a warrior be and still not break the stone?"

"Elf Flandrena is slim enough, Elf Gildor," answered

Brega, "but you are taller, heavier, and I would advise King Galen to send only those of Elf Flandrena's weight or less."

Again a murmur ran 'round the War-council, and Ubrik protested: "But Dwarf Brega, that would rule out most if not all of the Vanadurin. Aye, it is true that we Harlingar have little or no experience climbing stone, for we ride the flat grassy plains and come not often into the mountains. Still, your words would rule out all Men from this mission."

"Not all Men, Marshal Ubrik." The speaker was young Prince Igon. "I deem I fall under Flandrena's weight. And I have scaled many a wall."

At Igon's words a look of distress crossed Galen's face, but he said nought.

"But that is only three." The words came from one of the Vanadurin, Raiklen by name. "Who else can undertake this mission?"

Patrel stood. "We can go."

Ubrik groaned. "King Galen, I deem we send but lads on a Man's mission."

Brega growled and leapt to his feet, his dark eyes blazing in ire. "*I* am no lad, Man Ubrik! And Flandrena holds a hundred times your years. Prince Igon is young, it is true, yet I know of his feats and I would have him with me. And as to the Waerans, I have walked through darkness with one at my side, and no finer comrade, no better warrior, could I ask for." Brega stepped to Tuck and placed a gnarled hand on the buccan's shoulder. "This Waeran helped slay the Ghath—the Gargon. Have you warriors in your company who can say the same?"

Tuck felt embarrassed to be the center of all attention, and he was surprised at Brega's fervent outburst, yet at the same time a quiet pride filled his being, for Brega's words meant much to the buccan.

Tuck stood and spoke: "I would not debate that there are better warriors in this company than I am. Yet, as I understand it, this mission calls for those who can climb and are of slight weight. Among the Warrows are some who fill this need: Danner for one, and I, for many a time we have clambered up the stone face of the High Hill near Woody Hollow. And we are skilled with bow and arrow . . . and in a pinch I have been known to use this." Tuck flashed Bane from scabbard and held it on high, and the blade-jewel streamed blue flames down the sharp edges, shouting of the nearby fortress filled with evil Spawn from the Untargarda, from Neddra.

The Men of Valon gasped to see such a potent token of power in the hands of a Waldan, and they looked upon the Wee One with a new respect.

Tuck sheathed the blade. "There is this, too, Marshal Ubrik, said by one of your own riders upon the banks of the Argon. We are squatty, the likes of Rutcha . . . given the slightest disguise. Only we can hope to march upon yon ramparts—cloaks soiled, hoods up, snarling among ourselves—and stand a chance of reaching the gate unchallenged. For we will have the look of a squad of Rūcks—the Warrows and Dwarf Brega—and Prince Igon and Flandrena will be our Hlōk masters."

Tuck sat down, his words done, and none said aught for a time. Then King Galen spoke: "So be it, then. We shall try this plan. Captain Patrel, how many of the Waerlinga can ascend stone? And Marshal Ubrik, what diversion can we provide to distract the Spawn and give Brega's climb a chance? And lastly, Warrior Brega, how long will you take, and when should we strike? Tomorrow is the Darkest Day."

And so the planning went forth, and none but Tuck noted the quiet tears sliding down Merrilee's face, for she knew full well she had not the skills to make the climb, just as she knew that her buccaran did: Tuck would go without her.

In the end, along with Brega, Flandrena, and Igon, six Warrows were selected to go: Tuck, Danner, Patrel, Rollo Breed, Harven Culp, and Dink Weller. Of all that company, Flandrena had the least experience climbing stone, though he *had* clambered among the crags of Arden Vale; yet his skill was deemed enough for him to join the raiders. Too, his green eyes burned with an inner flame that cried out for the revenge of his lost comrades—Vanidor, Duorn, and Varion—and none would deny him the right to go.

And when all the planning was done, King Galen gave over the Atalar Blade to Patrel, the long-knife a sword in the Warrow's hand. "Take this edge, Captain Patrel, for it cleaves Evil. This was the blade that hacked into the

Krakenward to spare Lord Gildor. I deem you might need such a weapon upon those walls; it will serve you well."

Patrel took the silvery blade from its scabbard and gazed at the golden runes. "I will bear this sword in honor, King Galen," said the Warrow. And then he sheathed the weapon and girted it to his waist.

Ubrik barked an order in Valur to the Vanadurin in the War-council, and swiftly, long-knives were given over to all the Warrows, Ubrik's own blade going to Danner. And though the Wee Folk knew little of sword play, they graciously accepted the gifts, for they knew well that these edges would be needed ere their dangerous enterprise came to an end.

That 'Night, Tuck held Merrilee in his arms as she wept softly, for on the morrow he would depart with the raiders on their desperate mission to open the way. They would set out six hours ere the Sun-Death—a scant six hours ere the blackest depth of the Darkest Day. And no one, perhaps not even Adon, knew their destiny.

The time drew nigh, and before the High King stood the nine climbers: Brega, Flandrena, Prince Igon, Tuck, Danner, Patrel, Rollo, Harven, and Dink. Grime had been smeared on the faces of the raiders and filth splashed upon their clothes to give them a Rūckish look.

King Galen stepped to their ranks, and one by one he embraced them each, saying a few words to most. But when he clasped Tuck unto him, and then Igon, Galen said nought, for he did not trust his voice. Lastly, he gruffly hugged Brega and gripped the Dwarf's gnarled hand, saying, "Lead them well, Warrior Brega, for on this climb depends the fate of all Mithgar."

Tuck's heart hammered to hear such words—*the fate of all Mithgar*—but Brega merely grunted and nodded.

Now King Galen stepped back from the raiders and spoke to them all: "Once again the world is faced by the forces of darkness, and once again an alliance of Men, Elves, Dwarves, and Wee Folk is called upon to cast Evil down, and, yea, once again the fortune of the world pivots on the valor of but a few.

"The Evil One squats in his dark tower like a bloated

spider and spins his vile webs of doom to the woe of the world, for he would snare the hearts of all free things and bind them in despair.

"Yet Modru is but a shadow servant of the Great Evil, and perhaps it is Gyphon's will we see at work here.

"We know not what the darkest hour of the Darkest Day will bring, yet it will be utterly evil, of that we can be certain. And we must do all that is within our power to deflect Modru's vile plan, and in doing so, perhaps we can save Mithgar from a hideous doom.

"I cannot promise you that we will be victorious; yet hearken: If we are to suffer defeat, to perish, then let us rain havoc upon our foe as we ourselves fall. And if we can cause the ruin of Modru's evil scheme, even in defeat we will have won.

"I have but one more thing to say, and it is this: May your eyes be keen, your shafts fly true, and your blades be sharp. And may Adon go with you."

Galen fell silent, and no one spoke for a moment. Tuck looked to see Merrilee weeping, and unshed tears stung his own eyes. Yet there echoed through his mind High King Galen's words: *. . . the fate of all Mithgar . . . the fortune of the world pivots on the valor of but a few . . .* And Tuck thought, *Oh, Adon, this crushing burden, I have not the strength to bear it . . .*

Yet ere Tuck's thoughts could run on, Brega cleared his throat and growled, "We'll not ope' the gate if we stand here all day. Come, let us clamber through a black ravine and up a dark wall. The fortress awaits, but the Sun and Moon do not."

And as the raiders turned to go, Merrilee flung herself forward and fiercely embraced Tuck, and attempted to smile through her tears. And she tried to speak, yet all she could utter was "Tuck, oh Tuck, my buccaran . . ." before she burst into tears.

And Tuck tenderly kissed her and said, "Don't cry, my dammia," as tears slid down his own cheeks, "for I shall return. After all, I wear your favor, a silver locket, and it has borne me through much."

Lord Gildor stepped forward and knelt beside the dam-man and put an arm around her as Tuck gently disengaged. Merrilee buried her face in the Elf's chest and sobbed uncontrollably as Tuck turned and ran to catch up to the others on their way to save the world.

"See, there it is," said Brega softly, pointing at the far wall of the ravine. "There's where we'll make the climb up."

The raiders lay upon the backslant of an upjut of rock and stared across the wide abyss yawning just ahead.

Along with Ubrik and a scout named Aric and the buccan Burt Arboran, the nine climbers had ridden from Galen's camp west, away from the black fortress and out into the Shadowlight until they had gotten beyond the pry of the evil gaze of the warders upon the walls. Yet it was not only eyes upon the walls that they had sought to elude: Vulg spies, too, had concerned them, and a small force of Men had ridden out before the raiders to draw Modru's curs away. Hoping that no Vulgs watched them, the raiders then had circled to the eastern side of the stronghold, the steeds of the Warrows and Brega in tow behind Ubrik, Igon, Flandrena and Aric. They had come 'round to the point facing where they would climb, then had turned and ridden straight toward the distant ramparts until once again the eyes of the Men could just make out the distant bulk of the dark bastion; and all the raiders had dismounted and taken down their weapons and the long coils of rope, and had handed Ubrik the tethers of their steeds.

Ubrik had saluted each of the nine and then had spoken an ancient Vanadurin benediction: "May the smiling countenance of Fortune's three faces be turned your way." And so saying, he had spurred back out into the Dimmendark, the string of horses running after.

Leaving the scout and Burt behind—Burt's Warrow eyes to keep track of the mission from afar—the raiders had turned and begun making their way toward the stronghold, flitting silently and one at a time from rock outcropping to brush to mound to ground crevice, using whatever cover they could find. And they slowly had made their way to the crevasse bering the fortress walls.

And now the raiders lay upon the upjut of rock and peered through the Shadowlight at the gulf and, beyond, at the ramparts of Modru Kinstealer's holt.

"*Ssst!*" hissed Dink. "Up on the wall above: a sentry."

Tuck peered across and upward, and his heart plummeted, for high upon the rampart opposite he could see the distant form of a Rūck warder slowly pacing along the parapet, the sentry passing in and out of view as he trod along the castellated walls with its merlons and crenels.

"Rach!" muttered Igon, "we can't make the climb under his very nose. Can we not clamber through the ravine elsewhere?"

Slowly the Rūck paced to a corner, then turned and trudged back.

"Nay," growled Brega, his voice bitter. "It is here or not at all." A questioning look upon his face, the Dwarf turned to Flandrena.

"Your memory does not deceive you, Drimm Brega," Flandrena's soft voice answered the Dwarf's unspoken question. "The guard was not here when we surveyed the crevasse."

"Well, we're going to have to get rid of him or let him watch us climb," hissed Igon. Then the Prince turned to Patrel. "Captain Patrel, can your arrows reach him?"

Once more the Rūck turned and paced back the way he had come.

Patrel shook his head. "Mayhap if I had Grayling's fabled bow I could bring the Rūck down, but without that magic weapon, I have not the skill to make such a shot."

"Danner," said Tuck. "Only Danner might be able to do it."

"Wha—what?" hissed Danner. "Tuck, your mouth speaks what your mind knows is not true. No one can make that shot. Oh, aye, perhaps I can cast an arrow that far, but so can we all. Yet to loose it with accuracy . . . well, it cannot be done. Remember Old Barlo's words: 'The arrow as strays might well'er been throwed away.' Only in this case the straying arrow will clatter upon the wall or against a turret or into a courtyard. And *then* the maggot-folk *will* be warned of our coming."

"You have no choice, Waeran Danner," growled Brega. "We must make the climb, else all is lost. We cannot climb with the Grg there. You have the greatest skill with the bow."

Brega fell silent, his argument done, yet Danner's amber

eyes followed the distant guard and still the buccan did not take up his bow.

Flandrena's soft voice spoke: "Though you would not choose to do this thing, believing it will bring ruin, circumstance dictates no other course. It is ever so in War that choice oft is taken from us. Yet think on this: if you do not try, then our mission is ended here and now; if you try, and miss, and alert the *Rûpt,* then again our mission will have failed; but if you try, and succeed . . ."

Muttering under his breath, Danner slid over the slant of the rock to the level ground below. Tuck and Patrel jumped down to join him while the others remained above, watching the guard. Danner took all of his arrows from his quiver and sighted down the shaft of each, choosing this one, discarding that one, taking up another and comparing it to the one just selected. He winnowed and culled until at last he held but three arrows, and these he carefully scrutinized—point, shaft, fletching, nock, weight, balance— and in the end he made his choice.

Now Danner stepped to the edge of the upjut, and his eyes swept o'er the nearby 'scape and up to the patrolling Rūck. "I'll try it from that outcropping over there. It will give me a slightly better angle for this impossible shot."

"Do you want someone to go with you?" asked Patrel.

"No!" Danner's voice was sharp, then softened: "Ar, Paddy, no. It'll be hard enough keeping my concentration without someone breathing down my neck. Thanks but no thanks, Paddy, this one I'll do alone."

Danner turned to go. "Good luck," whispered Harven, and so said they all; and then Danner scuttled away while the Rūck's back was to them as he paced atop the wall.

Tuck and Patrel clambered back upon the stone and watched as Danner flitted through the Shadowlight across the snow to the nearby outcropping, where he slid into the darkness at the base of the stone. And then Danner paused long, seeming to do nought; but the Woody Hollow buccan was watching the Rūck sentry trod to and fro on his station, his form now shielded by a merlon, now exposed through a crenel, only to be shielded then exposed again as he slowly marched on. And Tuck knew that Danner was counting to himself, timing the Rūck's measured step, gauging the distance and reckoning the length of time the arrow would be in flight.

Now Danner took up his bow and set the selected arrow to string, and then the buccan stood beside the stone and drew the bolt to the full and aimed across the ravine and up toward the pacing guard.

But then Danner relaxed the pull and set the bow and shaft aside and removed his Elven-made cloak. Then he took up the weapon once more and again drew the quarrel to the full.

But again Danner relaxed his aim, for a thin chill wind had sprung up. Slight it was, yet it would deflect the arrow in flight, and the buccan had to take it into account.

Once more an eternity passed as Danner estimated the needed windage, but at last he again drew and aimed.

"Hsst!" Flandrena sharply drew a breath through clenched teeth and pointed northward along the base of the wall; and Tuck looked and saw one of the ravine patrols marching southward on the far flank of the chasm.

Danner, don't shoot! Tuck's thoughts silently cried, for he knew that if the warder atop the wall were felled, then the mission would be detected by the oncoming Rūcks.

"Patrel, Rollo, Harven, Dink," whispered Tuck urgently, "ready your bows. We may have to slay them all . . . if we can."

"If this patrol is slain," breathed Patrel, as all the buccen nocked arrows, "then others will come looking when this bunch doesn't report in. Let us pray that Danner does not shoot."

Yet Danner, too, had seen the ravine patrol, and he once more lowered his bow and slipped deeper into the darkness of his outcropping.

And at that very same moment, upon the wall a second figure, a Hlōk, stepped into view and watched as the Rūcken squad tramped nigh. "Har, yar!" the Hlōk called from the rampart to those below, his grating voice sounding down the wall and pitching outward to echo from the crevasse. "Has yer spotted anythin'?"

"Nar!" shouted up the Hlōk leader of the marching Rūcks. "Nothin's in this stupid hole in the ground!"

"Keep your gummy eyes open, then," yawped down the other. "They say somethin's astir on the far side, north of the gate." After receiving an affirmative grunt from below, the Hlōk above snarled at the sentry and spun on his heel and left the rampart, disappearing from view.

Grumbling and jostling and cursing one another, the ravine patrol marched below the sentry and to the south, passing opposite the raiders and going onward. And on the wall the Rūck warder glared over his shoulder in the direction his Hlōk master had gone, then leaned upon his hands in a crenel and watched the squad tramp away. And so, too, did the Elf, Man, Dwarf, and Warrows watch as the Rūcks marched on.

And time passed.

But at last the patrol tramped out of sight beyond a buttress, and once more the sentry took up his pacing.

And once more Danner took up his bow . . .

And arrow . . .

And counted time . . .

And gauged the distance . . .

And estimated the windage . . .

And drew . . .

And aimed . . .

And Tuck's eyes flicked from Danner to sentry and back again.

And the Rūck paced toward the corner.

And with his heart in his throat and his inner core wound tight as a spring, Tuck's mind screamed, *Shoot, Danner, shoot! For Adon's sake, shoot!*

Thuun! Danner shot. And the arrow was in flight, arcing upward through the Dimmendark. And the sentry passed from open crenel to shielding merlon. Now the arrow hurtled through its zenith and began hissing downward, and the eyes of all the raiders were locked upon the crenel where the Rūck would next appear, but had not. Now the bolt gathered speed as it sissed down, hurling toward the vacant slot . . . and it struck the Rūck in the throat as he stepped forth into the open! With a clatter, the sentry dropped the pike he had borne and clutched at his neck and staggered forward, toppling from the corner in the wall to fall silently down the rampart face to land with a sodden thud on the edge of the ravine. And then the corpse slid over the rim and down into the blackness below.

Danner had done it! He had made the impossible shot!

Behind the rock outcropping, Tuck and Patrel grabbed one another in rib-creaking hugs and clamped their jaws shut to keep from shouting for joy. Igon pounded Brega's back, and Flandrena's eyes sparkled, while Rollo and Dink and Harven held hands and danced around in soundless circles.

Then Tuck and Patrel flitted through the Shadowlight and across the snow to the outcropping where Danner stood. And there they found the buccan with his face buried in his hands.

"It couldn't be done, Tuck. It couldn't be done, Paddy." Danner's voice broke as the tears slid down his cheeks, the buccan weeping with the sudden release of unbearable tension.

"But you did it, Danner, you did it," whispered Tuck, embracing the Warrow.

Patrel took Danner's cloak up off the ground and gently draped it around the crying buccan and fastened it at the throat; and Patrel, too, embraced Danner, then softly said, "Let's go, buccoes, we've a ravine to cross, a wall to climb, and a gate to open."

And so, taking up their bows, the three buccen made their way back to the other outcropping, where they found Brega, Igon, and Rollo anchoring soft pliable Elven-made ropes to the rock—ropes brought from Arden Vale upon Flandrena's pack-horse and borne hence into Gron. For ere he had set out to venture again unto the Iron Tower, the Elf had suspected that another attempt to scale the wall of the crevasse might become necessary.

Three long lines were cast over the edge of the ravine to drop all the way to the bottom. Then, because only Brega knew the art of rappelling, he showed each of them how to wrap the line under one thigh, across the body, and over a shoulder so as to slip over the edge and walk backwards down the wall of the crevasse.

And while a fourth line was used to lower weapons and extra ropes into the blackness below, the raiders began their descent, three at a time, Tuck, Igon, and Flandrena going first. With his heart pounding and one hand high and one hand low and using his legs and feet to fend, Tuck stepped backwards over the lip of the yawning darkness.

It seemed to take Tuck forever, the rope slowly slipping

through his gloved hands and sawing around his body, his feet at times scrabbling upon the icy rock. And three times he lost contact with the stone and freely twisted and turned like a trapped insect on a spider's strand—or a victim on the gallows. But at last Tuck came to the bottom as Igon reached up in the darkness to brace him, while Flandrena untied the weapons and gear from the fourth line and shook it to signal Brega that all were down and safe.

The fourth line was hauled up through the ebon shadows, only to return with three more sets of weaponry as another trio of raiders rappelled down: Patrel, Dink, and Harven. And when they came to the bottom, once more Flandrena signalled Brega.

The last of the weapons were lowered and the final three raiders came down: Brega plummeting down the rope almost as if he were falling, while Danner and Rollo descended more slowly.

Armed once more and bearing Elven ropes, all followed Brega through the jagged boulders and stone rubble and scree bestrewn across the crevasse bottom; and slowly they made their way through the darkness to the opposite side to come to the layered outjut rising up to the distant rim.

Brega reached forth with a gnarled hand and grasped the stone, and it flaked and crumbled under his grip. "Bad rock," growled the Dwarf. "Worse than I thought. Yet still we must climb it. Use hands and feet to spread your weight, and move only one limb at a time while supporting yourself with the other three. And if we come to places where it is possible, lay your whole body against the stone to spread the load even more.

"We will rope ourselves together so that if one of us slips the others can support him; and let us hope that no single fall will carry all of us to our deaths.

"I will go first and test every step of the way. My instructions are to be passed back down the line as each of you in turn comes to the same place; and my words are to be followed to the letter.

"And this shall be our climbing order: I go first, followed by Elf Flandrena, then Prince Igon, Danner, Harven, Tuck, Rollo, Dink, and lastly Patrel.

"Roll your cloaks and sling your weapons across your

backs and shoulders; they must be out of the way and not
entangle you nor hamper your ability to climb.

"Now let us tie ourselves together and begin this journey
up the rotten stone."

Soon the cloaks and weapons—bows, arrows, swords,
long-knives, and axe—were secured across the climbers'
shoulders, and the nine were roped together. Brega turned
to the outjut and began the slow ascent, Flandrena and the
others creeping up after.

When Tuck started up, sixth in line, he could feel the
stone flake and crumble under his grip, and pebbles and
grains of rock slithered down from those above. And the
buccan felt as if at any moment the entire face of the ravine
could come crashing down. He wondered how those ahead
of him felt, for they were heavier than he. Then it was that
Tuck realized how Brega had selected the climbing order—
by weight, the heaviest first, the lightest last, for the stone
grew weaker with each passing climber. Yet at the same
time, Tuck knew that in any event Brega would have gone
first, for only he could lead this climb.

And slowly they crept up the crumbling outjut, now all
nine climbers upon the face of the ravine. And Brega
cursed, for the stone was much worse than it had seemed
from afar. At times the climb came to a complete standstill
while the Dwarf searched for a route onward. And these
were the worst moments for Tuck, for he could feel the
rock slowly disintegrating under his grasp, and he strained
to maintain his hand-and footholds, while at the same time
striving to stress not the stone. And as the nine inched up
through the rain of flakes and sand, whispered instructions
from Brega were passed back down the line as each came
to those same places: *Grasp the crevice to the left . . . Put
no burden on the round outcrop . . . 'Ware the slab, it is
loose . . . This ledge is solid and will bear all your heft . . .*

Time eroded past like the sand slithering down the face
of the ravine, moments gradually edging into minutes, and
minutes into hours. And still the raiders struggled on.

As he toiled upward, salty sweat ran down Tuck's forehead and stung his eyes, and his entire body was covered
with perspiration. His harsh gasping breath came through
jaw-clenched teeth, and his arms and legs trembled from
the agonizing strain. His stomach felt as if it were tied in

knots, for the stone crumbled and shifted under him, and the bottom of the ravine was lost in blackness some ninety or one hundred feet below. And his heart hammered in his breast, partly from the labor, partly from the strain, partly from the fear. All he wanted to do was simply rest; but even when he stopped there was no relief, for even then the wall eroded in his grasp. And the raiders continued the long upward struggle o'er the disintegrating rock, the lip of the crevasse now but yards above Brega's head.

Stop! The command relayed down the chain of climbers. Brega had come to an impasse: the stone just below the rim was the weakest of all. Long did the Dwarf search, carefully sidling both left and right, and the scree slithered down. Flandrena just below the Dwarf, clung to the face of the sheer, while Igon, next, stood on a narrow ledge. And those below the Prince clung to knob and crevice and slab while standing in cracks and upon outjuts.

At last Brega said, "*Kruk!* It is all of it more rotten than ever and may not bear my weight, yet here will I try it, for this place is least weak. May the spirit of First Durek guide my way."

And Brega started up the unsound stone, testing, probing, then slowly shifting his weight upon the crumbling rock. Pebbles rattled down upon those below as the Dwarf inched his way toward the top, now but a few feet above his reach.

Up he crept, and a rock gave way 'neath his right foot and crashed down. Brega threw himself flat against the wall and clung with two hands and his left foot while he sought purchase with the right. At last his boot found a crack, and he rested but a moment, then went on.

And the rim was nearly in his grasp.

Slowly his trembling fingers stretched for the lip—just inches away—and then his hand fumbled o'er the rim, and gripped it, and he began to haul upwards.

But at that moment, with a sharp *Crack!* the slab he stood upon gave completely away and hurtled downward, and the Dwarf was left dangling by the fingertips of his left hand. Yet whether or not Brega could have held on will never be known, for the slab tumbled down and knocked Flandrena from the wall; and the Elf fell, his rope jerking the Dwarf's grip loose, and they both plunged downward amid crashing stone and falling rock.

Prince Igon was next in line, and he braced himself as rocks and Flandrena and Brega tumbled past. The line between the Elf and the Man snapped taut as Flandrena plummeted to the limit, and the shock wrenched Igon's grip loose and jerked him down upon the ledge; then Brega hit the end of his line, and Igon was dragged over the jagged edge. But the youth's grip clutched a narrow crevice, and he held on with all the strength he could muster, for he knew that if he fell then all nine would be carried to their doom.

Now Igon got his other hand in the notch, and his left foot found purchase, and then his right. Grinding his teeth, he held on, concentrating all of his strength into clinging to the ravine wall. And below him—dazed—an Elf and a Dwarf swung pendulously, while Warrows watched as their lives and the fate of their mission hung in the balance, depending upon the strength and grit of a high-born youth.

And Igon not only held on, but slowly, *against the full weight of Brega and Flandrena,* pulled himself back upon the ledge! And he struggled to a standing position and, gasping, turned and took hold of the rope and braced his back against the ravine wall!

Danner and Harven, closest to Flandrena—one above, one below—began to sidle across the face of the ravine wall toward the stunned Elf, stone crumbling and showering down. But Brega—quickly recovering and finding a fingerhold here and a toehold there, hence taking much of the strain off Prince Igon—barked at the two Warrows, "Nay, move not on this rotten stone. Return to the path I climbed. I will aid Flandrena."

Testing each foot of the way, the Dwarf clambered up toward the dangling Elf; but ere Brega arrived, the Lian warrior came to his senses and grasped the layered stone, taking the last of the strain off the now-trembling youth above.

"Elf Flandrena," Brega's voice was low yet filled with anxiety, "how fare you? Are you injured?"

"Nay, Drimm Brega," answered the Lian, "I am not injured. Mayhap bruised, but nothing is broken."

"How fare the rest of you?" Brega asked the others.

"I feel as if I've lifted a horse," softly answered Igon, "yet I'm hale."

"Nought but pebbles rattled down on me," whispered Danner, now back upon the climbing path.

"Yar, me too," came Harven's quiet reply.

"I think my foot may be broken," gritted Tuck in pain. "One of the larger rocks smashed down on it."

"I'm all right," softly called Rollo, "and Dink and Patrel say they're fit, too."

"Tuck, you will just have to put up with it till we reach the top," hissed Brega, "then we will take a look."

Once more the Dwarf slowly inched up the ravine wall—Flandrena creeping behind—while all the other raiders held their positions on the crumbling face. After a long while, once more Brega came to the stone of the rim.

"Hmph," grunted the Dwarf, "the rock uncovered by the fall seems sturdier."

Now Brega began climbing the last critical few feet. Cautiously he went, again testing every grip, every foothold. And all eyes watched up through the falling sand and rattling pebbles; and suddenly the Dwarf was gone from sight as he crawled over the lip of the ravine and onto the rim beyond.

Now Flandrena began, and his climb went more quickly, for Brega, on firm ground above, hauled upon the line.

And as the Elf went up, Prince Igon advanced, too, and so did they all, Tuck climbing in spite of the excruciating pain in his left foot; and the Warrow could feel something *grind* each time the foot bore weight.

Now Flandrena and then Igon disappeared over the edge, and with the three—Dwarf, Elf, and Man—all pulling on the line, the Warrows swiftly went up the face of the ravine and over the top: Danner first, Patrel last.

Flandrena looked up at the raiders gathered 'round Tuck. "Indeed, it does seem broken," said the Elf. "Yet I cannot say for certain unless we remove the boot; but if we do, the foot will swell, so I deem it best to leave it shod. In any case, Tuck cannot go on. Our climb has taken overlong, for less than an hour remains until the Sun-Death—and we have much yet to do. I think . . . nay, I *know,* we must leave Tuck behind."

"What?" hissed Danner. "You cannot be serious. We can't leave him behind. The ravine patrols—"

"We have no choice, Danner," interrupted Brega. "We *must* go on. Up that wall." The Dwarf pointed at the nearby rampart. "True, it will be easier to climb than the ravine, for the wall has projections, and it is sturdy. Even so, it is beyond a broken-footed Waeran's power to mount it."

"No—" Danner started to object, but again he was interrupted:

"He's right Danner," said Tuck, smiling in spite of the fact that his heart was sinking. "They're both right. And though none has said it, for me to try to come with you would endanger the raid beyond measure. You've *got* to leave me behind. You *must* continue the mission. And none can stay with me, for all are needed to drop the bridge and raise the gate." Tuck raised his hand to forestall Danner's objections. "I know: the ravine patrols will come by, and soon. Well, help me to that jumble of rocks yon, and I will hide out as they draw nigh. But me no buts, Danner, for there is *no* other choice. Hurry now! For you all must be on your way."

And so the raiders carried Tuck to a pile of boulders next to the base of the wall. And with tears in his eyes, Danner fastened Tuck's cloak about the broken-footed buccan's shoulders. And Tuck hoarsely whispered, "Thanks, bucco . . . now go! I'll be all right."

At that moment there came to their ears the juddering howls of roving Vulgs. *"Hsst!"* breathed Flandrena sharply. "Modru's curs. We must hasten, for they may have spied us." With quick farewells to their injured comrade, the raiders swiftly returned to the corner and began to climb upward. And, blinking back tears, Tuck watched them go.

Upward the eight began to climb, the outjutting stones on the angle of the wall giving them easy purchase—for when the fortress had been constructed, Modru had not dreamed that any could gain these walls to scale. But suddenly the raiders froze, dark blots on a dark wall.

Wha—Tuck wondered why they stopped. Then he saw: a ravine patrol! Coming this way!

Pain lancing through his foot, Tuck scuttled backwards into the boulders. And the patrol came on: snarling, jostling Spawn. Tuck's eyes followed the Rūcks' progress. *Don't look up!* he willed the maggot-folk. *Keep your eyes down!*

And the dark shapes of the eight climbers moved not.

Onward came the squabbling patrol, now even with, now striding past the rampart corner, passing below the silent raiders frozen but a few feet above.

Then the quarreling *Spaunen* were beyond the corner, and they had not glanced up. Tuck breathed a sigh of relief and slithered further back among the jumble of rock, where he no longer could see the patrol.

Yet hark! It sounded as if the Rūcks—or at least some of them—were coming toward the rocks of the Warrow's hiding place!

Desperately, his foot shooting agony up his leg, Tuck scrambled even deeper among the boulders, squirming through small crevices between the huge stones, shoving his bow and quiver ahead of him. He crawled over a rusted iron grate lying between two huge rocks and squeezed forward into a black hole but barely large enough for him to enter.

Behind he could hear the muffled sounds of maggot-folk speaking the harsh Slûk tongue. Trying not to grunt, Tuck wriggled onward in the blackness, the hole so tight that he could not raise his head.

Ten feet he went, then twenty, the stone scraping along his chest and back; and he prayed that he would not get stuck as he pressed on; and there were places where he had to exhale just to go forward, but forward he went, for he knew that if he tried to back up, his own cloak and jacket would roll up along his body and jam him tight. And so, not really wanting to go ahead but afraid to back up, Tuck wriggled on.

Tuck did not know exactly how far forward he struggled to get through that long constricted hole—twenty, thirty, forty feet, or more—yet at last he hauled and pressed and wormed his way to its end. And when he emerged he found that he had been crawling through a channel, a drain channel, one that ran under the fortress walls, for when he emerged to painfully stand in a shallow recess along the bulwark, Tuck discovered that he was in Modru Kinstealer's holt. He had crawled under the cold stone walls of the dread fortress of the cruel Iron Tower!

*   *   *

The eight raiders held absolutely still upon the wall as the ravine patrol marched beneath them. Only the eyes of the climbers moved, following the track of the Rūcks below. Patrel, climbing last, did not even breathe as the maggot-folk tramped past not fifteen feet under, so close that the small buccan felt as if he could almost reach out and touch them. All that the Rūcks would have to do would be to glance up, and the raiders would be discovered. Yet the maggot-folk snarled at one another and cursed and jostled, so intent upon elbowing and shoving and squabbling that they saw not the eight Free Folk on the wall above.

Past the corner the Spawn marched and on toward the south. Yet wait! Two of the Rūcks swung wide of the squad, *and they strode toward Tuck's hiding place!*

Upon the wall the raiders watched in anguish, and Danner made as if to descend. But Prince Igon reached out and grasped the buccan's arm and whispered, *"No!"* and Danner froze once more.

Now the two Rūcks came to the rocks, and snarled in the foul Slūk tongue as they stood and relieved themselves. And then they turned and rejoined the squad, marching on southward.

The eight raiders breathed a collective sigh of relief, for injured Tuck had not been discovered. And when the Rūcks disappeared from view beyond the distant buttress, once more the eight began to climb.

Up they mounted the soaring ramparts, their hands and feet finding ready purchase upon the outjutting rock in spite of the hoarfrost and rime. And upward they climbed.

At last Brega came to just below the crenel, where he stopped, and so did all the others—for the Dwarf would signal if the ramparts were clear, and then the eight would o'ertop the walls.

But Brega gave not the sign to proceed, for there came to the Dwarf's ear the sound of scuffling Rūck feet as one of the Foul Folk came at the change of the watch; yet the guard he came to relieve was gone, lying slain at the bottom of the ravine. And below the slot at the lip of the rampart, Brega clung with only one hand to the stone while with his free hand he unslung the axe Drakkalan, for he heard the unseen Rūck mutter and pick up the dead guard's fallen pike and then step straight toward the opening.

As Ubrik came riding back into the King's camp, leading the long string of horses used to bear the nine raiders to the eastern side of the dark fortress, he found Galen and Gildor discussing the strategy of the Legion.

"Ho, Ubrik!" called Galen, seeing the Marshal return. "Fared they well?"

Ubrik dismounted and handed the tethers over to an attendant. "Aye, King Galen, as far as we went. Yet grave danger will face them not until they come to the ravine. The Waldan, Burt, and my scout, Aric, now watch the progress of the raiders and will report to us when the nine scale the fortress wall."

Galen grunted and handed over a warm cup of tea to the Reachmarshal. "Let us then review one last time the tactics of our ruse."

Their plan was simple: the Legion would ride to the north of the gate, where the ravine was narrowest. There they would send forth a force of Men in plain view with ropes and shields and escorts of archers, and this force would make as if to scale the ravine under the cover of arrows. In this, the remaining Warrows—led by Merrilee—would join the archers from Valon.

Meantime a second force, proceeding in apparent secrecy, would move even more northerly and act as if to cross over the crevasse and mount the walls. It was expected that here too the Men would be seen, and it was hoped that the Rūcks would think that *this* was the true mission to breach the fortress, and thus would not look elsewhere for raiders.

And while these things were going forth, Lord Gildor would hold a strike force on the southern flank of the main body of the Legion. This group would mill about as if part of the whole, yet its purpose was to drive across the bridge—if and when it was felled by the raiders—and through the gate where they would hold the way until the whole of the Legion arrived.

Lastly, during the entire ruse King Galen in his scarlet armor would ride Wildwind along the fore of the Host and draw *Spaunen* eyes to him and away from Lord Gildor upon the flank.

"Argh!" growled Ubrik. "I like not this plan of mine, for it accomplishes nought if the nine do not succeed. I think we have put too many, nay, *all* of our horses in but one byre, and if it should burn . . . My meaning is this: if the raiders fail, then there is nought can be done to halt the Evil One."

"Aye, Ubrik," responded Lord Gildor, "yet what else would you have us do? Were there siege engines, scaling ladders, and assault bridges, then would we act in a different manner. But there are none of these things at hand. This plan, as plain as it is, should draw the *Rûpt* attention to us and away from the eastern wall. Our only hope is that the *Spaunen* will flock to jape at us and taunt us and sneer at our feeble attempts. Pray that their eyes turn toward us and not toward their own ramparts."

"It is the sneering of the Wrg that bothers me most, Deva Gildor," rumbled Ubrik. "I admit it. I realize that drawing Spawn in great numbers to jape at us is at the core of what we do. But I do not have to like it."

"Yet you are right, Reachmarshal Ubrik," said Galen, "if the raiders fall, then so do we all."

Galen turned to the Lian. "Where stands the 'Day, Lord Gildor?"

"In but five hours, Galen King, comes the Sun-Death," replied the Elf.

"Then it is time to begin." Galen stood and girted Steelheart to his waist. "Like it or no, Reachmarshal Ubrik, now is the moment to draw Spawn jeers. Sound the signal to the Legion, for the hour has come."

Ubrik raised his black-oxen horn to his lips, and an imperative call split the air. It was answered over and again as company after company signalled that it stood ready.

Galen, Gildor, and Ubrik mounted their steeds and set forth at the head of the Legion, riding toward the Iron Tower: Ubrik on the left flank, Gildor on the right, and King Galen in the center. And just after Galen, rode the Wee Folk: Merrilee, Dill, Teddy, and Arch, all upon steeds being led by mounted warriors. Then came the widespread ranks of the Vanadurin, steel helms glinting darkly in the Shadowlight, spears couched in stirrup cups, sabers sheathed in saddle scabbards, and some warriors bearing bow and arrow. And far to the north rode fifty Harlingar: the false assault force.

Amid the jingle of armor and the rattle of weaponry and

the drum of hooves, the peals of black-oxen horns rang forth, calling challenges to the forces of Modru Kinstealer's holt.

Yet from the distant Shadowlight behind and to the north of the Host there came the chill howls of Vulg spies, calling unto the Iron Tower. A shudder ran through Merrilee, for she guessed that Modru's curs reported that a small band rode to the north—the false assault force—and the damman wondered if Vulgs had also seen the raiders. Did Modru know that Tuck and the others were coming, too? Or had the Vulgs been fooled, drawn off, missing the raiders altogether? Merrilee knew not the answer to her questions, and she could but hope that all had gone well.

Closer loomed the dark citadel, and Spawn could be seen rushing thither and yon atop the battlements. And an occasional arrow would be launched from the rampart as the *Spaunen* tested the range.

Still nearer drew the Legion, until they came to the limit of blackshafted Rūcken arrows. Reachmarshal Ubrik's horn call split the air to signal along the ranks, and the Legion ground to a halt.

In the fore-center, warriors with shields and ropes dismounted and marched toward the dark crevasse. Behind them came the bowmen, and in this company went the Warrows; and they took advantage of the great fangs of rock thrusting up through the land, using them for protection.

Closer they came to the black ravine, and closer still. Now the Men with ropes and shields came unto its edge. They tied their lines to jut and boulder and cast the loose ends over the edge and down into the blackness below.

And Rūck and Hlōk and evil Ghûl looked upon these Men in disbelief: Did these *fools* think to scale the ravine and breach the walls under the very eyes of Modru's Horde? Raucous jeering rose up from the *Spaunen* ranks.

Then a clamant blat of Rūcken horn sounded, and a sleet of blackshafted barbs hissed down upon the Men, thudding into shield and earth and flesh alike.

The arrows of the Host hissed up to the battlements in reply, the shafts for the most part to sail o'er the walls or to shatter against the carven stone, though a few bolts found foe.

A great prolonged shout rose up from the Legion, for the High King in a scarlet chain-mail corselet rode along the forefront of his Host, and Steelheart flashed in the Shadowlight as Galen exhorted the ranks.

Still the black-shafted quarrels rained down upon those at the ravine, and arrows flew back in return. But at last, at a signal from their Captain, the Men abandoned their ropes and retreated back to the Legion, the archers loosing shafts up toward the walls and backing away, too.

And along the battlements the *Spaunen* jeered in revelment, their strident wrawls, their japing shrieks, wauling out after the fleeing allies.

And along the left flank, Ubrik ground his teeth in rage at the fleering of the Wrg.

Yet all was going as planned.

Brega gripped Drakkalan's black helve, the Dwarf's eyes locked upon the open crenel just above. He could hear the Ûkh scuffling toward the opening. Brega grasped the stone of the wall with his left hand and thrust his feet deeper into the crevice supporting the bulk of his weight. Now he could hear the rasp of Ûkh breath, the scrape of pike along stone, the slap of hand down upon the sill; and then the Grg leaned out of the opening to look below.

Chok! Drakkalan sheared through the side of the Rûck's skull, sending bone and split helm whirling off below; and dark grume splashed upon merlon and wall and warrior. And the corpse slid backwards out of sight to collapse in a grotesque sprawl upon the ramparts.

Brega hoisted himself up and peered cautiously along the banquette. It was empty of guards! Signalling the ones below, the Dwarf quickly slipped over the top and onto the wardway; and the remaining climbers scrambled up after. As the others joined him, Brega raised the slain Rûck overhead, and with a heave of his powerful Dwarven shoulders, he flung the corpse out and away from the wall, hurling it into the ravine below, and then cast the two pikes after.

"We must hurry," hissed Flandrena, his voice filled with urgency. "Less than a half hour remains ere the Sun-Death, and we have far to go to reach the gate, and much to do once we get there."

Hastily the raiders donned their soiled cloaks and cast

their hoods over their heads. Then, falling into ranks—the Warrows and Brega to the fore, Flandrena and Igon coming after—they began marching along the wall toward the distant gate, jostling and snarling among themselves as would the *Spaunen* do.

I'm inside! Inside the fortress! Tuck's heart hammered wildly as he peered forth from the recess along the wall. Hundreds upon hundreds of Spawn swarmed across the courtyards before him, some carrying crates or kegs, others bearing weapons and marching up ramps to the battlements above, and still others jostling and snarling as they tramped 'round corners and away or marched toward the buccan. Among the teeming Rūcks, cruel Hlōks plied whips and snarled orders; deadly Ghûls sat upon Hèlsteeds and watched o'er all.

Tuck pulled his hood as far over his head as he could, hiding his face deep in a fold of shadow.

Out of the frying pan, thought Tuck. *Now what? Back into the hole? Nay! I came to get into the fortress, and I did—by an unexpected route, to be sure, yet I am in.*

Once again Tuck peered forth from the recess. The swarming of the maggot-folk had not abated one whit. And the dead black eyes of a nearby Ghûl swept across the courtyard before him. *All right, bucco, now that you are in, do you think you might get to the gate? The raiders will need you there, you know. Due west, the gate is due west . . . straight across the fortress from here, straight through a hold teeming with the enemy. All you have to do is pass undetected through the entire Horde. But first, you have to get past that watching Ghûl.*

Again Tuck peered out and ducked back quickly, for a snarling Rūcken company marched along the wall toward his hiding place. *Tramp, tramp!* Forward they came, and Tuck pressed deeper into the darkness of the recess and slipped his bow and quiver across his shoulders and back. *Tramp, tramp!* On marched the Rūcks, and Tuck could now hear their quarreling snarls. *Tramp, tramp!* Now the first ranks strode past the buccan, and he moved not in the darkness of the wall. *Tramp, tramp!* Hlōks grated orders, and the jostling Rūcks bore onward. *Tramp, tramp!* Rūcks streamed by, and Tuck prayed that none would peer in to see him. *Tramp, tramp!* Now the last of the ranks hove past.

This is it, bucco! Tuck thought. And when the final Rūck passed, the Warrow stepped forth from the shadows *and joined the marching Spawn.*

With each step he took, lancing agony shot up his left leg, and he could feel something *grinding* within his boot; yet he strode onward, his jaw clenched to keep from crying out in anguish, his heart hammering in fear—a lone Warrow marching at the tail end of a company of squabbling Rūcks. *Like a foolish lamb in Wolf's clothing,* Tuck's mind gasped between strides.

South they tramped, alongside the wall, and then they turned westward, following a stone-cobbled way between squat buildings and stark towers. At the rear of the company Tuck hobbled, refusing to yield to the stabbing torment of his foot, yet afraid that he would scream or collapse at each and every step.

Past the watching Ghûl they marched, his dead black eyes flicking but lightly over this jostling company as west they bore. Tuck kept his face down and hidden and held his hands beneath his cloak as he limped past the Ghûl. And the Hèlsteed snorted and grunted as the Warrow hitched by, and the buccan knew that the beast had scented him. Yet at that very moment the corpse-foe reined the 'Steed and rode away toward three companies of violently squabbling maggot-folk, the Ghûl paying no heed to the squeals and grunts of the creature that bore him.

On Tuck limped, at the rear of the tramping company of Spawn, passing across a courtyard, only to turn north. Tuck could see a way bearing west, and as the *Spaunen* swung 'round a corner, the Warrow stepped aside into a shadowed doorway as the maggot-folk marched on.

Savage pain shooting up his leg, Tuck hobbled back to the courtyard and across it, keeping to the darkened buttresses shoring up the buildings to the north side.

Into the western way he limped and found himself in a narrow twisting labyrinth of alleyways. Yet westward he strove, coming at times to dead ends where he would retrace his path and choose an alternate route. And with each step a sickening *grind* shot agonizing stabs of searing pain jolting through his frame.

Tuck hobbled along the narrow mews between the buildings and came to a great mass of stacked crates and kegs; slowly he worked his way through the wares to come at last to an exit from the twisting maze. Again he faced a courtyard teeming with Rūcks, and across the cobbles stood a great dark tower. Tuck glanced up and saw the black nimbus streaming forth from the top of the spire, wrenching at his Warrow eyes, and his heart hammered, for the buccan knew that he looked upon Modru's Iron Tower. And as he stared upward—

Ssshthack! The thongs of a scourge lashed across Tuck's shoulders and whipped under his hood to cut his lip and welt his face. The Warrow whirled, and there before him stood a snarling Hlōk. And as the buccan's hands under his cloak reached unseen for Bane . . . *"Theck dral, guth!"* rasped the Spawn, raising the cat-o'-nine-tails for another strike, and behind the Hlōk four Rūcks stepped forth from the shadows.

Thrice more the Legion sent warriors forth as if to scale the ravine, archers loosing arrows at the *Spaunen* upon the walls. Each time there came a hail of black-shafted bolts raining down from the ramparts; and the great crank-bow above the gate thrummed—*Thuun!*—and hurled the iron-pointed spears into the ranks of the Host. And thrice more the assault upon the crevasse was shorn off, the warriors and archers returning to the main body of the Legion while Yrm jeered and hooted in derision and blatted harsh calls upon brazen Rūcken horns. And Ubrik ground his teeth in rage.

Merrilee and the Warrows came back to stand at the fore-center of the Host and watched as King Galen and other riders of the Legion raced along the front and brandished weapons.

Thuumn! A spear arched northward from the gate to hurtle down and shatter 'gainst a stone upjut midst scurrying warriors.

And upon the walls, Spawn jittered about in revelment.

Yet Merrilee's eyes saw a large force of maggot-folk break off and race northward along the top of the rampart. And as Galen came back to the center of the Legion, a horse-borne scout thundered in from the north. "Hai, King

Galen!" shouted the warrior, hauling his horse to a stop. "The Wrg have seen the Vanadurin company sent north to scale the ravine, and now the black arrows fall upon those Harlingar, too."

"Then all goes according to plan," responded Galen. Yet his eyes turned south, seeking to see Aric and Burt bearing word of Brega's raiding party, but he saw nought. "Damman Holt, see you aught of scout and Warrow bringing news of the climbers to us?"

Merrilee turned her tilted sapphirine eyes southward and searched the distant Shadowlight, then shook her head no.

"Rach!" Galen smashed a gauntleted fist into palm. "We know not whether the raiders have succeeded or failed— or yet strive to scale the walls. But time grows dangerously short." The King tore his gaze away from the south and called, "Mount the fifth assault! Let us hold the *Spaunen* eyes upon us!"

And as a company of Harlingar took up their shields and started toward the ropes, the archers went forward with them; Merrilee strung arrow to bow and advanced, too. Her thoughts were a chaotic whirl as she agonized o'er the fate of Tuck and Danner and Patrel, of Rollo and Dink and Harven, and of Brega and Igon and Flandrena; yet how they fared she knew not as black-shafted arrows began to hiss forth from the walls.

The raiders, their features concealed deep within their hoods, tramped southwesterly along the high banquette atop the dark ramparts of Modru Kinstealer's holt. Below them, inside the walls, they could see swarms of maggot-folk rushing thither and yon upon the cobbles and marching in squads and companies to the harsh commands and lashing whips of Hlōk overseers. And here and there the dead black eyes of Ghûls watched over all.

Yet the gaze of the raiders did not dwell upon the mill within the courtyards nor on the teeming ways below; instead they stared across the hold past the great central tower—the tower that wrenched at Warrow eyes—and to the distant gate in the west wall. And their hearts plunged, for a great swarm of maggot-folk clustered atop the ramparts near the portal.

"They are gathered to repel the Legion," growled Brega.

"Look, to the north, another swarm," whispered Dink.

"The false raiders," said Flandrena softly as they now tramped westerly. "All goes according to plan: the Legion acts as if to cross near the gate, and 'round to the north the lone company of the Harlingar draws *Spaunen* eyes away from us."

"But there are too many Rūcks atop the gate itself," hissed Danner.

"Perhaps—" began Brega, but he broke off what he was about to say and began jostling and elbowing and snarling, as did they all while Flandrena lashed at them with a piece of Elven rope, cut to resemble a whip. And growling and cursing they marched past a Rūcken sentry, who gave them not a glance, fearing that if he took his yellow eyes from the ravine below, the whip would lash him, too.

Onward marched the raiders, tramping from angle to angle as they swung along the walls in a great zagging arc, bearing ever toward their goal. And they were not challenged as they passed warders and marching Rūcks alike along the high stone way. Now the eight of them marched upon the western wall, and they could see the Legion out on the moor beyond the crevasse, King Galen's scarlet armor drawing their eyes as he rode up and down the fore of the Host. There, too, they saw Gildor's strike force milling on the southern flank of the Legion, ready to charge across the bridge if and when it fell. Lastly they saw a small force of warriors dashing toward ropes hanging down into the ravine; some of the Men had already reached the crevasse, and black-shafted arrows rained down upon them while the quarrels of archers flew back in return.

But then the raiders saw no more, for now they were come upon the very rampart holding the gate itself, and they marched the last leg toward their goal. Before them they could see the huge Hlōk-driven crank-bow—*Thuun!*— and hear the clatter of gears as it was rewound and armed with another steel-tipped spear. And amid the raucous jeers of the maggot-folk, the raiders strode toward their prizes: the great winch of the iron drawbridge, and the hoist of the barred portcullis.

Thung! Clk-clk-clack-clk-clk-clk! The rattle of the ratchet on the great crank-bow clattered forth, and the Hlōks laid another spear in the groove. The captain of the gate guard turned to see a hooded squad step toward the drawbridge winch.

"Shugg du!" snarled the Hlōk, moving to block them, and the squad came to a halt. *"Shugg du!"* he barked again, only to be met by silence. *"Arg tha! Shugg du!"* The Hlōk stepped forward, rage upon his features, reaching for the cat-o'-nine-tails at his belt while at the same time shoving back the hood of the figure directly before him. *And the Hlōk's eyes flew wide, for he stared upon the forked-bearded features of one of the hated Dubh!* It was the last thing that the Hlōk ever saw, for Drakkalan clove the Squam's head from his body, and battle exploded upon the wall above the gate.

At sight of the four Rūcks behind the Hlōk, Tuck's mind raced, for he knew that he could not wield a sword well enough to slay them all before one would sound the alarm.

"Theck dral, guth!" snarled the Hlōk again, gesturing toward a group of kegs. Now Tuck saw that the Rūcks were bearing off toward the Iron Tower, and they had casks hoisted upon their shoulders.

He thinks I am a Rūck! Quickly Tuck limped forward, stooped and lifted a keglet to his own shoulder, and hobbled after the maggot-folk striding toward the spire, leaving the Hlōk behind overseeing other Rūcks coming to carry cargo.

Again excruciating pain jolted up his leg, and Tuck nearly fainted from the agony; yet onward he strove, sucking and spitting blood from his whip-cut lip, limping across the courtyard. And he saw that the Rūcks before him bore their burdens toward what appeared to be a feeding station. There two Hlōks oversaw the unloading of the casks, Rūcks breaking the containers open to dispense the food inside. In the background stood one of the dead white corpse-folk, the Ghûl's 'Steed at his side.

If that Hèlsteed catches my scent . . . As Tuck desperately looked for a means of escape, directly before the buccan a Rūck stepped forth through a door in the tower, coming down the three steps and past the Warrow and scuttling off across the courtyard.

The door! thought Tuck. *The Rūck left it open!* Without pause the buccan struggled up the treads and through the portal. As he pushed the panel to, a distant clash and clangor of weaponry fell upon his ears. But whence came these faint echoes of battle—from what direction—he could not say, for at that moment with a hollow *boom!* the door of the Iron Tower shut behind him and closed all sound away.

Tuck set the cask down and rested a moment, his eyes searching the gloom. Before him stretched a long hallway with guttering torches casting writhing shadows along its length, closed doorways to left and right. There too, yawning darkly, stood stone arches marking where cross halls bore away. To Tuck's left a staircase mounted upward, and to his right a stairwell led down to a closed door.

Suddenly enraged shrieks rang throughout the tower, and there came the slap of footsteps running toward him; and Tuck scrambled up the stairs to his left, pain crashing through his entire being as he hobbled upward. He came to a landing, and still the raging cries resounded. Rūcks and Hlōks raced down the hall toward him. Once more Tuck hitched up another flight of stairs, and maggot-folk ran past him down the steps, paying little heed to the hooded figure going upward.

As Tuck came to the next landing, the piercing shrieks fell silent. But more Spawn came toward the Warrow, and Tuck knew that if but one of them stopped him, he would be revealed. The buccan turned to the nearest door and shot back the brass bolt and stepped inside, slamming it shut behind.

Pausing but a moment to catch his breath, Tuck surveyed the room: a canopied bed, a fire, a doorway through which he could see the corner of a bathing tub, and heavy drapes covering what had to be a window. From the outside the buccan could hear skirl of battle muffled by the curtain, and, too, there came the sound of a great *Blang!*

The raiders! Have they reached the gate? Still breathing heavily, Tuck limped toward the window and reached to pull the drapery aside.

And as the cloth swung away from the wall, a figure dressed in quilted Rukken garb lunged forward out of the blackness and swung a heavy iron bar down at the buccan, the thick rod glancing painfully down Tuck's arm and back as the Warrow twisted and sprang aside, rolling on the stone floor, arrows spilling from his quiver, the bow across his back clacking against the flag, his cloak twisting around his body as he struggled to draw Bane.

And the hood fell back from his head, and he looked up with his tilted jewel-hued eyes to see the flaxen-haired female leap forward, bar raised for the killing blow.

"Princess!" he shouted.

Clang! Laurelin dropped the bar and threw herself to her knees beside the fallen Warrow. *"Sir Tuck!"* she cried, clasping him to her as he sat up. "Oh, Sir Tuck." Laurelin wept uncontrollably and rocked back and forth and fiercely held on to the buccan, and Tuck put his arms around her and stroked her hair and soothed her and wondered at the workings of Chance that had led his footsteps here.

Through the window came the trumpeting sound of a bugle, and Tuck knew that the silver call came from no other clarion than the Horn of the Reach borne by Patrel. "Come now, Princess," said Tuck, "we must get gone from here."

"Tuck, the Ghûls!" cried Laurelin, rocking back on her heels, then scrambling up. "We *must* get out of here and to my Lord Galen. I must warn him: a great force of Ghûls rides o'er the Wastes of Gron, coming to fall upon the Legion from behind."

"Ghûls? Coming across Claw Moor?" At Laurelin's nod, Tuck's face blenched. "You're right, my Lady, we've got to warn the Legion!"

Thuun! The thrum of the great crank-bow sounded through the window as Tuck painfully got up from the floor: broken-footed, lip whip-split, face wealed, and arm and back bruised by an iron bar. Quickly he inspected his bow—none the worse for having been rolled upon—and then he began gathering the arrows strewn on the stone and putting them in his quiver.

"And Tuck!" added the Princess. "Modru plans something horrible this 'Day. What it is, I know not, yet it is evil and concerns Gyphon . . . Gyphon's return!"

"Aye, Princess, we suspect as much. Our hope is to disrupt Modru's vile scheme." Tuck snatched up the last arrow and glanced at Laurelin. "Your hair, Princess," Tuck's voice snapped with authority, "hide it under your cloak and hood. We've got to pass through a Horde."

Quickly, Laurelin unfastened her cloak and shook her

hair down her back, then donned the cloak over it, pulling the hood up to hide her face. "We can leave by the window," she said. "Down a rope."

"The door is unbolted," responded Tuck, "and we are less likely to get caught walking down steps than climbing down ropes."

Laurelin scooped up her bar and stepped toward the door. "Let us be gone then, Sir Tuck, for I sense the Ghûls come even now."

The sounds of the black-oxen horns of Valon drifted in through the window as Tuck cast his own hood over his head and took his bow in hand and limped to Laurelin's side.

Taking a deep breath, he grasped the latch and looked up at the Princess, and at her nod he opened the door.

And there before them stood a figure dressed in black, with raging eyes glaring through a hideous iron mask. Ere the Warrow could move, *"Sssstha!"* hissed Modru, and he struck down with a whelming blow of metal gauntlet, the heel of his hand smashing into the Warrow's forehead, the clawlike fingers ripping down the buccan's face and neck and tearing through cloak and jacket to the silveron armor concealed below, one finger striking the catch of the silver locket and springing it open as the hideous hand ripped past. Tuck reeled back, stunned, and fell to the stone, his helm striking hard, his bow lost to his grip.

Laurelin lashed the bar at Modru with all of her strength, yet the Evil One threw up a hand and—*Chang!*—caught the thick rod and wrenched it from her grasp. Then, like a striking viper, his free hand whipped forward and clutched her wrist, and he jerked her toward him.

"So, you sought escape. *Fa!* Did you think the *runt* would save you from your fate?" Modru dragged the Princess toward the form of the fallen Warrow, who lay stunned on his back, face clawed and bleeding, cloak and jacket rent apart, and the silver locket bearing Merrilee's portrait lying open and glittering upon the buccan's armored chest.

Modru raised the bar. "We shall see which is stronger— this iron rod or your *rescuer's* head!"

As Laurelin wrenched and struggled in Modru's iron grip and screamed *"No, no, no!"* over and over again, the Evil

One leaned forward above the Warrow to smash the bar
down upon the buccan's skull.

And the pure silver mirrored side of the open locket
caught a small part of Modru's true reflection and cast it
back to the eyes of the Evil One.

With a shrill scream Modru flung the rod *blanging* away,
and threw his arm up over his face and reeled hindward,
unable to bear what he had seen in the argent speculum of
the locket—a locket crafted ages agone in the mystic land
of Xian, where it is said that Wizards once dwelled.

Yet even though the polished flat surface had struck
Modru a telling blow, the Evil One was not destroyed, for
the locket was diminutive and could cast back but a tiny
portion of his full image. Hence, as air sissed in through
Modru's gritted teeth, he recovered from the heavy brunt.
He clenched the gauntleted, taloned fingers of his free
hand, curling them into a black iron fist.

Once more he wrenched Laurelin along after him as he
stepped toward the felled Warrow, preparing to smash the
life from the Wee One. Yet Modru had reckoned not upon
the potency of the argent device warding the buccan; for
at that very moment Tuck groaned and feebly moved, and
the glittering silver of the locket shifted upon his chest, and
the sparkling plane of the mirror seemed to turn toward
the Evil One, as if seeking him out.

"Sssstha!" Again Modru reeled back, jerking his head
aside, away from the token of power lying open upon the
breast of the now-stirring Warrow, the Evil One unable to
face even this small part of his own true image, unable to
come at the helpless buccan.

"Ssss." Air raggedly hissed in and out of Modru's lungs
as he paused and gathered strength, and he did not look
toward the Warrow, did not look toward the silver bane.
And though Laurelin twisted and jerked, she could not pull
free, for the Evil One's dinted grip held her fast even as
his power swiftly returned unto him.

"Pah!" Modru spat at last, whirling away. "Whether it is
now or in but a span, it matters not, for the runt will die . . .
yess, die when I fetch my Master, and that moment is at
hand. Come, Princess, to the tower above. It is time to
meet your fate."

And hauling Laurelin stumbling behind, caught in his

grip of iron, Modru stalked from the room, jerking her toward the steps spiraling up to the chamber at the top of the tower, where lay the yawning ebon of the Myrkenstone.

Once again the Legion had been driven back from the ravine, and the Spawn hooted and jeered. And now even King Galen ground his teeth and cursed in frustration at their japing; he had known that the Yrm would fleer at the Host's feeble attempts, for that, too, was part of the plan, yet still their gibes grated upon him.

"Hoy!" cried Teddy Proudhand, one of the Warrows. "Here comes Burt and that Harlingar scout."

Galen upon Wildwind turned his eyes to the south, and hammering forth through the Shadowlight came two steeds bearing riders: Man and Warrow, Aric leading Burt. Along the forefront of the Legion they rode, thundering at last to a halt before the crimson-armored King.

While his steed pranced and curvetted, Aric struck a clenched fist to his heart. "Sire, the raiders are upon the wall at last." Aric gestured to Burt, the buccan having leapt to the ground as Merrilee and the other Warrows gathered 'round.

Burt looked up at Galen. " 'At's right, your Lordship, sir. Long we waited, till I thought as somethin' had gone wrong for certain. But then I saw 'em, climbing up the wall at last, though I counted only eight where there should have been nine . . . One of 'em was missin', and where he's got to, or what's happened, well, it's a mystery right enough. I watched till they topped the wall, then me and Aric hightailed it for here."

Merrilee's heart had plummeted upon hearing that one of the raiders was missing, and a deep foreboding washed over her being, but she did not dwell upon it, for Galen barked, "When did they top the wall? How long ago?"

"Mayhap a quarter hour past, King Galen," replied Aric, "for we rode swiftly and straight away."

Galen wheeled Wildwind. "Vanadurin!" he cried. "Now the moment draws at hand. Pass the word to stand ready, and let us pray that the raiders succeed. But now we must make one last sortie to draw all *Spaunen* eyes to us and away from their own walls." Galen flashed Steel-heart into the air. *"Hál Vanadurin! Hál Harlingar!"*

A great yell rose up from the ranks of the mounted war-riors, and Wildwind thundered up and down the fore—from the south flank to the north—rearing and pawing at the air as the High King came to each end. This was the signal to both Gildor and Ubrik to prepare, for it meant the raiders were upon the walls.

Once more a company of Vanadurin took up shields and ran toward the ravine, and with them went the Warrows and other archers. And a great jeering came forth from the Spawn upon the walls, for again these Men, these *fools,* sought to cross the crevasse in spite of the fact that they had failed six times before. And black-shafted arrows hissed downward.

Merrilee's eyes glanced up through the hail of barbed death, and southward—atop the wall above the gate—she thought that she glimpsed combat, struggle; but then she turned her sight once more upon the rampart before her, for her aim was needed here.

When Drakkalan sheared the Hlōk's head from his body, the raiders exploded into frenzied action: knife, sword, and axe, cleaving, stabbing, and hacking. The Hlōks manning the great crank-bow were caught completely unawares, and they fell in their own black gore, with throats cut, breasts split, skulls cloven, bodies gutted.

Nearby Hlōks and Rūcks turned at the sounds of the slaughter as Flandrena and Igon sprang to the great winch to lower the bascule. The two seized the spokes of the winch wheel as cries of alarm burst forth from the Spawn. The Man and the Elf threw their weight against the ra-dial arms, and maggot-folk charged toward them as War-rows loosed bolts to fell Rūcks and Hlōks in the fore of the oncoming enemy.

And the wheel moved not.

"It's jammed!" cried Igon, straining against the handle, and Dink leapt forward to aid—but still it did not move.

"Release the ratchet!" cried Flandrena but ere any of the three could make a move to do so, Rūcks and Hlōks sprang into the gate cap, and the Prince and Lian warrior took up their swords and began hewing while Dink loosed arrow after arrow.

Now the fighting was too close for bow and arrow, and

Danner and Patrel found themselves side by side with long-knife swords in hand, and there came the skirl of steel upon steel as they engaged *Spaunen* scimitars.

Chang! Shang! The Rūck facing Danner fell slain, and the buccan turned to see Patrel in a hand-to-hand struggle with a large Hlōken foe, the tiny Warrow straining to hold the enemy's dirk away from his throat.

Chonk! Danner's blade bit into the Hlōk's neck, and foul dark blood splashed into Patrel's face as the Spawn arched over backwards, dead ere striking the stone. But before either buccan could catch his breath, *Clang! Drang!* once more their swords engaged those of the Rūcks.

Driven by the strength of youth, Igon's sword cut a gory swath, black blood flying wide as the edge clove into the onrushing foe. And Flandrena moved like a wraith—side-stepping, whirling, dodging, swerving—and the Elf's blade licked out time and again, Rūcks and Hlōks falling dead. And Brega bashed scimitar and tulwar aside, Drakkalan chopping through steel, sinew, and bone alike.

Yet still the Spawn came on.

Rollo again managed to use his bow, and he felled a Rūck pressing Danner while Patrel slew another, and they glanced up to see great numbers of the foe rushing toward them, now aware that something was amiss atop the gate. Horns blatting, voices yelling, the enemy mounted a charge; and Harven fell, slain by steel pike.

Danner's eyes rolled white, and spittle foamed on the corners of his lips, and then an amber glare stared out from his distorted face, and dark gutturals snarled forth from his writhing mouth. He ripped off his cloak and jacket and flung his long-knife aside and scooped up one of the long iron bars from the grip of a dead Hlōk.

"Danner!" cried Patrel, but to no avail, for the tall buccan had leapt to the fore and stood in the mouth of the wardway leading into the gate area. And Danner swung the bar with an unmatched fury, for now he was a berserker.

And in the narrow wardway the foe was hurled back!

Brega sprang to the winch and swung Drakkalan overhead and down with all the strength of his massive shoulders. *Chang!* With a great shower of sparks the black-runed axe *bit completely through the haul chain.* And slowly at first, but with ever-gathering speed, axles squealing in protest, the great iron drawbridge slammed down:

BLANG!

And now Igon and Flandrena leapt to the portcullis hoist and began cranking the barway upward as Brega sprang to Danner's side, for the foe charged once more. Again the Spawn were hurled back.

But suddenly the portcullis stopped moving upward, and strain as they might, Igon and Flandrena could budge it not.

Patrel ran and peered downward.

Below, the great Troll warding the gate clutched the barway, stopping it dead in its track. And the wee Warrow knew that the Man and the Elf could not move the hoist with this monster holding it back. Patrel could see more maggot-folk racing across the courtyards in the direction of the gate.

Swiftly the tiny buccan leapt down the steps toward the gateway below. And when he came to the cobbles, he ran to the Troll and hewed the Atalar Blade into the creature's scaled shank. *Ching!* The golden-runed silver blade glanced downward and did not cut through the Ogru's stonelike hide. Yet the Warrow *had* caught the creature's eye, for with a snarl it swiped a great thick hand at the Wee One, just missing as Patrel sprang backwards.

Ching! Again the blade chopped at the Ogru's calf, and again the scaled hide turned the edge aside. Once more the Troll's evil red eyes glared at the buccan, and its huge hand clutched and missed.

Now Patrel danced out before the Troll, the Warrow slipping under the partially raised barway and shouting at the creature, "Hai! You big stupid oaf! You can't catch me, for I am the golden warrior!" And Patrel threw open his jacket, and the gilded armor shone forth gleaming.

With a snarl, the Ogru-Troll hurled up the portcullis and reached his great clawlike hands for the buccan. And Patrel ran out upon the iron drawbridge, the monster in pursuit—a huge iron club clutched in one thick hand, his great stride overhauling the Wee One's flying legs.

And up on the wall, Igon and Flandrena spun the hoist to the full and locked it in place, for Patrel's quick wits had loosed the barway from the grip of the Troll, and the portcullis was up and pinned.

Man and Elf turned to the battle, just in time to see Brega felled by Hlōk War-bar and Spawn leap forward to slay the Dwarf. But ere any maggot-folk could reach Brega's side, a black-armored buccan stood above the fallen Dwarf and lashed out with a great iron bar. As the mighty cudgel crunched Rūcken bones, the Warrow warrior cried, *"King of the Rillrock! King of the Rillrock! Danner Bramblethorn is the King of the Rillroc—"*

A black-shafted arrow hissed through the air to smash through the black chain mail and pierce Danner's side, and a spear burst into his shoulder, hurling the buccan backwards to crash unto the stone. Igon and Flandrena sprang forward, their swords lashing into the oncoming *Rûpt*. And Brega struggled to his feet, his forehead red with gore but Drakkalan in his hand. And Rollo and Dink loosed bolt after bolt, felling Spawn left and right.

Danner lay in a widening pool of blood, and the glazed berserker look faded from his eyes. He tried to struggle upward, but could not, and his cheek lay against the icy stone next to a machicolation. He gazed out through the hole and down upon the iron drawbridge, now spanning the black crevasse. And he saw Patrel out upon the iron, taunting a great Ogru that slowly stalked toward the wee Warrow.

As Patrel darted out through the gate, the Troll coming behind, the buccan's eyes saw Gildor's force flying along the ravine toward the downed bridge.

If the Ogru sees them, he may turn back and slam the portcullis to, thought the wee Warrow. *I've got to keep him from catching sight of the riders.* In the middle of the span Patrel stopped and turned, spreading his arms wide and shouting, "All right now, you overgrown lummox! See if you can catch me!"

Sensing a trap, the Troll came to a halt. Now he stalked slowly forward, the iron bridge shuddering under his massive tread, his dull wit searching for a snare, his red eyes locked upon this tiny warrior taunting him.

"Hai, jobbernowl!" cried Patrel, darting from side to side. "What's wrong? Am I too big for you?" And the Wee One took the Horn of the Reach—the Horn of Valon— from beneath his jacket, where he had borne it all along,

and raised the rune-marked bugle to his lips and blew a
lifting call into the air. The silver notes rang and echoed
from the crevasse and through the gate and over the walls,
and everywhere that Free Folk heard it, hearts were lifted
and spirits surged; but everywhere that the notes reached
the ears of the maggot-folk, the Spawn quailed back in
fright.

The Troll, too, snarled in fear and stared at this small
pest on the edge of the bridge. Then the huge Ogru roared
and raised the great iron club and strode forward. And
Patrel knew that he would not survive the blow.

Thuun! The huge crank-bow atop the gate hurled a steel-
pointed shaft with all the might of that great ballista, and
the spear flew through the air to crash into the Troll's back
and smash through his heart and burst forth from his chest;
and black blood flew wide, and where it fell a reeking
smoke curled upward from the iron. A look of surprise
came over the Ogru's features as he was whelmed to his
knees; and—*Clang!*—his club crashed to the bridge, lost to
his fingers. The Troll staggered to his feet and clutched at
his back, trying to reach the shaft; and, one knee buckling,
he stumbled sideways and fell silently into the black depths
of the crevasse below.

Stunned, Patrel looked up toward the wall atop the gate,
but he could not see who had loosed the great bolt that
had slain the Ogru. But a dire feeling of dread washed over
him, and he began to run back toward the open portcullis.

And the black-oxen horns of Valon sounded as Gildor's
strike force hurtled across the iron bridge and past the running buccan and through the gate of Modru's fortress.

Atop the wall, Man, Warrow, Dwarf, and Elf battled
against the Spawn. And a black-armored buccan released
his grip from the stock of the great crank-bow and slid
down to sit with his back to the pedestal. There was a faint
smile upon his face as the blood leaked from his body, for
he heard the horns of Valon sounding. And slowly the
golden light dimmed in his eyes and then was gone: Danner
Bramblethorn had loosed his last arrow.

When Galen King's signal came that the raiders were
upon the ramparts, Lord Gildor swept his gaze along the
wall above the gate. The Lian warrior's eyes searched for

sign of Brega's band, yet he was too far away to tell whether there were any members of that small party among the multitudes that swarmed there. Yet wait! Did his Elven eyes see sign of struggle upon the rampart? Perhaps. He was not certain. Yet he called a warrior unto him. "Stand ready with your horn, Captain Brate, for if we are to succeed or fail, the next few moments will tell."

The next few moments . . . Gildor's green eyes leapt to the sky where the faint glow of the Sun could just now be discerned as it swung toward the zenith. And most of the feeble disk was even now occluded, for the time drew nigh. There remained less than a quarter hour till the Sun-Death would come full. Gildor stood in his stirrups and then sat back down, and his knuckles were white, so tightly did he clench the reins, for still nothing seemed to be happening atop the gate.

Then, with a slow majesty that belied its hurtling rush, the iron drawbridge separated from the wall and toppled out and down across the chasm to fall to with a dinning *Blang!*

"Now!" cried Lord Gildor. *"Ride! For Adon's sake, ride!"*

Brate raised his black-oxen horn to his lips and blew a sundering blast that echoed across the moor. And, as one great body, Gildor's strike force wheeled and raced for the bridge, flashing hooves now flying along the edge of the chasm.

And behind, King Galen turned his warriors, too, and they hurtled after, with Reachmarshal Ubrik's brigade following.

Lastly, the company at the ropes broke off their ruse and ran for their horses, and with them came the archers— Merrilee and the buccen among the latter.

And as the ravine company fell in with the riders of Ubrik's force, now thundering past, Dill Thorven cried, "Merrilee, look! Out upon Claw Moor! A great array comes!"

Merrilee looked to where the buccan pointed, and there, hammering across the wastes, came thousands of riders, but whether they were friend or foe, she could not say. "Hoy, Degan!" she called to the rider who led her steed. "Find

King Galen! Or Reachmarshal Ubrik! A great force rides toward us across Claw Moor!"

Degan spurred forward, leading Merrilee's mount behind, racing to find King or Marshal.

In the fore Lord Gildor's steed ran full tilt for the bridge. The Elf's eyes saw a small figure run forth upon the span, followed by a Troll. *Run, Waerling, run!* cried Gildor's mind, and yet the small mite turned to face his hulking adversary. Gildor urged his steed to even greater speed, but he knew he would not arrive in time to aid the tiny buccan.

Thuun! The sound of the great crank-bow came to the Elf's ears, and his eyes widened as he saw the mighty bolt flash down from the wall and strike the Troll in the back. And as the monstrous creature fell into the ravine, Gildor plunged onto the iron bridge, the Harlingar thundering after, the span booming and ringing as the strike force hurtled across, the black-oxen horns of Valon blowing wildly.

Past Patrel they ran headlong and through the open gate, hooves striking upon hard cobblestones within the fortress walls. Black-shafted arrows rained upon them from the ramparts, but the Vanadurin thundered inward like an iron wave, their lances piercing Rūcks and Hlōks in the courtyard before them. Gildor wheeled and gave a cry. Harlingar flocked to him, and they spurred toward a ramp leading up to the banquette above.

Outside, the Vanadurin pressed toward the bridge, a bottleneck to their invasion of Modru Kinstealer's holt. Here Degan searched among the milling press for Reachmarshal Ubrik or High King Galen, yet he found neither. But there was no need, for Ubrik's eyes had seen the oncoming force thundering out of the Shadowlight upon Claw Moor, and they were near enough to identify: Ghûls upon Hèlsteeds. Modru's Reavers had come to fall upon Galen's Host.

Black-oxen horns rang, and Ubrik's brigade wheeled to meet this new threat. Again the horns sounded, and lances were lowered and sabers raised. And at a third signal, first at a walk, then at a trot, Ubrik's Vanadurin set forth in a spreading line. Their pace quickened—now a canter, now a gallop—and at a fourth and last horn call it became a headlong run. The two forces raced pell-mell toward one another, leering Ghûls astride squealing Helsteeds, grim-faced Harlingar upon the fiery belling steeds of Valon.

Across the iron drawbridge the remaining Vanadurin pressed, yet they could not come into the Kinstealer's holt, for within the gateway and athwart the entry now stood a second Troll—the one that had guarded the Hèlsteed stables. The monster wielded a great iron War-bar and roared in pleasure as he smashed aside warrior and steed alike. Though he was dressed in nought but black leather breeks, still the swords and arrows of Men harmed him not, but glanced aside notched or shivered asunder against his scaled hide. And the black-shafted arrows of the *Rûpt* rained down, striking shield and horse and Man alike; and warriors and steeds fell screaming into the abyss below.

Lord Gildor, leading the Vanadurin already inside, fought his way through Rūcks and Hlōks and Ghûls toward the ramps leading up to the walls above the gate, for it was the mission of the strike force to secure the drawbridge winch and the portcullis hoist and to rescue the raiders, if any yet lived.

At last the horses burst through the *Spaunen* and came to the stone incline, and Lord Gildor leapt from his steed and raced up the pitch, Men charging upward in his wake. Rūcks ran down at them, but Red Bale clove through their ranks, as did the steel of Valon. And Spawn fell slain or tumbled to their deaths below. But still the weapons of the foe took their toll, as cudgel and iron pole, scimitar and tulwar, and hammer and pike slew the warriors of the Legion.

Yet Gildor's strike force won to the banquette and fought their way to the gate cap, where they found Brega and Igon and Flandrena and Dink in furious battle, still holding the gate area atop the wall.

And when the Vanadurin charged into the fray, *Rûpt* fell back. Igon flicked a brief smile at Lord Gildor, and Flandrena and Brega each gave a nod, while Dink took up his bow and loosed arrows upon the Spawn. And then the maggot-folk struck once more.

Up the steps from the gateway below came a wee buccan: Patrel. And his sword—the Atalar Blade—was asplash with black gore. He came onward, through the clash of steel upon steel and the shouts and screams of battle twisting and dodging, trying to win through the press and come unto Gildor.

"Lord Gildor! Lord Gildor! To me! To me!" cried Patrel. And Red Bale hewed through a Hlōk, felling the Spawn, and in two strides the Lian was at the Warrow's side.

"Quickly, Patrel, speak," barked Gildor, his eyes upon the swirling battle.

"An Ogru blocks the way and thwarts the Legion below," panted Patrel, but he said no more, for at that moment the combat came upon them, and buccan and Elf fought for their lives.

Yet toward the steps Gildor battled, and at last he won free of the mêlée. Down the stairs the Lian warrior bounded, and now he could see the Troll at the gate. Scarlet fire blazed forth from the blade-jewel of Red Bale and leapt down its edge.

Chnk! Krch! The great Troll War-bar smashed into the fore of the Host, and horse and Man alike were slain. The mighty Ogru roared his laughter as steeds were reined back and the faces of Men blenched before this twelve-foot-high monster. And still the deadly arrows hissed down from the wall and into the milling warriors trapped upon the span.

Toward the hulking creature raced Lord Gildor, the lithe Elf running to come between the drooling Troll and the Ogru's victims. And as the Lian warrior finally came before the monster, so too did Galen King at last win his way through the press upon the bridge to push unto the fore of the Host. Galen raised Steel-heart and prepared to spur Wildwind forward, but Lord Gildor cried, "Nay, Galen King! This Troll is mine! For now I see his image through Vanidor's eyes!"

The Ogru blinked down at this *Dolh* before him, and a gaping leer spread o'er the monster's features, spittle dripping from yellowed tusks. Then he struck.

Clang! The great War-bar smashed upon the cobbles, but Lord Gildor darted aside, narrowly evading the blow.

Woosh! The bar slashed sideways through the air, driven by the massive thews of the twelve-foot-high creature. But the Elf fell flat, the iron pole lashing above him.

Chang! Once more the iron smashed to the stone, again barely missing as Gildor rolled away and sprang up and inward; and Bale flicked out to catch the twisting creature upon the thigh. Scarlet fire blazed out from the ruby blade-jewel as a great gash opened across the monster's leg and black blood gushed forth to fall smoking upon the cobblestone way.

The Ogru yawled in pain and fell back beyond Gildor's reach. And the moment the Troll gave way, Vanadurin surged forward, some to slip their steeds past the creature and into the fortress. Yet the monster moved once more to block the gate, lashing forth with the War-bar to smash aside warrior and mount. Yet again Red Bale flared up as it drank Troll blood, cleaving across the creature's fending wrist.

With a great bellow of rage, the Ogru struck at Gildor. *Krang!* The iron bar whelmed down upon empty stone, for the Elf was not there; he had leapt forward, under the blow. And impelled by all the force the Lian warrior could muster, Bale cut a great open swath across the Troll's abdomen. The Ogru roared in agony and stumbled to its knees as steaming entrails spilled forth amid a whelming gush of black blood. Gildor's sword lashed out, the blade-jewel blazing scarlet as Bale sliced through the Troll's throat, the Elf leaping aside as the huge Troll smashed facedown unto the cobbles, dead before striking the stone. And green fire blazed behind Gildor's eyes: Vanidor's killer had been slain.

King Galen spurred forward, Wildwind leaping over the great corpse. And with a glad shout, inward poured the Legion after.

And out upon Claw Moor, with a great juddering din of iron, Ubrik's brigade hurtled into the charging Swarm of Guula, lance thrusting against barbed spear, saber clashing against tulwar, horse lunging against Hèlsteed. And Men died, and corpse-foe fell slain, as the forces shocked through each other, driving beyond one another's ranks. Ubrik sounded his black-oxen horn, and the Vanadurin wheeled to meet the turning Guula. And Ubrik gave the call to mount a second charge, though he knew that in the end the battle could have but one outcome, for his fifteen hundred Harlingar rode against six thousand reavers. Yet the Reachmarshal also knew that King Galen and the Legion now pouring through the distant gate and into the Kinstealer's holt needed time to disrupt Modru's plan, and, by delaying the Guula that time could be purchased. The price would be deadly, yet it was a price Ubrik was willing to pay.

Back at the fortress, as King Galen and the Legion surged across the bridge and through the gate and into the court-yards of the dark citadel, a shuddering blackness seemed to jolt across the darkling sky above as a spreading ebon tide surged throughout the Shadowlight.

Lord Gildor raced back up the steps to the wall above, where battle still raged. He looked upward through the Dimmendark, though he knew what he would see. Slowly the dim glow of the Sun was fading away as the arc of the unseen Moon ate across the last of the feeble disk above. And the Elf's heart pounded as an ever-deepening gulf of blackness rolled forth across the land. The deep toll of a great Ruchen gong knelled through the darkling air: *Doon!. . . Doon!. . . Doom!* And Gildor despaired, for all about him *Spaunen* fought with growing strength . . . their time had come at last. Although the Men of Valon battled with fierce determination, still their eyes flicked to the dimming sky, and their faces were grim, for the darkest hour of the Darkest Day had come: it was the time of the Sun-Death.

South, in Grūwen Pass, Vidron and Talarin surveyed the pitiful remnants of the Host that had defied the Horde for *lo!* these many 'Darkdays. Attack after attack had they fended off, delaying the Swarm, buying time for King Galen. Yet the Horde had hammered time and again into the Men of Wellen and the Elves of Arden Vale, pounding them back with each strike. And now it was the fifth 'Darkday since the Battle of Grūwen had begun, and each 'Day more of the Wellenen had fallen, more of the Lian had been slain. Still, hundreds upon hundreds of the *Rûpt* had been slaughtered as the combat raged by frigid 'Day and bitter 'Night upon the heights of the icy col. But slowly the teeming Horde had battered the Host the full length of the narrow pass. And now, no longer did the sheer stone walls protect the Legion's flanks, for at last they had been driven backwards across the entire width of the Rigga Mountains; and exhausted Men and weary Elves and spent steeds stood on the margins of Gron and watched as Spawn poured through the notch and down into the land to hem the allies against a great bluff.

"Aye, Lord Talarin, I deem you counted well," growled Fieldmarshal Vidron. "I, too, make our number to be a scant six hundred or so. And though we've left five thousand Wrg lying dead in our wake, still there be another five thousand to come against us this last time."

Talarin merely grunted and said no word in reply as he watched the *Spaunen* continue to swarm forth from Kregyn.

As the last of the *Rûpt* joined the iron ring surrounding the trapped allies, raucous calls blatted forth from the brazen horns of the enemy, and scimitar, tulwar, hammer, and cudgel were brandished. The foe readied themselves to destroy the last of this stubborn Legion.

Vidron raised his black-oxen horn unto his lips, and its resonant call split the air, to be answered by the clarions of the surviving Wellenen. And four hundred or so weary Men, and half that number of worn Elves, mounted up onto exhausted steeds and made ready for one last battle.

Yet even as the allies girded themselves for the final charge, a great wave of blackness surged through the Dimmendark, and a loud wordless jeering shout rose up from the Horde. Talarin's eye caught that of Vidron. "It is the time of the Sun-Death, Hrosmarshal," said the Lian warrior, grimly. "It comes upon us even now, and I fear that Galen King's mission has failed."

Beyond the Grimwall and within the ring of the Rimmen Mountains in the Land of Riamon, furious battle raged before the gates of Mineholt North as Men and Elves and Dwarves alike fell upon the Swarm besieging the mountain where was delved the Dwarven Realm.

Swift horses bearing bright Elves shocked into the *Spaunen*, and the Men of Dael, on foot, struggled hand to hand with the foe. Forth from Mineholt North poured the black-armored Dwarves, hewing left and right with their double-bitted axes, cleaving a swath through the Squam.

Yet the Spawn, too, took their toll, as Free Folk fell slain by *Rûpt* weapon, and the vast numbers of the Horde pressed back in upon the allies.

Thrice had King Dorn joined his Men of Dael with the Elves of Coron Eiron to try to break this siege of Mineholt North and free the Dwarves of King Brek. Yet thrice had the Yrm hurled them back, leaving many dead in their wake.

Now this was their fourth attack, and its outcome teetered in the balance. The battle raged to and fro, but at last the Men won unto the Dwarves' side, splitting through the center of the ranks of the Horde. A great glad shout rose up from the allies, only to clog in their throats; for just as it seemed that finally they had the advantage, a great tide of darkness rolled throughout the Shadowlight—and the hearts of Men and Elves and Dwarves alike plummeted. And the Horde surged 'round them, beringing them in an evil clutch as darkness descended upon the land.

King Aranor of Valon sat upon his steed at the fore of a great Host, and at his side sat Reggian, Steward of Pendwyr. From concealment on the slopes of the Brin Downs they looked forth upon the vast throng marching into the plains of Jugo. The Lakh of Hyree had come north, skirting the Brin Downs, and now the swart Men of the south marched past the Host.

And overhead the Sun was bright.

Now Aranor turned to survey the Legion, perhaps half the numbers of the Lakh. And the King knew that the Host would be hard-pressed, yet they would not quail from this fight.

Once more Aranor swung his gaze to the distant enemy, and *lo!* they ground to a halt even as he looked *and fell prostrate upon their faces upon the ground . . . as if in worship!*

And a darkness commenced to fall upon the land. Aranor glanced to the sky, and the hidden Moon began to eat the Sun.

And south upon the waters of the Avagon Sea the fleet of Arbalin, along with the great Elvenship *Eroean*—a ship not seen in these waters for more than six thousand years—came to stand across the mouth of Hile Bay, where sat the ships of the Rovers of Kistan; yet the enemy made no move to break the blockade, for they moaned in ecstasy as an arc of darkness cut into the orb above.

*   *   *

Warrows wept as they fled back toward Littlefen. Rood was in flames, for once again the great Swarm of maggot-folk had razed a Bosky town. Captain Alver's Thornwalkers had not been able to divert the Spawn from their march of destruction down Two Fords Road. And the raids of the Wellenen upon the Horde had been of little effect, for the Men were hopelessly outnumbered. No other allies had come unto the Seven Dells, though a herald had lately ridden to Captain Stohl bearing news that more Wellenen were on the way—but they had not yet arrived. And now the Warrows tramped toward the refuge of the marshes—though it was questionable how long the fens would remain safe, for they were iced over and even Rūck and Hlōk could walk across the frozen morass.

And as the Wee Folk trudged north and west, the hard-edged darkness of the Shadowlight began to deepen.

Reachmarshal Ubrik wheeled his outnumbered brigade once more to face the Guula. But the corpse-folk did not array themselves to whelm down on the surviving Men. Instead, Guula sat unmoving upon Hêlsteeds and gazed at the sky above Claw Moor. And while a distant gong tolled *Doom!* a vast darkness slowly descended upon the land.

Merrilee, Burt, Dill, Teddy, and Arch—Wee Folks all—mounted upon horses led by Vanadurin, were among the last to cross the bridge and come into Modru's dark citadel. Yet even as they thundered through the gate and clattered forth upon the fortress cobblestone and raced deep into the holt, a great spectral blackness flooded the very air. Men cried and rubbed at their eyes, and those upon steeds reined to a halt and dismounted. They groped forward with outstretched hands, or felt their way with extended sword or lance, for the Men could not see.

Yet the maggot-folk, too, were blinded by the cloaking blackness and stumbled unseeing, fumbling and feeling as they went.

But still the fighting continued: hand-to-hand grappling, dirk and longknife against kris and yataghan, blind warrior versus sightless Spawn, the Legionnaires crying *Adon!* as each came to grips with another being, striking swiftly if they received no answer, or the wrong reply.

Yet one warrior did not need to reply, for his weapon blazed forth his identity; Red Bale's blade-jewel still flared scarlet, and the ruby shafts of light drove through the darkness. And Elven eyes were not completely baffled by the ebon radiance, for Gildor and Flandrena both could dimly see those around them.

But it was the Warrows whose jewel-hued Utruni eyes fared best, for they could still see by the wrenching black light that streamed forth from Modru's Iron Tower, though their vision was greatly curtailed, as if looking through a dark glass.

"They can't see!" cried Teddy, leaping down from his steed and running forth to take the hand of the warrior who had led his horse.

Dismounting, all the Warrows stepped to the riders they had followed. "Stick with us," said Arch. "We can see."

"I thought I'd gone blind," croaked Degan, and Merrilee squeezed the Man's hand.

"What should we do?" asked Dill, peering through the blackness.

"We can pick off Rūcks and such," answered Burt, "or we can try to do something about *that*." The buccan stabbed a finger upward toward the tower whence the darkness streamed.

"You're right, Burt," agreed Merrilee, "we must invade that spike, for there, I think, lies the foul heart of this evil blackness . . . and it must be destroyed. But I fear we cannot do it alone. Let us go forth, gathering more warriors along the way—and quickly, for the Sun-Death of the Darkest Day has come."

And so the Wee Folk moved swiftly into the dark fortress for an assault upon the tower, collecting allies as they went—Warrows leading Men. And among those mustered and led hand in hand toward the spire was the High King of Mithgar: Galen, son of Aurion.

And somewhere within the holt a great gong tolled: *Doon!* . . . *Doon!* . . . *Doom!*

Tuck groaned and rolled over, his mind struggling upward from darkness. Through the window came the blats of Rūcken brass and the resonant calls of black-oxen horns, the cries of Men and the snarls of Spawn in combat, and the din and clash of steel upon steel. *Got . . . got to get up,* he muzzily thought, and tried to rise; but with a sharp hiss of air sucked in through clenched teeth, agony lancing upward from his broken foot, the buccan sank back to lie upon the cold stone floor, his legs drawn up, his entire being laced with pain. And then he remembered the looming black figure in the hideous mask. *Modru! That was Modru! The Evil One!* A chill dread raced through the Warrow's veins. *The Princess!*

"My Lady!" Tuck gasped, his mind now fully alert as he sat up with a start and stared wildly about. Laurelin was gone, as well as Modru. *The tower!* Tuck vaguely recalled the Evil One's hissing voice . . . something about taking the Lady Laurelin to the tower above . . . *to meet her fate.*

Tuck scrambled to his feet, anguish jolting up his leg. Taking up his bow and gritting his teeth, the Warrow hobbled to the door left standing ajar. A swift look down the length of the torch-lit hallway revealed no maggot-folk. And so, casting his hood over his head and adjusting his cloak, and closing the leaves of the silver locket—that had *somehow* sprung open—and tucking it under his torn jacket, the buccan limped the few strides to the near end of the hall, where steps mounted, and up these he struggled.

The steps came up to a wide circular stone floor, nearly sixty feet in diameter. Around him the walls of the tower reared upward into high darkness, and a torch-lit open stairwell clung to the side and spiralled up into the shadowed vault above.

Clamping his jaws together, bow in hand, Tuck started upward, step by torturous step, the *grinding* in his boot sending waves of sickening *hurt* through his very bones. Yet up the stairs he struggled, flight upon flight, past landing after landing, each with a window slit, and the great stone floor became lost in the blackness below. And sweating, grunting in pain, the wee Warrow slowly neared the top.

"Guttra!" a harsh voice suddenly snarled out, and Tuck gasped in startlement as the word echoed down the stairwell, for there, just one flight above upon a wide landing before a massive door, stood two scimitar-wielding Hlōks.

"Guttra!" Again came the harsh challenge, and Tuck thought to himself, *Do it right, bucco, for if you miss, and*

if there are any more of these Spawn behind that door, it's all over here and now.

Swiftly the buccan plucked an arrow from his quiver and set it to string and drew, aimed, and loosed all in one motion. And ere that arrow struck, he was reaching for another. *Sssthock!* The first bolt struck one Hlōk full in the chest, and even as that Spawn pitched backwards . . . *Ssshthwock!* a second arrow pierced the other guard, this Hlōk to tumble down the flight of stairs and land with a sickening thud at the Warrow's feet as the scimitar spun down through the blackness toward the distant stone floor below.

Tuck paused, a third arrow set to string, the buccan listening, hearing only his own ragged breathing as he tried to determine if any foe behind the door above had detected the encounter . . . *ching* . . . The scimitar struck far below. As if that were a signal, Tuck began the ascent once more. And he painfully hobbled up the remaining steps to the landing and past the other dead Hlōk to come at last to the iron-banded door of Modru's chamber.

Tuck pressed his ear to the portal but could hear nought; the panel was too massive. Cautiously, the Warrow pushed at the door, and then shoved harder; but it did not budge, for it was barred on the inside. *I've got to get in there,* thought Tuck, *and see if this is where Modru has brought the Lady Laurelin.*

Hobbling past the dead Hlōk, Tuck painfully clambered upon a stone bench. Removing his quiver, he leaned out of the narrow window slit and peered along the outside tower wall. *There!* A short distance to the side and up was another, larger slit—and the eye-wrenching black radiance poured out through the opening. Tuck examined the stone. It was covered with ice and hoarfrost, yet projections outjutted from the wall just as they had on the angles of the ramparts beringing the fortress—and the buccan believed that he could reach the wide slit. Tuck glanced below but quickly jerked his eyes away, for the plumb drop down the sheer tower wall was frightening. He could only hope that he wouldn't fall, as he prepared to squeeze through the narrow slit and out upon the vertical height of the tower.

Tuck still had a short hank of Elven rope hanging from his belt. He tied one end 'round his waist and the other end to his bow and quiver, and he lowered the weapons out the window. Then he levered his body up and squeezed through the slit. Then, taking a deep breath and keeping his eyes upon the wall before him, Tuck grasped a frost-rimed stone and swung out upon the face of the sheer drop, his boots finding purchase on the icy juts, his left foot bearing weight in spite of the pain. And the broken-footed Warrow clung to the frozen stones on the side of the tower and began edging over and up toward the wide slit, his bow and quiver depending from a rope 'round his waist and swinging pendulously. And as he clambered across the sheer face, a great brass gong began dinning, the brazen sound pulsing throughout the holt: *Doon! . . . Doon! . . . Doom!* And a deepening pall of darkness descended upon the Iron Tower.

Laurelin yanked and twisted and pulled back in vain as Modru dragged her up the long well of steps and past two Lōkken guards and into the chamber atop the tower, for the Evil One's grip was like iron, and his wrenching strength was overwhelming.

Boom! The iron-bound door slammed to behind her.

Clang! The great bar fell into place.

And despite her struggles, Modru rent her cloak from her and hauled her past the ebon *blot* of the Myrkenstone and to a great dark lithic altar. He heaved her upon the raised slab and roughly locked her wrists and ankles into iron cuffs embedded in the stone.

The slab was canted, and Laurelin's head was lower than her feet. By arching her neck and tilting her face back, she could see the Myrkenstone looming nearby upon its pedestal. And her long flaxen hair lay in a channel that ran down from her shoulders to the edge of the stone. And Modru took up an iron knife and began hacking off her tresses, hissing, "We can't have these locks of yours soaking up the blood, for all of it will be needed: to *slake* my Master's thirst—upon His advent unto Mithgar—to invest Him with His full powers here in the Middle Plane; and to *quench* the Myrkenstone, closing the way behind, sealing forever the fate of all!"

Laurelin gasped, and again Modru's sissing laughter hissed forth as he sawed the blade through her hair. "*Ahh.*

At last you know your purpose, *Princess*. Recall! Once you pledged that you would never serve me—I remind you of your foolish words now that it is time for the throne of Mithgar to be mine. Never serve me . . . *tchaa!* It is *your* royal blood that my Master will quaff, *your* blood that will quench the 'Stone. I would have used the *Dolh's*—Vanidor's—but he was of Adonar; and here, the blood of one born to Mithgar is needed. Faugh! Any fool's would have done as well as yours, so long as he was of this world, but it *pleases* me to use the blood of a royal damosel."

Tears brimmed in Laurelin's eyes as Modru stepped back to survey his handiwork. "*Sss.* Excellent. My Lord Gyphon will be pleased, for though your hair is cropped, still you are . . . unblemished. *Yesss,* pleased, for it has been long since He has sipped the blood of one so fair . . . and He *thirsts.*"

Modru turned and took up a stone basin and set it upon a stand at the edge of the altar where it would catch the blood flowing down the channel. And beside the basin he set an iron chalice. Then the Evil One brought forth a tray covered with black velvet, and he set it down on the altar slab and unfolded the cloth, revealing an ebon knife crudely shaped of the same hideous matter as the Myrkenstone. Lastly, Modru laid open a great tome on the slab and then consulted a chart.

And there came to the great turret the knell of a massive gong: *Doon! . . . Doon! . . . Doom!* And through the window slits an utter darkness could be seen descending upon the world.

Modru turned to Laurelin and hissed, "It is time, for the Sun-Death has come."

And the Evil One removed his black gauntlets, and his great clawlike hands took up the 'Stone knife and held it on high; and he began chanting, reading from the tome, the guttural obscene words of power rolling forth—vile, malignant, evil.

Still the gong tolled, and Merrilee's heart hammered in dread to hear the ominous *Doom!* Yet she and Burt, Dill, Teddy, and Arch each led hand in hand a small group of Sun-Death-blinded warriors, five Warrows guiding eighteen

Men. And they veered between widespread groups of unseeing maggot-folk and struck for the tower.

At last they came to the great spire and made their way to a door. Whispered instructions were passed, and Men were cautioned to hold their places—to move not—and to be silent, for Spawn were near. And then, arrows nocked to bows, the chary Warrows slowly opened the door.

Torchlight streamed out, and the startled Men could see once more. *Har!* cried Rūcks to see the light streaming across the courtyard. Swiftly, sword in hand, Men rushed in after the Wee Ones and slammed the door behind.

Before them lay an empty hall.

"Quick now," commanded Galen, his voice low but urgent, "we must hurry. Spawn may be in these corridors, and surely those without come after. Let us to the top, for if the Wee Ones are right, the black heart of the Dimmendark lies in this pinnacle, and it must be destroyed."

Swiftly up the stairs they went, and no *Spaunen* did they see. One flight . . . two flights . . . and another and they came to the open stone floor above which reared the tower. They began the ascent up the long spiral staircase twisting upward inside the walls, King Galen in the fore with Steelheart in his grip, and Men and Warrows coming after.

Landing after landing they crossed, each with a window slit looking upon the Sun-Death blackness outside, as upward they pressed. Now they neared the top, and they could see a door at the head of the stairs. Another landing they came to, and a dead Hlōk lay in a pool of his own blood, a shortened arrow through his heart.

As they hastened up the last flight of steps, Warrows looked questioningly at one another, for they knew the Hlōk below had been slain by a bolt from the bow of a Wee One: Yet who could it be?

They came to the last landing, and *lo!* another arrow-pierced Hlōk lay slain before the iron-bound door—this bolt, too, from buccan bow.

With her heart pounding in hope, Merrilee knelt down to examine the quarrel, but ere she could do so—

The shrill scream of a Woman rang through the door, and a desperate anguished cry of words, their meaning muffled and lost.

Yet Galen recognized the voice. *"Laurelin!"* he shouted,

and hurled himself at the door, to no avail. Wildly his eyes cast about. "The bench! The stone bench!" he cried, leaping for the massive seat below the window slit. "We'll use it as a ram to batter down the door!"

And as Vanadurin sprang to help him, *Ssss-thunk!* a black-shafted arrow chunked into the door. Merrilee and the buccen scrambled to the edge of the landing. There below, clattering up through the torch-lit shadows, swarmed a band of maggot-folk. *Shssh!* . . . *Shssh!* More black-shafted arrows hissed upward, to be answered in kind by deadly Warrow bolts flying downward.

And behind, as the Men heaved up the heavy stone slab to whelm the door, another piercing cry rang forth from Modru's chamber.

Doon! . . . *Doon!* . . . *Doom!* Still the toll of the gong knelled out as Tuck slowly hoisted himself up and across, his fingers clutching at the frost-rimed stone, his feet pressing into crevices. His teeth were gritted against the pain, and his eyes were locked upon the sheer wall before him to keep from looking down from the dizzying height to the courtyard far below.

A great darkness blotted the land, yet Tuck's jewel-hued eyes saw by a different light than those of other Folk—a light seen only by the Wee Ones. And up through this blackness he crawled, edging toward a wide window slit out of which poured an ebon radiance.

At last he came to the opening, and guttural obscene mouthings hissed forth from the window and fell upon his ears, and he shuddered in revulsion to hear such malediction voiced. Yet into this slot he would climb. He hauled up his dangling bow and quiver and slid them onto the wide sill before him, and then he hefted himself up after, clambering into the eye-wrenching blackness.

Squinting against the ebon radiance, through the turret wall he crawled, pushing his bow and arrows before him. He came out upon a raised stone catwalk that encircled the round room below. Yet Tuck saw little of the chamber, for his eyes were *trapped*—held by a great, dark *blot* resting upon a pedestal in the center of the room. And although Tuck did not know it, this was the very piece, the very fragment of the Dragon Star that had cloven the immense burning gash as it slashed over the Boskydells and beyond the Northwood, beyond Rian . . . even beyond Gron. It had smashed to Mithgar in the barren wastes where was exiled Modru, *just as Gyphon had planned four millennia agone*. This was the Comet Spawn, the Myrkenstone, the vile eater of light, the source of the ebon radiance that spread throughout the Dimmendark. And it trapped Tuck's eyes and seemed to draw the vision out of them, steadily replacing sight with darkness. And the Warrow could not tear his dimming gaze away from the hideous eye-wrenching *hole,* for its vile power held him locked.

Yet other powers, other energies, were at work within the chamber, too, as guttural obscene runewords rolled forth from the mouth of the Evil One to shock through the room.

And the very air began to *gather,* to *ripple,* as if it were become a dark liquid into which the words *fell* as would ebon stones fall into black waters.

And through the undulation, a dim figure began to appear, as if a distant dark portal had opened and an indistinct shape had stepped toward the room, drawing nearer with every hideous word uttered.

Closer it came, and closer; and with each syllable, each step, the form took on substance, and it *glowed* with a dark halo—as did the Myrkenstone. And now the figure could be seen more clearly, as if through a fluctuant glass: a Man, some would say; an Elf, would claim others; yet He was neither. Instead, it was He who once held Adon's trust, who once stood next to the High One's throne, who once wielded power exceeded only by The One, who once fell from grace and was forgiven, who fell again . . . beyond the Spheres. It was Gyphon. And as He issued forth from the Great Abyss, the undulant air rippled less and less, for He came unto Mithgar, and finally His image took on a sharp definition and He could be seen clearly at last. And He was exquisitely beautiful, for He was the Great Evil.

It was Gyphon's darkly luminant form that pulled Tuck's eye from the Myrkenstone; and the buccan gasped, his spirit whelmed by the comeliness of the figure he saw; and he could but barely keep his eyes upon such fairness. The Warrow glanced away, and his heart lurched in horror, for there beyond the Myrkenstone was Laurelin, shackled upon an altar. Above her loomed evil Modru, chanting, foul words issuing forth from the hideous iron mask, his arms raised upon high, the vile 'Stone knife clutched in his left hand. And a stone basin and an iron chalice rested upon a stand at the end of a blood channel in the altar. *He's going to kill her!* Tuck's mind screamed.

His hands trembling in haste, the buccan untied his bow from the Elven rope, and his eyes sought an arrow. And there before him, resting in his quiver, was the red quarrel from Othran's Crypt: an arrow no longer a dull ruddy color, but instead now flaring scarlet in the black light streaming from the Myrkenstone, an arrow made of a strange light metal and borne by the buccan on an epic journey from Challerain Keep to the Weiunwood and thence to Arden Vale, through Drimmen-deeve and the Larkenwald beyond, down the Argon and back to Gûnarring Gap, and thence up the Grimwall and through Grūwen Pass into Gron, and finally across Claw Moor and under the walls of the fortress and up to this very room atop the Iron Tower. And Tuck's hands, as if guided by another's will, snatched up the crimson bolt and set it to bowstring.

But even as Tuck nocked the arrow, the ripples in the air vanished entirely, and now Gyphon—the Great Evil— stood at last upon Mithgar, corporeal but powerless until the quaffing of sacrificial blood and the quenching of the Myrkenstone. The fate of the world teetered upon the brink of doom.

And Tuck stood and drew the red shaft to the full.

And Laurelin screamed, *"No!"*

For at the same moment Gyphon stepped forth into Mithgar, the Princess saw the Warrow rise up out of the shadows upon the catwalk. By his clawed face and silveron armor gleaming through his torn jacket she knew him to be Tuck, and she saw that he aimed at Modru.

"No!" she cried again, with all the force she could muster. "Slay Gyphon! Slay the Great Evil!"

The Great Evil? And then Tuck knew. And his aim shifted to the fair luminant figure. *Yet how can such beauty be evil? And even should I kill Gyphon, Modru will murder Laurelin ere I can set another arrow to bow.*

Again Tuck's aim fell upon Modru, but the Evil One had spun around to see the Warrow, and the 'Stone knife now threatened Laurelin's throat, though the obscene chanting went on.

"Gyphon!" Laurelin's scream was rent from her very soul. "Slay Gyphon!"

In that moment, *Boom!* . . . *Boom!* . . . *Boom!* the iron-bound door shuddered from the impact of a ram, and splinters flew as the heavy planking cracked under the whelming blows, but the great bar staying the door held fast.

Once more the buccan's aim swung to Gyphon, but he could not bring himself to shoot, for if he did, Laurelin would die. Again he sighted upon Modru . . . yet Tuck realized that Modru was but a *servant* of the Great Evil, and to slay the serf and yet let *this* Master live would be the sheerest folly. And, too, it then would be the Master who would murder the Princess, perhaps to complete the ritual ere Tuck could set another arrow to bow.

Boom! . . . *Boom!* . . . *Boom!*

And as the Warrow's aim wavered, two memories stirred deep within his mind.

From Othran's Tomb:

> *Loose not the Red Quarrel*
> *Ere appointed dark time.*

And Rael's Rede:

> *"Neither of two Evils must thy strike claim;*
> *Instead smite the Darkness between the same."*

Suddenly the cryptic meaning of both of these riddles became clear to the Warrow, resolving his dilemma. And as the booming ram whelmed the door, and planks split and the bar cracked, Tuck swiftly aimed at the Myrkenstone, yet the ebon *blot* again wrenched at his Utruni eyes, and his remaining sight was gone: He could not see.

The voice of Old Barlo rang in his mind: *"The arrow as strays might well'er been throwed away."*

And Modru's chanting stopped!

And Tuck knew he had to shoot *now!*

Adon, guide my aim, fervently prayed 'Stone-blinded Tuck. *Red Quarrel, red arrow, fly true.* And he loosed the shaft.

Like a scarlet streak, the Red Quarrel hissed crimson across the room to strike the Myrkenstone square in the center, the strange metal arrow piercing deeply into the ebon *blot*. A blinding detonation shattered forth, dashing Tuck violently back against the window sill and blasting the batter-whelmed door into splinters and flying bolts of wood, hurling Galen and the others down upon the stair landing, their stone-bench ram smashing into shards as it fell ponderously to the deck and slid heavily down the steps. And a savagely intense glare flashed up to flood the room with a blazing incandescence so bright, so violent, that scrolls began to smolder and alembics filled with arcane liquids shattered.

For the Myrkenstone flared, radiance blasting forth, as if it yielded up the very sunlight it had stolen. And the ravening fulgor raged, blinding luminance blaring forth, great radiant beams blasting from the chamber.

And on the landing, amid the wrack of the iron-bound door, Galen and Merrilee and the Men and Warrows struggled up and shielded their eyes with up-flung arms and staggered toward the room. But they could not come into the glare, for it was too bright, and the wild light exploding through the door raged out like a furious gale ripping at weapons and armor and clothing and folk alike.

Blazing candescence lit up the interior of the tower, and stabbing beams shot through the window slits; and where the savage light touched, inside and out, Spawn were destroyed. Thus did some *Rûpt* perish upon the fortress walls, and so too died all the *Spaunen* upon the stairwell within the Iron Tower.

And in the fury-filled chamber atop the spire, raging light blasted forth from the Myrkenstone. And in this roaring fulmination, Tuck staggered to his feet, the unbearable brightness lancing into his 'Stone-blind eyes, *and the buccan could see once more!* Yet this 'Stone-light, too, ripped at Tuck's vision, hammering it toward oblivion. Still, the buccan's scathed sight saw Modru rise up from the altar where he had been flung over Laurelin. The Evil One stood and turned and held his clawlike hands out before him as if warding off an attack. Hoarse screams rang forth as he staggered back in horror against the stone slab, for the flesh on his taloned fingers was rent away by the savage light, and the very bones of his grotesque hands and wrists shone forth only to crumble into dust. His piercing screams chopped into silence as the flesh was rent from his throat. His chest and lungs were blasted away, his ribs collapsing into ruin. His desperate eyes *dissolved,* leaving empty sockets behind, which then disintegrated, too, as the remainder of his body pitched backwards onto the altar, destroyed ere he struck. And the hideous iron mask, now empty, fell to the floor with a hollow *Blang!*

And stricken by the scarlet bolt the Myrkenstone, too, fell toward ruin, its substance blazing away, perishing. And in the blasting glare as the 'Stone disintegrated, once more the air began to ripple. And a distant dark portal seemed to open, and Gyphon's features twisted into desperate rage; He screamed, yet no sound was heard. He began to recede, as if drawn back along the path whence He had come. And as the ripples became more intense, Gyphon's aspect began to *change:* His fairness, His comeliness, altered. His beauty fell away as if it were a mask removed, and a loathsome semblance stared forth. Yet this aspect, too, altered, shifting to a ghastliness beyond description as the figure of Gyphon rushed back toward oblivion. As the undulant air shuddered, once again Gyphon's features shifted, and Tuck could not face the hideous monster that fell down into the Great Abyss beyond the Spheres.

And the blinding flare died, for the Myrkenstone was destroyed, slain by a Red Quarrel loosed by one of the Wee Folk. And with its destruction, the Dimmendark collapsed.

Out in the courtyards and upon the walls of the fortress, hand-to-hand battle raged, and the passing of the Dimmendark was not then noted, for still the Moon hid the Sun, though a dim corona shone forth. But, of a sudden, beads of light sprang out from the rim of the unseen Moon, and slowly a fingernail-thin crescent of the Sun blazed forth. Rūcks, Hlōks, and Ghûls had time only to glance upward in horror ere the Withering Death struck; and they shrivelled to dust, arms and armor falling with a clatter to the stone.

On Claw Moor, Ubrik and his brigade waited grimly for the blackness to pass, knowing that when the battle began once more, they would fall to the tulwars and barbed spears of the Ghûls.

Yet when the darkness at last fell away, *lo!* the flaring edge of the Sun gradually emerged from behind the unseen Moon; and before the astonished eyes of the Vanadurin, Ghûls and Hèlsteeds collapsed into withered husks, and a chill wind gnawed through their ashes.

In Grūwen Pass, Vidron, Talarin, and the surviving Men and Elves girded themselves for the last charge, but suddenly the Dimmendark *vanished,* and an arc of the Sun shone forth, partially eclipsed; and the japing Spawn jeered no more, for they were fallen into ruination.

In the Land of the Thorns, the Struggles came to an end in a town called Rood—central to the Boskydells—for there raged the Horde when the Dimmendark collapsed and a curve of the Sun burned down upon the Spawn.

Dwarf King Brek of Mineholt North, King Dorn of Riamon, and Coron Eiron of Darda Galion came together upon the battlefield before the slopes of the Rimmen Mountains. They squinted upward at the emerging Sun and then at the War-ground, where Men and Dwarves and Elves wandered awestruck among the slain and wounded. And of the savage Horde there was no trace, except for tattered clothes and empty armor and fallen weapons . . . and dregs stirring in the wind.

In Jugo the land had not fallen into total darkness, for there the Moon did not eat all of the Sun. And Aranor and Reggian had watched as the Lakh of Hyree had fallen down in worship at the beginning of the fearful occultation. Slowly the hidden Moon had eaten across the disk of the Sun while Aranor and Reggian debated. The King of Valon thought to launch an immediate attack upon the prostrate Hyrania, while the Steward of Pendwyr argued to wait until the depth of the obscuration. Reggian prevailed, for he reasoned that the Lakh would be in the thrall of their canting when that moment came.

And so they waited, poised in the northern fringes of the Brin Downs, ready to launch the attack. At last the penumbral darkness reached its depth, and the horns of Pellar and Valon blew wildly as horsemen thundered across the plains.

Some among the Lakh looked up from their worship to see the Host charging down upon them, and they leapt to their feet, crying in alarm. Up swept the Hyrania, weapons in hand, ready to face the outnumbered Legion. And the swart Men looked to their Jemadars for orders, and the Jemadars in turn looked to the vacant-eyed slack-jawed emissaries governing their battles. But at that moment, the faces of the surrogates twisted in agony—eyes rolling white, spittle frothing from grimacing, clenched, shrieking mouths—and their muscles spasmed. And then, as if strings had been cut from puppets, the emissaries fell to the ground dead, as if the malignant will driving them had been slain.

Yet even though they knew that something was amiss in their vile chain of rule, perhaps in the Iron Tower itself, still the Jemadars turned to command their Men, for they would fight against their ancient enemies. And the Hyrani leaders shouted orders as the horsemen of Valon and Pellar crashed into their ranks. And a raging battle began, and the Lakh of Hyree fought with the faith and strength of zealots, for this was the day the long-held prophecy would be fulfilled.

Inward drove the Legion, spears and sabers meeting pikes and tulwars. And the Host sheered off, only to form and strike again.

And slowly the hidden Moon receded and the Sun grew toward fullness.

Again the Legion drove into the Hyrania, and once more steel skirled upon steel, and iron points pierced, and blades clove.

Men fell slain as the Sun crept from hiding.

Again the Host fell back to regroup, their ranks severely depleted. And Aranor and Reggian rode to one another to decide whether to press the fight once more or to withdraw.

And the Sun won free of the Moon.

And Gyphon did not appear among the files of the Hyrania: The prophecy was *false!* They had been *deceived!*

A moan of despair rose up from the Lakh, and many threw down their weapons and fled, while others went forth to the Legion and surrendered. Still others rent their hair and clothes and plunged knives into their own bosoms and fell dead, while a few—waving tulwars and screaming hoarsely—charged at the Host and fought to the death and were slain.

And the Battle of Jugo was finished.

In Hile Bay the fleeing Rovers of Kistan sailed upon the tide and into the blockade of the outnumbered ships of the Arbalina fleet. With ropes and timbers creaking, and canvass snapping in the wind, and waves *shsshing* upon hulls, the mighty armada of the south tacked and hauled toward the gap where lay the squadrons of the King's flotilla, and Aravan's ship, the *Eroean*. And catapults flung burning fire—*thwack!*—and timbers groaned against one another as argosy met flotilla. Some Rover ships burned, but so did craft of Arbalin, while others in each fleet sank, holed by great underwater ram beaks. Some Kistania craft were grappled and boarded, and hand-to-hand fighting ensued. Some brigand crews surrendered. But for the most part, the ships of the Rovers escaped, for their numbers were too many, and they sailed beyond the line of the Kingsvessels and away into the Avagon Sea, the swift *Eroean* in deadly pursuit.

Back at the Iron Tower, when the flare of the Myrkenstone died, Merrilee and Galen and Men and Warrows rushed through the sundered door and into the evil sanctum. And there, near a great scorched pedestal, they found Laurelin partially covered by a black cloak and shackled to an altar. And in the shimmering heat, Galen rent open the bonds and fiercely swept the Princess up in his arms.

And Merrilee glanced across the chamber and upward, and there on a stone catwalk stood Tuck swaying, his foot broken and his body bruised, his face clawed . . . and deeply seared, as if by the Sun.

"Tuck!" cried the damman, and she raced past the charred stand and to the far side of the room, and scrambled up the ladder to him, and caught him as he collapsed to his knees. And she wept and would have kissed him but did not, for she was afraid her touch would harm his burned face. "Oh Tuck, my buccaran . . . my buccaran." And she sobbed uncontrollably as she held onto him.

"Merrilee?" Tuck's voice was questioning, hesitant, and his seared hands fumbled out to touch her face. "Oh my dammia, I cannot see you, for I am blind."

At that moment out upon the ramparts a great glad shout rose up to greet the emerging Sun, for the foe was slain! The Shadowlight of Winternight was gone, the Winter War was ended; and here, as well as in all Mithgar, Free Folk rejoiced.

But there were those who did not join in the jubilation, for they stood among their slaughtered comrades and wept: in Riamon and Jugo, in Pellar and at Grūwen Pass, in the Boskydells, and upon Claw Moor in Gron.

And at the Iron Tower, atop the ramparts above the gate, stood five warriors, each of them wounded in some fashion—arm, wrist, forehead, side, leg—blood seeping unattended. They did not seek aid, but instead stood with heads bowed: a youth, a Man, Prince Igon; a buccan Warrow, Dink Weller; two Elves, Lian warriors, Flandrena and Gildor; and a Dwarf—bloody Drakkalan in hand, hood cast over his head—Brega. And they grieved. And before them sat a wee Warrow—Patrel Rushlock—weeping, keening, clasping the slain body of a black-armored buccan unto him.

CHAPTER 6

The Journey Home

Tuck was led down from the tower to suitable quarters below where he was undressed and put to bed. A healer was summoned to treat his and the Lady Laurelin's wounds, for she too had been burned by the searing light of the flaring Myrkenstone, though not as severely as the buccan. Modru himself—though not by choice—had shielded the maiden from that initial, most violent blast, for he had been standing between the Princess and the 'Stone at the moment the Red Quarrel had struck. And when the Withering Death had smote him and he had pitched backwards onto the altar, his empty cloak had fallen across Laurelin in such a way that only her hands had been directly exposed to the unbearable glare; yet she had been closer to the 'Stone than Tuck, and her hands had been terribly seared.

Even so, at Laurelin's behest the healer treated Tuck's wounds first. Herbs were dissolved in water and daubed upon the Warrow's burns, the healer using a sunscald remedy; Tuck's broken foot was bound; and cold compresses were set upon his bruised arm and ribs. Then the healer carefully looked at the Warrow's eyes and said, "There's nought I can do about this. Perhaps Elven medicine can help, but . . ."

As the healer fell silent and turned to treat the Princess, Arch Hockley darted down the stairs and out the door to find Lord Gildor or Flandrena. The buccan called to several Men, but none knew the whereabouts of the Lian warriors until the Warrow came upon a soldier who said he'd last seen the Elves above the gate.

The buccan turned and trotted to the wall and up a set of steps to the ramparts over the portal. There he found the Lian warriors, as well as Prince Igon, Dink Weller, Patrel, and Brega staring grimly out across Claw Moor, where rolling clouds of a gathering storm could be seen from the northwest across the Claw Spur of the Gronfang Mountains.

"Lord Gildor," Arch panted, out of breath, "I've come to fetch you or Flandrena or both. Tuck's been blinded—"

"Tuck?" Patrel interrupted, his face haggard, his emerald eyes swollen. "He's alive? . . . Blinded? . . . How? Where?"

"Why, at the top of the tower, Captain," answered Arch. "He lost his sight when he destroyed the thing that made the Dimmendark, and light just exploded out of it—the Myrkenstone, the Lady Laurelin calls it—"

"Laurelin?" blurted Igon, cutting Arch's words short. "You . . . you've found Laurelin?"

"Oh aye," responded Arch. "The Lady is with the King and Tuck—though she's got a bit burned, too, 'cause when Tuck slew the 'Stone and killed Modru—"

"Modru slain . . . by Tuck?" Lord Gildor now asked, his green eyes wide.

"Look," said Arch, exasperated, "we could stand here all day telling tales about how Tuck slew the 'Stone and caused the Dimmendark to collapse, and how he killed Modru and rescued the Lady and sent Gyphon back beyond the Spheres—"

Gyphon! gasped several at once, but Arch was not to be deterred.

"Yes: Gyphon," snapped the buccan. "But I'm not here to tell stories. The plain fact is, Tuck needs your help, Lord Gildor, Flandrena—if you have any—and the sooner the better. And if you are interested in Tuck's adventure, I'll tell you all I know on the way to his room—yet little enough that is."

"You are right, Wee One," said Lord Gildor. "We should not stand here listening to tales when there are those in need. Lead us; we will follow."

Arch turned to go, but at that moment the gruff voice of Brega came from beneath his hood: "Patrel, you go, too."

"I can't." The words choked out of Patrel, and he vaguely gestured with one hand. Glancing to where Patrel had motioned, tears sprang to Arch's eyes, too, for there among the dead the Warrow could see the forms of three slain buccen, buccen whom he had come to know and love.

"You *must* go," growled Brega. "You all must. I will

attend to things here." None could see the Dwarf's face beneath his cowl, yet they each knew that he grieved, too. They also knew that Brega was right: they needed to get away from the ramparts—away from the slain Warrows— to find peace . . . especially Patrel.

As Gildor and Flandrena, Igon and Dink, and Patrel all turned and followed Arch, hooded Brega stood upon the ramparts and watched the black clouds of the dark storm boil through the mountains and obscure the Sun, and a sudden blast of a frigid wind blew down upon the fortress.

Patrel was led weeping down the steps by Lord Gildor. And as they came to the bottom and crossed the cobbled way, behind them Reachmarshal Ubrik and his Men wearily rode across the iron drawbridge and in through the gate. It took long for the plodding horses to pass into the fortress, for their numbers were many; yet more than half the brigade had been left behind, slain upon Claw Moor.

In somber silence Arch led the five warriors across icy courtyards, and they followed the cobbled ways unto the central tower. They entered through a portal and mounted up a darkened stairwell and made their way along a torch-lit corridor to Tuck's door. Arch knocked softly, and then they all entered the room. There sat Laurelin wrapped in a blanket, and beside her sat King Galen, and Merrilee and the healer stood next to the bed where scalded Tuck lay.

Galen sprang to his feet, and he and Igon embraced one another, each glad to see that his brother lived. And then the Prince gently kissed Laurelin's bandaged hand. And she kissed Igon upon the cheek in her joy to see him once more; yet her happiness fled with quicksilver swiftness and tears brimmed in her eyes, for she had just moments before learned of Aurion's death, and it was as if her own father had died.

Merrilee turned to see Dink and Patrel, and she rushed across the room and gave both a hug and kissed Patrel. And she took Patrel by the hand and led him to the bed-side, where Lord Gildor and Flandrena spoke quietly with the healer.

"Tuck," she said softly, and the burnt-faced buccan turned his head toward the sound of her voice. "Tuck, I've a good friend here: it's Paddy, Paddy's come." To her con-

sternation Patrel began to weep, tears flowing down from
his viridian eyes.

"Why, Patrel." Tuck reached out a bandaged hand, and
Patrel took it gently. "This is a reunion, yet I hear you cry."

"Oh, Tuck . . . Merrilee," Patrel reached forth with his
other hand, gripping the damman's, too. "Danner . . . Danner is dead."

A great blizzard raged forth out of the Boreal Sea to
hurtle down upon Gron, shrieking wind wailing across the
wastes, driving snow before it. The storm hammered upon
the peaks and massifs of the Rigga and Gronfang mountains, whelming upon the Land. And its icy fist pounded at
the walls and turrets of the dark fortress. Legionnaires huddled inside, none to venture forth—not even into the
nearby courtyards—for Man, Elf, or Warrow could get lost
but a few paces into the blinding fling.

Yet Gron was not the only place hammered by the great
storm. It swept down along the Jillian Tors and across the
Dalara Plains to strike into Rian and the Lands below:
Wellen, the Boskydells, Harth, Rhone, Rell, Trellinath.

And it howled across the Steppes of Jord to vault the
Grimwall, and there savage fury mauled: in Aven and Ria-
mon, in Darda Erynian and Darda Galion, and in the
Greatwood.

And to the south, torrents of freezing rain and sleet
lashed down upon the Realms: Valon, Hoven, empty
Gûnar, Jugo, Arbalin Isle, and Pellar.

It was as if the Dimmendark had been holding back the
natural march of weather, for when the Myrkenstone had
been destroyed and the 'Dark had collapsed, wind and
snow and sleet and ice then had rushed in behind its fall—
to the woe of those now trapped in the blasts.

In Grüwen Pass, Vidron and Talarin and the other survivors of that epic stand grimly fought their way southward
through the shrieking blindness, pressing on for Arden
Vale, for they knew that if they stopped they would perish.

In the Boskydells, Warrows huddled in the Dinglewood,
and in Eastwood, and in Bigfen and Littlefen, and elsewhere,
for the Ghûls had destroyed many homes, and the Swarm
that had come after had levelled entire towns. Though no
Spawn remained alive, still they had done great damage,

and Wee Folk suffered for it, though the fens and the forests shielded them from the worst of the brunt.

In Riamon, the Men, Elves, and Dwarves entered through the great iron gates of Mineholt North and closed them fast behind to wait out the storm in the refuge of the carven halls of the Dwarvenholt under the Rimmen Mountains.

And all across Mithgar, wherever Free Folk dwelled, they took in friends and strangers caught in the blast and sheltered the homeless in bothy, cot, flet, burrow, lean-to, cavern, stone house, or whatever other haven they could offer. And whether it was meager or plentiful, food was shared. It was a time of great need, and few if any withheld their aid.

Though no one knew it at the time, the great storms were to rage without letup for nine days.

On the afternoon of the first day, Free Folk everywhere warily eyed the glowering skies and hurried toward shelter. In Gron, that shelter was in the dark fortress itself, where the Legion sought comfort and the wounded were treated. And one of those wounded was a blinded Warrow.

Lord Gildor, who was skilled in medicine, had examined Tuck's eyes; yet the Elf could not suggest any remedy to the healer concerning the buccan's sight, although Gildor did say that the Dara Rael in Arden perhaps could help, for she had more skill in healing than anyone else he knew. Gildor mixed a sleeping draught for Tuck to quaff later, for it could be seen that the buccan was in considerable pain and would need the potion to rest.

That night a fever came upon Tuck, and he alternately quaked with chills and burned with fire. His seared face and hands were ever hot to the touch, and his body at times was drenched in perspiration, while at other times it was parchment dry.

Warrows came to sit with him 'round the clock, and they daubed his face and hands with the solution of water and herbs.

Yet Tuck did not waken, though at times his eyes were wide open as he startled up in delirium to wildly cry out warnings and to call names and to implore that someone, *anyone*, give aid to those in need that only he could see—

phantoms from other days, other places: Hob, Tarpy, Aurion, Danner.

And outside, the great storm hammered at the ramparts and towers, ravening at the stone and hurling snow and ice down upon the fortress.

The next day fluid-filled blisters rose up on Tuck's face and hands. At times when he seemed partially awake the attending Warrows tried to get him to eat; yet he retched even upon water and could keep nothing down.

And still the storm raged across the wasteland and rammed into the fortress, clawing at the citadel.

On the fourth day Tuck's fever broke, and he spoke with a saneness that had been missing from his voice. Dink was with him at the time and had been in the process of daubing the sunscald liquid on Tuck's face when the bedridden Warrow whispered quite clearly, "Who is with me?" For although he looked directly at Dink, Tuck's eyes could not see.

"It's me, Tuck . . . Dink Weller," said Dink, daubing more solution on Tuck's right hand.

"Hullo, Dink." Tuck's voice was raspy. "Would you have something to drink? My throat feels as if all the burning sands of Karoo were inside."

Quickly Dink poured water into a cup and propped Tuck up and held the cup to the buccan's lips, and Tuck drank greedily.

"Whoa now, Tucker," cautioned Dink. "The healer said to take it slow—little nips over a time."

Sipping, Tuck finished that cup and another and then sank back upon the bed. "Merrilee . . . where's Merrilee?"

"Ah, Tuck, she's sleeping," answered Dink. "Day and night she's been here. And she ran herself into the ground. Some of us finally dragged her off to a bed of her own, and she was dead to the world the moment she laid down."

A small smile played across Tuck's cracked lips, and he closed his eyes and said nought else. And Dink slipped from the room and ran to fetch Merrilee, but when they returned, Tuck had fallen into a deep natural slumber.

Dink insisted that Merrilee return to her bed, and she went without argument, for now she knew that her buccaran was going to be all right. And the damman crawled back under her blankets with her heart lightened, while outside the wind moaned and howled and snow hurtled across the 'scape.

The next morning, with the aid of Arch and Burt, Tuck tottered out of his bed to relieve himself, refusing to spend one more moment being cared for, as he put it, ". . . as if I am a helpless babe." Yet it was all the buccan could do to keep from swooning when he first stood upright.

The healer came and pronounced Tuck fit to take meals, and Merrilee brought him breakfast, meager though it was: gruel and bread and hot tea. Yet to Tuck it was a sumptuous banquet, but he could not eat it all.

And Tuck rested propped abed, while Merrilee sat. They quietly talked—whenever the buccan was awake, that is, for Tuck frequently fell asleep even as they conversed. At these times Merrilee would sit lost in her own thoughts, listening to the storm and waiting for Tuck to awaken again, and then they would talk on. And they spoke of many things, some more important than others.

"The King has come every day, Tuck," said Merrilee, softly. "He's been most worried about you. They say he smiled for the first time in days when he heard your fever had broken."

"He'll make a good King, Merrilee," responded Tuck. The buccan fell silent a moment, then: "How's the Lady Laurelin? And Prince Igon? And the others . . . how do they fare?"

"Well," answered Merrilee, "the Princess is wan, for she too has been ill from the sunscalding of the burning Myrkenstone, though not as gravely as you, Tuck. But she's been up and about for the last two days, and she spends much of her time visiting the wounded.

"As for Prince Igon, his wounds—shoulder and wrist—are healing well. And he also has come to see you, as well as many others.

"Lord Gildor and Flandrena both are well, though Gildor was stabbed in the leg, and Flandrena took a cut across the cheek. He'll bear a scar the rest of his days . . ."

Merrilee fell silent as her words were drowned out by a rising howl of the blast hammering and clawing at the tower. And as the wind fell back to a sobbing moan, the damman stood and stepped to the fire, stirring up the blaze with an iron ere taking her seat once more.

"This storm is terrible, Tuck," she said, again pulling a blanket 'round her shoulders. "It has set everyone's teeth on edge, even the King's, for we've been trapped inside these squalid Rūcken quarters for five days now—the entire Legion—and all are restless and cross, nettled . . . everyone except Brega that is."

"Brega?" Tuck's voice was full of surprise, for he knew the Dwarf's bellicose nature, and if anyone were to have his hackles up, it would be Brega.

"Oh yes, Tuck," answered Merrilee. "Why, if it weren't for Brega no one could get between the buildings at all. I don't know how he manages to do it, but the storm doesn't seem to turn him around. Against all advice, he was the first to venture outside, and he's done it many times since. Yet Brega always seems to know how to get back safely. Why, they say he's even been outside the walls, through the gate and over the bridge and beyond. But why he went, what he did there, he will not speak of it.

"And he's guided King Galen, Prince Igon, and Princess Laurelin—as well as many others—between the buildings through that swirling white blast; but they say that Brega moves as if he's on a well-trodden path.

"Why, I do believe that the horses would have starved had Brega not led some Men to the stables to care for the steeds. And the horses, well, they too are skittish and cross, living in that Hèlsteed stink the way they do. I pity them in those foul stables. But at least Brega took the Men there to feed and water the poor beasts."

Tuck listened to the juddering wind. "So Brega goes out into the storm," mused the buccan, shaking his head, "and to care for horses at that." The shriek of the blizzard climbed higher, and Tuck fell silent while his memories slipped back to recall the howling whiteness along the edges of the Dimmendark, where nothing could be seen in the hurtling fling; and he knew that if the blizzard raging now was anything like that, then it was indeed a wonder that Brega could fare in safety.

Merrilee stood once more and stepped to the window and peered out through the heavy drapes. With a shudder

Tuck came out of his reverie at the sound of the curtains being thrust aside. "Is it gone, Merrilee?" he asked.

"Wha—what?" The damman turned. "I'm sorry, Tuck . . . the wind noise . . . I didn't hear what you said."

"The Dimmendark," responded Tuck. "Is it gone? Is it truly gone?"

"Yes, my buccaran, it is gone," answered Merrilee. "It is truly gone. The land is free of Shadowlight."

Tuck turned his sightless eyes toward his hands folded in his lap. "Oh . . . I would love to see that."

Merrilee faced once more toward the storm, and the sound of her weeping was lost in the wind.

Over the next two days, Tuck rapidly gained strength, and the sunscald diminished greatly. With the help of others to see for him, Tuck hobbled on crutches along the corridors. Too, he would sit in his room with his broken foot propped up and chat with visitors. And many came to see him: Galen, Igon, Laurelin, Brega, Gildor, Flandrena, Ubrik, numerous warriors of the Legion, and, of course, the Warrows. To all Tuck seemed of good cheer, and he spoke at length with each of them. Yet those who knew him best— Merrilee, Patrel, Galen, Gildor, Laurelin, even Brega— could see that Tuck was given to long lapses of deep introspection, and they spoke softly among themselves, voicing their concern for the Woody Hollow buccan; yet none knew of aught to do.

On the eighth day of the blizzard, the wind diminished somewhat, and the snow slackened to the point where dim shapes could be seen across the courtyards. Though the storm still raged, Legionnaires could now guide themselves without the aid of Brega. The spirits of many began to climb, for they speculated that the great angry tempest hammering upon the land out of the distant Boreal Sea was at last coming to an end. The crossness of the past few days began to melt away, and once again the talk was bright when Legionnaires grouped together.

All of the Warrows had gathered in Tuck's room, to sit and chat and speculate on how soon it would be ere the journey homeward would begin. Eventually the talk turned to the Winter War and the Struggles. And as is the wont of warriors everywhere, they began to tell stories of combat and danger, of heroism and hardship, and of feats both fearsome and foolish. And, too, as is also the wont of warriors, the Warrows laughed in one minute and grew sober the next and frequently talked all at once or fell into long silences. Yet at other times there were moments of unbearable poignancy.

"Ar . . . the worst part of being snowed in here," said Teddy Proudhand, "is the food—nothing but gruel, crue, hard bread, and tea."

There was a general murmur of agreement, but Tuck said, "Hold on there, at least we've now got the gruel, the bread, and the tea. When King Galen and I trekked from Weiunwood to Arden, all we had was crue and water."

Several Warrows groaned in sympathy, and a sharp laugh came from Patrel. "Hoi, you're right, Tucker. Let me tell you about the time in the abandoned town of Stonehill in the empty White Unicorn Inn when all that we had to eat was our crue with some leeks found by Danner . . ." Patrel's voice dropped into silence, and his green eyes clouded with tears. Without saying another word he arose and stepped to the fire and stood with his back to the others and stared into the depths of the flames.

For long moments silence reigned in the room, and then, to break the sad mood upon them all, Burt Arboran said, "Ar, Tuck, tell us about cuttin' the Gargon's leg. Be this the sword you used? What did you say as its name was?" Burt picked up the long-knife in its worn leather sheath.

"It is called Bane," responded Tuck, clearing his throat and wiping his cheeks with the heel of one hand.

Burt grasped the hilt and pulled the blade from the scabbard. "Oi!" exclaimed the buccan. "Does it always glow blue like this?" A cobalt flame flickered along the edges of the sword.

"Blue?" exclaimed Tuck. "Is it glowing? Does the blade jewel burn with an inner fire?"

Forgetting that Tuck could not see, Burt nodded, bobbing his head up and down, but Merrilee quickly said, "Yes, Tuck! The jewel is lit. The blade flames, too."

"Someone get Lord Gildor," snapped Tuck, "and King Galen. And hurry! Evil is about."

*   *   *

The voices of warriors and the rattle of arms and the jingle of armor sounded from the hall. Princess Laurelin and Merrilee stood as King Galen, Lord Gildor, and Brega came wearily into the room.

"Nought," said Galen, removing his gauntlets and dropping tiredly into a chair. "Though the Legion has searched high and low throughout this holt, still we've found nought." He turned a questioning eye toward Gildor.

"Evil is here, Galen King," said the Elf. "Both Bane and Bale whisper of it."

"Do they glimmer because this fortress itself is vile?" asked Tuck from his chair by the fire.

"Ah, nay, Wee One," answered Gildor. "Only to living evil will the blade-jewel glow, usually to creatures who are of the Untargarda—Ruch, Lok, Troll, Ghûlk, and the like—though now and again the gems will respond to a vile being of Mithgar . . . the Hèlarms, some Dragons . . ."

"Arr," growled Brega, sitting cross-legged on the floor, "no matter how long the list of foul things these blades can warn of, King Galen has said it: we found nought, though we searched high and low."

"The dungeons under the tower?" Laurelin's voice was strained. "When I was held within a cell there, a creature, a monster of the dark . . ." The Princess shuddered and stared into the fire.

Galen reached out and took her hand. "Aye, my Lady, we strode by torchlight through that most vile of pits. If ever a place could be said to be evil . . ." Galen's voice trailed off, and his lips pressed grimly into a thin line.

Silence reigned for a moment, then: "At the deepest level, the passages issue into a labyrinth of caverns," said Lord Gildor, "branching off in a myriad of directions. These we did not search, for they are dark and bodeful. I did not like their look, nor did I wish to tread them. Too, any mind mayhap would get lost in their twisting ways to never again come to the light of day."

"There you are not correct, Elf Gildor," objected Brega. "Neither I nor any Dwarf would get lost in any cavern. Even so, I agree with you on one point: I would not freely set foot in that foul place under, for it is a Squam grot . . . And now I know why it is said that the Utruni detest the Grg, for there below I saw how the Squam defile the living stone itself. But think you upon this thought: mayhap the blades glow because one or two Ukhs escaped and now hide in that abomination beneath."

Again silence fell upon the room, and about the dungeons no more was said, though the grim looks upon the faces of those who had been there spoke volumes.

Again there came from the hallway the sound of approaching soldiery, and Patrel, Igon, and Flandrena came into the room as other warriors of the Legion continued on down the passage.

Galen glanced up at Igon, and the Prince shook his head. "Fruitless," said the youth. "We found nought in the entire tower but this."

Laurelin gasped as Igon handed a hideous dark helm to Galen.

"What is it?" asked Tuck, unable to see.

"I don't—" Merrilee started to say, but she was interrupted by the Princess.

"It is Modru's iron mask, Tuck," said Laurelin, unable to tear her eyes away from the grotesque helm.

Galen drew his cloak over the iron vizard, concealing it from Laurelin's view. "Nothing else?" he asked.

Igon glanced from Flandrena to Patrel. "Nothing," said the Prince.

"But wait," spoke up Tuck. "What about Modru's 'Stone knife? Wasn't it there in the tower, too?"

"No, Tuck," answered Patrel. "And I especially looked for it, too, even though you warned me that it might draw at my vision. But it wasn't there."

"Perhaps it burned up with the Myrkenstone," suggested Flandrena. "The destruction of the one could have been the ruin of the other."

"You may be right, Elf Flandrena," rumbled Brega. "And you may be wrong. But it is in my mind that whatever creature it is that causes the swords to glow mayhap has taken the 'Stone knife."

At Brega's words Tuck's heart raced in his breast, for if the Dwarf was right, another feartoken was loose in Mithgar. Would it someday fulfill its evil destiny?

That night a double guard was posted, for none knew whether evil would strike in the dark. Bane and Bale were watched closely, yet their glimmers spoke only of a distant threat that came no closer in the night. And the talk among the Men was how fiercely the Warrows themselves guarded the blind one's room.

Throughout the ninth day the fury of the storm continued to abate. The howling shriek of the wind fell to a moan and then to a murmur, and by day's end only a gentle snow wafted lightly down upon the land.

Earlier in the afternoon, warriors had been put to work clearing a path from the stables to the gate, and scouts had been sent forth upon the moor. And as darkness fell they came riding in to report that huge drifts had accumulated near every great rock and tor and swale; but out upon the flats, the fierce blast had blown the snow across the moor and it had not foregathered to any significant depth—why, in some places the land had even been scrubbed bare by the wind.

Upon hearing this news, King Galen turned to Ubrik. "What say you, Reachmarshal? Should the waning storm come to an end tonight, as it seems likely, will the Legion be ready for travel on the morrow?"

"Aye, my King," replied Ubrik, with a fierce grin. "All are eager to leave this foul place and come once more to the wide lands and open skies of Valon, where the swift horses race free o'er the clean grass."

"Then so be it," responded Galen. "If the snow stops, on the morrow we ride."

Glad shouts rose up at such news, and all prepared for the long journey home. Litters had been made for those most severely wounded, and they would be drawn slowly southward upon travoises with healers and an escort in attendance. Yet it was incumbent upon the King to go swiftly to Pellar, for much needed doing to set the Kingdom right. And so he and the bulk of the Legion would ride ahead—though they would not fare south at the grueling pace that had borne them north.

And all of the Warrows would go with the King, for none of them bore major wounds, except perhaps Tuck, and neither his broken foot nor his blindness would significantly affect his riding.

*   *   *

That night guards again were posted against the distant vileness whispered of by Bane and Bale, yet no evil came to pass. And just after mid of night, the snow ceased to fall. The storm had ended.

The grey light of dawn found eight Warrows gathered around three cairns set upon the moor, out before the dark fortress. With them stood Brega, Bekki's son, Dwarf warrior of the Red Hills.

"I bore them here in the blizzard," said Brega his voice low, his hood cast over his head. "Harven, Rollo, and Danner. I could not leave them within the walls of that vile place, for they were my comrades in arms. And so I laid them here beneath these stones. Brave warriors were they all—brave as any Châkka—and they strode in honor. Nothing greater can I say of anyone."

Tears ran freely down the faces of all those gathered. Tuck knelt and reached forward with a hand, and Merrilee guided it to rest upon a stone of Danner's cairn. And Tuck spoke: "Once before—oh, it seems so long ago—I knelt beside a cairn like this. And I placed my hand upon a stone and swore an oath to avenge the comrade beneath it. And you, Danner, you swore that oath, too. And we kept it, you and I, and Patrel here . . . and all the rest. For the Evil that slew Hob and Tarpy and so many others is himself now dead. But oh, my friend, I would gladly give my own life if you could but have yours back . . ."

Tuck buried his face in his hands, and great sobs shook his frame. Brega tenderly lifted him up as if he were but a babe and bore him back toward the bridge. And weeping and leading the horse that had carried Tuck out to the cairns, so went all the Warrows—except Patrel, for the tiny buccan remained behind as the others walked back toward the fortress. And as they crossed the bridge, there came to their ears a sweet singing; and they turned at the sound, pausing, seeing a small figure in the distance standing alone in the snow before Danner's cairn. And Patrel's voice rose up into the clear early sky, but he was too distant for any to catch the words of his song.

In midmorning the Legion entire at last rode out of the fortress. Five thousand had ridden north, and but thirty-five hundred now fared south, for hundreds had fallen in

battle. And among the many Men that had survived rode
a Princess, two Elves, eight Warrows, and a Dwarf.

South they hammered across the wind-swept snow, leaving behind the abandoned hulk of Modru Kinstealer's holt,
the hideous iron mask nailed to the wall above the gate as
a mute warning to all who would follow Evil's path.

Southward they fared, day after day, the white miles
lengthening out behind them as they skirted 'round the edges
of enormous drifts, keeping to the wind-scrubbed flats.

Down across Claw Moor they rode, and at the end of
the second day they came to Claw Gap. The following
morning they struggled through great drifts to pass across
the Gap River valley, for there was no way around. And
when they had won beyond that barrier, onward they
pressed along the eastern margin of Gron. Past the great
Gwasp they rode to come to the long treeless barrens
wedged between the Rigga Mountains and the Gronfangs.

Late on the eighth day they came to the north end of
Grūwen Pass, where they pitched camp. And among the
drifts they found scattered heaps of Rūcken armor, as if a
great battle had ended here.

Dawn of the ninth day found the Legion pressing
through Grūwen Col; and time and again they rode past
the frozen bodies of slain Men and Elves, half buried in
the snow, the blue and white of Wellen and the Eld-Tree
flags of Arden Vale proclaiming the identity of the dead.
Here too lay a cluttered splay of empty Rūcken armor and
shattered scimitars and broken staffs bearing a scarlet ring
of fire on an ebon field: the windtattered standard of the
Evil One, who was no more.

Past the rimed carnage and frigid litter of War they rode,
now and again breasting through icy drifts; and it was late
in the starry night when at last they came down out of the
frozen pass to make camp in the Land of Rhone. Few, if
any, spoke of the bitter sights they'd seen this day. And
neither Lord Gildor nor Flandrena came to take a meal at
the fire; instead they stood at the edge of the night and
stared out across the bleak moonlit snow.

Just ere noon of the tenth day, as the weary Legion
wended along the northernmost flank of Arden Bluff, one

of the forward scouts galloped back toward the Host, and *lo!* riding with him came Elf Lord Talarin and Hrosmarshal Vidron. And as the scout turned and again bore off to the fore, the Lord and the Marshal reined their steeds in a wide arc to come alongside Galen, matching their pace to that of Wildwind.

"My King!" hailed Vidron, striking a clenched fist to his heart, a great smile beaming out from his silver beard. "Good news from the south: the War there is ended! We have won!"

Galen put his face in his hands, and long moments passed ere he looked up again.

"*Kel,* Galen King," said Talarin, his manner somber. "My eyes are glad to see you, yet my heart grieves for the dead."

"Aye," replied Galen, "many have fallen in this struggle against Evil. Yet it is finished at last."

At that moment Prince Igon thundered up on Rust, and in his wake rode Gildor and Flandrena and Reachmarshal Ubrik.

"Hai, Vidron!" cried the young Man, happy to see the warrior; and then, more gravely: "Hál, my Lord Talarin."

In response to the exuberance of youth, a brief smile flickered across the features of Talarin, and he nodded to the Prince; and the Elf's eyes sought those of Gildor and Flandrena as the Lian warriors and Ubrik joined the small foregathering. And they looked upon one another and were glad. And the talk turned to the ending of the War.

Yet Vidron raised in his stirrups and twisted to look back along the column bearing southward. But his searching gaze saw not what he sought, and, settling back into his saddle, he turned to Galen. "Sire, I must ask: the Lady Laurelin . . ."

"She is well, General Vidron," replied Galen. "She rides behind the vanguard in the company of Warrior Brega and the Wee Ones."

"Hai!" barked Vidron, a fierce grin upon his face. "And the Waldana, how fare they?"

"Three were slain, and Tuck was blinded," answered Galen. "Your Danner was one who fell."

Vidron turned his eyes out over the snow, and for long moments only the sound of hooves was heard. Then Talarin cleared his throat. "As you have said, Galen King, many have fallen in this struggle against Evil."

They rode along without speaking for a time, then again Talarin spoke, the Elf gesturing at the glittering brightness. "Once you pledged to bring the Sun back unto the world, and so you have, yet I pray that the price you paid to do so was not as heavy as the cost we bore in Kregyn."

"Our burden was most heavy—as was yours," responded Galen, his mind casting back beyond the trailing Legion and up into the frozen reaches of the mountains where lay Grūwen Pass, called Kregyn by the Elves. "We saw the signs of the brunt you bore."

"Long we held them," rumbled Vidron. "Yet each 'Darkday they hammered us deeper into the Pass. At last they drove us through, and we were trapped. As they mounted their final charge, a great blackness fell. But then, *whoosh!* the Dimmendark was gone! And they fell to Adon's Ban."

"But wait!" cried Galen in amaze. "That means you held them for . . ."

"Five 'Darkdays," interjected Vidron. "We held them five 'Days. Fifteen hundred Wellenen and five hundred Lian—"

"Against *ten thousand Spaunen!*" exclaimed Galen.

"Hai!" cried Igon. "This will be a saga the bards and tale-tellers will chant for ages to come."

Talarin nodded. "Aye, long will the harpers sing of Kingsgeneral Vidron, the Whelmer of Modru's Horde, for indeed it is a mighty tale. Yet let them not forget to sing of those heroes who did not ride away from the field when the battle was ended."

At last the fore of the long column of the Host had ridden nearly to the concealed entrance to Arden Vale. "Come," said Talarin. "Lead your weary Legion down into the Hidden Refuge to spend some days of quiet and rest. We have warm shelter and hot food and drink. And as you pause, you can speak to us your tale, for we would hear how you brought about the downfall of the Dimmendark."

As Ubrik raised his black-oxen horn to his lips and signalled unto the column, Galen said, "Ah, but it was not I who vanquished the Shadowlight, Lord Talarin. Instead it was Tuck who loosed the shaft that slew the 'Stone and freed the light to destroy Modru and hurl Gyphon back beyond the Spheres. It was Tuck who caused the collapse of the Dimmendark and returned the Sun unto the world to whelm the Spawn. Aye, it Was Tuck and none else who did this thing, and we did but help the Waerling along his fateful course."

And as Talain and Vidron listened in wonder to Galen's words, they led the Legion toward the bluff to ride through the hidden tunnel and down into Arden Vale.

Rael held a polished crystal in her fingers and peered through it and into Tuck's eyes. Behind her the light of a single candle shone over her shoulder, casting a dim glow within the darkened room. Long she looked, first into one eye and then into the other. And no one spoke. At last she stepped back and gave a sign, and window curtains were thrown open to let vivid sunlight stream through and fall upon the buccan sitting in the chair. As Rael continued her examination, watching the reaction of the Waerling's eyes to the brightness, Talarin continued a conversation he and Tuck had started earlier.

"And so," said the Elf Lord, "had Gyphon come to rule in Mithgar, the power would have swung to Him."

"King Galen once told me that Mithgar was like the fulcrum of a teeter-totter," responded Tuck.

"Aye, Tuck," answered Talarin, "although I had never thought of it in that light, Galen is correct. And as it is with any teeter-totter, at the critical moment, when the powers are within balance, the slightest impulse one way or the other can shift the equipoise for good or for ill.

"Such was the case with you, Tuck, for you tipped the balance, but the force you used was by no means slight . . . by any measure. For you see, although four thousand years apast Gyphon set into motion events none could stop, so too must have Adon started His own plan—and tokens of power were created upon Mithgar to find their way unto the Iron Tower for use at the critical moment.

"And you, Tuck, chose and were chosen to follow the course that would bring you to Modru's evil sanctum in that darkest moment of the darkest hour, where you could shift the balance away from Evil and toward Good, away from Gyphon and toward Adon."

Tuck seemed lost in thought. "Lord Talarin, this I have wanted to ask: Gyphon was so beautiful when I first saw Him, but then He changed to something ghastly. How can that be? How can it be that One so vile can be so fair to the eye?"

"Evil often comes with a fair face, Tuck," replied Talarin. "But beneath it all is a hideous monster."

Again Tuck seemed lost in thought. "There is something else that is puzzling me, Lord Talarin: In the moments just before I shot the Myrkenstone, Rael's rede and the inscription from the tomb of Othran the Seer came into my mind:

> *'Neither of two Evils must thy strike claim;*
> *Instead smite the Darkness between the same.'*

> *Loose not the Red Quarrel*
> *Ere appointed dark time.*

Now, in hindsight, the rede is clear: it told me to shoot the Myrkenstone instead of either Gyphon or Modru. But the tomb inscription still has me mystified. I thought it meant for me to shoot at *any* time during the Sun-Death, but I couldn't seem to loose that red arrow until Modru's chanting was ended. And I *knew,* as if someone compelled me so, that I had to shoot *then.* Why couldn't I shoot before? I mean, the Lady Laurelin was nearly slaughtered by my delay. Yet I did not, *could* not, shoot till the chanting stopped."

In the silence that followed, Rael stood and turned and stepped to the window and looked toward the distant pines. Merrilee, who had sat quietly during the examination, went to sit by Tuck's side, taking him by the hand. "Perhaps, Tuck," said the Elf Lord, then paused, "perhaps it was only *after* the incantation was completed that the Myrkenstone was vulnerable, open to attack. Mayhap *that* was the *appointed dark time* spoken of by Othran the Seer ages agone." Again silence fell.

Rael continued to gaze out o'er the sparkling snow, and in the stillness her voice spoke softly: "Tuck, say again how the Myrkenstone affected your vision."

"Well, when we first saw the black light streaming from the tower it *wrenched* at all of our eyes," responded Tuck, "all of the Warrow eyes, that is, for no other Folk could see it—not Man nor Dwarf nor even Elf. But the Wee Folk, we knew it was bad from the very beginning . . . yet none of us knew just how bad.

"When I first crawled into the room atop the tower where lay the Myrkenstone, it *trapped* my eyes: I couldn't look away from it. And my vision began to dim, to fade; and if Gyphon hadn't come, hadn't *pulled* my gaze to Him, I think I would have lost all my sight then and there.

"But He did come, and I looked away from the 'Stone first to Him and then to Laurelin and Modru. And I took up the Red Quarrel and set it to my bow. When I looked back at the Myrkenstone to shoot it, well, it took away the last of my vision. I could see nothing at all: My sight had been devoured by that terrible maw.

"I must have been looking right at the 'Stone when I shot it. And only in the unbearable glare of its burning did I have vision once more.

"And when the glare was gone, I was blind."

Tuck fell silent a moment, then said in a low, halting voice, "My last sight . . . was of an unendurably hideous monster . . . falling . . . falling into a pit beyond conception. If one is to . . . to lose his sight, he should last see something of beauty . . . a flower, perhaps . . ."

Merrilee squeezed Tuck's hand as Rael turned from the window to face the buccan. "I do not know what caused the damage to your eyes, Tuck. Whether it was the strange black radiance of the Myrkenstone—as seems most likely— or whether it was the furious blare of the 'Stone's destruction, I cannot say. But this I do know: your affliction is not unlike that of snow blindness . . . but I fear it is permanent." Rael paused, her eyes filled with a great sadness. "You who brought the Sun back to Mithgar may never again see the light of day."

Merrilee drew in a great sob of air, and she wept bitterly. Tuck drew her into his arms and stroked her hair and soothed, "Don't cry, my dammia. There's no need to cry. I may not live to see the Sun, but I can feel it on my face."

And Talarin and Rael quietly went from the room, leaving behind a blind buccan holding a weeping damman while sitting in a pool of golden sunlight.

*   *   *

A week fled quickly, and well the Legion rested, gaining in strength and haleness from the Elven provender. And in the quiet vale, spirits were renewed. Yet there was no celebration, for the Lian moved in a state of deep mourning. Although the number of their War-dead did not match that of the Men, still nearly half of the Elven warriors of Arden Vale had fallen in battle. And for a people said to be immortal, Death strikes an especially onerous blow. For with these Folk the Dark Reaper does not cut life short by a mere few years—instead an uncounted span of eras is lost.

On the seventh day the train of those wounded at the Iron Tower at last arrived from Gron, and they, too, were taken into the Hidden Refuge.

Their arrival seemed to be a signal to High King Galen: he would now fare south, and most of the Legion would go with him, for, as he told the council, "There is much to be done: The Realm is to be set aright, and I am needed in Pellar.

"Yet this also I say: I would that the Wellenen form an escort and return the Waerlinga unto the Land of the Thorns, for the Wee Ones have given more than any could ask, especially Tuckerby Underbank. None can ever repay him for the deeds he has done, for we owe him a debt beyond measure. Yet this is the way we will begin: Men shall come to help rebuild the Bosky, and Tuck's will be the first home restored. But that will not be all, for the Crown shall ever remember our obligation unto him, and he will want for nought.

"Now, if the Legion stands ready, we shall fare forth on the morrow."

Thus it was decided: Tuck and the other Warrows and the surviving Wellenen would strike west for the Boskydells while the Legion would fare south toward Valon, and beyond to Pellar.

But Brega—stubborn Brega—would not go with the Legion, for the Dwarf refused to mount a horse. "Hmph! Ride a horse? Nonsense!" grumbled Brega. "The War is over, and the only mount I will now sit astraddle is a pony. The Legion may ride south in haste upon their great beasts, but as for me, I will make my way back to the Red Hills at my own pace upon the back of a sensible steed—if any can be found. And if not, well then I will walk."

No amount of debate, no logic of argument, would sway the obstinate Dwarf from his decision: he would ride a pony or walk, nothing else would do. And the High King would not ask him to act otherwise, for although Galen did not know why Brega had taken this stand, still he respected the Dwarf's wishes.

In the end, a pony was located and given over to Brega. On the morrow the Dwarf would set out south for his beloved Red Hills, and with him would go Flandrena upon Swiftmane, keeping Brega company; for beginning with their mission to climb the walls of the dark fortress, the Dwarf and the Elf had become fast friends.

As for Lord Gildor, he would remain behind in Arden Vale for a while, for he too knew the healing art, and he would serve the wounded.

Thus were the Deevewalkers to be sundered, each to answer a calling of his own. On the morrow they would bid their farewells.

The dawn came bright and clear. The Legion stood ready to depart. So, too, stood the Warrows in the company of the Wellenen. Brega held the reins of a small grey pony, and at the Dwarf's side was Flandrena. Talarin, Rael, and Gildor stood before an assembly of Lian, and they faced Tuck and Patrel and Merrilee, and Igon, Laurelin, and High King Galen. And behind the King stood Vidron and Ubrik.

And the three Elves—sire, dam, and son—stepped forward to say their farewells, clasping hands and embracing these most honored guests.

"Fare thee well, Lady Rael," said Laurelin as they embraced. "You came to me and gave me comfort in my gravest hour of need, and drew forth my spirit from a dark place where it had fled. Those days in Gron I shall strive to forget, but I shall always remember your gentle love."

The Lady Rael kissed Laurelin and held her at arm's length, and they smiled one upon the other, and it was like unto the Sun looking upon the Moon, so fair were they.

Gildor came to Tuck and knelt and embraced him. And when Tuck once agan tried to return Bane to the Elf Lord,

Gildor said, "Nay, Tuck, it is for you and yours to keep forever."

Gildor then turned to Patrel. "When we were together in Challerain Keep, Wee One, and I heard you strum the lute, I knew that you could master the harp, too. And so I resolved that if we both survived the War, I would give you this." Gildor gave over to Patrel a finely wrought, black Elven harp with glistening argent strings. "It was mine when I was a youth, and I would that it be yours, now. Small it is, yet it will fit your reach, and the sound of its music is as sweet as the pure air."

Patrel took the gift and held it reverently, and a gentle vagrant zephyr caused a faint humming in the sheening web of silver. "Oh, my Lord Gildor, how can I ever take such a priceless gift? It deserves the sure hand of a master and not the clumsy fingers of a fumblewit."

Gildor laughed. "Fumblewit you are not, Patrel, else none of the Legion would have entered Modru's dark citadel. Yours was the quick wit that fooled the Troll at the portcullis, and caused him to use his own hand to fling up the grille. Nay, Patrel, take the harp—did I not say you could master it? I give you my word."

As Gildor and Patrel laughed together, Rael came to Merrilee, and the black-haired damman turned her sapphirine gaze up into the deep blue eyes of the Elfess. "Merrilee Holt," said Rael, smiling, "ever will I remember the 'Day I first met you, a gentle lady among warriors riding to battle. Tales will be told of your great courage and skill, long after the deeds of many of us are forgotten. Yours is a story most rare and beautiful—as are you yourself. Fare you well, Merrilee Holt, bright spirit."

A tear slid down Merrilee's cheek as she and Rael embraced; never again would the damman feel awkward in the company of anyone.

Talarin and Vidron gripped the forearms of one another in the clasp of Harlingar warriors. "We fought well together, you and I," said Vidron.

"Ah, yes," replied Talarin, "but I would that we never have to do so again."

Brega too, bade his farewells, brief to all but a few. Long did he speak to Tuck and Gildor and Galen, but what he said is not recorded. Yet when he came to Igon, these were his words: "My Prince, were it not for you, none of us would be standing here today. Yours was the strength that kept us from falling, there in that black ravine. And atop the walls, you were a mighty warrior. Should ever there come a time you are in need, send for Brega, Bekki's son, and I will come to your side."

At last Talarin stood before all and held up his hands, and when quiet fell o'er the assembly, he spoke: "Galen King, now you prepare to leave our peaceful vale, for much needs doing to set the Realm right again. Yet hearken: when last you came to Arden, the world was plunged into darkness, and Evil beset us all. But now the days are bright once more, and yours was the Crown to bring this wonder about. Oh, aye, it is true that you did not do it alone, but no one ever does. And it is also true that there are many heroes here among this Company—and one special hero. Yet let us not forget those who fell upon distant battle-fields, for they, too, heroes all, helped to achieve this victory—helped to return the miracle of light unto the world.

"We bid you farewell, Galen King, as well as those who set forth with you. May all who leave here find peace and happiness at journey's end."

Talarin fell silent, and now Galen took Tuck by the hand and led him to a dais, the buccan hobbling with the aid of a cane. And they stood together for all to see. And the High King spoke: "My Lord Talarin, all you have said is true: All of those who struggled against Evil are indeed heroes, and many fell in battle. Heed me: they shall not be forgotten.

"Too, this War was filled with the brave acts of many—some deeds of which we will never know.

"It is also true that none of us could have survived without the aid of others, many of whom now lie slain. And so I say that each of us who strove for Good can take great pride in our victory, no matter how large or how small our contribution.

"Yet there is one among us whose path led him straight to the destruction of Evil—and all of the rest of us but aided him along his way."

And now the High King of all Mithgar did an unprece-dented thing: he knelt upon one knee in high homage to a Waerling of the Land of the Thorns. And so, too, did all the assembled warriors of the Legion, as well as the Lian. And the only ones left standing were the Warrows of the Boskydells.

And King Galen cried, "All hail Tuckerby Underbank, Hero of the Realm!"

And thrice a great shout burst forth from the assembled throng: *Hál! . . . Hál! . . . Hál!*

Tuck stood a long moment without speaking as the last echoes rang forth through the pines. His great blue eyes gazed unseeing out beyond the Men and Elves, the Warrows, and the Dwarf. At last Tuck spoke, and his voice was filled with emotion: "Cheer for yourselves, brave warriors, for had any of you been thrust along the path that I trod, you would have done as well or better than I." And Tuck raised his voice in praise, and he was joined by all: *Hál! . . . Hál! . . . Hál!*

And as the last shout cleft the air, Galen stood, and so did the throng. Merrilee rushed to Tuck and led him limping back to the waiting Warrows. And Brega was overheard to grumble, "I will not reach the Red Hills with my feet stuck here in Arden. Are you ready, Elf Flandrena?" At Flandrena's nod, Brega mounted his small grey pony, and Flandrena vaulted to the back of Swiftmane. And leading a packhorse, the two set out.

As if that were a signal to all, Galen signed to Ubrik, and the Reachmarshal raised his black-oxen horn to his lips, and its resonant call pealed forth and was answered in kind by the horns of Valon.

So, too, sounded the calls of the clarions of the Wellenen. The Warrows were lifted to the backs of horses, and all of those departing mounted up as well.

And, amid the knells of horns and shouted goodbyes, slowly the cavalcade went forth, the pace quickening as the warrior companies fell into a long column faring southward. Swiftly they overtook Brega's plodding pony, leaving the Dwarf and Flandrena in their wake. And onward rode the great long train, through the pines along the banks of the River Tumble down through the Vale of Arden.

And as they rode, a southerly breeze sprang up—redolent with an earthen smell, scented with the promise of new life. And the step of the horses grew light and spirited.

It was the first day of spring.

Two days the column fared south, and on the morning of the third day the travellers departed from their camp near the Lone Eld Tree and passed through the hidden way under the waterfall and out into the Land of Rell.

Soon they came to the Crossland Road, and here the Wellenen turned west to follow the road while the Harlingar continued south, striking for the old abandoned trade road through Rell, for they had reached the parting of the ways: the Warrows to be escorted to the Land of the Thorns, while the High King's entourage fared to Pellar.

Yet ere they parted, sad farewells were said as damman and buccan embraced Man and Woman, and they kissed one another, and then it was time to go. Yet Laurelin whispered into Galen's ear, and the High King turned to Tuck and Patrel.

"I am told that Aurion, my sire, commanded that until he personally recalled it, the Dwarf-made armor you now wear was to remain in your hands or in the possession of those you would trust." Galen's eyes turned to the west and north toward distant Rian, where lay Challerain Keep and his slain father. And he raised his voice so that all could hear: "Hearken unto me as I reaffirm the command of my sire: unless the shade of King Aurion recalls it, the armor is yours—silveron for Tuck, gilt for Patrel, and in the northern Wastes of Gron, black for Danner Bramblethorn."

West went the Wellenen; south, the Harlingar. And as the columns parted and drew nearly beyond the sight of one another, Patrel took the argent Horn of the Reach from his saddlebag. He set the clarion to his lips, and a silver call split the air. And from the distant Harlingar came the answering sound of black-oxen horn. And then the two columns passed beyond the seeing of one another.

In midafternoon the Wellenen crossed the Tumble River at Arden Ford, passing from Rell into Rhone. The ford was still frozen, trapped under a sheet of ice, though here and there dark pools swirled where the chill grip of winter had begun to break.

That night the company camped within the eastern margin of the Drearwood. And Captain Falk set a double picket of Wellenen about the camp, saying, "We are in Drearwood, a place of ill repute of old. Here we will stand a double ward, for mayhap not all of the Spawn lie slain. Only those Wrg caught in the sunlight died the Withering Death. Those who perhaps were hidden in caverns and bolt-holes would not have fallen to Adon's Ban. And it is said that this dire wood harbors such places for the Spawn to escape the light of day. Hence, double guard, double caution, for I would deliver my charges safely unto their homes."

The next two days found the column pressing west through Rhone, spending the nights camped alongside the Crossland Road, still within the bounds of Drearwood. But early on the following day, the company crossed the Stone-arches Bridge over the River Caire to ride out of Rhone and into the Wilderland, caught between Rian to the north and Harth to the south; they had left the Drearwood behind.

Onward they rode, each day faring thirty miles or more, passing through the Wilderness Hills and across the open land north of the Wilder River, journeying through the Signal Mountains, where the Crossland Road skirted the northern flank of Beacontor.

The road then led them to the upper margins of the Bogland Bottoms, faring forty miles or so along its length, and here peat moss was gathered for the campfires.

On the eleventh day of travel, late in the evening, the column came to the rock wall surrounding Stonehill. Up to this bulwark rode the company, coming to a halt before the east gate. The barrier was closed.

"Who goes?" rang out a voice in sharp challenge.

"We are the Kingsmen of Wellen," called Captain Falk. "We escort the Heroes of the Iron Tower, and I ask that you give us shelter for the night—and hot food and drink for us all, if you can spare it."

"Don't you move none," called back the voice. "Just stand where you are till we fetch our Captain."

Minute after minute eked by, and the Men and horses grew restless, but at last a light could be seen atop the wall—a lantern held high in the grip of a Man, the yellow glow casting out to reveal the fore of the warrior column, the remainder of the Wellenen receding into the shadows before the gate and but dimly seen by the light of the half Moon.

"Here now," called down the Man, "just who did you say you were, and what's all this about Heroes of the Iron Tower?"

Although Tuck could see nought, still he recognized the voice of the speaker. "Hoy, Mr. Brewster!" called the buccan to the Captain of the Men of the Weiunwood Alliance. "It's me: Tuck . . . Tuckerby Underbank!"

Bockleman shielded his eyes from the lantern light as Tuck was led forward upon his steed. "Lor bless me!" cried the innkeeper. "Is it truly you, Master Tuck? . . . Well, so it is!" The Man turned to someone unseen by the escort. "Here now, Bill, open the gate straight away. These folks are all right if Master Tuck is with 'em."

As the heavy grind of the withdrawing gate bar grumbled forth, Bockleman turned back and called down to Tuck: "I did not expect you to come ridin' in with an escort of a couple hundred soldiers and all, Master Tuck. We can't be too careful hereabout these days. We're still on a War footing, you know, even though that awful Dimmendark and such seems to be gone. I mean, the Evil in Gron might be trying to fool us, I shouldn't wonder."

"Nay, Mr. Brewster," called back Tuck, "the Evil in Gron is no more: Modru is dead. The Winter War is ended."

Bockleman's eyes flew wide at these tidings. "Hoy! Now there's a good piece of news that I never thought to hear. Modru is dead! Well now, we'd got the word that the War in the south was won, but this is the first that we've heard of the Evil One. And better tidings we couldn't have hoped for!"

The gate swung open, and Men with bows and pikes could be seen, gathered to repel invaders if need be. "Bring in your company, Master Tuck," called Bockleman. "I can't put you all up at the Unicorn, but perhaps other folk in the 'Hill can spare a bed or so, and stables . . . and even a warm bite or two."

Slowly the column filed into the cobbled ways of Stonehill, and as the last of the Wellenen rode through, the gate was once again barred, for, as Bockleman said, "Though the War is done, and Adon's Ban rules the day, still it is

night and we can't be too careful of the Rūcks and such
that might be about."

The residents of Stonehill opened their hearts and homes
to the company. All of the Warrows and many of the Men
were put up at the White Unicorn, and the stables were
filled with their steeds. The rest of the Wellenen were taken
into private dwellings. And all were fed.

At the White Unicorn the food was hot and the ale was
good, and stories of combat and War were traded back and
forth. And only Patrel seemed withdrawn as he sat in a
corner by the fire and stared deeply into the flames. Merrilee quietly took him a mug of ale and gently asked him
if he felt well, and the wee buccan replied, "I was just
remembering the last time I was in the Unicorn." And Merrilee reached out and took his hand and squeezed it, a tear
sliding down her cheek for lost Danner.

All the next day the company rested in Stonehill, but the
dawn of the following day found the column once again
ready to set forth upon the Crossland Road.

"Well, Master Tuck," said Bockleman as he stood beside
the mounted buccan, "there's much you've told us that will
live long in the hearthtales of the Stonehillers. And your
name will stand at the top of the list of the Heroes of the
Winter War.—Here now, don't you go gainsaying me, for
without you we'd all be slaves of the Evil One, or some
such thing I shouldn't wonder. And we're sorry that you
had to lose so much—you bein' blind and all—but we're
glad that folks like you stood up to Evil and won. And
remember this: the hands of the Big Folk and the Wee
Folk of Stonehill—and I'm sure of Arbagon's Wee Folk of
the Weiunwood beyond—will always be open to you."

Tears glistened in Bockleman's eyes as he looked up at
the blind buccan, and the innkeeper took out a great kerchief from his pocket and noisily blew his nose and wiped
his eyes. Then he said, "Go on with you, now, Master Tuck.
The Boskydells are waiting. And if you don't hurry and
leave, I'm going to make a fool of myself crying before
my Men."

Captain Falk signalled to one of the Wellenen, and the
call of a clarion sounded. And slowly the column set forth,
hooves ringing on hard cobblestones as the company rode

toward the west gate; then out along the dirt dike they went, riding to the Crossland Road. And behind, Stonehillers cheered and waved. And Bockleman Brewster turned and went into the inn, and the sign of the White Unicorn squeaked in the breeze behind him.

Two days they fared, camping south of the Battle Downs the first night and then in the margins of Edgewood. And mid of morning of the third day they came to the great Spindlethorn Barrier. They rode through the thorn tunnel to come to the bridge over the Spindle River, where Thornwalker buccen opened the way to pass the column through.

West they journeyed, and in early afternoon they came to the town of Greenfields. Here Patrel with an escort of Wellenen was to turn south, heading for the East Ford, and Bryn, and beyond to his home near Midwood. Ere parting company, Patrel clasped hands with each of the buccen. He embraced Tuck and Merrilee, and the damman kissed him upon the cheek.

"I will come to Woody Hollow to visit you," said the wee buccan. "But not until my heart has rested from these grievous days—perhaps when the summer winds blow. Yet, today, be of good cheer, for after all is said and done, this is not a goodbye parting. And so I say, fare you well, until we meet once more."

In spite of Patrel's words, there were tears in Merrilee's eyes and a lump in Tuck's throat when Patrel and his escort fared forth down the Bryn Road. And just before he passed beyond seeing, the silver call of the Horn of the Reach drifted o'er the rolling hills.

And as the wondering citizens of Greenfields watched, the remaining Wellenen set out along the Crossland Road, striving for Raffin, where they spent the night.

The next day, westward fared the column, and at points along the way other buccen turned aside, one at a time, to journey with escort to their homes—Dink Weller, Arch Hockley, Burt Arboran, Dill Thorven, and Teddy Proudhand—some heading north and some south as the company rode west along the Crossland Road through Tillok and Willowdell and beyond. And everywhere the cavalcade passed, Wee Folk gathered and wondered who these Warrows were, and what they had done to ride high upon the backs of big horses and to be convoyed by a cavalry of Men.

It was late afternoon when the Wellenen turned north along Byroad Lane to ride through the burnt-out hamlet of Budgens. Still, the village was not abandoned, for tents were pitched alongside the charred remains as the citizenry prepared to rebuild their homes and places of trade. One tent even had a sign set before it—*The Blue Bull*—proclaiming the intentions of the owner of that Boskydell pub to reconstruct his tavern.

Beyond Budgens and along Woody Hollow Road they fared, plashing through Rill Ford and wending toward their goal. And as dusk fell, the escort crossed the bridge above the Dingle-rill to come into the town of Woody Hollow.

Up past the Commons they rode, Market Square and then Town Square on their left. And Warrows came forth to watch in silence as they passed. On up through the coomb they rode, soon to come to the wooded swale up at Hollow End. Yet they plodded beyond the curving lane to The Root—for Tuck's home, Tuck's burrow, had been burned by Modru's Reavers. Instead, the escort rode on to Merrilee's burrow, and there they stopped.

The two Wee Folk were helped down from their horses. And as the Wellenen turned to make camp in the End Field, Tuck and Merrilee moved slowly up the walk—the buccan hobbling with a cane and the damman leading him tenderly—and they went into the burrow and quietly closed the door behind. They were home at last.

And a soft warm wind blew gently from the south, and rills and streams sang with the sparkling waters of the snowmelt.

It was the fourth day of April.

CHAPTER 7

The Raven Book

In the days following Tuck's return to Woody Hollow, winter loosed its chill grip, and spring grew into fullness and passed into summer. And free people everywhere came once more unto their homes, and the work of clearing away the rubble of War's destruction began.

And, too, across the reaches of Pellar, Valon, Jugo, and Hoven, and in Grūwen Pass and out upon the plains of Riamon, great turved mounds were raised as the dead were buried at last.

Dwarves led by Brega marched north from the Red Hills into Rell to tenderly place the slain forty upon a fitting pyre. And as the only survivor of that mighty battle with the vanguard of a Horde, Brega spoke the somber speech of the Châkka ere he fired the great bier.

Along the Battle Downs the slain of the last waggon train were laid to rest, while farther north at Challerain Keep great mounds were raised among the barrows. The Tomb of Othran the Seer was set aright, though the Atalar Blade and the Red Quarrel were now gone—yet these two tokens of power had only been held in the keep of the Seer until needed upon the face of Mithgar.

And Aurion Redeye was placed under the earth in a small barrow central to the mounds of those felled in that great opening battle of the Winter War. And above his grave a dolmen was raised bearing carven runes stating: *Aurion, who chose freedom.*

Far to the north in Gron, out before the dark citadel, a great mound was raised where the slain Harlingar were laid to rest. There too, in later years, a tomb was built above three cairns. Heavy was the stone, and dark, that made up the blocks of this monument. And three names were carven deeply in the rock. And under one of the names, another phrase was added so that the whole of it declared: *Danner Bramblethorn. King of the Rillrock.* Who built this tomb, and when, it is not told—though some say that it was the work of Dwarves.

And in the Bosky, in each of the Seven Dells, simple ceremonies were held as the fallen were returned to earth; yet many Warrow families grieved for their kith lost to War in strange and distant Lands.

And in that summer of the year two thousand and nineteen of the Fourth Era waggonloads of Men, sent by the King, came to the Bosky bearing lumber and tools and other goods to aid in the reconstruction. And true to Galen's word, the first place rebuilt was Tuckerby Underbank's Warren— The Root—made larger, more spacious, with rooms to house guests who might be Men, so high were the ceilings. And the walls were panelled with rich-grained woods: walnut, oak, cherry, and the like. Furniture, large and small, was brought in, some of it made by the wicker weavers of Bigfen and Littlefen. Tables came from Thimble and chairs from Weevin, and cloth for curtains from the village of Preece. Too, gifts were sent from Stonehill and Weiunwood, and from Wellen in the west.

And when they were finished with Tuckerby's Warren, the men went to help others rebuild houses and stores and mills and barns and other buildings destroyed in the ravage of War. All told, this work would take three years to complete, though none knew it at the outset.

On Year's Long Day—or as some would call it, Mid-Year's Day—during Fair Time, Tuckerby Underbank was married to Merrilee Holt. Fireworks filled the air, and there was great celebration, for not only was it their wedding day, but this was also the annual celebration for all who had had a birthday or an anniversary in the past year—which, of course, included everyone—especially those who had passed from one age-name to the next, as had Merrilee, going from her maiden years to those of a young damman.

In August of that year the newlyweds moved into The Root, for at long last the work was finished. There was a great home-warming party, and nearly everyone in Woody

Hollow and Budgens came to see and to *ooh* and *ahh* over Tuckerby's Warren.

In September a Kingsman came to The Root, bearing a message from High King Galen, requesting the presence of Mr. and Mrs. Tuckerby Underbank at the wedding of Galen, son of Aurion, to Princess Laurelin of Riamon.

The wedding of the High King took place in the golden days of autumn. Caer Pendwyr had never before seen such pageantry and splendor. And every day in the last few weeks preceding the great event, it seemed as if some new and colorful retinue would come to the High King's holt in Pellar. Kingdoms from all corners of the world sent lavish gifts: from Gelen, Leut, Thol, Jute, Gothon, Vancha, Basq, Tugal, Alban, Hurn, and distant Lands unknown to most. And Kings, too, came by land and sea to attend the ceremonies. King Dorn of Riamon of course was there, for Laurelin was his daughter. King Aranor and Queen Alare of Valon came with a great entourage of Harlingar. Coron Eiron, sad-eyed Elf of Darda Galion, and Lord Talarin with his consort Rael came, as well as their son Gildor. And many looked on in wonder as the bright Elves and their escort came unto the castle. From Darda Erynian came Ural, a giant of a Man, Chieftain of the Baeron, and at his side was Lady Aska. Too, there came an unprepossessing Man from Stonehill, Bockleman Brewster, in the company of Elf Lord Inarion and one of the Wee Folk, Arbagon Fenner. Hrosmarshal Vidron and Reachmarshal Ubrik and other warriors too numerous to name were there. And Dwarves, too, marched into Caer Pendwyr: King Brek of Mineholt North and Del-fLord Borta of the Red Hills. And in this company strode Brega, Bekki's son. Additional guests came from Wellen and Trellinath and Rian and other places scattered o'er all Mithgar.

Yet it was one of the Wee Folk who drew a hush of reverent awe as he limped down the center aisle to take his place of honor, escorted on his right by a black-haired damman and on his left by a wee buccan in golden armor. Dressed in silveron mail he was, his sapphire-blue eyes staring sightlessly from a whip-scarred face. He was the Bearer of the Red Quarrel, the 'Stone Slayer; he was Sir Tuckerby Underbank, Thornwalker, Hero of the Realm.

All that day the bells of Caer Pendwyr and of all Pellar pealed in glorious celebration, ringing in the changes, for Galen, son of Aurion, resplendent in scarlet and gold, had taken radiant Laurelin of Riamon to be his wife.

On this day, too, there came into being the Realmsmen, chosen of the High King, defenders of the Land, champions of Just Causes. For as Galen said to Tuck and Merrilee and Patrel, "Never again shall a threat such as Modru steal upon us unawares. These trusted guardians shall ward the Realms, quietly, without fanfare. Perhaps in some small measure this will give Danner's death meaning—and meaning to all those slain in the Winter War."

There was a grand ball that evening, and many came to bid their respects to Tuck. And it was only afterward that the buccan realized just how many stalwart comrades he had come to know during the War, for as he said to Merrilee that night, "I began this quest in the company of strangers, but now I find that they were my brethren all along."

Throughout that year storms had raged with unprecedented violence, as if the weather of the world had been terribly disrupted by the Dimmendark. And the winter of 4E2019 was no exception.

Yet the Winterfest of Yule was especially bright—in spite of the blizzard that raged over much of Mithgar in the north, and in spite of the freezing rain in the south. For this was to be a *special* Yuletide: The High King had decreed that Modru's downfall had marked the end of the Fourth Era, and that this Year's Start Day was the beginning of the Fifth. And everywhere, Free Folk rejoiced.

On January 15, 5E1, a monument was unveiled in Budgens, commemorating this village as the place where began the Struggles. It was set upon a knoll at the north end of the hamlet, and the names of the nineteen Warrows slain in the Battle of Budgens were engraved upon it. So too were Merrilee Holt's words set into the stone: *Let it be said now and for all the days hereafter that on this day the struggle began, and Evil met its match.*

The damman Thornwalker was there with Tuck, and she made a speech at the unveiling. Captain Patrel Rushlock had come all the way from his home near Midwood, and he blew a rousing call upon his silver horn, and all the gathered Warrows cheered.

A week later, before setting out from Tuckerby's Warren to return again unto his home, Patrel gave over the Horn of the Reach into Tuck's keeping, saying, "Hold it for me, my old friend, and blow it at least twice a year: Sound it on the ninth of November, for that was the day you and Hob, Tarpy and Danner, and I all set out from Woody Hollow on a quest that ended with Modru's downfall; and sound it again on the fifteenth of January, the day when we began the Struggles. Here now, I see protests springing to your lips, but heed me: there may come a time when the weather forbids travel, yet I would have this horn blown here in spite of it."

Patrel then turned to Merrilee, and she hugged him and kissed him on the cheek. "You know, Merrilee, I don't think I've ever told you this, but you were among the very best warriors in or out of the Bosky—bar none—yet you are the most gentle soul I have ever known."

With that, Patrel stepped through the studded oaken door of Tuckerby's Warren and mounted his pony and set off for his distant home.

On February the twenty-second there was a general celebration throughout the Boskydells, for that was the day that the Dimmendark had collapsed, marking the end of the Winter War. Yet in a solemn rite he would perform on this day for the rest of his life, blind Tuck was led by Merrilee down to the Rillstones, where the buccan placed a burrow-grown flower upon the center rock, the Rillrock. And there, too, upon the bank, stood Hanlo and Glory Bramblethorn, watching Tuck's quiet ceremony, for on this date their son Danner had died.

On October 12, 5E2, Merrilee Underbank was delivered of a wee damman. Black was her hair, dark as night, and when he was told of it, Tuck named her Raven. The celebration at the One-Eyed Crow lasted far into the wee hours.

*   *   *

Over the next few years a quiet change came over Tuck, and he seemed to slowly, gradually, withdraw from the world around him. He was not exactly embittered by his blindness, yet he seemed to feel as if he was useless—or, as Tuck put it, ". . . not pulling my weight." Only when he was playing with Raven did he seem happy—and then for but a little while. Yet even during those times he would become moody, for he could not see his own child.

Merrilee quietly, without telling Tuck, posted a letter to Galen, High King.

Three months later a special courier came to the Bosky, bearing a missive for Sir Tuckerby Underbank. With trembling hands, Merrilee took the letter from the Kingsman, and, breaking the elaborate waxed seal, she opened the crackling parchment. Taking a deep breath, this is what she read to Tuck:

Sir Tuckerby Underbank

Woody Hollow, The Boskydells

My Dear Cherished Waerling:
   You have been much in my thoughts of late. My mind keeps returning to that long, grueling journey we made o'er the face of Mithgar. And I can still envision you scribing in that diary of yours by the light of the fires we kindled.
   It is about your journal that I write you, for it holds the tale of the Winter War—or a part of it at least. It is a tale that needs recording, not only for scholars to study, but also for folk the world over to hear.
   And that is why I am writing, for I recall a remark I once made as we spent a night in an abandoned house south of Challerain Keep. There it was that I said that perhaps one day I would ask you to scribe your diary into a Waerling history of the Winter War—some day when the fighting was done.
   Well, Tuck, that day has come, and I have a commission for you, if you will have it. I would that you write up your tale, and also tell the story of others who struggled in the Winter War. And when and if that work is ever done, I would have you gather other facts, other histories, other legends bearing upon Mithgar, and set them down, too.

Do not take on this task lightly, for it will take your life-time and more, for it never will be finished since history itself is never done.

If you accept, then with the funds I have set aside I ask that you choose scholars to aid you with the gathering, read-ing, study, and scribing of the text. But you, my cherished Waerling, must lead this endeavor, for I can think of no one more well-suited to the task.

> Galen, Son of Aurion,
> High King of Mithgar

Post Script: Laurelin is heavy with child, our first.

Merrilee's voice fell silent, and tears stood in the eyes of both Warrows; and it was long ere Tuck spoke: "Please pen a note to the King, my dammia. Tell him that I most graciously and humbly accept."

In the succeeding years, Raven grew from a youngling to a maiden and then to a young damman. And her hair was as black as ebony and her eyes as blue as the sea. And this beautiful damman spent her formative years in the company of scholars; and she herself worked tirelessly upon the great history of the Winter War.

Raven or one of the other scholars would read aloud to Tuck the terse handwriting from his journal, and the buccan would try to recall in full detail the events surrounding the entry, as scribes took down his words. And slowly a huge tome took form: *Sir Tuckerby Underbank's Unfinished Diary and His Accounting of the Winter War.*

Often the scholars would travel to other places, both within the Bosky and without, to speak to others concern-ing the events of the War. And many was the time that Tuck went on these journeys, to Stonehill and Vanar, to Challerain Keep and Arden Vale, and to Dael and Mine-holt North, and to many other places. And everywhere he went, Merrilee and Raven went with him, and they were welcomed with open arms.

It was during a journey to the Cliffs in Westdell that Raven met Willen Greylock, and she knew that she'd lost her heart to this handsome buccan scholar. But a time was to pass ere she would see Willen again, for the Underbanks set forth for the Red Hills to seek out Brega who was now DelfLord of those Dwarven halls, to speak to him of the dark trek through Drimmen-deeve.

Yet Tuck, Merrilee, and Raven spent much time in Woody Hollow, too, where historians quartered in Tuckerby's Warren. And as they compiled the epic tale, often one scholar or another would marvel at how near to triumph Modru and Gyphon had come. In one of these moments, Tuck was heard to say, "Time and events are like a field of grain, each stalk producing seeds of chance that fall unto the earth. Some seeds lie fallow, while others take root and grow into reality and produce seeds of their own.

"General Vidron once said that a long string of chance had led him to rescue the Warrows during the Battle of Brackenboro. And I know that a long string of chance led me to the evil sanctum atop the Iron Tower.

"Think of how history might have differed had other events, other realities, taken root."

Willen Greylock came to The Root to work on the history, and Raven walked about with her heart singing. Soon it became apparent that Willen, too, was smitten to the core, for he and the raven-haired beauty spent long hours gazing at the stars together—and if it wasn't the stars, it was flowers, or the Moon, or ants, or an endless number of other totally fascinating things.

And Willen came to Tuck and asked for the hand of Raven, and consent was granted. And one of the wedding gifts given to them was Tuck's original diary, and the first copy of the *Accounting of the Winter War.* As Tuck bestowed these precious books upon them, he said, "This account really ought to be called *The Raven Book,* for without Raven, it would not be what it is today."

After they were married, Willen and Raven Greylock moved to the Cliffs in Westdell.

Throughout the years, many a harper sang the deeds of the Heroes of the Winter War; yet sadly, the words and music of most of these songs never found their way onto paper. But in the Boskydells, Patrel Rushlock, a buccan bard playing a black Elven harp with silver strings, scribed two of the best-known lays:

The Loosing of the Red Quarrel

Loose not the Red Quarrel ere appointed dark time
When through the gate His beauty shines
As the portal of Evil's coming ope's
To crush the good and dash all hopes.
His beauty shields vile as Moon shields Sun.
Destiny asks, "Strike which one?"
An Evil so fair, and an Evil in iron,
High in the tower in the Wastes of Gron.
Neither of two Evils must thy strike claim;
Instead smite the Darkness between the same.
Loose then the Red Quarrel and free the light.
Loose then the Red Quarrel but lose thy sight.

The Lay of the Iron Tower

From frozen north
Comes Vile Power:

The Evil One in
The Cold Iron Tower.

His black Vulgs rave
Down through the Land;
Before their fangs
A bold few stand.

He calls the Hordes
Of evil kind;
By terror and fear
To him they bind.

The Swarms invade
To east and west.
The allies stand
To brave the test.

Dark Hordes come
Across the plains.
Many are felled;
Cold Death reigns.

Liege is slain
At the keep.
Few escape;
Many weep.

Challerain falls;
Winter is come;
Terror rules
The north Kingdom

The Hosts of the King
Are fettered in War,
As under the Mountains
Stride the Four.

The Horror is felled;
The Four win free;
To Larkenwald come:
The Land of Eld Tree.

South on the river
Ride the Four;
Then a swift gallop
To the Harlingar.

Vanadurin, Wellenen,
Fly toward the Wastes.
The Darkest Day comes;
Make all haste.

Wellenen and Elves,
Hold the way.
The Host races north
For the Darkest Day.

The Heroes come
To the Cold Iron Tower.

Nine are chosen
To assault the Power.

An arrow is loosed
With no chance at all,
Yet it fells the guard
Atop the wall.

The ravine is crossed,
The stone is climbed:
Eight go up;
One stays behind.

Under the wall
Crawls the one,
And wins to the tower
For the Death of the Sun.

The bridge is felled;
The iron teeth lift;
The strike force charges;
The horses are swift.

Swords are in
Among the Foe.
Brave friends die;
Sorrow and woe.

Darkness falls;
The Doom has come.
The Fate of the world
Depends on the one.

Through window slit
The Wee One tries;
Yet Myrkenstone
Traps Warrow eyes.

Evil chants fall
Upon his ears,
And Gyphon comes
From Beyond the Spheres.

Sped by the bow
Of the brave Wee One,
The Red Arrow is loosed
To strike the Myrkenstone.

The Myrkenstone dies
In a flare of light,
And the Wee One loses
His power of sight.

Yet Modru is slain,
And Gyphon cast below;
And the Dimmendark falls
To the Sun's bright glow.

The Hordes fall dead
By Adon's Ban.
And southward, too,
The War is won.

Many praised the victory;
Many mourned the slain;
Yet all prayed that nevermore
Would War come here again.

Yes once there was great Evil,
And darkling Shadowlight,
But thanks to many a brave one,
Outside the Sun shines bright.

These two ballads were ever popular in Mithgar, from King's halls to taverns, all across the Realm. And many a minstrel rendered them—but never so well as the wee buccan harper who always sang these lays with bright tears glistening in his viridian eyes.

In 5E35, Raven Greylock was delivered of a daughter, Robin; she was Tuck and Merrilee's first grandchild. The Underbanks travelled to the Cliffs to visit with the newest dammsel of the family. And Tuck was introduced to Willen Greylock's circle of historians, who called themselves the Ravenbook Scholars. In the limestone holts of the Cliffs, these historians had begun to gather books and scrolls in what was to become one of the greatest libraries of all Mithgar . . . but that would come several years hence. At the time, the Ravenbook Scholars were but a small circle of historians and scribes, and their great work was to produce illuminated texts of Tuckerby's epic tale. Why, already they had sent a marvelous duplicate of *The Raven Book* to the High King in Pellar, and he cherished it.

The years fled by, and Tuck and Merrilee gracefully aged. Part of Tuckerby's Warren became a museum, housing Merrilee's bow, Elven cloaks and ropes, the silveron armor and Bane, as well as Patrel's gilded armor and the Atalar Blade . . . and the Horn of Valon that was still sounded regularly on November the ninth in Woody Hollow, and on January fifteenth in Budgens. Helms and trews, arrows and quivers, flags and staffs, and other accoutrements and arms and armor bedecked the walls and rested in glass cases. Folks came from miles around to see them.

And Tuck was content, his life a most peaceful one— except for an occasional dream of terror from which he would start awake in a cold sweat, his blind eyes wide and again seeing the hideous monster Gyphon falling back into the Black Abyss beyond the Spheres. At these times Merrilee would hold him until the phantom of the past was dispelled.

In 5E46 word came that King Galen had died during a savage storm from the Avagon Sea that whelmed upon the walls of Caer Pendwyr. Gareth, eldest son of Galen and Laurelin, was now High King. Tuck and Merrilee made the long pilgrimage to far Pellar and stayed awhile with Laurelin, still beautiful though she was nearing her sixty-fifth birthday. And even though four and a half decades had passed since the end of the Winter War, still the castle was abuzz with talk of this wee limping guest: Sir Tuckerby Underbank, the blind buccan with the whip-scarred face who had slain Modru and saved Mithgar.

At the end of the summer, the buccan and the damman journeyed back to the Boskydells. And except for an occasional trip to Stonehill, the days of their long journeys were ended.

*   *   *

It is told that after Galen's passing, Talarin, Rael, and Gildor rode the Twilight Ride unto Adonar. It is said that none of the three ever fully recovered from the death of Vanidor Silverbranch—especially Gildor Goldbranch, whose eyes always harbored a deep look of sadness.

It is also said that many other Lian passed unto Adonar, too, for their hearts had long held much grief for those slain in the War.

Yet whether or not these tales are true, none knows.

In the winter of 5E73, December seventeenth, to be exact, Tuck took to his bed with a cold. And as the days passed to become a week, and then another, the granther buccan sank deeper into his illness, regardless of all that could be done. He was ninety-seven at the time, and only he and Merrilee and Brega in the far Red Hills remained alive of all the mortals who had survived that epic day at the Iron Tower. Patrel, Igon, Laurelin, Ubrik, all were gone. One by one they had sailed upon the Darkling Sea to join Vidron, Aranor, Reggian, Arbagon, Bockleman, Dorn, and countless other loved ones on the endless journey 'neath the Silver Suns. And now, in spite of the healer's herbs and simples, in spite of Merrilee's tender ministrations, on this Year's End Day the flame of Tuck's life waned and flickered as his spirit was irresistibly drawn away. And though Merrilee held tightly to her buccaran's hand, she could feel the silver cord of his life slowly slipping from her frail grasp.

And as she gripped Tuck's precious hand, she did not see before her a fragile ancient Warrow; instead she looked beyond the pale translucent flesh and snow-white locks, and her eyes saw the handsome young buccan that she first had fallen in love with.

And she wept, for she knew she could not stay the hand of the Dark One.

Tuck's thready breath softly filled the room with the sound of dying, yet now and again he would murmur a few words—some in the ancient Warrow tongue.

And as the hour neared mid of night, and Merrilee laid her weary head down and wept bitter tears, she felt Tuck stroking her hair. "Do not weep, my dammia," he whispered, "I will wait for you."

Long moments passed, and his breathing grew faint, and the yellow candlelight guttered, the flame wavering, as if someone had come into the room.

Merrilee felt Tuck's grip tighten, and the buccan's sapphirine eyes flew wide. "Adon, oh Adon, you have made it so bright and beautiful," Tuck breathed. And then his voice was filled with the strength and vigor of youth, and he called out, "Hiyo! Hiyo, Danner! Wait for me!"

And then he was gone.

And Merrilee wept for her lost beloved, while down in the swale of Woody Hollow, out beneath the turning stars, horns sounded and people cheered and someone began ringing the fire gong, for it was the beginning of a new year.

* * *

"But if for no other reason, Evil must be destroyed so that we can once more guide our own destinies."

—Rael of Arden
January 10, 4E2019

A Word About Warrows

Common among the many races of Man throughout the world are the persistent legends of Little People: Wee Folk, pixies, leprechauns, sidhe, pwcas, gremlins, cluricaunes, peris, and so forth. There is little doubt that many of these tales come from Man's true memories of the Eld Days . . . memories of Dwarves, Elves, and others, hearking back to the ancient times before The Separation. Yet, some of these legends *must* spring from Man's memory of a small Folk called Warrows.

Supporting this thesis, a few fragmentary records are unearthed once in a great age, records that give us glimpses of the truth behind the legends. But to the unending loss of Mankind, some of these records have been destroyed, while others languish unrecognized—even if stumbled across—for they require tedious examination by a scholar versed in strange tongues—tongues such as Pellarion—ere a glimmering of their true significance is seen.

One such record that has survived—and was stumbled across by an appropriately versed scholar—is *The Raven Book;* another is *The Fairhill Journal.* From these two chronicles, as well as from a meager few other sources, a factual picture of the Wee Folk can be pieced together, and deductions then can be made concerning Warrows:

They are a small Folk, the adults ranging in height from three to four feet. Some scholars argue that there seems to be little doubt that their root stock is Man, since Warrows are human in all respects—that is, no wings, horns, tails, or the like—and they come in all the assorted shapes and colors that the Big Folk, the Men, do, only on a smaller scale. However, to the contrary, other scholars argue that the shape of Warrow ears—pointed—the tilt of their bright strange eyes, and their longer life span indicate that some Elven blood is mingled in their veins. Yet their eyes do set them apart from Elvenkind: canted they are, and in that the two Folk are alike; but Warrow eyes are bright and liquescent, and the iris is large and strangely colored: amber like gold, the deep blue of sapphire, or pale emerald green.

In any case, Warrows are deft and quick in their smallness, and their mode of living makes them wood-crafty and nature wise. And they are wary, tending to slip aside when an *Outsider* comes near, until the stranger's intentions can be ascertained. Yet they do not always yield to intruders: Should one of the Big Folk come unannounced upon a group of Warrows—such as a large family gathering of Othens splashing noisily in the waters of the fen—the *Outsider* would note that suddenly all the Warrows were silently watching him, the dammen (females) and oldsters quietly drifting to the rear with the younglings clinging to them or peering around from behind, and the buccen (males) in the fore facing the stranger in the abrupt quiet. But it is not often that Warrows are taken by surprise, and so they are seldom seen in the forests and fens and wilds unless they choose to be; yet in their hamlets and dwellings they are little different from "commonplace" Folk, for they treat with *Outsiders* in a friendly manner, unless given reason to do otherwise.

Because of their wary nature, Warrows usually tend to dress in clothing that blends into the background: greys, greens, browns. And the shoes, boots, and slippers they wear are soft and quiet upon the land. Yet, during Fair Time, or at other Celebrations, they dress in bright splashes of gay, gaudy colors—scarlets, oranges, yellows, blues, purples—and they love to blow horns and strike drum, gong, and cymbal, and in general be raucous.

Some of the gayest times, the most raucous, are those which celebrate the passing from one Warrow age to another, not only the "ordinary" birthday parties, but in particular those when an "age-name" changes: Children, both male and female, up to the age of ten are called "younglings." From age ten to twenty, the males are called "striplings" and the females "maidens." From age twenty to thirty, males and females are called respectively "young buccen" and "young dammen." It is at age thirty that Warrows reach majority—come of age, as it were—and until sixty are then called "buccen" or "dammen," which are also the general names for male or female Warrows. (The terms "buccen" and "dammen" are plurals; by changing the *e* to an *a,* "buccan" and "damman" refer to just one male or female Warrow.) After sixty, Warrows become "eld buccen" and "eld dammen," and beyond the age eighty-five they are called, respectively, "granthers" and "grandams." And at each of these "special" birthday parties, drums tattoo, horns blare, cymbals clash, and bells ring; gaudy colors adorn the celebrants; and annually, on Year's Long Day, during Fair Time, bright fireworks light up the sky for all who have had a birthday or birthday anniversary in the past year—which, of course, includes everyone—but especially for those who have passed from one age-name to the next.

Once past their youth, Warrows tend to roundness, for ordinarily they eat four meals a day, and on feast days, five. As the elders tell it: "Warrows are small, and small things take a heap of food to keep 'em going. Look at your birds and mice, and look especially at your shrews: They're all busy gulping down food most of the time that they're awake. So us Wee Folk need at least four meals a day just to keep a body alive!"

Warrow home and village life is one of pastoral calm. The Wee Folk often come together to pass the day: The dammen klatch at sewings or cannings; the buccen and dammen gather at the field plantings and harvests, or at the raising or digging of a dwelling, or at picnics and reunions—noisy affairs, for Warrows typically have large families.

Within the home, at "normal" mealtimes all members of a household—be they master, mistress, brood, or servantry—flock 'round the table in one large gathering to share the food and drink, and to speak upon the events of the day. But at "guest" meals, customarily only the holtmaster, his family, and the guests come to the master's table to share the repast; rarely are other members of the holt included at that board, and then only when specifically invited by the head of the house. At meal's end, especially when "official business" is to be discussed, the younger offspring politely excuse themselves, leaving the elders alone with the visitors to deal with their "weighty matters."

Concerning the "hub" of village life, every hamlet has at least one inn, usually with good beer—some inns have the reputation of having better beer than the average—and here gather the buccen, especially the granthers, some daily, others weekly, and still others less frequently; and they mull over old news, and listen to new happenings, and speculate upon the High King's doings down in Pellar, and talk about the state that things have come to.

There are four strains of northern Warrows: Siven, Othen, Quiren, and Paren, dwelling, respectively, in burrows, fen stilt-houses, tree flets, and stone field-houses. (Perhaps the enduring legends concerning intelligent badgers, otters, squirrels, and hares, as well as other animals, come from the lodging habits of the Wee Folk.) And Warrows live, or have lived, in practically every country in the world, though at any given time some Lands host many Warrows while other Lands host few or none. The Wee Folk seem to have a history of migration, yet in those days of the *Wanderjahre* many other Folk also drifted across the face of the world.

In the time of the writing of both *The Raven Book* and *The Fairhill Journal,* most northern Warrows resided in one of two places: in the Weiunwood, a shaggy forest in the Wilderland north of Harth and south of Rian; or in the Boskydells, a Land of fens, forests, and fields west of the Spindle River and north of the Wenden.

The Boskydells, by and far the larger of these two Warrowlands, is protected from *Outsiders* by a formidable barrier of thorns—Spindlethorns—growing in the river valleys around the Land. This maze of living stilettoes forms an effective shield surrounding the Boskydells, turning aside all but the most determined. There are a few roads within long thorn tunnels passing through the barrier, and in generally peaceful times these ways are left unguarded, and any who want to enter may do so. During times of crisis, however, along the roads within the barrier Warrow archers stand guard behind movable barricades made of the Spindlethorn, to keep ruffians and other unsavory characters outside while permitting ingress to those with legitimate business.

In that cold November of 4E2018, when this tale began, it was a time of crisis.

Calendar of the Iron Tower

Events of the Second Era

In the final days of the Second Era, the Great War of the Ban was fought. On the High Plane, Adon prevailed over the Great Evil, Gyphon; on the Middle Plane, by an unexpected stroke the Grand Alliance won and vile Modru was defeated upon Mithgar. Adon set His Ban upon the creatures of the Untargarda who aided Gyphon in the War: they were forever banished from the light of Mithgar's Sun, and those who would defy the Ban suffer the Withering Death. Gyphon, swearing vengeance, was exiled beyond the Spheres. Thus did the Second Era end and the Third Era begin . . . and so matters stood for some four thousand years, until the Fourth Era.

Events of the Fourth Era

4E1992: Patrel Rushlock born near Midwood, Eastdell, the Boskydells.

4E1995: Tuckerby Underbank born in Woody Hollow, Eastdell, the Boskydells.

4E1996: Danner Bramblethorn born in Woody Hollow, Eastdell, the Boskydells.

4E1999: Merrilee Holt born in Woody Hollow, Eastdell, the Boskydells.

4E2013: Comet Dragon Star flashes through the heavens of Mithgar, nearly striking the world. Great flaming gouting chunks score the night skies, some pieces hurtling to earth. Many see this hairy star as a harbinger of doom.

The Winter War
4E2018

August: A cold month. Wolves sighted in Northdell, the Boskydells. Gammer Alderbuc begins organizing the

Thornwalker Wolf Patrols. Some days of frost in late August.

September: Gammer Alderbuc appoints Captain Alver as head of the Thornwalkers. Snow falls on the seventh of the month. Old Barlo begins archery classes in Woody Hollow, training a group of Thornwalker recruits; Tuck and Danner are students. Rumors come to the Boskydells of some dark Evil up north, reputed to be Modru.

October: Several Boskydell families disappear; none can say where. Cold grips the Land. Snow.

November 2: Old Barlo's archery class graduates. As Thornwalker recruits, Tuck, Danner, Hob Banderel, and Tarpy Wiggens are to join the Eastdell Fourth, guarding Spindle Ford.

November 9: With Patrel as their guide, Tuck, Danner, Hob, and Tarpy set out for Spindle Ford.

November 10: The five Warrows stop at the Huggs' farm, but the owners have disappeared. The Warrows discover evidence of evil Wolf-like Vulgs who apparently have slain the Huggs.

November 11: Vulgs attack the Warrows at Rooks' Roost. Hob is slain.

November 13–December 5: Tuck, Danner, Tarpy take up their Thornwalker duties in Patrel's company, standing Beyonder Guard at the Ford and riding Wolf Patrol. On December 3, a waggon train of refugees passes through bearing news that High King Aurion prepares for War at Challerain Keep. On December 4, a Kingsman arrives calling the muster at Challerain Keep. A Vulg attack upon the herald results in the drowning of the Man, the horse, and Tarpy. Tuck survives, rescued by Danner. On December 5, Tuck, Danner, Patrel, and forty other Warrows volunteer to answer the King's call.

December 6–13: The Warrows travel to Challerain Keep. On December 13, Tuck, Danner, and Patrel meet Prince Igon, Princess Laurelin, Elf Lord Gildor, Kingsgeneral Vidron, and High King Aurion. The Warrows learn of the Dimmendark, a spectral Shadowlight to the north where the Sun shines not and Adon's Ban does not rule, hence vile creatures roam free.

December 14–20: Warrows take up duties as members of the Castle-ward. Tuck becomes friends with Princess Laurelin, learning that she is betrothed to Prince Galen, who even now rides with a company of Men within the Dimmendark, scouting for evidence that Modru is gathering his evil Hordes of old.

Tuck, Danner, and Patrel attend the Princess's birthday eve feast, and as the celebration rises to its height, a wounded warrior comes bearing news that the dreadful pall of the Dimmendark has started moving south. The Winter War has begun.

December 21: First Yule: Princess Laurelin departs Challerain Keep on the last waggon train of refugees, escorted by Prince Igon, who is sent to hasten the King's Host from Pellar to Challerain Keep.

December 22: Second Yule: The Dimmendark sweeps over the Keep and beyond. The spectral Shadowlight baffles eyesight: Men see at most two miles over open plains, and even less in forests and hill country; Elves see perhaps twice as far as Men; Warrows, as if seeing by a new color, see farthest of all, as much as five miles.

December 23: Third Yule: The Warrow company is disbanded, and the buccen are posted among the King's Companies to use their Warrow eyes to see for the Men.

On this day the Horde, thirty thousand strong, lays siege to the Keep.

December 24: Fourth Yule: In the distance north of the Keep, Galen's Men set fire to a siege tower, yet other siege engines arrive to be used by the Horde. Catapults fling fire over the walls, and the city burns.

December 25: Fifth Yule: Challerain Keep continues to burn.

Laurelin's waggon train is attacked by Ghûls; Prince Igon is felled; Princess Laurelin, her arm broken, is taken captive; all others are slain.

December 26: Sixth Yule: The Horde attacks. The first and second walls of Challerain Keep fall.

Prince Igon, sorely wounded, takes up pursuit of Laurelin's captors.

December 27: Seventh Yule: The third and fourth walls of Challerain Keep fall.

The Battle of Weiunwood begins. Here, in this shaggy forest, the Weiunwood Alliance of Men, Warrows, and Elves fends off another of Modru's Hordes.

December 28: Eighth Yule: Challerain Keep is abandoned. The King's forces attempt to break free of the Horde. King Aurion is slain. Separated from the others, Tuck flees, taking refuge in an ancient tomb where he discovers the Red Quarrel and the Atalar Blade. By happenstance, Prince Galen comes to the same tomb. Together they flee southward, riding for a rendezvous in Stonehill with any others who might have survived.

Danner and Patrel, also cut off from the others, begin their own trek for Stonehill.

General Vidron and Lord Gildor, along with the pitiful remnants of the Kingsmen, break free and ride east toward the Signal Mountains.

The Battle of Weiunwood enters its second 'Day.

December 29: Ninth Yule: The Battle of Weiunwood enters its third 'Day. The Horde breaks off and marches east and south, skirting the borders of the shaggy forest.

December 30: Tenth Yule: Year's End Eve: Tuck and Galen discover the slaughtered waggon train and begin the long pursuit of Laurelin's captors.

December 31: Eleventh Yule: Year's End Day: Danner and Patrel come upon the slaughtered waggon train. Knowing that ponies are too slow to overtake the Ghûls, the pair decides to continue on to Stonehill and the rendezvous.

4E2019

January 1: Twelfth Yule: Last Yule: Year's Start Day: Snow covers the track of Laurelin's captors. Tuck and Galen arrive at the Weiunwood; they are given food and a place to sleep and are warded by members of the Weiunwood Alliance.

January 2–3: Seeking information about Laurelin's captors, Tuck and Galen travel through Weiunwood to meet the Alliance leaders: Arbagon Fenner (Warrow), Bockleman Brewster (Man), and Lord Inarion (Elf). Galen is told that the Ghûls passed by, heading eastward, perhaps riding for Drearwood. Tuck and Galen strike out for that dire forest.

Vidron and Gildor and the remnants of the Kingsmen of Challerain Keep come to the Weiunwood. Gildor turns aside to confer with his kith while Vidron continues on toward Stonehill. Gildor learns that Galen passed through the Weiunwood, and the Elf sets out in pursuit, one day behind.

January 4: The captive Princess Laurelin is borne through Grūwen Pass and into Gron. She knows now that she is bound for the Iron Tower, Modru's mighty fortress upon Claw Moor.

In her wake, Prince Igon, suffering dreadfully from his wound, collapses in the snow. He is discovered by a patrol of Elves who bear him to the Hidden Refuge of Arden Vale, where he is tended.

January 5–7: Tuck and Galen continue the long pursuit, crossing Drear Ford on the sixth and picking up the track of Laurelin's captors as it runs through Drearwood.

Danner and Patrel come to Stonehill; the town is deserted. They decide to wait two days, and if no one else comes, they will go west to the Boskydells and gather more Warrows and then fare south to Pellar to join the Host and be their eyes in the Dimmendark.

January 8: Tuck and Galen enter Arden Vale, where they meet Lord Talarin and Lady Rael, Elven leaders of the Hidden Refuge. Lord Talarin takes them to see the wounded Man the Elves found lying in the snow. It is Prince Igon, abed and delirious from his wound. At last Galen confirms that Laurelin is indeed a captive. Lord Gildor finally catches up to Galen and informs him that King Aurion is slain and that Galen is now High King. Galen must choose between love and duty: to pursue the captive Princess, or to rally the Host to War.

Danner and Patrel leave Stonehill for the Boskydells. Just as they ride out through the west gate, General Vidron and his force ride in through the east gate; they do not see one another.

January 9: Galen finds he has no choice; he must ride south and rally the Host to fight the enemy. With heavy hearts, he, Tuck, and Lord Gildor begin the long journey toward Pellar.

Vanidor, Gildor's twin brother, with three comrades—Varion, Duorn, and Flandrena—sets off north into Gron to spy out Modru's strength and, if fortune favors them, to rescue the Princess.

An ex-soldier named Jarek comes to Stonehill and tells Vidron that Gûnarring Gap, the key pass to the south, is held by the foe. Vidron decides to ride west to Wellen and muster troops to break the grasp of the enemy upon the Gap.

January 10: Danner and Patrel enter the Boskydells and discover that Modru's Reavers have laid waste to the village of Greenfields. During the night, General Vidron and his company gallop through Greenfields on their way to Wellen. Again, the two Warrows just miss encountering Vidron.

January 11: Princess Laurelin arrives at last at the Iron Tower. Modru imprisons her in a lightless, filthy cell.

January 12: Danner and Patrel arrive at Woody Hollow; Ghûls have set the hamlet aflame. Merrilee Holt saves Danner and Patrel from a reaver. Danner and Patrel learn that Tuck's parents as well as Merrilee's were slain by the raiding Ghûls.

January 13: Warrow archers meet in Whitby's barn to make plans to strike back at the Ghûls.

January 14: Tuck, Galen, and Gildor, riding south along the Grimwall Mountains, come upon Brega, Dwarf warrior, the only survivor of a great battle between a Dwarven company and the vanguard of a Rūcken Horde. Brega joins the trio and south they ride.

January 15: Battle of Budgens: Warrows ambush Ghûl reavers in Budgens, Eastdell, the Boskydells.

January 16: Fleeing before Ghûls, Tuck, Galen, Gildor, and Brega are forced to the Dusk-Door of Drimmen-deeve. There they are attacked by the Krakenward and flee into the dark, Gargon-ruled halls of the ancient Dwarven Realm.

Laurelin is taken from her cell and led to a high tower, where she finds Vanidor captive. Modru gloats over the Myrkenstone, a chunk of the Dragon Star used to create the Dimmendark. Laurelin is forced to witness Vanidor's murder. By an unknown Elven power, in the moment of his death Vanidor thrusts a Death Rede upon his twin, Gildor, who is far to the south at the Dusk-Door.

In the Boskydells, Budgens is burned.

January 17–18: Tuck, Galen, Gildor, and Brega trek through Drimmen-deeve, heading for the Dawn-Gate and freedom. The Gargon, a fear caster, discovers that they are in the caverns and pursues them, aided in the hunt by a

Horde of maggot-folk. The four Heroes manage to slay the Gargon and escape.

January 19–20: Travelling south, Tuck, Galen, Glldor, and Brega at last win free of the Dimmendark.

In the Boskydells, the Company of Whitby's Barn joins with the Eastwood Company, and on the twentieth they ambush a great gang of Ghûls in the Battle of Brackenboro. Danner, Patrel, and Merrilee are rescued by Vidron and warriors from Wellen who are on their way to free Gûnarring Gap from the Lakh of Hyree.

January 21: Tuck, Galen, Gildor, and Brega come to Darda Galion, Land of Eld Trees, Land of the Silverlarks.

Danner, Patrel, Merrilee, and seven more Warrows join Vidron to act as eyes for the Men as they set off for Gûnarring Gap.

January 23: Tuck, Galen, Gildor, and Brega speak with Coron Eiron in Wood's-Heart, Darda Galion. Plans are made to fare by boat to the Argon Ferry where, if the ferry is in friendly hands, they can find aid to lead them to the Host.

Vidron's Legion leaves the Boskydells, riding for Gûnarring Gap.

The vanguard of the Horde from Challerain Keep enters the Boskydells by the old abandoned Northwood tunnel.

January 24: Tuck, Galen, Gildor, and Brega set out by Elven boat for the Argon Ferry.

The main body of the Horde from Challerain Keep enters the Boskydells.

January 25: While speaking of an eclipse, Gildor at last remembers Vanidor's Death Rede: "The Darkest Day, The Greatest Evil . . ." Gildor surmises that during the eclipse coming February 22, Modru will attempt to bring Gyphon to Mithgar from beyond the Spheres.

January 28: Tuck, Galen, Gildor, and Brega arrive at the Argon Ferry.

January 29–31: Tuck, Galen, Gildor, and Brega, accompanied by Reachmarshal Ubrik, ride for Gûnarring Gap.

At the Gap itself a great battle rages between the Harlingar of Valon and the Lakh of Hyree. After three days, the Harlingar prevail.

February 1: Tuck, Galen, Gildor, Brega and Ubrik arrive at Gûnarring Gap. King Aranor of Valon commits five thousand Vanadurin warriors to ride north with High King Galen to the Iron Tower to attempt to disrupt Modru's plans on the Darkest Day, the 'Day of the eclipse.

Vidron at last comes to the Gap, and, believing it to be enemy-held, plans an attack.

February 2: Vidron, not realizing that the Gap is now in friendly hands, unknowingly launches an attack upon the Vanadurin. In the last moment both sides see that neither is the foe of the other, and each sheers off the attack.

Vidron's Legion joins High King Galen's quest.

Tuck is reunited with Merrilee, Danner, and Patrel.

At the pace of a Valanreach long-ride, the Host starts north for Gron in a race to arrive at the Iron Tower ere the coming of the Darkest Day.

February 5: Galen's Host comes to Gûnar Slot.

February 7: Galen's Host comes to the edge of the Dimmendark.

February 8: Galen's Host passes Ragad Vale.

The Horde attacking Weiunwood breaks off the assault and starts east from Stonehill to intercept Galen's Host.

February 9: The Host passes the road to Quadran Pass.

The Horde is at Beacontor.

February 10: The Host crosses Rhone Ford. The horses of Vidron's Legion are weary, for they have come all the way from Wellen, and they begin to have difficulty maintaining the hard pace.

The Horde continues east at a forced march.

Elf Lord Inarion sets out from Beacontor to warn Lord Talarin in Arden Vale of the Horde's eastward march.

February 11: The Host camps south of Drearwood. The horses of Vidron's Legion continue to grow weary.

The Horde nears the Wilderness Hills.

February 12: The Host comes to the Crossland Road near Arden Ford.

The Horde comes to the Stone-arches Bridge.

Lord Inarion arrives in Arden Vale.

February 13: The Host camps alongside Arden Bluff. Prince Igon, Elf Lord Talarin, Elf Lord Inarion, and Elf Flandrena come to High King Galen's camp. Inarion speaks of the Horde. Flandrena, the only survivor of Vanidor's ill-fated mission into Gron, tells of the strength of the Iron Tower. Galen asks Vidron and the Wellenen to delay the

Horde at Grūwen Pass. Talarin and the Elves of Arden join Vidron's force of Wellenen. Prince Igon, recovered from his wound, joins Galen on the mission to the Iron Tower.

February 14: The Host passes through Grūwen Pass to come into Gron.

Vidron's Legion and the Elves of Arden take up positions to defend Grūwen Pass.

The Horde comes to Arden Ford.

February 15: The Host continues north.

The cast is removed from Princess Laurelin's arm, now healed. Laurelin continues to seek a means of escape.

February 17: The Host comes to the south edge of the Gwasp.

The Horde arrives at Grūwen Pass.

February 18: The Host comes to the north edge of the Gwasp.

The Horde attacks the defenders of Grūwen Pass.

February 19: The Host comes to Claw Moor.

Second 'Day of the Battle of Grūwen Pass.

February 20: The Host arrives at the Iron Tower.

Third 'Day of the Battle of Grūwen Pass.

February 21: Galen and his War-council plan the assault of the Iron Tower.

Fourth 'Day of the Battle of Grūwen Pass.

February 22: The Darkest Day: The Host begins the assault on the Iron Tower. Brega leads a raid across a chasm and up the fortress walls to lower the drawbridge and open the gate. Injured, Tuck crawls through a drain under the rampart and slowly makes his way to Laurelin's prison chamber. Modru stuns Tuck and drags Laurelin to the top of the tower to sacrifice her and bring Gyphon to Mithgar. Brega's raiders drop the drawbridge. Patrel tricks a Troll into opening the gate. The Host invades the fortress. Danner is slain in the battle atop the gate. Tuck wins to the tower and slays the Myrkenstone, killing Modru and sending Gyphon back beyond the Spheres. Tuck is blinded. The Dimmendark collapses; Adon's Ban is restored and the Withering Death strikes down the maggot-folk. The Lakh of Hyree are defeated. The Rovers of Kistan flee across the Avagon Sea. The Winter War is ended.

February 23–March 3: Great storms hammer Mithgaŕ. A blizzard traps the Host in the Iron Tower.

March 4: The Host leaves the Iron Tower and begins the trek homeward.

March 13: The Host arrives in Arden Vale.

March 20: First Day of Spring: After a week's rest, the Host again resumes the journey homeward.

March 22: King Galen, Princess Laurelin, Prince Igon, General Vidron, and the Men of Valon continue south for Pellar, while Tuck, Merrilee, Patrel, and the surviving Warrows, escorted by the Men of Wellen, turn westward along the Crossland Road heading for the Boskydells.

March 30: The Warrows and their escort arrive at Stonehill.

April 1: The Warrows and their escort leave Stonehill.

April 3: The Warrows and their escort enter the Boskydells. Patrel Rushlock turns aside to journey to Midwood, Eastdell, the Boskydells.

April 4: Tuck and Merrilee arrive in Woody Hollow, Eastdell, the Boskydells.

June 21: Year's Long-Day: Mid-Year's Day: Tuckerby Underbank marries Merrilee Holt.

August: The Underbanks move into The Root.

Autumn: High King Galen marries Laurelin of Riamon. The Order of the Realmsmen is founded.

December 31: Eleventh Yule: Year's End Day: Last day of the Fourth Era.

Events of Later Years

January 1, 5E1: Twelfth Yule: Last Yule: Year's Start Day: First day of the Fifth Era (5E).

January 15, 5E1: A monument is unveiled in Budgens on the anniversary of the Battle of Budgens commemorating the village as the place where began the Struggles.

October 15, 5E2: Raven Underbank is born in Woody Hollow, Eastdell, the Boskydells.

Circa 5E7: Tuckerby Underbank is commissioned by the High King to gather and record the history of the Winter War, a work that is to take his lifetime and will be called *Sir Tuckerby Underbank's Unfinished Diary and His Accounting of the Winter War.* In the work Tuck will be assisted by many scholars and scribes, but mainly by his daughter, Raven. In later years Tuck will refer to the work as *The Raven Book*.

5E31: Raven Underbank marries Willen Greylock. They move to the Cliffs, Westdell, the Boskydells, where Willen founds the Ravenbook Scholars.

5E35: Robin Greylock born, the Cliffs, Westdell, the Boskydells.

Circa 5E40: Tuckerby's Warren, The Root, becomes a museum housing artifacts of the Winter War.

5E46: High King Galen dies at Caer Pendwyr, Pellar, during a raging storm. His and Laurelin's eldest son, Gareth, becomes High King.

Circa 5E47: Rumors abound of many Elves passing to Adonar upon the High Plane, leaving Mithgar behind.

December 17, 5E73: Tuck falls ill.

December 31, 5E73: Eleventh Yule: Year's End Day: Tuckerby Underbank, Bearer of the Red Quarrel, 'Stone Slayer, Hero of the Realm, dies at the age of 97.

5E91: Merrilee Holt Underbank dies.

5E193: Brega, Bekki's son, DelfLord of the Red Hills, dies at the age of 242. Thus passes away the last of the mortal Heroes of the Winter War.

The Long Journeys

In the course of the Winter War, several extraordinary, long, hard journeys were undertaken. Ravenbook Scholars summarize these journeys as follows:

The pony ride of the Company of the King from Spindle Ford to Challerain Keep: 175 miles in 7½ days (December 6–13, 4E2018).

The Hèlsteed ride of the Kinstealers from the Battle Downs to the Iron Tower: 600 miles in 18 days (December 25, 4E2018–January 11, 4E2019).

The pony ride of Danner and Patrel from Challerain Keep to Stonehill: 250 miles in 10 days (December 28, 4E2018–January 6, 4E2019).

The ride (on Jet) of Tuck and Galen from Challerain Keep to the Battle Downs and thence to Arden Vale: 400 miles in 11½ days (December 28, 4E2018–January 8, 4E2019).

The ride (on Fleetfoot) of Gildor from Challerain Keep

to the Signal Mountains and then to the Weiunwood and thence to Arden Vale: 350 miles in 11½ days (December 28, 4E2018–January 8, 4E2019).

The ride of Vidron (and Men) from Challerain Keep to the Signal Mountains and then to the Weiunwood and thence to the Battle Downs and on to Stonehill: 300 miles in 11½ days (December 28, 4E2018–January 8, 4E2019).

The ride of Jarek from Gûnarring Gap to Stonehill: 565 miles in 12¼ days (December 28, 4E2018–January 9, 4E2019).

The pony ride of Danner and Patrel from Stonehill to Woody Hollow: 125 miles in 5 days (January 8–12, 4E2019).

The ride of Vidron (and Men) from Stonehill to Wellen: 300 miles in 6 days (January 9–15, 4E2019).

The ride of Tuck, Galen, and Gildor from Arden Vale to the Dusk-Door of Drimmen-deeve (Brega joined the trio for the final 3 days): 325 miles in 8 days, the final 20 miles while being pursued by Ghûls on Hèlsteeds (January 9–16, 4E2019).

The ride of Vanidor, Varion, Duorn, and Flandrena from Arden Vale to the Iron Tower: 275 miles in 6 days (January 9–14, 4E2019).

The ride (on Swiftmane) of Flandrena from the Iron Tower to Arden Vale: 275 miles in 3½ days (January 16–19, 4E2019).

The ride of Vidron's Legion from Wellen to Brackenboro: 175 miles in 4 days (January 17–20, 4E2019).

The ride of Vidron's Legion from Brackenboro to Gûnarring Gap: 575 miles in 12 days (January 21–February 1, 4E2019).

The Elven boat ride of Tuck, Galen, Gildor, and Brega down the River Argon from Bellon Falls to the Argon Ferry: 750 miles over 4 days (January 25–28, 4E2019).

The ride of Tuck, Galen, Gildor, Brega and Ubrik from the Argon Ferry to Gûnarring Gap: 400 miles in 4 days riding horses with trailing remounts and obtaining fresh mounts at the Red Hills Garrison (January 29–February 1, 4E2019).

The ride of Vidron's Legion from Gûnarring Gap to Grū-wen Pass: 635 miles in 13 days (February 2–14, 4E2019).

[Note: Perhaps the three rides of Vidron's Wellenan Legion are the most remarkable of all. The horses of Wellen, bearing Warriors, arms, and armor, covered a combined total of 1,385 miles in 29 days (January 17–February 14, 4E2019) in an unremitting Valanreach long-ride from Wellen to Brackenboro to Gûnarring Gap to Grūwen Pass. It is little wonder that this grueling trek took its toll upon the steeds such that they at last could no longer keep up the pace.]

The ride of the Host from Gûnarring Gap to the Iron Tower: 900 miles in 18½ days (February 2–20, 4E2019).

The forced march of one of Modru's Hordes from Stonehill to Arden Ford and thence to Grūwen Pass: 350 miles in 9½ days (February 8–17, 4E2019).

The ride (upon Wingfoot and Wildwind) of Inarion from Beacontor to Arden Vale: 215 miles in 3 days (February 10–12, 4E2019).

The ride of the Host from the Iron Tower to Arden Vale: 275 miles in 9½ days (March 4–13, 4E2019).

The ride of the Warrows and Wellenen from Arden Vale to Stonehill: 375 miles in 11 days (March 20–30, 4E2019).

The ride of the Warrows and Wellenen from Stonehill to Woody Hollow: 125 miles in 4 days (April 1–4, 4E2019).

Thus were the remarkable journeys of both friend and foe during the Winter War, as recorded in *The Raven Book*.

The Eclipse of the Darkest Day

The Raven Book makes it clear that the solar eclipse of February 22, 4E2019, was a total one at the Iron Tower. Further, from the context it can be inferred that the duration was lengthy. But the text may be misleading, for if we assume that the celestial mechanics of the earth-Moon-Sun system of Mithgar of yore are the same as those of the earth-moon-sun system of today, then the duration of the totality at the Iron Tower could not have exceeded seven minutes thirty-three seconds (the maximum possible duration of totality at any given point on the earth's surface along the path of the umbra). And if a few simple assumptions are made about the probable latitude and longitude of Modru Kinstealer's holt, then it is more likely that the duration of the totality would fall somewhat short of this maximum time. Finally, if the eclipse was "typical," a totality time of two to four minutes seems reasonable.

Yet, two or four or even seven minutes does not seem to be enough time to carry out the actions known to have occurred during the totality at the Iron Tower. For example, after the darkness fell, could Merrilee and the Warrows have gathered together a force of warriors in the courtyards and then gotten to the top of the tower . . . all in seven minutes or less? It does not seem likely.

Three immediate hypotheses spring to mind: (1) the actions described actually took place in a very brief time; (2) the motions of the earth-Moon-Sun system of Mithgar of yore were not the same as those of our system today; or (3) the darkness fell within the Dimmendark prior to total occlusion.

Of these three hypotheses, the last one seems most likely: that is, somewhat prior to totality, the Sun's rays were eclipsed to the point that the remaining light simply was too feeble to significantly illuminate the Dimmendark. At this point the Men could no longer see, and the Elves, but dimly. This theory is supported by the fact that approximately two hundred miles southward in the Dimmendark, at Grūwen Pass—and for that matter, at Mineholt North in Riamon, as well as even further south in the Boskydells—where the eclipse was not total, darkness fell upon the combatants, and they, too, could not see. (Except, of course, wherever Warrows were, the Wee Folk saw by the "black" light of the Myrkenstone.)

Hence, it can be surmised that although the time of the totality at the Iron Tower was but two to four minutes in duration, the actual span of time that only the Warrows could see was perhaps fifteen or more minutes—certainly time enough for the described actions to have taken place.

Two other items of interest: (1) Based on *The Raven Book,* it can be surmised that the path of totality swept from the west across Rian, over The Rigga Mountains and into Gron, across Claw Spur and over the Iron Tower, past the Gronfang Mountains and into Jord, and thence over the Grimwall Mountains and through Aven and beyond. In Grūwen Pass, Arden, the Boskydells, Riamon, Valon, Jugo, Pellar, and the like, the eclipse was only partial. (2) The "beads of light" spoken of in *The Raven Book* that sprang forth from the rim of the unseen Moon as the eclipse was lifting were, no doubt, Baily's beads, which are described elsewhere in astronomical literature.

Finally, the latitude and longitude of the Iron Tower only can be speculated upon, and many scholars have tried to deduce its location (some have suggested that it was situated near Leningrad [30° east, 60° north], while others have selected a site near Warsaw [21° east, 52° north], and yet others have their reasons for selecting a diverse number of even different locales). Again, the reader is cautioned that it is sheer speculation as to the location of Modru Kinstealer's holt. *The Raven Book* states that Gron was in the north and was a cold barren Land; hence, any location above perhaps 50° north is suitable grist for scholars' mills. It would seem that astronomers specializing in solar eclipses are more likely to isolate the probable location of the Iron Tower than are historians and linguists.

The Effect of the Myrkenstone on Tuck's Eyes

Although the Ravenbook Scholars of Tuckerby's time speculated long over the cause of Tuck's blindness, they came to no firm conclusion. In the Sixth Era however, Warrow Historian Burmly Gribbs proposed that Tuck's sightlessness came about as follows:

It seems clear (postulated Burmly) that the Myrkenstone emitted a radiance beyond the usual range of vision, a radiance seen only by Warrow and not by Man, Elf, Dwarf, or even by Spawn. Hence, when Tuck confronted the 'Stone—standing but a few feet from it—his eyes were whelmed by the dark "glare" just as if he were staring at an extremely bright source of nearby ordinary light, a source so brilliant that close-by torches emitting normal light were lost to his sight in the darkling blare of the Myrkenstone. Tuck's "special" Warrow vision was blasted by this black radiance, rending him of his ability to see in the dark luminance. Yet, there is good evidence that he would have been able to see by normal light had he at that time been taken away from the vicinity of the 'Stone. Instead, he loosed the Red Quarrel, and when it struck the Myrkenstone a raging flare blasted forth. Now, in truth, Tuck was staring through a glare so bright, so intense, that his "normal" sight was destroyed, too. Hence (concluded Burmly), what vision the harsh black radiance did not sunder, the blaring bright radiance did, and Tuck was totally blinded as a result. No scholar since Burmly's time has set forth a more convincing explanation.

Songs, Inscriptions, and Redes

(Listed by: type; title; first line; book[s] and chapter[s] of appearance)

Old Barlo's Admonition: The arrow as strays might well'er been throwed away (Book One, Chapters 1, 5; Book Two, Chapter 3; Book Three, Chapter 5) Warrow Song: *The Thornwalkers' Song:* We are Thornwalkers (Book One, Chapter 2)

Warrow Dirge: *Sail the Endless Sea:* The Shadow. Tide doth run (Book One, Chapter 2)

Othran's Tomb Inscription: Loose not the Red Quarrel (Book One, Chapter 4; Book Two, Chapter 6; Book Three, Chapters 5, 6, 7)

Warrow Song: *The Merry Man in Boskledee:* Oh—Fiddle-dee hi, fiddle-dee ho (Book One, Chapter 4) Rael's Rede: Neither of two Evils must thy strike claim (Book Two, Chapter 2; Book Three, Chapters 5, 6, 7)

Warrow Dirge: *The Four Seasons:* In Winter's glade now cold and bare (Book Two, Chapter 3).

Budgens Monument Inscription: Let it be said now and for all the days hereafter that on this day the struggle began, and Evil met its match (Book Two, Chapter 3; Book Three, Chapter 7)

Rael's Sooth: Bright' Silverlarks and Silver Sword (Book Two, Chapter 6)

Vanidor's Death Rede: The Darkest Day (Book Two, Chapter 6; Book Three, Chapter 3)

Warrow Lay: *The Loosing of the Red Quarrel:* Loose not the Red Quarrel ere appointed dark time (Book Three, Chapter 7)

Warrow Lay: *The Lay of the Iron Tower:* From frozen north (Book Three, Chapter 7)

Translations of Words and Phrases

Throughout *The Raven Book* appear many words and phrases in languages other than the Common Tongue, Pellarion. For scholars interested in such things, these words and phrases are collected together in this appendix. A number of tongues are involved:

Châkur = Dwarven tongue
OHR = Old High tongue of Riamon
OP = Old tongue of Pellar
OR = Old tongue of Rian
Slûk = Spawn tongue
Sylva = Elven tongue
Twyll = ancient Warrow tongue
Valur = ancient War-tongue of Valon

The table on the following page is a cross-check listing of the most common terms found in various tongues in *The Raven Book*.

		Man		
Warrow (Twyll)	Valon (Valur)	Pellar (Pellarion)	Elf (Sylva)	Dwarf (Châkur)
Rūck	Rutch	Rukh	Ruch	Ůkh
Rūcks	Rutcha	Rukha	Rucha	Ůkhs
Rūcken	Rutchen	Rukken	Ruchen	Ůkken
Hlōk	Drōkn	Lōkh	Lok	Hrōk
Hlōks	Drōkha	Lōkha	Loka	Hrōks
Hlōken	Drōken	Lōkken	Loken	Hrōken

Warrow (Twyll)	Valon (Valur)	Man Pellar (Pellarion)	Elf (Sylva)	Dwarf (Châkur)
Ghû	Guul	Ghol	Ghûlk	Khōl
Ghûls	Guula	Ghola	Ghûlka	Khōls
Ghûlen	Guulen	Gholen	Ghûlken	Khōlen
Dread	Dread	Dread	Dread	Dread
Gargon	Gargon	Gargon	Gargon	Ghath
Gargons	Gargons	Gargons	Gargoni	Ghaths
Ogru	Ogru	Troll	Troll	Troll
Kraken	Kraken	Kraken	Hèlarmûs	Madûk
maggot-folk	Wrg	Yrm	*Rûpt*	Grg
Spawn	Spawn	Spawn; *Spaunen*	*Spaunen*	Squam
Dwarf	Dwarf	Dwarf	Drimm	Cnâk
Dwarves	Dwarves	Dwarves	Drimma	Châkka
Dwarven	Dwarven	Dwarven	Drimmen	Châkka
Elf	Deva	Elf	Lian;* Dylvan	Elf
Elves	Deva'a	Elves	Lian; Dylvana	Elves
Elven	Deven	Elven	Lianen; Dylvanen	Elven
Giant	Giant	Utrun	Utrun	Utrun
Giants	Giants	Utruni	Utruni	Utruni
Warrow	Waldan	Waerling	Waerling	Waeran
Warrows	Waldana	Waerlinga	Waerlinga	Waerans
Wee Folk	*Waldfolc*	Wee Folk	—	—

*The Elves consist of two strains: (1) the Lian, the First Elves, and (2) the Dylvana, the Wood Elves.

In the following text, words and phrases are listed under the tongue of origin. Where possible, direct translations () are provided; in other cases, the translation is inferred from the context { } of *The Raven Book*. Also listed is the name of the speaker [], if known.

Châkur
(Dwarvèn tongue)

Aggarath (untranslated) [Brega] {Grimspire}
Baralan (Sloping land = the Pitch)
Châkka djalk aggar theck! (Dwarven——-!) [Brega]
Châkka shok! Châkka cor! (Dwarven axes! Dwarven might!) [Brega]
Ctor (Shouter) [Brega]
Deôop (Deep) [Brega]
Drakkalan (Dark Shedder) [Brega]
Gaard! (untranslated) [Brega] (a Wizard word perhaps meaning Move!; Act!)
Ghatan (untranslated) [Brega] {Loftcrag}
Hyranee (Hyrani) [Brega] {one or more Men of Hyree}
Jarak (Courser) [Brega]
Khana (Breakdeath) [Brega]
Kistanee (Kistani) [Brega] {one or more Men of Kistan}
Kraggen-cor (Mountain-might) [Brega] {Drimmendeeve}
Kruk! (untranslated expletive) [Brega]
Mountain (Living stone) [Brega]
Rávenor (untranslated) [Brega] {Stormhelm}
Uchan (untranslated) [Brega] {Greytower}
Vorvor (untranslated name of a whirlpool) [Brega]

OHR
(Old High tongue of Riamon)
Zūo Hēlan widar iu! (To Hèl with you!) [Laurelin]

OR
(Old tongue of Rian)
Ahn! (horn call meaning, Ready!) [Jarriel]
Ahn! Hahn! (horn call meaning, Assemble!) [Jarriel]
Hál! Aurion ūre cynig! (Hail! Aurion our King!) [Captains of Challera Keep]

Hál! Hēah Adoni cnāwen ūre weg! (Hail! High Adon knows our way!) [Aurion]

Rahn! (horn call meaning, Prepare!) [Hogarth]

OP
(Old tongue of Pellar)

Cepān wyllan, Lian; wir gān bringan thē Sunna! (Keep well, Lian; we go to bring the Sun!) [Galen]

Hál ūre allience! Hál ūre bond! (Hail our alliance! Hail our bond!) [Galen]

Hōhgarda (High Worlds) [Galen]

Jagga, Rust! Jagga! (Hide, Rust! Hide!) [Laurelin]

Larkenwald (Lark Wood = Wood of the Larks)

Maeg Adoni laenan strengthu to ūre earms! (May Adon lend strength to our arms!) [Aurion]

Mittegarda (Middle Worlds) [Galen]

Poeir bē in thyne earms! (Power be in thine arms!) [Galen]

Rach! (untranslated expletive)

Untargarda (Under Worlds) [Galen]

Slûk
(Span tongue)

Arg tha! Shugg du! (untranslated) [Hlōk gate captain] {You there! Name yourself!}

Dolh (Elf/Elves) [Modru]

Dolh schluu gogger! (Elf——-!) [Modru] {Elf on rack!}

Dubh (Dwarf/Dwarves) [Modru]

Garja ush! (untranslated) [Modru] {Raise her up!}

Ghun (untranslated) [Ghol] {Gone}

Glâr! Glâr! (Fire! Fire!) [Drimmnen-deeve Horde]

Gluktu! (untranslated) [Modru/Hyrani emissary] {Attack!}

Glu shtom! (untranslated) [rebellious Ghûl] {I would stay!}

Guk klur gog bleagh. (untranslated) [Rūck] {Eating is better than fighting.}

Gulgok! (untranslated) [Ghûl emissary] {Master!}

Guttra! (untranslated) [Hlōk door guard] {Halt!}

Khakt! (untranslated) [Modru]{Here!}

Nabba thek! (untranslated) [Modru-Naudron] {Dead search! = Search the dead!}

Nabbu gla oth. (untranslated) [Modru/Naudron] {Death take you.}

Negus (Lord/King) [Modru] {Negus of Terror = Lord of Terror = the Gargon}

Rul durg! (untranslated) [Modru/Naudron] {Ready her!}

Schtuga! (untranslated) [Hlōk jailor] {Fool!}

Shabba Dūl! (untranslated) [Modru] {To the Pit!}

Shuul! (untranslated) [Modru] {Guard!}

Slath! (untranslated) [Modru] {Stop!}

Theck dral, guth! (untranslated) [Hlōk overseer] {Get to work, sluggard!}

Thuggon oog. Laug glog raktu! (untranslated) [Modru/Naudron] {Split in two. Half join the Horde!}

Urb schla! Drek! (untranslated) [Modru/Naudron] {All go! Ride!}

Ush (untranslated) [Modru/Naudron] {Up!}

Vhuul! (untranslated) [Modru] {Troll!}

Vulpen (Vulgs) [Modru]

Sylva
(Elven tongue)

Aevor (untranslated) [Gildor] {Grimspire}

Alor (Lord)

Aro! (untranslated exclamation) [Gildor]

Chagor (untranslated) [Gildor] {Loftcrag}

Cianin Andele (Shining Nomad) [Gildor]

Cianin taegi! (Shining days!) [Gildor; Vanidor]

Coron (Ruler/King) [Gildor] {Stormhelm}

Coron Eiron, va Draedan sa nond! (King Eiron, the Gargon is dead!) [Gildor]

Dara (Lady) [Elven healer]

Darda Erynian (Leaf-tree Hall-of-green = Greenhall Forest)

Darda Gallon (Leaf-tree Land-of-larks = Forest of the Silverlarks)

dele (porridge)

Draedan (Dread One/Gargon)

Drimm (Dwarf) [Gildor]

Drimmen-deeve (Dwarven-delvings) [Gildor]

Ealle hál va Deevestrīdena, slēanra a va Draedan! (All hail the Deevewalkers, slayers of the Gargon!) [Eiron]

Eborane (Dark Reaver) [Eiron]

Eryn (Green: e.g., Eryn Ford = Green Ford) [Eiron]

Falanith (Valley Rising = the Pitch)

Fian nath dairia! (May your path be ever straight!) [Inarion]
Gralon (untranslated) [Gildor] {Greytower}
Hál, valagalana! (Hail, valiant warriors!) (Havor; Eiron and Lian escort]
Kel! (untranslated greeting) [Talarin]
Kest! (Stop!) [Duorn; Tuon]
Kregyn (untranslated) {Grūwen Pass}
Lianion (First Land) [Talarin]
mian (waybread)
Nond? Va Draedan sa nond? (Dead? The Gargon is dead?) [Eiron]
Talarn (Steel-heart) [Eiron]
Va Draedan sa nond . . . (The Gargon is dead . . .) [Gildor]
Vanil (silvery)
Vani-lērihha (Silverlarks)
Vio Gildor! (I am Goldbranch!) [Gildor]
Vio ivon Arden. (I am come from Arden.) [Gildor]
wela (mead)

Twyll
(ancient Warrow tongue)

Chelga! (Stand still and speak your name!) [Baskin]
Ellil! (Friend!) [Tuck]
faer sylva (fair forest)
Hai roi! (untranslated exclamation, probably Valur in origin) (buccen of the Eastdell Fourth]
Hanlo's Reya (Hanlo's Foxes) [Danner]
Hlafor Galen, tuon nid legan mi hinda! (Lord Galen, do not leave me behind!) [Tuck]
Hyranan (Hyrani) [Tuck] {a Man of Hyree}
Mandrak (Man-Dragon)
Skut! (untranslated expletive) [Danner; Luth]
So ho! (untranslated ancient hunting call, perhaps meaning, Here!) [Tuck]
Taa-tahn! Taa-tahn! (Warrow horn call meaning, Rally! Rally!) [Patrel]
Ta, tahn! Ta, tahn! Ta, tahn! (Warrow horn call meaning, Attack! Attack! Attack!) [Patrel]
Thuna glath, Fral Wilrow. (Go in peace, Friend Wilrow.) [Tuck]
Wanderjahre (Wandering Days)

Valur
(ancient battle-tongue of Valon)

daemon (demon) [Borel]

Garn! (untranslated expletive) [Vidron]

Hahn, taa-roo! (Valon horn call meaning, Return!) [Vidron]

Hai roi! (untranslated exclamation) [Borel]

Hál, Deva Talarin! Vanada al tro da halka! (Hail, Elf Talarin! Together we shall be mighty!) [Vidron]

Hrosmarshal (Horse Marshal)

Waldfolc (Wood Folk = Folk of the woods)

Zlye pozhirately koneny! (Vile gluttons of horseflesh!) [Vidron]

About the Author

Dennis L. McKiernan was born April 4, 1932, in Moberly, Missouri, where he lived until age eighteen, when he joined the U.S. Air Force, serving four years during the Korean War. He received a BS in electrical engineering from the University of Missouri in 1958 and an MS in the same field from Duke University in 1964. Employed by a leading research and development laboratory, he lives with his family in Westerville, Ohio. His Iron Tower Trilogy—*The Dark Tide, Shadows of Doom* and *The Darkest Day* brought him instant acclaim. He is also the author of the bestselling Silver Call Duology—*Trek to Kraggen-Cor* and *The Brega Path*—and *Dragondoom*.

Return to the world of Mithgar!

Dennis L. McKiernan

SILVER WOLF, BLACK FALCON

Dennis L. McKiernan's newest epic takes you back to Mithgar in a time of great peril—as an Elf and an Impossible Child try to save this ravaged land from a doom long ago prophesied....

"Once McKiernan's got you, he never lets you go."
—Jennifer Roberson

"McKiernan's narratives have heart and fire and drive."
—Katherine Kerr

❑ 0-451-45786-2/$23.95

Prices slightly higher in Canada

Payable by Visa, MC or AMEX only ($10.00 min.), No cash, checks or COD. Shipping & handling: US/Can. $2.75 for one book, $1.00 for each add'l book; Int'l $5.00 for one book, $1.00 for each add'l. Call (800) 788-6262 or (201) 933-9292, fax (201) 896-8569 or mail your orders to:

Penguin Putnam Inc.
P.O. Box 12289, Dept. B
Newark, NJ 07101-5289
Please allow 4-6 weeks for delivery.
Foreign and Canadian delivery 6-8 weeks.

Bill my: ❑ Visa ❑ MasterCard ❑ Amex _____ (expires)
Card# _____
Signature _____

Bill to:
Name _____
Address _____ City _____
State/ZIP _____ Daytime Phone # _____
Ship to:
Name _____ Book Total $ _____
Address _____ Applicable Sales Tax $ _____
City _____ Postage & Handling $ _____
State/ZIP _____ Total Amount Due $ _____

This offer subject to change without notice.   Ad # MCKN 2 (4/00)

Dennis L. McKiernan
HÈL'S CRUCIBLE Duology:

In Dennis L. McKiernan's world of Mithgar, other stories are often spoken of, but none as renowned as the War of the Ban. Here, in one of his finest achievements, he brings that epic to life in all its magic and excitement.

Praise for the **HÈL'S CRUCIBLE Duology:**

"Provocative...appeals to lovers of classic fantasy—the audience for David Eddings and Terry Brooks."—*Booklist*

"Once McKiernan's got you, he never lets you go."—Jennifer Roberson

"Some of the finest imaginative action...there are no lulls in McKiernan's story."—*Columbus Dispatch*

Book One of the **Hèl's Crucible Duology**
❑ **Into the Forge** 0-451-45700-5 / $6.99

Book Two of the **Hèl's Crucible Duology**
❑ **Into the Fire** 0-451-45732-3 / $6.99

Prices slightly higher in Canada

Payable by Visa, MC or AMEX only ($10.00 min.), No cash, checks or COD. Shipping & handling: US/Can. $2.75 for one book, $1.00 for each add'l book; Int'l $5.00 for one book, $1.00 for each add'l. Call (800) 788-6262 or (201) 933-9292, fax (201) 896-8569 or mail your orders to:

Penguin Putnam Inc.
P.O. Box 12289, Dept. B
Newark, NJ 07101-5289
Please allow 4-6 weeks for delivery.
Foreign and Canadian delivery 6-8 weeks.

Bill my: ❑ Visa ❑ MasterCard ❑ Amex _____ (expires)
Card# _____
Signature _____

Bill to:
Name _____
Address _____ City _____
State/ZIP _____ Daytime Phone # _____

Ship to:
Name _____ Book Total $ _____
Address _____ Applicable Sales Tax $ _____
City _____ Postage & Handling $ _____
State/ZIP _____ Total Amount Due $ _____

This offer subject to change without notice.   Ad # MCKN (9/00)

Penguin Putnam Inc.
Online

Your Internet gateway to a virtual environment with
hundreds of entertaining and enlightening books
from Penguin Putnam Inc.

*While you're there, get the latest buzz on
the best authors and books around—*

Tom Clancy, Patricia Cornwell, W.E.B. Griffin,
Nora Roberts, William Gibson, Robin Cook,
Brian Jacques, Catherine Coulter, Stephen King,
Ken Follett, Terry McMillan, and many more!

**Penguin Putnam Online is located at
http://www.penguinputnam.com**

PENGUIN PUTNAM NEWS

Every month you'll get an inside look at our upcom-
ing books and new features on our site. This is an
ongoing effort to provide you with the most
up-to-date information about
our books and authors.

Subscribe to Penguin Putnam News at
http://www.penguinputnam.com/newsletters